M

WHERE TIGERS
ARE AT HOME

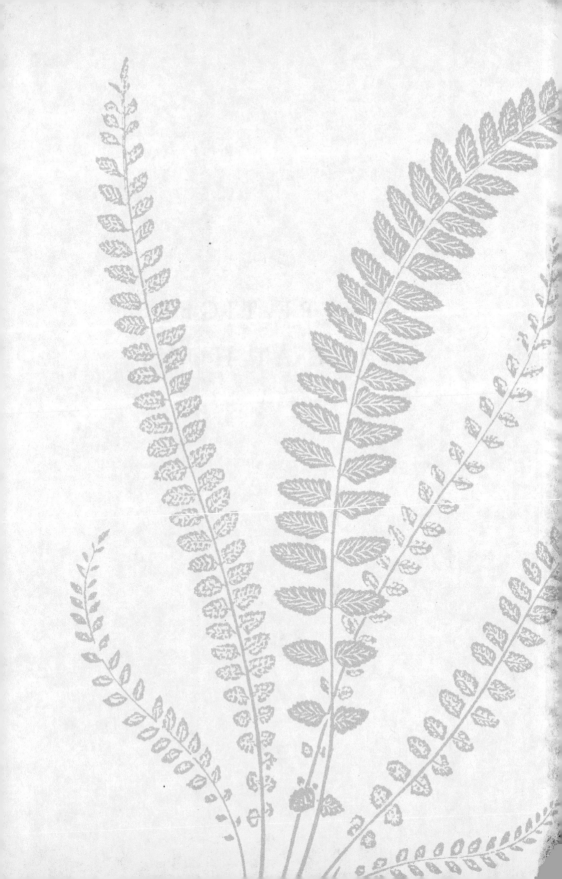

WHERE TIGERS
ARE AT HOME

JEAN-MARIE BLAS DE ROBLÈS

Translated from the French by Mike Mitchell

Other Press • *New York*

Library of Congress Cataloging-in-Publication Data

Blas de Roblès, Jean-Marie, 1954–

   [Là où les tigres sont chez eux. English]

  Where tigers are at home / Jean-Marie Blas de Roblès ; translated from the French by Mike Mitchell.

      p. cm.

  ISBN 978-1-59051-562-4 (hardcover : acid-free paper) — ISBN 978-1-59051-563-1 (ebook) 1. Foreign correspondents—Brazil—Fiction.   2. French—Brazil—Fiction. 3. Kircher, Athanasius, 1602-1680—Fiction.   4. Science—History—Fiction. I. Mitchell, Michael, 1941-   II. Title.

  PQ2662.L354L313 2013

  843'.914—dc23

2012015748

For Laurence
Virgile, Félix and Hippolyte

In memory of Philippe Hédan

No one can walk beneath palm trees with impunity,
and ideas are sure to change in a land where
elephants and tigers are at home.

—GOETHE
Elective Affinities

PROLOGUE

ALCÂNTARA: *Whipping-post Square*

"**M**an's swelling his pointed dick! Squaaawk! Man's swelling his pointed dick!" Heidegger's harsh, nasal, drunken-sounding voice echoed around the room.

Eléazard von Wogau looked up from his reading in sudden exasperation; half swivelling around in his chair, he grabbed the first book his hand lit on and threw it as hard as he could at the bird. At the other end of the room the parrot, with a vigorous, multicolored ruffling of feathers, rose from its perch just enough to avoid the missile. Father Reilly's *Studia Kircheriana* landed with a crash on the table beyond it, overturning the half-full bottle of *cachaça*. It shattered on the spot, soaking the book that had fallen apart.

"Oh, shit!" Eléazard groaned.

For a brief moment he wondered whether to get up and try to save the book from further damage but then, catching the Sartrian look of the large macaw, which was pretending to be searching for something in its plumage, its head thrown back in an absurd attitude, its eye crazed, he decided to return to Caspar Schott's manuscript.

It was pretty remarkable, if you thought about it, that such a find was still possible: a completely unpublished manuscript that had come to light in the course of an inventory at the National Library in Palermo. The librarian had not thought the contents worthy of anything more then a brief article in the library's quarterly bulletin together with a note to the director of the local Goethe Institute. It had taken an exceptional concatenation of circumstances for a photocopy of this handwritten manuscript— the biography, written in French by an obscure German Jesuit, of another, equally forgotten Jesuit— to reach Brazil and Eléazard's desk. In a sudden access of zeal, the director of the Goethe Institute had taken it upon himself to communicate the discovery to Werner Küntzel, the Berliner who for several years had been attempting to demonstrate how the binary language of computers was rooted in the scholasticism of Ramon Llull and its later variants, notably that of Athanasius Kircher. Always inclined to get carried away, Küntzel had immediately proposed it to the Thomas Sessler publishing house. Balking at the cost of translation, the publisher agreed in principle to a subscription edition and, on Küntzel's advice, had commissioned Eléazard to establish the text and provide a commentary.

You old bugger, Werner, Eléazard thought with a smile, you've really no idea . . .

He hadn't seen him since the distant days, already disappearing in the mists of time, of their meeting in Heidelberg, but he well remembered his weasel face and the nervous twitch causing the obscene quiver of a little muscle in his cheek. It suggested repressed tension, ready, it seemed, to explode at any minute, with the result that it sometimes made Eléazard forget what he was saying, an effect perhaps more or less consciously intended by Küntzel.

They had corresponded from time to time, although in fairly formal tones on his part, and Werner had never received more than a postcard, occasionally two, in response to the long letters in which he went into detail about his life and his successes. No, really, he didn't realize to what extent his own life had changed, nor what resources he had had to find to return to his old love. No doubt he knew Kircher's works better than anyone—fifteen years of close acquaintance with a famous unknown are generally sufficient to procure one that useless privilege—but Werner had no idea how far behind he had left his youthful ambitions. Eléazard had long since consigned the thesis he had been working on in Heidelberg to oblivion, even though he continued to evoke its shade as the sole motivation for an obsession that kept surprising him a little. He had to admit: he collected anything closely or distantly connected with the life of that grotesque Jesuit with the same obsessiveness as some people collect bottles of whiskey or cigarette packets long after they've stopped drinking or smoking. First editions, engravings, studies or articles, scattered quotations, everything was grist to his mill to fill the void left by his long-ago abandonment of university life. It was his way of remaining faithful, of satisfying, even if at the same time mocking, an appetite for knowledge of which, long ago, he had not shown himself worthy.

"Soledade!" he shouted without turning around.

It wasn't long before the young mulatto's strange, beaming clown's face appeared. "Yes, *Senhor*?" she said in her velvety voice and with the intonation of someone wondering what could be wanted of her so abruptly.

"Could you make me a *caipirinha*, please?"

"*Pode preparar me uma caipirinha, por favor?*" Soledade repeated, imitating his accent and errors of syntax.

Eléazard repeated his request by raising his eyebrows, but she just wagged her finger at him, as if to say, "You're incorrigible!"

"Yes, *Senhor*," she said before she went, not without making a face from which the tip of a pink tongue protruded.

A mixture of African and Indian, a *cabocla* as they said here, Soledade had been born in a village of the Sertão. She was only eighteen but from adolescence she had had to move to the town to help feed her overnumerous brothers and sisters. For five years the interior regions everywhere had suffered from drought; the peasants were reduced to eating cactus and snakes, but they could not bring themselves to abandon their patch of land and preferred to send their children to the large towns on the coast where they could at least beg. Soledade had been luckier than most: with the help of one of her father's cousins she had found work as a servant with a Brazilian family. Shamelessly exploited and thrashed for the least failure to carry out her employers' orders, she had been delighted to accept an offer of work from a Frenchman whose eye she had caught at a *feijoada* given by his colleagues from the office. Denis Raffenel had been more attracted by her smile, her silky black skin and her beautiful young girl's body than by her domestic skills; but he had treated her kindly, not to say respected her, so that she was perfectly content with the double wages he paid and the minimum work she was asked to do to earn them. Three months ago Eléazard's divorce had happened to coincide with the departure of this heaven-sent Frenchman and he had asked her to come and work for him, partly to please Raffenel but mostly because he was alone. Since she knew him from having seen him several times when he visited Raffenel and since he was French as well—she would have died rather than go back to work for the Brazilians—Soledade had accepted immediately, though she did demand the same wages, a pittance to be honest, and a color television. Eléazard had agreed and one fine day she had moved in.

Soledade did the washing, the shopping and the cooking, cleaned the house when it suited her, which was rarely, and spent most of her time watching the insipid soaps on TV Globo, the national channel. As for the 'special' services she had provided for her previous employer, Eléazard had never requested them. He had never even entered the little room she had chosen for herself, out of indifference rather than thoughtfulness, for which Soledade seemed grateful.

He watched her as she came back, once more enjoying her casual gait, her very African way of sliding over the ground with the irritating slap of her bare feet. She placed the glass on his desk, made a face at him again and left.

Taking a sip of his drink—Soledade got the perfect balance between *cachaça* and lime—Eléazard gazed out of the window in front of him. It gave directly onto the jungle or, to be more precise, the *mata*, that luxuriance of tall trees, twisted lianas and foliage that had retaken possession of the town without anyone objecting. From his first floor Eléazard had the feeling he was plunging straight into the heart of organic life, a little like a surgeon bent over a stomach open to his curiosity alone. When he had decided to leave São Luís to buy a house in Alcântara he had been spoiled for choice. The old baroque town, the jewel of eighteenth-century architecture in Brazil, was falling into ruin. Ignored by history since the downfall of the Marquis de Pombal, engulfed by the forest, insects and damp, it was inhabited by a tiny population of fishermen too poor to live anywhere but in shacks made from corrugated iron, clay and cans or in tumbledown hovels. From time to time a grower would appear, wild-eyed at having stepped out of the great forest so abruptly, to sell his harvest of mangoes or papayas to the dealers who went to and fro between São Luís and Alcântara. It was there that Eléazard had bought this immense, dilapidated house, one of the *sobrados* that in former times had contributed to the beauty of the town. He had acquired it for what seemed to him next to nothing but which represented a substantial sum for most Brazilians. Its façade looked straight out onto Pelourinho Square, with the abandoned Church of São Matias on the left, and on the right, also open to every wind that blew, the *Casa de Câmara e Cadeia*, which is the town hall and prison. In the middle of the square, between the two ruins, of which only the walls and roof were left, the *pelourinho* still stood, the ornate stone column where refractory slaves used to be whipped. A tragic symbol of civil and religious oppression, of the blindness that had led some to massacre thousands of their fellow men with a clear conscience, the whipping post was the only one of all the monuments of the town that had remained intact. Even though they allowed their pigs to wander freely inside the church and the town hall, none of the *caboclos* who lived there would have allowed the least indignity to be inflicted on this testimony to thousands of years of suffering, injustice and stupidity. For nothing had changed, for nothing would ever shake those three interlinked pillars of human nature, and in that column, which had defied the ravages of time, the locals saw the symbol of their poverty and degradation.

Elaine, his wife, had never been able to bear this place where everything bore, like a stigma, the mold of deterioration, and this epidermal discharge had doubtless played a part in their separation. One more item in the multitude of faults that had been hurled at him out of the blue one evening the previous September. All the time she was talking, his mind had been filled with the standard image of a house eaten away by termites that suddenly collapses without the least sign of the impending disaster having been visible. The idea of trying to vindicate himself never entered his head, as it doubtless never enters the head of all those who are surprised one day by a slap in the face from fate: can you imagine justifying yourself when faced with an earthquake or an exploding mortar bomb? When his wife, suddenly an unknown woman,

had demanded a divorce, Eléazard had submitted, signing everything he was asked to sign, agreeing to all the lawyer's requests,
just as people allow themselves to be transported from one refu-
gee camp to another. Their daughter, Moéma, was no problem,
since she was of age and led her own life, that is, if one can call
her way of shirking all obligations day in, day out, "leading a life."

Eléazard had chosen to remain in Alcântara and it was only
recently, six months after Elaine had left to go to Brazilia, that he
had started to go through the debris of his love, less to see what
could be salvaged than to find the cause of such a mess.

Thinking about it, Werner's proposal had come at just the right
time. The work on Caspar Schott's manuscript would be a kind of
safety rail, forcing him to concentrate and persevere in a way that
would be therapeutic. And even though there was no question of
forgetting, nor ever would be, at least it would allow him to make
the intervals between upsurges of memory longer.

Once more Eléazard leafed through the first chapter of the *Life
of Athanasius Kircher*, rereading his footnotes and certain passages as he did so. God, wasn't the opening terrible! Nothing more
irritating than that stilted tone, the tone of all hagiographies, to
be sure, but which here scaled the heights of platitude. The pages
stank of candles and cassocks. And that tedious way of reading
into childhood the signs of future "destiny"! In retrospect it always worked out, of course. A real pain in the ass! as Moéma said
of anything, however minor, that got in the way of what she called
her freedom but which was basically nothing but irrational and
pathological egoism. The only one he felt attracted to was Friedrich von Spee, despite the inanity of his poems.

"Man's swelling his pointed dick! Squaawk, squaaaawk!" the
parrot screeched again, as if it had waited for the moment when
its utterance would have the greatest effect.

As resplendent as it's stupid, Eléazard thought, regarding the animal with disdain. A common enough paradox, alas, and not only in the great macaw of the Amazon.

He'd finished his *caipirinha*. A second—a third?—would have been welcome, but the idea of bothering Soledade again made him hesitate. After all, in Portuguese *soledade* meant "solitude." "I live alone with Solitude . . ." he said to himself. There are pleonasms that have a kind of excess of truth in them. It could have been a quotation from the *Romance of the Rose*: "When Reason heard me, she turned away and left me pensive and mournful."

CHAPTER 1

In which we hear of the birth & early years of Athanasius Kircher, the hero of this history

O N T H I S D A Y, dedicated to Saint Genevieve, the third of the year 1690, I, Caspar Schott, sitting like some student at a desk in this library of which I have charge, undertake to relate the life, exemplary in every detail, of the Reverend Father Athanasius Kircher. Out of modesty this man, whose edifying works have put the stamp of his intelligence on our history, hid behind his books; people will, I am sure, be grateful to me if, as is my heartfelt desire, I gently lift this veil, in all propriety, to throw light on a destiny which glory has rendered immortal now & for evermore.

Setting out on such an arduous task, I put my trust in Mary, our mother, whom Athanasius never invoked in vain, as I take up my pen to bring back to life the man who was my master for fifty years & who bestowed on me, I make bold to assert, his true friendship.

Athanasius Kircher was born at three o'clock in the morning of the second day of May, the feast of Saint Athanasius, in the year 1602. His parents, Johannes Kircher & Anna Gansekin, were fervent & generous Catholics. At the time of his birth they lived in Geisa, a small town three hours from Fulda.

Athanasius Kircher was born, at the beginning of a period of relative concord, into a pious & close-knit family & into an atmosphere of study & contemplation which, I am sure, was not without influence on his future vocation, especially since Johannes Kircher possessed an extensive library so that as a child Athanasius was constantly surrounded by books. It was always with emotion & gratitude that, later on, he would mention to me certain titles he had held in his hands in Geisa, in particular the *De Laudibus Sanctae Crucis* of Rabanus Maurus, through which he had practically learned to read.

Favored by nature, learning even the most difficult of subjects was literally child's play for him, but despite that he showed such application that he outshone his classmates in everything. There was never a day when he did not come back from school with some new decoration pinned to his coat, rewards with which his father was justifiably well pleased. Appointed class prefect, he assisted the master by explaining Canisius's catechism to the first-years & heard the juniors' lessons. At eleven he could already read the Gospels & Plutarch in the original. At twelve he won all the disputations in Latin hands down, could declaim better than anyone & wrote prose & verse with astonishing facility.

Athanasius was particularly fond of tragedy & at the age of thirteen his father gave him, as a reward for a particularly brilliant translation from Hebrew, permission to go to Aschaffenburg with his classmates to see a play: a company of wandering players were putting on *Flavius Mauricius, Emperor of the East* there. Johannes Kircher sent the little band in the care of a local farmer who was going to the town—two days' walk away from Geisa—by cart & was to bring them home once the performance was over.

Athanasius was carried away by the talent of the actors & their truly magic ability to bring to life a figure he had always admired. On the boards, before his very eyes, the valiant successor to Tiberius once more defeated the Persians amid sound & fury; he harangued his troops, drove the Slavs & the Avars back over the Danube, eventually reestablishing the greatness of the Empire. And in the last act, when the traitor Phocas killed this model Christian most horribly without sparing either his wife or his sons, the crowd very nearly tore the poor actor playing the role of the vile centurion to pieces.

Athanasius took up Mauricius's cause with all the hotheadedness of youth & when it was time to return to Geisa our madcap refused to go in the cart with his companions. The farmer who was in charge of the children tried in vain to hold him back: aspiring to an heroic death & ablaze with desire to emulate the virtue of his model, Athanasius Kircher had decided to go alone, like a hero of Antiquity, to face the Spessart forest, which was notorious not only for its highwaymen but also for the wild beasts that were to be found there.

Once in the forest, it took less than two hours for him to get lost. He spent all day wandering to & fro, trying to find the road they had taken on the way there, but the virgin forest grew thicker & thicker & he was seized with dread as night approached. Terrified by the phantasms his imagination saw in the darkness & cursing the stupid pride that had sent him on this adventure, Athanasius climbed to the top of a tree so that he would at least be safe from the wild beasts. He spent the night clutching onto a branch, praying to God with all his

heart, trembling with fear & remorse. In the morning, more
dead than alive from weariness & trepidation, he plunged deeper
into the forest. He had continued like that for nine hours,
dragging himself from tree to tree, when the forest started to
thin out, revealing a large meadow. Joyfully Kircher went to find
out where he was from the laborers who were gathering in the
harvest—the place he was looking for was still two days' walk
away! Furnishing him with some provisions, they set him on the
right path & it was five days after leaving Aschaffenburg that he
returned to Geisa, to the great relief of his parents, who thought
they had lost him for good.

Having exhausted his father's patience, Athanasius was sent to
continue his education as a boarder at the Jesuit college in Fulda.

True, discipline there was stricter than in the little school
at Geisa, but the masters were more competent & were able to
satisfy the young Kircher's insatiable curiosity. There was also
the town itself, so rich in history & architecture, the church
of St. Michael, with its two asymmetrical towers, & above all
the library, the one founded with his own books by Rabanus
Maurus so long ago & where Athanasius spent most of his
free time. Apart from Maurus's own works, in particular the
original copies of *De Universo* & of *De Laudibus Sanctae Crucis*, it
contained all sorts of rare manuscripts, for example the *Song of
Hildebrand*, the *Codex Ragyndrudis*, the *Panarion* of Epiphanius
of Constantia, the *Summa Logicae* of William of Ockham &
even a copy of the *Malleus Maleficarum*, which Athanasius
could never open without a shudder.

He often talked to me about that last book, every time he
recalled his childhood friend, Friedrich von Spee Langenfeld.
He was a young teacher at the Fulda seminary &, recognizing
in Kircher the qualities that distinguished him from his fellow
students, it was not long before he became attached to him. It

was through him that Athanasius discovered the darker side of the library: Martial, Terence, Petronius . . . Von Spee introduced him to all these authors, whom propriety insists should not be read by innocent souls; & if the pupil emerged from this dubious trial strengthened in his aspiration to virtue, that still does not exonerate his master, for "vice is like pitch, as soon as you touch it, it sticks to your fingers." We are, however, all the more willing to forgive him this slight bending of the rules of morality because his influence on Kircher was solely beneficial: did he not go out with him every Sunday to the Frauenberg, the Hill of Our Lady, to relax in the abandoned monastery & talk about the world as they contemplated the mountains and the town below?

As for the *Malleus Maleficarum*, Athanasius well remembered his young mentor's anger at the cruelty and arbitrariness of the treatment inflicted on those supposedly possessed by the devil who were caught in the net of the Inquisition.

"How can you not confess to having killed your mother & father or fornicated with the devil," he said, "when your feet are being crushed in steel shoes or they're sticking long needles into you all over your body to find the witches' mark, which does not feel pain and which proves, according to the fools, that you have had dealings with the devil?"

And it was the student who felt the need to calm his master down, urging him to be more prudent in what he said. Then Von Spee would start to whisper, out there on the hillside, quoting Ponzibinio, Weier or Cornelius Loos in support of his outburst. He was not the first, he insisted, to criticize the inhuman methods of the inquisitors; in 1584 Johann Ervich had denounced the ordeal by water, Jordaneus the witches' mark, & as he said this Von Spee got carried away again, raising his voice and striking terror to the heart of the young Athanasius, who admired him all the more for his reckless courage.

"You see, my friend," Von Spee cried, his eyes shining, "for one genuine witch—& I am prepared to doubt whether there ever was one—there are three thousand feeble-minded simpletons & three thousand raving madmen whose problems fall into the competence of doctors rather than inquisitors. It is the pretext that these things concern God & religion that allows these cruel supposed experts to have their way. But all they reveal is their own ignorance & if they attribute all these events to supernatural causes, it is because they are ignorant of the natural reasons governing things!"

Throughout his life Kircher repeatedly told me of his fascination for this man & the influence he had had on his intellectual development. Occasionally the young teacher would read him some of the magnificent poems he was writing at the time, those that were collected after his death under the titles of *Counter-nightingale* & *Golden Book of Virtue*. Athanasius knew several of them by heart & on certain evenings of anguish in Rome, he would declaim some in a low voice, as you would say a prayer. He had a marked preference for *The Idolater*, a poem the Egyptian coloring of which he found particularly delightful. I feel as if I can still hear his resonant voice reciting it in a solemn, restrained style:

> *O mighty pennate Ishtar, adorèd, benefic,*
> *Wellspring, lunar brilliance, cat-queen edenic!*
> *With the salamander, live adornment of thee,*
> > *Fluorescent sea!*
>
> *Androgynous, its lip tingled: Tutankhamun,*
> *Hermes, puppets, sibyls lie carolling welcome*
> *loyalties, elders deploying stichomythia.*

He would finish with his eyes closed & remain silent, absorbed by the beauty of the lines or some memory connected with the text. I would take advantage of that to slip away, sure as I was that I would find him on the morrow back in his usual high spirits.

In 1616 Von Spee was transferred to the Jesuit college in Paderborn, where he was to complete his noviciate, & Athanasius, suddenly tired of Fulda, decided to go to Mainz to study philosophy. The winter of 1617 was particularly hard. Mainz was buried beneath the snow, all the rivers around were frozen over. Athanasius had flung himself wholeheartedly into the study of philosophy, above all that of Aristotle, which he loved & assimilated with astonishing rapidity. But having learned from his experiences at Fulda, where his fellow students had sometimes reacted brutally to his subtlety of mind, Athanasius worked in secret & refused to reveal how much he had learned. Feigning humility & even stupidity, he was looked upon as an industrious pupil limited by his lack of understanding.

A few months after his arrival in Mainz, Kircher expressed the desire to enter the Society of Jesus. Since he was not, to all appearances, intellectually gifted, it took an approach by his father to Johann Copper, the Jesuits' superior in the Rhineland, before the latter accepted his candidacy. His departure for the noviciate in Paderborn was put off until the autumn of 1618, after he had taken his final exams in philosophy. Athanasius was delighted by the news, doubtless in part at the prospect of seeing his friend Von Spee again.

That winter ice-skating was all the rage; Athanasius developed such skill in this activity that he derived sinful satisfaction from showing off in front of his companions. Filled with vanity, he liked to use his agility & the length of his slides to leave them behind. One day, when he was trying to skate faster than one of his fellow students, he realized he could not stop on the ice: his legs went in different directions & he took a severe fall on the hard-frozen ground. This fall, which was a just punishment for his conceit, left Kircher with a nasty hernia & various abrasions to his legs, which the same pride made him keep hidden.

By February these wounds had become infected. Not having been treated, they started to suppurate badly & in a few days poor Athanasius' legs had swollen so much that he could only walk with extreme difficulty. As the winter intensified, Athanasius continued to study in the worst conditions of cold & discomfort imaginable. Afraid of being rejected by the Jesuit college, where he had only been accepted with great difficulty, he remained silent about his state, with the result that his legs got progressively worse, right up to the day he was to leave for Paderborn.

His journey on foot across the Hesse countryside was veritable torture. In the course of the days & nights of the walk Athanasius recalled his conversations with Friedrich von Spee about the tortures inflicted by the inquisitors on those accused of witchcraft: that was what he was having to endure & it was only his faith in Jesus & the prospect of soon being reunited with his friend that helped him to withstand as best he could the sufferings of the flesh. Limping terribly, he reached the Jesuit college in Paderborn on October 2, 1618. Immediately after they had expressed their delight at seeing each other again, Von Spee, who was there to receive him, squeezed his secret out of him. A surgeon, who was called urgently, was horrified at the state of his legs; he found them already gangrenous and declared Kircher beyond hope. Thinking an incurable sickness was enough in itself, Kircher said nothing about his hernia. The superior of the college, Johann Copper, came to tell him gently that he would have to return home if his health had not improved within the month. However, he called all the novices together in prayer to ask God to relieve the poor neophyte.

After several days during which Athanasius's agonies only increased, Von Spee advised his protégé to appeal to the Virgin, who had always watched over him. In the church in Paderborn there was a very old statue of the Virgin Mary, which was said to have miraculous powers. Its fame was widespread among the ordinary folk of the region. Kircher had himself taken to the church & for a whole night he begged the Madonna to look down mercifully on the affliction of her sick child. Toward the twelfth hour he tried out his limbs to see if his supplication had been granted & was filled with a wonderful feeling of satisfaction. No longer doubting that he would be healed, he continued to pray until morning.

Waking a few hours later from a dreamless sleep, he found that both legs had healed & that his hernia had gone!

Look as he might through his spectacles, the surgeon was forced to admit the miracle had happened: to his great astonishment he only found scars & no trace of the infection that ought to have utterly destroyed his patient. Thus we can well understand the special devotion Athanasius retained throughout his life for Our Lady, who had succored him in his ordeal, indicating how Kircher was predestined to serve God within the Society.

ON THE WAY TO CORUMBÁ: *"The Death Train"*

Uncomfortable on the hard seat in her compartment, Elaine looked out of the window and watched the landscape passing by. She was a beautiful woman of thirty-five, with long, brown, curly hair that she wore in a loose, artistically tousled chignon. She was wearing a lightweight, beige safari jacket and matching skirt; she had crossed her legs in such a way that, without her noticing or perhaps without thinking it important, revealed rather more than she should of the suntanned skin of her left thigh. She was smoking a long menthol cigarette with the touch of affectation that revealed her lack of experience of that kind of thing. On the other seat, almost opposite her, Mauro had made himself comfortable: legs stretched out under the seat across the compartment, hands behind his neck, headset over his ears, he was listening to the cassette of Caetano Veloso, swaying his head in time to the music. Taking advantage of the fact that Elaine was turned to the window, he looked at her thighs with pleasure. It was not every day that one had the opportunity to admire the more intimate anatomy of *Profesora* Von Wogau, and many students at the University of Brazilia would have liked to be in his place. But he was the one she'd chosen to accompany her to the Pantanal because of his brilliant performance in his defense of his doctoral thesis in geology—passed with distinction, if you please!—because he had the handsome looks of an unrepentant Don Juan, and also perhaps, though to his mind it really didn't come into consideration, because his father was governor of the state of Maranhão. *"Cavaleiro de Jorge, seu chapéu azul, cruzeiro do sul no peito . . ."* Mauro increased the volume, as he did every time his favorite tune came on. Carried away by the beat of the song, he started humming the words, drawing out the final "oo" sound as Caetano used to. Elaine's thighs quivered a little every time the train jolted; inwardly he rejoiced.

Disturbed in her daydream by her companion's irritating chirping, Elaine suddenly looked over and caught him examining her thighs.

"You'd do better to show an interest in the landscape we're passing through," she said, uncrossing her legs and pulling her skirt down.

Mauro switched off his Walkman at once and took out his ear-phones. "I'm sorry, I didn't hear. What did you say?"

"It's not important," she said with a smile, touched by Mauro's worried expression. He was sweet with his dishevelled hair and the embarrassed look of a child caught in the act. "Look," she went on, pointing out of the window, "there are geologists who come from all over the world to see that."

Mauro glanced at the lunar landscape moving almost imper-ceptibly across the window frame; bizarre lumps of red sandstone looking as if they'd been dropped there, haphazardly, by some gi-gantic creature. "Precambrian ruiniform reliefs, highly eroded," he said with a slight frown, as if reciting a lesson.

"Not bad . . . But you could have added, 'A magnificent prospect with a savage beauty that gives humans a sense of their fragility here on Earth.' Unfortunately that's never in the geology manu-als, not even in another form."

"You're just making fun of me, as usual," Mauro sighed. "You know very well that I'm sensitive to that aspect of landscape; otherwise I'd have chosen history or math. To tell the truth, I'm starting to get tired."

"Me too, I have to admit. This journey's interminable, but re-member that we're going back to Brazilia by plane. The Depart-ment hasn't a lot of money, so we had to come to a compromise. Having said that, I'm not at all unhappy that we're taking this train, it's something I've been dreaming about for ages. A bit in the same way as I dream of going on the Trans-Siberian Railway some day."

"The Death Train!" said Mauro in funereal tones. "The only train in the world where you never know if it's going to arrive . . ."

"Oh, don't start that, Mauro," Elaine said with a laugh. "You'll bring us bad luck."

The Death Train, so called because there were always accidents happening or an armed attack, linked Campo Grande with Santa

Cruz in Bolivia. Just before the border it stopped at Corumbá, the small town where the two travellers were to meet up with the rest of the team, two professors from the University of Brazilia: Dietlev H. G. Walde, a specialist in palaeozoology, and Milton Tavares, Jr., head of the Department of Geology. To economize on cost, Elaine and Mauro had gone by van to Campo Grande, the last town accessible by road before the Mato Grosso. They had left the van in a garage—Dietlev and Milton, who had done the first stage by plane, were to pick it up on the way back—and waited at the station until dawn. The train was a veritable antique on wheels, with a steam engine worthy of the Far West, slatted-wood carriages in faded colors and arched windows. The compartments resembled ships' cabins with their mahogany veneer and a tiny cubicle with a little washbasin in pink marble. In one corner there was even a nickel-plated steel fan mounted on a universal joint, which at the time it was built must have been the height of luxury. Now the tap, eaten away by rust, merely managed a hint of moisture, the handle for opening the window went round and round without engaging, the wires of the fan seemed to have been torn off years ago and there was so much grime everywhere, and the felt of the seats was so badly torn it was impossible to imagine at what distant time in the past all this could have been the very latest in up-to-date comfort.

The heat was starting to get uncomfortable; Elaine wiped her forehead and unscrewed her water bottle. Under Mauro's amiable gaze she was trying to avoid spilling water over herself every time the train jolted when they heard angry shouts from the corridor. Drowning out the racket from the axles, a woman's voice seemed to be trying to rouse the whole world. They saw several people rush toward the rear of the train, followed by an obese conductor, uniform unbuttoned, cap askew, who stopped for a moment, panting, by the open door of their compartment. The shouts continued even louder, until they were cut off abruptly by two dull thuds that shook the partition and made the window and the fan vibrate.

"I'll go and have a look," Mauro said, getting up.

He pushed his way through the luggage blocking the corridor and came to a small group of people around the conductor. Armed with a little ax—"only to be used in case of fire"—he was trying to wreck the carriage, starting with the lavatory door.

"What's going on?" Mauro asked one of the peasants watching the scene impassively.

"Nothing. Just a *desgraçado* who's robbed a woman. He's shut himself in there and refuses to come out."

For a good ten minutes the conductor continued to attack the locked door. He took a step back, struck the door a powerful blow with the ax, sending an aftershock through the fat of his double chin, paused a moment to catch his breath, then continued. Mauro was dumbfounded by the profound serenity of the violence and, even more, by the appreciative nods of the audience.

When the door had finally been broken down, they saw a poor drunk asleep on the lavatory, a wallet on his knees. After having checked then pocketed the stolen item, the conductor set about extracting the sleeper from his hideout. With the help of one of the passengers, he carried him out onto the open platform at the end of the carriage, waited a few seconds, then pushed him off. Mauro gasped as he saw the body fall onto the embankment like a sandbag. The man turned on his side, as if making himself more comfortable, put his hand over his face and continued to sleep.

"If I could only get my hands on the bastard who stole my passkey!" the conductor muttered as he replaced the ax. Then, turning to Mauro, he said, "It was a good door, solid, they don't make them like that anymore."

FORTALEZA: *Avenida Tiburcío Cavalcante*

Querido, Papa!

Don't worry, it's nothing serious. On the contrary. But I need a little extra this month, just two thousand dollars. (Write me a check, you know I can exchange it at unofficial rates thanks to my Greek in Rio . . .) The thing is, my friend Thaïs and I have had the idea of opening a nice little bar not far from the beach. A young place with music ao vivo every night (Thaïs knows all the musicians in the town!) and with an ambience that will enable us to attract both students and artists. If it goes as planned we're even thinking of having poetry evenings and exhibitions of paintings. Brilliant, don't you think?

To set ourselves up in the place I've found we need precisely the sum I'm asking, half for the first month's rent, the rest for tables, chairs, drinks, etc. Given the enthusiastic response of everyone we've told about it, after that the bar will pay its way, no problem. What's more, I read the tarot pack three times and three times in a row the Chariot turned up. So there you are!

I can already hear you grumbling that it'll affect my studies . . . Don't worry, I've got into the second year of ethnology and since we'll take turns at the bar, Thaïs and I, I'll have all the time I need for classes when the new semester starts.

I had a letter from Mama saying she was off to the Pantanal to search for some fossil or other. I'm really envious of her!

I hope you're better and that you're managing all right—you know what I mean. I'll try to come over and see you some time, promise!

How's Heidegger?

Love and kisses, beijo, beijo, beijo!

Moéma

All the visible space outside the French window in the living room was filled by the royal-blue night, which had a strong smell of ozone and jasmine. Sitting, naked, on the large straw mat that covered the floor, Moéma's teeth chattered as she reread her letter. Sudden shivers ran down her spine; she was sweating copiously. She'd have to do something about that pretty quick. She put the letter in an envelope, stuck on a stamp then wrote her father's address, forcing herself not to tremble. Going back into the bedroom, she stopped on the threshold a moment to look at Thaïs stretched out, naked as well, on the sheets. Her eyes were closed and her full figure was prey to the same icy waves that were making Moéma's own skin contract from time to time. Through the Persian blinds, the moon cast soothing stripes over her body.

Moéma sat down on the edge of the bed; she ran her fingers through the girl's thick hair.

"Have you done it?" Thaïs asked, opening her eyes.

"Yes, that's it. I'm sure he'll send me the dosh. After all, he never refuses me anything."

"I'm speeding a bit, you know."

"Me too, but I'll sort it out."

Moéma turned to the bedside table and took out the little ebony box containing the coke. With a strip of cardboard she took out a pinch of powder and poured it into a soup spoon; *the* spoon with the twisted handle that kept it perfectly horizontal. Deciding the quantity was too great, she put some of it back in the box before mixing the rest with a little water from a dropper.

"You'll be careful, yes?" Thaïs whispered, watching her.

"Don't worry, I've no desire to die, even less to kill you," Moéma replied, heating the contents of the spoon over a lighter. "I'm not as crazy as I seem."

After having drawn up the mixture, Moéma gave several taps to the fine syringe they had used four hours ago, gently pressed the plunger, checking that there were no air bubbles left, then picked up the delicate dressing-gown belt lying on the floor.

"Off we go, sweetheart."

Thaïs sat up and held out her chubby arm. Moéma wrapped the belt twice around her biceps, then pulled it tight until a vein swelled up in the crook of her arm.

"Clench your fist," she said, leaving Thaïs herself to keep the tourniquet tight. She soaked a piece of cotton wool in perfume then rubbed it over her arm. Holding her breath in an attempt to curb her trembling, she cautiously brought the needle up to the chosen vein.

"How lucky you are to have such large veins; with me it's always a big production . . ."

Thaïs closed her eyes. She couldn't stand the sight of the last part of these preparations, the moment when Moéma drew out the plunger a little: a tiny jet of black blood spurted into the syringe, as if life itself, escaping from her body, were spreading out in there in thin, deadly curls. The first time, two months ago, she had almost fainted.

"Now, unclench your fist slowly," said Moéma, starting the injection. When she'd half emptied the syringe, she pulled the needle out and bent Thaïs' arm over on a wad of cotton wool.

"Oh my God! Oh, the shit, my God, the white shit!" the girl repeated, slumping down on her back.

"Are you OK, Thaïs? Say something! Thaïs?!"

"It's OK . . . Don't worry . . . Come and join me, quick," she said, articulating with difficulty.

Reassured, Moéma put the belt around her left arm, holding it in place with her teeth. Now her hand was trembling uncontrollably. Clenching her fist as tight as she could, she pricked herself several times without managing to find a vein in the bluish network scarcely visible under her skin. In desperation, she ended up sticking the needle in a blood-filled bulge in her wrist.

Even before injecting the rest of the syringe, she had a strong taste of ether and perfume in her mouth; and as the aperture on the world gradually closed, she felt herself cut off from the living, cast back into the darkness of her own being. A metallic rumbling swelled up abruptly inside her head, a kind of continuing echo, muffled, such as you hear during a dive when your cylinder hits the rusty metal of an old ship. And along with this shipwreck's wail came fear. A terrible fear of dying, of not being able to turn back. But right at the bottom of this panic was a couldn't-care-less attitude to death, a sort of defiance that was almost clear-headed, despairing.

Sensing that she was coming close to the very mystery of existence, she followed the progressive disappearance of everything that was not of the body, of her body and her own will to merge with another body eager for sensual pleasure, with all the bodies present in the world.

Moéma felt Thaïs' hand on her chest, pulling her down. She stretched out, immediately concentrating on the exquisitely voluptuous enjoyment the contact gave her. Thaïs bit her on the lip, at the same time stroking her clitoris and rubbing her own genitals against her thigh. Life exploded in all its restored beauty; it had a lovely smell of Givenchy.

FAVELA DE PIRAMBÚ: *L'aleijadinho*

A nasty play on words between *aleijado* (handicapped) and *alijado* (reduced) meant that he was called "Reduced Nelson" or, more often, simply "Reduced." He was a boy of about fifteen, perhaps older, who seemed to have the gift of ubiquity. Wherever you went in the streets of Fortaleza you always ended up seeing him between cars, in the middle of the road, begging for a few cruzeiros. Down as far as the groin he was a complete and, if anything, attractive boy with his shoulder-length hair, his big brown eyes and the beginnings of a mustache; he was only "reduced" in his lower limbs: with the bones of his two legs fused and his feet just stumps, he moved around like an animal, using his arms. Always dressed the same in a shapeless loincloth, like someone being crucified, rather than shorts, and a striped football shirt that he rolled up above his breasts, in the fashion of the *Nordeste,* he popped up everywhere, dragging himself along quite nimbly through the dust of the streets. Forced by his disability to perform ungainly acrobatics, from a distance he looked like a velvet crab or, to be more precise, a robber crab.

Since the heat in the town forced people to drive with their windows open, he would take up position at the main crossroads and wait for the lights to turn red before launching his attack on the vehicles. Suddenly two callused hands would grasp the bottom of the window, then a head with a fearsome look would appear while repulsively crooked limbs thumped the windscreen or threatened to invade the interior of the car. "Have pity, for the love of God, have pity!" the *aleijadinho* would cry, in menacing tones that sent shivers down your spine. Springing up from the depths of the earth, this apparition almost always produced the desired effect: the drivers would fumble with their wallets or rummage around nervously in the jumble of the side pockets to get rid of the nightmare as quickly as possible. And since his hands were occupied, Nelson would order them to place the grimy banknote they'd managed to unearth in his mouth. Then he would slip down onto the road and transfer the money to his trunks after having given it a quick glance.

"God bless you," he would say between his teeth as the car was about to set off again; and such was the scorn he put into the words that it sounded like "Go to the devil."

He filled women drivers with terror. But when you got to know him a bit and handed him his alms even before he had to beg, saving him having to climb up onto your car, he would thank you with a smile that was worth any number of blessings.

On bad days he would go thieving rather than fight with the vultures at the municipal rubbish dump for a piece of rotten fruit or a bone to gnaw. Usually he only stole things he could eat and that was a real torment for him because of his great fear of the savage violence of the police. The last time he'd been caught, for the theft of three bananas, the pigs had humiliated him until he couldn't take any more, calling him a half-pint; they'd forced him to take off all his clothes, supposedly to search him, in reality to mock his atrophied organs even more cruelly and to tell him again and again that Brazil ought to be purged of such unnatural monsters. Then they locked him up for the night in a cell with a *cascavel*, one of the most poisonous snakes of the region, in order to cause "a regrettable accident." By some miracle the serpent had left him in peace but Nelson had spent terrified hours sobbing and vomiting until he fainted. Even now the *cascavel* still haunted his nights. Fortunately Zé, "the truck driver," had come in the morning to bail him out, so he had escaped the worst.

Nelson's admiration and gratitude for this odd fellow knew no bounds. Zé, always in a jovial mood, had befriended him and came to the *favela* to see him from time to time. He always had some new story to tell and even took the *aleijadinho* in his truck for trips to the seaside. Not only was Zé—Uncle Zé as he called him—tall and strong and drove around the world in his huge, brightly colored truck, he possessed what in Nelson's eyes was a genuine treasure: Lampião's nephew's car! It was a white Willis that Zé had shown him one day. It didn't go anymore, but he looked after it carefully; Nelson had never been so happy as the day he had been allowed to sit inside it. Famous spoils of war! Virgulino Ferreira da Silva, alias Lampião, who had become an outlaw after his father was killed by the police and spent almost twenty years leading them by the nose, had taken it from Antônio Gurgel, a rich landowner who had ventured into the Sertão. Lampião had attacked it on horseback with his band as if it were an ordinary stagecoach and Gurgel had only come out of it alive by paying a large ransom. Nelson knew all the history of the *cangaço* and of the men who were called *cangaceiros* because they carried their rifles across their spine, the way harnessed oxen bore the *cangalho,* the yoke. They had thrown off the yoke of oppression to live the life of free men in the Sertão, and if their Winchesters weighed heavy on their shoulders, at least it was in a good cause, the cause of justice. Fascinated, like all the boys in the *Nordeste,* by the figure of Lampião, Nelson had done everything he could to collect material about this Robin Hood of the great estates. The sheet-metal and plywood walls of his lair in the *favela* of Pirambú were papered with numerous photos cut out from *Manchete* or *Veja.* They showed Lampião at all ages and in all aspects of his career, also his companion in his adventures, Maria Bonita, and his principal lieutenants: Chico Pereira, Antônio Porcino, José Saturnino, Jararaca . . . all of whose exploits Nelson knew by heart, holy martyrs whom he often called upon for protection.

Zé having promised he would come by that evening, Nelson had gone back to the *favela* a little earlier than usual. He'd bought a litre of *cachaça* from Terra e Mar and filled the two little paraffin lamps he'd made out of old tin cans. Performing contortions, he had even managed to level out the sand in his room, after having cleared away all his cigarette butts. Now, as he waited for Uncle Zé, he looked at his father gleaming in the half-light. Oh, no one could say that he neglected him: the steel bar had been cleaned as if it were a silver candlestick; oiled and rubbed day after day, it reflected the flame of the night-light on it that he kept lit all the time.

Like many men from the *Nordeste*, his father used to work in a steelworks of the Minas Geraís. Every evening he would tell him about the hell of the blast furnaces, of the dangers the workers were exposed to because of the rapacity of the owner, Colonel José Moreira de Rocha. One day he didn't come home. At nightfall a fat oaf in a suit and two foremen had come to see him in the shack, unfit for human habitation, that the boss generously granted each of his employees. They talked of an accident, describing in detail how his father, his own father, had fallen into a vat of molten metal. There was nothing left of him apart from this symbolic piece of rail, which they had insisted on bringing with them. There were sure to be a few atoms of his father spread through it, they said; it weighed 143 pounds, exactly the same as his father, so it could be given a church funeral. And for good measure they added that, since he no longer had any claim on the house, he was being asked to quit the property.

Nelson was ten years old. His mother had died when he was born and having no other family, he found himself on the street at a moment's notice. Through all his trials and tribulations he had held on to the piece of rail and lavished care on it as his most precious possession.

The Colonel was a bastard, a son of a whore eaten away by the pox.

"Don't you worry, Daddy," Nelson murmured, turning to the steel bar, "I'll get him, you can be sure of that; sooner or later that swine will feel the vengeance of the *cangaço*.

CHAPTER 2

Which takes us to the terrible war that lasted for thirty years
and turned the kingdoms of Europe upside down; and in
which Athanasius displays rare courage on the occasion of a
misadventure that could have ended very badly

ATHANASIUS HAD JUST started his
study of physics when war came to Paderborn. When, on
January 6, 1622, Johann Copper gave his flock the order to flee,
it was almost too late: the rabble had already surrounded the
buildings. Relying solely on his courage & his faith in Our Lord,
the principal of the college went out to meet the mercenaries
& urge them to show mercy. They flung a flaming torch in his
face. He managed to avoid it but the Lutheran fiends threw
themselves on the holy man; he was given a thorough thrashing,
insulted & humiliated before being tied up like an animal &
dragged off to prison. He was fortunate not to be taken straight
to the scaffold, on which many other Catholics no more culpable
than he ended their days.

While this was going on & to obey the orders of their superior, the eighty Jesuit pupils—not including five priests who decided to stay—left the college in small groups disguised as ordinary men. Fifteen of them were captured & taken to join the principal in prison. Accompanied by another student, Athanasius & Friedrich managed to leave the town with no problem.

On February 7, 1622 they reached the banks of the Rhine, in the vicinity of Düsseldorf. The river had frozen over only recently but the locals indicated a section where the ice was thicker & it was possible to cross—which was a brazen lie dictated solely by the desire to save money! The custom was to pay some poor devil every year to cross the river & thus test the ice. The three strangers were a godsend for the country folk & it was solely to save a few coppers that these miserly peasants showed no mercy & lied to then. In those times of misery & hardship men's lives, & *a fortiori* the lives of strangers who seemed to be vile deserters, were not worth a cabbage stalk. The skinflints showed them a path by which, they claimed, everyone went across without mishap.

With the hotheadedness of youth & his experience of skating, Kircher took the lead & went on, twenty paces ahead of the other two, to make sure they at least would be safe. The weather was worsening rapidly. Masses of fog drifting down from the north were threatening to hide the shore. Athanasius hurried on. When he reached the middle of the river, he saw to his horror that the ice was melting there. He immediately turned around in order to rejoin his companions & warn them of the danger, but with an ominous cracking noise the ice split between him & his friends with the result that the part he was standing on started to drift on open water. Carried along by the current, shouting himself hoarse on his ice floe, Athanasius disappeared in the mist.

Fearing for his life, the young man threw himself wholeheartedly into prayer. After sweeping perilously downstream, by a happy chance the ice-raft came close to the frozen part of the river & Kircher nimbly jumped onto it &, without wasting a moment, set off for dry land & the completion of the crossing. However, at about twenty cubits from the bank, while he was still thanking Our Lord for letting him escape from such a dangerous situation, & fairly comfortably too, the ice split in front of him again. Blue with cold, covered in bruises from his repeated falls, Athanasius did not hesitate for one second but threw himself into the icy water & after a few strokes, which called on all his experience as a swimmer, managed to pull himself up onto the bank, more dead than alive.

Soaking wet, teeth chattering, he set off for the town of Neuss where there was a Jesuit college. After three hours of agony, he rang the bell of the college & collapsed in the porter's arms. When he came to, he rejoiced to see his travelling companions, who had managed to cross the river at another place &, having assumed he had died, now wept tears of joy to see him safe & sound.

After three days of well-deserved rest they were fit enough again to reach Cologne without a stop. It was in that city that Von Spee had been ordained & on his advice Athanasius decided to abandon his façade of humility: even though they might offend some people's susceptibilities, his knowledge & skill at reasoning were too important to be concealed. In a few months Athanasius completed his degree in philosophy with distinction, all the while continuing to study physics, languages & mathematics on his own. Impressed by his exceptional abilities, his teachers decided to send him to the college at Ingolstadt in Bavaria to complete his studies of the humanities & to teach

Ancient Greek. In obedience to his superiors, Athanasius left
Cologne toward the end of 1622, but he was sick at heart: he was
leaving Friedrich von Spee behind & with him all the joy of his
youth & of learning. They were never to see each other again.

Kircher spent three years improving his knowledge in
numerous disciplines. Under the direction of Christoph
Schreiner, whose reputation is firmly established, he studied
astronomy & mathematics without respite & was soon as
outstanding in them as his master. He achieved the same in
physiology, in alchemy & in many other subjects, at the same
time deepening his knowledge of languages. At the age of
twenty-three Kircher easily outshone all his colleagues, who
agreed that he had a remarkable gift of memory in addition to
an inventive mind & extraordinary mechanical skills.

At that time Ingolstadt was under the jurisdiction of Johann
Schweickhardt, Archbishop of Mainz and Elector of the Holy
Roman Empire. Now it so happened that a delegation sent by
His Grace was announced for the beginning of March. Such
visits were not at all frequent and the town received the visitors
with great pomp & ceremony.

The Jesuits, & Kircher in particular, were called upon
to contribute to the festivities. Athanasius devised several
spectacular events of his own invention that were much admired
by the bishop's delegates. To the amazement of the audience, he
created optical illusions in midair, projecting fantastic shapes
onto the trees in the park & the clouds—chimeras, sphinxes &
dragons; he presented distorting mirrors that showed you upside
down, aged or rejuvenated by several years, & concluded with
a lavish fireworks display in which the rockets, as they burst,
formed the imperial eagle & other emblematic animals. Accused
of black magic by some simple or jealous people, Kircher had to
demonstrate the mesoptic, catoptric & parastatic instruments

that he had used to create the spectacle & show the legates how they worked; they were all instruments of his own invention, which he later described in detail in his *Mundus Subterraneus* & his *Ars Magna Lucis & Umbrae*. The ambassadors were so delighted with the entertainment that they insisted the young prodigy stay with them until they left.

Charmed by the reports of his envoys, Johann Schweickhardt urged Kircher to come & see him without delay. Athanasius therefore went to see the old man in Aschaffenburg & made an excellent impression on him. Immediately taken into his service, he spent a large part of his time inventing & constructing numerous curious machines to amuse the archbishop during his leisure moments. Thus he made a speaking, moving statue, which appeared to be alive, &, among other marvels, explained the miraculous properties of the lodestone, showing how it could be used to cure nervous illnesses or transmit thoughts over a distance. At the request of Johann Schweickhardt he started to write down his reflections on magnetism, which a few years later were the subject of his first book, the *Ars Magnesia*.

The archbishop also charged Kircher with making a topographical survey of certain parts of the principality. He took only three months to complete it & was preparing to extend the task when his patron was suddenly called to meet his Maker.

At the end of 1625 Kircher returned to Mainz to follow a course in theology there. He studied the sacred texts rigorously & assiduously, but not without continuing his scientific work. Having bought one of the first telescopes in circulation, he spent a large part of his nights contemplating the stars. One morning he shut himself away in his cell to observe the sun. Following the instructions of Schreiner & Galileo, he had placed his telescope against a hole made in the shutter of his window and put a sheet of white vellum under the concave glass so as to be able to see the image of the sun clearly on that piece of paper. As he watched the stormy sea of flames on the paper, he noticed numerous spots contrasting with it, appearing then disappearing. The sight filled him with amazement & from that day on astronomy became one of his main fields of study.

One morning in May 1628 he was scanning the shelves of the college library when he came across Mercati's book about the obelisks erected by Pope Sixtus V. His curiosity was immediately aroused & he started to speculate on the meaning of the numerous hieroglyphs reproduced in the illustrations to the volume. Initially he took them for recent ornamentation, but on reading the book he soon learned that these figures or inscriptions had been carved on Egyptian obelisks since time immemorial & that no one had ever been able to decipher them. Put in his way by Divine Providence, this enigma was to demand twenty years of uninterrupted effort before finally coming to a happy resolution.

In December 1629, at the end of the last year of his course, Kircher was sent to Würzburg to teach mathematics, ethics & Biblical languages. It was at that college, where I was starting my noviciate, that I met him for the first time.

Sitting in our classroom, my fellow students and I were waiting for our new mathematics teacher, a certain Father Kircher, who had been greatly praised, but of whom we were already making fun, biased against him because of his excessively high reputation. I remember that I was not the last to snigger at him, outdoing the others in ironic remarks about this 'Father Churcher' coming down from the heavens with his extravaganzas. However, when he came in & ascended the rostrum silence fell without him having to utter a single word. Father Athanasius was twenty-seven & if ever a face showed the harmony that arouses immediate attachment, as if by sympathy or magnetic attraction, then it was his: a noble and intelligent forehead, a straight nose such as you can see on the David of Michelangelo Buonarotti, a finely delineated mouth with red lips & the faintest downy shadow of an incipient beard—which he kept trimmed very short throughout his life—&, below thick, almost horizontal eyebrows, big, deep-set black eyes with the fascinating sparkle of an inquiring mind, always ready for repartee or debate.

He introduced himself to us in Latin worthy of Cicero & began a lesson the least details of which remain imprinted on my memory. The subject of that lesson was to work out how many grains of sand the Earth contained, supposing that was what it was made of. Kircher walked along the rows of desks, giving each of us a pinch of sand that he took out of the pocket of his cassock & having done that told us to draw a line in our exercise books a twelfth of an inch long. Then he instructed us to place as many grains of sand side by side on the line as it would take: we were amazed to see that each time the line contained exactly 30 grains of sand. Following on from this experiment, which he assured us could be repeated with all the grains of sand that might be found throughout the world, he proceeded with his demonstration. If we imagined a sphere a twelfth of an inch in diameter, it would contain 27,000 grains of sand; a sphere one inch in diameter would contain 46,656,000, one a foot in diameter 80,621,568,000, one a league in diameter 272,097,792,000,000,000,000, hence if the whole Earth consisted of grains of sand it would contain 3,271,512,503,499,876,784,3 72,652,141,247,182 & 0.56 for it is 2,290 leagues in diameter & contains 12,023,296,769 & 0.3 spheres a league in diameter . . .

One can easily imagine our amazement at such knowledge & above all at the ease with which he dispensed it. From that day on my admiration & respect for Father Kircher knew no bounds & nothing has happened since then to lessen them. I ceaselessly sought out his company & he favored me, if not with his friendship, then at least with his generous patronage. His favor brought me the jealousy of my comrades & various annoyances, which are not relevant here but which I am happy to forgive in view of the immense honor that was granted me.

Two happy years passed in this way. Kircher enjoyed Würzburg & tirelessly continued with his own work alongside his duties as a teacher. Through his correspondence with the greatest names of the time & the missionaries of the Society scattered over the globe, he was kept informed of all the new developments in the sciences. And protected as we were in a profoundly Catholic kingdom, the war raging between Reformers & the partisans of the Counter-Reformation seemed a long way away, although we regularly heard the most terrible reports.

It looked as if everything was going to continue in studious tranquillity when Athanasius Kircher had a strange experience: one stormy night, suddenly wakening with a start at an unusual noise, he saw a crimson light at his window. Jumping out of bed, he opened the skylight to see what was happening. To his great surprise he saw that the college courtyard was full of armed men drawn up in ranks! Horrified, he ran to his neighbor's cell, but found him so fast asleep he could not wake him & it was the same with all the other Jesuits he tried to warn. Worried that he was suffering from hallucinations, he came to get me and took me to a place overlooking the courtyard. The armed men had disappeared.

During the following two weeks Gustavus Adolphus, King of Sweden, joined the war on the side of the Reformers. Reverses for the Catholic side came thick & fast, & after the battle of

Breitenfeld & his victory over Tilly, the Swedish army entered
Franconia: we received news that the fiends were marching on
Würzburg! Kircher's worst fears were being realized . . . We
only had time to gather a few belongings together & fly.
Würzburg having no garrison, no reserves, no help of any kind,
the college dispersed within twenty-four hours. The enemy was
approaching & it was said that the Swedes showed no mercy
toward Jesuits. We were caught up in unspeakable chaos; we
had to flee to Mainz & on October 14, 1631 we set off with little
more than what we stood up in. My master had to leave behind
the manuscript of his *Institutiones Mathematicæ*, the fruit of
several years' work & a loss it took him several months to get
over.

ALCÂNTARA: *An intelligent piece of ass,*
a very intelligent piece of ass!

Whenever Eléazard felt dazed from having spent too long sitting
at his computer, he would put his machine into sleep mode, watch
the constellations moving across the star-studded night on the
screen for a moment, then go and sit down in front of the large
mirror in the living room. There he would practice manipulat-
ing the ping-pong balls with which his pockets were now filled.
There was nothing that could empty his mind so well as repeating
the precise movements governing the appearance and disappearance of the objects. He would watch the balls emerge between
his fingers, or multiply, correcting the positioning of his hands,
trying his utmost to make their dexterity more automatic. This
fad had started only a few months ago, the day when he had admired the astonishing dexterity of a juggler in an alleyway in São
Luís: a grubby, skinny little *matuto* with a mouth devoid of teeth,

but who was sticking an unlikely number of very long nails up his nose. More than the act itself, Eléazard had admired the man's perfect control over his body and the almost mathematical elegance he gave his movements. Spurred on by a feeling of urgency, he had scoured all the bookshops in the town to buy an introductory manual on these skills. He had been disappointed at how poor the books on that subject were. Most of those devoted to conjuring went no further than to reveal the secrets of a few ploys that might fool children. What he wanted to learn was how to be able to produce pigeons out of hats or pull miles of scarves out of someone's ear, tricks that bordered on the miraculous. Having exhausted all the possibilities, he wrote off to France for a book that would meet his demands.

In reply to his letter, Malbois had sent him a fine copy of the only book ever written by Robert-Houdin plus a *Fundamental Techniques for Conjurers*, which had so many illustrations of hands and palming maneuvers that it looked like a manual for the language of the deaf and dumb. The two authors emphasized that the only way to achieve true mastery was by a long period of exercises to make the fingers supple and their movements automatic. Eléazard, therefore, was training himself according to these principles, repeating conscientiously every little exercise of a system that, for him, was quite close to martial arts.

He was annoyed by Moéma's letter. Not that the money she was asking for was a problem—he spent hardly anything on himself— but he objected to his daughter's casual attitude. To write just when she wanted something from him was OK, even if it hurt him; after all, it was a father's function to help a child he'd been selfish enough to bring into the world. But for a bar! She who wasn't even able to manage a simple student's budget! He would have preferred it if Moéma wheedled money out of him to go off on a trip or to buy new clothes. Why not? That was the way of things, especially at her age, but every time she had to invent some new project even more unreasonable than the previous one. The worst thing was that she seemed to believe in her idea of a bar as firmly as she had been enthusiastic, two months ago, about the career of a model that was "beckoning her" and of which he had heard nothing since. Three thousand dollars for a portfolio and incidental expenses . . . Just a kid, really! he thought with a smile, suddenly touched by her ingenuousness. Or perhaps it's me crossing the threshold: once you start noticing the follies of youth, whether to be offended by them or simply to forgive them, it means you're already old. So bear with her. He'd sent the check that morning and he would continue to give in to his daughter's whims until she found her vocation. It was the only way of ensuring she never had the feeling she'd missed out on something because of others or lack of money, of allowing her at some point to develop her own sense of responsibility in the course of her life. Was that not the way one *became*?

At this point in his disenchanted reflections he was overcome with hunger. He felt like seeing, talking to people, so he decided to go out for dinner. Soledade was annoyed when he told her. She'd already prepared his evening meal and immediately made a face. Eléazard tried to cheer her up, but to no effect; her only response was a scornful pout before flouncing out of the kitchen. Glancing at the stove, he saw an omelette swimming in oil; she had gone to the trouble of making a dish that Raffanel had taught her. Not a great teacher, he thought, as he surveyed the contents of the frying pan, unless it's just that she's not up to it. He shrugged his shoulders helplessly.

Evening was falling over Alcântara, a sort of disturbing grayness, thicker and blacker than the overcast sky that had darkened the afternoon. There was a threat of rain for the night. Eléazard hurried on, taking care to avoid the zebu droppings that booby-trapped the poorly paved alleyways in places. He turned left, behind Sâo

Matías church, and was soon in the *Rua da Amargura*, the street of sorrow, so called because Viscount Antônio de Albuquerque, the former owner of the palace he was walking past, had been in the habit of making his slaves lie down in the mud so that his wife and daughters could cross with dry feet when going to mass on Sundays. Moth-eaten fabric hung in the wide windows, which destructive weeds were doing their best to take apart stone by stone; there were only scattered and cracked fragments left of the elegant blue-and-white *azulejos* that used to decorate one of the most beautiful residences in the town. Let the leprosy of time finish its work, Eléazard thought, let it peel off the façade of this obscene testimony to the barbarity of man to the very last tile.

When he reached the *Rua Silva Maia*, he glanced at the Church of the Rosário. It stood out in its white and green against the leaden sky. Placed there, right in the middle of a strip of ground reclaimed from the forest—but invaded by weeds because it hadn't been paved—it seemed to be trying to suck up all the humidity of the soil, as could be seen from the spreading patches of red ochre that soiled the lower half of the façade. Shutters closed, a blind pediment, it oozed fear and neglect. Behind it the fur coat of the mango trees swayed heavily, disturbed by audible quivering that shook the foliage from one end to the other.

Eléazard pushed open the door of the Caravela Hotel—*Clean and comfortable. Seven well-appointed rooms*—making the lengths of bamboo hanging from the ceiling clatter against each other. A young creole immediately came to greet him, arms stretched out toward him, his face radiant with a broad, happy smile.

"Lazardinho! What a lovely surprise . . . *Tudo bem?*"

"*Tudo bom.*"

Eléazard felt real enjoyment offering these ritual words of welcome; afterward, as if soothed by their magic, life immediately seemed more attractive.

"So how's things?" Alfredo asked after having given him a friendly embrace. "If you want to stay and eat I've got some fresh prawns. I went to get them from the boat myself."

"Prawns are OK . . ."

"Take a seat. I'll tell Socorró."

Eléazard went into the interior courtyard of the hotel. A few tables spread around under the vast roof of the veranda constituted the restaurant. Three immense banana trees and an unknown bush on the patio partly concealed the stairs to the rooms. A naked bulb was already lit, casting a yellow glow over the bare courtyard.

Once he had sat down, Eléazard checked the brief typed menu lying on the table; unchanged for months, it was very simple:

> *Filé de pescada, Camarão empanado,*
> *Peixadas, Tortas, Saladas.*
> *Preço p/pessoa: O melhor possível*
> FAVOR FAZER RESERVA

Alfredo's whole charm was contained in the basic level of catering. Three dishes with fish or prawns, tarts and salads. Even the plural was a harmless exaggeration since apart from exceptional cases *booking advised!* there was nothing but the *plat du jour*, that is, what Alfredo himself and his young wife were having. As for the prices—*The best*, the cheapest *possible*—they simply depended on inflation (300 percent per year) and what Alfredo felt about the customer.

After a meager inheritance had left them with this dilapidated house, Alfredo and Eunice had decided to transform it into a hotel. They were motivated not so much by the idea of making a fortune, though that was an illusion they had harbored during the first euphoric days, than by the love of a simple way of life and a desire to bring back some life to Alcântara. Proponents of an *alternative* solution—the word came to their lips frequently as a panacea for *bourgeois self-interest* and *American imperialism's hold on the planet*—they managed to get by in their haven of peace and humanity. During the season a few tourists, whose passion for colonial architecture was such that they forgot the time of the last boat, would end up in their hotel, the only one in Alcântara, and that brought in enough to allow Eunice and Alfredo to struggle through with the restaurant for the rest of the year. Out of the goodness of their hearts rather than necessity, this likeable couple employed old Socorró as cook and to help do the rooms.

Alfredo reappeared carrying two glasses and two large bottles of beer. "Ice-cold! Just the way you like it," he said, joining him at the table. He cautiously filled the glasses then raised his to Eléazard:

"*Saúde.*"

"*Santé,*" Eléazard replied, clinking glasses with him.

"By the way, have you heard the news? We've let a room!"

It was remarkable enough, right in the middle of the rainy season, for Eléazard to show his surprise.

"It's true, I swear it is," Alfredo assured him. "An Italian woman. She's a journalist like you, and . . ."

"I'm not a journalist," Eléazard insisted, "I'm a correspondent. It's not the same thing." To his mind, at least, it was different, but he was annoyed with himself for instinctively putting on this air and immediately qualified it. "Although both are a similar species of vulture . . ."

"You're too hard on yourself," Alfredo went on, "and on your profession. Without you, without journalists, who would know what's going on here? Anyway, she's called Loredana, and she's quite a girl, I can assure you. If I wasn't married . . . phew." This was accompanied by a wink and a burst of finger-clicking.

"You'll have to teach me how you do that one day."

"You just have to get the knack," Alfredo replied. "Look: you let your hand go quite limp—that's the secret—then shake it as if you wanted to get rid of it. Your fingers knock against each other and that's what makes the noise of castanets."

As Alfredo looked on with an amused air, Eléazard tried to imitate him without success. He admitted defeat when Eunice appeared with a tray.

"Good evening, Lazardinho," she said, putting a plate of breaded prawns on the table. She leaned down and gave him a friendly embrace on both cheeks. "It's ages since we saw you, you rascal."

"Two weeks," said Eléazard in his defense, "not even that, twelve days, to be precise."

"Love doesn't count the days. But you're forgiven. Now tell me what you think of these little beauties," she said, pointing at the prawns.

"Succulent, as usual," said Eléazard, his mouth full.

"Good. I'll let you get on with it."

"Me too," said Alfredo, getting up at a brief sign from his wife.

"No, no, you stay. Go on, keep me company. Eunice, bring us another plate of prawns, please, and a bottle of white wine."

Alfredo sat down again with an evident air of satisfaction and he didn't need to be asked twice when Eléazard offered to share his prawns. Peeled and fried in breadcrumbs with just the tail fin sticking out, you could use your fingers to dip them in a kind of very spicy red mayonnaise then pop them in your mouth. They were delicious.

At Alfredo's instigation the conversation soon came around to the government project of setting up a rocket-launching site somewhere in the surrounding forest. So far the information they had was sketchy, gleaned with difficulty by a Communist newspaper in São Luís, *Defense of Maranhão*, but it looked as if Brazil was preparing to sacrifice the Alcântara peninsula to the *higher interests of the nation*, as the newspaper editorial put it with a forest of ironic quotation marks.

"Rockets! I ask you!" Alfredo said in disgust. "People are starving to death in the streets, the national debt's strangling the country to such an extent that we're only working for the bloodsuckers of the IMF—and they want to send rockets into space! It's the Americans again. But we'll fight, you can be sure of that. If not, it's the end of Alcântara . . ."

Eléazard loved the ease with which Alfredo fell into a rebellious attitude. He appreciated it in his daughter as well, although secretly and in a more selective way, without managing to find the core of innocence that would have allowed him to embrace their optimism. True, he shared the sense of the absurdity of the project that had brought a quiver to the Brazilian's voice, he approved of his anger and his determination, but not for one moment did he feel able to believe in the possibility of holding up the course of events in any way. Not that he had become fatalistic, at least not in his own eyes, nor reactionary or conservative; he had simply lost the hope that alone can move mountains, or at least let you believe it's worth trying. Even if he didn't see it as such, his outward resignation worried him. But how can we call into question our feeling of being clear-sighted when, unfortunately, we are so taken with it? Humanity, he believed, was an indifferent species and anyone unfortunate enough to have sensed that obvious fact can do nothing about the innumerable mass of those who provide the evidence. Alfredo wasn't a friend and would probably never become one, with the result that Eléazard kept to himself that extreme and contagious despair that must only—can only—be acknowledged within the protective sanctuary of friendship.

To get back to the "rockets," Alfredo didn't know whether they were talking about strategic missiles or a civilian base for launching satellites. Not that it mattered much for in either case the forest would be destroyed, the inhabitants expelled from their homes, the ecosystem endangered; this vague project had provided a focus for all his disapproval, as if it were an imminent threat to the world, and that, in its very excessiveness, was admirable.

The veranda bulb suddenly started to flicker and crackle. "The storm won't be long coming," Alfredo said. "I'd better go and find some candles."

STRETCHED OUT ON her bed in bra and panties, Loredana watched the unsettling fluctuations of the electric light on the ceiling medallion. She found its slow and constantly postponed death fascinating. In the humid, stifling atmosphere of the room, her hair was releasing the water of her body drop by drop. She wondered how long it would take before she liquefied completely, leaving nothing below the death rattle of the bulb but a large dark patch on the sheets.

Tormented by an increasing irritation in her crotch, she got off the bed and undressed. As they fell to the floor, her underclothes almost captured a large, honey-colored cockroach, which scuttled behind the skirting board. The folds in her groin were smarting in a very unpleasant way. One foot on the washbasin, she rinsed herself down with her facecloth, taking great care and grimacing with pain, before smearing cream over her raw skin. Standing in front of the mirror, she spent a long time fondling her breasts while she waited for the burning sensation, which was forcing her to maintain that uncomfortable posture, to subside. God knows how long she would have to spend moldering away here . . . Moldering, that was the word, she thought, brooding

over the fungal infection that was starting. And could she trust
her go-between? Nothing was less certain. The guy had seemed
odd to her, those sidelong glances he'd been giving her all the time
she'd been negotiating with him. That he'd wanted to be paid in
advance was understandable, but what she found difficult to accept was the fact that he'd revealed so little of the process that
was under way, simply making her wait in this hotel. Two to three
weeks, he'd said, perhaps a bit longer, but it would all be done by
the end of the month. She might as well go and have something
to eat, it would take her mind off things. Having failed to find any
clean underwear in her suitcase, with sigh of exasperation she put
on a skirt and T-shirt over her bare skin.

When she appeared on the veranda, emerging from the gloom,
Alfredo broke off. "There she is," he whispered. "I'll be back in a
minute . . ."

Eléazard watched him dash over to the Italian woman who
had had such an effect on him. She must be about thirty-five or
forty, to go by certain signs that stopped him putting her age at
less, but without showing the beginnings of biological decline one
would expect at that age. Eléazard's experienced eye noted her
firm breasts, unconfined under her T-shirt, long, slender legs and
a slim, elegant figure. Having said that, she was far from being as
beautiful as that rogue Alfredo had suggested. As far as Eléazard
could tell, her almond-shaped eyes and her mouth were a little too
big for her emaciated face; and her excessively long and pointed
nose added to the lack of proportion.

When, led by Alfredo to a nearby table, she passed him, he
gave her a smile of welcome; her sole response was a slight nod
of the head. Ignoring that, he added a delightfully rounded pair
of buttocks to her assets. "An intelligent piece of ass," he told
himself, slightly annoyed at her indifference, "a *very* intelligent
piece of ass."

In fact Loredana had not been as uninterested in him as he assumed. Of course, it was impossible for her not to notice the presence of a person in the otherwise deserted restaurant. Even before he had become aware of her, she had observed him for several seconds and judged him attractive, that is to say dangerous, which explained her wariness toward him and her reserve when he greeted her with a smile. Not that he was physically especially attractive—in that respect Alfredo came out an easy winner—but she had seen in him, in his look and his way of moving, an unusual "depth of field," an expression that to her mind defined the sum total of criteria that made a human being more or less worthy of interest. Even though she was still susceptible to the physical charm of a person, be it a man or a woman, it came a long way behind a quality of being, or at least its probability, that she believed she was capable of perceiving at first glance.

Sitting two tables away from Eléazard and placed so that she was looking at him in profile, she examined him at leisure: the self-confidence of a forty-year-old, black hair, just a touch of silver at the temples but high on his forehead in a way that promised some nasty surprises in the future; what was most striking was his nose: a hook nose, not really ugly, but one she had never seen before except in Verrocchio's *condottiere* in Venice. Without being exactly delicate, the stranger showed no other of the statue's warlike aspects. He simply seemed sure of himself and cursed with rigorous and redoubtable intelligence. Dante seen by Doré, if she had to choose another artistic resemblance. Moreover, he could even be Italian; Loredana didn't speak Portuguese very well, but well enough to have noticed a strong foreign accent when she heard him talking to Alfredo.

Suddenly sensing the persistent look directed at him, Eléazard turned toward her. He silently raised his glass to her before putting it to his lips. This time Loredana could not repress a smile, but it was to excuse her unrelenting stare.

Alfredo had just served the food when the light went out. After having lit several candles, he came to sit with Eléazard again to open a second bottle. It was the moment the mosquitos chose to emerge. As if there were a link between their appearance and the power-cut, they invaded the veranda in invisible clouds and attacked the diners, irritating Eléazard, who was very sensitive to their bites.

"*Pernilongos*," said Alfredo as he saw him squash one of the insects on his neck. "They don't worry me but I'll go and get an incense coil. They're supposed to drive them away."

Eléazard thanked him. As Alfredo disappeared into the interior of the hotel he glanced at the other table. Better prepared than he, Loredana had taken out a little bottle of insect repellent from somewhere or other and was rubbing it over her arms and ankles. Seeing Eléazard watching her, she offered him the repellent and came over to hand it to him.

"I bought it in Italy," she said, "it's very effective but it smells awful, really awful."

"You can speak Italian," Eléazard said, putting on his best accent, "I'm better at that than at Portuguese. And thanks again, I was being eaten alive."

"You speak Italian?" the woman said in surprised tones. "I never expected that. And then, you're French . . ."

"How do you know that?"

"When a foreigner speaks Italian, even as well as you, I can generally tell. Where did you learn it?"

"In Rome. I lived there for a while. But please sit down," he said, getting up to bring over a chair. "We can chat more easily like that."

"Why not," she replied after the briefest hesitation. "Just a moment while I go and get my glass and plate."

Loredano had not sat down when Alfredo returned with his incense coil. He put it in a small dish and lit it, then quickly sat down with them. Eléazard noted his pleasure at finding the Italian woman sitting at his table. She, on the other hand, seemed annoyed at seeing him joining in the preliminaries of their encounter. For a moment he shared her unexpected vexation: Alfredo had become a nuisance. How human, he thought, to repudiate him in this way; a few words with an unknown woman were enough and a man, for whose company he had expressly come, was suddenly *de trop.* Feeling guilty toward Alfredo, he decided to accept the unfortunate situation.

"Let me introduce myself," he said to Loredana in Brazilian, "Eléazard von Wogau. I think it better to use the language that allows all three of us to join in."

"Of course," Loredana replied, "but you'll have to make allowances for me. I'm Loredana . . . Loredana Rizzuto," she added, grimacing with disgust. "I'm still a bit ashamed of my name, it's so ridiculous . . ."

"But not at all," Alfredo broke in fervently. "I think it's very beautiful, very . . . Italian. I'd prefer to have a name like that instead of 'Portela.' Alfredo Rizzuto, God, doesn't that sound great . . ."

Eunice's mocking voice was suddenly heard. "Alfredo Rizzuto?! What is it you've found now to attract attention to yourself?" She had appeared behind her husband carrying a tray with a slice of tart and a few mangoes. "You must excuse him," she said to Loredana, "but as soon as he sees a pretty girl he can't control himself. And now, *Senhor* Rizzuto, stop drinking and come and help me—there's no more water. The pump must be on the blink again."

"OK, OK," said Alfredo in resigned tones. "Don't worry, I won't be long."

Once Alfredo had left, Eléazard and Loredana burst out laughing; his expression when he heard his wife address him like that had been downright comic.

"A funny lad," Loredana said, reverting to her mother tongue. "Nice, but a bit . . . clingy, no?"

"It depends. He doesn't often have the chance to talk to people from outside, so he takes advantage whenever the occasion arises. And then I think he was a bit intimidated by you. That said, he's far from stupid, you know. He's not what I'd call a friend, but I like him a lot. Will you join me?" he said, lifting up the bottle. "It's slightly fizzy, you could swear it was Chianti . . ."

"With pleasure," Loredana said, holding out her glass. "Oh, Chianti . . . You're going to make me feel nostalgic. But just a minute, let's go back to the beginning, I'm starting to get things mixed up. How come you're French with a name like that?"

"Because my father was German and my mother French, so I have dual nationality. However, since I was born in Paris and studied there for the most part, my German roots don't mean very much."

"And may one ask what you're doing in this hole? Are you on holiday?"

"Not exactly," Eléazard replied, "although my work does leave me plenty of free time. I'm a foreign correspondent, I just have to send a report to my agency from time to time. Since no one's interested in Brazil, it goes straight into the wastepaper basket and I still get paid. I've been living in Alcântara for two years now. You're a journalist too, from what Alfredo told me . . ."

Loredana, somewhat flustered, blushed to her ears. "Yes . . . That is, no. I lied to him. Let's say I'm here on business. But please don't go shouting it from the rooftops. If it came out, that is if some Brazilians got to know, it could work against me."

Loredana was furious with herself. What had got into her? The *shady* lawyer in São Luís (the term she always used for that in-dividual with the manner of a con man) had made her promise to keep it absolutely secret and here she was telling the first per-son she came across. She had caught herself just in time, but if he started asking questions she wouldn't be able to keep up the new lie for long. God, what an idiot, what a damned idiot I am, she told herself, going even brighter red.

The blush made her look like a little girl. Eléazard almost paid her a compliment along those lines, but then changed his mind. Nothing was worse than being in a situation like that.

"What business would that be?" he asked with a touch of irony. "If I'm not being indiscreet, of course."

"Gold, precious stones . . ." (Stop, Loredana, you're mad. You'll never get out of it! a voice screamed inside her head.) 'But I prefer not to talk about it. It's an operation that is—how shall I put it—on the borderline of legality . . . I hope you can understand."

"Don't worry, I won't bother you with that anymore. But take care, the Brazilian police are no angels and I'd be sorry to see you in their hands." He refilled her glass and then his own. Without quite knowing why, he added, "Don't worry. I know it's wrong, but it's the way things are: if I had to choose I'd always be on the side of the smugglers rather than the police."

"That's all right, then. So I'm a *contrabbandiere*, for the mo-ment . . ." Loredana said with a laugh. Then, with a change of tone but without it being clear whether the remark was connected with what had gone before, she said, "You certainly like a drink. It's almost . . ."

Eléazard pursed his lips. "A bit too much perhaps. Is that what you mean? In Brazil the water's more dangerous than wine and since the idea of drinking Coca Cola fills me with horror . . . Joking apart, avoid tap water like the plague; even filtered, it's still dangerous. There's new cases of hepatitis every day."

"I know. I've already been warned."

A flash of lightning followed by a particularly resounding clap of thunder made her start. The echo was still fading in the distance when the downpour hit the patio. It was heavy, violent rain, pattering on the polished leaves of the banana trees with force. The unexpected deluge created a kind of intimacy between Eléazard and Loredana, an enclosure of quiet and togetherness where they were happy to take refuge. The candle dribbled little transparent pearls, the mosquitos sizzled in the flame, bringing a momentary warm tone to the light. To the strong odor rising from the soil, the candle added unusual fragrances of church and of sandalwood.

"Perhaps we could call each other *tu*?" Loredana suggested, after a few minutes of silence enjoying the rain. "I'm fed up with having to make the effort."

"I was going to suggest the same," Eléazard agreed with a smile. Abandoning *Lei*, which suddenly brought them closer together, gave him an almost physical sensation of pleasure. "Your repellent really works," he said, picking a mosquito out of his glass, "I haven't had a bite since that one ages ago. But it's true that it stinks to high heaven. I'm sure it would keep off policemen as well . . ."

Loredana laughed, but it was a slightly forced laugh. She felt guilty at having fooled Eléazard with her silly story of smuggling. The wine was starting to go to her head.

"So what do you do all day when you're not sending your despatches, which don't seem to take up much of your time anyway?"

"I live, I dream . . . I write. Recently I've been spending quite a lot of time at my computer."

"What kind of things do you write?"

"Oh, nothing exciting. I've been commissioned to prepare a seventeenth-century manuscript for publication. The biography of a Jesuit father I've been working on for several years. It's a piece of research rather than writing."

"You're a believer?" she asked, surprised.

"Not at all," Eléazard assured her, "but this guy no one's heard of is an interesting oddity. He wrote about absolutely everything, claiming each time and on each subject to have the sum total of knowledge. That was fairly standard at the time, but what fascinates me about him—and I'm talking about a man who was a contemporary of people like Leibniz, Galileo, Huygens and was much more famous than they—is that he was entirely wrong about everything. He even thought he'd managed to decipher the Egyptian hieroglyphs and everyone believed him until Champollion came along."

"Surely you're not talking about Athanasius Kircher?" Loredana broke in, visibly interested.

Eléazard felt his hair stand on end. "It's not possible . . . It's just *not* possible," he said as he looked at her, dumbfounded. "How come you know that?"

"I haven't told you everything, far from it," said Loredana in a tone of mystery and enjoying her advantage over him. "I've more than one string to my bow."

"Please . . ." said Eléazard, putting on a hangdog expression.

"The simple reason is because I'm a sinologist. Well, not quite; I studied Chinese, a long time ago and I've read one or two books that talked about Kircher because of his work on China. *Cazzo!*" she suddenly exclaimed. "*Puta merda!*"

"What's the matter?" Eléazard asked, taken aback by her swearing.

"Nothing," she said, blushing again. "I've been bitten by a mosquito."

SÃO LUÍS *Swollen lips, the yielding fruit of the mango tree . . .*

"Yes . . . Right . . . I want all of them, every last one . . . It's of vital importance, I hope you understand that. Who? . . . One moment, I'll check."

The telephone wedged between his shoulder and his right ear, in a posture that made his cheek bulge around the receiver, Colonel José Moreira da Rocha unrolled a little more of the cadastral map spread out on his desk.

"What was it you said? . . . 367 . . . N.P. . . . B? N.B. . . . 40 . . . There, I've got it. Why is he refusing to sell? It's nothing but forest and marshes. My God, what a load of cretins! Offer him twice the price and let him go hang. It all has to be sorted out within the fortnight . . . No . . . I said no, Wagner! I don't want any trouble, especially not at the moment. And you know I don't really like those methods anyway . . . How does he earn his living? . . . OK, I'll see to it. Don't you worry, it'll go through even quicker than we thought. By the way, they've moved the meeting up: tomorrow, three o'clock . . . I don't want to know! Be there without fail, I'm counting on you . . . That's right . . . That's right . . . OK, call back if there's the least problem."

As soon as he'd replaced the receiver, the Colonel leaned over to the intercom. "Anita, get me *Frutas do Maranhão*, please. And then I wouldn't mind a little coffee."

"Right, Colonel . . . Who do you want to speak to?"

"Bernardo Carvalho, the CEO . . ."

The Colonel leaned back in his chair to light a long cigarillo, savoring the first puffs with evident enjoyment. Behind him a little colonial-style window, the lower half with small yellow and green panes, cast a slightly acid light on his off-white suit. With his broad, clear forehead and wavy, black Franz Liszt hair hanging down over his ears, Governor Moreira da Rocha's face was like a picture of a politician from the previous century. The impression was confirmed—or perhaps it was the detail that created it—by the presence of a pair of huge white side-whiskers encroaching on his cheeks to the corners of his mouth, setting off in a way that bordered on the obscene a heavy chin split in two by a cleft. With this frame, all eyes were drawn to his mouth; seen by itself, its fullness and the sensual pout of disdain that twisted it slightly made it look youthful. Meeting the Colonel's eyes after that, lodged like two pieces of lead shot between the reptilian folds of his lids, one became aware of the cynicism accumulated in their deep, grainy, blackish rings and it became impossible to say whether one was dealing with a fairly well-preserved old man or one prematurely aged by overindulgence. Moreira was aware of the unease caused by his expressive features and he always made skillful, sometimes even cruel, use of it.

The intercom crackled briefly. "That's Bernardo Carvalho on the line, Colonel, extension three."

The Colonel pressed a switch and settled back in his chair again. "Hi there, Nando? . . . Fine, and you? How are things with you, old chap? . . . Yes . . . Ha ha ha! You'd better watch out, at your age getting up to that kind of lark could cost you! You'll have to introduce me to her so I can show her what life's really about. But let's get down to serious stuff. There's a little shit, name of Nicanor Carneiro, who owns some property and who's giving me problems. You know who it is? . . . No, nothing serious, but I'd like to give him a lesson, teach him good manners. You're going to forget him for a while when you're purchasing fruit . . . Just long enough for his bloody mangoes to rot. That's right, yes . . . And do it so he can't pass them off to someone else, eh . . . OK, *amigo*, don't worry, I owe you. And I expect to see you at my little party, don't forget. See you soon . . . Yes, that's right . . . That's right . . . *Ciao*, Nando, got to go now, there's someone on the other line . . . *Ciao* . . ."

He relit his cigar when his secretary came in carrying a silver tray. Closing the door with her hip, she crossed the room carefully so as not to spill anything on the crimson wall-to-wall carpet.

A translucent, fine linen suit, boxwood pearls on her tanned skin, austere bun and stiletto heels. A woman to tempt all the saints of Bahia! Certainly something different from those frumps of the Nordeste.

"Your coffee, sir," she said hesitantly, suddenly embarrassed at finding herself mentally undressed by the governor.

Moreira moved some papers that were right in front of him. "Put it down there, please."

To put the tray down where he had indicated, Anita had to go around the desk to his right-hand side. The Colonel felt her body brush against his shoulder. Just as she was about to pour the coffee he slipped a hand up her skirt.

"No . . . Not that, sir . . ." she said, trying to move away. "Please . . . Don't . . ."

His hand clamped to the flesh of her thigh, unmoving like a handler subduing a dog, he maintained his hold, relishing the way the young woman stiffened and the waves of panic running across her skin.

The ring of the telephone caught them in this petrified stuggle. Without letting go, the Colonel picked up the receiver with his free hand.

"Yes? No, darling . . . At the moment I still don't know when I'll be able to get away. But I'll send the driver if you want . . . *The sudden capture of the crotch, swollen lips, the yielding fruit of the mango tree* . . . Now don't be silly . . . Of course I love you, where did you get that idea . . . *Earthy moisture, the jungle of the genitals, spongy under the kneading fingers* . . . But of course, my love, I promise . . . Put on your glad rags, there'll be quite a crowd . . . Go on, I'm listening. I've said I'm listening, now be reasonable, please."

Tears in her eyes, leaning forward as if being searched by the police, Anita desperately scrutinized the bust facing her. *Antônio Francisco Lisboa . . . Antônio Francisco Lisboa . . .* With an absurd sense of urgency, she read and reread the inscription on the plaster, gorging on it as if it were an exorcism that could purify her.

CHAPTER 3

*The happy chance that took Kircher to Provence,
the distinguished figures he met there & how he achieved
his first successes*

HARDLY HAD WE reached the security of
the Jesuit college in Mainz than the superiors of our
Order decided to send Athanasius Kircher far away from
the war and the German states. This favor was due solely to
his renown, which was already considerable both within our
Order & in learned societies the world over. He was given
letters of recommendation to the College of Avignon & I was
granted permission to accompany him in the capacity of private
secretary.

In Paris, where we arrived without mishap, we were received
with open arms by the Jesuits of the *Collège de la Place Royale.*
There Kircher was to meet some of the learned scholars with
whom he had been in correspondence for several years: Henry
Oldenburg, first secretary of the Royal Society in London, who

was visiting Paris, La Mothe Le Vayer & the Franciscan Marin Mersenne. With the latter he had long disputations on all kinds of questions that at the time were beyond my understanding. He also saw Monsieur Pascal, who seemed to him a peerless mathematician but a sad specimen of humanity & one whose faith smacked of heresy. The same was true of Monsieur Descartes, the apostle of the New Philosophy, who made a mixed impression on him.

He likewise met Monsieur Thévenot de Melquisedeq, who had travelled to China & had returned with an inordinate taste for oriental philosophies. Fascinated by Kircher's knowledge of these difficult subjects, he invited him to spend several days at the *Désert de Retz*, a property he owned on the outskirts of Paris. I was not allowed to accompany him & am therefore not in a position to say what happened there, especially since Athanasius always maintained a discreet silence on the subject. But on the pretext of religion or some Chinoiseries, my master was compelled to witness scenes decency forbade him to describe, for every time he mentioned an example of human lechery or excesses to which idolatry or ignorance can lead, he would cite the *Désert de Retz* as the principal source of his experience.

After just a few weeks spent in Paris, we finally arrived at the Collège d'Avignon, where Father Kircher was to teach mathematics & Biblical languages. A Northerner brought up in the Germanic mists, Athanasius was immediately taken with the brightness of the South. It was as if the world were opening up again for him, as if he could suddenly see its divine light. More than a simple star to observe through the telescope, the Sun proved to be the lamp of God, His presence & His aura among men.

Discovering in the plain of Arles the wonderful predisposition of the sunflower to follow the course of the sun, my master conceived and immediately constructed a clock based on this singular principle. He filled a small, circular basin with water on which he floated a smaller disc bearing a pot containing one of those plants. No longer held back by its fixed roots, the sunflower was free to turn toward the daystar. A needle attached to the center of its corolla indicated the hours on the fixed ring which crowned this curious device.

"But above all this machine," Kircher said when he presented it to the college authorities, "or, to be more precise, this *biological engine* in which art & nature are so perfectly combined, shows us how our soul turns toward the divine light, attracted to it by an analogous sympathy or magnetism of a spiritual order when we manage to free it from the vain passions that impede this natural inclination."

The heliotropic clock was soon known through Provence & contributed greatly to the spread of his fame.

My master also found it a valuable advantage to be living close to the port of Marseilles. Thus it was that he had the good fortune to meet David Magy, a merchant of Marseilles; Michel Bégon, treasurer of the Levant Fleet in Toulon; & Nicolas Arnoul, master of the galleys, who had been commissioned to go to Egypt & bring back various objects for the King of France's collections. It was through these people, who purchased all the curiosities the Jews & Arabs could bring them, that Kircher saw any number of little dried crocodiles & lizards, vipers & serpents, scorpions & chameleons, stones of rare color engraved with ancient figures & hieroglyphs as well as all sorts of Egyptian images made of glazed terracotta. He also saw some sarcophagi & a few mummies at the house of Monsieur de Fouquet, idols, stelae & inscriptions, of which he always begged to be allowed to make an impression. Athanasius never wearied of going around the country to visit these people and admire their collections. He bought, exchanged or copied everything that was directly relevant to his researches, especially Oriental books or manuscripts that reached the continent in Provence. Thus it was that one day he had the great good fortune to exchange an old astronomical telescope for an exceedingly rare Persian transcription of Saint Matthew's Gospel.

Conjecturing that the Coptic still spoken in Egypt was like the petrified language of the ancient Egyptians & that it would be useful in penetrating the secrets of the hieroglyphs, Kircher immediately started to study it & became very knowledgeable in it within a few months.

My master seemed to have forgotten Germany & all his ties with Fulda; he never ceased to learn, nor to put his astonishing ingenuity into practice. Thus it was that, shortly after our arrival in Avignon, he had the idea of illustrating his knowledge of catoptrics by constructing an extraordinary machine. Working day and night in the tower of the *Collège de la Motte* he assembled, with his own hands, a device capable of representing the whole of the heavens. On the appointed day he astounded everyone by projecting the entire celestial mechanics onto the vault of the grand staircase. As if impelled by their own motion, the Moon, the Sun & the constellations moved in accordance with the rules established by Tycho Brahe, & by a simple & swift contrivance he was able to reproduce the precise state of the sky at any date in the past. In response to requests from teachers and students he thus presented the horoscopes of Our Lord Jesus Christ, of Pyrrhus, of Aristotle & Alexander.

It was on that occasion, as Pierre Gassendi recounts in his memoirs, that Nicolas Fabri de Peiresc, councillor at the parliament of Aix and a native of Beaugensier, was informed of Kircher's researches. When he learned that my master was

already well known for his knowledge of hieroglyphs, he insisted
on meeting him.

A strange man, this Provençal country squire: fascinated
by the sciences & the friend of some of the most distinguished
scholars, he had conceived a passion for the antiquities of Egypt
and their enigmatic script. He spent a fortune acquiring any
object of importance in that area. Not long previously Father
Minutius, a missionary in Egypt & the Levant, had offered him
a papyrus roll covered in hieroglyphs that had been found in a
sarcophagus, at the feet of a mummy. Peiresc had great hopes
of Kircher's ability to translate the pages and wrote inviting
him to stay with him in Aix, at the same time sending him, as a
gift, several rare books and a copy of the *Table of Isis*, also called
the *Bembine Table*. As a postscript he asked him to bring with
him the famous manuscript of Barachias Abenephuis, which
Athanasius had been fortunate enough to acquire.

Kircher was flattered by this keen interest & one day in
September 1633 we travelled to Aix, with said manuscript in our
luggage as well as various specimens of the Hebrew, Chaldaean,
Arabic and Samaritan languages.

Peiresc welcomed us with a charm & delight such as is rarely
seen. He was proud to meet my master & did everything he
could to make himself agreeable to him. Kircher, for his part,
was very impressed by the collections his host revealed to him
little by little, making the most of its effects & enjoying our
sincere admiration. His house was crammed full with all kinds
of dried or stuffed animals, but equally with a multitude of
Egyptian artifacts & books. There for the first time we saw a
phoenicopterus, an aspic, a horned viper, a lotus & any number
of dried & mummified cats. In his garden he showed us several
pink laurels, which he had grown from a shoot given him by
Cardinal Barberini, as well as a pond with graceful papyrus

all around from which he made paper in the manner of the Egyptians. We also admired a kind of little rabbit, the size of a mouse, which walked on its hind legs & used it front paws, which were shorter, like monkeys to hold the food it was given, & an angora cat Father Gilles de Loche had brought back from Cairo for him as well as various manuscripts obtained at great expense from the Coptic monasteries of Wadi el-Natrun.

Peiresc, now completely won over by Athanasius, finally revealed his two human mummies of which one, notable for its size and state of conservation, was the corpse of a prince, as was proved by its richness of ornamentation. It was at the feet of this mummy that the little book in Egyptian hieroglyphs had been found that Peiresc had mentioned in his letter to Athanasius. The book was made up of pages of old papyrus written in hieroglyphic characters like those on the obelisks. There were bulls & other animals & even human figures together with other smaller characters, like those in the *Bembine Table*, but no Greek letters.

Kircher's eyes were sparkling with excitement. He had never held a genuine example of this mysterious writing in his hands & could not stop himself immediately starting to study it. Peiresc asked him as a special favor to think out loud & Kircher obliged without batting an eyelid. Thus it was that once more I had the opportunity to observe my revered master's singular genius & his wealth of knowledge.

It was at this juncture that we heard the news of the condemnation of Galileo Galilei by the Holy Office. Peiresc, who was a close friend of the astronomer & had sure information from his contacts in Rome, asked Kircher to come & see him in Aix to discuss the matter. We went at once, though my master remained so silent and seemed so morose that it was impossible for me to tell what he thought about it.

Peiresc was aghast at all this; he was foaming with rage & railing against the horrendous ignorance of the inquisitors. In the argument that followed, Athanasius employed all his rhetorical skill to defend the verdict of the Holy Office & to advocate blind obedience to its authority, especially during that grievous period of schism & religious discord.

However, given Pereisc's manifest disappointment & the proofs cited in support of the movement of the Earth, Kircher eventually admitted that he regarded the opinion of Galileo & Copernicus as true, as, moreover, did Galileo's accusers, Fathers Malapertuis, Clavius & Scheiner, though they had been put under pressure & compelled to write in support of Aristotle's assumptions & were only following the Church's directions by force & out of obedience.

When he heard him express these views, Peiresc embraced my master, overjoyed to see him return to the path of reason. As for myself, until then educated to respect Aristotle absolutely, I did not conceal my disagreement with the result that the two of them made great efforts to show me where the infallible philosopher was mistaken. I was easily convinced—young people are malleable—but this abjuration left me with the uncomfortable feeling of belonging to a secret brotherhood that favored heresy. On the way back I was quaking in my shoes, so convinced I was that people would recognize my seditious opinions & deliver me up to the Inquisition. Kircher was amused at my disquiet, but calmed me a little by suggesting I outwardly adopt, as he did himself, the system of Tycho Brahe, which was recognized by the Church & was intellectually satisfying insofar as it constituted a neat compromise between the *unmoving paradise* of Aristotle & the universal movement of the Italian.

A few days later an order came that we were to go immediately to Vienna & we had to make hasty preparation to leave Avignon.

CORUMBÁ: *A little fish, a tiny little fish*

Dietlev and Milton were there to meet them when their train arrived at Corumbá station. Elaine was glad to see the cheerful face of her German colleague. Small and tubby, he sported a bushy salt-and-pepper beard, as if to compensate for the sparse crown of hair that was still resisting the encroachment of baldness. Known for his good nature, his hearty appetite and his love of puns, he hardly ever seemed to lose his infectious good humor. He laughed so easily that Elaine could not imagine him without seeing the gleam of his teeth behind his tousled mustache. His scalp, badly burned by the sun and brick red, proved that he had not been inactive while waiting for them.

Much more reserved than Dietlev and therefore less accessible, Milton's severity was legendary and made him an imposing figure. Despite his lack of experience of the terrain, or more probably because of that, he made a point of showing reserve and punctilious formality in all things. His political connections and the great favor in which he was held in the upper echelons of the university gave him hope of being appointed rector the following year. Anxious to show how much he merited the position, he was already cultivating a cold and pretentious façade. All in all he was something of a pain in the neck and Dietlev would have been happy to do without him but had been forced to yield to his prerogative as head of department and his power as a member of the commission allocating research funds.

During the taxi ride Mauro was the object of much solicitous attention on the part of Milton. Questioned more assiduously than Elaine about the events of their journey, he was forced to recount the episode of the wallet-thief in detail, which he did with a light, humorous touch.

Once they reached the Beira Rio Hotel, Dietlev left the new arrivals to settle in, arranging to meet on the terrace for lunch. Elaine's first concern was to take a shower. She was exhausted from the train journey and felt dirty from head to toe. She had never realized there were still steam locomotives in the country, even less that the smoke was so grimy! Brand new when she had left Campo Grande eight hours previously, her clothes were ready for a thorough cleaning.

She was just coming out of the shower when there was a knock at the door. It was Dietlev. Since she was on familiar terms with him, she just wrapped the bath towel around her before going to open the door. He seemed worried.

"You're not ashamed to let someone into your room when you're half-naked?" he joked.

"Not if it's an old friend," she replied with a laugh, "and one who's seen me without a stitch more than once, if I remember rightly."

"You just be careful, my girl. One day the devil slumbering inside me might well wake up. Especially when lured by such charms . . ."

"What is it you want, you nincompoop?"

"I wanted to see you alone. Without Milton, that is. You know that he gets shit-scared as soon as he feels obliged to leave his office. He's only come with us so he can reap the glory of my discovery and flatter Mauro's father by looking after his son personally. If he hears what I've got to tell you he'd be quite capable of cancelling everything on the spot."

"There's a problem?"

"There is. The simple fact is that the guy I'd made an agreement with to go upriver has changed his mind. He won't hear of hiring out his boat to us anymore. And do you know why? You'll never guess. They say there's some crazy guys blocking the river above Cuiabá. Even the police won't go there—they fire machine guns at anything that moves . . ."

"But that's ridiculous!"

"Traffic in crocodile skins, it appears. A whole gang of them from Paraguay. They've even got a little landing-strip in the forest. And since it's a pretty lucrative business, they don't hesitate to use any means to make sure they're left in peace."

"You believe all this, do you?"

"I don't know. Everything's possible out here."

"But the police, dammit?"

"Simple—they'll get a slice of the cake."

"And there's no way of going around the area? Really, it's beyond belief."

"None at all. I've studied the maps with Ayrton, the fisherman who brought me the fossil last year. The arm of the river with the deposit starts twelve miles higher up and it doesn't connect with anything negotiable. The only way of getting there would be to disembark downstream and walk through the jungle for forty or forty-five miles . . . It's out of the question."

Elaine was devastated. Knowing Milton, it would be the next plane back to Brazilia. "What are we going to do, then?" she asked, stunned.

"For the moment nothing. But we keep quiet. Not a word to Milton; nor to Mauro, either. You never know. I've made some other contacts and I'll have a reply this afternoon. OK?"

"OK," Elaine said with a disappointed expression.

"Go and get dressed. We're meeting on the terrace in ten minutes."

LEANING ON HIS elbows at the window of his room, Mauro was drinking in the unfamiliar landscape he was seeing for the first time. The Beira Rio Hotel stood beside the river, on the short strip of old structures bordering the bank at that point. From his look-out post the student could see the Pantanal marshes stretching out forever to the east. Twittering flocks of unfamiliar birds flew across a sky that was cloudless, but of a hazy blue. The silty and perfectly smooth water of the Rio Paraguay looked like a yellow-ing mirror, tainted in places with rust or suspicious patches of mold. It was difficult to believe that this loop of still water could be part of the great river by which the lumberjacks sent their huge rafts of timber down to Buenos Aires or Montevideo. Floating as if by some miracle were small craft made up of bits and pieces, an old two-decker gunboat and the patrol boat of the river police, all moored to trees or worm-eaten posts driven into the bank. Long aluminum barges turned over on the grass among dugout canoes and ropes threw off a dazzling light.

Like every geology student, Mauro had taken part in numer-ous field studies during his course but this was the first time he was part of a real research project, and, what is more, with the cream of the university. Dietlev Walde had become famous two years ago by discovering, together with Professor Leonardos and other German geologists, an unexpected fossil in a Cormubá quarry: a polyp comparable to *Stephanocyphus*, which had already been identified in certain regions of the world, but distinguished from it by important structural differences, notably by the pres-ence of secondary polyps. After analyses carried out by various specialists—of whom Elaine von Wogau was one—on the samples brought back to Brazilia, it had been dated back to 600 million years ago and they had shown that the fossil belonged to a primi-tive branch in the evolution of the *Scyphozoa*: it was not only the first Pre-Cambrian fossil ever to be found in South America but also one of the most archaic. Named *Corumbella wernerii, hahn, hahn, leonardos & walde*, it immediately gave Dietlev and his team an international reputation.

The previous year Dietlev had returned to the Mato Grosso to collect further samples. The rumor having gotten around that there was a mad German who was looking for rocks with impressions and was prepared to give a good price for them, a fisherman had brought him a stone he had picked up by chance high in the north of the Pantanal. Analysis had confirmed that it was a Pre-Cambrian fossil that predated the *Corumbella* and, what was even better, of an echinoderm that had never been found before, not even in the rich deposits of the Ediacara Hills in Australia! This had led to the idea of the expedition, which promised excellent results.

If the prospect of having their name associated with an animal species gets most scientists worked up, it had turned Milton into a veritable wild beast: obsessed with the idea of promotion, he had intrigued to take the place of Othon Leonardos on this expedition. Like Dietlev and Elaine, Mauro despised him for this attitude, unworthy of a true scientist, but his influence was such that one had to put up with him or give up the very idea of working at the university.

After all, the only thing that was really important was to advance our knowledge of the world. This fossil, coming in a direct line from "primordial fauna" promised a fantastic advance in our understanding of our origins and Mauro too was seething with impatience—why be ashamed of it?—to be part of this triumph.

Not counting the fact that it would shut his father up, shut him up for good, he hoped.

At the agreed time, the four of them met on the terrace on the top floor of the hotel. Dietlev went over their objectives again and the role each would play on the expedition. From the logistical point of view everything had gone as planned apart from the problem of obtaining a supply of petrol for the boat. He'd only managed to get half the necessary fuel, but the problem was solvable if they would accept a slight additional cost. Milton having told them that they had sufficient funds to buy up all the reserves of Corumbá, they enjoyed an untroubled lunch.

Toward three Dietlev took them to the quarry so that they could familiarize themselves with the geological layers associated with *Corumbella wernerii* and, if possible, collect further samples. After having shown them the thin stratum of gray-green clay on which they were to concentrate their efforts, he left them, saying he would see them at the Ester at the end of the afternoon.

Before he got into the taxi, he turned around and saw Elaine and Mauro on their knees, using their hammers on the slope. Hands in his pockets, panama pulled well down over his ears, Milton was watching them work in the white dust.

WHEN DIETLEV ENTERED the Ester, the café-restaurant where he had arranged to meet the man who represented his last opportunity of finding a boat, the owner dropped his brush to greet him with a great show of friendship. *"Holà, amigo,"* he said, embracing Dietlev, "it's a pleasure to see you again. What have you been doing all this time?"

"Hi, Herman," Dietlev said, without a reply to a question that didn't expect one, "still painting, then?"

"I'm afraid so. I'm just giving these old walls a bit of decoration, but this time it's going to be a portrait. Look what I unearthed," he said, picking up a postcard that was lying on the table: "Otto Eduard Leopold von Bismarck. Not bad, eh? I'm just making a copy of it, it's going to be fantastic!"

Dietlev turned toward the large niche where Herman had started to color in an amateurish sketch of the photo. "Indeed . . ."

he said. He felt ill at ease: as always at some point this individual would suddenly make him feel violently sick. Herman Petersen spoke German and behaved like a German but he was . . . Bolivian. If one expressed surprise, he would produce the remnants of a passport to prove it. Having married an obese mulatto, who was horribly marked with smallpox (he can't have found her disgusting since he had given her three kids), he claimed to have Brazilian nationality as well. When he was drunk, which happened every day after a certain time in the evening, he would become voluble and go on about his nostalgia for order and even his sympathy for the great *Reich*. "True, he overdid it toward the end," he would say, without ever mentioning Hitler by name, "but all the same! The ideas are still there and they weren't all bad, far from it, believe me!" The only information Dietlev had been able to extract from him during his two previous visits to Corumbá was that Petersen had arrived in Bolivia in 1945, after the defeat— "But I was just a simple soldier, a little fish, a tiny little fish."

"OK," said Herman, "what can I offer you to celebrate your return? I've got a new draft beer, a real treat."

"Later," said Dietlev seeing the man he was waiting for enter the bar. "I've got some urgent business with this guy."

"No problem, *amigo,* make yourself at home."

The Brazilian approached Dietlev with a false air of humility, an ominous sign. "*Senhor* Walde," he said, avoiding his eye, "it's impossible, absolutely impossible. I would have liked to take you, but I can't risk losing my boat, as I'm sure you'll understand. You can't get past there, they shoot you like rabbits. No one will take you, you can be sure of that."

Dietlev felt his face flush with anger. "I'll double the price! Think carefully: two hundred thousand cruzeiros!"

The Brazilian squirmed, as if electrified by the immensity of the sum, then his eye suddenly fixed on something behind Dietlev's back. Instinctively he turned around; Petersen was calmly drying a beer glass, his head bowed over the towel.

"Well?" Dietlev asked.

"I'm sorry, really sorry. I can't do it, it's too dangerous. Next year, perhaps . . ."

"There'll be no next year," Dietlev said furiously. "It's now or never. My funds can't be carried over to next year, can you understand that?"

"Take it easy, *senhor*. Losing you temper won't change my decision. I've seen *Seu* Ayrton . . ."

"Ayrton? The fisherman?"

"He left for Campo Grande this morning. He asked me to tell you that he couldn't go with you. You see, his mother's ill . . ."

"That caps it all!" said Dietlev, clenching his fists. "*Scheisse!* Did you hear that, Herman?"

"Hear what?"

"This guy!" he said, turning to point to the Brazilian with a grand theatrical gesture. But he had grabbed the opportunity to slip away and Dietlev just had time to see him disappear through the bead curtain over the café entrance. With a look of despair, Dietlev went over to the bar and leaned on it: "I think the time has come to have a beer. The way things are, there's nothing left to do but get thoroughly plastered."

"Look at that," said Herman, putting a huge beer mug under the tap, "it comes from Munich, from the Café Schelling. I got it out specially in your honor. So you've got problems, it appears?"

"And how! You can't imagine what a mess I've got myself into."

Elbow on the bar, chin on his hand, Herman listened as Dietlev outlined the situation. He must have once had a fine Nordic face such as people imagine it in Latin countries, with blue eyes, blond hair and pink cheeks. Over the years the alcohol had remodeled his features: lumpy skin, sagging face, puffy in places, and eyes so pale they looked as if they were veiled by cataracts. His white hair, drawn back, seemed to have been combed with a mixture of fat and nicotine, his cheap false teeth gave him a waxworks smile and, apart from a belly like a child suffering from malnutrition, his body was skinny and disappeared inside his wide shorts and a short-sleeved shirt.

"This fossil you're talking about," he asked, "what is it exactly?"

"The one I'm looking for? A kind of sea urchin, if you like, but without spines."

"And all this bother just for a sea urchin? You're mad, *amigo!*"

"You don't realize, Herman, it's something no one's ever seen. There are institutions and collectors who'd pay a fortune just to have one."

"A fortune? How much, for example?"

"I couldn't really say. It's simply beyond price. A bit like a stone brought back from the moon. A few of these fossils would finance our research for several years . . ."

"And the one you've got?"

"It's not worth a penny. Without identifying the deposit it comes from we're left with nothing but assumptions; as with any erratic."

"Erratic?"

"Yes, that is something that's not in its original site any longer. For example, if you open a pharaoh's tomb and find some grains of wheat in the sarcophagus, you can deduce that the wheat is at least as old as the mummy, that it has a value in the cult of the dead because it symbolizes rebirth, et cetera. If you find those same grains of wheat out in the desert, or if someone brings them to you, they give you no information at all, not about the grains themselves or about anything else. They'll be of no interest whatsoever."

"I see . . . And you're sure this deposit of yours exists?"

"Absolutely sure. That's the worst thing about it. I questioned Ayrton at great length, I showed him the satellite maps I'd been able to get: everything agrees. It's a hill between the junction of the Rio Bento Gomes and that of the Jauru, a bit before you get to Descalvado."

"I know it."

"What d'you mean, you know it? Have you been there?"

Wrapped in thought, Herman ignored his question. "And you think you could find the place, even without Ayrton?"

"I'm convinced I can. Once there I can guarantee I'd manage, I'm used to it. Ayrton would just have helped me save time."

Herman looked Dietlev straight in the eye, as if he were weighing the pros and cons one last time. "Good," he said after his brief reflection, "I think I'm going to give you a second beer."

"No thanks. I don't feel my usual self as it is."

Despite that the old German took the two mugs and leaned over toward the pump.

"No. Please, Herman. I haven't—"

"I might have a boat," Herman said without raising his eyes from the beer running into the mug.

"What was that you just said?"

"You heard. I said I might have a boat, a pilot and everything you need. But it's likely to cost you. It's up to you."

Dietlev started thinking fast. Just one word and hope was re-born, stronger than ever. Milton wasn't worried about money, he'd pay anything to make sure the expedition went ahead. As for Herman, it didn't look as if he was trying to put one over on him.

"Who will I be dealing with?" he asked with a haste he imme-diately regretted.

"With me," said Herman, placing a full mug in front of Dietlev. "It's a good boat. I bought it from the State Property Office ten years ago. Ninety-one feet, steel hull, 300 hp engine. And your captain is here before you."

"Are you pulling my leg? What would you do with a thing like that?"

Herman seemed annoyed. "I'm no more stupid than the next man, you know. I can't keep a wife and three children on what I earn from the bar. There's lots you can do with a boat around here: take tourists out fishing during the season, transport goods from one *fazenda* to another, or hire it out . . . to geologists, for example."

"OK, OK. Sorry. It's just so unexpected . . . But out with it now, this story of crocodile hunters, it's a load of nonsense, isn't it."

"Not at all, they weren't lying."

"But you're not afraid?"

"With me it's different. You see, I do a bit of business with them. I take fresh supplies to them from time to time. They're not so bad if you leave them in peace. But that's my business. You know nothing, see nothing, and there'll be no problem."

"How much do you want?"

"Ah, now that's the question," Herman said, baring all his false teeth in a laugh. Becoming serious again, he went on, "I want 400,000 cruzeiros and . . . 30 percent commission on the sale of the first fossils."

Dietlev was struck dumb by the enormity of his demands, less because of the sum of money he wanted, they could always come to an agreement on that, but the crazy idea of a commission.

"It seems to me you haven't quite understood, Herman," he said, trying to remain calm. "It's not gold nuggets I'm looking for. If I do find these bloody fossils, if my hypothesis isn't mistaken and if foreign scientists are interested in them, then we might perhaps think of selling some. But in that case it will be the department that deals with it and all the money will revert to the

university. To the u-ni-ver-si-ty! I won't get anything at all out of
the business."

"There's always ways and means, aren't there? There must be a
trick somewhere. You're not going to get me to believe . . ."

"But I'm telling you it's impossible, Herman. Unthinkable
even."

"Then it's no, *amigo*. Find yourself another boat."

"You can't do that to me, Herman. Just think a little about what
I've told you. I'm happy with the 400,000 cruzeiros and that's one
hell of a good deal, isn't it? As for the fossils, we don't even know
if they exist. What you're basing your demand on is nothing but
thin air. If everything goes as planned you'll be the only person
to know where they are and there'll be nothing to stop you going
back and helping yourself. The only thing I could promise is to
send collectors to you . . ."

Herman sipped at his beer, a vacant look on his face. He was
about to reply when Elaine came in, followed by Mauro and
Milton.

Dietlev made the introductions as the little group settled at
the bar. Captivated by the charms of Elaine, Herman's smile returned. She had been back to the hotel to shower and change. In a
plain, almond-green cotton dress, her hair still damp, she exuded
freshness.

"What are you drinking?" Dietlev asked.

"I don't like beer," Elaine said, seeing the empty mugs. "Would
it be possible to have some wine?"

"But of course! Herman Petersen has everything, especially for
a pretty girl like you. Here, try this, you'll like it," he said, taking
a bottle from under the bar. "Valderrobles red. It's Bolivian and,
just between ourselves, a cut above the stuff you find in Brazil."

Mauro having asked for wine as well, Milton decided he would
join them.

"How did it go?" Dietlev asked Elaine.

"Not bad. Mauro and I found three excellent examples of *Co-rumbella*. The impression is very clear, we'll get some nice casts."

"But it was Mauro who found the most interesting one," Milton interrupted in a sugary voice. "The boy has talent."

Turning his back on Milton, Mauro raised his eyes heavenward to show Dietlev how irritating he found this obsequious solicitude.

"A truly auspicious start to our expedition!" Milton added, rubbing his hands. "So when do we leave, Dietlev?"

Elaine saw a glint of panic in her colleague's eyes. He turned to Petersen, who had just finished pouring the wine. He put down the bottle and said, smiling at Elaine, "Whenever you want." He spoke slowly, as if replying to a question from her. "I'm at your service."

Relieved, Dietlev held out his hand to thank him for his decision. "The day after tomorrow, that OK?"

"The day after tomorrow's OK, *amigo*," Herman said, shaking his hand warmly over the bar. His insistent look said: we're in agreement on the conditions, aren't we? Reading a positive reply in Dietlev's wink, he added, "I think it's your turn to buy me a beer."

"To buy *us all* a beer," said Dietlev. "That calls for a celebration."

"Excellent!" Milton exclaimed. "I'm keen to get on to the serious business."

Without mentioning their negotiations or the crocodile hunters, Dietlev introduced Herman as a member of the team. The next day would be devoted to stocking the boat and making their final preparations.

"What kind of boat will we be going on?" Mauro asked.

"The finest boat in the whole of the Pantanal! Come and have a look, it's moored just outside," said Herman setting off for the door. "Look, it's the *Mensageiro da Fé*. The one next to the Customs launch."

"That one!" Mauro exclaimed, recognizing the old gunship he'd seen from his bedroom window.

"That one," said Petersen, ignoring the disparaging tone. "It's not much to look at, true, but it's a marvelous little boat. And with me at the helm you'll be quite safe, trust me."

"The *Messenger of the Faith* . . . it's a nice name," said Elaine with a smile.

"I wanted to call it the *Siegfried* but my wife was against it. Oh, and that reminds me, I must warn her—you're staying to eat here, aren't you? You'll see, she cooks piranhas like no one else."

Dietlev having indicated his agreement, they went back in and sat down at the bar again while Herman shouted for Theresa at the top of his voice.

Eléazard's notebooks

WITTGENSTEIN: "In philosophy a question is treated like a disease." Which means starting out by looking for all the symptoms that would allow diagnosis. Use this framework to deal with the "Kircher" question?

ONE COULD SAY of his books what Rivarol said of Court de Gébelin's *Monde primitif*: "It is a work that is out of proportion with the shortness of life and that demands a summary from the very first page."

MOÉMA'S LETTER . . . The magnificent arrogance of youth, the beautiful, hip-swaying, unconcerned freedom of those whose future still lies ahead. Something so obvious it makes, as if inadvertently, the old ones get off the pavement, where they no longer have a place.

REGARDING THE TRACKS OF FOSSIL FOOTPRINTS overlapping each other that have been found on the Eyasi Plateau in Tanzania: they show that in the Pliocene, three million years ago, a young woman amused herself by walking in the footsteps of the male who was going in front of her. Elaine saw it as reassuring proof that the hominids of the distant period already resembled us. The fact that I, on the contrary, saw it as a sign of a depressing sameness of our species, was something she found irritating.

NEVER, PERHAPS, has the transition from one century to the next been so lackluster, so drearily full of its own self-importance.

LOREDANA . . . When she speaks she makes the pleasant murmuring of an onion roux in the frying pan.

TRUTH is neither a path through the fields nor even the clearing where the light mingles with the darkness. It is the jungle itself with its murky profusion, its impenetrability. For a long time now I haven't been looking for a way out of the forest anymore but rather trying not to get lost in its depths.

NOTHING IS SACRED that managed, if only once, to breed intolerance.

WRITE A SENTENCE with sugar water on a white sheet of paper, put it down by an ant-hill and film it as it appears, with the deviations in form and perhaps in meaning the insects make it undergo.

FOR THE INFORMATION OF ELAINE, last night, from a deep sleep: "You are requested never to speak to me, not even in my dreams."

PIRANHA: *etymologically "gate of the clitoris." In Amazonia its teeth are used to make scissors.* Doubtless that would have struck a chord with Dr. Sigmund, but I cannot believe for one moment that such images can be explained by the "castration anxiety." I prefer to think that when it came to naming things, mankind instinctively chose the most bizarre, the most poetic expressions.

THE WAY I SEE HIM, Kircher is fairly close to the character of that name in Heimito von Doderer's novel *Ein Umweg*: a mandarin imprisoned within his own indiscriminate erudition, a mere compiler full of his own importance and his authority, a man still believing in the existence of dragons . . . in short, a kind of dinosaur whose disciple the young hero of the novel quite rightly refuses to become.

KIRCHER FASCINATES ME because he's a crank, a veritable artist at failure, at sham. His curiosity was exemplary but it took him to the very edge of fraud . . . How could Peiresc continue to trust him? (Write to Malbois to check details on Mersenne, etc.)

ST. AUGUSTINE'S VORTEX: "I do not fear the arguments of the philosophers of the Academy who say, 'But what if you are mistaken?' If I am mistaken, I exist. Anyone who does not exist cannot be mistaken, therefore if I am mistaken, I must exist. And since being mistaken proves that I exist, how can I be mistaken in believing that I exist, since it is certain that I exist if I am mistaken . . . Since, therefore, I must exist in order to be mistaken, then even if I am mistaken, I am not mistaken in knowing that I exist." (Saint Augustine: *The City of God*) As complicated, Soledade would put it, as making love standing up in a hammock . . .

CHAPTER 4

In which we hear how Kircher made the acquaintance of an
Italian who carried his wife's corpse around for four years . . .

AS GERMANY WAS too risky for people of our
order, it was decided we should go to Austria via northern
Italy. We therefore set off for Marseilles where we embarked
on a fragile vessel that hugged the coast as it sailed for Genoa.
Having been blown off course by storms, we only managed to
reach Civita Vecchia. Since we felt sick at the very idea of going
back to sea, we did the sixty leagues to Rome on foot.

A big surprise was awaiting Kircher there. By the strangest
of coincidences, since our presence in Rome was due to the
vagaries of the wind alone, the superiors of the Society were not
at all surprised to see Athanasius when we presented ourselves
at the Roman College. On the contrary, they welcomed him as
one impatiently expected. During our eventful journey, Peiresc's
efforts had finally borne fruit & Kircher had been appointed to
the chair of mathematics at the College, in place of Christoph

Scheiner, who had left for Vienna to take over Kepler's
position. As well as teaching mathematics, it was specified that
Athanasius was to devote himself to the study of hieroglyphs,
a requirement in which it was easy to see the good offices of his
Provençal colleague.

It is difficult to describe Kircher's satisfaction on hearing this
news: at the age of thirty he had a personal chair at the most
renowned Jesuit college & could treat the most learned men of
his time, those he had admired since he began his studies, as
equals.

When we arrived in Rome in November 1633 Galileo had
just been imprisoned for the first year of his incarceration; my
master took it upon himself to go and see him whenever his
work allowed.

With the room he had been given on the top floor of the
Roman College Athanasius Kircher had a unique view of the
city. Down below he could see the teeming population of Rome—
which at the time had more than a hundred and twenty thousand
inhabitants!—he could view the domes or capitals of the most
beautiful buildings ever raised &, above all, he could make out
some of the tall obelisks Pope Sixtus V had started to restore.

On Peiresc's advice he struck up a friendship with Pietro della
Valle, the celebrated owner of the Coptic-Arabic dictionary,
translated by Saumaise. Between 1611 & 1626 this indefatigable
traveller had scoured the Indies & the Levant. From his
investigations of the tombs of the pharaohs he had brought back
a number of mummies, objects & manuscripts that could be
found nowhere else, not counting the valuable information an
educated traveller can harvest during such journeys. He was
best known for having seen the ruins of the Tower of Babel from
which he had brought back a fine granite stone, which he later
gave to Athanasius.

Father Giovanni Battista Riccioli, who had been present at his return from the Indies, never tired of recounting his exploits. "You must know," he said, "that in 1623 della Valle had married a Persian woman, a Christian according to the Eastern Rite. Sitti Maani Gioreida, as she was called, combined within her all the beauty of a woman & of the East but only a few months after their marriage she died following a miscarriage. To his despair at losing his young companion was added that of having to bury her in unconsecrated ground & Pietro della Valle decided to have her embalmed by the most reliable methods, in order to bring her back to Rome. For four years he travelled accompanied by the mummy of his wife & as soon as he arrived back, he organized a magnificent funeral ceremony for her. A funeral that was perhaps excessive for a simple Persian woman, but certainly reflected the love he felt for her. The funeral car was pulled by twenty-four white horses and on it was a catafalque with four pedestals bearing statues of Conjugal Love, Concord, Magnanimity & Patience. Each of the statues had one hand pointing to the glass coffin of Sitti Maani & in the other they held a cypress to which were attached the poems that all the Academicians of Rome had written on the death of the lady."

Athanasius Kircher was dazzled by this figure. At their very first meeting he had no hesitation in confiding all his ideas & projects to him; he described the festivities he had organized in Ingolstadt & quickly convinced Pietro della Valle of his superiority in the matter of hieroglyphs. Impressed by the knowledge of a man who had only traveled in Europe, if at all, & charmed by his nature, della Valle agreed to entrust to him the dictionary that was the envy of all scholars. A detailed study of it convinced my master that Coptic was an indispensable stepping stone to deciphering the hieroglyphs, with the result that at the death of Thomas de Novare in 1635 Pietro della Valle, with the support of Cardinal Barberini, commissioned him to prepare the work for publication on his own.

Sadly, the following month Athanasius was plunged into mourning by the death of Friedrich von Spee. He had stayed in Germany, where he had continued to fight against the fanaticism of the Inquisition, & he had been carried off by the plague, following the taking of Trier by the Imperial army during which he had treated the wounded who had been struck down with that terrible disease. My master was much affected by this too early death & and it was from that day on that he occasionally kept his sadness at bay by recounting to me the happy episodes connected with the memory of his friend.

In 1636, after two years of unremitting work, Kircher published a little quarto volume of 330 pages, the *Prodomus Copticus Sive Ægyptiacus,* in which he set out his ideas on the mysterious language of the Egyptians & the method that would guide his future work. After having established the relationship between Coptic and Greek, he demonstrated the necessity of going through the study of the former if there was to be any hope of one day completely unravelling the hieroglyphs. And he asserted for the first time the great truth that was to bring the success we all know, namely that the hieroglyphs were not some form of writing but a symbolic system capable of expressing the theological ideas of the priests of ancient Egypt with great subtlety.

The *Prodomus* was a resounding success; Kircher received enthusiastic letters from all erudite persons of his time, notably the hearty congratulations of Peiresc, who was constantly telling people how, through his mediation, he was to a small extent responsible for my master's discoveries.

The year came to a dramatic end: the astrologer Centini and his little entourage of disciples were accused of having plotted

to assassinate Pope Urban VIII during black masses, which my
sense of propriety forbids me to describe in detail & then tried
to poison him. Kircher was charged with analyzing the poisons
found in Centini's house & in the Holy Father's food. This gave
him the opportunity of familiarizing himself with certain
remarkable poisons & their degree of toxicity, experience that he
later turned to account in one of his publications on the subject.
Centini & his acolytes were condemned to death & hung from
gallows erected in St. Peter's Square for the edification of the
populace. I almost fainted at the sight of the poor wretches
wriggling at the end of their ropes, but Kircher, who was taking
notes, reprimanded me sharply:

"What's this!" he exclaimed. "You're trembling like a leaf
at a scene that is quite natural. These men schemed to bring
about someone else's death & their just punishment is the fate
they planned for him. The more they suffer as they die, the
more favorably Our Lord will hear their prayers, especially
since they confessed to their crimes & therefore deserve all the
mercy due to those who have repented. Instead of bewailing
what is nothing more than a swift passage to a better life, you
would do better to observe, as I do, the process of asphyxiation
& the signs accompanying it." Thus admonished, I found the
courage to watch the execution of these unfortunates to the
end, though without managing to remember anything apart
from the horrible rictus in which their faces were twisted &
and the slate-blue color of their tongues jutting out like the
bladder of a fish that has been dragged up from the depths too
quickly.

A few minutes after the death of Centini, as the crowd was
already dispersing, Kircher went over to the hanging bodies.
Authorized by his ministry, he felt their breeches one after the
other. Very satisfied, he made me note the dampness of each

body at that place & promised to explain one day how that
observation confirmed some of his most secret research.

But if the year 1636 finished tragically, 1637 began with some
important news: the return of Frederick of Hesse, the governor
of Hesse-Darmstadt, to the bosom of the Catholic Church.
Kircher rejoiced at the news: Fulda was part of the Grand
Duchy of Hesse & the conversion of the Grand Duke promised
to bring peace to a region that was close to his heart but plunged,
alas!, in darkness because of war & privation.

Thus Frederick of Hesse came to Rome, where he was
received with all honor by the Supreme Pontiff & Cardinal
Barberini. The Grand Duke having decided to travel through
Italy to Sicily & Malta, Kircher was officially appointed his
confessor & travelling companion. This time again, my master
managed to arrange it so that I was attached to him for the
journey.

A few weeks later, while we were making our final
preparations, Athanasius heard that Peiresc had died & at the
same time received a letter, a copy of his will. The old Provençal
scholar had bequeathed him his entire collection which, duly
listed and parcelled, was already on its way to Rome.

My master was deeply moved as he broke the seal on
his friend & protector's final letter. Having been told of his
forthcoming voyage to the south, Peiresc urged him to measure
the elevations of the pole down there, to observe Mount Etna
& to bring back for him a list of the books in the principal
libraries of Sicily, most especially a list of the manuscripts in
Caeta Abbey. Athanasius hardly needed these suggestions,
having himself worked out a very full program of research, but
Peiresc's posthumous encouragement went straight to his heart
& he decided to carry out his observations not as if they were his
own, but as a response to the wishes of his dear departed friend.

As for his collection, which was to arrive in Rome after our departure for Sicily, it filled Kircher with joy. Determined to create his own *Wunderkammer,* he obtained, thanks to Cardinal Barberini, several rooms in the Roman College to house it. The crates were to be deposited there until he could organize what was later to become the *Kircher Museum,* which is the most famous collection of curios that ever existed.

FORTALEZA: *O indio não é bicho*

In dark glasses, leather ski pants and a long-sleeved T-shirt to hide the needle marks on her arms—the branch of the *Banco do Brazil* where she had opened an account was on the university campus— Moéma waited her turn. After having received the check from her father she had quickly sent it on to a certain Alexander Constantinopoulos, the Greek in Rio whose PO Box number she'd gotten from a friend and who undertook to double the amount of any check made out in foreign currency. The bank had just telephoned to say that a transfer had been made to her account by fax. It was magic! Like playing roulette and winning every time. A vaguely guilty feeling brought the note accompanying the check back to mind: *"I do worry . . . Too much, I'm sure. But you're still my little girl, I can't change that. Look after yourself, my dear, and remember that I love you more than my own life."* Despite her efforts to keep them down, these words kept rising to the surface, black and swollen, like drowned bodies. Her father hadn't mentioned the money, nor the bar, but it was precisely his discretion that aroused her indignation. He couldn't care less what I might be doing, she thought. A few nice words, the dough and that's it. He's just a stupid old fool. So sure of himself, especially when he pretends to be in doubt. He'll never understand anything about anything . . ."*I love you more than my own life . . .*" When I think that he even managed to pull out that old chestnut! I wouldn't be surprised if he made a rough copy first.

However, this flood of complaints did not manage to suppress her sense of being in the wrong. *"Heidegger's fine, as far as you can say that of a stupid parrot who's getting old. He continues to repeat his favorite sentence and to peel anything he can get his beak on, as if it were extremely important for the universe not to leave the least scrap of skin on anything. To be honest, though, I'm starting to resemble him a bit . . ."* Reading this rather involved confession, Moéma had almost jumped on the first train to go and console her father. But now, standing in the queue that wasn't moving, she stamped her foot impatiently to help bring back her feeling he was not being straight with her. What an idiot! Would the day ever come when he could say things simply, instead of always hiding behind this literary veil. Why didn't he write, "I love you, Moéma, I miss you, but I'll only send you the dough when you've proved you're able to face up to life without having to rely on me . . ." She immediately realized that didn't make sense: if that were the case, she wouldn't be asking him for money, *porra!* What about: "Give up all these fantasies, Moéma. Grow up, if only for my sake." That didn't work either. She had no desire to "grow up," to be a woman like her mother or like all those adults who progressed step by little step, all buttoned up in their pretension and their certainties. My God, if he knew! she said to herself with an enjoyable shiver of perturbation. A lesbian and a drug addict! Imagining his reaction, she saw herself in her room, with Thaïs, the syringe and all the paraphernalia . . . and her father arriving without warning. He didn't say a word but sat down on the bed, beside her, and took her in his arms. Then he stroked her hair, for a long time, and hummed, his mouth closed, with a throaty sound that made his chest resonate like a drum. And there was great comfort in listening to his lullaby, a sweetness that opened all the gates, all her hopes. And then, at the moment when this feeling of accord was at its strongest, her father said:

"Yes, Madam? I do have other things to do . . ."

Caught in her daydream, Moéma had a slight dizzy turn at the counter.

"Is something wrong? Don't you feel well?"

"No, no . . . I'm sorry," she said, forcing herself to smile, "I was miles away. I'd like to take out some money."

SHE WAS COMING out of the bank when she heard a familiar voice. *"Tudo bem?"* Roetgen asked, coming over to her.

"Tudo bom . . ."

"You've become a stranger . . . Have you decided to drop out of my course?"

"No, no, not at all. And if I was going to drop out of a lecturer's course, it wouldn't be yours."

"So what's going on?"

"Oh, nothing. I've got a few minor personal problems at the moment. And the year's almost over, isn't it? There can't be a lot still going . . ."

"That's true," Roetgen said with a laugh. "But that's not a reason for my best student to desert me." Feeling uncomfortable at not being able to see her eyes, Roetgen took off her glasses. "You know it's very impolite to keep these on when you're talking to someone, especially to one of your teachers?"

He said it in a friendly tone and to tease her a little, and was surprised at the way she shrank back. For a brief moment she seemed so thrown by it, he felt as if he had undressed her. Her big blue eyes looked even stranger than usual; like those of a nocturnal bird suddenly exposed to the full sunlight, they had fixed in a disturbingly vacant and terrified expression.

"What do you think you're doing?" she said in a harsh voice. "We haven't slept together as far as I know."

Roetgen felt himself blush to the roots of his hair. "You must excuse me," he said awkwardly, "I don't know what came over me. But it's a pity to hide such pretty eyes."

"Oh, these Frenchmen, they're all the same," Moéma said, smiling at his embarrassment.

"Don't think that or you could come in for some unpleasant surprises." Then, with a glance at the clock on the bank, "*Oh là, là,* I'm going to be late, I must be off. By the way, there's an event at the German Cultural Institute this evening, d'you feel like coming? We could have a chat . . ."

"All this organized stuff's just a pain in the ass, nothing but speeches and youth-club entertainment."

"This time it'll be different. You don't know Andreas, he really wants to get things moving. But if the students don't come, there's no point."

"I'll see."

"Great. See you this evening then, I hope."

Roetgen was what in Brazil is called a *profesor visitante,* that is, a lecturer on a fixed-term contract within an exchange with a foreign university. A recent graduate—he was almost the same age as his students—with a passionate enthusiasm for the ethnology of the *Nordeste,* he had come to Fortaleza during the year to give a series of seminars on the "methodology of observation in rural areas." Somewhat shy and reserved, he had made friends with Andreas Haekner, the director of the German Cultural Institute. And since they were always seen together, the rumor had gone around that they had unmentionable feelings for each other. Moéma laughed with the others at the stream of innuendo the sight of Roetgen could set off, without, however, having seen any signs that would indicate a tendency to homosexuality. He wasn't *one of the family*, as she put it, and if by some unlikely chance she was wrong, it was truly a pity for Brazilian women.

GETTING OFF THE bus at the sea front, just opposite the side street where Thaïs lived, Moéma stopped for a moment. Transformed by her tinted glasses, the Atlantic looked like a lake of molten gold fringed with coconut trees made of tin and leather.

"They should force people to wear dark glasses," she said, parting the bead curtain that led directly into Thaïs's main room. "It might help them use their imagination properly . . ."

From the mattress and the cushions they were lounging on, Virgilio, Pablo and Thaïs applauded her assertion. As she joined them Thaïs gave her a querying look. Moéma reassured her with a wink: she'd got the money.

"*Maconheiros!*" Moéma said, making a deliberate show of sniffing the air. "You've been smoking, you bastards."

"We *were* smoking," Pablo said with a roguish grin. He turned his right hand so that the palm was facing her and showed her the joint he was holding between his thumb and forefinger. "Would you like some?"

"I wouldn't say no," Moéma said, delicately taking the spliff from him.

When she'd finished inhaling the smoke from inside her hands cupped around her face, Virgilio couldn't wait to show her the first issue of the journal he'd been boring them with for several weeks. Its title, with its Shakespearean allusion—*Tupí or not Tupí*—referred to the Tupí-Guaraní, natives "unsuitable for work" whom the conquistadores had systematically massacred then replaced with slaves brought from Africa. The pamphlet was not particularly large, but it was properly printed and had numerous black-and-white illustrations. In his editorial entitled *O indio não é bicho* ("The Indian isn't an animal"), Virgilio set out the aims of the little group around him: to protect the Indians of Brazil—those of Amazonia as well as those of the Mato Grosso—from extermination; to defend their culture, their customs and their territories from invasion by the industrialized world; to assert their history as the best way for Brazilians to resist the takeover of their country by the great powers. This wide-ranging program embraced all the popular cultures of the interior, which had inherited, according to Virgilio, the customs of the indigenous tribes and also included an active defense of the language and oral traditions of Brazil.

"So what do you think of it?" Virgilio asked, a little anxiously. His thin face covered in acne did him no favors, but he had doe-like eyes behind the lenses of his little gold-rimmed glasses. Moéma had a very high opinion of him.

"Fantastic! I never thought you'd actually get it out. It's brilliant, Virgilio, something to be proud of."

"You must write an article for the next issue. I've already got ten subscriptions, not bad for the first day, eh?"

"And I make eleven. You must tell me how much I owe you." Then, leafing through the journal, she went on, "The paper on the Xingu tattoos is great. Who is this Sanchez Labrador?"

"Me," said Virgilio in apologetic tones. "Also Ignacio Valladolid, Angel Perralta, et cetera. I did everything, including the drawings. You know how it is, you get promised lots of articles, but when the time comes, no one's to be found. Of course, now the first issue's out, I'm snowed under with offers. It makes me sick. People really are unreliable."

"That's true," said Thaïs as she burned her fingers on the tiny butt from which she was trying to take one last puff.

"If you want," Moéma said, "I could do something on the Kadi-wéu. We took them as an example this year to study the concept of endorsement. Did you know that they feel responsible for everything, even the sun rising?"

"Christ, the fools!" said Pablo, bursting into laughter. "I don't envy them . . ." Then, seeing Moéma's furious look, "OK, OK. If you can't even take a joke! I know nothing about all that old stuff."

"Well you ought to make an effort. It's the present that's at stake, your present. Every time a tree disappears, an Indian dies; and every time an Indian dies it's the whole of Brazil that becomes a bit more ignorant, that is, a bit more American. And it's precisely because there are thousands like you, who couldn't care less, that the process continues."

"Oh, come on, I was only joking . . ."

"So was I," Moéma snapped.

"You always have to get on your high horse whenever we start talking about Indians. You're getting tedious, sweetheart, you really are."

"OK, that's enough you two," said Virgilio in conciliatory tones. "That doesn't get us anywhere. While you're getting in each other's hair our dear president has sold a part of Amazonia the size of the Netherlands to a Texas mining company."

"How big is the Netherlands?" Thaïs asked, her speech slurred by the cannabis.

"Roughly the size of Ceará."

"A mining company!" Moéma said in disgust, her whole body racked by a wave of anger.

"I heard it this morning. On the radio, so it must be official."

In the profound silence that followed Moéma felt terribly impotent. She felt like being sick.

"Right," said Pablo, "then we'll have to get up our strength for the fight. Can I have this thing, Thaïs?" Without waiting for a reply, he took a little clip-frame with a picture of Saint Sebastian bristling with arrows off the wall.

"What are you doing?" Thaïs asked, uneasy. Without being religious herself, she didn't like people playing with religious objects. Such color prints could be found in all the shops selling religious bric-a-brac, but she was fond of this Saint Sebastian because of his sad smile and beautiful androgynous face. Less innocent was the way the drops of crimson blood dripping down from his wounds secretly excited her to the extent that she always saw this image at a particular moment of pleasure during lovemaking.

"Don't worry, sweetheart," said Pablo, carefully opening a film-roll box and pouring the contents onto the clip-frame, "it's on the house."

"Wow!" Thaïs exclaimed, seeing the large lumps of cocaine rolling a cross the glass. "It's Christmas, *Mãe de Deus!*"

"Goodness!" Moéma said, just as fascinated by this sudden abundance. "Where did you find that amazing stuff?"

"I've just got it. When it's like that, in little crystals, it means it's not been cut. It's the purest of the pure, ladies."

Closely watched by the two girls, Pablo started by crumbling up the lumps with a razor blade. Once the cocaine had been reduced to powder, he divided it up into four equal parts, which he then deftly drew out into a number of parallel lines.

"Leave me out," Virgilio said suddenly, standing up. "Sorry but I have to go."

"See you this evening, at the *Casa de Cultura Alemã?*"

"Yes—if you're still in a fit state to go anywhere by then."

"Don't worry, I'll be there."

"Good. See you, then. But be careful, that stuff's shit."

He hadn't even left before Pablo had shifted his share of the powder to the other three lines. "Your little journalist doesn't know what he's missing. Is he afraid or what?"

"Leave it, Pablo," Moéma said icily, "he's OK."

"Fine, fine, I didn't say anything. Off you go, you lead the way."

He handed her the clip-frame and the 100-cruzeiro note he had just rolled up into a tube. Leaning over the picture of Saint Sebastian, Moéma put the improvised straw up one of her nostrils, blocking the other with her forefinger. She snorted half the line steadily and confidently, then repeated the process. After having sniffed it all back, she tapped the glass to pick up the last crystals on the tip of her finger and rub them vigorously on her gums.

"*Que bom!*" she said, closing her eyes. The heat came in stronger and stronger waves; an odd taste, slightly bitter, was making her mouth numb.

"Well then?" Pablo asked, while Thaïs hurried to go through the same ritual.

"You're right, it's good stuff, very good stuff."

"If you want some, tell me now. It's going to disappear very quickly."

"How much?"

"For you, the price is the same as the last time: ten thousand a gram."

Cooled down by a burst of guilty conscience, Moéma almost refused the offer, but the idea exasperated her. The feeling it gave her of being under surveillance, judged in advance by the paternal tribunal. When was she going to make up her mind to accept the choices she'd made? With the money she'd exchanged she'd enough cash to renew her supply of coke—she'd almost none left since the other night—and to pay the first expenses for setting up the bar. She calculated that two grams would be sufficient to see her through to the end of the month. And she suddenly felt so good, so much mistress of herself and her destiny . . .

"Share mine with me, I already snorted a bit too much for today," Pablo said with a smile.

Thaïs quickly took her share, as if to stop him changing his mind.

"Three grams, can you do that?" Moéma said, as if it was nothing.

"Can do," Pablo replied with a knowing wink. "Four o'clock at your place, OK?"

"OK."

"I'll get it done right away. Just as long as it takes to go around to the safe and then back to my place to weigh it."

"To the safe?" Moéma asked, surprised.

"You don't think I keep my stock in my parents' house, do you? With a safe deposit box at the bank I'm not running any risks. Even if I get nicked with some stuff on me, they can't accuse me of dealing. You've got to look after number one, sweetheart, it's the only way of surviving."

Moéma waited until he'd gone before snorting the coke Thaïs had left. Shifted around by the various operations on the glass, most of the powder had accumulated in the middle of Saint Sebastian. She spent a long time over that part, revealing little by little the flesh of his thighs, the bulge of his groin, as if removing the linen concealing his nakedness thread by thread.

AFTER THE TRANSACTION with Pablo the two girls had "tested" the new coke and gone to bed. They only got up toward seven, to have a shower and go out to eat—extravagantly, Moéma invited Thaïs to the Trapiche, the best restaurant in town. Exhilarated at the idea of shocking the strait-laced clientele of the establishment, they spent more than an hour making up and choosing their dresses. Thaïs painted her fingers with mauve varnish, tending to black, and put on bright red lipstick and her favorite dress: a loose-fitting smock in almost transparent pink muslin, pulled in at the waist and dotted with little stars of metallic blue plastic. Moéma just put on a man's suit with a tie and a white shirt, but she slicked back her hair in a very tight bun, before drawing on a thin mustache à la Errol Flynn with a stick of greasepaint.

One last pinch of coke, "to pep them up," and they were braving the *Beira-mar* and the crowds of young people who frequented the sea front once night had fallen. Thronging the terraces of the bars or drinks stands, which stretched out for miles along the shore, clustering around parked cars with their doors open and music going full blast, they moved about, danced on the spot, laughed, shouted abuse at each other sometimes, clutching a glass or a bottle, a constantly milling, gaily colored mass. Street peddlers were selling all kinds of craft items, necklaces, "handmade" jewelry, leather and lace from the *Nordeste*, as well as half-open sharks' jaws, shells bristling with spines, crab fritters, *acarajé*, in a heady smell of fried coconut oil. Thaïs and Moéma plunged unhesitatingly into this dark, heaving mass. Despite their familiarity with carnival dressing-up, or perhaps because of it, people turned around as they passed with amused expressions, wolf whistles or even off-the-cuff compliments. Feigning total indifference, the two of them strolled along slowly, determined to behave naturally and forcing themselves to stop from time to time on the pretext of examining a stall or to kiss each other tenderly on the neck.

When they entered the restaurant like two schooners with the wind behind them, the maître d'hôtel, who came to greet them, had a brief moment of hesitation. Holding his gaze with composure, Moéma asked for a table for two and inquired with a polished turn of phrase about the freshness of their spiny lobsters. Doubtless influenced by her confident tone, the maître d' led them to one of the last free tables deep in the rich, air-conditioned half-light that is the hallmark of a great establishment. Thaïs was intimidated by it. Struck dumb by a formality she was encountering for the first time, terrorized by the unrelenting attentiveness of the waiters, she was only her old self again after her second aperitif. The effect of the alcohol combining with that of the cocaine, she quickly forgot her provincial unease and, following Moéma's example, concentrated on the restaurant's customers. The two girls thought up lots of scabrous stories behind their conventional appearance, mocking one person's face or mimicking another's mannered gestures with an inventiveness that sent them into uncontrollable giggling fits. The waiters for the most part colluded in their high spirits, giving them big smiles, taking care not to be seen by the maître d'hôtel; his black looks showed how much he was annoyed with himself for having let these overexcited customers in.

Exasperated by remarks of which he was the target, one diner with heavy jowls and a pot belly cut short his meal; trailing his wife and children behind him, he left in high dudgeon. Highly amused, Thaïs and Moéma saw him take the maître d'hôtel to one side and rail against their behavior, with much wagging of his finger and spluttering. The maître d' threw up his arms, clasped his hands and made one low bow after another, but his profuse apologies could not stop the customer from venting his rich man's anger on him before stalking off.

They were then served spiny lobster tails au gratin in half a pineapple brimming with a creamy sauce flavored with ginger and cardamom. And since Thaîs was worried about having to use her fish knife and fork, Moéma led the way by starting to eat with her fingers. Under the now disapproving glances of the waiters, who were very unhappy with this insult to the speciality of the restaurant, they persisted in the affront, smearing their glasses and serviettes with their greasy fingers and mixing long draughts of beer—Moéma had ordered some just to see the look on the sommelier's face—with the excellent chablis he had recommended.

They had reached the dessert when Thaïs, completely tipsy, decided she had to write a poem on the tablecloth. After a long rummage around in her handbag, she took out a large fountain pen, which she showed off to her friend. The first word she wrote on the cloth remaining invisible, she swore at the recalcitrant implement, unscrewed it and squeezed the cartridge so hard that a jet of ink spurted out onto her dress, over her thighs. She shot to her feet and saw that the damage was done: a huge black stain was spreading through the fine muslin, beyond repair. They both burst out laughing at the same time, then ordered a bottle of champagne in an effort, they claimed, to ward off ill fortune.

"And a pair of scissors, please," Thaïs said to the waiter as he was going off. He made her repeat her request, assuring her, with a weary look, that he would do his best.

When he came back he had the scissors she'd asked for. As he was undoing the wire around the champagne cork, Thaïs suddenly climbed up onto her chair. "Off you go," she said, handing Moéma the scissors.

Moéma got up and, walking around her friend, cut off the dress above the ink stain, making it into a mini skirt. Out of the corner of their eyes, or openly looking at them, the other customers observed the operation in a profound silence broken by the clatter of forks and whispers. Mesmerized by the agreeable view of Thaïs' panties that his position gave him, the waiter had watched the scene without moving, his hand rigidly clasping the neck of the bottle he was preparing to open. It was the sudden explosion of the cork that broke the spell.

Delighted with the exploit and having decided that the shortened dress was much more becoming than previously, Thaïs and Moéma sat down again and drank the champagne right down to the last drop.

When the moment came to present them with the little box containing the bill, the maître d'hôtel did so with the satisfied expression of a man finally giving his worst enemy a bomb that was bound to have a devastating effect: the bill reflected their extravagance and he was hoping, with all his flunkey's soul, that it would be beyond the means of these dykes. After a quick glance, Moéma counted out the sum on her lap, so that Thaïs couldn't see how much it was, then put it in the box without batting an eyelid.

"I presume you're going to give us a cigar," she said with a haughty smile, casually dropping a large tip on the table.

The maître d'hôtel swallowed his ill humor and gave the order. Puffing their Havanas aggressively, they got up from their table, walked across the restaurant like a royal couple, responding to the forced thanks and farewells of the staff with a slight nod, and left the restaurant.

The bar project would have to be put off a little longer, then, Moéma thought as she counted what was left. But the evening with Thaïs was well worth the sacrifice. They had passed through the darkness of the Trapiche like two nameless comets heading for outer space, leaving a scattering of little blue metal stars behind them in evidence of their passing.

"What would you say to spending a few days at Canoa?" she suddenly asked Thaïs. "I've still got enough money to pay for you as well."

"Great! You're fantastic, really," said Thaïs enthusiastically. "I've been dying to go back there for ages."

"Tomorrow, then?"

"No problem, count me in. Oh, what a great idea."

Once more caught up in the lively crowd along the shore and laughing at their inability to walk straight, they somehow managed to reach the *Avenida Tibúrcio Cavalcante*. It was only while searching for her keys that Moéma remembered the meeting at the German Cultural Institute. It was eleven o'clock.

"Shit, shit and double shit. I completely forgot about that."

"Me too," said Thaïs, bursting out laughing.

"I have to go. I promised Virgilio."

"Forget it. Anyway, it's too late and I can't take one more step, the state I'm in."

"You wait for me here, then. I'll be right back."

"Oh, no, I don't want to be left all alone," Thaïs simpered.

"Rest assured, I won't be long. I promised, Thaïs, I have to go."

Thaïs embraced her and gave her a long kiss on the lips; balancing on one leg, she rubbed herself up against Moéma's thigh. "Look, she's already crying because you're going away," she said, guiding Moéma's hand toward her groin.

"Don't worry, my love, I'll console her when I get back. There, take the keys, I'll be back in no time at all."

"You're sure?"

"Sure as sure can be. I don't want you snorting all my coke."

FAVELA DE PIRAMBÚ: *Life is a hammock rocked by fate . . .*

Blue and red against the setting sun, Zé's truck suddenly appeared on the swelling dunes of the horizon. Driven at full speed and distorted by the heat haze, it looked like a knight in armor in his final charge against the dragon. Its dazzling chrome shot off more flames than the sun itself and, like the shield of St. George, gave rise to indescribable hope.

It came to a halt right in the middle of the shanty town, not far from Nelson's shack, after one last whinny and a couple of shudders that sent up a cloud of sand and dust.

Zé Pinto got down from the cab nimbly, but Nelson realized there was bad news coming when he started to walk toward him with tentative steps. His shoulders more hunched than usual, his smile with a hint of sadness, he couldn't say exactly what it was, but he was so accustomed to reading the anguish in other people's expressions that something told him the day would not finish without some new blemish. Despite his truck driver's tan, Zé looked gray; dark rings under eyes glassy with fatigue said more than his speedometer about the number of miles he'd driven in the last three days.

"Hi, son," he said with feigned cheerfulness. "How's tricks?"

"*Tudo bom*, the Lord be praised," Nelson replied, holding out his hand.

Zé slapped the boy's palm, then their thumbs engaged, the other fingers wrapping themselves around their wrists. After a double rotation, allowing each in turn to clasp a clenched fist, the strange ritual gesture finished with the four hands intertwined, a Gordian knot that sealed their friendship.

They went into the hut. Bending his head so as not to hit the corrugated iron ceiling, Zé strung up a second hammock beside Nelson's then started to empty the plastic bag he'd brought. "Just a few bits and pieces . . . I don't know what to do with them myself."

He put a tin of olive oil on the floor, three loaves of *rapadura,* the raw cane sugar the *aleijadinho* was fond of, an enormous mango and some eggs. Zé had bought all this for him but Nelson merely muttered his thanks in order to keep up the pretense. They both appreciated this basic restraint, a kind of lightning conductor for any effusiveness.

"Where've you been?" Nelson asked, filling the glasses with *cachaça.*

Zé shook his head in disapproval. God knows how much they made him pay for that bottle, he thought. "You shouldn't have," he said. "You know it's bad for you."

"Where've you been," Nelson repeated, his eyes fixed on Zé's.

"Juazeiro. I was delivering twenty tons of cement to a firm. I stopped in Canindé on the way back. The people are starving out there, they told me there were forty cases of plague."

"Plague?!"

"The black death. The doctors in the hospital wanted to close the town, but the mayor doesn't want the news to get out because of the elections. It's always the same old story! *The poor don't grow, they swell* . . . I read that on a Mercedes tractor-trailer, a *pau de arara* that was coming from the plantations."

All over Brazil the long-distance truck drivers thought up a "maxim" and had it painted on a decorated piece of wood they fixed to the front and back of their vehicle. Some showed a humorous or poetic touch, others were happy to add their bit to the prevailing misogyny, but the majority had one sole theme: inexhaustible variations on the curse that is life. It was from the gaily colored aphorisms speeding along the roads that Zé had derived his whole philosophy. At fifty—he looked much older, as did the majority of the lower classes in the *Nordeste*—he had hundreds of different adages stored in his memory. Whenever he passed trucks as he drove around, he made sure to learn their anonymous maxims parading their modicum of irony, mysticism or suffering below the windscreen. After having meditated on them for hours, sometimes for days, he made the most caustic ones his own and peppered his conversation with them. Nelson looked on him as a fount of wisdom, especially as his own truck bore a sentence that utterly perplexed him: *A vida éuma rede que o destino balança*, life is a hammock rocked by fate.

"By the way, I almost forgot," said Zé, rummaging around in his pocket. "Look, I've got these for you as well. I found them in Petrolina."

He handed Nelson two little booklets of *literatura de cordel*, those long popular poems that could be found almost everywhere in the Sertão. Written and illustrated by the *violeiros*, wandering guitarists who printed them themselves on poor-quality paper, they were sung by their authors at markets, in the streets or cheap restaurants. To display them to potential customers, the *violeiros* were in the habit of tying them around the middle, like any old cloth, and hanging them from a cord strung between two trees. Thus the name "cord literature" for all such chapbooks.

Nelson could manage to decipher a text word by word, but it demanded too intense an effort for him to read normally.

"There's *The cow that started talking about the present crisis* and *João Peitudo, the son of Lampião and Maria Bonita*," Zé went on. Would you like us to sing them together in a while?"

Nothing gave Nelson more pleasure. He had a guitar and he'd learned to play the monotonous rhythm needed to chant these poems; he only needed to hear them once or twice for them to be imprinted on his memory for good.

"Why not right away?" he asked, twisting around to get his instrument. "Shall we start with the *Son of Lampião*?"

"There's something I have to tell you first. You know," he said, lowering his eyes and fixing them on his large, scarred hands, "a few years ago all the truck drivers had a dog in their truck but today any dog can have a truck ... It's getting harder and harder to get a load, so I couldn't pay the installments on my Berliet ... Well, I've been forced ... I really have been, I assure you. I've ... the Willis, you understand. I've sold the Willis."

Not far away, behind Nelson's shack, a dustcart could be heard tipping a load of refuse on the rubbish dump.

CHAPTER 5

The Italian journey: of Morgan le Fay, of Atlantis & of the
fumes of Mount Etna

WE WERE ONE day's journey away from the
Straits of Messina, riding slowly in the oppressive heat of
Calabria, when Athanasius opened a missive with green wax
seals that were unknown to me. Drawing my attention with a
smile and a little gesture, he read out the letter to me, now and
then absentmindedly wiping away the sweat dripping down his
forehead with a handkerchief:

> *On the morning of the Assumption of the most Blessed Virgin,*
> *standing alone at my window, I saw such numerous and such new*
> *things that I cannot—nor will not—stop thinking about them be-*
> *cause the most Blessed Virgin caused a vestige of the paradise that*
> *she entered on this very day centuries ago to appear in the light-*
> *house where I was. And if the eye up above possesses, like the intel-*
> *lect, a mirror in which, of its own volition, it can make anything*

it wishes appear, then I can call the one that I saw the mirror of that mirror! In an instant the sea that bathes Sicily swelled up and became, over a distance of about ten miles, like the spine of a black mountain. Then there appeared a very clear & transparent crystal; it resembled a mirror, the top of which was resting against the mountain and the foot on the Calabrian shore. This mirror suddenly showed a succession of more than ten thousand pilasters of equal height; & the bases between pilaster & pilaster were of the same bright clarity, of the same shadow. One moment later the said pilasters lost height and curved to form arches, such as the aqueducts in Rome or the foundations of Solomon have; & the rest of the water remained a simple mirror, even to the mountain pools of Sicily. But after a short while a large cornice formed above the arches & on it there appeared a number of veritable castles, all set out in this immense glass & all of the same form & the same workmanship. Then the towers turned into a colonnaded theatre; then the theatre split along a double vanishing point; then the alignment of the columns became a very long façade with ten rows of windows; the façade changed into a forest of pines & cypresses of equal height, then into other species of trees . . . At that everything disappeared & the sea, hardly rougher than before, became its former self. That is this famous Fata Morgana, which for twenty-six years I had believed improbable & which I have now seen, more beautiful & and more real than what had been described to me. Since that hour I believe it is real, I believe in this way various fleeting colors have of appearing, more beautiful and more vivid than those of art or of nature. I desire Your Reverence, who live surrounded by the glories of Rome and contemplate from close to the divine verities, to tell me who the architect or the craftsman is & with what art & what material he gathered together these varied and numerous glories in one place. While waiting, I pray God may ever look favorably on me and I commend myself to His most holy sacrifices.

Reverend Father Ignazio Angelucci of Reggio. S. J.

This letter, dated August 22, 1633, had been given to Athanasius by Father Riccioli who had admitted he couldn't understand a word of it. Concerned about Father Angelucci's mental health & because Reggio was one of the places where we had to stop, he had asked my master to clarify this enigma.

"Well, Caspar," Kircher said, handing me the letter, "what do you think of it? Madness? Mystical visions? Authenticated miracle? Is our Ignazio a gentle simpleton or a holy man the Lord has touched with his finger?"

"*Blessed are the poor in spirit,*" I replied without hesitation. "The chosen ones of God have often been seen as fools or madmen in the eyes of their fellow men. However, the things that Father Angelucci describes with such sincerity seem to me to be so far beyond understanding that I believe he has been fortunate enough to witness a true miracle."

"A correct reply," said Athanasius, "but wrong. Correct in logic, but wrong in truth. The author of this letter is neither mad nor one of the elect; he is, like you my dear Caspar, simply a victim of his own ignorance. What Father Angelucci witnessed, the famous Morgan le Fay, over which so much ink has been spilt, is not a miracle but a *mirage*. The columns this fellow from Reggio saw were doubtless those of the Greek temples of Agrigento or Selinunte, infinitely multiplied and pleasingly distorted by progressive transformation through the vapors rising from the sea. Having said that," he added with a smile, "I would give anything to be able to witness such a fantasmagoria & above all . . . to be able to verify what I have just put forward."

He wiped his forehead & immersed himself once more in his notes, without making anything of my defeat, for which I was grateful: once again a few words had been enough for him to resolve a mystery that had ever thwarted the most learned

scholars & to make me aware, by comparison, of my own
immeasurable ignorance.

As soon as we reached Reggio, we went with Father Angelucci
to the lighthouse from which he had seen the *Fata Morgana*.
He confirmed the details of his letter point by point & and
we found him to be of perfectly sound mind, if a little rustic.
Kircher explained the agencies of the spectacle he had witnessed,
but even though the reverend father pretended to accept them,
we could see that he didn't believe a word of it & by far preferred
miraculous explanations to those of physics.

During the week we spent in that town we went to the
lighthouse every day without being granted a sight of the mirage.
And, to be honest, it would have been rather unfair if a privilege
that had cost our host twenty-six years of his life should have
been granted us after so little effort. As the marine landscape
we saw from that window was charming, it at least gave rise to
pleasant conversations.

From Reggio we put out to sea &, skirting the coast of Sicily,
reached the port of Valletta. Together with Frederick of Hesse
we were given rooms in the palace of the Knights of the Order
of Malta. The government of the island was seriously concerned
about the presence of Turcoman pirates in the Tyrrhenian Sea
& there was much disquiet. But Kircher, unaffected by all that,
immediately set about organizing a tour of the island in order
to carry out his program of observations. He started to study
the plants & animals, also collecting a quantity of geological
specimens.

From information supplied by one of the knights of the
Order, we went to the east coast to view a cliff that had been
sculpted by nature into a gigantic human figure. It was a
woman's face, which fascinated both of us by its beauty. I knew
that nature, by definition, was capable of such marvels, but it

is quite a different matter to contemplate the product of this magnificent art *de visu*. Kircher ran this way and that to vary his viewpoint, lifting up his cassock to climb the rocks more easily. He pointed out to me a very precise spot where the face could be seen but disappeared at the slightest change in the angle of observation, merging once more into the surrounding rock. He was talking to himself, laughing out loud, in one of those transports of delight that were customary with him every time he discovered something new.

"Jesus Maria! Only a few cable-lengths away from Africa, from Egypt! It's proof. All the pharaohs and their wives in this emblematic figure! *Natura pictrix,* Caspar, *natura pictrix!* I'm on the right road, no doubt about that. Natural anamorphosis is only one of the forms of the universal analogy! I've never been so close to the goal . . ."

I had too often seen Athanasius in these states close to ecstasy to be particularly worried, but it was always amazing to see a man normally so level-headed in such a fever of excitement. When he had finished prancing around, my master sat down in the shade of the rock in question & started to write. I passed the time patiently cutting his quills, knowing that sooner or later he would tell me the result of his meditations.

Never having been so close to Egypt, Kircher confessed to me that he regretted that the Grand Duke had not asked to visit that land that in his eyes was so important for the understanding of the universe. In Valletta Athanasius was often absent for hours on end, sitting by the sea, his eyes fixed on the southeast, in the direction of the Nile, travelling in thought through those cities that are almost as old as the world. He would spend whole mornings wandering round the harbor, talking to sailors returning from Africa, avidly gathering all the information or curios these people might possess. But the time came when we had to leave Malta & start the return journey, which promised so many marvels.

After a calm passage, we disembarked at Palermo where we lodged in the Jesuit college. Frederick of Hesse having numerous official obligations to fulfill, we were free for several weeks, but before starting out on our planned tour of Sicily, Kircher had to demonstrate his talents to the teachers at the college and to the local notables, who already knew him by reputation. For several days, in this library where I am at the moment, he answered his colleagues' questions with consummate ease, developing all the topics as they were submitted to him. He had a prodigious memory & could quote most of his sources *in extenso* or do extremely complex calculations without referring to a single note. His lectures were so successful that they were the talk of the town & soon he had to receive a number of aristocrats attracted by a man whose erudition was such a contrast with his youth & attractive features. The Prince of Palagonia, who prided himself on his knowledge of the sciences & astrology, attended several of these lessons & eventually invited us to go and stay at his palace on the outskirts of the town. Kircher accepted this gracious invitation, but he was so keen to begin his studies on the land of Sicily that he put it off until near the end of our stay. And that was what was agreed.

Finally the moment came when the two of us set off for Mount Etna, an expedition Athanasius had made a priority in memory of Peiresc, though it was also his own. Despite my fear of the Sicilian bandits who infested the roads, we reached Caeta Abbey unmolested. In the library Kircher and I set about making a complete inventory of the manuscripts. We were fortunate enough to find several extremely rare items such as the *Hieroglyphica* of Horapollon, the *Pimander*, the *Asclepius* or *Book of Perfect Speech*, the Arabic text of *Picatrix* dealing with

talismans and sympathetic magic & a number of papyri that
Kircher had me copy. It was an unexpected harvest & it was
with light hearts that, a few days later, we undertook the ascent
of Etna.

As night was falling after a long day's walk, we came to a
dilapidated cottage that was a stopping place for travelers. We
had a bed for the night there & a meal as well as a guide for
the last part of our venture. After supper, a frugal meal but
accompanied by a good red wine from Selinunte, from the
very same hills where the ancient Greeks used to grow vines,
we sat down by the hearth & Kircher, a little mellow from the
wine, happily agreed to explain his ideas on geology to me. Like
Monsieur Descartes, he accepted the presence of a fire at the
center of the terrestrial globe, miners at the coal face testifying
that the heat increased with depth.

We went on talking until late into the night. Stimulated by
my questions, Kircher dealt one after the other with the biggest
problems set by the formation of the Earth, confiding in me
that what I was hearing were the premises of a book he was
preparing in secret—having been officially instructed to devote
himself to Egyptology—& which he would doubtless call *The
Subterranean World*. When we thought about getting some sleep,
it was already four o'clock in the morning & since we had to rise
at dawn to continue on our way to the summit, we decided to
stay up. Our conversation turned to volcanoes again. Athanasius
never tired of describing the fantastic upheavals the central fire
could cause when it escaped by those chimneys.

"According to my calculations, Atlantis was somewhere
between the New World & North Africa. When its highest
peaks started spewing out fire, when the ground started
trembling & caving in, spreading terror & death, the Atlantic
submerged the whole land. But when it reached the volcanoes

it succeeded in cooling their heat & consequently in arresting the progressive collapse of the land. The few peaks that were thus spared are the islands that today we call the Canaries & the Azores. And such was the power of these volcanoes, which must assuredly have been some of the major chimneys of the central fire, that even today they still display a certain amount of activity: all those islands smell of sulphur, & from what I have been told one can see numerous little craters & geysers where the water that escapes is boiling. It is therefore not impossible that one day the same phenomenon that made a whole world disappear could suddenly make it reappear, with all its ruined cities & and its millions of skeletons . . ."

Even though imaginary, this vision made my blood freeze. Kircher fell silent, the fire was dying out in the hearth & I shut my eyes in order to see with my mind's eye the emergence of the terrible graveyard from those far-off times. I saw the alabaster palaces slowly rise from the depths, the towers truncated, the huge statues broken, lying on their sides, decapitated, & I seemed to hear the sinister creaking noises accompanying this nightmare apparition. But suddenly the sound took on a quite different quality, it became so real that I made an effort to throw off my drowsy imaginings; I woke at the very moment when a terrible explosion made the walls of our lodging tremble & cast a red light over the room where we were.

"Up you get, Caspar, up you get! Quick!" Kircher yelled, a transformed man. "The volcano has woken! The central fire! Quick!"

As I stood up, terrified, I saw Athanasius rushing toward our luggage as one explosion followed the other. "The instruments! The instruments!" he shouted to me.

Taking that to mean he was urging me to help him save our precious equipment before fleeing, I did my best, despite my shaking legs, to help him gather up our things. The innkeeper, who was to be our guide, & his wife did not take such precautions; they cleared off, not without having advised us to join them at the foot of the mountain as quickly as possible.

We soon came out; even though it was night, the sky was ablaze & we could see as if it were daylight. My spirits revived somewhat when I saw that the track by which we had arrived had not been affected by the eruption. But my terror returned when I saw my master setting off in the opposite direction, the one that led toward the crater the color of incandescent embers.

"This way! This way!" I screamed to Kircher, thinking his agitation had made him go the wrong way.

"Stupid ass!" was his reply. "It's an unexpected chance, a present from heaven. Come on, hurry up! We're going to learn a lot more today than we could by reading all the books ever written on the question."

"But our guide!" I exclaimed, "we haven't got a guide! We're going to certain death!"

"We've got the best guide possible," said Kircher, pointing to the skies, "we're in His hands. If you're too frightened, go down & get yourself another master. Or follow me & if we must die that's just too bad, but at least we'll have seen."

"By the grace of God," I said, crossing myself, & ran to catch up to Kircher, who had already turned away & set off for the summit.

ALCÂNTARA: *A bird flies off, leaving its call behind it*

"What do you think of Kircher from the point of view of Sinology?" Eléazard asked. "Do you think he can be considered a precursor, in one way or another?"

"I don't know," Loredana replied, "it's odd. And then it all depends on what you mean by a 'precursor.' If you mean someone who put forward, before anyone else, some basic principles for understanding Chinese culture that were sufficiently penetrating to open the way to the understanding we have today, then the answer is definitely no. On that level his book is nothing more than an intelligent—and often dishonest—compilation of the work of Ricci and other missionaries. And every time he takes it upon himself to interpret these facts, he gets it badly wrong, just as with the Egyptian hieroglyphs. His theories on the way Asia was peopled or on the influence of Egypt on the development of Chinese religions are completely crack-brained. And it's the same with his approach to the formation of ideograms ... On the other hand, his book has been a fantastic tool, the first of its kind, for the understanding of the Chinese world in the West: he's never prejudiced, except in religion of course, and all things considered presents a pretty objective vision of a world that until then simply didn't exist for Europeans. And that, despite everything, is not bad at all."

"That is what I think too," said Eléazard, "but in my opinion it goes even farther. In his way he does more or less the same as Antoine Galland did for Arab culture when he produced the first translation of *A Thousand and One Nights*: he creates a myth, a mysterious China, supernatural, inhabited by wealthy aesthetes and scholars, a baroque exoticism that Baudelaire, or even Segalen, will recall in their fantasies of the Orient."

"It's difficult to prove," Loredana said reflectively, "but it's an interesting idea. Kircher as the unwitting initiator of Romanticism. It's close to heresy, isn't it?"

"To bring in Romanticism is going a bit too far, but I really think that by providing, for the first time, an overall image of China and not a simple traveler's tale, he determined the string of prejudices and errors under which that country continues to suffer."

"Poor Kircher, it sounds as if you really do have it in for him," Loredana said with a smile.

Eléazard was surprised by this remark. He had never seen his relationship with Kircher from that angle and even as he was collecting his thoughts to deny it, he realized that this way of formulating the problem opened up disturbing prospects. Looking at it more closely, there was certainly a touch of resentment in his constant denigration of the Jesuit. Something like the hatred with which a discarded lover reacts or a disciple unable to fill his master's shoes.

"I don't know," he said earnestly, "I find your question disturbing . . . I'll have to think about it."

The rain was still pouring down on the patio. Lost in thought, Eléazard peered at the candle flame as if the light would provide him with an answer to his questions. Amused by his attitude, the unusual importance he seemed to accord the meanings of words, Loredana felt her prejudice against him crumble away a little more. It was perhaps because of the wine, but she found her defensive reaction just now—when she had reprimanded herself for lowering her guard, even just a little—exaggerated. One ought to be able to confide in him without being afraid of his pity or a lesson in morality. It was good to know that.

"I think I have it in for him for having been a Christian," Eléazard suddenly said, without noticing how the few minutes of silence made his statement sound absurd. "For having betrayed . . . I can't say what exactly at the moment, it's the dominant impression despite my sympathy for him. His whole life's work's such a mess!"

"But who would have dared to be an atheist at the time he lived? Do you really think that was possible, or merely thinkable, even for a layman? Not out of fear of the Inquisition but because of the lack of the appropriate mind-set, because of an intellectual inability to imagine a world without God. Don't forget it was three more centuries before Nietzsche managed to express that denial."

"I agree with all that," Eléazard said, shrugging his shoulders, "but no one is going to persuade me that Descartes, Leibniz or even Spinoza had not already got rid of God, that in their writings the word is nothing but a term for a mathematical void. Beside them Kircher looks like a diplodocus."

"I don't think it's that simple," Loredana said with a doubtful look. "Anyway, I'd quite like to read this biography if you could lend me a copy."

"Can you read French?"

"Well enough, I think."

"No problem, then. I have a duplicate of my working copy, though you won't be able to see my notes, I've only got a rough draft of those. You could come round to my place, tomorrow morning, for example. It's not far: 3, Pelourinho Square."

"OK. My God, just look at that rain . . . I've never seen it like that. I feel all clammy, it's very unpleasant. I hope Alfredo's managed to get the water working, I'm dying to have a shower."

"I've no idea what he's doing, but he must have some problem. With the pump or with his wife."

"Oh, I hope not," said Loredana with a smile. "I wouldn't like to be responsible for a domestic squabble."

Something about the corners of her smile, or perhaps it was just the ironic glint in her eyes, convinced Eléazard that, on the contrary, she was flattered to have aroused Eunice's jealousy despite herself. This coquettishness suddenly made her seem desirable. Fixing his eyes on hers, he found he was imagining her in his arms, then devising various strategies to produce that result: suggesting she came to collect the Kircher biography that evening; taking her hand without a word; just telling her straight out that he wanted her. Each of these ploys generated a fragmentary scenario, hazy and with infinite ramifications that led nowhere except back to the acknowledgment of his desire, the image of their two bodies coming together, the urgent, suddenly vital need to touch her skin, to smell her hair . . .

"The answer's no," Loredana whispered with a hint of sadness in her voice. "I'm sorry."

"What are you talking about?" Eléazard said, realizing she had read him like an open book.

"You know perfectly well," she told him with a mild reprimand.

She had turned her head away to look at the rain. Without appearing nervous, she was rolling little balls of warm wax in her fingers and then putting them on the table, a faraway look in her eyes and the sulky expression of a little girl disheartened by an unwarranted reproof on her face.

"And may one ask why?" Eléazard went on, in the conciliatory tone of one who accepts defeat.

"Please . . . Don't ask anymore. It's not possible, that's all."

"Forgive me," he said, moved by the sincere note. "I . . . It's not something that happens to me every day, you know . . . That is, I mean . . . I meant it seriously."

When she saw him getting himself into such an awkward situation, she was a whisker away from telling him the truth. It did her good to see his desire for her in his eyes; two years ago she would already have dragged him off to her room and they would have made love while listening to the rain. But why should she, she told herself, since her openness—and it wasn't something she wanted to try again—disconcerted people more than it brought them closer.

"It's too soon," she said to give herself one last chance. "You need to give me time."

"I can wait, I'm good at that," Eléazard said with a smile. "It's one of my rare qualities, apart from . . ." (with a look of surprise he took the ping-pong ball that had just appeared in his mouth and put it in his pocket) "a certain acquaintance with Athanasius Kircher, Esq . . ." (a second ball, like an egg that insisted on being regurgitated) " . . . a modicum of intelligence and, of course . . ." (as a last ball was expelled more slowly, his eyes wide, like someone preparing to spew out the whole contents of his gut) "my natural modesty . . ."

Loredana had burst out laughing as soon as the first ball appeared: "*Meraviglioso!*" she said, applauding. "How do you do that?!"

"Secret," Eléazard whispered, putting his finger to his lips.

"How stupid of me—it's the same one each time, isn't it?"

"What d'you mean, the same one each time? You can count them if you want," he said, taking out of his pocket the three balls he always carried with him to practice with.

Loredana was still astonished. "Well I'm flabbergasted! With a trick like that you'd be made king of the Papuans."

Now it was Eléazard's turn to burst out laughing. She had never seemed so attractive as in her artless amazement.

"If you tell me how you do it, I'll read your future," she offered in mysterious tones.

"From the lines of my hand?"

"Not at all, *caro* . . . That's a load of bullshit. I read the *I Ching,* now that's something else, isn't it?"

"That's debatable, but OK," said Eléazard, delighted at having managed to revive her spirits.

"So?"

"So what?"

"The trick. That's our deal: you tell me how you do it . . ."

When she knew how to conjure the balls away—the trick was all the more deceptive for being simple, once you knew—Loredana took a booklet out of her bag and three little orange pottery discs.

"The sticks are too much of a bother to carry round, so I use these things . . ."

"What is it?" Eléazard asked, picking up one of the discs.

"It's called a St. Lucia's eye, a little plate that covers the entrance to some seashell, but I don't know its real name. Have you seen the spiral? It's almost the sign of the Tao. Right. Now you have to ask me a question."

"A precise question?"

"That's up to you. A precise question gets a precise answer, a vague one, a vague answer. That's the rule. But take it seriously or it's not worth the effort."

Eléazard took a sip of wine. Elaine had immediately appeared in his mind's eye. Elaine as a question. Not surprising, given the circumstances, but the contradictory questions that almost immediately clamored to be asked made him think: Was there a chance she might come back and everything would be as it was before? If she came back, would I be able to love her again? Will I know love with another woman? Does something else start once something has finished, or is that just an illusion to ensure the survival of the species? All this, he realized sadly, could be summed up in the one question: When will I be free of her?

"Come on. Is it so difficult?" she said, growing impatient.

"The two of us . . ." said Eléazard, looking up at her.

"What do you mean, the two of us?"

"The two of us. What will be the consequences of our meeting?"

"Clever," said Loredana with a smile. "But that could well make the answer complicated. Shall we start? OK. You've to throw the shells six times while concentrating on your question. That's the 'heads or tails' that allows me to determine the nature of the lines, but I imagine you know that."

Having tried to concentrate but having produced nothing but Elaine's distorted face, Eléazard threw the discs. After each throw, Loredana noted down the result, said some numbers and marked the lines of the hexagram with whole matches or ones that had been broken in half, as necessary.

"This first *Gua*," she said when the figure had finally been completed, "represents the current possibilities of your question. From that I will derive a second one, which will give you some elements of a reply for the future. You will know that there are some 'old' and some 'new' lines; an 'old' line always remains itself, while a 'young' line can become the opposing 'old' line. Thus a young *yin* changes into an old *yang* and a young *yang* into an old *yin* . . ."

"Aha . . . It's not exactly straightforward then, is it?" Eléazard mocked, amused by the earnestness with which she explained these distinctions.

"It's even more complicated than you think. I'll spare you the details. According to the numbers you have thrown, your hexagram has three 'young' lines, so I will transform them into their opposite, which gives us . . ." She opened the booklet, looking for the first of the two diagrams. "Ah, here we are: *Gou,* the Meeting. *Below: the wind; above: the sky. In the meeting the woman is strong. Do not marry the woman.*"

"Well now!" said Eléazard, genuinely surprised.

"I'm not making anything up. You can read it yourself, if you like. Put in everyday terms it says you will meet again something you had expelled from your mind. Which means a big surprise . . ." Loredana continued to read, wrapped in thought, then said, "That's incredible! Listen: *The meeting is an assault, it is the flexible one who takes the firm one by assault. 'Do not marry the woman' means that a long-term association would be pointless . . .*"

"Not very encouraging by the sound of it," said Eléazard scornfully.

"Wait, that's the overall sense of the hexagram. Now we have to interpret the lines that are susceptible to change and compare their meaning to that of the second hexagram. It's only after that that we can get a resolution. And the first one says . . . Just a moment. Yes: *In the presence of a fish in the net, the duty implied by this presence does not extend to visitors at all.*"

"And the fish is me?"

"Wait, I tell you. For the second we have: *A melon wrapped in branches of a weeping willow. It contains a brilliance that indicates the descent of celestial influences to the terrestrial plane . . .*"

"Aha! That's you! An angel come down from heaven . . ."

"And the third," Loredana added, as if replying to Eléazard's mischievous comment, "specifies that: *To meet a horn, that is something humiliating. But you incur no blame in this.*"

"If you mean I've hit a snag, thank you for nothing, I'd already noticed that."

Loredana shook her head regretfully. "We can stop if you've had enough. I really have the feeling I'm wasting my time."

"Please go on. I won't do it again, promise."

She leafed through her booklet for a while to identify the second hexagram. "That one's the *Xiao Guo*, the Little Excess . . . *Below: the mountain, above: thunder. A bird takes flight, leaving its call behind it. It ought not to rise higher. It ought to come down. In that case, and in that case alone, there will be happiness.*"

"It leaves its call behind it . . ." Eléazard repeated, taken with the sudden poetry of the image.

"Which means you are too excessive, even in things of little importance. *If the bird rises higher and higher, its cry will be lost in the clouds and become inaudible. If it came down, the others would hear it. Hearing the bird's call symbolizes listening to one's own excesses, becoming aware of them and carrying out a prompt adjustment.*"

Loredana continued to read silently. People of high society, the book said, are excessively polite in their conduct and excessively sad in their mourning . . . It was one of the oddest of the *I Chings*, one of the most explicit she'd ever read for someone, doubtless because she had been involved in the questioning. She knew very well why her meeting with Eléazard could not go beyond certain limits fixed inside her by her fear, even if that were exaggerated. This result must fit him one way or another . . . She decided to drive him into a corner.

"For whom or for what are you in mourning?" she asked him point-blank, aware that this unexpected question shook him.

Eléazard felt his scalp tingle. He had reached the point of seeing the previous metaphor as representing his attitude to Elaine and of trying it out at random on the thousand and one aspects of his anguish, and with one word this stranger had hit the bull's eye.

"You're amazing!" he said with genuine admiration.

He thought: I'm in mourning for my love, for my youth, for an unsatisfactory world. I'm in mourning for mourning itself, for its twilight and for the soothing warmth of its lamentation . . .

But what he said was: "I'm in mourning for everything that has not succeeded in being born, for everything we do our best to destroy, for obscure reasons, every time it puts out a shoot. How can I put it . . . I can't understand why we always see beauty as a threat, happiness as degradation . . ."

The rain stopped, replaced by a silence spattered with drops and sudden trickles of water.

"We haven't gotten anywhere yet," said Loredana, screwing up her eyes.

ELÉAZARD GOT UP around eight, a little later than usual. He found his coffee being kept warm in the kitchen and his piece of toast on the table beside the bowl and some *maracujá* juice. Soledade never appeared before ten, the television programs having kept her awake for a good part of the night, so she made a point of preparing his breakfast before going back to bed. With a muzzy head from the excesses of the previous evening, Eléazard took two soluble aspirin. "What a strange woman," he thought as he watched the tablets swirling round in the glass of water, "but she certainly knew how to twist me round her little finger . . ." To the very last moment he had hoped to finish the night with her and, thinking about it, he had come very close: at the end of the *I Ching* session there had been a moment, he was sure, when she'd been thinking seriously about the possibility, but that idiot Alfredo had appeared to announce his victory over the pump. Loredana had seized the opportunity and used her desire for a shower as an excuse to get away. She fled, Eléazard told himself, without understanding the motives for her escape or being able to do anything about the frustration it caused him. A little later, with the help of the aspirin, he was blaming himself for having succumbed to the lustful promptings of alcohol; mortified to think he must have cut a ridiculous figure, he decided to repress the memory of the evening. What a bad idea it had been to go out for dinner!

Before sitting down at his desk, he poured some sunflower seeds into the parrot's feeding dish. Heidegger seemed to be in a good mood, rocking back and forward and making his back ripple like a plumed serpent. Eléazard picked up a seed and went up to the bird, speaking softly to it, "Heidegger, Heidi! How are you today? Still not decided to speak normally, eh? Come on, come and get the seed, my beauty." The parrot came toward him by shuffling sideways along its perch, then let itself topple over and came to a stop head down in a bat-like pose. "Well then, what do you think of the world? You really think there's some hope?" Eléazard was moving his hand toward the enormous beak when the bird, like a spring suddenly released, bit his index finger and drew blood. "Oh, go fuck yourself, you stupid bastard," Eléazard yelled in pain. "You're mad, sir, stark staring mad! One day I'll pop you in the saucepan, d'you hear, you moron?"

Squeezing his cut finger, he was heading for the bathroom when Soledade appeared in front of him.

"*Que passa?*"

"What has happened is that that stupid parrot's bitten me again! Just look at that, he almost cut my finger off. I'll release him in the forest, then he'll learn what suffering is . . ."

"If you do that, then I'll leave as well," Soledade said solemnly. "It's your own fault, you don't know how to go about it. He doesn't bite me at all."

"Oh, really? And could you tell me what you have to do to please him? Get down on your knees? Crawl over to give him a seed? I'm really fed up with the creature."

"A parrot isn't like other animals. Xangó shines like the sun, there's fire inside him; if you don't show him respect, he'll burn you. It's as simple as that."

"You're as crazy as he is," Eléazard said, disarmed by this reasoning. "And why do you insist on calling him Xangó?"

"It's his real name," she said with a stubborn look, "he told me himself. He doesn't like the one he's been given at all. Come, I'll bandage that for you. That kind of thing can be dangerous, you know."

Eléazard gave in, overcome by the girl's touching naïveté, Brazil really was a different world.

"You got back late yesterday," she said, pressing some cotton wool soaked in alcohol on the wound.

"That hurts! Be gentle now."

"Gentle doesn't get you anywhere," she said, giving him a strange look, a mixture of sweet revenge and irony. "The disinfectant has to get to the bottom of the wound. What's her name?"

" . . . Loredana," he said, after a brief pause of surprise at her perspicacity. "She's Italian. But how do you know?"

"My little finger told me. Is she beautiful?"

"Not bad. That is, yes, curves in all the right places. She's got a superb ass," he added to provoke her a little.

"You're all the same," said Soledade as she finished wrapping the Band-Aid round his finger. "But when you go fishing at night, all you catch is eels."

"And what's that supposed to mean?"

"I know what I mean. Right, there, that's done. I'll go out and do the shopping."

"Get a bit more in than usual, we might have a guest."

Soledade nodded like the parrot and gave him a black look.

"*Si senhor*," she said, mimicking absolute servility. "But I warn you, don't expect me to serve at table, *O meu computado não fala, computa!*"

God knows where she heard that, Eléazard thought as he went back to his study. Spoken in a tone of contempt, it was a sentence that could be understood differently depending on the stress on the last word, either "My computer doesn't speak, it computes," or: "My computer doesn't speak with *puta*" (i.e., whores). He certainly felt that Soledade was a bit too free and easy, but he liked the pun and tried unsuccessfully to translate it into French in a way that retained its marvelous concision.

Then he immersed himself in Caspar Schott's manuscript. Rereading his notes on the computer, he decided they were too succinct and slightly prejudiced. The problem was to know whom they were aimed at: an academic familiar with the seventeenth century would doubtless consider them adequate but an ordinary reader wouldn't find enough in them to satisfy his curiosity fully. But how far should he go? He felt he had so much to say about Kircher's century, to his mind one of the most notable since

Antiquity, that he could easily double or even triple Schott's text with his notes. As for his prejudice against the man himself, that was something new, resulting entirely from his conversation with Loredana. There was a happy medium to be observed between unquestioning praise and systematic hostility, a balance in which his rancor toward Kircher was muzzled in the right way.

Still stormy, the weather was piling all the sadness of the world on Alcântara. Eléazard wondered whether Loredana would come and see him that morning, as she had promised. The woman was pretty unique of her kind. Now he remembered the night in the Caravela as something intense and poetic, one of those he would like to revive in his life. If she should come that day, he would offer her a genuine apology and tell her how much he wanted her friendship. He found himself imagining her in the alley she would have to go down to come to his house. Impatient, almost anxious, he watched out for her like a teenager on his first date.

I'm like an old child, he told himself with a smile. It's Moéma who's right. Down to work, then. In his archives—he'd have to get round to cataloging them one of these days—he'd finally managed to find the article by François Secret that had been missing since he'd edited the notes to chapter three. Secret, what a name for someone who'd devoted his life to hermeneutics! It was enough to make you think surnames could sometimes determine the destiny of those who bore them. Having said that, the study in question, *A forgotten episode in the life of Peiresc: the magic sabre of Gustavus Adolphus*, did not do much for Kircher since, in the light of the writings of George Wallin, it proved that the sabre he had examined was false. To make matters worse, Wallin quoted *De orbibus tribus aureis* by the Strasbourg scholar Johannes Scheffer, a book in which Kircher was accused of total ignorance in matters of interpretation for having talked of magic characters when, out of malice, someone had shown him what were merely samples of the Danish language. Of course, as thoroughgoing antipapists, Wallin and Scheffer were trying to rehabilitate Gustavus Adolphus and, through him, Protestantism as a whole; their accusation, along with many other similar ones, cast doubt on the Jesuit's competence. And this all the more so since his attempts at deciphering the hieroglyphs ended, unquestionably to our eyes, in abject failure.

Eléazard wondered how a person could be so blind. Without being able to say why, he was convinced that Athanasius Kircher had never knowingly cheated. If he could be accused, for his part, of supporting the cause of the Counter-Reformation with a white lie, that motive did not come into question for the Egyptian hieroglyphs. It followed, therefore, that the man must either have been deceiving himself—by autosuggestion? out of madness?—about his abilities or have taken Machiavellianism and a love of fame to a point where it became truly monstrous.

Eléazard edited the note relating to the "magic" sword then continued with the task of putting the text on the computer. He could not, however, stop himself from going to look out of the window from time to time, on the pretext of smoking a cigarette.

Toward ten Soledade came back from shopping with the mail and the newspapers she had gone to collect from the first boat. There was nothing of interest in the dailies. Always the same reports on murders or muggings more or less everywhere in the big cities, all largely drowned in the slush of articles on football, pop singers, provincial social events and ministerial bombast. A VASP plane crashing in the mountains near Fortaleza was the front-page news. *Nada restou!*—"Nothing left!"—was the expressive summary in one headline. "A hundred and thirty-five dead and two babies" proclaimed another with involuntary cynicism, as if the fact of having avoided the adult sufferings of human beings meant the babies did not have the right to be counted among the dead. There followed, in order, the usual photos to tickle their readers' taste for blood and gore, a description of the pillage of the wreck before the rescue party arrived, and posthumous praise for the crew.

Eléazard's attention was drawn by the plundering of the airplane: one more symptom in the long list he kept faithfully up to date. Two months previously several hundred destitute youths had left the favelas of Rio and poured onto the well-known Copacabana beach. They had cleaned out the place to such an extent, leaving the practically naked tourists to get on with their tan, that they had been dubbed *grilos*, "the locusts." More or less all over the country gangs were getting together to rob banks, supermarkets, hotels and even restaurants. In the filthy and overfull jails the prisoners were rebelling in such large numbers that the police had started shooting on sight. Every time they were called in it ended with dozens of dead. Corruption had spread to the highest levels of the state and while the mass of people was getting poorer by the day, suffering an alarming resurgence of diseases such as leprosy, cholera and bubonic plague, a tiny number of the *nouveaux riches* could watch their assets grow in the Miami banks. Brazil, as they say of white dwarfs, was collapsing in on itself and no one could say what "black hole" would be the result of the implosion.

Day after day Eléazard kept sending this prognosis of disaster to his news agency but the old world was too preoccupied with the symptoms of its own breakdown to feel sympathy for the misfortunes of a nation that neither the media nor international travel had managed to bring close to it. Without being pessimistic by nature, Eléazard was starting to have his doubts about the future. Following successive breakups, Europe was becoming volatile to the extent that it was beginning to resemble the continent that had been torn apart by the Thirty Years' War. Even worse, actually, since in those days the religious dissension was limited to Catholics against Protestants. And even if the current upheavals should be interpreted as announcing a radical metamorphosis of the West, what could be seen of it at the moment was hardly something to get enthusiastic about.

Eléazard was feeling depressed. He lit a cigarette and was about to read his mail when a voice made him start.

"Eléazard?"

It was Loredana.

"My apologies," she said, blushing, "the front door was open wide and since no one answered, I took the liberty of coming up."

"And quite right too," he said, disturbed by her sudden appearance. "I . . . I've gone native. What the locals do is to clap their hands to announce their presence. It's more effective than knocking on the door, especially when they're always open. But please sit down."

"Isn't he beautiful!" she said, noticing the parrot. "What's his name?"

"Heidegger . . ."

"Heidegger?!" she said with a laugh. "You don't do things by halves, do you! Hi, Heidegger. *Wie geht's dir, schräger Vogel?*"

Reacting to its name, the parrot shook its feathers, puffing out its crop, and uttered the only words it knew.

"What's he saying?"

"Nonsense. The man who gave him to me, a German friend, had tried to teach him a line by Hölderlin: 'Man's dwelling is poetic' or something like that, but it didn't work. The stupid bird insists on repeating that 'Man's swelling his pointed dick,' and there's no way of making him correct it."

"But why would you want to correct him?" she asked with a glint of irony in her eyes. "He's only telling the truth. Aren't you, Heidegger?"

As she spoke, she went over to the animal and now she was scratching its neck in a gentle friendly fashion, something Eléazard had never managed to do in the five years they'd been living together. More than anything else, he found this quiet feat alluring.

SÃO LUÍS, FAZENDA DO BOI: . . . *nothing but* *the indubitable present moment*

When the Colonel's limousine appeared at the entrance to the *fazenda,* the guard acknowledged it with a nod of the head as it went through and hurried to close the heavy wrought-iron gate behind it. Then he telephoned the butler to tell him the master was about to arrive home.

The Buick drove silently along the newly asphalted three-mile drive leading to the Governor's private residence. Through the smoked-glass windows Moreira watched the green expanse of the fields of sugar cane pass, darkly gleaming in the twilight. The long stalks had benefited from the rain and grown even more—twice the height of a man, he thought proudly—and it promised to be a fine harvest, even if it only brought in a supplementary income. He kept this crop out of sentimentality, in memory of a time that had made the reputation and fortune of his family, and enjoyed watching the canes grow to maturity every year. They could reach a height of as much as sixteen feet and he never looked at them without seeing them as the jungle of giant beans they had represented when he was a child. But the days of fairy tales and of agriculture were long gone. He had preferred to invest his money in mines and prawn fishing, while pursuing the political career his ambition demanded. Of the huge stretches of arable land bequeathed him by his father he had agreed to lease a few plots to some ignorant *matutos*, still in thrall to their out-of-date customs, less for the rent they paid—those peasants were more cunning than foxes and stole from him without batting an eyelid!—than for the sight of them, when he was out on his horse, bent over in his father's fields. The rest of his property was left lying fallow or used for raising cattle. Like the country squires who were his ancestors, he prided himself on not eating anything that did not come from his own estate.

The Governor closed his eyes. The vision of his land worked like an analgesic, dispelling the tiredness of the day as he came closer to the *fazenda*. His sense of well-being would have been complete were it not for the prospect of seeing his wife's sullen face and having to deal with her regular hysterical fits brought on by alcohol. She hadn't been the same since Mauro had gone off to university in Brasilia. Or perhaps since *Manchete* had published that photo of a tipsy "Governor Moreira," shirt undone, nibbling the breast of a second-rate dancer? Carnival fever, the cocktails at the education offices and the stupid challenge of Sílvio Romero, the minister of public works . . . Yet he had explained the circumstances that had led to his behavior to his wife. At the time she had pretended to understand, to pardon his infidelity and the humiliating scandal that had ensued, but that same evening she swallowed a whole tube of Gardenal with her whiskey. They'd just managed to save her. *Menopause problems, it happens more often than you think. Be patient with her, Governor, it'll only last a few months . . .* Too optimistic, as always, Dr. Euclides, the business had been going on for three years now and the annoying thing was that it was getting worse. Recently Euclides da Cunha had had the idea of advising them to undergo psychoanalytic couples therapy! Not a bad idea for her, certainly, but what was it to do with him?! The doctor was getting old, he'd have to think about consulting someone else. Discreetly, of course.

The Buick had stopped by the flight of steps leading up to the *fa-zenda*. The liveried chauffeur came around the car to open the door but the Colonel stayed on the seat for a few moments, contemplating the white façade of the family home, a dreamy look on his face. In the classical style—Moriera maintained, without a shred of evidence, that it had been built to a plan by the French architect, Louis Léger Vauthier—the house was like a little palace. Flanked by two symmetrical wings linked by a covered gallery, the main building had a balustraded upper floor and a triangular pediment. Coming out toward the steps, an imposing portico with three arches emphasized the seigniorial aspect of the building. Lengthened by the setting sun, the shadows of the royal palms were slanting across the pale pink roughcast of the walls, creating a harmonious geometrical network with the semicircular arches of the windows.

On the wide grass borders with their elegant groves of hibiscus, acanthus and laurels, the sprinklers suddenly started their *staccato* operation, sending out their fine, swirling spray over them. The Colonel checked his watch: seven thirty precisely. Order and progress! The *Fazenda do Boi* looked good, an image of the opportunities offered by Brazil, the symbol of a success that was open, as in North America, to the lowliest of its citizens, provided they believed in their country more than in their gods and worked to combat Nature's irrepressible tendency to disorder. What his father had done and his father before him, and what he was doing, in his own way, even more than his forefathers.

"Tell the gardener to mow the grass," he suddenly said to the chauffeur, who had remained standing stiff, his cap in his hand, beside the portal. "I want a proper lawn, not a meadow."

Without waiting for a reply, he got out of the car and went up the white stone steps leading to the main entrance.

Ediwaldo, the butler, was there to greet him as he entered the vestibule. "Good evening, sir. Have you had a good day?"

"Exhausting, Ediwaldo, exhausting. If you knew the number of problems I'm supposed to sort out in this state and the number of imbeciles who get together to complicate matters every time they're in danger of getting a bit too simple . . ."

"I can imagine, sir."

"Where is Senhora Moreira?"

"In the chapel, sir. She wanted to collect her thoughts before dinner."

The Governor's lips pursed in annoyance. *That fucking chapel! Another way of avoiding me . . . She who never used to set foot in it . . . Fucking God, dammit! Fucking shit of a woman!*

"Has she been drinking?"

"A little too much, sir, if you'll forgive me saying so."

Ediwaldo saw the Governor's jaw set. He hurried to strike a match under the cigarillo that had suddenly appeared between his lips.

"Thank you. Go and tell her that I want to see her at once in the drawing room. And have a whiskey sent up while you're at it."

"Cutty Sark, as usual?"

"As usual, Ediwaldo, as usual."

The Colonel slowly climbed the marble staircase leading to the second floor. On the landing he avoided looking at his own reflection in the large baroque mirror with the deep vista of golds and crimson velvet of the reception rooms; purring, with a noise like a crackling fire, a jaguar came crawling toward him.

"Jurupari, my beauty! Juruparinha . . ." he said lovingly, abandoning his hand to the animal, which licked it eagerly. "Come, *querida*, come, my lovely."

Moreira sank back into an ornate sofa—jacaranda wood, arms carved with passion fruit and star fruit, all bought at an exorbitant price from an antiques dealer in Recife. The jaguar had put its front paws on his knees to let him stroke its neck, eyes closed, quivering with pleasure. "Yes, *carinha*, yes . . . you're the loveliest . . . the most powerful . . ." Nothing moved him like the taut muscles under its tawny coat, hypnotic, speckled with eyes fixed on him alone. *In its universe there are no names, there's no past, no future, nothing but the indubitable present moment.* To think that it needed an Argentine to write that, to tell the truth about wild animals . . . His fingers could feel the warm gold of the collar in the animal's fur and, thinking of Anita's receptive thighs, her secret bush, he put one hand to his nostrils to try and bring back a memory.

Its spine suddenly twisting in a spasm, its ears flattened, the jaguar raised its head, turning its yellow eyes toward one of the drawing-room doors.

"Now, now, Jurupari. Calm down, calm down," Moreira said, keeping a firm grip on its collar. "It's only my aperitif."

"Yes, sir, of course, sir, will that be all, sir?" came his wife's slurred voice.

"Oh, it's you," said Moreira, turning toward her. "But what . . ."

Wearing a faded dressing gown—the one she preferred, as if out of revenge because he couldn't stand it—a cheap, pastel pink, padded nylon dressing gown that parted at every step to reveal her fat thighs, his wife came toward him, a glass of whiskey in each hand. "I ran into Imelda on the stairs and I thought I might as well serve the drinks myself."

"And took the opportunity to get one for yourself . . . You drink too much, Carlotta, it's bad for you, the doctor told you. You ought to make an effort, at least for your health."

Putting her husband's glass on a little low table, Carlotta flopped down on the other end of the sofa, spilling some of her drink on her chest. Without seeming at all concerned, she took a handkerchief out of her sleeve and wiped herself nonchalantly, revealing a flaccid breast, pitifully neglected.

"I've already told you not to walk around dressed like that," Moreira said irritably. "It's . . . it's indecent, for God's sake! If you won't do it for me, at least do it for the servants. What are they going to think of you? Not to mention the chapel. Since it seems you've become pious . . . I don't think it's really appropriate to pray half naked."

"You can go to hell," she said calmly. "Countess Carlotta de Souza's telling you to go to hell, Governor."

A look of dismay on his face, her husband shrugged his shoulders. "Just look at yourself, darling, the state you're in. You don't know what you're saying anymore."

"You wanted to speak to me," she said in an aggressive tone, "so get on with it, I'm listening. Come on, out with it."

"I don't think it's the right moment, you're in no state to listen to anything."

"Get on with it, I said . . . or I'll start screaming."

Startled by the raised voice, the jaguar started to growl, trying to escape from its master's grip.

"Quiet! Calm down, my beauty!" Then, in a lower voice, to Carlotta: "You're mad! I don't believe it! Do you want to get eaten up or what?"

"I warned you," she said, apparently unconcerned at the jaguar's growing agitation.

"I'm having a reception here, in a fortnight," the governor said. "Fifty people. It all has to be perfect, it's important for business. I'm counting on you to organize it. I'll give Ediwaldo the guest list . . . and we'll talk about it tomorrow, when you're sober. And now, with your permission, I'm going to take a shower. I advise you to do the same and to make yourself presentable for dinner, you look like . . . like an old whore, *querida*, an old whore!" He came so close to her he was breathing over her face. "You understand?

You understand that I'm starting to get fed up with your whims? I've had it up to here, *caralho!*"

Carlotta watched him leave the room, followed by his lousy jaguar. She was going to finish her drink but irrepressible sobs, all the more convulsive for being silent, made her double up with grief on the sofa.

CHAPTER 6

Continuation of the journey through Italy: in which Kircher
examines the central fire & vies with Archimedes

WE MADE RAPID progress toward the frightful
fireworks in front of us. After we had been walking
for half an hour the vegetation, already sparse, disappeared
completely & we were faced with a desert landscape of black and
ochre rocks, porous like pumice stone. It had become extremely
hot, we were sweating under our clothes, while from time to
time brief gusts of wind enveloped us in stinking fumes. The
continuous rumbling of the volcano made it impossible to utter
a word without having to shout oneself hoarse; the polluted air
was full of ash and sulphur . . .

All the time I was praying to God that Athanasius would
decide to turn back, but he kept going on, imperturbable, using
his hands to climb the warm slopes & jumping from rock to
rock like a kid goat, untroubled by the weight of baggage he was
carrying. At the time when dawn should have been breaking, it

was still night, with that kind of darkness that properly comes with a total eclipse.

At a turn in the path we suddenly found ourselves before one of the most monstrous spectacles it has been my lot to observe: three hundred paces to the right, below the spot where we were standing, a broad torrent of incandescent matter was pouring down, ravaging the ground as it swept by & appearing to dissolve everything it met in its bubbling stream. As for the source of this dazzling river, it was surmounted by gigantic flames, as if coming from hell itself, & produced an immense plume of smoke rising up into the sky until it was lost to sight. I was begging Kircher to go back down when a more violent explosion made the whole mountain shake; we saw a large number of molten rocks thrown up into the air, very high in the sky, before raining down around us. Since we were still far enough away from the diabolical furnace only the tiniest of these particles hit us & we were peppered with glowing embers. Believing my moment of death had come, I fell to my knees to beseech the Lord to have mercy on me but Kircher pulled me up, slapping me vigorously all over to put out my cassock. Then he dragged me to up a higher place, under a sort of rocky overhang where we were finally sheltered from the projectiles. Once there, he saw to his own cassock, which was burning in places, without, however, taking his eye off the marvelous scene before us. Then he took out his chronometer to measure the intervals between eruptions, calmly dictating figures and comments to me. The heat was almost unbearable and we were finding it difficult to breathe when dozens of crawling things suddenly started to pour through our refuge: all sorts of snakes, salamanders, scorpions and spiders scuttled between our legs for a few moments that seemed close to an eternity to me. Flabbergasted by this phenomenon, we did not think of using our equipment to collect some specimens. Kircher, who had observed the process with his usual concentration, immediately drew the most unusual of these creatures in his notebook.

"As you see, Caspar," he said when he had finished, "we have not wasted our time coming here. Now we know from the evidence of our own eyes that certain creatures are born of the fire itself, just as flies are engendered by manure & worms by putrefaction. Those there had been created practically before our very eyes & we can, or at least *you* can bear witness to it to the world at large, since, for my own part, I have decided to take a closer view of this original matter. Make sure you note down everything you hear & if anything should happen to me you must go back down to deliver to the world the posthumous fruits of my sacrifice."

I begged Kircher not to do anything so foolish, but he half covered himself up with his cape, poured our supply of water over himself &, carrying his bag & his instruments, set off at the same moment as a further explosion shook Etna.

"Be with me, Empedocles! And do thou hear me, Caspar, son of wise Anchites," he cried, rushing toward the stream of lava. I watched him, under a blazing deluge, approach the fiery matter, gesticulating & skipping about like a whole litter of mice; he looked like a man possessed suffering the torments of hell & I crossed myself several times to ward off this evil omen. From where I was standing, my master appeared to be enveloped in embers & his clothes were giving off white steam & I yelled at him to make him come back . . .

God finally answered my prayers: Kircher was coming back. However, his feet seemed to be so itching to get back that his biretta fell off as he ran & it was bare-headed that my master rejoined me, safe & sound, in the shelter of the rock. His cassock was in tatters & scorched by the fire, his boots were sizzling, which partly explained the capers I had seen him perform & I had to put out his hair, patches of which were burning, with the skirt of my cassock.

After having thanked me with a fraternal pat on the shoulder, Athanasius borrowed my chronometer to continue his observations. When he established that the interval between each eruption was increasing regularly, he finally decided to quit the pandemonium.

We returned without any major difficulties to the town where we had left most of our luggage. Kircher, whose feet, hands & face had some nasty burns, was in a pitiful state, so we granted ourselves several days' rest, which my master used to copy out his notes.

As soon as Athanasius's injuries had healed, we set off for Syracuse. Our program included a study of the ancient monuments of the city as well as visits to the Dominican libraries in Noto & Ragusa, but, without informing me, Kircher had concocted other plans: Syracuse being the town where Archimedes was born, I should have realized my master would not waste the opportunity of measuring his genius against that of the famous mathematician.

We walked on the ramparts of Ortygia, above the sea, for several hours without my being able to understand the point of the measurements Athanasius was constantly making with the astrolabe, or of the sketches that were filling his notebook. Then he locked himself in his room for two days & one night, forbidding anyone to disturb him. When he came out, radiant with joy, he immediately went to see various craftsmen, who were given very precise tasks to carry out without delay. During the next two weeks we did our planned tour of the libraries of the area.

In Ragusa my master bought various books in Hebrew on the *Cabbala* from the Jew, Samuel Cohen, & from the musician,

Masudi Yusuf, a manuscript containing the first *Pythian Ode* by
Pindar, accompanied by a system of transcription that made it
possible to reproduce the original melody! After having studied
it, he made a present of this inestimable work to the Monastery
of San Salvatore in Messina.

But the day came when, all the pieces ordered by him having
been delivered, Athanasius condescended to explain the purpose
of these mysterious preparations. When Syracuse was besieged
by the Consul Marcellus, in 214 before the birth of Our Lord,
Archimedes's inventions delayed the Roman victory for a long
time. According to Antioch of Ascalon & Diodorus of Sicily
this admirable scholar even managed to set enemy vessels on fire
by shooting the rays of the sun at them from a burning mirror.
Declaring it physically impossible to construct such a powerful
mirror, most of the commentators & scholars of the present age
had declared the story a legend; contrary to this general opinion,
Kircher intended to rehabilitate Archimedes in the very place
where, almost two thousand years ago, he had proved the
incomparable power of his genius.

"You see, Caspar, all these ignoramuses, for example
Monsieur Descartes, to quote but one, all these asses are
quite right when they claim it would be impossible to light a
fire from so far away with mirrors: a flat mirror would not
concentrate enough of the sun's light since it sends the rays
back perpendicularly to its surface. Circular or parabolic
mirrors are certainly capable of setting combustible material
on fire, but only from very short distances, that is, at the point
of convergence of the rays. Given this problem, the first task
was to work out precisely where Marcellus's ships were. Given
the configuration of the town ramparts, the depth of water
at their perimeter and the closeness necessary to besiege the
town effectively, factors that I calculated with you recently, the

Roman galleys must have been operating at thirty or forty paces from the walls. Now to satisfy these conditions, a parabolic mirror would have to be a league in diameter, which is indeed scarcely conceivable, even today. But the resources of the human mind are are boundless &, thanks be to Heaven, I conceived the idea of an elliptical mirror which, I am sure, will succeed where the others have always failed! The Duke of Hesse will be here in three days' time. I have informed him of my project & he has invited the most notable personages of Sicily to witness the occasion. They will, therefore, have first sight of this new *speculum ustor*, which we are going to construct together, my dear Caspar, if you will agree to assist me . . ."

We set to work without delay & after two days of uninterrupted labor, during which we glued, nailed & pinned numerous pieces of wood, a cart came to transport our machine to the place on the harbor where the demonstration was to take place. Once there, we installed it & covered it with a cloth in the colors of the Grand Duke & His Majesty the Viceroy of Sicily. Then we waited.

Once all the guests were assembled, Athanasius Kircher—who was pacing up and down the rampart in a fever of anxiety about a result that would make or break his reputation—gave a review of the historical facts, explained his theory at length & elaborated a little on possible uses of his machine, if it should work; he pretended to have his doubts about that, given the limited means at his disposal & the aging of the sun, which must necessarily have lost some of its power in the 1848 years since Archimedes's feat. At the agreed time, eleven o'clock in the morning, a large fishing boat, purchased with the help of Frederick of Hesse, anchored at forty paces from the place where we were. A Roman she-wolf had been painted on the stern to serve as a target. After having placed some model—but perfectly

copied—legionnaires here & there on the deck, the sailors left
the ship. Kircher raised the cloth & uncovered his machine to a
general murmur of astonishment.

It consisted of a wide truncated cone, open at either end, the
interior of which had been made into a mirror; a fairly simple
system of wheels & gears allowed it to be deployed precisely
in all directions. Turning several handles one after the other,
Athanasius focused the mirror so that the patch of light it
produced struck the center of the target. Then came the wait.
There was absolute silence and one could hear the lapping of
the waves below. A quarter of an hour and still nothing had
happened. The guests started to whisper among themselves.
Kircher was sweating profusely, constantly adjusting his ray,
his eye fixed on the roman she-wolf. Attracted by the unusual
spectacle, the common people had gathered behind the cordon
of guards & were commenting out loud on what they could
see, laughing & joking as is the custom among these people
of the south when faced with something that is beyond their
understanding. A half hour had already passed with no result &
even the guests were beginning to grow impatient at the time it
was taking when a seagull, doubtless attracted by the brightness
of the mirror, let go a dropping which splattered on the machine,
only just missing my master. It was all that was needed to set
off general hilarity. *Lazzi* directed at Athanasius came from all
sides & I heard a Sicilian noble comment in a tone of profound
contempt:

"*La merda tira la merda!*"

I saw Kircher flush at the insult, but he continued to busy
himself with his machine as if nothing had happened. I started to
pray that it might all be over quickly, this way or that, & I could
already see definite signs of irritation on the Grand Duke's face,
when a bellow from my master made all the spectators jump.

"*Eureka!*" he shouted again. "Look! Look, O ye of little faith!"

Motionless & in a theatrical pose, he was pointing at the target with a vengeful finger: a thread of black smoke was coming from it, rising straight up into the blue sky.

A hum of admiration rose from the whole audience. Simultaneously, or almost, the wolf burst into flames, crackling, & set off, as if by a trail of gunpowder, fires at several points on the boat. As I gave Kircher a look of astonishment at this development, he gave me a quick wink & I realized that he had taken care to make sure the vessel was prepared. Aware of my master's expertise in this area I got ready for more surprises & they weren't long in coming. As the felucca went up in flames, numerous rockets started shooting out of the hatches, exploding in the sky with great noise. Then Bengal lights turned into fountains of fire spouting up around the hull like the petals of many-colored flowers & catapults sent the blazing bodies of tailors' dummies flying across this marvelous show. The Greek fire had not gone out when, with a piercing whistle, further rockets flew up very high to form as they exploded the three-legged symbol of Sicily, the "S" of Syracuse & the four letters of the Hebrew word for Jehovah. To finish, an uninterrupted volley of shots could be heard as the boat went straight to the bottom in a thick cloud of smoke.

Warm applause greeted Athanasius's success, accompanied by hurrahs & shouts of joy from the people of Syracuse. I rushed to embrace my master, who had the kindness to make a gesture including me in his success. The Duke of Hesse came to congratulate him, granting him on the spot a very large sum of ducats to fund the later publication of his labors. Then all the guests filed past us to congratulate Kircher & admire the fiery machine. The Sicilian gentleman who had had the presumption to make such an insulting remark only a few minutes previously also had to pass through these Caudine Forks. When the puffy-faced tub of lard came to pay his respects, with much ridiculous posturing, Kircher spoke to him in his most flowery Italian:

"Verily Your Lordship was speaking words of wisdom this afternoon, excrement does indeed attract excrement & for that reason you, more than any other, should take care . . ."

Now it was the Sicilian's turn to flush red as a lobster. He muttered a few words & put his hand on his sword; if the Duke of Hesse had not been there, his presence forbidding any outburst of violence, the affair would doubtless have taken an unfortunate turn for my master, even though he was a man who would defend himself & possessed of strength rare among men of the cloth. Emboldened by Kircher's attitude, I pretended to fan myself, as if to get rid of a bad smell, which made this charming provincial braggadocio furious, so that he turned his back on us, though not without having made a sign at me with his hand & teeth, the precise meaning of which escaped me. For the first time I enjoyed a rare feeling of pleasure that follows any unexpected victory, "the joy of delayed triumph," as Athanasius dubbed this category when we discussed the matter that same night. Nevertheless I felt guilty for having shown a lack of magnanimity toward the poor Sicilian, but my master reassured me by asserting that to have behaved in any other way would have been to demonstrate hypocrisy, which sin was worse than the—after all rather venial—one of a deserved & innocuous retort.

CORUMBÁ: *The hoarse double cry of the caymans*

The engine at half speed, the *Messenger of the Faith* made its way up the river with the noise and the blind obstinacy of a stubborn tractor digging up the earth. The whole team had got up at dawn to load the crates of equipment that had been sent from Brazilia, while Petersen and his deckhand saw to the food and the engine. After a last meal at the Beira Rio, washed down with plenty of wine to celebrate their departure, they had embarked without ceremony and cast off. Leaving the tiller to Yurupig, the Indian who lived on board, having accumulated the functions of mechanic, guard and cook, Petersen had flopped onto one of the benches in the saloon, where he had been snoring like a pig for hours. Milton was doing the same in his cabin; as for Dietlev and Mauro, they were leaning on the rail, discussing a point of palaeontology that seemed to preclude any other preoccupation.

Lying face down on the warm roof of the gunboat, carried along by the river and hypnotized by its immense labyrinth of arms and channels, Elaine abandoned herself to a delightful drowsiness. Soothed by the absolute calm of the Pantanal—though the previous evening Petersen had assured her that the wind and floods could set off huge waves on this glossy plain—she played a game of focusing, as if with a camera, on various images in the exuberance of the virgin forest. The blood-red splash of a pair of parrots in flight, the delayed take-off of a white heron, very high up on the top of a tree, the gap-toothed smile of a naked child, squatting behind his father in the pirogue gliding along the riverbank, an unmoving swirl of yellow mud right in the middle of the river . . . And each time she made a little click with her tongue, taking delight in the fact that she hadn't thought of bringing her camera: for one second later the parrots set off a flight of budgerigars in a cacophony of vivid greens and screeches; the white heron suddenly opened its wings like flapping sails and gave a long cry, its neck stretched out toward the sun; the kid's smile vanished; when he saw her, his father, with a feverish look, paused in his paddle stroke; the wake of the boat released the clawed skeleton of a tree stump that had been held up in its journey to the south. Even a camera would have misrepresented these free images of the River Paraguay by isolating them from their coexistence with all the other observed moments. Eléazard would approve, she thought, he who made it a matter of principle never to capture anything on film.

Elaine closed her eyes, lulled by the regular throb of the engine. Suddenly she felt once more the extreme weariness that, one day, had alienated her from Eléazard. There was nothing specific that had motivated her departure, unless it was her final survival reflex that had compelled her to flee a man being slowly but surely killed by his cynicism. Eléazard was being eaten away by his excessive clarity about people and things. She was angry with him because he didn't believe in anything anymore, not even in his own abilities. His dissertation on Kircher had long since been abandoned, his desire to write anything other than dull agency dispatches had long since withered, and if he still seemed to be interested in what was going on in the world, it was simply in order to make a list of its defects. How often had he mocked her for claiming to understand it, to define the laws by which it operated? She thought she could still hear him: 'Science is just one ideology among others, neither more nor less effective than any of its fellow ideologies. It just works on different areas but misses the truth by as wide a margin as religion or politics. Sending a missionary to convert the Chinese or a cosmonaut to the moon is exactly the same thing: it derives from the same desire to govern the world, to confine it within the limits of doctrinaire knowledge that each time presents itself as definitive. However improbable it might have appeared, Francis Xavier went to Asia and really did convert thousands of Chinese; the American, Armstrong—a soldier, by the way, if you see what I'm getting at—trampled the old lunar myth underfoot, but what do these two actions give us, apart from themselves? They don't teach us anything, since all they do is confirm something we already knew, namely that the Chinese are convertible and the moon tramplable . . . Both of them are nothing more than the same sign of men's self-satisfaction at any given moment in history."

One day she couldn't bear these cracks in the blind wall of certainties any longer. Alcântara had come to seem like the exact reflection of Eléazard: a heap of contagious ruins she had to get away from at all cost. She felt herself threatened by her husband's morbid interest in that sad failure, Athanasius Kircher. That was what she had fled from, that insidious sense of abandonment. Divorce had doubtless been going too far, but it had been a necessary step on the way to breaking once and for all the spells that kept her captive, to be alone, in tune with life, with the very ordinary happiness at being alive.

The noise of the engine stopped abruptly. As the boat continued to drift along in silence, Elaine could hear the clamor from the aviary of the jungle. From her post she watched Yurupig go to the prow and release the anchor chain. For a moment the clatter of the links halted the chatter of the invisible monkeys on the bank. Herman Petersen appeared on deck, carrying a bucket and a basket.

"What's up?" Dietlev asked, a look of concern on his face. "Some problem with the engine?"

"Nothing to get worried about, *amigo*. It's just that night falls quickly and round here it's not a good idea to keep going in the dark. We could have gone for maybe an hour, but we wouldn't have been sure of being able to anchor. And anyway, there isn't a better place for *dourados* on the whole river."

"What are they, *dourados*?" Mauro asked.

"*Salmidus brevidens*," Dietlev replied immediately, as if it was obvious. "A kind of golden salmon that can weigh up to forty-five pounds. I had some last year, it's delicious."

"To work, then," said Herman, taking several lines out of his basket. "If you want some for supper, now's the time to show what you can do."

"Can I try?" Elaine said from up on her perch.

"But of course, *senhora*. I was wondering where you'd got to."

"I have to tell you," she said as she came down on deck, "I've never fished before."

"It's easy, I'll show you," said Herman. "That's the bait," he added, pointing at the bucket. "*Piramboias*, there's nothing better."

Elaine came to look. She shrank back slightly when she saw the short, compact creatures it was teeming with. "Snakes?" she said with a look of disgust.

"Almost. But you'd better not stick your hands in," he said, wrapping a cloth round his hand to grasp one of the eels.

With one slash of his knife he cut it in two and stuck one of the wriggling pieces on a hook. After having thrown it in the river, just a few yards from the boat, he handed the line to Elaine. "There you are. All you need now is patience. If there's a tug, you pull it in; there's nothing more to it than that."

"Do these things stay alive for long," she asked, pointing with her chin at the pool of blood where the *piramboia* tail was still writhing.

"For hours. They're indestructible, that's what makes them so attractive—no fish can resist a bit of meat like that. Especially the females . . ."

He said it in suggestive tones, his dull, watery eyes fixed on Elaine's breasts. She pretended not to hear and turned to look at the river.

"What about you, Mauro? D'you feel like a go?"

"Why not? I'll try anything once."

"Come and get your line, then."

Dietlev having declined the same offer, Petersen went to fish with the others.

They only had a few minutes to wait. Elaine suddenly had a violent bite but when she pulled in her line, it was empty—it had been cut off just above the hook. The same thing happened almost immediately to Herman and Mauro.

"Shit!" Herman exclaimed in disgust. "Piranhas. The fishing's over, guys. When they're about it's no good for catching anything else. Too greedy, the little bastards . . . But just a minute, my dears. Since that's the way things are we'll get a few for the soup. I'll put some steel hook lengths on the lines, that'll give them something to think about."

The first to have one of these, Elaine was soon struggling with a catch; the line was stretched almost to breaking point, zigzagging unpredictably through the yellow water.

"Go on, pull," Herman shouted, also busy trying to land a fish. "It won't break, pull, dammit! But be careful when it's on the deck. Let Yurupig deal with it, they can cut off your fingers, no problem."

Flashes of gold appeared in the disturbingly opaque river. With a great heave into which she put all her strength, Elaine brought a gleaming piranha flying onto the deck. The Indian rushed forward: two powerful blows with his club and that was the end of its convulsive twitchings she was trying awkwardly to avoid.

"Look, *belleza*," Herman said. He had just landed a piranha and had managed to get it on his left hand, still alive, so that Elaine couldn't tell whether he was taking a liberty in the way he addressed her or talking about the fish. She watched as Petersen inserted the point of his knife into its prognathous jaw; the two rows of triangular teeth—truly monstrous fangs—quickly closed on the blade, several times in succession, like a little stapler. With a cracking of bone that sent shivers down her spine, and with the help of Herman levering with his knife, the piranha broke its teeth one by one on the metal.

"After that he won't have to go to the dentist again," Herman guffawed, proud of his demonstration. "Just imagine what they can do under water . . . A shoal of them can eat up an ox in no time at all. D'you know what *piranha* means in Tupi-Guarani? It means 'scissors fish.' Not bad, eh?"

Despite the fish's repulsiveness, Elaine was appalled at the pointless torture Petersen was inflicting on it. She corrected herself immediately: it was oafish, obnoxious or anything you like from the catalog of human stupidity, but certainly not "pointless," given that the word suggested there were tortures that were sometimes justified. She was about to tell Herman to stop his cruel sport when Yurupig went up to him.

"Let go of it," he said calmly, but in a threatening tone. "At once!"

The two men stared at each other for a moment. Herman decided to smile as if it were nothing. "I'll do even more than that," he said, turning to Elaine, "I'll let it go free. Just to please the fair lady . . ." And with an affected gesture, he threw the bleeding piranha back into the river.

Yurupig turned toward the concentric circles on the surface of the water that were already becoming less distinct and, holding up the palms of his hands to the sky, muttered a few incomprehensible phrases. Having done that, he went back inside without a word.

"I've got one, I've got one!" came a sudden shout from Mauro, who had missed the whole incident. Herman took the opportunity to turn his attention to him. When the fish was on the deck, he simply clubbed it without further ado.

"Come on then," he said cheerfully, "two or three more and that'll be our soup."

While he was baiting more lines, Elaine went to him. "What did he say?"

"Who?"

"Stop acting stupid. Yurupig, of course!"

"A load of nonsense. Indian stuff . . . It's not important."

"He was praying for the fish," Dietlev suddenly said solemnly. "I couldn't understand everything, but he invoked the *law of the river* and asked to be forgiven the death of the poor animal."

"But it was still alive," Elaine said. "I saw it swim off."

"That's the worst thing about it. It was alive, but injured from the hook and incapable of catching its prey thanks to this . . . to this 'gentleman.' We can only hope the others ate it at once, otherwise it'll spend days dying."

Elaine gave Herman a look of contempt, her eyes flashing angrily. "You knew that, didn't you?"

"So what? What does it matter? Don't give me all that crap for a lousy fucking piranha! You'll have to calm down a bit, the whole lot of you . . . Otherwise . . ."

"Otherwise what?" Dietlev asked, looking him straight in the eye. "I must point out that you've already been paid, so it's you who're going to calm down, and pretty quick too."

Herman's eyes seemed to clear under the impact of his rage. He said nothing, just shrugged his shoulders and turned his back on them. The saloon door slammed shut behind him.

"I DIDN'T KNOW you could speak Tupí," Elaine said to Dietlev after this outburst. "Where did you learn it?"

"I can't really speak it properly," Dietlev said, "just enough to deal with any situation with the Indians. I did some courses at the university in Brazilia, it's often helped me to locate a deposit or collect fossils in the back of beyond. You should think about learning it too."

"You're right. I'll see about it when we get back."

Yurupig's attitude had made a deep impression on her. She only realized now that it was the first time since they'd left that she'd heard his voice. In her mind's eye she could see a sharp image of his profile as he confronted Petersen: his copper complexion, almond eyes, slightly slanting under the bulge of his lids, a very flat nose, without any obvious cartilage but which made you feel like kneading the flesh to give it shape, and thick lips that he hardly moved when he spoke. Dressed in overalls thick with dirt and grease, he never seemed to be without a baseball cap worn back to front with a quiff of hair sticking out like a tuft of black feathers over his forehead. Elaine thought he was utterly beautiful, especially when he made his moving prayer to the piranhas.

"What's happened?" Mauro asked, intrigued by Herman's abrupt departure and the look of annoyance on his teachers' faces. Elaine told him briefly what had happened.

"Hmm, not the best of starts, then?" he said, scratching his head. "The swine deserves to be thrown in the water himself and we'll carry on without him."

"I don't really trust him . . ." said Elaine, as if talking to herself. And turning to Dietlev: 'You know what? He's hanging around me all the time and it's obvious why. I get suggestive remarks every couple of minutes."

"I don't believe it!" said Mauro, in a blaze of anger. "That drunkard! That . . . that Nazi bastard!"

"Be careful what you say," Dietlev said firmly. "It's only a rumor, I really ought to have held my tongue. Anyway, don't forget that our expedition depends on him and on his boat. That goes for you too, Elaine. We're going to be together for the next two or three weeks so we'll have to soft-pedal a bit, all of us. I don't know what there is between him and that Indian, but it's none of our business."

"You saw how he humiliated him!" Elaine objected, outraged.

"Yes, I did, and it's not to his credit, but for the moment let's not exaggerate: it was just a piranha put back in the water."

"That's worst of all!" said Mauro, clenching his fists.

"That's enough! I don't want to hear any more about the incident. And not a word to Milton, understood?"

"What's this, what's this? Hiding things from me, from what I hear." Milton's voice was suddenly heard behind them. "I don't like that, you know . . ."

During a couple of seconds of guilty silence, Dietlev desperately looked for a way out of the situation, then Elaine came to the rescue. "OK, OK," she said, with a disappointed look, "that's our surprise down the drain. It's a pity, but since you heard everything . . ."

"What surprise?" He stifled a yawn. "Pardon me, I slept like a log. Too much wine at lunch, it's never a good idea. So what is it you're not to tell old Milton, guys?"

"That we're having piranha soup for dinner . . ." said Elaine, not knowing how she was going to get out of it.

" . . . ?!"

"Yes," she went on, seized with consternation at the difficulty of thinking up anything convincing, " . . . and, well, Petersen maintains that piranha soup has a certain . . . aphrodisiac quality . . ."

Mauro leapt in. "And we'd decided to do a 'blind' experiment, as they say," he said, putting on an embarrassed look. "A student joke, it was my idea. We'd have come clean about it tomorrow . . ."

"I see you're enjoying yourselves behind my back," said Milton with a chuckle. "But I can assure you I've no need of that kind of thing, thank God; despite my age, I'm still perfectly capable in that respect."

A little later, when Milton had gone off with Dietlev, Elaine thanked Mauro for his contribution. "I'd no idea how to extricate myself from the lie," she said with a laugh. "I'm really very grateful."

"It wasn't much," said Mauro, blushing. "I surprised myself, I'm not usually known for my quick-wittedness. I'm still wondering how he managed to swallow it."

"The brilliant idea was to take everything on yourself. I have the impression he'd forgive you anything."

Mauro thought over the comment for a moment. Put like that, it seemed obvious. "I don't like him very much, you know," he said.

"Don't worry, neither do I," she replied in confidential tones. "He's not a bad guy, but his career comes before everything and for me that's not worthy of a scientist."

Mauro contemplated the river. The sun, having gone down, had set the whole sky ablaze: the giant trees stood out against docile cumulus clouds with fiery outlines. The louder and louder chirring of insects was gradually replacing the wailing of stray birds, expressing one last time their apprehension of the night. On the bank, only a few yards from the boat, furtive rustlings in the bushes kept exciting his alert senses. A burst of exultation, inexplicably combined with a feeling of sadness, loosened his tongue. "On the other hand, I like you very much," he said to Elaine, without daring to look at her. "Well, a lot, I mean . . ."

Moved by this disguised avowal, Elaine ruffled his hair, as she would have done to Moéma in similar circumstances. And at the very moment when, both delighted and offended by this disconcerting response, he felt her hand in his hair, they heard for the first time the hoarse double cry of the caymans.

HALF-STRETCHED-OUT on his bunk, his back against the metal wall of the cabin, Herman Petersen tried to grab the bottle of *cachaça* he'd been making every effort to finish for what would soon be two hours; just the attempt set a dizzying rotation of his field of vision in motion and, seeing the storm lantern swirling around him for no good reason, he accepted that he was drunk. Resisting the desire, irrepressible though it was, for another swig, he closed his eyes in the vague hope it might stop his head spinning. The images continued to harass him.

He'd started drinking with Dietlev and Milton, some time before the meal when the two came down to join him in the saloon. Relaxed, smiling, a glass of aperitif in his hand, Dietlev had inquired about the piranha soup. Herman had noted their submission. Without showing the ill feeling he still harbored, nor his pride in having made them submit so quickly, he'd ordered the stupid Indian to prepare their meager catch then amused himself by explaining the supposed virtues of the soup to Milton. When she came with Mauro, Elaine had asked him nicely for a *caipirinha*, signalling that she too was determined to forget their recent altercation. In the course of the meal she had even consented to take a sip of the much-vaunted soup and even went so far as to make a complimentary remark about its taste. This ultimate sign of goodwill would almost have mollified him if it hadn't been for Mauro's sympathetic look: the snotty-nosed kid was sorry for her because she had to swallow such an affront. *Comedia, comediante!* They were all mocking him . . . Seething with rage, he dreamt of the nasty things in his vengeance he would mete out to these shits one by one.

He'd make Yurupig eat his own balls, then he'd throw him to the piranhas, since he was so fond of them. As for Elaine, that would be longer, more complicated . . . like what he'd seen done to that activist tart, in the good old days of the dictatorship. The cops had taken her out of the van and dragged her off to the Tavarez brothers' piggery, on the edge of the town. Damned patriots, they were, real *varones*, with some real meat inside their trousers! If there'd been a few more of their kind, Brazil would never have become this country of beggars and queers. It'd be like Chile . . . you should see how things worked down there! The Switzerland of South America. Everyone kept their nose clean, everything worked. Even their wine was great . . . When she went in, the girl had insulted them. They locked the door and got their cocks out.

"Get your clothes off, slut! First of all we're going to fuck you up the ass to teach you some manners, then you're going to suck us all off, we're going to put gallons in your tank. Maybe that'll make you think before talking crap like that." She'd started to blubber, standing there, surrounded by the guys. She was shit-scared, the stupid bitch, she implored them, but they put a gun to her head and she'd no choice but to do everything they wanted. Everything. You have to give it to them, they carried out their program to the letter! She screamed, she cried, and they screwed her every which way, and the *cachaça* flowed—it was ages since they'd had such fucking fun!

Herman closed his eyes tight, concentrating on the visions of horror that were piling up inside his head. He would never forget that girl's face, but Elaine's replaced it, fading in and sometimes getting bigger until it filled his whole field of vision. He could see her trembling all over, like the other woman, begging them on her knees, her body filthy, with the swellings from the kicks and cigarette burns. And he lay back, happy just to watch and insult her, inventing new humiliations, new abuses, giving free rein to fantasies from the deepest cesspit of human nature. That would teach her to come and piss people off with her little ass and her film-star tits, shaking it all about as if it were nothing, while talking about her stupid fossils. The other had been just the same, a stuck-up little bitch going on about her "democracy," her high-falutin ideas, but she let the bastards of her own kind screw her.

Mauro's type, precisely . . . Long hair, nothing in his pants but goes around shoving his opinions down real men's throats. That one could wait, with his nancy-boy looks and his bloody Walkman thump-thumping all the time . . . djim boom boom . . . djim boom boom . . . It was enough to drive you mad.

She'd made less of a fuss when Waldemar brought the dog. It was even more excited than the guys, the Doberman was. It had a huge erection, as if it had been trained for that. The cops had tied the girl up in the pigsty with a damned neat system that kept her on all fours, her arms behind her back, legs apart, and there was a thing on her eyes, like they put on pigs when they cut their throats. She was begging them to kill her . . . There always came a point where they preferred death to all the rest, even to the hope of escaping; that was when it became interesting. And while the dog was screwing her, while she was half suffocating, her mouth and nose in the shit, they'd jerked off on her again. After that, when they'd got fed up with sticking anything they happened to find up her cunt, with pissing on her and whipping her with barbed wire, they'd stopped to have a smoke. No one had any idea how long they'd been there. "Do you know how they kill jaguars without damaging their skin? D'you know that, you cow?" one of the Tavarez brothers asked, the one-eyed one, the one who'd caught the pox in a brothel in Recife. "They trap them alive then stick a white-hot poker up their backside. It hisses, it sizzles, it smells like a *churrasco*. It's a beautiful sight . . ."

He'd started heating the barrel of his hunting rifle right in front of her—a Springfield double-trigger rifle! He must've been bombed out of his skull to do that . . . and he stuck it up her socialist asshole, forcing it as far as he could. Then he calmly fired his two shots—buckshot. After that they all went off to bed. But he'd still had the strength to fuck his negress till the evening. The socialist comrade had ended up in the Tavarez's lime kiln, no one had come to ask any questions, it was as if she'd never existed. It would be the same for Elaine, exactly the same . . . As for the others, he wasn't bothered about them. A bullet in the head, two for Mauro and *auf Wiedersehen, Johnny* . . .

Herman shivered. Drenched in sweat, his shirt was sticking to the metal partition. Visions of snow-covered landscapes and battlefields overcame him without warning . . . abandoning the Mauthausen concentration camp before the Russians arrived, the collapse, the blackish corpses frozen to the road . . . then all the months in captivity in Warsaw, sick with fear, in the sheet-metal huts the cold made ring like old U-boat hulls. Sobs came, choking him until it hurt in the back of his throat. The images suddenly blurred and from a particular flush on his cheeks, an intolerable feeling of remorse and self-pity, he knew that Esther's face was going to return to torment him and that neither alcohol nor hate would keep the night free from his recurring nightmare.

Eléazard's notebooks

IF KIRCHER CLAIMS TO BELIEVE IN the existence of giants, it's solely so as not to contradict Saint Augustine: one couldn't cast doubt on the words of one of the fathers of the Church without casting doubt on the Church herself, etc. Willful blindness and lies, comparable on all points with those of Marr or Lysenko in other fields. It's this kind of terrorism that religions or ideologies lead to that makes me want to puke. Take up the question with Loredana . . .

REPEATING SIMPLE FACTS: that religion is the opium of the people, the hard drug that for six thousand years has stopped all the pricks from rising up and confronting heaven; that Jesus, the man with the nails—*that criminal from a Western kingdom during the Han period* as Chinese scholars of the seventeenth century called him, outraged at seeing such a scoundrel deified—has laced our drinks with bromide forever and ever; that our civilization is dying from having learned to feel sorry for itself, to give positive value to defeat and its victims.

THAT WE MUST RETURN to the sources of the sacrifice, to the perception of the right moment and of a balanced relationship with the world. Reinvent the crudest paganism and deny the *defixio* that nails our penises to the lead curse tablets of the graveyards. That a religion founded on the decaying carcass of a crucified man will inevitably have a worm-eaten view of the world.

A GOLIATH COMPLEX: the giant of Holy Scripture only exists in relationship to David, he is only strong and gigantic so he can die at the hand of the small, weak man. Merely to name any being or object Goliath will of necessity bring the David into the world who will do away with him or it. By its name alone the Titanic was destined to go down with all hands.

FROM A TRIBUTE TO JOËL SCHERK: "How could a beautiful theory be false?" The danger of symmetry and simplicity as arbiters of elegance. Since it's beautiful, it's true: a theory of everything or a metaphysical ragbag? If beauty consists of economizing on concepts, why should asymmetry or complexity be incapable of that? The fact that we find economy of means more satisfying than profusion doesn't mean it has a greater truth value.

ALL THAT REMAINS of the astronomical observations made by Kircher is the crater that bears his name today. A rut on the surface of the Moon.

LOREDANA TALKING TO HEIDEGGER: "How's things, you funny old bird?" Her eyes, her Ferdinand Knopff smile. My conjuring tricks seem to work.

AT THE BEGINNING OF THE nineteenth century, at the moment when Egypt became a target for conquest, Buonaparte's scholars recalled Kircher's fanciful conjectures. "For the first time, I entered the *archives of science and the arts*," Vivant Denon wrote after the discovery of the temple of Dendera. With hindsight, it looks as if the sole purpose of the Egyptian expedition was to unearth the Rosetta Stone and with it the supposed origin of Western Christian wisdom.

"AMONG THE FOUNDING FATHERS OF OCCULTISM" wrote Dr. Papus, "a very special mention is due to Athanasius Kircher, a Jesuit who was clever enough to get his works printed by the Vatican; on the pretext of attacking occultism, he gave a very full account of it." Off the mark, but symptomatic—one charlatan recognizing another. Kircher's outdated hermeticism, his assertions on the initiatory meaning of the hieroglyphs, his taste for the fantastic, the extraordinary, the mysterious establish esotericism well before Court de Gébelin or Eliphas Levi.

CREDULITY: Against religion, astrology, spiritualism and other twaddle, those varieties of stupidity in which the minds of our contemporaries continue to take refuge.

ARREST OF FRANÇOIS DE SUS: "Condemned to have his hand cut off, then his head, for having, with evil intent, struck a paper crucifix with a dagger two or three times ... The same for a Jew for having poured a pot full of piss on a cross that a Christian was carrying in a procession."

THE ARREST OF ESTIENNE ROCHETTE: "Condemned to the strappado then strangulation and then his body to be burned and his ashes scattered outside said church, for having broken the arms of two or three statues of saints in the church of Saint Julian in Pommiers en Forez."

IF A BELIEVER FEELS INSULTED because the statue of his god has been mocked, it is at best because he still has doubts about whether his god exists, at worst because he's stupid enough to identify with him. But when he finds weapons to avenge this offense in the laws of a society, or in going against them, that makes him into a sworn enemy, a wild beast to be locked in a cage.

KIRCHER IS A PERVERSE POLYMATH ... He devotes himself to the encyclopedia. An attempt to enumerate the universe. Analogical technique: the whole is contained in each part, as in holograms.

FLYING VISIT TO QUIXADÁ: The night in the monastery of São Esteban, the room where President Castello Branco spent his last night before the airplane accident that wiped him off the surface of the earth once and for all. The pretty nun who showed me all the objects that had been faithfully kept, his sandals, the candle, the bar of soap, the last chair he sat in, the last sheets, covered in transparent plastic, etc. Without having any idea that there was only one thing I wanted: to screw her there, beneath the portrait of Saint Ignatius.

SPALLANZANI: he put trousers on frogs and proved that they had to copulate together to reproduce ...

THE WIT OF HINDSIGHT: What I ought to have said to Loredana: "Liu Ling often gave himself up to wine. Free and in high spirits, he would get undressed and walk around his house naked. To those who came to see him and rebuked him for it, he would reply, "I take the sky and the earth for my house and my house for my trousers. What do you think you are doing, Mademoiselle, coming into my trousers like that?"

CHAPTER 7

In which Kircher tames swordfish & the difficulties
that led to . . .

WE FINALLY RETURNED to Palermo,
where Kircher was received with great honor. His feat
at Syracuse was on everyone's lips, with the result that all the
academies in the town were vying with each other to have him
speak to them. He took up his courses at the university again,
tackling all subjects as they were suggested to him. In particular
he showed how many hairs each man could have on his head—not
more than 186,624 for the most fortunate, less than half that for
the majority—& that if it was easy to imagine an infinite number
by using addition, it was much more difficult, on the other hand,
to imagine a similar number using division, for if one accepted
that a hair could be divided infinitely, then one would also have to
accept that the whole was less than the sum of its parts . . .

When an old Sicilian scholar rebuked Kircher for his
propensity to count hairs & to divide them by four, Athanasius

shut him up by reminding him that a good Christian should
not be afraid to imitate Divine Providence & that there was
nothing on earth or in the heavens that was so tiny or so vile
that it did not merit profound speculation. And if the gentleman
would like to come to Rome, he would show him, thanks to a
magnifying glass of his own invention, how one could enlarge
a hair until it looked like a tree, with branches & roots, & how
understanding this phenomenon alone merited several whole
books. Kircher had won over his audience & the old scholar was
left without a leg to stand on.

My master also commented on the assertion of Father Pétau
& others that God had started to create the world on October
27 of the year 3488 before Christ, at eight hours and forty-seven
seconds after midnight, demonstrating with ease by examining
radically different theories about the day & the year that it was
presumptuous to decide on that date &, by extension, on that of
the Apocalypse.

The Prince of Palagonia had come to attend my master's
lessons again, together with the Duke of Hesse & people of
standing in the town. There were various rumors circulating
about him & scandalmongers wasted no time in accusing him
of the seven deadly sins. They claimed the prince, being of a
very jealous nature, kept his wife captive & that his palace was
more like a castle inhabited by demons than a true Christian
residence. We were also told of various fads that made him sound
brain damaged but we paid no heed to them. The prince, like
my master, was courtesy itself &, indeed, appeared to be more
intelligent and cultivated than most of his fellow citizens. It was,
therefore, with pleasure that Athanasius agreed to go & stay with
him when he repeated his invitation for Christmas 1637.

There were a few days left before the date appointed by the
Prince of Palagonia, when my master, in his insatiable curiosity,

decided to cross the sea to Messina. The rector of the university having told him that the fishermen of the district used a certain song to tame the swordfish & thus lead them toward the net, Kircher was absolutely determined to verify this marvel for himself. My reservations, dictated by my fear of seasickness & of Turcoman pirates, had no effect whatsoever; there was nothing for it but to yield to his whim.

I will pass over the details of our crossing to get to the moment when we reached the fishing grounds, marked out by some buoys. Once our boat had anchored, we transferred to one of the six small boats we had been towing, the one belonging to the *raïs* or captain. He was the only one, we later established, who had the ability to formulate the magic words that attract the fish. The sailors began to row & we had not gone a quarter of a mile when the *raïs* started to sing. It was an uninterrupted melodic line, sad & haunting, following the cadences of the oars & the rowers' responses. As soon as the song started, Kircher leant over the gunwale to observe the depths & soon he grasped my arm insistently to force me to look: under the water, which was clear & transparent as crystal, I saw a number of large, silvery fish, moving along slowly, keeping up with our boat. It was such a magnificent spectacle that I did not tire of watching it . . . As for my master, he feverishly started to note down the marvelous song. After some time, silence suddenly fell. Looking up—Kircher from his notebook, I from the depths of the sea—we were surprised to see that all the little vessels were gathered in a wide circle. The sailors had stopped rowing, they were drawing in a vast net rhythmically, pulling it up foot by foot. The captain began a new song to encourage the fishermen in their exertions & from the way the nets sloped toward the center of the circle, I realized it was a huge pocket in which the fish were now caught.

The bottom of the net was soon horizontal below the surface: tuna and swordfish, half out of their element, were making the sea boil with their wild thrashing. I was wondering how the fishermen would get them on board, when they secured the net, to keep it in place, & grasped strong pikes that ended in broad hooks. The *raïs* intoned a third song, the solemn poignancy of which, chanted like a *Dies irae*, accorded fully with the slaughter that ensued.

Retching with revulsion, I observed Kircher. His eyes bulging, his hair dishevelled, spattered with blood & water, he was deeply affected by the carnage. I could sense that his every nerve was tingling, & looking at his broad hands gripping the side of the boat, I saw the knuckles go white.

"Pray for my soul, Caspar," he murmured abruptly, "& stop me if I ever pick up one of those pikes."

Convinced my master was tempted to berate the men for their cruelty, I gathered all my strength to beg the Lord to protect him &, thanks be to Heaven & perhaps to my prayers, Kircher did not yield to the impulse. Fortunately, for I would hardly have been able to hold him back & save him from eternal damnation given the wretched state I was in.

When all the fish down to the very last one were on board, we climbed back onto the ship & set sail for Messina. Once there, we embarked again almost immediately & it was only when we saw the splendid cliffs above Palermo that my master finally unclenched his teeth.

"Caspar, my friend, you have seen me in a very delicate situation & I will make confession about it to my superiors as soon as we are back in Rome, but before that I am anxious to explain to you what happened. That will perhaps help me to dissipate the shadows clouding my mind . . ."

CANOA QUEBRADA: *An astronomer's dream*
of a barbarous, devastated planet . . .

Every time Roetgen felt overtaken by circumstances he would, as he put it himself, "go cataleptic." After a period of intense concentration he would manage, without great difficulty, to paralyze his faculty of judgment and keep himself in a state close to complete detachment. Having put himself, by his own decree, in a position where anything could happen without him consenting to appear affected by it, nothing did actually affect him anymore. The worst worries simply slid off the invisible walls of his apparent serenity. He could have been in a Boeing in free fall or facing a raging lunatic armed with a gun and not a muscle in his body would have twitched; he would have died, if that should happen, with a lemming-like indifference.

Standing in the aisle, toward the back of the bus, his arms fused in a cross to the tarnished steel bars, squashed on all sides by the passengers clustering around him, jostled and jolted, dazed by the heat and the noise, Roetgen held his course like a sailing ship heading into a storm. Each time the driver was forced to suddenly slow down to avoid animals, kids or objects that appeared in front of his vehicle, as if on the screen of a video game, he sent a battering ram of the flesh and sweat of fifty people thumping into Roetgen. The desert landscape of the Sertão, occasionally glimpsed through the heaving mass, filled him with a sense of its desolation.

He felt a gentle tug on his shirt. "Are you OK? You wouldn't like to sit down a bit in my seat?" Moéma managed to say, craning her neck to see him.

"No problem," he said in resigned tones. "I can last a good five minutes before I collapse."

"It's almost over," she said with a sweet smile, "we get there in half an hour."

When Moéma had arrived at the German Cultural Institute she had appeared surprised to see Roetgen helping Andreas and a few other lecturers putting the chairs away.

"But what time is it?" she'd asked Roetgen when he came over to her.

"One o'clock. I'd given you up. So had a certain Virgilio. He left just ten minutes ago."

"Damn! I'm hopeless, really. I just wasn't aware of the time passing. She seemed stranger than when she'd been coming out of the bank, her breath smelled of alcohol.

"Would you like a drink? Andreas always has a bottle of whiskey in his desk."

"No thanks, I can't," she replied after a brief moment of hesitation. With a glance at the little group of women lecturers bustling about under the mango tree, she went on, "They'd have a fit, it would be very bad for your reputation. In Brazil the teaching staff aren't in the habit of having a drink with their students, especially not their *female* students."

"I couldn't care less about my reputation, so if that's all it is . . ."

"No, no, it's not possible," she said. "Anyway, I don't . . . Tell me, what do you do on weekends? In general, I mean?"

Roetgen had resisted smiling at the young girl's obvious embarrassment. Was she getting in a tangle at the last moment as she was about to go on to something she'd prepared in advance or was this first step that defied the conventions an improvisation. He had already been drawn to her by her wild side, the glint of revolt and irony in her look when he met her eye at the back of the class, everything that calls attention to a person to the point where they intrude on our dreams, our thoughts, infiltrating them, casting a mysteriously persistent light on them; he was beside himself with joy at this stumbling approach.

"On weekends? Not much. I read, play chess. And then there's Andreas, you know him, we often go for walks together with his two children."

"Where?"

"More or less everywhere. In the "Interior," as you call it here, more often to Porto das Dunas. We have a glass of wine, we talk . . . Nothing very original, as you can see."

"Do you know Canoa Quebrada?"

"I've heard of it."

"It's a little fishing village, completely isolated in the dunes, about two hundred miles from here. It's preserved, you know . . . *cool*. No hotels, no tourists, no electricity even. The most beautiful spot in the *Nordeste* in my opinion. I'm going there with a girlfriend tomorrow, d'you feel like coming with us?"

He'd grabbed the chance. Moéma had arranged a rendezvous, advising him to bring a hammock, then slipped off into the fragrant darkness of the campus.

Very early the next morning Roetgen had met the two girls at the *Radoviária*, the huge bus station in Oswaldo Studart Street. Thaïs had seen to the tickets, so all he'd had to do was get on the Fortaleza-Mossoró bus that was sputtering in the square. Even before leaving the town, the bus had filled up with a boisterous motley crowd whose one topic of conversation was the airplane accident on the front page of the newspapers. Just a quarter hour into the journey Roetgen had given up his seat to an old lady—he would have put her at sixty until Moéma convinced him she was pregnant!—and for three hours now he'd been trying to ignore his nagging regret at his own courtesy.

Iguape, Caponga, Cascavel, Beberibe, Sucatinga, Prarjuru . . . presumably Moéma had told the driver, for shortly after Aracati the bus stopped out in the middle of the countryside, where the road crossed a little track, rutted but dead straight, which rose imperceptibly toward a horizon of scrub and gaunt *carnaúba* palms.

"So that's that," said Moéma when the bus had left in a cloud of dust. "An hour's walk, and we'll be there."

"An hour's walk?!" Roetgen protested. "You didn't mention that."

"I thought it might put you off," said Moéma, putting her sunglasses on. Then, with her most disarming smile, "I did warn you that it was off the beaten track. You have to earn paradise."

"Off we go to paradise, then. I hope at least we can bathe when we get there."

"And how! You'll see, it's the best beach in the *Nordeste*. But first of all we've got to prepare ourselves for the walk. You . . ." she hesitated, then went over to the familiar second person, "you've nothing against a little joint, I assume. You must excuse me, but I'm fed up with addressing you so formally. Here we're on my territory, too bad if I've got it wrong."

"*Vixe Maria!*" Thaïs exclaimed, stunned by her friend's brazenness. "Have you gone completely bonkers, it's not possible . . ."

"Don't worry," Roetgen hastened to assure her, excited all the same by Moéma's cockiness. "I'm perfectly capable of differentiating between the university and the rest. The proof is that I came with you, isn't it?"

"If I'd had the least doubt, I'd never have suggested it," Moéma said without looking up from the cigarette she was carefully pulling to pieces, collecting the tobacco on the top of her rucksack.

Roetgen watched her make up the joint. Despite what he said and his studied nonchalance he was sufficiently disturbed by the procedure to feel out of place. Uncomfortable with the drug—he'd smoked only once or twice, without enjoying it and without being able to understand how his generation could have developed such a taste for bouts of nausea—it was with apprehension that he saw the moment approaching when he'd have to either cross the threshold or look ridiculous. However, it did help him understand the girl's occasional vacant air during his classes, her dark spectacles and her characteristic way of jumping from one subject to another or bursting out laughing for no obvious reason. Believing he had fathomed the obscure mechanism of his liking for her, he abruptly felt a kind of disapproval.

"You first," said Moéma, handing him the joint she'd just rolled, still damp with her saliva.

Roetgen lit it, trying to inhale as little as possible. He could already see himself getting dizzy, about to throw up, a human wreck abandoned to the filth of the gutter. At the same time he was worried the girls might accuse him of pretending, or of wasting precious puffs through his inexperience. He was angry with Moéma for having put him in this embarrassing situation.

He came out of it unexposed, either because he'd managed to fool them or because they were intelligent enough not to make a fuss about his faking it.

"Off we go, then," said Moéma when the joint came back to her, "the worst is yet to come."

As they set off, the sun blazing down on them, Roetgen tried to get to know Thaïs, but she didn't seem interested in making conversation. Discouraged by her monosyllabic answers, he let silence return. Ten minutes later he was pouring with sweat. "Isn't it hot," he said, wiping his face with his handkerchief.

"You should have worn sandals," Moéma said, glancing at his shoes. It's the first time I've seen anyone going to the beach in shoes and socks."

"It's unbelievable," said Thaïs, suddenly livening up at this heresy. "I hadn't noticed. *Meu Deus,* it must really be smelly in there!"

"Worse than that," said Roetgen, laughing as well. "But I would beg you to show my feet a little more respect. I am, after all, one of your teachers."

"A teacher who smokes *maconcha* with his pupils. That could set tongues a-wagging!" said Moéma in insinuating tones.

Roetgen realized how thoughtless he'd been. Of course Moéma was joking, but if she should decide, for one reason or another, to reveal the episode, that would be the end of his position at the university. For a second a look of panic flitted across his face.

"There's no need to worry," she said, in a serious voice once more, "I'd never do that, whatever happens. And then you could always say it wasn't true and we'd be the ones who were accused of lying, not you."

"I should hope so," he said earnestly. "And to change the subject—there's not a lot of people on this track. We haven't seen a soul for the last half hour."

"Wait till we get to the coast and you'll soon see why."

When they reached the top of the rise, Roetgen was surprised to see a completely different landscape: still dead straight, the track sloped gently down to a barrier of high dunes where it quite simply disappeared.

"It was the road to Majorlândia," Moéma said, "the dunes covered it three years ago. They shift a lot around here. But we wouldn't have been following it for long, that's not where we're heading."

"It's crazy!" Roetgen said. "You'd think we were in the middle of the Sahara. You're sure the sea's at the other end of it?"

"Of course I am."

They went on to the point where the road became invisible. From close up it looked even more astounding, as if the mountains of sand had been deliberately dumped on the road.

"What now?" Roetgen asked at a loss at the dead end they'd reached.

"We keep straight on," said Moéma, pointing at the dunes. And with a hint of irony in her smile: "You think you can manage it?"

"I'm going to have to, aren't I?"

The two girls set off up the slope ahead of him. Outlined briefly against the cloth of their baggy shorts, their rumps bobbed up and down in front of him before moving off. Using their hands, Thaïs and Moéma climbed with disconcerting ease, setting off avalanches of loose sand that hid the ground before him. Encumbered by his shoulder bag, which kept slipping, blinded by sweat, sinking in then suddenly sliding down several yards, Roetgen reached the top long after the girls, who were highly amused at his comically exhausting efforts.

But the vision awaiting him took all the mockery out of their laughter, transforming it into a chorus, a joyous celebration of the beauty of the world. The Atlantic had appeared, turquoise blue, shining like Mozarabic pottery. As far as the eye could see along the crescent of the coast, an interminable plateau of dunes curved gently down toward a shore edged by a broad white expanse of waves. Not one tree, no insects or birds, nothing to suggest the presence of men: an astronomer's dream of a barbarous, devastated planet, forever motionless beneath the searing heat of the sun.

Roegten gave a soft whistle of admiration.

"Not bad, eh?" said Moéma. There was a touch of pride in her voice. "I was sure you'd like it. Look, the village is immediately below."

In the direction she was pointing there was just a sweep of rocks that looked like ruins, their ochre making a slight contrast with the surrounding fawn color. Looking more closely, Roetgen could make out the sails of five or six *jangadas* merging with the white horses of the sea. Hurrying up, they soon caught sight of some straw huts that had so far been concealed by a patch of dunes. A scrawny dog started to come toward them; it gave a feeble bark, as if in a fit of conscience, then a donkey loaded with blocks of ice passed in front of them. Led by a little girl, it left a long trail of dark drops behind it.

They had reached Canoa Quebrada.

BUILT IN AN elevated position, directly on the sand of the dunes, the village was merely a collection of rudimentary houses facing each other across the slope and forming a single lane running down to the sea. Mostly built of clay and straw, crudely whitewashed and supported on thin props of faded wood, twisted and knotted, reflecting the niggardly vegetation of the Sertão, they were embellished with improvised awnings bristling with twigs and dried palms. The poorest of them were nothing but huts imitating the shape of more permanent structures, simple shelters where one went straight from the sand of the lane to the sand of the single room made even smaller by the crooked interweaving of the framework. None of the windows had frames or glass, the people there were apparently happy enough with simple, poorly fitting shutters. Standing lopsided in the middle of the lane, ten or so worm-eaten poles still carried a flimsy network of slack electric wires and bulbs with tin shades; the generator had been broken down for so long they had given up hope of it ever being repaired. Here and there a few stunted palms and slightly more tamarisks, which seemed to resist the salt-laden wind better, rustled in the sea breeze. Hens and pigs were running free, scouring the piles of rubbish that had accumulated here and there behind the shacks in their search for food.

A single well supplied brackish water to the population of fishermen that survived in this out-of-the-way place, turned in on itself, huddled up in its isolation like a decimated tribe.

Moéma's first concern was to go and see Néoshina in her house at the end of the road, just where the slope down to the beach began. For a few cruzeiros they could sling their hammocks in one of the two huts her son had built not far away, solely for travelers.

"They don't get a lot of visitors here," she explained to Roetgen, "but there are people who come from Aracati or farther away to bathe in peace. Us, for example. Néoshina makes a little money like that, fair enough. When I'm by myself I stay with my friend João, he's a fisherman. But with three of us it's impossible. We'll go and see him in a minute, he's great, you'll see. I've never met anyone so kind."

"Oh come on," said Thaïs, "let's just dump our bags in the hut and go and have a swim. OK?"

"We can do the bags, OK, but then I'd like to go to João's first. It'll only take five minutes."

"If you must," said Thaïs, slightly irritated, "but I've had enough. I'll see you in the water."

They left their bags on the sand inside the hut. While Thaïs was changing, Moéma and Roetgen set off back up the lane.

"What's the matter with her?" Roetgen asked.

"It'll pass. She's a bit jealous, that's all."

"Jealous! Really? Jealous of whom?"

"Of you, of course. She's very possessive and you weren't exactly on the agenda."

Enjoying this back-handed compliment, Roetgen looked at her with raised eyebrows. A smile formed on his lips which said, *"How stupid! Jealous of me when there's never been anything between us,"* but which at the same time betrayed a certain smugness and the unspoken desire to confirm Thaïs's suspicions.

"Don't go imagining things," Moéma said sharply. "If I invited you yesterday it was because I felt sorry for you with your little-lost-dog look. You looked so out of place among all those stupid lecturers. So sad. You're not where you belong there. It's so obvious, I'm surprised they don't see it. I felt like taking you out and showing you something else, the real Brazil. People who're alive."

Roetgen fixed his eyes on her as if he were trying to unravel the true sense of this confidence. For a moment he regretted having come to Canoa.

They had stopped outside a hut like the one they were staying in, although less fresh, as if it had withered. Put out to dry on top of a tiny awning, shark fins gave off a powerful acrid smell. Squatting in the shade, a man was meticulously dismantling a piece of fishing equipment with the composure and nimble fingers of a dressmaker. He only noticed them at the same moment as Moéma hailed him in a clear voice: "*Tudo bem*, João?"

Frozen for a moment in a pose with the gravity of a scribe, his face lit up with a gap-toothed smile as touching as that of little girls whose exposed gums disfigure them without making them ugly.

"Miss Moéma!" he said, getting up to embrace her. "What a lovely surprise! *Tudo bom*, my girl, *tudo bom*, thanks be to God."

"And this is . . ." She stopped and turned to Roetgen. "What is your first name, anyway?"

"Forget it," he said in an odd tone. "Just Roetgen, I prefer that, if if doesn't bother you."

"I couldn't care less," said Moéma. "OK, this is Roetgen, *just* Roetgen . . . a French friend, he teaches at the university in Fortaleza."

João tried to say the unusual name, mispronouncing it in a different way each time. "I'll never manage it, *francês*, it's too complicated," he said with an apologetic gesture, "but hello all the same."

Moéma handed him the plastic bag she been carrying since they'd dropped their bags in the hut. "There you are," she said,

"I've brought you a few things I don't need. Also some aspirin and antibiotics."

"God bless you, my dear. Fishing's not what it used to be, I can't even feed my children anymore. And Maria's pregnant again . . ."

"They've got eight already," said Moéma with an expression mingling irritation with compassion. "Crazy, isn't it?"

"I'll give José a banana right away," said João. "He needs vitamins after his accident."

"How is he?" Moéma asked as they went into the hut.

"Not too bad. It's almost healed over, but there are still some abscesses. Néoshina's making him some cow-dung poultices. She says they kill off infections."

"You must promise me you'll stop that and give him the tablets I brought you. Two of each, morning and evening. OK?"

"I promise. Don't worry."

A thin partition of woven palm leaves separated the kitchen from the rest of the hut. Roetgen had the time to observe the tiny seats arranged around the stove—a circle of stones on the sand— two or three smoke-blackened earthenware jugs, strips of dried fish hanging from the roof and, standing on the ground, a little rack of shelves with a can of oil and a meager stock of tins.

All there was in the other room was a jumble of mats and hammocks slung from the branches of the framework. João cautiously went up to one of them and looked in. "He's asleep," he said in a whisper. "That's better for him."

Snotty nosed, his skinny body naked, a baby of one or two was lying on his back, across the canvas sheet. From the elbow down his left arm was bandaged with rags sticky with suppuration.

"You must change that, João, it's dangerous."

"I know. Maria's gone to do the washing, she'll bring back some clean cloths.

"What happened to him?" Roetgen asked in a low voice.

"A pig," João said, gently rocking the hammock.

"All the kids play on the landfill," Moéma explained, "even the little ones. A pig chewed his arm. Hunger makes them fierce, it's not the first time it's happened."

He felt sick, with a lump in his throat as if he'd just eaten a piece of meat his taste buds had suddenly told him was rotten. "*C'est abominable,*" Roetgen said. "And the pig? They didn't . . . I mean, what did they do with it?"

"And what would you do in their place?" she asked in harsh tones. "Just think a bit before you speak. Do you really believe they can afford to have qualms? Eat or be eaten, there's no alternative."

NOT LONG AFTERWARD they headed back toward their hut to change. Roetgen had withdrawn into a reproachful silence; his expression somber, his eyes fixed on the Atlantic at the bottom of the lane, he abandoned himself to the surrounding desolation.

"I'm sorry," Moéma suddenly said without looking at him, "that was unfair of me just now, but there are some things I just can't take. You can understand that, can't you?"

"What should I understand?" Roetgen mumbled, still ashamed of having reacted in such a stupid way.

"Oh come on, stop sulking . . . You know very well what I mean, it wasn't you I was getting at. The fact that such situations can exist at all and no one bats an eyelid, everything goes on as usual, that's what makes me furious. And then I can't stop myself being annoyed with João for accepting everything that happens as inevitable. It's stupid."

"He has no choice, but you're right, you can't do anything on your own. It's a cliché, but no one seems to want to know nowadays. Everything is geared to make that obvious truth look old hat. It's the same with the class struggle, resistance, trade

unionism . . . they threw out the baby with the bathwater of Soviet communism. It was perhaps necessary in order to get things
back on a sounder basis but until that happens, it stinks . . . it
stinks to high heaven."

They'd reached the hut and, inviting him to go in, Moéma
placed her hand on his shoulder. She increased the pressure of her
fingers until he looked at her in acknowledgment of her gesture
of complicity.

"We'll have to talk about all that some time. For now we'll go and
have a *caipirinha* on the beach. That'll help us to think, won't it?"

A sudden twist of the head brought a whole shock of hair tumbling down and she started to rummage in her bag. "OK," she
said, taking out her swimsuit, "you'd better turn around, it's not a
sight for a teacher."

"I'm not so sure about that," said Roetgen, tantalized, "but
since that's the way things are, you turn around too and we can
get changed together?"

"OK."

They got undressed back-to-back. Less sure of himself than
his jokey tone had suggested, Roetgen hurried up as if—as he
noticed with amusement—he were afraid of being caught in the
act. Once naked, however, he stopped, deliberately prolonging
the erotic sensation of being naked back-to-back with a young
woman who was also undressed. His tacit promise not to turn
around gave way beneath the growing weightlessness of his penis
and its untimely twitching; without moving his chest, he took a
quick glance and was surprised to see his reflection caught in the
mirror of a symmetrical movement. Moéma's mocking eyes left
his and slowly went down, lingered. "Not bad, for a teacher," she
said with a smile. "What about me?"

With both hands, she gathered up her mane, uncovering the
back of her neck. The pose brought out her small, white breasts,

with the pallor of flesh, he thought, *that has been too long compressed*, and the contrast with her skin, tanned everywhere else, made her even more desirable. Her frail, gauche body—you could almost call it prepubescent—had the gracile curves of an Eve by Van der Goes.

"It'll do," said Roetgen, making every effort to maintain the relative propriety of his posture, "for a student, of course."

PUTTING ON THEIR swimming things was the work of a moment.

"You didn't bring any sandals?" Moéma said in concerned tones when they were ready to go out.

"No. I like walking barefoot."

"It's my fault, I should have told you. It's not really advisable here because of the filth all around the village. And then there's the *bicho-do-pé* . . ."

"What's that when it's at home?" Roetgen laughed.

"A minuscule worm, a parasite, if you prefer. The female gets under your skin, through the pores on your toes, and digs tunnels as it goes deeper. If you don't spot them right away it can be very difficult to get them out; especially since they lay eggs and—"

"Stop!" said Roetgen, with a look of revulsion. "And does this thing hurt?"

"Sometimes it itches a bit, that's all. But they can pass on an awful lot of diseases.' Seeing genuine uncertainty in his expression, she hastened to reassure him: 'Don't worry, I get some every time I come here and I've never caught anything. The important thing is to pick them off as quickly as possible and you can trust me, I'm a real expert. Try not to walk in the crap too much and it should be OK . . ."

"I don't intend to walk in the crap *at all*."

"You'll tell me how you do, OK? All right, let's go."

Towels over their shoulders, they set off in the sun. The blazing heat made them hurry toward the steep path through the sand leading down to the shore. They'd hardly reached it when Roetgen started to cry out and hop up and down: "The sand! It's burning my feet."

With a sudden idea he threw his towel down and immediately jumped onto it. "It's unbelievable," he said after a "Whew!" of relief, "I've never come across that before. The sand's sizzling, I'm sure you could cook an egg on it."

"It does happen sometimes," Moéma said, bursting out laughing.

He looked ridiculous, stuck on his towel.

A fisherman walked past, a cluster of sparkling bonitos at either end of the rod he was balancing on his shoulder.

"So what now?"

"I've no choice," he said with a shrug. "Everyone ought to have to cross a desert at least once. See you in the water, if I haven't been barbecued first. Would you look after my towel, please?"

Without waiting for a reply, he plunged off toward the sea, elbows tucked in, back arched. Moéma watched him go; graceful as he set off, his descent quickly started to look like flight as he went down, yelling and taking irregular leaps and bounds.

Mad, he's stark, staring mad!

She laughed.

FAVELA DE PIRAMBÚ: *his face covered in blood, his mouth opened exaggeratedly wide and full of clots of blood*

The sale of the Willis left Nelson feeling he'd been robbed. It was as if his hero had been assassinated a second time, as if injustice had triumphed over the whole of the Earth.

"Talk to me, son," Zé said after a long silence. "Tell me you're not angry with me."

"It's not your fault," Nelson replied. "I know you'd have kept it if you could. But I want to know who you've sold it to."

"A collector from São Luís. It seems he already has a dozen vintage cars, Jaguars, Bentleys . . . The guy at the garage refused to tell me his name."

"I'll find out, I promise you I'll find out. It was Lampião's car, don't you see? Our car. He doesn't have the right!"

"Oh, come on, you know people have every right when they're rich. As for me, it lets me keep my truck. I'll buy it back one day and give it to you. I swear I will, on the head of *padre* Cícero."

"How much did you get for it?"

"Three hundred thousand cruzeiros. Peanuts!"

"That's the problem . . . And when you can buy it back—if that ever happens—it'll be worth three million, perhaps even more. If only they'd all just fucking drop dead. I really wish they'd all just die and good riddance!"

"Don't say things like that, son. You're the one they might bring bad luck. Have a drink instead. To the Willis!"

"To the Willis," Nelson said sadly.

They drained their *cachaça* and spat the last mouthful on the floor.

"For the saints," said Zé.

"For my sainted aunt!" said Nelson, refilling the glasses.

"Don't mock. You know I don't like it. The saints have nothing to do with it."

"Oh, yes?" said Nelson with tart irony. "And what do they do, apart from drinking *cachaça*? I shouldn't think they've been sober for centuries. They don't care, your saints, they're not interested in us."

Zé shook his head with a look of exasperation, but he couldn't find an answer to the boy's bitterness. Eventually he said quietly,

"When the sea's fighting the sand, the crab's the one that gets the worst of it."

The expression just came to him—all at once he could see the Super Convair DC-6 that displayed it in yellow letters in the dust of Piauí—but it contained something of what he would have liked to express more clearly. Looking at Nelson's atrophied legs and his scabby arms, it suddenly occurred to him that the image of the crab might have been hurtful. "I'm not saying that about you, of course . . . the crab, that's me, that's all of us. Just like the crab, all men are in God's hand. You see what I'm getting at?"

Nelson didn't reply. They continued to get drunk in silence. Later in the night at the request of the *aleijadinho*, who, however, refused to accompany him on the guitar, Zé started to chant *João Peitudo, the Son of Lampião and Maria Bonita*:

The Earth goes round and round in space,
The sun's rays' heat is like a stove,
Some men's blood is spilled for cash,
While others meet their end from love,
But whether poor or reprobate,
No man can escape from his fate.

The story I'll recount today,
I wouldn't call it sentimental,
But it tells, in its own way,
A tale to thrill, both fierce and gentle:
The words and deeds of Lampião,
The legend of the wild Sertão.

It had more than a hundred and fifty verses . . . *No one can change his destiny* was the conclusion of the author of this classical tragedy, *no man can live happy in the Sertão when he's the son of Lampião.*

Half asleep, Nelson was remembering. As every evening, a few minutes before going to sleep he saw the farm at Angicos where the army had finally succeeded in surrounding Lampião and his band. They had been gunned down, one after the other, and when the massacre was over the soldiers had posed for photographs in front of the mutilated corpses. One day he had seen in one of these old sepia photographs—they were regularly exhibited at fairs, along with other equally morbid attractions—the naked and dismembered body of Maria Bonita. Between her splayed legs the huge stake the soldiers had driven up her vagina was sticking out. Beside her, placed on a stone to be in the front row for the performance, Lampião's head could be seen: his face covered in blood, his mouth opened exaggeratedly wide and full of clots of blood from his shattered jaw, he seemed to be screaming out his hatred for all eternity.

CHAPTER 8

*The conclusion of Kircher's confession followed by a description
of the Villa Palagonia, its enigmas and its strange owners*

"I HAVE TO admit, Kircher went on, that the
sight of those men & the bleeding tuna made me lose
my head; I had the feeling I was watching a pagan festival &
was considering the unreal side of such a spectacle, when I
was almost caught up in something I condemn. Remember,
Caspar, there was the fish, the symbol of Our Lord, the blood
of sacrifice, love & death mingled in a furious joy & with all
the solemn incantation of a sacred ceremony. Suddenly I could
understand the trance of the Maenads the classical texts talk
of & how they identify with the darkest forces of our being. The
intoxication of the senses to the point of madness, Caspar, the
obliteration of everything that is not the body & solely the body!
For a moment everything else seemed empty to me. In the man
who was singing I saw the only priest worthy of that name &
in the fury of the sailors the only religious way of belonging to

this world. Our Church had lost its way in losing this immediate, sensual contact with things, we could only approach the divine in the real violence of life, not in a puerile simulacrum of it. The one we are struggling against, the frenzied god, the "twice born," he alone was worthy of our respect, despite our efforts to make him look ridiculous. Dionysus, yes, it was Dionysus whom we ought to worship, just as our ancestors before us did, & I should pick up a pike, lose myself in the mass of bodies, forget myself in the spurting blood until the complete consummation of the sacrifice . . .

Athanasius's admission left me with my head in a whirl. My master had always been very assured in matters of religion; the doubts he had just revealed to me showed, even though they were the product of an oversensitive imagination, that he was as vulnerable as ordinary mortals. His acceptance of human weakness only made me love him all the more.

Three days after our return to Palermo, a carriage came to the Jesuit College to take us to visit the Prince of Palagonia.

In keeping with his reputation as an eccentric, the Prince lived outside the town, close to a village called Bagheria, where there was nothing but peasant hovels. When, after several hours, we saw his residence, we could not but admire its style. What the people of Palermo called a villa was a little Palladian palace, such as could be seen in the area around Rome; in truth, however, it was not that that drew our attention: the first thing to strike us was the height of the surrounding wall & the monstrous figures overhanging it for the whole of its circumference. It was as if the house were being attacked by all the demons of hell. The closer we came, the better we could make out these misshapen beings carved out of the porous rock that looked as if they'd come from the imagination of a man possessed by the devil. I crossed myself, calling on the Blessed Virgin while Athanasius seemed greatly perplexed.

Our astonishment reached its height when we saw the two gnomes flanking the entrance gate. The one on the right above all impressed by its obvious barbarian nature; as far as one could tell from the unspeakable bulge jutting out from its lower abdomen, it was a seated Priapus, but crooked & distorted. Like the headless Libyans mentioned by Horace, its chest took the place of its head; a huge head, out of proportion & prolonged by an absurd Pharaoh's goatee! And if the face's two almond-shaped eyes looked like two slits opening onto the dark the tiara on top made up for it by being decorated with four pupils, arranged in a triangle, whose evil look made my blood curdle. The Egyptian inspiration for this horrible idol was manifest, but this one made me feel uneasy in a way that none of the sarcophagus figures had, nor the Egyptian grotesques I had seen at Aix-en-Provence in the collection of the late Sieur Peiresc. This disagreeable sensation was only increased by the way the servants hastened to lock the wide wrought-iron gates as soon as we had passed through. All this boded ill for our stay & I found myself deploring my master's rashness in accepting this invitation.

"Come, Caspar," my master said, "summon up all your courage. If my intuition is correct, you're going to need it to face up to what's in store for us." He said this with a little amused smile that frightened me more than all the rest.

Having driven around the villa, the carriage stopped beside a fine double staircase & we got out. A lackey invited us into the house while another unloaded our baggage. We were taken to an antechamber that was rather dark but richly decorated.

"I will inform the prince of your arrival," the servant said, "please make yourselves comfortable."

He went out, closing the door behind him; it imitated the marble of the walls so perfectly I would have found it difficult to find my way out of the room if I had been invited to do so.

"Whatever happens, don't say a word," Kircher whispered surreptitiously. I acknowledged this with a nod of the head, repressing my desire to tell him of my concern.

Athanasius started to stroll around the room. All around us were cartouches, painted in fresco & charmingly rendered, depicting numerous very strange emblems, mottoes or riddles; there were so many it would have taken several days just to read them all.

"Look, Caspar, what do you think of this one: *Morir per no morir?* Nothing? Really? You must have forgotten the phoenix, which has to be consumed by fire in order to be reborn from its ashes. That is really quite childish, I would have expected more wit from the Prince. But let us continue: *Si me mira, me miran . . .* That's hardly less elementary, because of the double meaning, a gnomon could say it of the sun or, equally well, a courtier of his sovereign. Ah, here's a more difficult one, but more amusing as well: *Entier nous le mangeons, mais ô prodige étrange, reduit a sa moitié ce coquin nous mange.* Come on, my friend, rack your brains a bit, what can we eat when it's whole but half of which eats us."

That was precisely what I had been doing for a while with no other result that a growing headache & once more I had to admit defeat.

"A chicken, Caspar, a *poulet*, a *pou-let!* Don't you get it? That's why the riddle's in French," my master said with a smile. When I looked baffled, he pretended to be looking for a flea in his hair. "Well try this one, since it's written in our own language," he went on, hardly giving me time to catch my breath: "*Ein Neger mit Gazelle zagt im Regen nie . . .* Well?"

I puzzled over this for five minutes but I could not work out why a negro with a gazelle never despaired in the rain or what it might signify.

"This time you're quite right, the sentence has no hidden meaning; on the other hand, it is a perfect palindrome & can be read equally well from right to left. This kind of frivolity was much in fashion in Rome during the days of her decline & I only wish Egyptian writing was as easy to decipher as these lame riddles.

"When it spotted me it was the one who was spotted . . ." he went on. "What do you think, Caspar? Is it not a witty way of painting with words the leopard's coat?"

My master was about to tackle a further puzzle when the valet returned to say that his Highness would soon be there but in the meanwhile he asked us to be patient & to take a seat. As he said that, the servant gestured toward several chairs arranged around a picture showing the Prince in hunting dress.

Hardly had I sat down than I felt a sharp pain in my posterior: the cushion on my armchair was bristling with tiny pins causing unbearable discomfort. I immediately stood up again, in as natural a manner as possible &, following my master's order, without saying anything. He, I think, immediately realized what the difficulty was.

"Oh, do forgive me, Caspar," he said, also standing up, "I'd forgotten your hernia and that you shouldn't sit in chairs that are too comfortable. Take mine, you'll be better there."

He immediately sat in the chair I had left without appearing to feel any pain at all. I admired the strength of character through which he could suffer a torment I had not been able to bear for five seconds. The armchair I was sitting in was not lacking an uncomfortable feature: the front legs were shorter than the back ones so that I kept sliding forward & had to tense my leg muscles to stop myself falling. The back sloped forward, aggravating the awkwardness of my posture, but compared with the other chair, it was a bed of roses & I was grateful to Kircher for having suggested this unfair exchange.

"But let's get back to our puzzles," my master said. "*Legendo metulas imitabere cancros*. Oho! Latin now & some of the very best. It's your turn, Caspar—"

At that moment the lackey reappeared behind us as if by magic; he announced the Prince of Palagonia. I was not in the least unhappy to leave my torture chair. The Prince was already approaching us with his limping gait. He was a small, very dry man, at most fifty but his uncombed wig and several bad teeth made him look as if he had one foot in the grave. His dress, of green silk, was rather austere in style & even somewhat dusty, betokening a man who cared little for his appearance.

"Good, good, good, that is good. My unworthy house is proud of your presence," he said to Kircher in the bad German he insisted on speaking to the end of our stay.

My master bowed without returning his compliment.

"Good, even better like that. I like men who do not put on false modesty, especially when they possess the means to it. But come, come, I must myself excuse & to see is better than to speak . . ."

As he said that, he led us out of the room by a concealed door. After going along several corridors, we came to a library, well stocked, as it seemed to me, where he locked the door behind us. Going over to the shelves, he made as if to take out *The Golden Ass* by Apuleus—I remember the book because I could not see why he should suddenly want to talk to us about that author—but in fact by so doing he released a mechanism which opened a little window in the books, revealing the back of a painting. The Prince invited Kircher to put his eye to a tiny hole. My master did so & let me take his place after a few seconds.

"Amusing but rudimentary," he commented without a muscle in his face expressing anything other than profound indifference.

I looked in my turn. The aperture gave a view of the room where we had been before.

"You understand," the Prince went on, "that I show out of sincerity that & to prove to you how much I your worldly wisdom greatly value. I offer you all my excuses for this modest examination. It allows me to judge human honesty & you are first to succeed. Believe me that I great opinion of your abilities have & trust you not to reveal little secret of mine."

Kircher assured him that we would never reveal the device to anyone, adding that the Prince's suspicion was fully justified: there was, he said, no limit to human hypocrisy & if one were going to waste one's time with people, it was best to take precautions in choosing those one was going to deal with."

"Good, good, good," said the Prince, nodding. "You permit me congratulate you for decipherment of decorative enigmas. It prove great knowing never before seen. But we speak later. I beg you first visit your habitation and rest you a little your travails. We see each other at lunch if that agree with you."

Athanasius nodded his agreement & a servant came to take us to our apartments, where we found our luggage. They were extensive and comfortable, with flowers in beautiful arrangements, a bottle of malmsey ready to drink and crystal glasses. In an open box we found a set of surgical instruments with everything we needed to treat the wounds caused during our wait. I encouraged my master to make first use of it, since he had suffered the torture of the armchair longest, but he waved my offer away. I was dumbfounded by such stoicism, but Kircher lifted the back of his cassock &, after having untied a few tapes, revealed a sheet of thick leather so well placed that it remained invisible from outside.

"Yes, my friend," Kircher said, giving my shoulder a friendly squeeze, "concerned by the rumors about the Prince, I took further advice & . . . several precautions. I'm sorry I didn't tell you about these preparations but our good faith had to be absolutely convincing. I suspected we would be observed & you, with your innocence & your usual courage, were the one who served that objective. I only intended to inflict the sloping chair on you, but you immediately sat down on the worst one of all. Let me tell you very sincerely how much I admire the way you reacted."

"But what about the riddles, the pictures?"

"Yes, Caspar, yes, I had done my homework on those as well, so as not to appear unworthy so close to our goal. But don't ask me any more questions, it's still too early to explain all that to you. All I ask is a little patience & you'll see yourself how justified this mystery-mongering was."

I assured Athanasius I would obey him implicitly & started to put my things away. You can imagine how dumbfounded I was at my master's cleverness & the way he took all possible steps to achieve his ends! His undertaking must be of some importance, I thought, as I swore to myself to do my best to support him in his projects. My unease regarding the Prince & his house had disappeared & I was full of impatience to take part in this unexpected adventure. My master was resting on his bed, his beard sticking up, his eyes closed, august & majestic, like a statue recumbent on a tomb. I almost knelt down before him, such was the effect of his strength of mind & superhuman intelligence on me.

Toward midday a servant came to take us to the room where luncheon was served. The Prince and his wife were waiting for us, sitting at a table whose setting showed perfect taste. He introduced us to Princess Alexandra, whose splendid beauty & youth were very much at odds with her husband's decrepit appearance. With her blond hair arranged in a complicated chignon, her blue eyes & her small, red mouth & dressed ravishingly in silk & organdie, she looked like a goddess come straight from Olympus. Unlike her husband, she spoke perfect German, a legacy, we later learned, of her Bavarian roots. Refined even in her movements, she walked & did everything extremely slowly, as if the least abruptness on her part would have brought the villa tumbling down about her ears. But this idiosyncrasy only made her all the more graceful & I blushed, tongue-tied, whenever she cast a glance in my direction.

"Good, good, good . . . ," said the Prince as the servants busied themselves about us, loading the table with the most exquisite dishes. "Do honor to this meager repast, I beg you."

Deaf to this invitation, Kircher stood up to say grace &, not content with this piece of impertinence, took a long time consecrating the bread. I could see that our host was not accustomed to such ceremony & that he raised an eyebrow at the liberty my master had taken.

"Since the bread we have before us," he said with a glint of malice, "could you me tell, Reverend Father, if its weight be lighter, after it taken out of the oven, when warm it is or cold?"

"Nothing easier to prove," Athanasius replied, starting to eat, "when one has done the experiment oneself. Bread is heavier when it is warm & has just come out of the oven than when it has cooled down. A half pound of risen dough is two and a half ounces lighter cooked than raw & and even lighter when cooled. Which demonstrates that those who maintain that it is lighter raw than cooked are mistaken. One should never write, nor base oneself on anything other than genuine experiments, especially when they are as easy to prove as this one. Even Aristotle is sometimes wrong: in the fifth problem of the twenty-first section of his physics he claims that a salted loaf is lighter cold than warm & an unsalted loaf heavier. A simple experiment showed me however that the two loaves remain the same weight, whether cold or warm, whether they are salted or not."

"Excellent, my sir, excellent," the Prince said, sucking a chicken leg. "I did not expect less from you."

Princess Alexandra turned to me &, matching action to words, said, "These gentlemen are too learned for me. And

I have to admit, lighter or heavier, it is a matter of complete indifference: I prefer my bread with butter anyway."

"Quite right too," my master agreed, also helping himself.

As for me, I kept my eyes fixed on my plate.

The meal continued on the same bantering tone. Wines & dishes followed each other without interruption & Athanasius did justice to them, much to the satisfaction of our hosts. When large slices of grilled swordfish were served, my master begged me to recount our adventures at Messina. Despite feeling intimidated, I still managed to describe our fishing excursion in detail, though naturally omitting the episode that had led to Kircher's confession. When I came to the death of the fish, I became so impassioned at the revolting memory that the Prince laughed at my sensitivity. But his wife had turned quite pale . . . Without a word, she put her hand on mine & I could tell that she shared my feelings. The Prince noticed the gesture, brief though it was, & abruptly stiffened.

After the meal we were served a very bitter liqueur based, so the Prince told us, on herbs from the mountains. He seemed to have become very heated & kept pestering my master with his questions. Then the Prince appeared to hesitate for a moment & after he had whispered a few words in Athanasius's ear, the two of them went to the other end of the room, where they continued to converse in low voices.

Left alone with the Princess, I did not know how to behave, so moved I was by her beauty. I asked her a few questions about God & the nature of the soul, to which her replies showed intelligence & good sense. Since the subject did not seem to interest her particularly, I brought the conversation to the twisted statues we could see through the windows, asking her to tell me what they meant. She went very pale & appeared to waver before answering.

"I feel you are a young man I can trust & I am happy to tell
you a story of which I have no need to be ashamed but which
was the cause of both those monsters & my misfortune. As you
perhaps noticed during the meal, my husband is of a very jealous
nature; a few years ago, not many months after our wedding,
despite myself I gave him occasion to feel his suspicions were
justified. A cousin of mine, Ödön von Horvath, came to visit me
here. He excelled in the art of composing airs for the lute or the
spinet & this inestimable gift was only equaled by his beauty.
As we were the same age & my interests were closer to his than
to those of my husband, I was very happy to see him here & we
passed whole days playing music together or discussing all kinds
of topics. I enjoyed listening to him talk about the country of my
birth & the loved ones I had left there. Alas, under the influence
of youth and loneliness, he fell so passionately in love with me &
declared his love so sincerely & so sensitively that I was moved
by it. All I felt for him was affection & a sister's love for her
brother but I have to admit that I was secretly flattered by his
attentions & his insistence might perhaps have eventually borne
fruit. Chance, or Providence, if you prefer, saved me from the
unfaithfulness without sparing me the shame. One evening after
supper, when the Prince pretended to go to bed on the pretext
that he had drunk too much during the meal, my cousin, even
more aroused than usual because of the wine, abandoned
himself to transports he normally managed to repress. He
begged me to grant him a kiss & since I refused, threatened to
go & kill himself on the spot; he was a man to carry out such
a piece of madness, especially given the state he was in, with
the result that the idea frightened me. I resisted less . . . he put
his arm around my waist & took advantage of the moment to
steal the kiss he seemed to have set his heart on. That was the
moment when my husband surprised us. He didn't say a word,

but the coldness & cruelty I saw in his eyes made my blood run cold much more than if he had lost his temper. Ringing for the servants, he had my cousin dragged out of the room & locked me in my bedroom without giving me a chance to explain.

"Since that ill-fated evening, I have been shut away in this house, which my husband has transformed into a prison. As for my cousin, I have not had any news of him, but I know that he has not returned to Bavaria & I cannot stop myself constructing the worst hypotheses about his fate. Three months later workers started raising the walls around our park & installing on them the devilish statues that are intended to remind me ceaselessly of my supposed sin. But that would be nothing without the excessive cruelty with which my husband carried out his undertaking: if you look at these statues closely, you will see that many of them represent musicians; everything about them is grotesque, distorted, monstrous, everything apart from their faces, they are always the same, calm & angelic, as if surprised to find themselves in such company. The face," the Princess quickly wiped away a large tear from her cheek, "is that of my cousin."

I sympathized profoundly with this unhappy woman & felt so sorry for her misfortune that I poured out my sighs. I was speechless at her husband's malevolence. I was trembling as I took her hand & squeezed it firmly as it seemed the only suitable way of consoling her a little.

"Excuse me," she said, thanking me with a wan smile & withdrawing her hand slowly, "but I must go and rest."

She gave me her arm & I accompanied her to the door. As she took more precautions than before, I thought she was about to faint and asked whether she felt strong enough to walk by herself.

"You needn't worry," she said with an artless smile, "it's just that the glass harpsichord in my stomach is vibrating a little more than usual. To hurry would risk breaking it & not all the skill of Father Kircher would be able to save me from a horrible death."

At that she went, leaving me in a state close to stupor.

ALCÂNTARA: *Euclides at his keyboard adjusting the slow motion of the stars ...*

A few days passed, days entirely devoted to work on Caspar Schott's text and Loredana's occasional but regular visits. Despite her initial hostile reaction, Soledade had immediately adopted the Italian, or rather, Eléazard thought, had been won over by her open nature and by the exemplary way she was interested in everything, people as well as things, without distinction. She had refused to come and stay with him—*there's plenty of unoccupied rooms*, he'd told her without any ulterior motive, *at least it would mean you wouldn't have to pay for the hotel, it's up to you*—but she had taken him at his word when he'd said she could come to Pelhourinho Square whenever she liked, to use his library or take advantage of a shower that worked more or less properly. He would run into her as she came and went in the house, reading on one of the chaise longues on the veranda or, more often, sitting at the kitchen table with Soledade. He was entirely satisfied with her unobtrusive, unpredictable presence; it was as if Loredana had always been living there and a spontaneous, transparent intimacy had quietly arisen in the course of both their lives.

She seemed to enjoy his guided tour around the town, putting a name, an anecdote to each dilapidated façade, reconstructing against the gray sky every ruined edifice with grand gestures and builder's jargon. In his enthusiasm he had even taken her to see the moving little church—one of the first the missionaries built in

Brazil—hidden on a tiny uninhabited island in São Marcos Bay. An unbelievable number of snakes had taken up residence there and, in a kind of fiendish revenge, subjected every nook and cranny of the battered walls to their interference. He decided, however, not to take her to the *island of the short-sighted* or to that *of the albinos*, such was Loredana's nauseated response to these examples, fairly banal, after all, of the dangers of inbreeding.

She still refused to go into detail about her own life and her reasons for being in Alcântara—and he had no desire to know more than she wanted to tell him—but proved to be inexhaustible on everything concerning China, a subject on which she had profound and first-hand knowledge. She had conscientiously set about reading Schott's manuscript, in small doses and, as he understood it, more to satisfy her curiosity about him than about Athanasius Kircher. She told him her thoughts about it and emphasized the difficulties she came across, which allowed Eléazard to refine his notes or even to add a comment on certain passages he had not considered worth dwelling on. Without her he would never have thought it necessary to explain to a potential reader the scourge the Thirty Years' War had been nor how exotic the simple discovery of Italy had been in the seventeenth century. It came to the point where he was writing his notes purely for her, not giving the matter final approval until it had been tempered by her comments.

For all that their rapport was something of a miracle, it still remained a provisional pact. Eléazard refused to see the problem from that point of view; he made sparing use of it, with the happiness it brought, as if it would last forever. Afterward he was to reproach himself for not having taken full advantage of what he knew from the start was to be a short-lived encounter.

He had told her so much about Euclides, his only friend in the area, that she had agreed in principle to meet him. That morning, however, when he wanted to take Loredana to lunch at the doctor's, neither Alfredo nor Soledade knew where she was. Eléazard had taken the ferry to São Luís with a feeling of irritation that even he eventually saw as both absurd and excessive.

"I ASSURE YOU the man's perfectly well mannered. A touch rustic, perhaps. Lacking good taste for certain, but that's more widespread than anything throughout the world and I would say you couldn't pride yourself on being the opposite without demonstrating a smugness that is even worse."

Eléazard looked doubtful.

"Yes, I know, I know," Dr. Euclides went on with a smile. "He's not really a left-winger, that's what's putting you off, isn't it?"

"That's going beyond euphemism, doctor, it's sarcasm," Eléazard said, smiling too. "And you're probably right, I can't see what I could do if I visited a man like that except insult him right in the middle of the party."

"Oh, come now . . . You're far too well brought up to indulge in anything so foolish. Just remember I'm asking you as a favor. You can believe me when I say from experience that you won't regret it; it's a very instructive milieu, especially for a journalist. And if my company alone isn't enough, bring your fair Italian, at least it'll give me the opportunity of meeting her . . ."

Eléazard watched the doctor as he took off his pince-nez and cleaned them meticulously on an immaculate handkerchief. Without the magnifying lenses, which made them look unnaturally large, grotesque, like some joke spectacles, his almond-green eyes suddenly revealed their great humanity once more. They had a cheerful look without showing any sign of the amaurosis—*Ah, morose is he! Amoroso . . . a nice name, don't you think, for the atrophy of the optic nerve*—that would soon dim their light entirely.

Euclides never combed his hair except with his hand; his thick, unruly gray hair, in a fairly short crew cut, stuck out in all directions, giving the impression of being constantly blown about by invisible gusts of wind. His perfectly straight nose contrasted with a tousled mustache and goatee, yellowed by the tar from his Egyptian cigarettes; the whiskers concealed his mouth and moved mechanically when he spoke, as on a puppet's face. Chubby without being fat, he always wore dark suits, made to measure, a starched white shirt and a sort of four-leaved bow tie; Eléazard wondered where he managed to get such an old-fashioned item of neckwear. The only extravagance he allowed himself in his dress was in his choice of vests, luxurious accessories with facings embroidered in silk or gold thread, with buttons of mother-of-pearl, marcasite or even delicate enameled miniatures; he had an impressive collection of them. For the rest he possessed an affability *à la Flaubert*—at least such as his devotees ascribe to him—combined with an unfailing calmness and courtesy. His encyclopedic and perceptive erudition was fascinating.

"You will be my eyes," he said, replacing his pince-nez on the hollow the glasses had dug out on the bridge of his nose. "The young eyes of an aging Milton on the decrepitude of this world. *O loss of sight, worse than chains, or beggary, or decrepit age!*" he said in impeccable English. "*A living death, myself my sepulchre.*" Or something like that, isn't it? You must find me very pretentious, comparing myself with such a great poet, but at least we share the same disease and that's something, you must agree."

"How is your sight doing at the moment?" Eléazard said, with a smile at the roguish twinkle in his eye.

"It's fine, don't worry. I can still manage to read, more or less accurately, and that's the only thing that matters. It's not the darkness that worries me." He gathered his thoughts for a moment, eyes closed. Then, pointing to the shelves covering two large walls of the room up to the ceiling, he said, "It's the silence, their silence . . . I couldn't bear it, you know." He stifled a laugh. "Fortunately I've lost my faith, otherwise I might think it was punishment from Bigbeard for what I've done. Just think, that would really be real hell, wouldn't it?"

Eléazard found it difficult to imagine how Dr. Da Cunha could have been a Jesuit, even in his young days, so far the person smiling before him was from the image we have of a man of the cloth. There was, of course, his biblical knowledge, so rare among laymen, and the fact that he was perfectly at ease with Latin and Greek, but that was not enough to distinguish him from a good teacher of classical languages.

"One day," Eléazard said, "you must tell me why you left the profession . . ." Immediately he tried to correct himself, embarrassed by the unfortunate choice of word. "That is, I mean . . ."

"No, you put it very well," Euclides broke in. "The 'profession,' it's the only word that can take account of the faith—that of a certain Savoyard vicar, if you see what I mean—and the occupation itself, which is too often just a job rather than a state." He lit a cigarette after having carefully taken it out of his box. "Have I really left it?" he wondered in sincere tones. "I'm still asking myself that. Do you know what word the Jesuits use to describe one of their order who has renounced his vows? They say he has become a 'satellite,' by which they mean that despite himself he remains in orbit around the Society, in a trajectory in which the forces of repulsion are in equilibrium with an attraction that he will never manage to eliminate. One doesn't leave the Society, one moves a greater or lesser distance away without ceasing, basically, to belong to it. And I have to admit that there is some truth in that way of looking at things. One can escape from slavery, although with difficulty, but never from several years of domestication; and that is what it is: training the body and the mind with one aim in view, obedience. So 'to disobey,' you know . . . Under those conditions the word doesn't make much sense. All it expresses is a mere temporary rejection of the law, a digression to be condemned, true, but that is remissible within the body of obedience itself. And if you think about it, you will have to admit that it's more or less the same for everyone. Breaking a rule, all the rules, always comes back to choosing new rules, that is, to returning to the bosom of obedience. You have the feeling you are liberating yourself, profoundly changing your being, when all you have done is to change your master. You know, the snake biting its own tail."

"Certain masters are more demanding than others, aren't they?"

"I agree, my friend, and I do not regret for one second the decision I made at a certain point in my life. I am the better for it in all respects, believe me. But if it is easier to follow laws one has freely chosen—and the very possibility of that choice is far from being as obvious as it seems—the fact remains that they imply submission, obedience, which is all the more dangerous for seeming less restrictive. I think it was Étienne de La Boétie—in fact, I'm sure it was," he said, correcting himself with a wink—"who spoke of 'voluntary servitude' to castigate the submission of the nations to the tyranny of a single man. But in his argument in favor of freedom, he distinguishes between *serving* and *obeying*, that is, between the, to his mind, reprehensible subjection of a serf to his lord and the obedience of a free man to a just government. It is a distinction I have never been able to embrace myself, despite my sympathy for the man. Even when accepted of one's own free will, and perhaps even more because of that illusion of freedom, all obedience remains servile, humiliating and, more importantly to my mind, sterile. Yes, sterile . . . The older I grow, the more I am convinced that revolt is the only genuine free and, accordingly, poetic act. It is insubordination that brings about progress in the world because it and it alone produces the poets, the creators, the naughty boys who refuse to obey a code, a state, an ideology, a technique, whatever . . . to obey anything that presents itself as the ultimate, as the indisputable and infallible outcome of an age."

Euclides took a long draw on his cigarette and then, in a cloud of the smoke that was recognizable among all others from its scent of honey and cloves, went on:

"If there is a concept we ought to analyze a bit more before jettisoning it, as we have done with such haste and relief, it is that of 'permanent revolution.' It's an idea I would prefer to call 'criticism' or 'permanent rebellion' to avoid the circularity inherent in the first term."

Eléazard never loved the old doctor so much as when he poured out his innate anarchism. He saw in it an innocence, a humanism and a youthful spirit that would have seemed exemplary in anyone but were even more so in a man of his age.

"I didn't know you had Maoist sympathies," he said in a jocular tone. Then, more seriously, he went on, "I've often thought about the same question myself, but I cannot see an idea that has caused millions of deaths as other than suspect, to say the least."

"And that is where you are wrong," Euclides said, feeling for the ashtray on the table. "It isn't ideas that kill, it's men, certain men who manipulate others in the name of an ideal that they consciously betray, and sometimes without even realizing it. All ideas are criminal the moment we persuade ourselves they are absolutely true and set about making everyone share them. Christianity itself—and what could be more inoffensive than the love of one's fellow man?—Christianity alone is responsible for more deaths than lots of other theories that, on the face of it, are more suspect. But the fault is entirely that of the Christians and not of Christianity! Of those who transformed what ought to have remained just an impulse of the heart into a sectarian doctrine . . . No, my friend, an idea has never hurt anyone. It is only the truth that kills. And the most murderous truth is certainly one that claims to be rigorously worked out. Metaphysics and politics in the same basket and let's add the scientistic creed or that smug, blasé despair that nowadays justifies the worst excesses . . ."

Every time Eléazard had a discussion with him there came a point where the old man shook him, less by his arguments, however, than by the vehemence with which he put them forward. Without sharing his view of the world, he always ended up yielding to its magnetism, its cold, enduring force.

"But what a doddering old fart I am," Euclides said, extricating himself from his armchair with difficulty, "I didn't even think to get us a glass of cognac. Give me two minutes and I'll rectify that."

It was no use Eléazard protesting, the doctor hurried off to get the necessary from the room where they had had lunch not long before. While he was away the library took on a new, disturbing quality, as if all the books, all the comfortable, old-fashioned bric-à-brac scattered around, had only been waiting to make it clear to the visitor that he was an intruder. The somber light, deliberately maintained by keeping the Venetian blinds closed, so fresh and friendly when emphasizing Euclides's slow gestures, now seemed aggressive, surly, Cerberus-like in protecting its master's solitude.

Situated not far from the Rosary Church, in the seedy part of São Luís, Euclides da Cunha's house was no different from the other run-down dwellings reeking of boredom and cellars, whose colonial style gave the *Rua do Egyto* its old-fashioned charm. Eléazard was only acquainted with the hall, which, being very long and having a huge number of chairs neatly arranged along the walls, each with its crocheted antimacassar over the back, resembled nothing more than a waiting room; the library, even more spacious but made to seem cramped by the dark, brocade hangings, the rocking chairs, the heavy neo-Gothic sideboards topped by mirrors, the pedestal tables, the ornate vases, succulent plants, they, too, old-fashioned by mimicry, dusty fans and daguerrotypes of old, chubby-cheeked babies and old folk mesmerized by the lens; and the dining room, smaller but that too cluttered up with the stifling hotchpotch aping the fine linen of bourgeois households of the previous century.

"Ignore this ghastly stuff," Euclides had said the first time I visited him, "it's my mother's world rather than mine. She made me promise to keep it the way it is until she dies and, as you will have noticed, the dear lady is still alive and kicking. Nothing has changed here since I was a child, which, paradoxically, has helped me become aware of my own evolution: as a boy I adored the décor here, I idealized it to the point where I saw it as the ultimate yardstick of aesthetic quality; as I grew up my eyes opened to its sad reality, I came to hate it as the very mark of bad taste—of course, all I was cursing was my transition to adulthood—and then one day I stopped judging, with the result that this ugliness has become familiar, precious to me, and now that it has merged into the mist with the rest of the world, indispensable . . ."

Dr. da Cunha's mother was a very old lady, tiny, bent, dry and twisted as a tree in the Sertão. She was always the one who welcomed Eléazard with a few kind words, made him sit in the hall and insisted he drank a glass of tamarind juice, without which she would have departed from the laws of hospitality. Then she would show him into the library before disappearing into the progressive darkness of a corridor. For all Eléazard knew, she looked after the house on her own, watching over her son like a nun attached to a holy man.

Hearing the clink of glasses falter in the other room, Eléazard got up to go and help his host.

"That's kind of you, thank you," Euclides said, allowing Eléazard to relieve him of the tray. "I took rather a long time, but my mother absolutely insisted you try her angel's sighs. It's a great honor, even I don't get them every day, you know."

They sat down on their sofa again. "Look," said Euclides, "while you're seeing to the drinks, I'll play you a little piece, the score of which I received the other day. If you can guess the compose . . ."

"If I guess the composer?" Eléazard asked as Euclides walked slowly over to the piano.

"You won't guess it anyway," he said with a laugh. "But *if* you should guess it, I'll put you on an interesting track. Yes indeed, very interesting . . ."

Without further ado he lifted the lid of the old Kriegelstein and started to play.

From the outset Eléazard was surprised by the odd repetitive, staccato rhythm the left hand produced in the low register. When the melody came on top of this strange bass, he very quickly recognized the loose-limbed rhythm of the tango, but a tango that was off beat, retarded, almost parodistic in the way it prolonged the wait, exaggerated the syncopated panting of the music. *One, two, three, drowning, oh fan-tastic, yes, two, three, four, a trip to asphyxia* . . . The words emerged, bursting on his lips like bubbles. *Sick at heart, sadness weary and profound* . . . Euclides at his keyboard adjusting the slow motion of the stars, regulating it, setting it up for other demands.

Without being a virtuoso, Euclides played somewhat better than the average amateur—several times Eléazard had heard him give a very decent interpretation of the more difficult pieces of *The Well-Tempered Clavier* or certain sonatas by Villa-Lobos that were equally difficult—but it was the first time he had shown such an ability to overturn the secret order of things in his playing. When the piece stopped on a harsh chord, immediately damped, Eléazard had that feeling of sudden disorientation that we sometimes get on waking after the first night in a strange bedroom.

"Well?" Euclides said, coming back to sit beside him.

"As expected, I give up. It's very beautiful, genuinely very beautiful . . ."

"Stravinsky, opus 26. There are certain little pieces like that, beyond categorization like all true masterpieces, that defy understanding. Another time I'll let you hear what Albéniz or Ginastera managed in the same vein. But have one of these delicious treats," he said, offering Eléazard the plate of little cakes he'd brought. "They're very special, something between a host and a meringue, but with orange-flower flavor. Their taste almost matches their pretty name." Then, without transition, he went on, "Since I'm a decent fellow, although you failed the test lamentably, I'm still going to alert you to the fact that Governor Moreira is preparing something. I don't know exactly what, but it's a bit fishy."

"What do you mean?"

"Some people are going around buying up the whole of the Alcântara peninsula, even the uncultivated parts and the properties that don't bring anything in. I have good reason to believe that it's Moreira who is behind the various intermediaries carrying out the operation."

"But why would he do something like that?" Eléazard asked, suddenly interested.

"That, my friend, is up to you to discover." There was a glint of malice in his eyes as he added, "When you accompany me to the *Fazenda do Boi*, for example."

FAZENDA DO BOI: *Alcântara International Resort*

"Good. I'll read that again: *Governor José Moreira da Rocha and his wife request the pleasure of the company of*—then a blank space, and please allow plenty of room, there's nothing more annoying than having to squeeze something in between two words—*at a reception they are giving on the 28th of April, from seven o'clock onward. Fazenda do Boi and the usual address* . . . Yes, a hundred. Someone will come to collect them tomorrow afternoon. Thank you . . . Goodbye."

Carlotta replaced the receiver with a sigh of relief. She held out her hands over the telephone and watched them trembling with a faint mocking smile. *You drink too much, old girl . . . Where's it going to get you? Don't you think getting old's enough in itself?* And immediately the irrepressible desire came to pour herself a glass, the first of the day, just so she felt better, just to escape the nagging fear the only answer to which was an infinity of questions. An abyss was opening up before her, making her heart beat irregularly, accelerating the unbearable collapse of her whole being. In a compromise with her morning resolutions, she swallowed a quarter of a Lexomil tablet and dropped into an armchair, opposite the beheading of Saint John the Baptist that took pride of place in her bedroom. It was a large picture, too academic, despite certain qualities in the treatment of light, to retain attention apart from by the signature: Vítor Meireles, the Brazilian painter who had devoted his work to the glorification of the Empire and brought out for the first time certain Indian motifs, though very discreetly and without calling into question the validity of the conquest of souls by the Christian religion. Of all the pictures she had inherited from her family it was Carlotta's favorite, her great-grandmother, Countess Isabella de Algezul, having posed for the figure of Salome in 1880. When she was young, Carlotta's resemblance to her great-grandmother had been so striking, had given rise to so many rapturous comments, that as an adolescent she had taken delight in doing her hair in the same style as the Jewish princess in the picture, imitating her regal bearing and lowering her eyes with the same disgusted sadness on the plates of cocktail

snacks she was offering her parents' guests. Yes, she had so resembled her in body and spirit that she had made some doubt the
authenticity of the picture and brought some others to the brink
of madness . . . Salome victorious and Victorian, the nymph Echo
from a dream in moist collodion with her heavy chignon of red
hair, her ghost's face in which emotion expressed itself in sickly
blotches; for a long time her only way of blushing had been this
sort of allergic reaction to the brutal contact with stupidity.

There was not much left of this remarkable beauty. Up to the age
of fifty Carlotta had managed, with creams and diets, to maintain
a certain similarity to the image of her younger days—for her son,
for his look of pride when he talked of the passions she aroused
in his classmates. Then Mauro had left and his departure had coincided with evidence of the lack of consideration for her that her
husband showed when away from home. To be honest, the photo
published in *Manchete* had shocked her less by the actual content,
as José wanted to believe, than by its revelation of a tragedy that
had been played out well before that execrable scene. Carlotta had
married Moreira da Rocha for love at a time when he was nothing more than a charming con man, shutting her eyes, against
her parents' advice, to his lack of culture, his thirst for money
and power. Alone in the *fazenda,* her eyes fixed on the photo that
made him look so ugly, she had realized that she no longer loved
him, probably never had loved him. That was the hardest to take:
thirty-five years together with a man she despised, a man whom,
she now saw, she had always despised . . . because he prided
himself on only reading the financial sections of the newspapers
and, without having ever opened one of his books, called Marcel
Proust a "dirty little queer."

This obvious fact, revealed too late and magnified by bitterness, had become a torrent, sweeping away everything in its path,
leaving its traces everywhere, even in Carlotta's own reflection

in the mirrors. Foundation creams and other artificial aids can never mask the body's decrepitude: as long as love persists, in whatever form, they embellish, they protect a beauty that exists beyond the contingencies of old age. They are part of a game with strict rules, the game of affection in which one knows there is nothing to gain but the pleasure of being able to keep on playing it. For those such as savages and children, whose eyes have not yet been opened by skepticism, reality is unvarnished because their trust is limitless. Once they learn the extent of their credulity, the magic of the world is spoiled, it turns into illusion, that other word for the impossibility of belief. Carlotta was vaguely aware that no cosmetics could disguise the unsightliness brought about by the withdrawal of faith.

Her mind a blank, she ran her hands over her tired flesh, feeling her flabby muscles, rolling the layers of fat under her distended skin. Bizarre the way the body had of producing fat when not enough demands were made on it . . . As if it were noting down our least abdication of responsibility toward life in order, by way of compensation, to provide richer nourishment for those that will continue the cycle after its death. Benumbed by the Lexomil, a rather stupid smile spread across her face at this new idea: accelerate the process, stuff herself, drink more and more, not to "forget"—nothing nor anyone could soothe the pain of a failed life—but to put on weight, get fat, as a way of making one last offering to the forces of life. She got up and looked through her address book, then rang La Bohème, the best restaurant in São Luís.

"Good morning . . . This is Countess Carlotta de Alzegul, could you put me through to Isaac Martins, please . . ." Seeing the bottle of whiskey she hadn't managed to finish the previous day, she stretched the telephone wire until she could reach it.

"Yes? . . . How are you, my dear Isaac? . . . Oh, I'm all right, even if it's not much fun being a governor's wife sometimes. But

that's precisely why I'm ringing: my husband is having a reception at the *fazenda* in a fortnight's time and I was wondering if
you would be willing to organize the food ... About a hundred,
perhaps more, you know how these things are, people imagine they're obliged to bring a companion, quite often one who
would have been better left at home ... You'll need to allow
for a full meal, something pretty lavish: lobster, shellfish, roast
meat ... Stuffed crabs? Yes, why not? ... Add to that anything
that comes into your head, I leave it entirely up to you. Expense
no object and you'll make sure there's plenty of everything, won't
you? We'll have to think in terms of three or even four identical
buffets, so hire all the extra help you think necessary, I don't want
any complaints about having to wait to be served ... Could you
come out to the *fazenda* tomorrow so we can get together to final-
ize the arrangements? Preferably in the morning ... Perfect. See
you tomorrow, Isaac ... Goodbye."

Carlotta hung up and drank her first mouthful of whiskey that
day. It all looked pretty promising, José was right to continue to
trust her in these matters; few women would be capable of organizing such an important social event and without the least show
of panic. She wasn't doing it for him, but for the honor of the Al-
zeguls, well aware that even if her husband had completely ex-
empted her from the task, the least mistake would still be blamed
on her and her alone. It was not unusual for José to organize this
kind of party, especially at election time, but he usually held them
at the governor's palace, reserving the honors of the *fazenda* for
a few privileged guests. Where the hell had the butler said he
would leave the guest list?

Her glass of whiskey in her hand, Carlotta left her bedroom and
headed for the study, where Moreira spent the better part of his
evenings. She quickly found three typed sheets, clearly visible on a
green leather blotter. As she sat down at the desk, in the "master's"

chair, she realized she hadn't been in the room for years, out of fear
of disturbing her husband when he shut himself away with his files
and then out of lack of interest in his affairs. *I won't bore you with
it, darling, it would take too long and you wouldn't understand much
anyway.* Nothing had changed since she'd seen to the decoration of
the room, apart from the addition of a huge map of the Alcântara
peninsula in garish colors that clashed with the eighteenth-century
engravings she'd had such difficulty tracking down all those years
ago. As she drank, she scanned the guest list. Dr. Euclides da Cunha
hadn't been forgotten, fortunately . . . two ministers, one ambassador, a few worthies . . . Suddenly she came across a series of names
indented, as if to emphasize their importance:

Yukihiro Kawaguchi

Susumu Kikuta   —Sugiyama Bank

Jason Wang Hsiao   —Everblue Corporation

Matthews Campbell Junior
Henry McDouglas   —Pentagon

Peter McMillan
William Jefferson   —Forban Guaranty Trust Co. of
                    New York

Accustomed to her husband's business relations, the only thing
to strike Carlotta about this collection of unknown names was the
mention of the Pentagon, but she felt a sort of irrational uneasiness. Having decided to ask her husband about it, she looked for a
pen to annotate the list and as she opened the large drawer in the
desk her eye was caught by the headings on a file:

CONFIDENTIAL
INFORMATION MEMORANDUM

Alcântara International Resort

1.   Project Description
1.1. Overview
1.2. Infrastructure
1.3. Marketing

2.   Financial Plan
2.1. Structure
2.2. Term Sheet

3.   Economic Analysis
3.1. Assumptions
3.2. Base Case
3.3. Conservative Case

4.   Co-agents
4.1. Sugiyama Bank
4.2. Forban Limited
4.3. Countess C. de Alzegul

Astounded to see her name on such a document, Carlotta looked up the relevant section. For a few seconds indignation made her stomach churn: she was involved in this project as "owner" of all the pieces of land on the Alcântara peninsula that were listed for development!

CHAPTER 9

The night of Christmas & the mysteries of the camera obscura

I T O C C U R R E D T O me that it wasn't just the Prince's mind that was wandering but his wife's as well & I convinced myself that she had merely claimed she had this harpsichord in her stomach in memory of her cousin & as a metaphor, so to speak, of the sufferings she had to bear.

Kircher & the Prince came back to join me with the satisfied expressions of men who have made great plans. Our host having taken his leave, we retired for a siesta.

"Everything is going as planned, Caspar," Athanasius said when we were safely in our room. "The Prince & I understand each other perfectly; our agreement should have consequences the scope of which you cannot imagine."

I felt I had the right to tell him what the Princess had revealed to me a few minutes previously. Kircher seemed not in the least surprised & merely calmed me with a smile. Then, placing a hand on my shoulder, he said, "It would be a good idea, I think, if you reread your Ignatius . . ."

Accepting his advice, I immersed myself in the *Exercises* for several hours. It made me regard the Prince slightly more indulgently, without freeing me from a certain hostility toward him. Furious with myself, I tied a hair shirt tightly around my torso, chastising my bodily appetites; this persistent pain finally released my mind & I managed to pray & thank Heaven for all its goodness.

On the evening of that December 18, 1637 we met in the same room for dinner. My master, who was always the center of the conversation, was in sparkling form. Abandoning his usual humility, he seemed to take pleasure in parading his knowledge & surprising our hosts with many curious facts and delightful anecdotes that the vagaries of the conversation brought to mind.

He assured us he had himself generated frogs from a little dust taken from the ditches, as he had scorpions by mixing some powder from that insect in a decoction of basil. Similarly, quoting Paracelsus, he said it was possible to resuscitate a plant from its own ashes, although that was much more difficult. From there we came to talk about the strangest animals nature had ever produced, that is, dragons, the progeny of the eagle & the she-wolf. He spoke of the small specimen that could be seen in the Aldrovandi Museum in Rome & of the one he had caught a glimpse of in 1619, flying out of a cave on Mount Pilatus near Lucerne, but also of all sorts of unthinkable animals that proved the infinite capacity of divine creation. Thus Kircher reminded us of the cock with a snake's tail or with a crest of plumes, one of the curiosities of the Boboli Gardens in Florence, which was the fruit of a chance mixture of sperm; the ostrich or "strontocamelo," whose name & appearance prove that it comes from the coupling of a camel with a fowl; the rhinobatos, the offspring of the ray & the angelfish mentioned by Aristotle; & numerous other exotic animals of which his correspondents in the Indies or in America sent him detailed descriptions.

Then the Prince, who was very much interested in the sciences, brought the discussion around to astronomy & questioned Kircher so passionately about the conflicting theories that were current at the time that they were soon at it hammer and tongs. Seeing that the Princess was enjoying these difficult subjects less, I decided to make conversation with her. Since I knew, from what she had told me before, that she liked music, I talked about the musicians who were all the rage in Rome, in particular Girolamo Frescobaldi, whom my master and I regularly went to hear in the Lateran church. She had a high opinion of all of them, she said, but she preferred the more spiritual compositions of Monteverdi, William Byrd & above all of Gesualdo, whose name she spoke in a murmur & with a quick glance at her husband. I nodded, to indicate that I had understood her allusion & fully approved of & shared her tastes. She seemed delighted by this accord &, with shining eyes & flushed cheeks, she drank in every word I said, so much so that I had to rub my back against the chair to make the prickles of my hair shirt work more effectively & call my flesh to order. I decided it was time to return to subjects more appropriate to my calling.

"How do you imagine God?" I asked her without further ado.

She gave me an affectionate smile, obviously unsurprised by the point-blank nature of my question, as if she clearly understood its motivation. "I cannot imagine Him," she replied almost immediately, "that is to say I cannot visualize Him as similar to men or to anything human. I believe there is a God because I cannot think that I or all the things around me are the product of chance or of some creature. Also, since the direction of my affairs is not a result of my own wisdom & since success rarely comes by the means I have chosen, Divine Providence must be involved in the matter . . ."

I was very pleased with this reply & admired her for not saying, as most women did, that she imagined God as a venerable old man.

"And since it has so happened that I am talking to you about myself in a way I have never before talked to anyone, I can admit that, were it not for the sacred bonds tying me to my husband, I would joyfully place my life under the yoke of Jesus Christ. Not in a convent, where the cross is too easy a burden, but in a hospital that accepts patients with all kinds of ailments, wherever they come from and whatever their religion, to serve them all without distinction &, following the example of the only husband worthy of the name, to take their infirmities upon myself. I know that my eyes are able to bear the most horrible sights, my ears the oaths and cries of the sick & my sense of smell the stench of all the infections of the human body. I would take Jesus from bed to bed to these wretched people, I would encourage them, not by empty words but by the example of my own patience & charity, & I would do so much that God would have mercy on them . . ."

The tears were welling up in the Princess's eyes at the evocation of her secret desire. Of perfect beauty, she seemed great & noble, free and majestic in her bearing, honest in her demeanor, with the soft, pliant voice of a saint. This young woman was admirable in every respect & her husband the most abominable—

"Extraordinary!" the Prince suddenly exclaimed, turning to me. "Caspar, I envy you: your master the most considerable is of scholars! We together realize soon great things . . ."

I blushed at this, as if I had been caught in the act & the Prince had been able to read my thoughts.

"You exaggerate," said Kircher, "knowledge alone is magnificent & that alone deserves your compliments. But you must excuse me, my lady, for having monopolized your husband for so long; I seem to have forgotten that our conversation was hardly of a nature to enthrall you."

"Do not worry, Father. We conversed on religious matters with Father Schott & it is I who have forgotten my duty as hostess. I have to admit that I didn't hear a single word of your discussion & I am sorry about that, even though I doubtless would not have understood much of it."

Kircher politely assured her she was mistaken in that & then, as if on a sudden inspiration, offered to divert us: "As we have finished this excellent dinner, it seems a suitable moment to follow it with an amusing experiment. What do you think, are we lighter before or after we've eaten?"

"Good, good, good," said the Prince, rubbing his hands in satisfaction. "I take up challenge! We must have method, always method, as say Monsieur Descartes. After meal I feel me more light, although I swallow at least four pound of food. This idea clear & distinct in my *intellectus*, therefore true: inside force of body transform chicken, fish and other nourishments in heat; heat produce intimate vapor, & vapor lightness . . . We eat too much we fly away, no?" he added with a laugh.

The Prince immediately rang & ordered the scales to be brought from the pantry. A few minutes later several servants appeared, struggling under the weight of the instrument.

"How much do you normally weigh?" Kircher asked.

"A hundred and twenty-two pounds," the Prince replied, "I not change weight since former youth."

"Good. Then if you have eaten four pounds of food, you ought to weigh a hundred and twenty-six pounds now."

"We soon see," said the Prince, climbing onto the pan.

Kircher moved the weights until the scales were in balance
& read off the result: "A hundred & twenty-seven pounds, three
marks & two ounces! You ate a little more than you estimated
this evening."

"Unheard of!" the Prince exclaimed, highly amused.

AFTER HAVING CHECKED the accuracy of the weights, he
wanted all of us to try. Kircher climbed onto the pan; it turned
out that he had eaten seven pounds of food, which he explained
away by claiming that he must have underestimated his weight
because he hadn't weighed himself since leaving Rome. I was
not surprised to find that I had only put on one pound, hardly
having given a thought to the food during the meal. As for
the Princess, she refused to submit to a trial that would have
offended the natural coquetry of her sex, but she was readily
pardoned her refusal. She retired soon afterward & I followed
suit when the Prince intimated that he would like to discuss
certain delicate matters with my master.

Once in my room, I examined my soul & realized how
much the Princess was bewitching me. Her virtue & her purity
seemed exemplary & I felt great satisfaction in being able to
recreate her face in my thoughts. I said lengthy prayers and read
the *Exercises* until late into the night. Obeying Saint Ignatius,
who says that it is a sin to take less than the adequate amount of
sleep, I took off my hair shirt, which was very uncomfortable, &
fell asleep.

When I woke next morning I saw that *lintea pollueram*[1] &
the thought of having yielded to the devil during the night, even
though I had no memory of it, filled me with horror. I put my

---

1 I had soiled my sheets.

hair shirt back on & began the day by examining my conscience thoroughly.

That day & the following days up to Christmas I hardly saw Kircher & the Prince at all. They shut themselves away in the library, where they were engaged in mysterious activities; several times workmen came from outside to work with them, which made me suspect some new machine was being invented. Left to my own devices, I had the pleasure of keeping company with the lady who occupied my thoughts; we discussed all kinds of topics, read the new books that had been sent to her or made music. And the Princess seemed to enjoy these innocent pastimes so much that I felt no guilt at all in doing this to lighten her spirits. Every day she became a little more determined to carry out her decision to take the veil with the Sisters of Mercy as soon as Providence gave her the opportunity & I encouraged her in this resolution with all my heart.

The meals did not last as long as on the day of our arrival, the Prince & Kircher ate quickly—when they deigned to leave the library—to return as soon as possible to whatever they were doing. But while the Prince appeared merry as a lark, Kircher seemed to me to be nervous & preoccupied. On the evening of December 23 he came to see me in my room, a little after ten in the evening. His expression was even more serious that usual.

"The die is cast, Caspar, & I fear for the consequences of my actions. The Archenemy can take so many different forms. Accustomed though I am to sniffing out his ruses, I'm not sure I'll succeed this time. But enough of this faintheartedness! The Prince has invited several people to supper tomorrow night, after midnight mass, which the priest from Bagheria will come to celebrate in the chapel here. You know the Prince's devious mind & I must repeat the advice to be prudent I gave you when we arrived. Be careful not to pass judgment on the things you will see, nor to offend anyone with overhasty reactions & remember, whatever happens, I take your sins upon myself. It is for the good of the Church that I am doing this, if I am mistaken I alone will take the punishment."

Alarmed by this, I swore to my master that he could trust me & that I would rather die than disobey his orders.

"You're a good fellow," Kircher said, ruffling my hair, "& a better man than I am. But prepare yourself for the worst, my child, & do not forget: it is the salvation of the Church that is at stake."

Then he knelt down & we prayed for two hours without stopping.

The morning of December 24 was so gray and cold that the fires were lit throughout the house. The kitchen staff had set to work, the servants were going backward & forward between the house & the park gate, from which they returned loaded with provisions, the whole building seemed to vibrate with the bustling preparations for the festival. Kircher was chatting with the Prince in the library; as for me, I was meditating on the Nativity, preparing myself as best I could to celebrate the arrival of Our Lord.

I was at peace with myself when my master came to fetch me in the middle of the afternoon.

The guests started to arrive, some had already gathered in small groups in the various drawing rooms. The great hall had been opened up & I could not but be astounded by it: imagine a vast rotunda with a cupola covered in hundreds of mirrors attached side by side to make a concave surface. Five large crystal chandeliers covered in candles hung down from it. The walls were composed of genuine & perfect imitation marble with niches containing polychrome busts of the most famous philosophers of Antiquity. And the Prince had had no qualms about placing busts of himself & his wife in a slightly more richly decorated recess above the entrance, together with a motto: *"Reflected in the remarkable magnificence of these mirrors, contemplate, O mortals, the image of human frailty."* I also saw a number of coats of arms painted in fresco with various devices of the type Kircher had deciphered when we first arrived. The floor, inlaid with mahogany & rosewood, shone splendidly. All this, however was not quite in the best of taste: there was a little too much ostentation & not enough genuine beauty; but the mirrors, multiplying colors, lights and movements ad infinitum, created a truly magical atmosphere. A small orchestra, with the musicians dressed as characters from a Roman tragedy, was playing quietly.

When the Prince saw us, he bustled over &, requesting silence, introduced Kircher to the assembled company; this was a new Archimedes, the glory of the age, & he was honored by his presence & his friendship. There was some discreet applause then the conversations resumed, even livelier than before. We sat down on one of the benches in the hall & the Prince told us about those he had invited for that evening.

There was Sieur La Mothe Le Vayer, known for his dialogues in the style of Latin & Greek authors; Count Manuel Cuendias de Teruel y de Casa-Pavòn; Denys Sanguin de Saint-Pavin, whose reputation for debauchery went ahead of him; Jean-Jacques Bouchard, a notorious libertine; a few poets & scholars & a swarm of ladies & petty marquis whose titles would have choked even the most robust master of ceremonies. All were intimate enough acquaintances of the Prince to be spared the usual humiliating tricks.

When the night was well advanced, the Prince, without a word, finger on his lips, shepherded us all into the hall of mirrors & suddenly had all the candles snuffed & the doors closed.

Hardly had we been plunged into total darkness than the Virgin
Mary appeared to us, life-sized & radiant with light, as if she
were floating on one of the walls. We could clearly see the blue of
her shawl & the rosy hue of her face—she seemed alive! Murmurs
of amazement could be heard all around me. The Princess,
startled, had taken my arm & was gripping it very tightly. I was
already wagering that my master was not without involvement
in this miracle, when his voice was heard, greatly amplified by
some device or other & echoing all around the cupola.

"Do not fear, all you who can hear me, there is nothing in
this apparition that cannot be explained by the simple laws of
nature. Our host, the Prince, has seen fit to prepare us all for the
celebration of the Nativity, let us give him our thanks."

Immediately another image appeared showing Mary &
Joseph on the road to Galilee. After the nativity, then the
adoration of the Magi, we were given a summary of the life
of Jesus. The music accompanying it suddenly took on such
poignant tones at the image of Our Lord dying on the cross,
that it brought tears to my eyes, as it did to those of most of the
company. After the Ascension, we were plunged into darkness
again. The musicians broke into a terrifying piece, rising in a
crescendo, & at its peak, at the very moment when the brass &
the drums were threatening to bring the house down around
our ears, the Devil appeared, surrounded by moving flames,
horned, grimacing, horrible to look at!

"The Archenemy!" Kircher bellowed, his stentorian voice
drowning out the cries of fright from the audience, "The
Tempter! The fallen Angel! The foul Fiend! Repent, all ye
sinners, to escape his clutches & the torments his army of
demons is preparing for you in hell! Here come Beydelus,
Anamelech, Furfur & Eurynome! Baalberith, the head of the
archives of evil! Abaddon, the exterminating angel! Tobhema,

Satan's cook! Philotanus, whose very name fills us with disgust!
And then Lilith, Negal & Valafar! Moloch, Murmur, Scox,
Empousa & Focalor! Sidragasum, who incites shameless women
to dance! Belial, O lewd seducer, Zapam, Xezbeth, Nysrak &
Haborym! Get thee away from here, Asmodeus! And thou,
Xaphan, return to thy cauldrons! Shades & Striges, fairies,
furoles & undines get ye out of our sight!"

The pictures of these demons appeared then disappeared
as my master named them, only increasing the terror around
me. I felt the Princess trembling against my arm. After them
it was hell, depicted with gripping realism. Myriads of naked
bodies were being subjected to the most abominable tortures,
suffering through that by which they had sinned. We could see
all types of depravity punished appropriately without being
spared anything of the torments awaiting the damned in the
world beyond. But however deep an impression the images of
the demons had made on the audience, the depiction of the
vices & their punishment appeared to excite them equally.
I found the chuckles and laughs I could hear around me
offensive, everywhere I could see smiling faces &, here and there,
wandering hands . . .

But soon, as the music cut off a last image of the torments
with the common chord, Athanasius asked everyone to join him
in reciting the *Anima Christi*. Without further ado the text of
this beautiful prayer appeared on the wall, translated line by
line into seven languages:

> *Soul of Christ, sanctify me,*
> *Body of Christ, save me,*
> *Blood of Christ, inebriate me,*
> *Water from the side of Christ, wash me,*
> *Passion of Christ, fortify me,*

O good Jesus, hear me,
Within Thy wounds hide me,
Never let me be parted from Thee,
From the evil enemy defend me,
In the hour of my death call me,
Command me to come to Thee,
That with Thy saints I may praise Thee,
World without end,
Amen.

And the fervor with which the prayer was said by everyone there, the emotion welling up from the voices resounding under the mirror cupola was certainly the most satisfying of rewards for Athanasius.

ON THE RIVER PARAGUAY: *A kind of red flash*
among the Nile-green palisades of the jungle

Scattered over the saloon table, several books on micropaleontology, five or six specimens of *Corumbella*, a powerful magnifying glass and drawing materials had easily created a familiar working environment. For the umpteenth time Mauro was reading Dietlev's report to the Brazilian Academy of Sciences.

Elaine's voice came from behind him: "Still at work, then?"

Mauro smiled and shook his head. "Not really ... I was daydreaming. We've been on this boat for a week now and I'm starting to feel I've been here forever. A bit as if we're never going to arrive anywhere, nor ever get back ..."

"I must be less of a romantic," she said with a hint of mockery, "because I can't wait to get to our destination. God knows what we'll find up there. The fossil Dietlev got his hands on is so much older than *Corumbella*; if we find the deposit, it's more or less certain we'll discover other species from the same period. It would revolutionize the whole of paleontology."

"I know that, but it doesn't have to stop me enjoying the present moment, does it?"

"*Carpe diem*, you mean? It's a bit difficult when even the shower water's moldy and we've been eating nothing but piranha . . . And then"—she glanced over his shoulder—"I don't like this Petersen. He's obnoxious, even when he's making an effort to be nice. I can't stand any more of him."

"I agree with you there. I've hardly ever met anyone I've taken such an instant dislike to. I could do without—"

Mauro was interrupted by a dull rattle followed by a longer burst that made the metal side of the boat ring.

"What was that?" Elaine asked in an automatic reflex.

Mauro didn't reply but she could tell by his expression that he too had identified it: the sound of an automatic rifle. With two minds but a single thought, they ran up on deck. A flight of frightened birds was still pouring out of the jungle, like a pillow case being torn open.

"Quick! Lie down!" Milton screamed, flat on his front along the rail. "They're firing at us!"

"Don't panic, don't panic, *Senhor Professor*," said Petersen calmly as he came out of the wheelhouse. "They didn't fire *at* us, they fired *in front* of us, it's a signal from my Paraguayan friends. You can get up. I'll go and have a chat with them and it'll be OK, you'll see. It'll take an hour at most . . . There's no need to worry," he said, seeing Mauro and Elaine, "you're under my protection. Stay calm and nothing'll happen to you. I'll go in the dinghy, it won't take long."

Dietlev's deep voice was suddenly heard. "I'll go with you?"

Herman turned around, looking furious, as if no one had ever asked him anything so unreasonable. "But of course, come and have a cup of tea, they'll be delighted to make your acquaintance . . . Now could we be serious? You help that stupid Indian keep the gunboat in the current. We can't anchor here, the riverbed's too unstable."

Without waiting, Petersen went to the stern. They watched him climb over the rail to get on the dinghy, then heard him start the outboard motor. The inflatable soon appeared and went past them at great speed upriver, toward a little beach concealed among the tangle of mangroves. After having landed, Petersen quickly moored his boat and immediately vanished, as if swallowed up by the undergrowth.

"Where were you?" Elaine asked Dietlev.

"In the wheelhouse with Herman and Yurupig."

"Can someone tell me what's going on?" Milton broke in irritably. He was still pale from the fright.

"I assure you it's just something very . . . *South American,*" said Dietlev, keeping his tone light. There's some hunters around here, guys from Paraguay who smuggle out crocodile skins. From what I've heard, they're also dealing in cocaine to supplement their income. Our dear captain has gone to see to his business with them and until we hear otherwise, it's nothing to do with us."

"Crocodiles!" Mauro exclaimed, suddenly angry. "The bastards! And no one comes to check up on this illegal trade?"

"Not really, no. They're real professionals. They were parachuted in two or three years ago and cleared a portion of the jungle, enough to make a landing strip for their Piper, then they set about their dirty work. It you must know, they hunt with Kalashnikovs. Since several boats, including one from the customs, came under fire from heavy machine guns, no one comes up here. No honest people, anyway. And as they grease the palms of certain local officials, it's not going to change in the near future . . ."

"It's unbelievable! Unbelievable . . . I can't get over it," said Milton, stunned. "And you brought us here! How did you find out about all this?"

Dietlev hesitated for a fraction of a second before replying, just long enough for Mauro to realize he wasn't telling the whole truth.

"From Petersen, of course. He knew we were going to a zone they control; the landscape changes very quickly around here and it's practically impossible to find a precise spot from one week to the next. As I'm the one who hired him, he warned me he might have to pick up some parcels around here . . ."

"At least you could have warned us."

"I didn't realize they would give us such a noisy welcome. There was no reason to be afraid, and there still isn't. As soon as Petersen gets back, we'll be on our way as if nothing had happened. It's not our job to uphold the law out here, is it? So we'll just calm down and wait, without pointless recriminations." Then, with a pleasant smile, he added, "Fix us a drink, I'm going to go and see how Yurupig's getting on."

"Just a moment," said Elaine in a strange voice. "What's that thing supposed to mean?"

All eyes turned in the direction she was pointing: a hundred yards behind the boat, where the banks made a bottleneck, a tree trunk had been thrown across the river. Pregnant with silent threat, its inexplicable presence meant there was no way back down the river.

YURUPIG HAVING NO need of anyone with him at the helm, they went down to the saloon to establish their position. First of all Dietlev showed them where they were on the satellite maps he had brought: "I've been checking our position as we've proceeded. That's where the river narrows and that white patch there, a little to the northeast, is probably their landing strip. We can't be more than three days away from our destination. OK, let's summarize the situation: Petersen's been gone more than an hour and there's no way of turning back—which is somewhat disturbing, I agree, even if it's probably no more than a simple protective measure—"

"A simple protective measure?!" Milton broke in, close to hysteria. "Are you joking? We're trapped and all you can say is: 'a simple protective measure!'"

Dietlev made an effort to remain calm. "Just think about it, Milton. They know it's Petersen's boat, but they don't know who's on board. They must know what type of person they're dealing with; just imagine if Herman double-crossed them, if the authorities made it worth his while to bring the police up here, or even the army. What would you do in their place? These guys are well organized, their survival depends on it."

"And if Herman doesn't come back?" Elaine asked calmly.

"He *will* come back. Or, at the worst, they'll come. Whatever, there's nothing we can do, so there's no point in making ourselves scared stiff while we wait. Tomorrow we'll all be laughing at the whole business."

"We're at their mercy," Milton said, "and you couldn't give a damn. Well I do. It's all your fault and I can assure you, Dietlev, as soon as we get back you're really in for it. I'll have you thrown out of the university."

"Good! Now you're thinking about what to do when we get back, which proves you're not entirely stupid. As for changing university, I didn't wait for you to consider that: I've been offered a chair at Tübingen and another at Harvard. I'm spoiled for choice . . . And I'm ready to do anything not to have to see your ugly mug anymore."

"Dietlev, please!" said Elaine, worried by the turn the discussion was taking.

"I know, I know," he said, grinding his teeth, "but he's really starting to get on my nerves."

"I can tell you, all this will be reported. The rector is one of my closest friends and I'm sure that—"

At this Dietlev exploded. "That what?" he asked, grabbing Milton by the collar. "You're sure that what? One more word, just one, and I'll smash your face in."

Milton's glasses misted over with fright and he restricted himself to several "Oh my goodness"es like a shocked old maid. With a contemptuous push, Dietlev sent him tumbling onto a bench.

"I'm going out for some fresh air," he said to Elaine with a reassuring wink. "Don't worry about me, I've wanted to tell that stupid ass what I think about him for ages."

"I'm coming with you. You're right, it is rather stuffy in here."

"Did you see that?" Milton said, turning to Mauro. "You're a witness. That foul fellow laid hands on me, he insulted me."

Mauro slowly adjusted the headphones of his Walkman over his ears. "I saw him calm you down, showing great tact, I have to say, after you had a hysterical fit unworthy of a university professor, but I didn't hear much, apart from your threats. My Walkman, you know . . ."

"You as well! You're on their side. Let me tell you, my young friend, you will never—"

Elaine put her head into the gangway. "I don't know if you're interested," she said to Milton, "but Petersen's just getting into the Zodiac. So leave the lad in peace and come and make up with Dietlev. It seems you need to apologize to him."

When Milton came up on deck, Herman was still on the bank together with a group of three men. Dietlev was observing them through his binoculars.

"It looks as if there's some problem," he said, not taking his eyes off them, "they all look pretty excited . . ."

Elaine knew him, he would never have feigned such unconcern if he hadn't been genuinely worried. For the first time since they'd left Corumba, she suddenly felt afraid.

"A problem, what problem?" Milton asked, whining already. "I knew, I just knew things would go wrong."

"Oh shut up, for God's sake," Dietlev barked, still glued to his binoculars. "Ah, that's it, he's getting in the boat. Or rather, *they're* getting in the boat. Petersen's not alone, there's one of the guys with him."

He turned to face Milton. "Armed," he said tonelessly, looking him straight in the eye. "Right, everyone stay calm, it's not the moment to screw things up."

"JUST GIVE ME a couple of minutes," Herman begged as soon as he was on board, "then I'll explain everything. Don't worry, it's OK. Just a little hitch . . ." He was sweating and seemed concerned despite the alcohol he'd obviously been drinking.

The man with him was a real brute, the kind you sometimes see on American motorcycles: mustache, stubble, greasy hair, a bandanna around his forehead, he seemed perfectly at ease in his ragged fatigues. Dietlev observed the belt with compartments he wore slung over his shoulder. Automatic rifle over his stomach, he sized them up one by one with a satisfied look, as if he'd ascertained Herman hadn't lied to him. Subjecting Elaine to a longer scrutiny, he gave a knowing smile revealing an impeccable set of carnivore's teeth. "*Puta madre!*" he said in a hoarse voice, automatically touching his testicles.

Humiliated, Elaine looked away toward the river.

None of them could have said how long the inspection lasted, so petrified were they by the man's very physical arrogance. All

Elaine could remember afterward was his powerful smell like that of a wild beast.

"And the Indian?" he asked in Spanish.

"At the wheel," Herman replied, clearly concerned to reassure him. "Don't worry, *amigo*, there's no one else."

"OK, lead the way," he said, taking hold of his rifle, "you're going to show me around." He followed Herman inside with disdainful self-assurance.

Milton was completely demoralized. Eyes wide, he sought a comforting word or look. Dietlev was desperately but vainly making an effort to think. He tried to analyze the situation, to see the data as if it were a problem in science, without managing to get rid of the stupid images that kept getting in the way of his reasoning; the most insistent was an obsessive one of an overfull mug of beer with the foam constantly trickling down onto the bar. Elaine, suddenly struck with the irrepressible desire to go to the lavatory but equally paralyzed by her refusal to confess to the need and her fear of having to pee where she was, concentrated on her bladder, entirely taken up with her dilemma.

Out of bravado more than unconcern, Mauro had switched on his Walkman; leaning against the rail, his eyes fixed on Milton, he was humming away assiduously.

Herman reappeared on deck and hurried across to Dietlev. "I assure you it's not my fault," he said right away. Their plane's broken down, there's no way they can repair it. They want us to take their mechanic to Cáceres to buy some replacement parts; there's an airport there."

"To Cáceres!" Dietlev exclaimed. He immediately saw in his mind's eye the two branches of the river a few miles upstream. "But that's not our route, it's even the opposite way."

"I know," Herman said, putting on a dismayed look. "Don't complicate things. I swear I've tried everything. I even proposed to leave you where you want to go first and pick you up on my way back. But they won't listen. They're in a hurry, a great hurry, if you see what I mean."

Dietlev realized they'd have to bring the mechanic back here, which dashed any hope he still had of completing their mission. At best, counting just three days in Cáceres to find the parts—and that was a minimum—they could only get back to this point at the end of their scheduled time in the Mato Grosso. "It's piracy!" he muttered. "Do you realize what that means? A whole year of preparations down the drain because of these bastards."

"I couldn't foresee this, *amigo*, I swear it."

"And there's nothing we can do about it? I don't know, what if we offer them money if they agree to leave us on the deposit with the fossils?"

"Money?" Petersen said genuinely amazed. "But these guys have a thousand times more than you, they're literally wallowing in dollars. You don't realize, Dietlev, you're lucky still to be alive. They don't care a fuck about the lot of you, about your mission or your bloody fossils."

"We just have to do what they say, and that's that," said Milton, still terrified. "I've had enough of . . . of all this. I'm canceling the mission, d'you hear. We'll take the plane from Cáceres. I'm cancelling everything."

"What plane?" the Paraguayan asked in mocking tones, putting down a large cardboard box full of tins of food and bottles. "And the little lady, is she ready? You haven't told her the news yet, eh, yellow belly? Come on, get on with it, I've got to take the Zod' to collect the mechanic."

"Please, Hernando," said Petersen in a tearful voice. "There's no point, I've given you my word. I'll bring your guy back, whatever happens. I've got to come back by this route anyway."

"Herman?!" Dietlev growled. His voice had deepened a tone, as if he had a premonition of what the old German's reply would be.

"They want to keep *Professora* Von Wogau until we come back. As security."

"No question!" Dietlev exclaimed without a moment's pause for reflection. Turning to Hernando, he said, "We'll take your mechanic to Cáceres, or even to Cuiabá if necessary, we'll do everything you want, but she stays with us, understood?"

"All right, that's enough," the man said, pointing his gun at Dietlev. "Herman, you put the supplies in the dinghy and you, *guapa*, you get on board double quick. We won't do anything to harm you, believe me."

There was a lecherous glint in his eye that said everything about what he had in mind for her.

Elaine was sitting on the deck, her legs tight together, shaking her head from side to side, unable in her panic to express her refusal to go with him in any other way.

Mauro faced up to the Paraguayan. "She's not going," he said in a tremulous voice. *"No venga, non viene!* What language do we have to say it in? I'll stay here, if that's what you want."

"Well he's got balls, the little cockerel," Hernando said with a smile, "I like that . . ." And with a swift blow with the rifle butt he hit him in the face. Mauro collapsed like a rag doll.

Dietlev was already coming forward, fists clenched.

"But he says they won't harm her," Milton yelped, pulling him back. "There's nothing for it but to leave her with them. Is there, Elaine? Tell him you'll stay. As you can see, he's not joking."

"Pansy!" Dietlev said, spitting on his mouth.

Hernando stuck the barrel of the Kalashnikov in Dietlev's throat. "You're getting to be a pain in the ass, you idiot. Come on, little lady, in the dinghy or I blow his head off."

Despite all her efforts, Elaine just could not stand up. She'd started crawling toward them, when the engine, suddenly put on full speed, made the gunboat leap forward.

Off-balance for a moment, Hernando realized what Yurupig was doing. "He's going to kill the lot of us, the stupid cunt," he screamed, rushing toward the wheelhouse.

At the same moment Dietlev saw the boat set off on a slanting course toward the bank. Without bothering about the others, he ran for the upper deck as well. He was just climbing the accommodation ladder when the gunboat changed course and boldly made its way back into the middle of the river. Then there was a sort of orange flash, on the extreme edge of his field of vision and, above the din of the engine, a kind of simultaneous discharge in which the white noise of war mingled with the screaming of the monkeys. Dietlev threw himself to the floor, covering his head with his hands. He felt his leg slap against the metal by itself, becoming one with it. Instinctively he tried to pull it back into a more natural position and, astonished at its lack of reaction, lost consciousness.

Staggered at Yurupig's reaction, Petersen had dropped onto the deck as soon as he saw that the boat was continuing its course and, despite Hernando's efforts, would pass the invisible limit set by the crocodile hunters. Dumbfounded, sucked into his deepest fears, he observed the ensuing events with a hypnotic sense of déjà vu: Milton, waving his arms and shouting demands for a cease-fire, the jig that the repeated impact of the bullets made him dance on the spot, the red gashes in his linen suit; Elaine on all fours relieving herself on the deck, eyes closed, with the expression of a saint undergoing a visitation.

Imperturbable under the hail of bullets, the *Messenger of the Faith* continued to glide up the river, forcing its way, with a kind of dogged voluptuousness, between the Nile-green palisades of the jungle.

Eléazard's notebooks

METAPHYSICIANS OF TLÖN: Kircher is like them, he is not looking for the truth, nor even the probable, he's looking for the amazing. It never occurred to him that metaphysics is a branch of literature of the fantastic, but his work belongs entirely to fiction and therefore also to Jorge Luis Borges.

THE ESSENTIAL CLOSENESS to death, a fleeting insight from this homemade hell where my struggles take place.

DRAGONS: If God is perfect, Kircher asks himself, why has He created these hybrid creatures that appear to cast doubt on the natural order of things? What is the meaning of these breaks, these departures from the norm? In that way God manifests His omnipotence: He can unmake what He has made, he can dismantle what He has set up. For however long it has been our experience that a stone thrown up to the sky falls back down, nothing can assure us that one day it will not disappear into the clouds, on a divine whim and to remind us that it is He who makes the laws.

This simple deduction forbids Kircher any pretension to knowledge: he chooses to believe the unbelievable, systematically, because it is absurd and that is what should make a true believer believe.

FAITH IN A WORLD created for the human theater and at times not merely theatrical. Kircher has an innate sense of the theatrical, a *quasi-Borrominian art of vertiginous asymmetries* (thanks, Umberto!). Reason's elastic vision, a tendency toward the picturesque, toward reminiscence, flights of the imagination, a taste for the raw forms of life, for theatrical machinery, for illusion:

Kircher is baroque, quite simply baroque (*Barocchus tridentinus, sive romanus, sive jesuiticus* . . .).

SERTÃO is a deformation of *deserto*: the desert. They also say the Interior. *Sertanejo*: someone who lives in the desert, who is himself deserted . . .

ADD A NOTE on the "anemic machine" invented by Kircher. Ineffective but charitable. Ineffective to the point of charity? At least it makes him more human.

INDISPENSIBLE MACHINES:
  for brushing monkeys
  for licking the soap clean
  for recovering the energy of copulation
  for growing old more quickly
  for delaying the millennium
  for blackening albinos
  for cooling down tea
  for demoting soldiers

NOTE. If you're going to get it wrong, do it with precision! Kircher and his contemporaries allowed our world a princely 4,000 years of existence; but at the same time the survivors of the Mayas were counting in millions of years and the Hindus calculating the cycles of successive creations of the universe in periods of 8.4 billion years . . .

CHAPTER 10

In which are recorded word for word the licentious
conversations of the guests of the Prince & various ignominious
acts that put Caspar Schott in grave danger of damnation . . .

WHEN WE RETURNED to the great hall,
we discovered that a very large table had been set in our
absence. Kircher was given the place of honor, opposite the
Prince, & I was happy to discover I was seated on the left hand
of his wife. The banquet started immediately. To describe the
profusion of dishes we were given is beyond the weak power of
my memory, especially since I was paying particular attention
to what my master & the Princess were saying. I do remember,
however, that there was a large amount of seafood, shellfish &
lobster, as well as poultry & joints of game, which the guests
despatched indifferently. As I was hardly touching the pieces
that arrived on my plate, being careful to avoid the sin of
gluttony, my master lectured me on the matter, telling me it was
a feast day & that there was no harm in rejoicing both in body &

in spirit at the birth of Our Lord. I must confess that I followed
this advice enthusiastically & did full justice to our hosts' meal.
Our glasses were refilled as soon as they were emptied, the
crystal sparkled & the whole table was abuzz with laughter &
witty ripostes; the Princess was gracious & amusing & I was
happier than I could have imagined when I arrived at this place.

The conversation turned on trivial topics & every time they
looked to Kircher for, if not the last word on the question, at
least the most authoritative opinion. This turned into a kind
of game among the guests: to see who could put forward an
argument that my master would then confirm, reveling in his
approval. Since the profusion of dishes suggested it, we discussed
the relative qualities of various foods & the strange habits of
ancient or far-off peoples. La Mothe Le Vayer reminded us
of the abstinence from all meat practised by Pythagoreans &
the Brahmins of the Orient, the latter leaving even grass unless
it had been dried, the reason being that the soul is in all green
growth; the rhizophagi, spermatophagi, hylophagi & foliophagi
of Africa, who live solely on seeds, leaves or the heads of plants
& leap from branch to branch as nimbly as squirrels. We can
read in Mendès Pinto, someone said, that the flesh of asses, dogs,
tigers & lions is on sale in the butchers' shops of China & Tartary.
And in Pliny, another said, that the Macrobians owed their long
life to the fact that they fed exclusively on vipers, as we know do
certain European princes, who have them swallowed by poultry
whose flesh they are going to eat subsequently. And what would
you say, Kircher added, trumping the lot, of the cynomolgi, who
live on the milk of bitches, which they suck? The struthophagi of
Deodorus the Sicilian, who eat ostriches, the acridophagi who eat
locusts or even the Asian phthirophagi mentioned by Strabo—
who are perhaps Herodotus's Budini—who swallow their lice
with great pleasure?

The ladies cried out in disgust at such habits, but it was even worse when La Mothe Le Vayer started talking about the anthropophagi . . .

THESE PEOPLE, WHO prided themselves on being philosophers, knew their classics well. References to Latin & Greek authors flew from all sides & the ladies were not slow to stand up for their sex with erudition. Only the Princess remained silent. I saw that she blushed whenever certain remarks reached the limits of propriety & I pressed my leg against hers to show that I shared her embarrassment & agreed wholeheartedly with her disapproval.

Arguing that love was a passion & that this passion could be satisfied either by ourselves or with the help of others, Sieur Jean-Jacques Bouchard analyzed that hoodwinking of the nerves they call "masturbation," which is an abomination but which he justified with numerous famous examples. In support he called upon Diogenes, of course, Zeno and Sextus Empiricus, who all swore by this method alone because of the independence of others it gave them, & also the entire population of Lydia, which practised this manual operation in broad daylight.

Count Manuel Cuendias, a young Spaniard with a pockmarked face, condemned such conduct, but only to defend love between men. He deluged his audience with a flood of Greek & Latin figures who in the past had all extolled what today we look upon as an act of depravity. Olympus was full of the likes of Ganymede and Antinous, Hercules only had eyes for his Hylas or his Tarostes, Achilles for his Patroclus; the wisest & most highly respected philosophers swore by their catamites: Plato indulged every whim of his Alexis, his Phaedo or his Agathon, Xenophon those of his Clenias; Aristotle went weak at the knees at the sight of Hermias, Empedocles at the sight of Pausanias; Epicurus courted Pytocles, Aristippus crawled for Eurychides . . .

The female part of the company cried out in indignation at these customs, objecting that humanity would quickly die out if such vile practices should spread excessively; love was really only to be found in the difference between the sexes & not in the androgyny vaunted by that debauchee Plato to justify his vices.

The Prince took up the argument in his own language. "If we are to believe you, mesdames," he said, "it is only among animals that true love is to be found, for they have the advantage over you of a greater difference & of not philosophizing . . ."

The Prince said that in such a tone that it was difficult to say whether he was joking or talking seriously. Since he started to smile, however, the assembled company chose to regard it as a witticism & roared with laughter, while the Princess, with tears in her eyes, dug her nails in my hand under the table.

"In that too," her husband said, "Greek mythology provides us with many examples of this zoophilia, of which I will only mention Pasiphae with her bull, Leda with her swan & Apuleius's matron with her ass. Which is nothing compared with reality. Any of our shepherds will prefer his nanny goats to the fair sex & in the town of Mendes in Egypt, where the god Pan was revered, the billy goats commonly coupled with the women. It is so widespread in Muscovy that Cyril of Novgorod, when asked if one could drink the milk & eat the flesh of a cow that had been known by a man replied that everyone could, apart from the one who had had commerce with it. In the East Indies the Portuguese enjoy dugongs as if they were women & the negroes of Mozambique are said to find great relief in abusing them even when they are dead. One cannot say that such copulation is simply a result of human depravity, for other animals have the same feelings toward us & the same combinations among themselves. Remember what Pliny has to say about the gosling from Argos that conceived a passion for a girl called Glauce who played the guitar and who was at the same time wooed by a ram that had fallen in love with her. We could also mention the trouble caused by an elephant for the woman who kept a shop in Antioch & that caused by a great ape of Borneo for a priest. As for lions, being in season at the beginning of winter & at their most dangerous then, everyone knows they will spare a woman if she hitches up her skirt & shows them her private parts . . ."

There were more roars of laughter. Whipped up by the Prince, the badinage became a hubbub of erudite obscenities. Incest was added to the stories of illicit love & for a long time all they would talk about was the demands of Caligula, Nero or Chrysippus, who thought it did not matter if he lay with his mother, his sister or his daughter. Strabo was quoted, who insisted that the magi of Persia & the Egyptians did the same in their temples; Amerigo Vespucci, who maintained that in all the West Indies there was no degree of kinship that forbade fornication; the Emperor Claudius who, having married his niece Agrippina, made the senate authorize incest . . . Then they set about sullying lawful love & modesty itself, saying they were nothing but an invention of weary nations, since they did not exist in the New World or the Far North, where the tribes willingly lent their wives or daughters to visitors without showing the least shame & copulated in public, just as the Cynic Crates used to screw his Hipparchia right in the middle of the Agora . . .

Faced with this flood of filth, which made me blush as much as the Princess, I kept giving my master imploring looks, unable to understand how he could retain such regal calm. Not a muscle in his face moved; he wore a good-natured smile, as if

he happened to be listening to mere childish prattle. The parish
priest had not stayed that long & had made his excuses some
time ago on the pretext of his great age & the lateness of the
hour. Finally, when I was despairing of ever hearing Kircher
speak out against this catalogue of loathsomeness, his voice was
suddenly heard:

"I have myself read everything to which you have alluded
but, while recognizing your knowledge, I am saddened that no
voice has been raised against all these vices, which, even though
they exist & continue to proliferate, are no less reprehensible. I
would report you all to the Holy Inquisition, as is my duty"—he
paused for a moment surveying the company with an icy look.
The blue of his eyes had gone pale & I saw several of the guests
among those who had previously been most voluble wipe their
brows, filled with irrepressible fear—"if I thought for a moment
you all held those opinions. But it is, perhaps, worth making
certain points clear. The more I extend my knowledge of new
things, the more I find confirmed what the wisest of mortals
says in *Ecclesiastes*: 'There is no new thing under the sun.' What
has happened? The same as will happen again. Persistence in
evil, that is, the Fiend, is the cause of all this licentiousness
because his sole aim is to fill the world with his vileness. The
Evil Architect is still building the house of ancient wickedness.
He uses all means, he tempts all persons & all ages. His principal
way of deceiving souls & taking them for himself has always
been to use their curiosity to attract them & to bring about
their downfall with tricks full of superstition and lechery. What
can be said is that if the Fiend has captured so many men, it
is because he has always used the same means, since the very
beginning of time: I am talking about magic & enchantment.
Our experience shows that all the gods venerated by the
Egyptians & their heirs are still those of the modern barbarians,

among whom we can see the signs of the transformation of
Isis & Osiris into the Sun & the Moon, & we can still find
Bacchus, Hercules & Aesculapius, Serapis & Anubis & monsters
similar to those of the Egyptians, although worshipped under
other names. Even in China we see children burned alive as
an offering to Moloch, blood spilt in disgusting sacrifices &
that obscene part of the body the Greeks called the "−φαλλο"[1]
held in particular veneration. These barbarians of the Orient
worship certain animals as if they were gods & the example of
the Egyptians has been so important for the outlook of those
people that they filled their lands with idols similar to theirs.
All the examples you were discussing just now are the fruit of
idolatry, the horrible product of the Enemy of human nature.
The Fiend is God's monkey, his serpent's tail trailing everywhere
his spirit of diabolical perversion appears. And although we
should not close our eyes to the distorted reflections his mirrors
permanently present to us, we must be careful not to take them
for reality & to expose his evil snares, which lead straight to
eternal damnation . . ."

ONCE MORE I admired the calm & simple manner in which my
master defended our religion & its holy principles. I despaired
of ever acquiring such moral strength, which, if truth be told, is
that of the chosen ones of God.

Held in restraint for a while by Kircher's speech, the guests
soon let their tongues, loosened by the wine, run free once more.
But since we had long since finished eating, the Prince invited us
to rise from the table & the company dispersed in small groups
in the salons while the servants cleared away.

1 Phallus.

Princess Alexandra took me to a sofa somewhat apart from the rest. After having discussed the evening's conversation & expressed in words the disapproval we had conveyed to each other by gestures, we spoke once more of music & harmony. Unaccustomed as I was to drinking that amount of wine, my mind was confused & all I can remember of our conversation was a feeling of sweet communion & the perfect accord of our opinions. Later, when we were once more comparing the respective merits of William Byrd & Gesualdo, the Princess wanted to show me the score of a motet I was unacquainted with & which one could not read, she said, without hearing the most marvelous music there ever was. I therefore followed her eagerly to an alcove not far away, where she kept her music. Hardly were we there than she double-locked the door to stop us being disturbed. I acquiesced in this, flattered by her preference for my company. She quickly found the score & we sat down side by side.

The score did indeed have an extraordinary grace & ardor, so that I was soon humming in a low voice, conquered by the delightful emotion it stirred within me. After a few minutes I felt as if my cheek on the side where the Princess was sitting was on fire. I looked up at her & immediately stopped singing: it was the fixed look in her shining eyes, burning like a glowing ember, that had pierced my skin. Without taking this frighteningly adoring gaze off me, she slowly brought her hand to my face and caressed my lips tremblingly.

"Caspar," she murmured, "Caspar . . ."

Her breathing had become irregular, her nostrils were quivering, her lips parted, as if she were trying to moisten her dry throat. Assuming she was about to faint, I half rose to assist her. With a gesture, she indicated she needed air, urging me to unlace her. Since she appeared to be suffering from the stuffy air, I started to open her dress, becoming irritated at all the ribbons

I was not used to. No sooner had I undone her bodice a little
than she finished loosening her dress herself. But she did not
stop where decency & the demands of her faintness would have
required, continuing to open her clothes in a kind of frenzy until
she displayed her chest to me completely naked! I was stunned
by the sight. Never having seen a woman's breast other than on
the corpses we dissected with my master, it seemed to me I had
never seen anything so beautiful in my whole life. To my alarm,
however, the Princess *molliter incepit pectus permulcere. Papillae
horruere, et ego sub tunica turgescere mentulam sensi.*[2] The Archenemy! This woman was possessed by the Fiend & I was within
an inch of being dragged into the abyss. I crossed myself while
reciting an exorcism, but the Princess, no longer herself, *divaricata
stolam adeo collegit ut madida feminum caro adspici posset.*[3] Both
my mind & my senses were in turmoil. On the one hand I was
horrified at the transformation of this woman, to whom I had
until then ascribed the virtues & modesty of a saint, & on the
other I felt more attracted to her than I had before. With one last
spurt of conscience, I moved away from her &, trembling, quaking
at the knees, I begged her to return to her senses.

"Stop it, my lady, for pity's sake," I said with all the conviction
I could muster. "You are risking damnation! You are dragging
me to damnation!"

But this reaction seemed to arouse her even more, for she
passed her tongue over her lips in an obscene manner. Realizing
the door was locked, I rushed over to the bell pull, threatening
to call for assistance.

2 (...) started to caress her chest voluptuously. Her nipples became erect
and I felt my member swell under my cassock.

3 (...) spread her legs and hitched up her dress until I could see the moist
flesh of her thighs.

CANOA QUEBRADA: *Like a bastion against the madness of the world . . .*

After a long swim, Moéma, Thaïs and Roetgen met on the beach again in the shade of a straw hut where *Seu* Juju, an ex-fisherman, served stuffed crabs and a *cachaça* with lime that was so warm it was almost undrinkable. No one had managed to explain to him why young city folk had started visiting this out-of-the-way place, but he accepted his good fortune all the more philosophically in that it enabled him to earn a living without too much effort. Leaning back on palm logs, three young men in swimming trunks were teasing each other amid great bursts of laughter. Wrestlers at leisure, their bodies gleaming with suntan lotion and drops of water, they were playing at anointing their shining skin with sand. Roetgen met the eye of the most voluble of them, a mestizo with perfect teeth who had his hands gracefully draped around the necks or shoulders of his companions and laughed in a shrill voice.

"*Eita, mulherzinha!*" he exclaimed, standing up immediately to embrace Moéma. Then, taking a step back as if to get a better view of Roetgen, "Where did you find this pretty boy? I'm already getting quite moist . . ."

"Calm down, and don't be coarse," said Moéma, slightly embarrassed. "He's my professor, so go easy."

"At least you could introduce me, can't you? I'm not going to eat him, although . . ."

"OK . . . Roetgen, this is Marlene," Moéma said with a smile. "Just ignore him or he won't let go of you."

"Don't listen to her," the young man said, holding the hand Roetgen held out to him for longer than necessary. "I'm as gentle and obedient as a little pet lamb. Isn't that so, girls?"

The two boys he spoke to said nothing but gave him black looks.

"Anaïs and Doralice," he said with an icy smile. "They're just jealous and that makes them impolite. It's always the same old story, not enough hormones . . ."

It was the first time Roetgen had heard a man speak of himself and his friends in the feminine form. Despite his openness of mind, he felt it as a provocation and didn't know whether to go along with the game or pretend to ignore it. Despite that, he had a kind of naive admiration for a person who dared to express his sexual preferences so openly. However, in a stupid automatic reaction, a mixture of panic and an old remnant of male pride, he felt the need to differentiate himself.

"I must be a bit odd," he said, "but I prefer girls . . . Having said that, it needn't stop us from having a drink together."

He immediately bit his tongue, furious with himself for having given way to such easy condescension, surely more offensive than a real insult.

"Pity . . . You can't recognize a good thing when you see it," Marlene said with a touch of contempt in his voice. "If you make the change, come and see me first, I'll open up a whole universe for you . . . Come on, girls. Last one in the water's a woman-fucker."

As one the three young men immediately set off for the sea.

"I meant no offense," said Roetgen, dismayed.

"You were quite right," Moéma assured him, "if you'd given him the least encouragement he'd have been unbearable. He'll get over it. He'll do anything for a free drink . . . Talking of drinks, a glass for each of us, please, Juju."

After one glass all three were tipsy.

WITH JUST A touch of pink in the distance, the beach disappeared on either side of their field of vision in a vast, dazzling haze. On the washed-out blue of the Atlantic, long rollers broke slowly with the sound of a torrential stream. A few *jangadas* drawn up high on the shore, a sparse scattering of bathers—there was nothing to impinge on their sense of being away from it all, at the back of beyond, in one of those moments outside time when the mind, at peace and with memory miraculously erased, is suddenly at one with itself.

"You know," said Moéma, "I could spend the whole of my life like this. It's true, all my sodding life watching the waves, a *cachaça* in my hand . . ."

Thaïs had cheered up. Stretched out, with her head on Moéma's stomach, she told Roetgen about their project for a literary bar, getting worked up about the ignorance of the age and the contempt the Brazilian middle classes had for poetry. She got carried away, almost slipping into a condemnation of the whole universe— *O que é isso, companheiro?* Don't tell me you've never heard of Fernando Gabeira?—then, brought back by Moéma's hand, which was stroking her hair, sang in a low voice the bossa novas of João Gilberto and Vinicius, wallowing in the notable melancholy of the lines. *Tristeza não tem fin, felicidade sim* . . . Had he read, not just listened to, but properly *read* the poems of Vinicius de Moraes, Chico Buarque, Caetano Veloso? He had to make the effort. And Mário de Andrade? And Guimarães Rosa? He would never understand their world at all if he hadn't read *Grande Sertão: Veredas* . . .

Roetgen mentally noted the titles, despite the instinctive reserve the presence of singers on the list aroused in him.

Marlene returned with his friends and some new faces as well. Not a man to bear a grudge, he demanded the promised drink, bombarded them with quips and smutty insinuations then told Roetgen that three or four hundred yards away there was a secluded part of the beach where the true lovers of Canoa met to practise nudism, play the guitar, smoke joints—a genuine liberty zone! Talking of which, he could supply him with *maconha* if he wanted. Good stuff, no problem. The *cachaças* followed one after the other until eventually he climbed up onto the table of the hut and, wrapped in several bathing towels, performed a striptease which sent all those who formed the audience of the improvised show into shrieks of laughter.

When, at the end of the afternoon, Roetgen woke in his hammock, on the floor of their hut, his memory seemed to have disintegrated after that scene. He had a vague recollection of having made love to Moéma, but he couldn't swear to it. All the rest had been swallowed up in a black hole from which all that managed to escape was a few hazy images and an incomprehensible feeling of resentment toward the young girl. Just as he was wondering about his strange position, he saw the grotesque slanting branch hanging down from the roof to the tangle of rope spread over his toes.

Then he heard a voice from a little above him: "Had a good sleep, Dionysus?"

Thaïs's beaming face appeared from her hammock, followed almost immediately by Moéma's. Curled up lovingly against her friend, she also appeared to be in a joival mood.

"WHEN WE DECIDED to have a siesta, you marched up the dune like a robot without faltering or hurrying up. And the sand was twice as hot as going down. You immediately commandeered my hammock and started to talk about Dionysus . . . Everything came out, Nietzsche, myth and cult, 'sacred violence,' you just went on and on!"

"I hope at least it was interesting?" Roetgen asked, with a doubtful look.

"Super, I assure you," Thaïs said. "And you were speaking perfect Portuguese, without an accent or anything. Crazy, isn't it?"

"It was unbelievable," Moéma said. "It was as if you'd been hypnotized."

"And then?"

"Then we smoked a joint and . . . You're not trying to tell me you can't recall anything of all this?"

"I swear," Roetgen lied. "Everything stops with Marlene's striptease."

"Well, you jumped me while Thaïs was still talking to you . . ."

"I did that?!"

"And how!" Thaïs muttered with a laugh. "The worst thing was, she seemed to be enjoying it!"

"Oh, my God, the shame," said Roetgen, genuinely conscience-stricken. "I would never have thought I was capable of doing something like that, even blind drunk as I was."

"Don't take it to heart," Thaïs said in affectionate tones. "I've seen plenty of others with her. She's one hell of a girl, you know. I did try to sleep, but it was impossible, you were making the hut shake with all your humping and grinding, a real earthquake. So then I went to join you and that's when the branch gave way . . ."

"We all fell on top of each other . . . and you just dropped straight off to sleep. For a moment we thought you'd fainted, but then you started snoring. We almost died laughing."

"So we left you on the floor and got into my hammock . . ."

"You have to be careful with *cachaça*, Professor," Moéma joked. "Especially here, with the sun."

"I should have eaten something," Roetgen said, "that's the real reason. I didn't drink all that much."

"Fourteen *caipirinhas* . . ."

"Fourteen?!"

"Exactly. You can trust *Seu* Juju; he's well capable of serving a few free drinks but he never forgets a single one of those you ordered."

THEIR CLOTHES UNDER their arms, they went to Neosinha's. She hired out her well and a shack used for ablutions. Roetgen was disappointed by a procedure that clashed with Moéma's much vaunted "natural hospitality" of the fishing community, never mind having to queue with a dozen other young people. It was like being in a children's holiday camp or, worse still, a campsite. Since Moéma and Thaïs seemed perfectly at home in these surroundings, he spared them his thoughts.

To save time, they showered together, each in turn filling an old food tin from the oil drum one of Neosinha's sons had brought them. Still somewhat under the influence, Roetgen felt no embarrassment in joining in the game that suddenly brought them all together, naked and close enough to brush against each other, as if it were something quite natural.

Moéma, long legs and muscular buttocks, slim, animal, with her boy's body and bronze bush; Thaïs with her heavy breasts, more than plump but just as attractive with the luxuriant black triangle emphasizing the creamy skin of her belly . . .

Teasing like children in the bath; he never knew whether he was the only one to see its very subtle depravity.

Moéma having suggested they invite themselves to João's for dinner, they bought some fish, fizzy drinks and flat bread before going back through the village. The sky was turning black and a wind off the sea was raising swirls of sand as they walked. On either side of the street little lights swayed in the dark holes of the windows.

"Oh, sugar!" Thaïs exclaimed, "we forgot to buy a *lampadinha* . . ."

Turning back, they bought a liter of paraffin and a tin oil lamp marked with the red and gold logo of a brand of butter.

"These basic lamps are made from old tins," Moéma explained, "they're all different. In the Interior you can unearth some very beautiful ones, really."

They found João and his wife swinging idly, each in their own hammock, their children playing in a cluster below them. Maria welcomed the little group effusively and hastened to get the fire in the kitchen going. João came to join them by the hearth a little later. He had a long face: one of the four sailors of the *jangada* was ill with the result that the fishing trip planned for the next day had been canceled. Roetgen was surprised at the decision. Why not go out all the same?

"It's not possible with just three," the fisherman replied. "It's a question of the balance of the boat, there'd be a risk of capsizing."

"No one can take his place?"

"The young men don't want to go out fishing anymore and the others are busy, either on land or on their boats. That's the way things are, there's nothing that can be done. In the meantime we'll continue to go hungry."

"I could go in his place, if you want . . ."

Moved by the desire to help the family, Roetgen had spoken without thinking. At João's disbelieving look, he insisted he had plenty of experience of regattas and sea fishing.

"There's nothing in the world I like better," he concluded, as if that were one more argument.

"We go out for one night and two days, *francês*, it's not a pleasure trip."

"I'm used to it. Take me and you'll see. At the very least I can be a counterweight, since that's the problem."

Moéma joined in. "You can trust him," she said, "I know him. If he offers to come it's because he's able to do it."

"OK, then, we'll try it," João said, suddenly offering him his hand across the hearth. "I'll have to go and tell the others, I'll just be two minutes."

When he came back a little later, his face was wreathed in smiles. "It's on," he said, sitting down again. "We meet here, five o'clock in the morning."

They ate the fish with their fingers out of battered aluminium bowls. Every time Roetgen met Moéma's eye during the meal, while João was telling the latest news of the village, he saw in her look the respect and admiration his gesture inspired.

"YOU DON'T REMEMBER that either?" Moéma said as they left João's. "You really are incredible. You even asked him to teach you to dance! I'm sure he'll be getting ideas . . ."

Weary from the all the drink, Roetgen would have preferred to go straight back to their hut, but from what the girls said, he'd promised Marlene and the others he'd meet them at the *forró*, behind *Seu* Alcides' bar.

"I managed to say a lot of totally stupid things," he groaned, furious with himself. He found the prospect of having to face Marlene revolting.

"Don't worry," Thaïs said, seeing he was in such a bad mood, "he'll have sobered up as well."

"And if you dance with us, no one will bother you. You'll see, it's a super place."

"Led by Moéma down the dark street, they walked slowly, passing silent silhouettes or noisy little groups they greeted without identifying them. The wind spattered their bare skin with sand, bringing with it the smell of seaweed or a burning landfill. They started to pick up snatches of frenzied music.

"The *forró*," Moéma said, "is a sort of popular or, rather, rural dance, which only exists in the Sertão. It would be interesting to make a study of it, but that's just by the way. The word is used for both the event as a whole and the particular dance. That's why you can get into a muddle; in the *Nordeste* you can say "to go to the *forró*" just as well as "to dance" or even "to play a *forró*."

"*Forró, forrobodó, arrasta-pé, bate-chinela, gafieira* . . ." Thaïs chanted the list with evident enjoyment. "They're all the same thing. See the looks on your colleagues faces when you tell them you've been to such a den of iniquity. It's the height of vulgarity, dangerous and all. Nothing in the world would persuade them to set foot in one."

When they entered *Seu* Alcides's tiny bar, they took a moment to readjust to the light. In contrast to the profound darkness in which the rest of the village was plunged, the few paraffin lamps scattered around gave the room the air of a reredos from a museum. *Seu* Alcides, an old, potbellied mestizo wearing a pair of glasses without side-pieces held on with a rubber band, lorded it over the place from in front of two sets of shelves that, when necessary, transformed him into a grocer; the ones on the left had a disconcertingly monotonous collection of bottles—on principle Alcides only served *cachaça*—while those on the right were piled high with household essentials: cans of soya oil, tinned butter, *feijão*, soap powder, *rapadura*, all the goods behind him gleaming like gold.

Leaning on a counter of bare earth, half a dozen *caboclos* were systematically getting drunk, downing their drinks in one and letting long trails of saliva drip down onto their flip-flops; on a small billiard table that looked as if it had been dredged up from the bottom of the sea, three young men from the village were playing game after noisy game of *sinuca*, a local version of snooker. Projected onto the wall, their shapeless shadows swayed this way and that with every draft.

The drinkers shifted to make room for them at the counter.

"*Meladinha* for all three of us," Moéma ordered after being greeted by Alcides like an old friend.

"Are you sure?" he asked, raising his eyebrows. "I know you and Thaïs can take it, but him"—this with a doubtful look at Roetgen—"do you think he can stay the course? It's strong, and when you're not used to it . . ."

"He'll just have to learn. He can't drink it in Fortaleza."

"And mine is the best in the Sertão," *Seu* Alcides declared, pouring a finger of a reddish, treacly substance into the bottom of the glasses. "Pure *jandaíra* honey, it's my cousin who makes it . . ."

"A kind of bee," Thaïs explained in a whisper to Roetgen while *Seu* Alcides filled the glasses with a good three ounces of *cachaça*.

"That's one hell of a measure," Roetgen said apprehensively.

"A man's measure," was Alcides's lapidary reply as he stirred the mixture with the point of his knife. "That's how we drink it around here. But you'll see, son, it does you good where you feel bad."

The men beside them burst out into hoarse laughter, each of them making a ribald remark or an obscene gesture.

All this insistence on virility, Roetgen thought, as if the only consolation for ignorance and poverty were in the obsessive over-emphasis on the male sex organ.

Imitating his companions, he emptied his glass in one go but without being able to bring himself to spit, as they did with an impressive nonchalance. It was sweet, slightly sickly but certainly better than pure *cachaça*. By the time he'd turned back to the counter the glasses had already been filled again.

Nobody seemed bothered by the booming music of the *forró*, which was scarcely muted at all by the wind: accordion, triangle and tambourines accompanied by voices that were husky, rasping, but softened by the drawling inflections of the *Nordeste*.

"It works on car batteries," Moéma said in reply to a question from Roetgen. She was playing a game with Thaïs to see who could be the first to name the group and title of each song

as it came. Dominguinho: *Pode morrer nessa janela* . . . Oswaldo
Bezerra: *Encontro fatal, Destino cruel, Falso juramento* . . . Trio
Siridó: *Vibrando na asa branca, Até o dia amainsá* . . . Like most
of the drinkers, they joined in the words without realizing, were
ready with the chorus, dancing on the spot. And Roetgen, who
would have been incapable of singing a single French song right
through, was disturbed by the extraordinary human heat given
off by this fusion of everyone with the music, a cohesion that did
not come from folklore but from the secret energy of a community
of pioneers.

Now there were incessant comings and goings; young folk
drenched in sweat came in from the *Forró da Zefa*, downed their
drink and returned to the dance. Hot from the dance, necks red,
hair awry, the young women crossing the bar looked like hallu-
cinating madonnas. Ravishing or hideous, they looked as if they
had made love just before coming in. Roetgen was surprised to
find he desired them all.

There was a brief period of silence between two records and,
highlighted by the pause, an unusual individual made his entrance. It was an Indian of around twenty whose hairstyle, in imitation of the Xingu tradition, would have been sufficient to make
him stand out: cut on a level with his eyebrows, his thick black
hair curved in a fringe above his ears before spreading out over
his back. Dressed in white—wide trousers knotted at the waist
and a very low-cut vest over his smooth, brick-colored chest with
delicate tattoos running down from his chin in a symmetrical design of braided cords—he bore his race and his beauty like a flag.

Looking for someone to share his astonishment, Roetgen
turned to Moéma; eyes riveted on the newcomer, she seemed to
be absorbing his image. Sensing her look, as if drawn by it, the
Indian pushed his way through the crowd until he was beside her.
On his shoulder was a smudge of blue ink, the mark stamped by

Dona Zefa on dancers going out of her dance hall. He drank his *cachaça* without a word. The music started up again . . .

"Alcéu Valença!" Thaïs exclaimed, abruptly carried away by the opening bars of the song. She started to sing: *"Morena tropicana . . ."*

"Eu quero teu sabor," the Indian went on, looking Moéma straight in the eye. Then he sketched a smile and left the bar.

"Funny guy, eh?" Alcides said. He'd missed nothing of the little scene.

"Who is he?" Moéma asked, as if she wasn't really interested in the answer.

"His name's Aynoré. He's been hanging around here for two weeks now." And, spitting on the floor to emphasize his contempt, *"Maconheiro,* for all I know . . ."

"Let's dance," Thaïs begged, still taken up with the music and jigging to the rhythm.

Once out in the street they went to the left of the bar and came to the *Forró da Zefa.* It was a sort of barn made of clay bricks with a corrugated iron roof proclaiming the relative affluence of its owner. Small windows—without glass, as everywhere in Canoa Quebrada—all along the front let out more hubbub than light. At the only door to this edifice they found *Dona* Zefa herself, an old mulatto stinking of alcohol and tobacco who immediately attached herself to Roetgen muttering what was clearly a flood of obscenities in a weary voice. She let go of him as soon as he'd managed to extract the few cruzeiros entrance money from his pocket. Behind her, in a hall about thirty yards long on which two gas lamps hanging from the ceiling cast a dim light, a milling crowd was concentrating on criss-crossing all available space on the beaten-earth floor in every direction. Like an intoxicated, teeming swarm, the couples, swift, earnestly bound to their partners, were gyrating their hips rhythmically, feet held to the floor by audible magnetism. Their serious expressions, their uniform gestures in perfect accord with the rhythm of the music, astonished Roetgen more than anything he'd seen so far: a dance in the catacombs, one last cheek-to-cheek before the curfew, acutely aware of their bodies and the imminence of war. Beneath the human voice and the instruments was the constant background noise of sandals on the ground, an incessant rhythmical pulse with all the menace of a silence of the primeval world.

All at once Marlene popped up in front of them. *"Que bom!* Welcome to the three of you in the haunt of night," he said in a grandiloquent manner. "Things are heating up, eh? Now who'm I going to invite to dance?"

"Me," said Thaïs giving Roetgen a conspiratorial wink.

"Now us," said Moéma as soon as the other two had been absorbed by the Brownian agitation on the dance floor, "two steps to the right, two to the left, try to do the same as me." Pressing up against him, she dragged him off into the turbulence.

Roetgen did quite well, at least from what Moéma said. Doing everything he could not to make himself look ridiculous, he gradually became aware of his surroundings: in the dark mass of dancers, who avoided each other with the dexterity of elementary particles, he only saw gaunt, gap-toothed faces and scrawny bodies mostly a good head shorter than he; every time a taller silhouette than the others caught his eye he recognized without a shadow of doubt one of the young city dwellers who had come to Canoa to "recharge their batteries." They radiated good health, laughed with their white teeth, enjoying themselves as if they were in some nightclub. There were two species there or, worse, two stages of the same humanity far apart in time. Cut off from both sides, but put in the position of the strong despite himself, Roetgen felt he was as wrong, as absurdly comic and out of place, as a parrot in the middle of a flock of crows.

"It's not quite there yet," Moéma laughed, "you're treading on my toes. You'll have to get in training if you're going to try and pick up girls in a *forró*."

"I'm stopping. I'm beat."

"OK, let's go and have a drink."

They were heading for the exit, their straight line disturbing the mechanics of the swirling eddies, when the Indian appeared. "You dancing?" he asked Moéma coolly, without for a moment seeming to doubt what her answer would be.

"Why not," she replied with a touch of arrogance in her voice, enfolding herself in his arms with a promptness and ease that gave the lie to her little coquetry.

Somewhat disoriented at being left high and dry, Roetgen watched the couple drift along the edge of the whirling mass, ready to be carried away. A moment before they disappeared, he saw Aynoré paw Moéma's buttocks in a harsh, obscene gesture, pulling her shorts up over her thighs, and her nails digging into the tattoos on his back.

Roetgen felt as if they had left a symmetrical claw mark on him. He had no right to be jealous, but allowed himself to wallow in a feeling of contempt that encompassed all the women in the world. His mind preoccupied with a thousand variations on his hurt pride, he left the dance hall, duly stamped by *Dona* Zefa as he passed, and went back to *Seu* Alcides's bar.

This mood affected his view of the drinkers, who seemed to him to have reached the depths of degeneracy. One guy who'd fallen asleep on the billiard table woke with a start every three minutes to offer his cigarettes to no one in particular; another, determined to humiliate himself, was making *pipoca* to order, blowing out his cheeks excessively to make the sound of popcorn bursting, as if this pitiful buffoonery were the whole justification for his existence. *Seu* Alcides himself appeared too fat to be honest, especially in comparison with the living skeletons thronging his bar.

He forced himself to swallow a *meladinha*. In a direct relationship of cause and effect, the drink set off a fit of stomachache that left him paralyzed, close to fainting. Panicking at the thought that he might not be able to control the disaster in his bowels, he left the bar, urgently hurrying to get to the dunes. Rummaging through his pockets without finding anything to substitute for toilet paper, he ran off into the darkness, sick and despondent.

When he was sure he'd never reach the sea in time, he turned to the right and walked straight ahead, determined to get as far away from the houses as possible. In the faint light of the stars, a no-man's-land of rubbish spread out, an unspeakable dump running along the whole length of the road. Plunging into the filth, Roetgen suddenly broke out in a cold sweat and was then overtaken by cramps that bent him double and sent him tumbling to his knees, like someone in despairing prayer. And there, alone, oblivious to everything, overwhelmed by the way his whole being was spinning, he thought he was going to die and that a pig would find him in the morning, bare-assed amid the steaming garbage of the village, a foul thing among the foulness.

His last banknotes were hardly enough to wipe away his anguish.

When he was able to get up, he wiped his sticky hands with sand and went back to the road, guided by a twinkling light that was in more or less the right direction. He came to a little window and stopped for a moment: gilded by the chiaroscuro of her lamp, an old black woman was slowly doing a piece of embroidery on a large frame of dark wood. Seeing Roetgen, she gave him a timid smile, pausing in her work. This snapshot of Flemish painting encapsulated the infinite gentleness of mothers and, with that, the sole bastion against the madness of the world.

THE TOWN OF PACATUBA: *The VASP airplane*

When Zé had offered to take him to visit his sister in the little house she had in the mountains, not far from Fortaleza, Nelson had been so dead drunk that he couldn't remember either his friend carrying him out to his truck, or having traveled through the whole night. So when he woke in the middle of a forest of banana trees, he thought it was a dream, one of the most calm and beautiful ones he'd had for a long time. Since he felt a bit cold, he pulled his hammock over him and went back to sleep.

"Come on, up you get, lazybones," he heard an hour later. "There's no point in coming to the mountains if you spend all the time sleeping."

Emerging from his hammock as if from a chrysalis, Nelson saw the smiling face of Uncle Zé. "Just have a look at this paradise," he said, pointing out of the window. "A bit of a change from Fortaleza, isn't it?"

Outside there were indeed the banana trees of his dream, a clear sky and the croaking of the buffalo frogs.

"Where are we?" Nelson asked, rubbing his eyes.

"At my sister's place, for God's sake! In the Serra de Aratanha. You were in some state last night."

"I must have been, my head feels like a watermelon."

"The mountain air'll sort that out in no time at all, you'll see. Get up, Firmina's made us a real country breakfast."

After a *mingau* of tapioca—a thick porridge of sweetened milk and flour—a good slice of sweet-potato omelette and two bowls of coffee, Nelson felt much better. Then Zé carried him piggyback to a large pond down below where they went fishing. Despite his lack of experience, the *aleijadinho* proved to be more skillful than his teacher and caught two catfish that looked monstrous to him.

When they went back for lunch, around one, it had clouded over, suggesting there would be a heavy shower during the afternoon. They hadn't finished eating when the storm broke, keeping them inside for the rest of the day. After the siesta, they stayed in their hammocks on the veranda, watching the rain. Then Zé sang from memory the adventures of Prince Roldão, which they'd gotten from a recent *cordel* by João Martins de Athayde. A naive mixture of the *Iliad* and *Orlando furioso*, the story told how the nephew of Charlemagne had managed to rescue his Angelica from the clutches of Abdul Rahman, king of Turkey and thoroughgoing infidel, by hiding, together with his weapons, in a gold lion designed by Richard of Normandy . . .

When the sun set, the rain finally stopped, leaving a frayed veil of mist. Nelson and Zé went inside to escape the evening humidity and opened a bottle of *cachaça* while old Firmina put the fish they'd brought back a few hours earlier on to stew.

They were in the middle of the meal and—remembering it later, Firmina saw it as a coincidence pregnant with meaning—laughing much too loud, when the sound of jet engines made the glasses on the table tremble, getting louder and louder until they had to draw their heads down into their shoulders, and finishing in an explosion that blew out all the windows in the house: the VASP Boeing 727, coming from Congonhas, had crashed spectacularly in the Serra de Aratanha.

The only one to react, Zé rushed outside. A little farther up the mountain, in the light of trees transformed into torches, a huge plume of black smoke was rising from a new gap in the forest.

"*Meu Deus!*" he said, realizing what had happened, "it almost fell on us." Then, turning to Nelson and his sister, who had followed him out onto the veranda, "You wait here, I'll go and see if I can do anything."

With that, he started to run toward the place where the disaster had happened.

Despite Firmina's loud cries and without really thinking about what he was doing, Nelson followed, hauling himself along the ground.

When, exhausted and covered from head to toe in red mud from sliding along the path, he reached the place where the plane had crashed, Nelson was petrified at what is generally called an "apocalyptic scene" but of which the horror for him was contained in the simple sight of a woman's torso still attached by her belt but now apparently sitting on her abundant entrails. All around, scattered over a very large area and highlighted by the fluorescent yellow of the life jackets, the smoking debris of the plane, disembowelled suitcases, an unrecognizable jumble could be seen. And then things that held a grisly fascination: horribly mangled bodies, scraps of flesh hanging from the trees like Tibetan prayers, limbs or organs scattered haphazardly over the soaked ground, obscene in their unaccustomed solitude . . . a feast of human flesh suddenly delivered to the hungry beasts of the forest. It was as if it had been raining blood, steak and offal, Nelson thought.

Woken by the sudden blaze, the vultures were already fluttering over this manna, nibbling at bared stomachs with their beaks, pecking at the eyes, fighting over the most appetizing carcasses with shrill cries. Nelson was hardly surprised at the number of silhouettes—some armed with torches—who were already busying themselves about the site of the tragedy: with little room for pity for those whom death had released from all need, these poor mountain folk were searching through the remains meticulously, picking out anything of value, with no sense of disgust: money, rings and jewelry but also clothes red with blood, odd shoes and even some pieces of the machine, of which it was impossible to say what use they intended to make.

For a brief moment he had been taken with the prospect of finding a well-filled wallet, but Nelson refused to join those robbing the corpses. Looking around for Uncle Zé, he made his way through the debris, The ground was nauseating, saturated with secretions and dubious matter. Crawling around a thicket, he came across what was left of a policeman, a decapitated cop who, absurdly, was still wearing his belt and holster with its pistol.

"You don't look too clever like that," Nelson muttered. "Fuck you, son of a bitch."

Like a divine response to this blasphemy, he felt two hands grasp his shoulders and rolled over, screaming.

"What the hell are you doing here, for God's sake? What the hell are you doing here?" Uncle Zé bellowed at the shock. "My God, have you seen yourself? You . . . you . . . I thought you were a survivor."

"I followed you . . ." Nelson stammered, he too trembling.

"I can see you followed me. I told you to stay in the house."

"Are there any injured?"

Uncle Zé shook his head sadly. "They're all dead. It's not possible after a crash like that. I'll keep looking until the rescue party arrives. And you're going straight back to the house, understood? I'll come as soon as I can."

Nelson stayed by the corpse for a few more minutes, surprised at the perfection of the plan that had formed in his mind. That was the way it would be, that and no other way. There was no other way it could be . . .

Back at the house, while Firmina, horrified at the state he was in, was heating some water to wash him, Nelson took the loaded gun out of his T-shirt and quickly stowed it in the bottom of his bag.

A little later, in the washtub where *Dona* Firmina was scrubbing his back while mumbling prayers for the victims, he had an amazing erection, the first hard-on he'd had since his father died.

CHAPTER 11

Containing the conclusion, ad majorem Dei gloriam, to the story of the Villa Palagonia

"DO THAT & YOU will be lost," this new Potiphar's wife said calmly. "I will say you tried to violate me & I can assure you that you will feel the whole weight of my husband's fury."

I was stunned, realizing the truth of what she said. For a moment I almost rang despite everything, preferring scandal, disgrace & even death to this shameful temptation; recalling *in extremis* my promise to Kircher, I knelt down, face to the wall, & begged God to grant me His aid.

I felt the Princess come over and wrap her arms around me tenderly. "Now don't be silly. You haven't taken your final vows yet & there's no sin in yielding under duress . . ."

Having said that, she pulled me down onto the carpet. My sight became blurred & my heart was pounding, obliterating any attempt at resistance, & I pressed my body against hers while repeating the name of Jesus like a man possessed.

Even today I blush at the memory of our unbridled lasciviousness; but I will drain this bitter cup to the last drop & confess the full extent of a sin that I am not sure I have expiated by my subsequent conduct. For, not content with abandoning myself to debauchery with the Princess, I did not refuse the perverted embellishments she taught me that night . . . *Lingua mea in nobilissimae os adacta, spiculum usque ad cor illi penetravit. Membra nostra humoribus rorabant, atque concinebant quasi sugentia. Modo intus macerabam, modo cito retrahebam lubricum caulem. Scrotum meum ultro citroque iactabatur. Nobilis mulier cum crura trementia attolleret, suavissime olebat. Novenis ictibus alte penetrantibus singulos breves inserui.*[1] The Princess's chignon had become undone, long locks half concealed her imploring looks . . . *Pectoribus anhelantibus ambo gemebamus.*[2] I was doing everything I could with my hands and my legs & *semen meum ad imam vaginam penetravit.*[3] But the Princess was insatiable, I soon had to start again. *Tum pedes eius sublevandi ac sustinendi fuerunt humeris meis. Pene ad posticum admoto, in reconditas ac fervidas latebras intimas impetum feci. Deinde cuniculum illius diu linxi, dum irrumo. Mingere autem volui: "O Caspar mi, voluptas mea, inquit,*

---

1 I pushed my tongue into the Princess's mouth and my lance penetrated her womb. Our limbs were dripping with our fluids, they made the same sucking noise. Sometimes I let my slippery rod macerate inside, sometimes I pulled it out quickly. My scrotum was tossed hither and thither. The princess raised her quivering legs, giving off a most sweet smell. I punctuated novenas of deep thrusts with single short ones.

2 We both groaned, our chests heaving.

3 And my semen flowed into the depths of her vagina.

quantumcumque meies, tantum ore accipiam!"⁴ Which it did, as *liquore meo faciem eius perfundi* . . . ⁵

She taught me other depraved acts that were equally abominable; by now I was indulging in them with pleasure without thinking for a moment that we were wallowing in mortal sin. However, the Princess, even while enjoying licentiousness such as had never appeared even in my worst nightmares, kept insisting I should take care not to brush against her navel or her stomach for fear of breaking the glass harpsichord she imagined was in there. It was a request I had some difficulty complying with, given my frenzied state.

When we were satiated, which was only after two hours of unbridled lust, she showed me an unobtrusive passage by which I could return to my room without being seen. Once there, I immediately fell asleep, drunk on wine & sensual pleasure. It was the early morning of December 25, 1637.

When I woke, feeling sick and bloated from my night of debauchery, it was to suffer the most excruciating torments of guilty conscience. There was no hope of redemption for my sin & already I was burning in the fires of a hell as terrible as the real one. Such were my sufferings and my self-hatred, such the sting of shame, that all I wanted was to confess my sins to my master & then bury myself in some hideous desert.

I had reached that stage of my torment when a lackey came to ask me to join Kircher in the library. I followed him like a man being taken to suffer the pain of martyrdom.

---

4 I had to lift up her feet and place them on my shoulders, then I placed my penis on her anus and plunged into the interior of that hidden and burning retreat. Then for a long time I enjoyed fellatio as she sucked my member. I needed to urinate. "O my Caspar," she said to me, "however much you piss, my mouth can take it!"

5 I flooded her face with my water . . .

270

Athanasius was alone among the books & an expression of profound compassion appeared on his face when he saw me. I immediately threw myself down at his feet, incapable of uttering a word, mumbling my desire for confession between sobs.

"That is not necessary, Caspar," he said, helping me up. "Whatever you have done, you are already pardoned. Look . . ."

He took a weighty folio tome down from the shelves & opened it in the middle at two blank pages. He placed the book, open, on a tall lectern facing the place from which it had been taken down, then asked me to put out the two candelabra lighting this windowless room.

"Pluck up your courage, Caspar, & look."

I went over to him to see, to my amazement, that the book now showed a luminous picture in color, as clear as the reflection in a mirror. But my astonishment at this piece of magic was as nothing compared with my stupefaction when I recognized the alcove where I had condemned myself to eternal torment the previous night. Crying out, I fainted.

I regained consciousness soon after, Kircher having applied some smelling salts he always carried with him. In the meantime he had relit the candelabra & I could see that the pages of the book were blank again.

"Sit down & listen, without asking any questions. I have a lot more to confess than you. First of all you must know that there is no sorcery in what you have just seen. It is just one of my inventions, a camera obscura, which I would have preferred to reveal to you under better circumstances. But God, for it can only be Him, has decided otherwise. I was here, with the Prince, when you went into that alcove with his wife yesterday evening; I spied on you until I was sure you would obey my orders without fail. I don't know what you did with the Princess, that Devil's spawn, & I don't want to know; it is the price that had to be paid for an enterprise in which we are both nothing but blind instruments. Your submission to my orders, far from sending you to eternal damnation, allows you to enter Paradise; by your sin, Caspar, you have quite simply saved the Church!

"I knew about this volume," he went on, grasping a thick roll of parchment, "even before I came to this house, but the horror of reading it surpassed everything I had been told."

Constituting as it did an inestimable piece of good fortune for the enemies of the Christian religion, the very existence of that work was a catastrophe in the troubled times in which we lived . . .

"This morning the Prince, in accordance with the pact I made with him, gave me this book, which could be such a dangerous weapon in the hands of our adversaries. I will have no regrets about burning it, Caspar. May your sins & mine be consumed in the same fire."

With these words Kircher cast the volume into the hearth & gave me absolution as the parchment buckled and twisted in the flames. He poked the fire until the manuscript of Flavius Josephus had been completely rendered to ashes, then looked me straight in the eye. I had never seen him so earnest & so moved. "Come," he said gently, "let us go and leave this lair of the Fiend as quickly as possible. Everything has been accomplished, we have done our duty."

We left the Prince's residence without taking our leave of him & I had the consolation of not having to see again the woman who had taken me so far into the labyrinth of lust.

In the hired carriage that was taking us back to Palermo, Athanasius went into more detail on the adventure of which I had been the willing victim. Our hosts were unmitigated libertines, so confirmed in their vice that they were only aroused by lascivious refinements. The Prince was almost impotent from all the Spanish fly he had taken & the Princess half-crazy since a miscarriage the previous year had deprived her of the child she had so longed for, which explained her *idée fixe* about the glass harpsichord she believed she had in her womb. She was a willing participant in her husband's lecherous schemes & knew very well when we were together in the alcove that her husband was spying on us. Although intelligent & cultured, these people were a prime example of the moral chaos resulting from skepticism; deprived of the support of faith, they sank a little deeper into depravity every day without concerning themselves with a future judgment of their actions. God's pity being infinite, sincere repentance could save them from Gehenna, but that, alas, was very unlikely. The manuscript of Flavius Josephus had been the sole reason for our presence in the Villa Palagonia. A knight of the Order of Malta had had it in his hands during an audience there & had taken it upon himself to tell Kircher about it & had supplied all kinds of useful details about the habits of the Prince & Princess.

My master continued to try & persuade me that I merited the plenary indulgence attached to the holy cause, which my unwitting efforts had supported. He kept repeating that I was, if not a martyr, then at least a hero of the Church; nevertheless, the delight I had felt while I disported myself with the Princess, the unreserved pleasure I had taken in the sin, precluded me from accepting that justification. What is more, my pride was hurt & I suffered less from having left the path of virtue than from having been a mere pawn in the vile schemes of those two libertines. But for Athanasius all this seemed to belong to the past already . . .

Once back in Palermo, in the studious calm of the Jesuit college, I helped my master file his notes & materials, after which we started to construct, for the Duke of Hesse, a new machine on the principles of the camera obscura, the first model of which I had unwittingly tested out. It was a wooden cube with arms, as on a sedan chair, & enough room for two people inside. We made an aperture in each of the sides in which a lens was later fitted. In this perfectly dark box we placed a second, smaller cube made of translucent paper fitted to a frame. It was so arranged that this screen was sufficiently far from the lenses to show a clear image of the world outside. An opening at the bottom of the machine allowed one to slip inside the framework & thus observe, by means of the transparent paper, the images of things or people that were outside.

Once the machine had been constructed, we had ourselves carried through the city & its surroundings by four servants. We saw city streets & country landscapes, people, objects, hunting scenes & the most fantastic sights, all reproduced with such *maestria* that no pictorial art could have matched their perfection. Everything appeared on the sides of our little compartment, flights of birds, gestures, looks, teeth moving, even words themselves, & in a way that was so vivid & natural that I cannot remember having seen anything so wonderful in all my life.

Duke Frederick of Hesse, who became acquainted with this portable chamber a few days later, was full of enthusiasm. Paying out of his own pocket, he asked us to construct a much larger one so that he could take his friends in it. Kircher set to work &, with the help of several craftsmen, had the new model ready for February 1, 1638. It was in the form of a galleon on carriage wheels & looked as imposing as a real ship. Magnificently decorated with stucco nereids covered in gold leaf, it contained inside all the comforts of a luxurious drawing room. Numerous lenses placed in the portholes created a magical spectacle on the white silk walls. Pulled by twelve piebald geldings, this magnificent vessel, the fruit of my master's art & ingeniousness, traveled up & down the avenues of Palermo for days on end without the Duke and those who intrigued to have the honor of accompanying him tiring of this marvel.

Believing it to be a new style of procession, the citizens followed these outings with cries of delight. The favor Kircher enjoyed knew no bounds.

As the date of our departure was approaching, we concentrated on making all the new curiosities the government of the island had given my master in return for his services ready for the journey. When we set off, at the beginning of March 1638, the Grand Duke's baggage train had been increased by five wagons solely for the carriage of all the various finds & samples we were bringing back from Malta and Sicily.

When we reached Messina, we had to wait three days for the weather to improve, the storm being so great no pilot was prepared to take us across to Calabria. When we got under way the wind & the sea were still so unfavorable the sailors themselves were frightened by the crossing. At Kircher's request we had to make a detour toward the rocks of Scylla & Charybdis to see what it was that made them so dangerous, but the captain refused to approach close enough. By way of compensation, my master was delighted to see Mount Stromboli throwing its plume of smoke and lava debris up into the stormy sky.

We resumed our journey north &, after several days of forced march, caught up with the equipage of the Duke of Hesse in the little village of Tropea, on the banks of the Tyrrhenian Sea.

SÃO LUÍS: *Everywhere there was the glint of little stupid eyes inside dark rings*

"I've seen quite a few things in my life, but that . . . It's nauseating! It's disgraceful!"

He had never seen Loredana in such a state. Lips pursed, white with anger, she gave vent to her indignation:

"An American couple with a seventeen-year-old daughter. They arrived at the hotel this morning, with the first boat. I was having breakfast downstairs with Socorró. Three monsters, I can tell you! Fat as pigs, badly brought up, swaggering, a caricature of all that's worst in that type. Neither a good morning nor a smile, nothing, not even making the effort to say a couple of words in Portuguese. Poor Socorró was petrified. I had to translate what they wanted: "Two rooms and some beer," just like that. She had to make several journeys to take up their cases without any of them lifting a finger. They started to get sloshed right away, all three of them, father, mother and daughter. You can just see it. When I left they'd already knocked back three cans each. They may be thick, ugly, impolite and like a drink, OK, but Socorró told me how it went on. They spent all the morning there, doing nothing but drinking and pissing; after lunch the two women went upstairs for a siesta but the guy insisted on having a mattress put down under the veranda and—you'll never believe it—ordered Socorró to fan him while he was asleep."

"Surely she didn't agree?" Eléazard said, eyes wide.

"Of course not, at least at the beginning. But he offered her ten then twenty dollars to do it and since she has a grandson at boarding school in São Luís and she's the one who looks after him . . ."

"I don't believe it! And what was Alfredo doing? You can't let that kind of thing go on!"

"He and his wife had gone to São Luís for the day. I can't tell you how angry he was when he heard all about it. He wanted to get rid of them right away, kick them out, literally, but Socorró begged him not to make a scene and to let her earn a bit more money this month. To cap it all, the guy's armed, he's got a revolver stuck between his trousers and his skin, Socorró saw it when he unbuttoned his shirt. Alfredo couldn't get over it. It really cooled him down, especially since they pay well, the bastards."

"We can't have this," said Eléazard coolly. "I'll talk to Socorró. I'll pay her what she would have got from fanning him, if necessary, but we can't allow that."

"If you'd seen her. She can hardly move her arms this evening."

"I'll speak to her tomorrow," said Eléazard, "but just now we'll have to hurry if we don't want to miss the boat."

SITTING IN THE back seat of the vehicle—an old Ford convertible that hadn't been driven for decades but that looked as if it were straight out of the showroom—Loredana enjoyed the close of the day. Driven smoothly by Eléazard, the car seemed to be heading for the red glow of the setting sun as if to merge with it in a gaudy apotheosis. Hair all disheveled, Dr. Euclides kept turning to her to chat about this and that or to comment, by guesswork, on a landscape he apologized for not being able to see. Though following the dictates of an out-of-date code of behavior, his attentions nevertheless had the unaffected charm of a long habit of courtesy.

"You will see," he said as they approached the *fazenda*, "Countess Carlotta is a very refined, very cultured person . . . quite the opposite of her boor of a husband. I'm still wondering what it was about him that could have attracted her. God knows what chemistry presides over the mystery of affinities, especially in their case! Have you read Goethe's little book, *Elective Affinities*? No? It's worth making the effort, believe me . . ."

Dr. Euclides da Cunha took off his glasses. As he wiped them mechanically, he turned even farther around toward Loredana:

"*Es wandelt niemand ungestraft unter Palmen,*" he declaimed in a quiet voice, "*und die Gesinnungen ändern sich gewiß in einem Lande, wo Elefanten und Tiger zu Hause sind!* No one can walk beneath palm trees with impunity, one might translate it, and ideas are sure to change in a land where elephants and tigers are at home. We have here, as I'm sure you'll agree, a good number of those males who combine the heaviness of a pachyderm with the ferocity of a big cat . . ."

Eléazard broke in: "You're embroidering, as always, Doctor." He fell silent for a few seconds, suddenly occupied with the demands of the road. "I would go even farther: you're misrepresenting what Goethe meant. If I remember rightly, poor Ottilie only writes that to encourage the men to concern themselves with the world around them. To her mind, it is a matter of condemning the unhealthy attractions of the exotic. Or am I wrong?"

"You will never stop amazing me, my friend," the doctor said, raising his voice in order to be heard. "I should have realized you would have your Goethe at your fingertips. It was only a little quip, but I'm standing by it. No one's going to stop me making words say a bit more than they appear to allow. But since it's cropped up, you must remember the whole of the passage in question, and you'll see that far from misrepresenting, I'm remaining absolutely faithful to it. It all starts out from a reflection on the relationship between man and nature: we ought to know, or seek to know only those living things in our immediate environment. To surround ourselves with monkeys and parrots in a land where they are mere curiosities is to prevent us from seeing our true *compatriots*, the familiar trees, the animals or persons who have made us what we are. The tree that stops us from seeing the forest, in a way . . . and the symptom of a serious disturbance. Uprooted from their natural environment, these foreign creatures are carriers of anxiety, of a distress they will transmit to us, as if by infection, and that will transform us profoundly: *It takes a gaudy and boisterous life*, Goethe says, *to be able to put up with monkeys, parrots and Moors around one*."

"He says 'Moors'?" Loredana broke in.

"Yes, but without racist undertones, as far as I'm aware. Don't forget that it was very common at the time to have black slaves as servants. He writes about them in the manner of Rousseau, if you see what I mean."

Loredana smiled tenderly; Dr. Euclides had won her over from his very first words of welcome two hours previously; his hair and goatee flattened by the slipstream, he looked like a terrier, its pointed nose sniffing the wind . . .

"And the converse is equally true. It's the precise meaning of the passage I was quoting just now. Removed from his native land and cast, willingly or not, on a foreign shore, a man becomes different. However much he mixes with parrots, monkeys and . . . let's say the native population, he still remains someone who doesn't belong, whose only alternatives are either the despair resulting from his lack of points of reference or complete integration in this new world. In either case, he becomes the 'Moor' of whom we were talking: a poor soul incapable of becoming acclimatized to this world where everything is beyond him and, soon, a cripple incapable of renewing his ties with his native land, at best a traitor who will spend his whole life aping a culture that even his children will have difficulty acquiring."

"If you insist," said Eléazard, in a tone that contradicted his agreement. "Though you could hear that opinion from the lips of a fanatical nationalist or a fascist opposed in principle to the horrors of interbreeding. Times have changed, nowadays we can move from one end of the world to another much more easily than from Weimar to Leipzig in Goethe's day; whether we deplore it or see it as an achievement, the fact is that cultural differences are becoming less marked, eventually they will give way to a blend hitherto unknown in the history of the world . . . But what's the connection with Moreira?"

"None whatsoever, my friend," said the doctor, bursting into a little silent laugh. "And why should there be? After all"—once again he turned to Loredana—"I'm not the one who lives with a parrot."

"One-nil to you," said Loredana, laughing too.

"You're lucky we're there," said Eléazard, turning into the main drive of the *fazenda*, "or I'd have shown you what I'm made of." He gave the old man an affectionate smile, but Loredana saw a flush on the back of his neck that hadn't been there a few seconds before.

"DO COME IN," said Countess Carlotta after the doctor had introduced them. "Follow me, we'll try and find José. After that you can do as you please." She took Euclides by the arm and firmly pushed her way through the groups crowding the hall right up to the stairs.

. . . six-four, six-love! He was never in the game. So I'm in the quarterfinals. I must admit I didn't think I could do it . . . If you'd seen the look on his face! Getting beaten by a veteran, he couldn't get over it . . .

The rustle of silk, the swirl of cigarettes, slow, grudging sidesteps to allow them through.

. . . Carlotta, darling, your lobster's quite simply sublime! You must tell me where you get them, the telephone number itself's worth it's weight in gold!

. . . I recognized it right away. Just imagine, a Vasco Prado by itself, in the middle of a pile of rubbish! And this imbecile who didn't even know what it was . . . I even haggled! It's not a masterpiece, of course, but it's a first edition, it's got something . . .

. . . he's a bastard, there's no two ways about it. I lost my temper, I know, but if there's one thing I can't stand, it's lies. A promise is a promise, and nothing will persuade me otherwise . . .

Women's bare arms, immaculate shirt collars with damp necks trying to wriggle out of them, sighs at the heat, shining skin, a sudden surplus of Dior or Guerlain under an armpit blue from the razor. Like a priesthood, blacks in white suits were strolling around gravely, magi offering their gifts of crystal and salmon canapes to the gods.

"Ah, there he is," said Carlotta, going toward the large mirror beneath which her husband was strutting, champagne glass in one hand, the other placed in a familiar gesture on the shoulder of a surly old man with whom he was conversing in a low voice. "José, if you please . . ."

The governor turned around automatically, looking annoyed. But when he saw Loredana his face lit up. "Good evening, Doctor, how are you? It's good of you to come."

"Very well, thank you. Don't let us interrupt, I just wanted to introduce the friends I told you about: Loredana Rizzuto, an Italian who happens to be visiting our region—"

"A pleasure," said the governor, bending over Loredana's hand.

"—and Eléazard von Wogau, Reuters correspondent . . ."

"Delighted to meet you. I've been hearing a lot about you."

"Only good things, I hope," said Eléazard, shaking his hand.

"Don't worry, our dear Euclides is unrivaled as a doctor but he is also an excellent advocate. And of course your articles, which I read regularly, speak for themselves . . ."

"Really?" said Eléazard, unable to keep a slight touch of irony out of his voice. No signed article by him had appeared for a year; the man must be either a hypocrite or a fool. Both, probably . . .

"Every time I come across one, anyway. My work hardly leaves me any time for decent reading. But if you will forgive me"—this with a glance at the old man behind him who was making no attempt to conceal his impatience—"we can continue our conversation a little later. Show them the buffet, darling, they must be thirsty in this heat." And as one of the waiters was just passing he took a glass of champagne off his tray and handed it to Loredana. "See you soon," he said, addressing her alone and with a smile that made her feel uneasy.

The smile of a man, she thought, who spends a fortune on his dentist.

"That was Alvarez Neto, the Minister for Industry," Euclides whispered to Eléazard as they went away.

"That antique! How did you manage to recognize him?"

"You wouldn't believe me if I told you."

"Try me."

"From his smell, my friend. That gentleman stinks of money as others do of excrement."

Led by Carlotta, they weaved their way between the dinner jackets and evening dresses that the gilded decoration on that floor—or was it just the presence of the governor?—seemed to have attracted to that spot. Seeing Loredana, the women's looks sprayed her with a toxic cloud of contemptuous rivalry; the men's, beneath an affectation of indifference, were meant to be eloquent. Wearing tight jeans and a crocheted crossover top, her hair hurriedly done up in a chignon that was threatening to fall apart, she made her sinuous way between them without deigning to notice the fissures caused by her passing.

"I'm going to deprive you of the doctor for a few moments," the Countess said, "make sure you get a few nibbles before these greedy pigs clear the buffet. It's always the same," she said to Euclides, watching the crowd obstinately gather in one corner of the room, "to see them, you'd think they hadn't eaten for days . . ."

In a hurry to get out in the open air, Eléazard and Loredana went back down to the ground floor. A servant took them to the French window leading out onto the patio: enclosed by the walls of the chapel, the *fazenda* and its outbuildings, was a huge garden with trees and grass. Concealing the sky behind a shimmering veil, a profusion of torches set the shadows dancing beneath the massive daturas and frangipanis skillfully arranged in sparse disorder.

"Can you tell me what the hell we're doing here?" Loredana asked reproachfully.

"What a load of cretins," Eléazard said, wiping his neck with his handkerchief. "It's unbelievable! If it was up to me, we'd leave straightaway."

"What is there to stop us?"

"I promised Euclides I'd make an effort. Anyway, it's his car so we'll have to wait to take him home."

Loredana seemed to hesitate a moment, frowning.

"Please," Eléazard said gently, as if he had heard her sharp words of objection.

She gave him a searching look and eventually smiled, twisting her lips in a comic manner to show how much she was having to force herself. "OK, But I warn you, I'm going to need champagne, lots of champagne."

Eléazard had been prepared for the worst. "No problem," he said, relieved, "I'll see to it."

He sat Loredana down at one of the little rattan tables scattered around under the trees and strode off toward the buffet.

Eyes half closed, Loredana watched him heading for the other end of the garden: his linen suit too big for him, his way of walking a touch too lithe, too nonchalant . . . this strange guy was pleasantly out of place in this milieu. Blotchy-faced apes, irritating females with flabby arms, décolletés marked with liver spots; out-of-breath divers only deigning to plunge into the night out of physiological necessity, for a breath of fresh air, and manifestly concerned to return to the glories of the center of the *fazenda* as quickly as possible; wizened corpses of first communicants, mummies in christening dresses, a velvety nightmare from a painting by Goya . . . It was crazy to be out here, in the middle of the Sertão, in the ostentatious, antiquated luxury of this grotesque house of the dead! And all because a fairly good-looking Frenchman had taken her under his wing and she'd gone along with it, because she had nothing better to do rather than out of weakness. Still no news from the lawyer. Yesterday morning, on the telephone, his secretary had sworn to her that he was actively pursuing "her affair," but she was beginning to have her doubts, wondering about the steps he was taking, suspecting they were just another way of getting out of it, of disguising the fear that had taken his breath away in the blazing sun, in Rome, only a few yards from the hospital exit.

Eléazard reappeared with two glasses and a bottle of champagne. He was accompanied by an amused waiter carrying a tray with enough to satisfy their appetite and more.

"Ah, there you are, 'the beautiful Italian who's dying of thirst,'" he said putting the plates on the table. "Help yourself, miss, there's everything you need," adding, with a wink in the direction of the bottle, "I've put three others on the side, just in case . . ."

"Thanks again, *rapaz*. And don't let them push you around," said Eléazard, slipping a banknote into the boy's pocket. "They're white, but it's because they're shit-scared."

"You're one of a kind," said the waiter, bursting out laughing. "I've never seen any like you before." With conspiratorial look, he pretended to sew up his mouth, gave them another wink and went back to the buffet.

"You know him?" Loredana asked, surprised and amused by the little scene.

"For all of ten minutes. I got to know him behind the buffet table."

"And what did you say to him to get all this?"

"Oh, not much. A lot of good things about you, and a load of obscene things about the old fogeys around us. But I was preaching to the converted, he and his pals had already noticed you; if you must know, they think you've got curves in all the right places, you're something else and not the least bit of a prude . . ."

"You're making it up."

"Not at all. They don't miss a thing, you know. It's a matter of practice. Those are the people—I mean the assistants, the café waiters, barmaids—for a psychological assessment of our world, they know more about it than anyone else."

"You can add the check-out women in the big stores, hairdressers, grocers, doctors, priests . . . it all adds up to quite a few 'experts' at the end of the day. A few too many, perhaps?"

"Not at all," Eléazard objected with a smile. "I agree about the doctors; they even have one advantage over barmen in that they don't just lay bare their patients' secrets but actually strip them naked. Ask Euclides and you'll see. Nudity has the same effect as alcohol, it produces a state of intoxication that encourages confession, a mental and linguistic brazenness analogous to the body's lack of modesty. The priests have missed the boat; if they'd compelled their flock to enter the confessional drunk and naked, they wouldn't have had to yield their prerogatives. The dimmest of waiters or doctors know more about their fellow citizens than the most charismatic of confessors. The psychoanalysts have got the right idea, but they stopped halfway. They put their clients on a couch to encourage them to speak, but they really ought to make them strip."

"Come on," Loredana broke in, "open the bottle instead of talking rubbish."

"It's not rubbish," Eléazard said, doing as she asked. "Just think about it and you'll see that I'm right."

"I'm not saying you're wrong. It just that I simply believe no one ever knows anything about anyone. There's no mathematics of the human brain; it's not an area with true or false, just masks and fancy dress. Anyone who can look at others believing, honestly or dishonestly, he can escape manipulation is putting on an act; anyone who lets others look at him is putting on an act as well. There's no way out of it . . ."

"It seems to me you're pretty much a pessimist." He poured the champagne, careful to check the flow as the foam rose. "Anyway, it's not something that can be proved either way. But there is at least one thing I know about you, you're even more beautiful in the torchlight." As if to stop her replying, he stood up on tiptoe, fiddled with a branch above him and placed a stalk with three long, blood-colored flowers in front of Loredana.

She was very close to thinking him corny. However, she decided to assume the compliment was naive and merely shrugged her shoulders, as if to say "isn't that just typical of you" and clinked her glass lightly against his.

"To Brazil," she said, without much conviction. Then, briefly looking him in the eye, "And to Father Kircher."

"To Brazil," Eléazard repeated, a shadow suddenly passing over his expression. Without really knowing why, though fully aware how absurd his insistence was, he refused to toast the poor Jesuit.

Loredana made no comment and he was grateful for her show of tact. Elaine wouldn't have hesitated to rub salt in the wound, putting forward all sorts of explanations, going on at him until she made him say something or other, anything just to get rid of her obstinate determination to find a reason for his silence.

They drank at the same time and as Loredana seemed resolved to empty her glass in one gulp, Eléazard did the same, after a brief moment of hesitation.

"*Ancóra*," she said, wiping her lips with the back of her fingers. "That was just for the thirst."

AN HOUR PASSED, devoted entirely to knocking back champagne and running down others. Then they talked about Socorró again and her dealings with the unsavory family of Americans who had just moved into the hotel, wondering what would be the best way of putting an end to such an awkward situation. The second bottle of champagne was almost empty when Loredana held the flowers up to look at them against the light.

"You know what they are?" she asked, her thoughts elsewhere.

"No," Eléazard admitted, "but they're not grown for their fragrance, that's for sure."

"*Brugmansia sanguinea*, a tropical species of datura. It's hallucinogenic, fatal in large doses. Some Indians still use it to communicate with their ancestors; in the past they also used to employ it to drug the women who were to be burned alive on their husband's funeral pyre . . ."

"You mean all I managed to give you was some poison?" Eléazard joked, putting on a look of annoyance. "And may one hear how you come to know such things?"

Their conversation was cut short by the Countess's voice behind them: 'Here I am again. You must excuse me for having monopolized Euclides for so long . . . He's waiting for you in the garage." With a grimace of contempt and looking up at the heavens, she explained, "My husband absolutely insists on showing his collection of cars to anyone who hasn't seen it before. It's tedious, but he does it every time. I'll take you there, if you don't mind."

As they stood up to follow her, Carlotta gave the bottle of champagne a quick glance and smiled at Eléazard. "You're French, I believe?"

While congratulating himself on having hidden the first bottle in the bushes, Eléazard felt a sudden itching sensation in his scalp.

"Don't worry," she assured him, taking his arm, "the champagne's there to be drunk. I'm just glad it's appreciated." Her breath stank of alcohol, showing that she, like them, had drunk more than was sensible.

"Tell me, Monsieur Von . . . Wogau—I hope I've got it right?" And after he had confirmed she had not mispronounced his name, she went on, "Would you be related to Elaine von Wogau, a professor at the University of Brazilia?"

Eléazard felt his heart start to pound. A sour taste came up into his mouth. Making an effort to control his voice, he replied in an offhand way, "We're in the middle of a divorce. If we ever were a 'family' it's in a pretty bad way now."

He saw the amused look in Loredana's eyes.

"Oh, do forgive me," the Countess said looking seriously embarrassed. "It's . . . I just thought . . . Oh my God, I really am sorry."

"No harm done, I assure you," he said, smiling at her consternation as if it had surprised him. "It's ancient history by now, or at least well on its way. You know her?"

"Not personally, no. It's my son who spoke about her, he works with her, at the university. But if I'd known, really . . ."

"There's no need to apologize, it's not important, believe me. So you've a son who's a geologist?"

"Yes, and a brilliant one, from what people say. He was chosen to take part in an expedition to the Mato Grosso with your . . . I mean with his professor—Oh, God, I really am confused!—and we've had no news from him since they left. I know there's nothing to fear, but you know how it is, you can't stop yourself worrying."

"I hadn't heard about it. My daughter doesn't tell me anything about her mother. Doubtless she thinks she's being diplomatic, at least that's what I tell myself. But there's no need to worry, my wife—after all, she is still my wife—" he added in a bantering tone, "my wife is very competent, your boy's in safe hands with her . . ."

Loredana observed all this as if she were watching a drawing room comedy. She followed in their wake as a path opened up for the Countess and Eléazard through the crowd of guests. The atmosphere had relaxed: stimulated by the wine, the penguins of both sexes—she clearly recalled their affected airs behind the misted glass in Milan Zoo—seemed less stiff. Having established a sort of territory, they cackled and prattled away with gay abandon, chests puffed out, beaks half-open. They strutted around, they choked with laughter, subject to quiverings and sudden flushes, they confronted each other, crop against crop; under the impassive gaze of the waiters, they revealed important penguin secrets, enjoying a delightful feeling, a mixture of the sense of their own superiority and the pleasure of cornering others in the sad servility of gratitude. The ladies were talking breeding, hatching and nestlings, preening their feathers with knowing looks. A glass accidentally dropped opened up a crater in the throng from which shrill cries flew out but which closed up again almost immediately, like a viscous bubble on the surface of the magma. They discussed strategies for the ice floes, while quaking at the thought of the invisible proximity of killer whales, they worked themselves up into fears as great as the hole in the ozone layer, as torrid as the greenhouse effect, as drenching as global warming. Some were up in arms against the policies of the bears, others, flapping their wings in argument-clinching fashion, denounced the fishes' unreasonable demands or expressed paternal sympathy with the distant and pathetic caricature of the species on the other pole. But they were unanimous in their admiration for the gulls' fantastic ability to fly, not without hinting that there was no doubt that with a little more order, morality and conscientiousness the penguins themselves would have taken flight . . . Everywhere there was the glint of little stupid eyes inside dark rings.

Leaving the entrance hall by a side door, they walked along under the arcades of a gallery covered in the pink effervescence of bougainvillea. With the servants keeping people out, this part of the *fazenda* was deserted and hardly lit, so that the Southern Cross could be clearly seen, isolated amid myriads of less bright stars.

The Countess stopped for a moment to look at the sky. "All these people make me feel sick," she said to Loredana, taking a deep breath of the night air, as if to clear her mind and body of the fumes of the party. "I wouldn't mind a glass of champagne . . . I don't imagine you're in a hurry to see those bloody cars?"

Eléazard offered to go and get a glass and the two women sat on the little wall between the columns. "He's nice," the Countess said when they were alone. "I'm annoyed with myself for saying the wrong thing back there."

"Don't worry, I don't think he was offended. Having said that, he never talks about it, which shows it must still touch a raw nerve."

"Are you an item?"

Surprised by such a direct question, Loredana put her head on one side slightly. "You don't beat about the bush, do you?" she smiled, knitting her brows. After a short pause for thought, she went on, "No, at least not at the moment . . . but to tell the truth, I like him well enough for that to be conceivable . . ."

This declaration left her speechless. She had just expressed, out loud and to someone who was more or less a stranger, a desire she had never admitted so directly to herself yet. While recognizing the reality of her attraction to Eléazard, she was annoyed with herself for having forgotten, if only for a moment, the impossibility of a liaison with him.

"I must be more drunk than I thought to say things like that," she admitted with an embarrassed laugh.

"Don't worry, you're still less drunk than I am," the Countess said, taking her hand. "that's one of the advantages of champagne, it loosens your tongue, or rather, it frees it from the bars imposed on it by convention. I like you, both of you, you'd make a lovely couple."

Almost completely cloaked in the bougainvillea, the governor's wife seemed like a pagan idol, a calm and thoughtful prophetess whose words had the force of an oracle. She must have been very beautiful, Loredana thought, scrutinizing the lines of her face.

"If you knew how weary I am, sick and tired of everything," the Countess suddenly said in a tone of profound helplessness. "I've only met you this evening, but these are things one can only admit in the combined intoxication and miracle of a meeting of minds. My husband doesn't love me anymore, or not enough to stop me from hating him, my son's far away and I'm getting old"—she gave a smile of self-deprecation—"like a pot in a corner of the dresser."

Guessed, other people's distress is almost always moving, even if the emotion only results in purely formal compassion; brazenly expressed, it inevitably provokes irritation. How feeble, Loredana thought, how self-indulgent! What was the bitterness of a grand lady compared with the threat that had been hanging over her for months? Did we have to be irrevocably deprived of our freedom before we could finally see its workings, before we could discover the value of the simple fact of being alive, of still existing?

Disconcerted, she abruptly lit a cigarette in an attempt to prolong the silence rather than continue a conversation she was no longer interested in. However, Carlotta eventually managed to get her to look at her. "Please don't get me wrong," she said in friendly tones, "I'm not looking for your pity. If you'd said the least word along those lines, I'd have left you right away. I'm well aware that we all have to sort out our own problems."

"What is it you want, then?" Loredana asked, somewhat brusquely.

With a smile on her lips, the Countess gave a long sigh expressing maternal patience and indulgence. "Let's say some Italian conversation. Would that suit you?" But her look begged, "Frank, open, irreverent conversation. Young conversation, my child."

CHAPTER 12

In which are described the Kircher Museum &
the magnetic oracle

KIRCHER RESUMED HIS studies, only
breaking off from them to receive people who brought
him curious animal, vegetable or mineral objects, knowing he
was making a collection of them. It was thus that he extended
his harvest of anamorphic rocks considerably; he was given
stones or sections of minerals in which nature herself had
depicted many easily recognizable shapes: dogs, cats, horses,
rams, owls, storks & snakes; men & women could also be clearly
seen in them, sometimes whole towns with all their parts,
their particular domes & belfries. Similarly there were certain
sections of branches or tree trunks that had emblems, portraits,
even scenes illustrating precisely all the fables of Aesop
beautifully engraved on them without recourse to art. The most
precious find in Kircher's eyes was without doubt that series of
twenty-one flints where one could very distinctly see each of the

letters of the Hebrew alphabet formed by the internal structure of the stone!

"The unique language," Kircher said, "the memory of the universal language given by God to Adam, with its magnificent descriptive power & the thousand & one arcana of its numerological structure. See what we can find in the most ordinary pebbles of the road, Caspar. In His divine goodness, the Creator had given us the means of finding Him in objects themselves; for nature has certainly drawn for us this symbolic Ariadne's thread to help us find our way in the labyrinth of the world."

Thanks to Kircher I came to see how the cosmos had been made on the analogy & in the image of the supreme archetype. From the summit down to the tiniest being everything was in absolute proportion and reciprocal conformity & yet, as Saint Paul testified, things invisible could be perceived by our intellect through material things . . .

From that day onward I put my heart even more fully into my work & into our search for the emblematic letters that would help us to go back in time to the origin of things.

"Research," said Kircher, "is collecting. It is to gather together as many of these undeciphered wonders in order to reconstitute the perfection of the initial encyclopedia; it is to reconstruct the Ark with the same concern for completeness & urgency as Noah showed. And I will accomplish this holy task, Caspar. With your aid & God's."

My master confided in me more & more, exhibiting a trust in me of which I ever strove to prove myself worthy. I can testify that at that time, at the age of just thirty-six, he had a view of the world that had reached a state of clarity & complexity that he then simply proceeded to develop. Henceforth *omnia in omnibus*, "everything is in everything," was his motto, meaning that there was no thing in the world that did not correspond to all the others according to a certain proportion & analogy.

We returned to Rome at the end of the summer of 1638 with no adventures worth mentioning apart from our discovery, as we left Calabria, of the fatal effects of the venom of the tarantula & the detailed study of its alexipharmakon. During the few months of our peregrinations, Kircher had acquired incomparable experience and knowledge. He brought back a phenomenal quantity of unique materials to the Roman College & his sole desire was to get down to studying them. During our journey back he had talked to me of the two books that were going through his mind & described his plans in great detail: a *Mundus subterraneus*, dealing with geology and hydrology, & an *Ars magna lucis et umbrae*, which would eclipse, in the field of optics, Kepler's *Paralipomena* & even the *Dioptrique* of the previous year, in which Monsieur Descartes made bold to assert so many arrogant & foolish ideas.

But Pope Urban VIII insisted he give priority to applying his genius to Egypt and deciphering the hieroglyphs. Thus Athanasius had to wait several years before being able to write the works in which he uses the results of our explorations.

During our stay in the south, the collections of the late Sieur Peiresc had finally reached Rome. We spent several months organizing them & arranging them on the floor of the Roman College the Father General of the College had put at Kircher's disposal. Together with everything my master had amassed during our recent voyage, it made a considerable accumulation of all kinds of rarities, especially since the Jesuits in the missions regularly sent him some from the East and West Indies.

Kircher wanted his museum to be the finest & most complete in the world. Not just a more extensive collection of curiosities than those of Paracelsus, Agrippa, Peiresc & others, but a veritable concrete encyclopedia, a display that would give each visitor the possibility of surveying the whole of human knowledge since the origins. The gallery where it was housed was resplendent with costly marble; Athanasius added some Greek & Roman columns, transforming the place into a portico where one could philosophize while walking up & down in the manner of the Stoics. Several classrooms opening off the sides were used to teach various arts & sciences.

My master had five oval panels painted in fresco on the vaults of the vestibule. The first, which greeted the visitor when he entered the museum, showed a salamander surrounded by flames.

"The salamander is me," Kircher told me when I asked him about the meaning of the allegory. "It says that I urge visitors to brave the fire of difficult studies . . ."

I found that entirely appropriate, especially since I had seen my master so at ease in the blazing infernos of Etna and Vesuvius.

The whole of 1639 was spent opening crates & setting the contents out in the embellished gallery. A ship had arrived from China, its hold packed with treasures sent to Kircher by Father Giovanni Filippo de Mariani, a missionary to Japan & China. Rhinoceros horns, ceremonial regalia embroidered in gold, belts adorned with rubies, samples of paper, statues of idols, saints, mandarins, inhabitants of those countries; flowers, birds and trees painted on silk, various drugs unknown to our doctors, especially the one called "Lac Tigridis," various books, manuscripts, grammars, etc.; all these riches poured into the Roman College, increasing the wealth of the museum. As well as that, there were numerous letters sent to Athanasius by his distant & faithful correspondents.

In particular Manuel Diaz, Deputy Provincial of the Order in China, mentioned the recent discovery of a stele, which was going to prove of major importance. On this stone, dug up by chance in 1623 in the course of excavations outside the city of Sian Fu, there was a text written in two languages, Syrian and Chinese. According to Diaz, it was an inscription carved in the year 781 after the death of Our Lord that proved that Nestorians had established themselves in China by that date. Kircher was extremely excited by the discovery that Christians, if only Syrians, had been present at such an early date at the heart of the Chinese Empire. He did not think it necessary to explain why this fact seemed so crucial to him but I did not for one second doubt that this simple letter had helped him take another step in the establishment of a doctrine that he was elaborating day by day.

Beside this letter from Manuel Diaz, our correspondence also included missives from Johann Adam Schall von Bell, the official in charge of introducing a calendar at the court of Emperor Ch'ung-chen, from the painter Johann Grueber, from Michal Piotr Boym & other equally famous missionaries, all of which were packed with marvelous information about that country. They were full of things such as magic or metamorphic mountains that could change or even move to another place, of sea dragons & extremely rare animals, of idols possessed by an evil spirit, of monuments & impassable walls. The missionaries also emphasized the power & antiquity of the Chinese Empire. They seemed fascinated by a people so different from ours & yet so advanced in numerous fields while still immersed in the most odious idolatry. The Jesuit who had accompanied the cargo on the boat had managed to keep an 'ananas' plant alive by giving it his own ration of water; Kircher pronounced the fruit absolutely delicious. The flesh beneath the skin is a little fibrous, but it dissolves entirely into juice in the mouth. Also its taste is so pronounced & so distinctive that those who tried to describe it precisely, finding it impossible to do so without having recourse

to comparison, cited everything that was most exquisite about
the aubergine, the apricot, the strawberry, the raspberry, the
muscat grape & the orange pippin, & having said that, they were
forced to admit that in addition it has a certain taste that could
not be expressed & that is restricted to it alone.

All that, combined with the perpetual persecution to which
the Jesuit missionaries were subjected in their work of propagating
the faith, convinced my master that he should go & join them. At
the beginning of 1640 he asked the Father General to authorize
him to leave for the East to devote himself to the conversion of the
Chinese. I was as excited as Athanasius at the idea of devoting my
life to God & to the Church, but Providence decided otherwise:
Kircher's request was refused on the express order of the Pope,
who did not want to lose such an estimable man at any price.
Despite what he admitted to me was a great disappointment,
Athanasius submitted to the orders of his superiors with good
grace while showing even greater interest than ever in everything
he could learn about these distant countries.

At the age of thirty-eight my master seemed at the pinnacle
of his powers. He was working on several books at once, mixing
all subjects, throwing light on all the disciplines of human
knowledge without, for all that, giving up his teaching of
mathematics & oriental languages, or forgetting the practical
application of his discoveries. Professor, astronomer, physician,
geologist & geographer, specialist in languages, archaeologist,
Egyptologist, theologian, etc., he was the man all the great
minds of his age wanted to talk to & none came to Rome
without asking for an audience with him.

The porter was therefore constantly climbing the College
stairs to his study to inform him of the presence of this or
that visitor. Since this brother was old & decrepit, Kircher
thought up a device to spare him such exertions, which were

incompatible with his age. He installed a copper pipe going from the porter's lodge to his desk six floors up; fixed to each end was a metal funnel to amplify their voices. Running down inside the pipe was a wire, which the porter could pull to sound a Javanese gong close to the place where my master was, informing him that the porter wished to speak to him. This invention worked perfectly & the porter thanked Athanasius a thousand times for his generosity. But my master had to remonstrate with him several times: he took such delight in using the machine for trivial reasons that he was disturbing Kircher in his studies.

In 1641 *Magnes, sive de Arte Magnetica* appeared, a book of nine hundred and sixteen pages in which Kircher returned to the questions he dealt with in his *Ars Magnesi*, published in Würzburg in 1631, augmenting it with numerous other examples, making it a definitive treatment of the subject. This attraction, which is so clear to see between beings & things, & so similar to the mysterious force present in the lodestone, Kircher attributed to universal magnetism. Once more analogy turned out to be invaluable, the sympathetic power drawing a magnetized needle to the north being merely an illustration of the far greater power uniting the microcosm with the macrocosm, as Hermes the Egyptian had established in far-off times. The irresistible attraction or repulsion that sometimes appears between a man & a woman, the force that guides the bee to the flower or makes the sunflower turn toward the Sun showed the same phenomenon at work on earth & in the skies: the power of God, the absolute magnet of the universe.

"The world," my master said, "is protected by secret ties & one of them is universal magnetism, which governs both the relationships between men & those that exist between animals, vegetables, the Sun & the Moon. Even minerals are subject to this occult force."

In this book Kircher also describes the "magnetic oracle," which he had designed for the Supreme Pontiff & had constructed in advance so as to be able to give it to him at the same time as the description. I was there the first time this curious machine was put into operation, in the presence of Cardinal Barberini, whom my master had asked to come and judge whether such a gift was appropriate.

You must imagine a hexagonal table with, towering up in the center, the reproduction of an Egyptian obelisk containing inside it a very big lodestone. Arranged around the table, one at each side, were six large crystal spheres, each harboring a cherub made of wax & hanging free on a thread. Between these spheres were a dozen smaller ones, constructed on the same model but with figurines representing mythological animals. These twelve figures also had a magnet inside them & each was in balance with the others in relation to the central stone. Finally, different systems such as the Latin alphabet, the zodiac, the elements, the winds & their directions were painted around each of the large spheres. A cursor on the edge of the table made it possible to turn the lodestone in the obelisk to a greater or lesser extent, which disrupted the balance between the figures & made them move until the balance of their magnetism was restored in a different position. The outstretched arms of the "putti," or cherubs, would then point to a particular constellation or letter of the alphabet, thus answering the questions the operator had asked.

"It's just a toy," Kircher told the Cardinal, "but I maintain that a man who is truly in harmony with nature, that is to say at one with the magnetic forces controlling it, could make excellent use of this machine & produce oracles worthy of belief."

"I can readily believe that," said Cardinal Barberini, his sparkling eyes showing his interest in my master's machine, "but it is a dangerous gamble for anyone who tries it; the machine only has to give a nonsensical reply to some question & the one who asked it would be consigned to the herd of the uninitiated, not to say ignoramuses."

"True," Kircher said with a smile, "but such an unfortunate person would always be free to blame the machine itself, in which case its inventor would defend it by arguing that it was only designed for amusement & that God alone knows the purposes of Providence."

"Indeed, my friend," the Cardinal said, also smiling. "Still, out of pure curiosity I would very much like to see you try it out."

"Your wish is my command, Monsignore. Now let us see, what question shall I ask this glass pythoness?" Kircher concentrated for a while, then his face lit up. "Does this toy, produced by my imagination to illustrate the secret powers of nature, have access to the truth? That is my question. I will therefore put it to the alphabetical sphere in order to get a written response. Caspar, a blindfold, a pen & some paper."

I hurried to fetch the objects my master had asked for from a servant. Then I had to blindfold him &, after the Cardinal had checked that he could not see, sit him down facing the cursor. Athanasius moved it. All the little figures started to revolve jerkily. When, after a few seconds, they were back in balance, the Cardinal announced the letter "N." I immediately noted it down, while my master operated the cursor a second time.

After a half hour of this, Kircher, exhausted by the effort of concentration it demanded, declared that he would stop there & removed his blindfold. Cardinal Barberini took the sheet of paper from me &, in a half-amused, half-sardonic voice, read out the following as if he were reading a verse from the Gospel: "*natu ranatu ragau deth . . .*"

"There, Reverend Father," he said, handing the paper to my master, "is a perfect illustration of what I was saying just now. I'm afraid you are not quite in tune with the Universal Lodestone."

Kircher frowned & I blushed for him, less at his failure—which was, after all, foreseeable—than at the prelate's acid remark.

In silence, my master read again the sibylline text the machine had produced &, still without saying a word, calmly took up the pen, drew four lines on the sheet & handed it back to the Cardinal.

However, dear reader, if you want to learn the surprising consequences of this action, you will have to wait until the next chapter . . .

ON THE RIVER PARAGUAY: *For a moment it seemed as if the forest were crying for her*

Once the gunboat had passed the nest of machine guns, the burst of fire became less accurate, then stopped: overconfident, the hunters only controlled the river downstream; the straight arm of the river, which widened out up to their camp, curved upstream of it, reducing the firing angle. It took a few seconds before Petersen realized he was confusing the hammering of the motor with the sound of automatic rifles. Recovering from the shock of the attack, he cautiously stood up. The boat was now out of range, but a plume of thick smoke was rising from the rear deck . . . *the fire extinguisher!* He dashed off toward the bridge, stumbling over Dietlev, who was lying on the floor, grimacing and groaning, clutching in both hands a bloody mass of pulp which he seemed to be trying to compress with all his strength . . . Herman swore silently, then leaned over the guardrail: "Up here, you two," he shouted to Mauro and Elaine. "Dietlev's been wounded, he needs a tourniquet. Get your asses up here, for God's sake."

Petersen continued on his way. The sheets of steel all around him were vibrating as if the whole structure were about to fall apart at any moment. "Slow down, you stupid bastard!" he yelled as he came to the wheelhouse. "Shut off the engine!"

Since Yurupig, paralyzed at the helm, didn't move, he reduced the throttle himself.

The gunboat continued to make headway, wallowing in the water.

"Where's Hernando?" Petersen asked, taking down the fire extinguisher. Almost simultaneously he saw the body of the Paraguayan: in the shadow on the other side of the wheelhouse, his eyes apparently staring in wonder into space, the man was lying on his back, his throat cut.

"I don't believe it," Herman stammered, feeling sick. "Fucking hell, what on earth got into you?"

Yurupig turned his head toward him, but just stared at him for a few seconds like a delirious priest, a madman on the edge of catalepsy.

"We'll sort that out later," Petersen said, all the more viciously, as he felt intimidated. "For now you leave it in gear and continue to go upriver slowly. Understood?"

Back on the rear deck, he wrapped an old cloth around his hand before opening the hatch to the hold. At the indraft the fire, which was smoldering under the deck, flared up, but Petersen sprayed the contents of the extinguisher on it until the blaze was put out. *A piece of luck this old thing worked . . .*

"Right, that's that," he muttered. *Inspect the tanks once the smoke's dispersed . . . For the moment he had to see to Dietlev. In a bad way, if you wanted his opinion.*

Milton's body, all twisted from the bullets, came to mind. He'd seen enough corpses in his life to recognize the improbable angle of death. *He'd had it, he could wait . . .*

"Herman!" Mauro shouted, running to meet him. There was urgency in his voice.

"What is it now?"

"A leak! Follow me, quick!"

Petersen followed him as he hurried to the top. One glance told him the extent of the damage: the water had reached the table in the cabin.

"The bastards, the fucking bastards! That was all we needed!"

"Get a move on," Mauro urged. "Where are the pumps?"

"Too late. We'll never manage to stem the inflow . . . We'll have to run aground, and quick."

Mauro grabbed Petersen by the arm. "The life jackets?"

"There aren't any. Warn the others and let me get on with it, OK?"

Once back in the wheelhouse, Petersen took the helm from Yuru-pig and examined the river in front: on that section of the Rio Paraguay the right bank's nothing but a marsh, a vast expanse of gorse and aquatic plants, impossible to land there; on the other bank, however—for a hundred yards at most—the whitish color of the water indicated shallows, alongside the forest. Wondering what was the best way of landing, Herman turned the wheel and accelerated to force the boat, already too heavy to be maneuverable, to point its prow in that direction. The gunboat was so slow to respond, he opened the throttle fully and headed straight for the sandbank.

WHEN PETERSEN CALLED for help, Elaine was still in a state of shock; huddled up in Mauro's arms, she was drifting, immersed in a flood of disjointed images, her sole sensation that of her skirt wet at the crotch. Dietlev's name in combination with a tourniquet had the effect of a slap on the face; on her feet at once, she rushed over to the gangway ladder, acting instinctively but determined to face up to the challenge.

"Go and find the first-aid kit," she said to Mauro as soon as she'd examined Dietlev's leg. "In trunk 6, with the maps . . . But do hurry, please!"

Without paying him any further attention, she undid her blouse and, with a trick only women can manage, pulled out her brassiere. She then proceeded to tie this improvised tourniquet around Dietlev's thigh, fairly high up underneath his shorts, and pulled it tight until it stopped the spasmodic flow adding to the pool of blood around him.

"It'll be all right," she said, taking Dietlev's hand.

Clenching his jaws, his face flushed with pain, he managed to sketch a smile. "It's bad?"

"Impressive, that's all. No need to panic."

She kept her eye open for Mauro; finally she saw him coming back with the first-aid kit.

"It's a real mess down there," he said, showing her his soaking trousers. There's water up to the berths, I'll have to go and tell Petersen . . ."

"OK," she said, opening the bag Dietlev had prepared in Brazilia.

To think she'd made fun of the obsessive care with which he'd gone about choosing and organizing the contents . . . *That thing's a real Pandora's box! We'll be in a pretty bad way when we get back even if only a hundredth of the mishaps you're preparing for happen . . . Now then, don't be negative, he'd replied with a laugh. God is great, as they say in Brazil, but the forest's even greater. I'll remind you of that, when the time comes. You'll be glad you can find what you're looking for, even if it's only for a scratch . . .*

She knew the procedure more or less; all those pages on first aid were perhaps going to be some use after all. Nervously tearing open several envelopes with sterile compresses, she moistened them with antiseptic and bent over the wound. *Clean it, find the artery, bind with a ligature, don't touch the nerves . . .* At the first contact Dietlev could not repress a cry. She pulled her hand away and looked at him with concern.

"Go on," he managed to say. "Ignore me."

She continued cleaning, concentrating on the bloodiest part of the knee. The joint was crushed, transformed into bloody pulp. *Meu Deus! They'll never be able to stick that back together again . . .* She was getting annoyed, swearing in a low voice.

"Get the clamp," Dietlev said with a grimace. "The pliers that look like a pair of scissors . . . That's it. Now loosen the tourniquet, you'll see it better . . ."

The wound started to bubble in brief spurts.

"It looks as if it's coming from behind," she said, sponging up the blood as it came, "No . . . Ah, there it is!"

She'd just noticed the section of pink tube, fluted like a chicken's esophagus, out of which the blood was pumping. Concentrating on what she was doing, she slipped one of the jaws under the artery, checked she wasn't taking anything that looked like a nerve, and closed the clamp until the catch engaged. The hemorrhaging stopped.

Mauro returned just at the moment when the boat started to go at full speed again. "We're going to run aground," he warned.

"Help me hold his leg," she said immediately, not without noticing his somewhat stunned look.

"Elaine . . ." Dietlev said in a faint voice.

She leaned close to him so she could hear better.

"Have I told you before you've got beautiful breasts?"

Blushing to her ears, she clumsily tried to close her blouse. His eyes fixed on her chest, Mauro was smiling, a stupid look on his face, like a child who's just seen Father Christmas.

PETERSEN WAITED UNTIL the last moment before disengaging the clutch. Its impetus took the gunboat three or four yards onto the sandbank, where it listed slightly to starboard before coming to a standstill.

"A neat piece of work," the old German said, proud of his maneuver. Then he cut out the engine and switched on the electric pumps. "Go forward," he said to Yurupig, "and try to find these blasted leaks."

When he came back down to the gangway, Elaine was just finishing binding Dietlev's artery with the ligature. "How is he?" he asked.

"He'll pull through," she said coldly, "but it was less a . . ."

She took a syringe out of its case, pierced the rubber stopper of a little vial with the needle and started to draw up the contents. Dietlev had noted the nature and method of administering the medicines on all the labels so that she'd had no difficulty finding what she needed.

"What about Milton?" Dietlev asked as Elaine injected the morphine in his arm.

"Dead," Petersen replied curtly. "I've just been to have a look."

Elaine paused for the fraction of a second. A painful silence took hold of the little group in which the feeling of guilt at having forgotten Milton mingled with the sudden awareness of his tragic death.

"Mauro, could you boil some water for me please? I've got to finish cleaning this. Then we'll have to take him down and make him more comfortable."

"Right," said Herman, "I'll go and have a look around to check the damage before night falls."

"One moment!" said Elaine. "That guy . . . I mean the Paraguayan?"

Petersen indicated his fate with an extremely expressive gesture. "Yurupig . . . He didn't have a chance."

FOLLOWING THE INDIAN, Herman went around the holds with a torch. He was furious when he emerged: the machine guns had made an unbelievable number of holes and tears that were impossible to plug. It was a miracle they'd stayed afloat for so long. Even with welding equipment it would take several days to patch up the boat. Herman hurried to the stern, but once he saw the condition of the rubber dinghy—a shapeless mass three-quarters submerged—he immediately sized up their situation. "Help me," he said to Yurupig, "we'll haul it aboard."

It was like a sieve, beyond repair as well. As for the outboard motor, it had not only been stuck under water, a direct hit had torn it apart. Yurupig shook his head. "Nothing we can do. The cylinder head's split."

"A fine mess you've got us into!" Petersen exclaimed. "Stupid fucking *indio*! What are we going to do now, eh? You tell me that."

Mauro's calm voice was heard behind them: "Stop your bickering and come and help us. We need a piece of wood or something rigid to immobilize his leg."

"I'll see to it," said Yurupig. "Start bringing the mattresses up to dry them out. The hammocks too . . ."

"And what else?" Herman said, beside himself. "I'm the one who gives the orders on this boat."

"Stop shouting, for God's sake," said Mauro, taking him by the arm. "He's right. As for giving orders, that's all over. I'd say you've shown us what you can do . . ."

Taken aback by his firmness, Petersen followed him down into the interior. There was no water left in the saloon, but everything was higgledy-piggledy: books and papers transformed into revolting sponges, splinters of glass, soaking cushions . . . countless objects swept away by the flooding were scattered around in the most unlikely places. The cabins hadn't been spared either, but on the top bunks they found three foam-rubber mattresses and a few blankets that were almost dry. The rest they spread out on the rail.

Meanwhile Yurupig had brought two small planks cut out of a crate lid and one of the webbing straps used to keep the tin

WHERE TIGERS ARE AT HOME

trunks tightly closed. Once she had the splints, Elaine set about seeing to Dietlev's leg. As a result of the morphine he was so fast asleep that she had no difficulty immobilizing it satisfactorily. Then Yurupig made arrangements to move him: after having tied both ends of the strap together, he pushed it under Dietlev's buttocks, leaving a broad loop on either side; then he lay on his back between Dietlev's legs, slipped his arms through the loops, as if he were putting on a rucksack, and turned over onto his front. Once in that position, with all the weight of Dietlev's body on his shoulders, he used one knee to lever himself up and got slowly to his feet. Not long after, he performed the same maneuver in reverse to put Dietlev down on a makeshift bed at the rear of the boat.

Elaine flopped down beside Dietlev. She had started to tremble and felt she was going to be sick. For a moment it seemed as if the forest were crying for her.

Under a blazing sky, the evening breeze began to raise little waves on the river.

"WE HAVE TO talk," said Herman with a somber air. "The boat is beyond repair, the same goes for the Zodiac. We're all of us up shit creek, I can tell you. It's no use waiting here, no one'll come . . . It would be possible to build a raft to go back down to Corumbá, but you know what's waiting for us a bit downstream. Those guys would shoot us like rabbits, that you can be sure of. That leaves the forest, which is at least as dangerous . . . but it's the only solution if we want to get out of here."

"Why not continue upstream on a raft?" Mauro asked.

Petersen gave a contemptuous shrug. "The current's too strong. Even if we did manage to build a raft that would more or less float, we'd never be able to go upstream on it."

"But they will eventually get worried," Mauro went on. "They can always send someone in from the north, from Cáceres, for example, or even from Cuiabá, can't they?"

"Who are 'they'? Here it's every man for himself. And my wife won't get worried, sometimes I'm away for several weeks on business. By the time she does, we'll all be long since dead."

"But we've enough provisions for quite a length of time," Elaine broke in, "and afterward we can always get by with fishing, or even hunting . . ."

"Oh, that's no problem, missie. It's not the grub I'm worried about, it's the water. When the jerricans are empty—and quite a few have bullet holes—all that'll be left will be river water, which leaves us the choice: die of thirst or of dysentery. That's for certain."

Elaine had read enough about tropical diseases to see that he was right. "And what are our chances of getting through the forest?"

"For you, none at all. It would be too hard, you're not used to it; him either," he said with a glance at Mauro. "Not to mention our friend; disabled as he is, it's unthinkable. No, what I suggest is that I go with Yurupig to find help. The fork in the river isn't that far, three or four days on foot, perhaps less, and once we're there I'm sure there'll be no problem finding someone to come and fetch you. At the very worst we'll have to go up as far as Pôrto Aterradinho."

Elaine hadn't even started to consider the disaster from this angle, but the arguments Petersen put forward seemed irrefutable. Relieved at not having to face the jungle, she was about to accept this solution, when her eye met Yurupig's. Slightly behind Petersen and without moving a muscle of his face, he was shaking his head rapidly to tell her to refuse.

"You keep out of this, I warn you," Herman immediately said, turning to the Indian. "Well," he said to Elaine, "what do you think?"

310

"It's not a decision I can make alone. I'll have to discuss it with Dietlev first, once he's woken up. And Mauro will have his say too, of course."

"As you wish," Petersen said with a suspicious look. "But there's nothing to discuss, believe me. I'm off tomorrow morning, anyway."

"You'll do what you're told to do and that's that," Elaine said in a steady voice. "That's what you've been paid for, and pretty generously paid too, from what I understand."

A flash of anger appeared in Petersen's eyes, but he merely gave a silent laugh, as if he'd glimpsed a comic sequel to the discussion. "I'm going to have a bite to eat and then get some sleep," he said, controlling his temper. "And you'd be well advised to do the same, *senhora* . . . Oh, by the way, I've put Milton's things in your trunk."

"What things?"

"What he had on him. I chucked them both in the water, him and the other bastard. A matter of hygiene, you understand."

Necrosis, the stench of corpses, caymans and piranhas falling on a naked body . . . She felt a quiver of disgust run across the back of her neck. "How could you!" she burst out indignantly. "Who authorized you to do a thing like that?"

"No one, *senhora*," Petersen said in honeyed tones and as if he were talking to a madwoman, "no one at all, I assure you . . ."

Eléazard's notebooks

KIRCHER's a common manipulator. He tampers with facts until they make sense. His clear conscience is no excuse. The propagation of the faith, propaganda, distortion of history, etc.—the sequence is only too well known. The certainty of being in the right is always a sign of a secret vocation for fascism.

I ASKED SOLEDADE IF, out of the goodness of her heart, she could give the library shelves a quick dusting: a categorical refusal. Even though it's dead she's terrified of the bird-eating spider I brought back from Quixadá.

A STORY FROM LOREDANA: A young Italian, on holiday in London, being taken home by car after a boozy night. It's summer and he opens his window and sticks his arm out to drum his fingers on the roof of the vehicle. The car goes into a spin, overturns. After the accident, there's nothing wrong with him apart from a bit of blood on his sleeves; he feels no pain, his pals are unharmed. Relieved, he shakes his hand in the gesture of a person who's got off lightly and his fingers fly off onto the tarmac.

KIRCHER'S COLLECTION as an anamorphosis of Kircher himself. Less of a museum than a curiosity shop, like that of Dr. Azoux with his papier-mâché models.

LETTER TO MALBOIS: add confirmation of details on La Mothe Le Vayer.

A HISTORIAN, historians say, is at least capable of grasping the style of an age, something that could only arise at a certain time and in a certain place. But that is an illusion; a historian can only grasp the difference from the reflection of his own times. He holds up a bronze mirror to the past, eagerly looking for distortions.

"COPULATION with animals," Albert Camus notes, "eliminates our awareness of the other. It is 'freedom.' That's why it is attractive to lots of minds, even including Balzac."

THE VERY END OF THE SIXTEENTH CENTURY: "In consideration of the criminal proceedings, charges and information, the interrogations, replies and confessions of the accused, confrontations with witnesses, conclusions of the aforesaid prosecutor; of the replies and confessions of the accused made in the presence of his lawyer and everything that has been placed before us, we declare the aforesaid Legaigneux guilty in fact and in law of copulation with a female donkey belonging to the same. As public atonement for this crime we condemn him to be hanged and strangled by the executioner, from a gallows that will be erected in such and such a place; and before this death sentence is carried out, the aforesaid female donkey will be stunned and killed by the aforesaid executioner at the aforesaid place, in the presence of the accused."

If the animal is punished it is because it shares responsibility for the act with the man: the man guilty of sodomy has stooped to the level of brute beasts, but the donkey committed the unpardonable crime of raising itself to the level of thinking beings. They are both "against nature." By betraying the laws of their species, they equally endanger the order of the world.

THE VERY END OF THE TWENTIETH CENTURY: "Accused of attempted sodomy with a dolphin called Freddie, Alan Cooper, 38, justified the act by saying that he was only masturbating the animal to gain its friendship. His lawyers based his defense on the fact that dolphins are notoriously licentious and are some of the rare animals who indulge in the sex act purely for pleasure. Alan Cooper risks ten years in prison if the charge of *clear intention of rectal or vaginal penetration* is accepted and life if sodomy is *proved beyond reasonable doubt*." (Newcastle upon Tyne, England.)

WHY DOES SCHOTT use Latin for the lewd passages when the language was understood by the majority of readers of his time? This false sense of decency is indecent.

IN GENERAL THE PROBLEM of the labyrinth is posed in terms of escaping: once one is in it, one has to find the way out. The labyrinth designed by Kircher seems to invert the question in that it doesn't lead anywhere. The heart is inaccessible. The pointlessness of Ariadne's thread: a true labyrinth should be devised from the center, it is a space that is totally cut off from the outside; an allegory of the brain, of its convolutions, of its impenetrable solitude. It takes a Daedalus to fly away from the labyrinth, but it also takes a Daedalus to kill the Minotaur in it.

THE XIAN STELE: For Kircher it's absolute proof that China was Christian before becoming Buddhist or Confucian. The remains of an Atlantis of the true faith suddenly appearing on the surface of the earth, it's enough just to point at them and the idolators will remember their lost paradise. The utopia of the perfect city is not situated in the future, as it is for More or Campanella, but in the most distant past.

TO BRING THE INVISIBLE INTO EXISTENCE: Euclides asking me to imagine an unfathomable abyss between us and finishing up crossing it with one great stride to join me. "You never know, do you . . ."

CHAPTER 13

In which is shown how Kircher surpassed Leonardo da Vinci
& caused the feline race to contribute to the most marvelous
of concerts . . .

"N A T U R A / N A T U R A / G A U D E T / H /,
natura natura gaudet!" the Cardinal read out in great
surprise, "'nature rejoices in nature' . . . That is truly marvelous
& I beg you to forgive me the irony I permitted myself just now.
Send your machine to the supreme pontiff within the hour, he
will be charmed by it, of that I'm sure. As for myself, I can only
beg you to make another one of the same ilk for me. You can rest
assured I will not be ungrateful . . ."

Athanasius promised the Cardinal he would do his best
& seemed very satisfied with the outcome of this meeting.
His credit continued to grow among the highest echelons of
the Church, ensuring that he had the freedom & resources
that were essential for his work. My master made me more
and more of a partner in it & during the two following years

I assisted him every day in his research into the meaning of
the hieroglyphs; except in 1642 when, for my glory and a few
minor aftereffects, my master developed a passionate interest
in the science of the air.

This adventure originated in a conversation with Nicholas
Poussin, who had come to see him in order to improve his
command of the difficult art of perspective. Leafing through one
of the codices of Leonardo da Vinci, which had most graciously
been lent him by Sieur Raphaël Trichet du Fresne, the librarian
of Queen Christina of Sweden, Kircher was struck by the flying
machine devised by the Florentine.

"Despite my great admiration for Leonardo," Poussin said, "I
have to admit that he sometimes flouted the most elementary
laws of physics. He was a dreamer of genius, but a dreamer all
the same—it's obvious that the air is too sparse & too weak to
support the weight of a man's body, however big his wings."

Kircher shook his head. "No, Monsieur, definitely not! Just
consider the way geese & other large birds flap their wings when
they want to take off & fly, & the weight of paper and wood that
can be made to glide by pulling them with a string, & perhaps
you will change your mind. I am convinced a man can rise
up into the air, provided he has wings that are large & strong
enough & has sufficient strength to beat the air as needed;
which could be done with certain springs, which would make
the wings move as quickly & as strongly as necessary.

"It is a persuasive argument, Reverend Father, but you will
allow me to dispute it as long as, like Saint Thomas, I have not
seen a man rise up into the air with my own eyes."

'That doesn't matter," my master said, "I will take up the
challenge & we will meet again in three months, the time it will
take me to carry out certain preliminary experiments. But I
insist that it is definitely no more difficult to fly than to swim;

& just as that seems child's play once it has been learned—even though one would have thought it impossible—we will consider the art of flying quite natural once we have practiced it."

Monsieur Poussin left that evening, dazzled by Athanasius's self-assurance, but far from convinced. For my part, I had such confidence in my master that I did not doubt for one moment that he would succeed. I was in a fever of excitement at the idea of flying up into the skies & I pestered Kircher so much that he agreed to grant my desire to be the first man to perform that feat.

The few weeks that followed are the most beautiful I can remember. We abandoned our studies to devote ourselves entirely to this project. Cardinal Barberini and Signore Manfredo Settala were enthusiastic about my master's undertaking; they advanced the funds necessary & the craftsmen set to work. Three weeks sufficed for the completion of the most astonishing thing seen for decades: it was like a huge bat with no body, an eighteen-foot wingspan covered in white feathers fixed to a framework of canes. The device was fitted to my shoulders by a system of straps & once it was on my back I realized I was able to move the wings without too much effort, though slowly.

"The great eagles of Tartary are like that," Kircher assured me, "they only take off slowly & with dignity, using the strength of the wind. Don't worry, Caspar, this machine has been designed not to lift itself up from the ground by its own force, but to move though the air once it has been carried up there."

One week later everything was ready. Kircher summoned Poussin, Cardinal Barberini & Signore Settala to the top of Castel Sant'Angelo, from which, it had been decided, I was to take off. It was a pleasant June day; a gentle breeze hardly made the leaves stir & I was very excited at the idea of being the first man finally to achieve this old dream of the human race.

"I chose this particular place," Athanasius explained to his guests, "so that my brave assistant, Father Schott, can land without harm in the waters of the Tiber, in the unlikely case— although a setback can never be excluded—that some adversity will force him to break off his flight. Father Schott being unable to swim, I have provided him with balloons filled with air, which will easily support him in the liquid element."

Having said that, he had two translucent waterskins—pigs' stomachs, as it seemed to me—which he tied on either side of my waist. Then I was harnessed & had to beat my wings several times while my master checked they were working properly. The three men were enraptured at the ingenious arrangement of this mechanism.

For the first time I became aware of the serious position in which my thoughtlessness had placed me: a fearful abyss yawned beneath my feet & the Tiber down below seemed tiny . . . Pictures of my previous fall, during one of the first trials, crowded my memory; I was sweating abundantly & as the strength drained from my arms, my legs began to tremble piteously. I was terrified.

"Off you go, Caspar," my master suddenly cried in grandiloquent tones, "& may the day come when your fame will outshine that of Icarus!"

For a fraction of a second the mention of that unfortunate hero seemed an ill omen, but as Athanasius had accompanied his words of encouragement with a friendly & vigorous push on my calves, I lost my balance &, rather than simply fall, I launched myself into the void.

It was the most extraordinary feeling of my whole life: freed from the fetters of my body, I was gliding like a seagull, or like a sparrow-hawk circling above its prey. However, this pleasurable sensation did not last long; I realized that I was in

fact rapidly losing height & that, far from gliding, as I thought,
I was well & truly falling, although more slowly than if I had
not been wearing my false wings. The waters of the Tiber were
approaching rapidly &, terrified, panic-stricken by the horror of
my situation, I tried to beat my wings with the energy of despair.
My fear was so great that I managed to move them several times
without, however, raising myself higher at all. The only result
of my efforts was, thanks be to Heaven, to slow down my fall a
little. Not enough, though, to stop me plunging into the Tiber in
a manner that I would have wished were more dashing. My last
conscious act was to recommend my soul to God before I had
the sensation of crashing into a surface as hard as marble . . .

When I came to, several hours later, I was lying in my bed in
the Roman College with both legs fractured in several places &
numerous bruises. The tormented expression on Kircher's face
told me that coming to my senses was more of a resurrection
than a simple awakening.

When I was fully conscious again, my first words were
to express my concern about the Cardinal's reaction and to
apologize to Kircher for a failure that would do such damage to
his reputation. It was not the machine that was at fault, but the
weakness of my constitution & the panic that had paralyzed me,
thus ruining the hopes founded on this project; I was unworthy
of the trust my master had placed in me & I could not forgive
myself for the boastfulness with which I had claimed a role
so obviously beyond my modest powers, & to tell the truth it
would have been better had I perished during my fall as a just
punishment for my sin of pride . . .

Kircher would not let me go on: I was wrong about everything,
since the project, far from being a setback, had succeeded beyond
his wildest hopes. After expressing their natural concern about
my fate, his guests had commended my exploit. A body thrown

from the ramparts of Castel Sant'Angelo would have fallen
straight down & crashed into the moat, while the artificial
wings had allowed me to make progress through the air &
reach the Tiber. So flight had been achieved, thus proving that
man could rival the eagles; all that remained was to add certain
improvements to the machine & train future pilots sufficiently.
The problem was no longer one of physics, but of technology,
& the human mind had always shown its skill in surmounting
problems of that order. The years to come would see to it that they
perfected what had been merely sketched out in this experiment:
one day we would fly as far, as high & as swiftly as the most agile
birds of prey. And I was the one who, through my courage & my
faith, had procured this certainty for our century . . . Moreover,
Cardinal Barberini had sent his personal physician to care for me
&, combining charity with generosity, proposed to continue to
fund from his own purse the flight trials with prisoners who had
been condemned to death, thus offering those poor wretches an
unhoped-for opportunity of saving their lives.

These comforting words gave me the strength & the patience
to endure being confined to my bed. Monsieur Poussin came
to see me several times, bringing me albums of sketches or
prints, & we spent many pleasant hours chatting about painting.
The Cardinal himself once did me the honor of coming to see
me. He repeated word for word what Kircher had told me &
congratulated me again on my bravery and selflessness. As
for my master, he came to see me as often as his numerous
occupations would allow. Nothing that would make my life
pleasant was too much for him: he read to me, told me stories
about China or the Indians of Maranhão & kept me informed
about his progress in deciphering the hieroglyphics. He even
went so far as to invent an unusual musical instrument with the
sole aim of amusing me.

Thus it was that one fine morning, toward the end of my convalescence, I was taken from my room to the Great Hall of the College. All the fathers & their students were gathered there & I was greeted with an ovation worthy of a person of consequence. It was only after I had settled down on a sofa that I noticed the imposing organ case that had been brought into the hall. Oddly enough, no pipes could be seen jutting out above the case, which was elaborately decorated with rustic scenes. Kircher sat down at the console and played a lively air by our old friend Girolamo Frescobaldi: the sound that came from the organ was that of a harpsichord & I was wondering why such a sizeable piece of furniture was necessary to house a mechanism that was, after all, not particularly bulky, when my master, with an amused look on his face, announced, "And now the same composition, but using the bioharmonic pedals!"

His feet immediately started flying over the pedals &, to general hilarity, produced the strangest concert of caterwauling that had ever been heard. Even stranger was the fact that this arrangement of animal cries reproduced the graceful air he had previously played; it was perfectly recognizable, including the most subtle harmonies. Like all my colleagues in the hall, I was enraptured.

Once Athanasius had finished there were many who wanted to try this instrument, the fruit of my master's inexhaustible genius. Each piece that was played produced new comic effects & nothing was more hilarious than to play in the upper registers. Afterward Kircher showed us some compositions of his own, asking Johann Jakob Froberger, the most gifted musican among us, to play them on the harpsichord.

Even in this simple amusement, Kircher had employed all his knowledge & skill. Once opened, the organ case revealed an exceedingly complex mechanism. When one of the pedals was depressed, an excellent transmission system operated a kind of hammer that suddenly came down on the tail of a cat strapped to a wooden plate. All the cats making up the two octaves of this instrument had been carefully selected by Athanasius for their natural ability to meow on a certain note. They were enclosed in little boxes, which only allowed their tails to stick out, & even if they did not seem particularly happy at the treatment to which they were subjected, they played their part perfectly.

If I had not already been well on the way to a complete recovery, such a concert would have cured me, I believe, as effectively as a tarantella!

I resumed my studies with gusto & toward the end of 1643 Kircher published his *Lingua Aegyptica Restituita*. This book of six hundred and seventy-two pages contained, apart from the Arabic-Coptic dictionary brought back many years ago by Pietro della Valle, a complete grammar of that language & confirmation of the thesis put forward in his *Prodomus Copticus*: namely that the hieroglyphs were the symbolic expression of Egyptian wisdom, the priests having refused to use the common language, that is Coptic, to express their most sacred dogmas . . .

Kircher now had no doubts that he had mastered the hieroglyphs. He did not provide the key to them in this publication, but acknowledged that he had advanced toward it thanks to the assistance of a mysterious corespondent, to whom he dedicated the book, as he also did to all Arab and Egyptian scholars, the sole heirs to & possessors of the ancient language.

The year 1644 was decisive. After the death of Pope Urban VIII, Cardinal Pamphilius succeeded him under the name of Innocent X. To celebrate his election, this worthy son of an illustrious family, whose palace had since the fifteenth century been in the Circus Agonalis, the former Stadium of Domitian, decided to complete the restoration of that place & to make it a memorial to his family & to his name. To that end he commissioned the famous Lorenzo Bernini to design a fountain, the center of which would be the great obelisk that had been lying along the Appian Way since time immemorial.

Our Superior General, Father Vincent Caraffa, had taken it upon himself to inform the Pope of Kircher's learning & it was naturally to him the Supreme Pontiff turned to design this project.

"Reverend Father," the Pope had said during their interview, "we have decided to erect a very tall obelisk & it will be your task to study the hieroglyphs carved on it. We would like you, who have inherited so many talents from God, to give yourself heart & soul to this task, doing everything in your power to ensure that those who are amazed at the scale of this project, will come to understand, through your agency, the secret signification of the inscriptions. In addition, you will guide the architect, Bernini, in the choice of symbols that will be the theme of this fountain, taking care to see that the work is carried out with the appropriate spiritual rigor. May God go with you."

CANOA QUEBRADA: *With no other*
cutting edge than fire and flint

When the alarm on his wristwatch woke him, the first thing Roetgen did was to look at Moéma's hammock: it was hanging there, slack and empty as a snake's slough. Thaïs's face appeared from hers, puffy and smeared with eyeliner. There was a look of panic in her eyes and she started to spew on the sand with the uncontrollable retching of a dying cat.

Outside the world was bathed in that silvery light the night leaves behind after its initial withdrawal. A slug's trail, Roetgen thought looking at the sea. The wind could not be felt anymore, it was pushing the blackness, sweeping it into rough piles, out toward the distant horizon. A cock crowed, then broke off right in the middle of a vibrato, as if strangled by the outrage of its own voice.

Roetgen hurried over to João's hut, wondering where Moéma could have spent the night. Soiled by disgusting objects that had been thrown away—there was even what looked like a sanitary napkin wrapped up in a pair of panties—the street was like a damp beach churned up by some foul storm. As he passed *Seu* Alcides's bar, Roetgen felt a twinge of regret and looked away.

João was squatting under his awning, checking his fishing equipment. He seemed pleasantly surprised. "*Bom dia, français* . . . I was worried you wouldn't come," he said with a smile. "You look like death warmed over."

"Slept badly . . . The sea air'll soon put me right."

"Well off we go, then. There you are," he said handing him what looked like a red plastic cannonball, the same as the one he had slung over his shoulder, "I've got your things ready. Put everything you've got in your pockets in there, everything you don't want to get wet."

Looking at it more closely, Roetgen realized that it was an old mooring buoy, probably picked up off the beach; at the top a broad cork stopper had been fitted into a circular opening. A cord attached to either side made it into a waterproof bag.

They walked down the road until they came to a little blue house, which they entered without knocking.

"Morning!" said João to the *caboclo* still half-asleep behind his counter. "Get a move on, the wind's going to turn."

Without bothering to reply, the man stood up, muttering indistinctly. With the slowness of an iguana, he gathered together a slab of *rapadura*, a piece of candle, a box of matches and a paper cone of *farinha*.

"Who's he?" he asked, pointing to Roetgen with his chin.

"Luís's replacement," said João irritatedly. "Give him his share."

"You're sure?"

"Don't try to understand. We've made an agreement with Luís, I tell you . . . Get on with it, we're in a hurry."

The iguana got moving again and, with a suspicious look, placed the same list of objects as before on the counter.

"Put that in your ball, *rapaz*, we're off," João said to Roetgen.

They left without paying, but once they were out in the street, the fisherman explained: the "cooperative" belonged to the owner of the jangadas, a guy who lived in Arcati; for every fishing trip, each of the men was given these paltry supplies free of charge, but on their return their share in the fish was exchanged for credit in the same shop. The system worked without money, increasing the fishermen's bondage and the owner's profits.

Appalled, Roetgen wanted to learn more about the owner, but he came up against João's fatalism: it was the same all along the coast, there was nothing to do but thank God and the guy for giving them the chance to survive.

When they reached the dunes they went along the crest until they came to a place where some scrubby plants grew. Using his machete, João started to chop up the dry brambles.

"It's for the brazier," João said, handing Roetgen the first part of his harvest. "There's already some on board, but it's better to take a full load. You never know."

They were going from bush to bush when João pointed out a long trail in the sand, the kind of winding mark you'd leave if you were pulling a garden hose behind you.

"*Cobra de veado*," he muttered, following its indistinct course. Then he went over to a spiny bush and cautiously pulled the branches aside: coiled up, a fair-sized python was doubtless digesting that night's catch. The animal didn't have the time to wake up before João had decapitated it.

"*Matei o bicho!* I've killed the beast," he exclaimed with a kind of childish pride.

Dumbfounded by the presence of such a snake in the dunes and by the fisherman's reaction, Roetgen watched as he picked up the corpse, still twisted in impossible knots, and whirled it around like a sling before sending it flying through the air to crash to the ground several yards away.

Saint George killing the dragon, prouder at having overcome his fear than at having triumphed over evil for a brief moment . . . Or was it rather a sacrifice, a propitiation come from the depths of time to haunt our self-obsessed century?

From the spot where the dunes were spattered with blood they went down to the beach.

The two other fishermen had just finished pushing a coconut log under the spatula-shaped prow of the jangada. Fairly young, with no teeth—Roetgen could never remember Brazil without visualizing these toothless mouths created by starvation—they didn't seem very communicative: Paulino, bulging muscles, woolly hair browned by the salt; Isaac, frailer, hollow chest caused by a congenital malformation of the sternum.

João put the wood in a basket, checked the position of the log and the four men braced themselves against the boat until it was balanced on the cylinder of wood, keeping it in that position while Paulino placed a second roller under the prow then hurried back to help the others push. As soon as one roller emerged at the back, he took it around to the prow, continuing to do so all the way to the edge of the water. Once the jangada was afloat, Isaac took all the heavy logs far enough back on the sand to be out of the way of the incoming tide, while they held the boat on the waves, immersed up to the waist. As soon as he returned they all heaved themselves up into the boat together. Grasping the rudder, João immediately hauled on the mainsheet and the jangada started to glide across the sea with the ease and grace of a sailing dinghy.

Behind them the dunes were turning pink as other jangadas, sails unfurled, seemed to be hurrying after them, bumping across the shore like crumpled butterflies.

IN A CROSSWIND the jangada headed straight for the open sea, with the characteristic lapping of the water against the hull and the gentle swaying that forces the body to adjust its balance all the time. Standing at the stern, his buttocks propped on a sort of narrow bench, João was concentrating on steering, both hands glued firmly to the steering oar. Roetgen was sitting with Isaac and Paulino on the windward side; he'd started nibbling his block of *rapadura*, less from hunger than to fit in with the others. Happy to be at sea, he examined the boat with the keen appreciation of a sailing enthusiast.

About seven yards long and two yards wide, the jangada was of a marvelous technical elegance. Shaped like a decked barge with no handrail or cockpit, the hull narrowed elegantly at either end, making it more like a sailboard than any flat-bottomed vessel. Apart from the thwart, at the stern, and a sort of trestle just in front that was used to wind the sheets around or to lean against when standing up, the only other component was a beam of solid wood supported by rods into which was fitted a detachable, un-stayed lateen yard, slender and supple, like the rib of a leaf.

On the dark brown sail, spotted with holes and patches, was an advert in large black letters: *Industria de Extração de Aracati*.

The most astonishing aspect for Roetgen, however, was the ex-emplary absence of all metal on the sailing boat. Not a shackle, not a nail in the construction . . . everything was tied or pegged; even

JEAN-MARIE BLAS DE ROBLES

the lateen yard and the boom, each made of several pieces were simply whipped together with fishing line!

The ultimate praise of vegetable matter, an out-of-date hymn to that age of gold that came before the sword, the arquebus, the helmet and armor. There was a time when the Indians of this coast begged forgiveness of the trees before felling them with no other cutting edge than fire and flint.

As João explained afterward, however fragile the whole might be, it did mean they could repair any damage very quickly with the means on board. This was especially the case since any ruptures always came at the weak points created by the joints and as the rope always gave way before the wood, all they had to do was to lash the pieces that had come apart together again and the boat was as good as new. The same was true of the hull, its simple construction meaning it could be repaired without the need of a carpenter. Nothing escaped this disregard of things metal, not even the anchor, the *tauaçu*, the stone nucleus in a framework of wood hardened by fire: four branches tied together at one end with two others forming a cross to secure the cage and grip the sand or seaweed. Always the same principle—was it economy or did it derive from something unconscious and more decisive?—governing the least of their technical productions: three branches would not have been enough to hold the stone, a fifth would have been superfluous ... A theorem to explain why the principal proportions of timber had not changed an inch for thousands of years: a Roman villa or a Provençal farmhouse, a Cathar castle or a Venetian *palazzo*, for comparable buildings the same size of beams and rafters would be found, too thin and the wood gives way, too thick, it's wasted. Thus the rules of these builders were founded, before all the mathematics of the resistance of materials, on a happy medium that a certain number of lost moorings or collapsed roofs had helped to establish.

328

A SUDDEN BURST of activity interrupted Roetgen's reflections. At an order from João, who immediately unhitched the clew of the mainsail, the two fishermen handed the sail, then quickly spilled the wind by bundling the sail around the mast with the topping lift. Once that was done, João came to help them un-step the lateen yard and lay it down with the boom along the center of the boat. Its wings clipped, the jangada came to a halt on the green water, nothing more than a frail raft encumbered with spars, a piece of flotsam hardly fitted to brave the rigors of the Atlantic. They cast anchor. The sun was rising; all the land around had disappeared.

Paulino and Isaac were sitting on the same side, feet dangling over the edge of the platform; instinctively Roetgen went to the other side, two yards from João. He was wondering what kind of bait they were going to use when he saw him unwind his line without bothering about his hooks at all. The line having quickly reached the bottom—there could only have been about twenty yards of depth—João took it in his fingers and pulled it up and down, as if fishing with a jigger.

"You've nothing to use as bait?" Roetgen asked, amazed.

João was surprised anyone could even ask the question. That's the way it was, no one did it any other way. Attracted by the jerks and the glitter of the hooks, some creature always took it eventually; once they'd hauled it up, it was used as bait for larger catches.

Hours passed, silent, somnolent hours during which the four men pursued the same quest beneath the sun. It was like the summary of an avant-garde play, Roetgen thought, reflecting on the absurdity of their situation: all alone on the Atlantic, four ship-wrecked sailors dip their unbaited hooks in the water.

A slack sea, the sun burning their necks, the creak of wood, marionnette-like contortions, out of sync, abrupt at times, like sleeping bodies twitching . . .

Toward noon they regretted having eaten their supply of sugar so quickly. Imitating the others, Roetgen put pinches of manioc flour in his mouth, just enough to stave off the pangs of hunger and to increase his desire for another drink from the jerrican. As time passed, the expressions on their faces became more feverish, their gestures more febrile, furtive, as if the better to conjure up hope from the depths. They changed arms more often, their muscles growing numb from repeating the same action.

Racked by hunger, four shipwrecked sailors beg the god of the oceans to take pity on them, but in vain . . . Twitching with nervous tics, four schizophrenics try to trap flies with vinegar . . . Petrified, four seamen insult God, the sea and fish before deciding to eat the cabin boy . . .

"Put that over your head," João said, handing him a piece of damp sacking, "you'll get sunstroke." Only then did he notice the straw hats the three of them were wearing.

Toward three in the afternoon, João let out an oath and pulled in his line as quickly as possible. He'd finally managed to spear a silvery fish hardly bigger than a sprat by the tail. Eight hours, eight hours for this small fry! Immediately there was an amazing bustle of activity on the deck: while João cut his catch up into thin slivers, careful to skim the backbone, Paulino and Isaac lit a fire in an oil can that they placed on the lee side. As soon as the wood was burning, they placed an old billycan filled with seawater on this improvized brazier. You would have sworn the men were going to cook their anchovy to eat it right away. Roetgen would have swallowed it raw, so tormenting were the pangs of hunger he felt. But João shared out the strips of fish he had prepared, so that they could all now bait their lines.

Scarcely five minutes later, a strong bite tugged at his arm. Striking the fish, he started to pull in his line cautiously, terrified he might make a wrong move. João came rushing over, bellowing advice, ready to take the line out of his hands. Mortified by this lack of confidence in him, Roetgen almost yielded to the fisherman's mute command, but his instinct took over and he started to talk to the fish in French, mixing insults and cajolery, going along with its attempts to escape, all the better to halt them smoothly after a while, oblivious to everything beyond the living tension at his fingertips.

"*Cavala*," said João when he saw the flash zigzagging up toward the surface. "And a fine one!"

One last jerk and a sort of long bonito landed on the deck with a dull slap. Paralyzed for a moment at this change of environment, it opened its mouth before struggling blindly. If paradise or hell existed, that would be the way the dead would wriggle when they arrived in those murky nightmare regions . . . João disembowelled it live, chucked its entrails overboard and chopped it up into large quivering slices. Keeping back a few for renewing the bait, he put the rest in the pot to boil.

They all watched it cooking. Once it was done, Paulino took out the slices with a piece of wood and placed them in front of him. The three fishermen fell on the food, burning their fingers to roll pieces in their bag of *farofa*, spitting out the bones into the sea with obvious pleasure, constantly congratulating the *francês* on such an excellent first catch. Roetgen did the same, appreciating each mouthful, convinced he had never tasted anything so delicious.

When they were full, they could finally start fishing. It was four in the afternoon.

Sea bream, albacores, rays, dogfish, dorados . . . they gathered in the fish in a sustained rhythm. Sometimes it took five or ten minutes, but the line never came up empty. Roetgen discovered a very different world from the one he was familiar with: here there was no pleasure taken in the act of fishing, hauling in a scad was like extracting ore, with no waste of emotions or of time. True, there were occasional exclamations at an exceptional catch, but they were those of miners discovering an unexpected seam of coal, richer, easier to take out. The animal was knocked on the head and thrown into the basket; when it was full to overflowing, one of the fishermen would wedge his line to the deck and set about salting them: scale and clean them out, cut off the heads, remove the fillets and pile them up in a crate in the prow of the jangada, cover them with a layer of coarse salt . . . Roetgen made an effort to assimilate this expertise; soon he was able to take his turn with the others. This essential task took a good half hour, at the end your back was aching, your hands scratched and smarting from the salt, but you felt pleased with yourself and a job well done.

Concentrating on his every movement, anxious not to lose the respect of the fishermen, Roetgen made it a point of honor to keep to their rhythm. This gave him no respite, he wasn't even thinking anymore but fell into the catatonic state he'd been in on the bus ride to Canoa. Moéma, Thaïs, Brazil, everything had gone; his mind clear, he wallowed in work and amnesia.

At sunset the fish became more difficult to take. The sea wind had started to blow, gradually raising a heavy, dangerous-looking swell around the jangada. A bank of leaden cloud, very low on the horizon, seemed to be approaching very quickly. It was an ominous sign, but the fishermen didn't seem particularly worried about it. Making the most of the last of the light, Paulino and João made fast every last object on the deck, while Isaac was cooking a second bonito they'd kept for themselves. It was put to cool while each rolled up his line and replaced it with a stronger one with larger hooks.

"At night it's only the big ones that bite," João explained, "sharks, swordfish, that kind of thing, so just two of us fish, to avoid getting in each other's way."

Paulino and Isaac had a bite to eat with them, then went to lie down in the hold. Seeing a hand wedge a bit of cloth between the

hatch cover and the coaming—presumably to let in some air—
Roetgen wondered how the two men had been able to squeeze
into such a restricted space: as far as he could tell, there was only
about twenty inches headroom! At a sign from João, he sat down
with his back against the sampson post and, following his example, tied himself to it around his waist and checked his bowline
before starting fishing again.

The sea had gotten up to such an extent that occasionally long
breakers swept over the boat. Roetgen could see the phosphorescent crests running along high above him in the black of the night,
mountains of foaming water that the jangada finally topped just at
the moment when it seemed certain they were about to engulf it.
Constantly undulating and dragging its anchor—as an experienced
seaman, João had made sure he doubled the length of the anchor
cable—slipping sideways or brought up suddenly into the wind
by the abrupt tautening of the cable, the prow half disappearing
into the water, the boat somehow managed to ride out the squall.
When the deck was submerged beneath a bigger wave, the two
men were left sitting in foaming water like a bubble bath—without
the rope cutting into their waists, they would certainly have been
swept away—then the exhausting rodeo started up again until another breaker came crashing over them. Soaked from head to toe,
eyes stinging, blinded by the spindrift, Roetgen lived through the
worst watch of his life. Hardly reassured by *Seu* João's morose im-
passibility, he forced himself to fish without managing to free himself from a degrading animal fear. Frozen stiff and deafened by the
wind and the roar of the Atlantic, he saw monsters.

WHEN PAULINO AND Isaac came to relieve them around one
in the morning there were hardly any fish in the basket: three
swordfish for Roetgen and two for João, plus a hammerhead

shark of about thirty pounds. There was still a heavy sea but the wind was slackening.

"The tide's turning," João said to Paulino, "They should start biting a bit more. Don't forget to take in the anchor cable bit by bit."

He crawled over to the hatch and held the cover half open and Roetgen slipped inside. "Go on, there's plenty of room," he said, seeing Roetgen hesitate. Once he had disappeared, João followed him into the hold and pulled down the hatch behind him, taking care not to close it completely. During the few seconds in which he was shrouded in darkness, in that sea-tossed coffin, he had to keep a grip on himself not to go back up on deck.

João struck a match and lit a little piece of candle wedged in between two sacks of salt, then wriggled to get in a more comfortable position. "*Puxa!*" he muttered, "What filthy weather!"

Stretched out on their sides, on either side of the centerboard case, they were closer to each other than they would ever be up in the open air. João's face looked as if it were carved from old wood, each of his wrinkles being a separate curve of the grain. The hold had a strong smell of fish and brine.

"Is it often like this?" Roetgen asked.

"From time to time, when the moon's in the wrong quarter. The problem is that the sharks don't like . . ."

"They sell well?"

"Like the others, but there's more meat on them. And then there's a bonus for the liver and the fins."

"What do they do with them?"

"The liver goes to the laboratories. I don't really know but it seems it's good for medicines, creams . . . It's the Chinese who buy the fins. They're very partial to them from what people say. Are there some in your part of the world too?"

"Sharks or Chinese?"

"Sharks."

"Not as many as around here. And they're farther down, well away from the shore."

"And sea bream?"

"There's hardly any left. They've been overfished. It's the same with all the others, certain species have even disappeared entirely."

"How is that possible?" João cried, suddenly frightened by that prospect.

"I tell you: too much industrial-scale fishing, pollution . . . it's a real disaster."

João clicked his tongue several times to express his disapproval. "God, it's not possible, things like that! Is it far away where you come from?"

"France, you mean?"

"How should I know? Where you come from, I mean."

"Three thousand miles, more or less."

João frowned. "How many hours by bus would that be?" His serious expression made it clear that he had no idea where France was and couldn't imagine a distance until it was converted into the only yardsticks he was familiar with: days on foot for shorter distances, hours on the bus for longer ones. Caught unprepared, Roetgen gave him a journey time in hours by plane, but the lack of response told him it meant nothing to the fisherman. He therefore made a mental calculation of the distance the jangada could cover in a day and told João: two months sailing to the east, provided there was a constant favorable wind during the whole of the voyage.

"Two months!" João repeated, visibly impressed this time. He was silent for several minutes, thinking it over, before coming back to the subject: "Where you live are there jaguars in the *mata* as well?"

"No."

"And armadillos?"

"No."

"Boas, anteaters, parrots?"

"No, João. We have different animals, but it's a bit the same as with the fish, there aren't that many left."

"Oh, right," João said, disappointed at a land so lacking in the essentials. "Not even caymans? And mango trees, at least you must have some mango trees?"

We've got high-speed trains, the Airbus and rockets, João, computers that can do calculations more quickly than our brains and contain complete encyclopedias. We have an impressive literary and artistic past, the greatest perfume makers, dress designers of genius who make such magnificent negligées if you lived three times over you still wouldn't have enough to pay for them. We have nuclear power stations that produce waste that will remain deadly for ten thousand years, perhaps more, we don't really know. Just imagine, João, ten thousand years! As if the first Homo sapiens *had bequeathed us rubbish bins that were so contaminated they'd still poison everything around them to this day. We also have tremendous bombs, little marvels capable of wiping out your mango trees, your jaguars and your parrots forever. Capable of putting an end to your race, João, to the whole of the human race! But, thank God, we have a very high opinion of ourselves.*

Roetgen knew he would never be able to describe to him a reality that only stood out, he suddenly realized with a feeling of bitterness and deprivation, by its arrogance. Called on to justify Western civilization, and himself with it, he failed to find a single feature likely to interest this man. A man for whom the natural riches of the earth, the warmth of the sun on it, the influence of the moon on this or that animal or plant, still had meaning and value; an intelligent, sensitive person, but living in a world where culture still retained its proper sense, like humus, a piece of land.

Feeling ashamed, humbled before João, like a guilty man facing the judge, he invented an environment that could match up to
his. Combining the stories of his childhood with some memories
of medieval history, he told of wolves attacking the villages on
winter nights and howled, there in the dark hold, as they were
supposed to across the snow in the valleys of the French countryside. Encouraged by the fisherman's continuing attention, he
embroidered his story with their shining eyes, their monstrous
fangs and even ended up telling the fable of the shepherd boy who
cried wolf, at length, as if it were a true story.

"He got what he deserved," said João after briefly reflecting
on the tragic end of the shepherd boy. "It's sad to say, but that's
the way it is. By lying all the time you end up making the lie into
a truth . . . It's like my son-in-law. For two years he kept telling
people his wife was unfaithful, just to attract attention. Until the
day she really did cuckold him. But tell me, *françès*, your family,
where do they live, in a village?"

"No, in a city. In Paris. Have you heard of it?"

"I think so, yes . . . But I never went to school, you know. It's
near *Nova-York*, isn't it?"

"Not exactly," Roetgen said, fascinated by a view of the world
in which geography played such a minor role. "I'll explain . . ."

It was no use, however. Neither the map of the world he drew
on the floor, nor his attempts to simplify it brought the least sign
of understanding on João's face. He had never traveled anywhere,
apart from the three hours' walk to Aracati to see the jangada
owner and, once when he was a child, a pilgrimage to the shrine
at Canindé, to thank Saint Francis for having saved his mother
from smallpox. Eight hours in a bus, of which his memory was
confused but filled with wonder. Unable either to read or write
and never having seen a television but for a few moments in the
town, his knowledge derived from his own experiences and from

the *cantadores*, who even came as far as the bars of Canoa to sing their laments. He could not imagine that the earth was round either, nor that men had gone to the moon, though he listened to these new facts with perfect politeness. Anything beyond his village, his work or what he had been able to see of Brazil for himself, was enveloped in a hazy mist in which things and places were associated by chance, in the jumble of names that happened to have stuck in his memory: São Paulo, New York, Paris . . . that is, the Otherworld; a world isolated from his concerns, a beyond with no fixed abode, a blurred virtual world that he assumed it was impossible to know.

SERRA DA ARATANHA: *Human fat to protect space shuttles from cosmic rays!*

"But I've told you, it's impossible to be in one piece after such an explosion. Look, Firmina, be reasonable, even oxen, even elephants would have been made into mincemeat."

"That's what *you* say, but I'm telling you it was the headless mule that caused the massacre. And I know very well who it was, you can trust me . . ."

It was four in the morning. Since Uncle Zé had come back an hour ago, Nelson and Firmina had been plying him with questions about the disaster. When the emergency services arrived, the corpse-robbers had disappeared as if by magic. From the passenger list it was known that there was a celebrity on board the plane, a poet whose name Zé could no longer remember but whose body the rescue party wanted to identify at all cost. At certain gruesome details she dragged out of her brother, Firmina crossed herself with a terrified look: she had recognized the infernal mark of the *mula-sem-cabaça*.

Only that creature of the devil could have torn them apart like that, and there must certainly have been several of them!

"The headless mule?" Nelson asked, turning to the old woman.

"What?! You've never heard of it? Well, when a girl does it before she's married, or a married woman sleeps with her father, she turns into a headless mule. She appears on Friday nights and starts wandering around the *mata*. Whenever she meets a living person, she swallows their eyes, nails and all their teeth; sick or dead people she tears apart and scatters the bits along the way. But the result's the same, no one can escape her."

"But how can she do that when she hasn't got a head?" Nelson asked, visibly alarmed.

"No one knows, and that's the most frightening thing. But never go past a cross at midnight, you'll make her come right away. And if you should meet her one day—God protect you from that misfortune—roll up in a ball, close your eyes and mouth, hide your nails between your thighs and she'll leave you in peace."

"Don't listen to that nonsense, son," Uncle Zé said wearily. "She's old, she doesn't know what she's saying anymore."

"Oh really," Firmina objected vehemently. "Because Conceição doesn't sleep with her father, perhaps? Everyone here knows that. It's difficult not to since he tells everyone who's willing to listen whenever he's had one too many."

"That may be true, but it doesn't prove anything."

"And that doesn't prove anything, all those poor people crushed to a pulp? You'll see, some of them'll be found without eyes, without nails and without teeth; and we'll know they were alive when the headless mule came to take them."

In the face of his sister's senile obduracy, Zé gave up, emptied his glass of *cachaça* and spat on the ground. That way of talking just didn't make sense, but how could you make her see reason?

The old woman always had an answer to everything, he couldn't see any way of convincing her she was wrong.

"It's like the *sacaolhos*," Nelson said, reflectively. "They come to the favelas, even in broad daylight, and tear out children's eyes."

"God forbid!" said *Dona* Firmina, crossing herself. "The things there are!"

"What's all this now?" Uncle Zé muttered.

"It's true. One day in Pirambú I saw a little girl with empty eyes and her mother, a Peruvian, told me that's who it was. They's *gringos*, always three of them together, two men and a blonde woman, with white coats, like doctors. They drive slowly into the middle of the favelas, in a Nissan Patrol with tinted windows, and when they see children alone, they offer to buy them a lemonade or a *guaraná*, then they take them to a quiet place and remove their eyes or the fat from their bodies, sometimes both . . ."

"The fat?" Uncle Zé asked in disgust, his skepticism suddenly shaken. "But whatever for?"

"Beauty products for the Americans and their friends. The oil from *caboclos* is very good for white people's skin, it makes it look younger, smoother, you see. But it's also used to grease precision instruments and to protect the space shuttle from cosmic rays. NASA need tons of it, it costs more than gold. So our government lets them get on with it, to pay off their foreign debt. It's like that all over Latin America. Before they didn't used to take the skinny ones, but now they're less choosy."

"And the eyes?"

"The eyes are for transplants. My neighbor's little girl was lucky, they didn't take her fat. Otherwise she'd be dead. When they found her, her eyes were bandaged and the orbits stuffed with cotton wool; and she had a fifty dollar note stuck down her underpants."

"God in heaven!" Firmina said, close to tears. "Fifty dollars for a person's eyes!"

"I was also told they took hearts or kidneys, and that there were even expensive restaurants in São Paulo where they serve human flesh to policemen and soldiers."

"It's the end of the world," said Uncle Zé gloomily. "I can't believe it. If that's the way things are, then there's no hope: none at all . . ."

"Don't worry, Zé. I watch out for them, for Nissan Patrols, and the day I see one I'll fucking well send it up in flames, the car and the bastards inside it!"

His lips were twisted in a horrible grimace that persisted for a while after he stopped speaking. *Dona* Firmina crossed herself again to help make it disappear.

CHAPTER 14

*The Fountain of the Four Rivers: how Kircher forced
his detractors to make restitution. Which also deals
with the symbolism of shade & light*

BERNINI WAS A bright, perspicacious &
extremely courteous man, despite an inclination to let
himself get carried away that his immense talent did not justify
but almost always made forgivable. Short & stocky, simply dressed
on all occasions, he scarcely spoke at all & was regarded as a
hypochondriac by those who did not have the rare honor of being
one of his friends. When he did manage to overcome his natural
shyness, he spoke freely & with such charming volubility that
he enchanted his circle of friends with his imaginative & lively
mind. He was attracted by Kircher's erudition, as Kircher was by
the skill he demonstrated in his art. The two men very quickly
became friends, which was of great advantage in the development
of the plans for the fountain.

After several weeks' work Kircher showed Bernini & the
Pope an initial design, developed from a sketch by Francesco
Borromini. Its aim was to represent the four regions of the
world through the biggest known rivers, thus subtly recalling
the four original rivers of the Garden of Eden. The Ganges, the
Danube, the Nile & the Plate were to be personified by four
marble colossi, each accompanied by emblematic animals. As
for the obelisk at the center of the monument, it would in itself
encapsulate all theology & sacred knowledge. Kircher was also
proposing to channel the water from Rome's best spring, the
Acqua Vergine, to it, thus giving the fountain a natural meaning
of purification.

These preparatory sketches aroused fierce discussion & my
master had to defend every one of his ideas, point by point.
But the design was accepted without amendment & Bernini
immediately set about conceiving a composition worthy of the
marble & chisel. That left, however, several physical problems:
the restoration of the obelisk, its transport to the Circus
Agonalis, its erection & the deciphering of the hieroglyphs.
The obelisk found in the Circus Maximus was in a very poor
state. Abandoned for centuries to the vagaries of the weather,
it had suffered serious mutilation. For days we scoured the area
around the stone needle looking for missing pieces, but we did
not, alas, recover enough to complete the inscription we were
working on. Moreover, certain passages that were still in place
had been erased by the weather, leaving us with the question of
whether to reconstitute the inscription by intelligent guesswork
or to accept these ugly blemishes. The former seemed, if not
impossible, then at least rather bold to Athanasius.

We therefore sent out an appeal to all the antiquaries of the
city to buy back, out of the funds provided by Innocent X, any

inscribed fragments of the obelisk, if they could be found. Kircher recovered a certain number but he encountered several wily collectors who refused to sell them, or even to provide my master with a copy. From an indiscreet remark by Signore Manfredo Settala, I learned that this rebuff did not come from a desire to push up the price, but from the machinations of those who, doubting my master's abilities, were challenging him in his efforts to restore the lost hieroglyphs. They hoped to be able to unmask him as an imposter by comparing his figures with those they had kept in their possession.

I informed Kircher & Bernini of this cabal. The sculptor fell into a rage, inveighing against those who had the effrontery to disobey the Pope & weave such malicious plots. Kircher remained thoughtful. "Perhaps," he said at last, after we had gone on at him about this, "perhaps it would be better to leave the few lacunae in the inscription blank . . . Not that I am afraid to take up the challenge thrown down by these doctors of doltishness, but there is a great difference between translating a text and restoring it. As in any language, several signs can express the same thing, save for a slight shade of meaning. Just imagine I made a mistake, however minor, & a scandal ensued, tarnishing my name, that of the Church & even the favor our Order enjoys with the Pope."

In an impassioned outburst Bernini insisted my master should confound his detractors & he did this in such friendly & confident terms that he managed to persuade him. Kircher took a copy of all the legible characters on the obelisk & on the retrieved fragments, then shut himself away in his study. As for Bernini, he fitted the obelisk into a device allowing it to be turned horizontally around its axis and started repairing the breaks. In order to avoid disfiguring it at all, he refused to use any cement or even iron pins &, in stone similar to that of the Egyptian monument, sculpted replacements so ingeniously that they fitted their respective places precisely.

Invited to assess the result of these efforts, Kircher went into raptures over Bernini's skill. Never at any time had such perfect work been seen! All that was left was to have the missing hieroglyphs carved, those copied from the fragments in our possession, which it would have been impossible to reinsert into the obelisk without damaging the beauty of the whole, & those, fewer as it happened, that Athanasius had to rewrite. This task was given to the sculptor Marco Antonino Canino & finished in 1645; Kircher's detractors were routed, for the symbols he had drawn corresponded exactly to the originals they had refused to divulge to him. They were therefore compelled to make a virtue of necessity & agree that my master, guided by the Holy Ghost, had truly uncovered the key to that enigmatic language.

The year 1646 saw the publication of *Ars Magna Lucis et Umbrae*. This heavy folio tome of 936 pages was dedicated to Athanasius's patron, Johann Friedrich, Count Wallenstein and Bishop of Prague.

Kircher began by describing the sun as the principal source of light, without avoiding the question of the spots, which could sometimes be observed on it surface, & their unhealthy influence. As proof of that he took the invasion by the Swedish armies in 1625, but also the death of the Ming emperor, that of Louis XIII & various catastrophes, the occurrence of which coincided with an inexplicable multiplication of the maculae.

After that, my master looked at the moon, that second source of light in the world, but which only works as a reflector of the sun. He continued with numerous pages on the heavenly bodies, gave for the first time a picture of the planet Jupiter & the rings of Saturn, & continued with a study of the colors: when pure light passed through a prism of a veil of raindrops, he wrote, it was contaminated by the contact, thus producing yellow, red and violet, which are degradations of white, which is the color of light, just as black is that of its absence.

In this connection my master wrote at length on the chameleon & its talent for coloring itself to resemble things it is close to. He added a few remarks on octopuses & other marine creatures with a similar ability, then considered a very curious Mexican species of wood sent to him by Father Alejandro Fabiàn. After having had a bowl carved from this *tlapazatli* wood, as Father Fabiàn had suggested, Kircher, in my presence, poured some pure water into it. Soon, & with no obvious reason for this change, the fibers of the wood being clean and clear like cherrywood, the water started gradually to turn blue until it took on a magnificent purple hue. Reduced to a powder, the wood continued to produce the same effect, although losing the capacity little by little in the course of time. Kircher gave the bowl to Emperor Ferdinand III, who regarded it as one of his most precious treasures.

From *tlapazatli* wood, the book went on to the internal structure of the eye & to human vision, emphasizing how everything worked in a similar way to the camera obscura he had tried out in Sicily, to my misfortune. All one needed to do to convince oneself of this, Kircher said, was to take a bull's eye—or a human eye, should the opportunity present itself—remove the vitreous humor & put it on the box in place of the artificial lens. Everything outside would then appear inside the black box with the precision of a most excellent painting.

Dealing with anamorphosis, he showed how to distort a drawing mathematically so as to make it appear monstrous to the eye, but unexceptional when seen reflected in a cylindrical mirror. Similarly he went through the various means of arranging trees, plants, vines, arbors & gardens so that from one particular viewpoint they would present the image of a man or a dragon, of which there would be no trace from any other point.

After a chapter in which Athanasius gave exhaustive lists of all the lunar months in the form of a "dragon with lunar knots," by which one could predict all the eclipses, he presented the picture of a man within a dial, showing the zodiacal relationships connecting each part of the body & each illness to each simple or sympathetic remedy that will cure it.

In conclusion, my master embellished his work with a splendid chapter on the metaphysical symbolism of light, crowning his efforts with a new philosophy & recalling the imperishable truths of our religion.

If I have taken the trouble to go through the matter of this *Great Art of Light and Shade*, it is not for my well-informed readers, who will be perfectly familiar with it, but to give an example to the younger among them, who will hardly be acquainted with Kircher's work, if at all, with his phenomenal knowledge in all things & with his very individual manner of disentangling the most difficult subjects in a way that is both pleasant & useful. My master never ignored any aspect of the world & whether he was interested in light, in Egypt or in any other specific subject, every time he felt compelled to embrace the whole of the universe before returning to its Creator to praise Him for all these many marvels.

As soon as it was published, this work enjoyed remarkable success. No praise was loud enough to express the admiration of scholars, who devoured it with relish, as if it were a great delicacy. Copies were sent to all the Jesuit missions throughout the world.

Meanwhile, intrigued by the frontispiece & unable to grasp all its subtleties, I went to see Kircher in his study. He welcomed me as usual & interrupted his work to explain the marvelous allegory that the Burgundian, Pierre Miotte, had engraved to his order.

I admitted to Kircher that, although I could understand a good number of these symbols, I had difficulty relating them to each other & that consequently the deeper meaning of the picture escaped me.

"Sit down," my master said in kindly tones, "there's nothing very mysterious about it, a little more effort & you would have understood all this mumbo jumbo. But first of all pour us some of this excellent Burgundy that the good Father Mersenne has sent to me, it will perhaps enlighten your mind, provided it doesn't cloud it entirely . . .

FAZENDA DO BOI: *A real car for the ladies' man . . .*

"There it is," said the Countess, stepping aside at the entrance to a large, isolated building a hundred yards or so from the main part of the residence. "I'll leave you in my husband's clutches. Don't join in his game," she advised with a smile, "or you've had it. See you later, I hope . . ."

With a meaningful glance at Loredana, she turned and left.

"So what do you think of her?" Eléazard asked. "Nice, don't you think?"

"Odd, I'd say," Loredana replied without knowing what she really thought of the Countess. "She can certainly knock it back. She was close to making a declaration of love! Good thing you came back with the champagne, I didn't know how I was going to get out of it."

Eléazard raised his eyebrows in surprise. She was annoyed with herself for summing up the Countess's attitude to her in such an off-hand way, with this habit she had of always wanting to get the upper hand, to dismiss others with a single defining comment for the sole reason that she'd been deeply moved by them and didn't know how to assess the feeling. She immediately made amends: "I'm just talking off the top of my head. The truth is, I liked her. Very much, even. She asked me to give her some Italian lessons and I think I'm going to agree. What do you think?"

"Why not?" said Eléazard, glancing inside the garage. "You can even tell her to come to my place, if that suits you better. Shall we go in?"

"OK," she said, her mind elsewhere.

They entered what had been the heart of the *fazenda* when it had been a working farm, in the days when José Moreira's father was still growing sugarcane on his land: a vast, circular construction where two pairs of oxen went round and round continuously to operate a mill with vertical rollers. Preserved by the Colonel, the mill was prominently displayed in the middle of the shed. Radiating from it, a circle of twenty or so old cars shimmered under halogen lamps that bathed them in a museum light. There were red carpets between the vehicles. A small group of people, among whom several Asian faces could be seen, were gathered around the tall figure of the governor.

"Come and join us," he said when he saw Eléazard and his companion. "You've taken your time, I can say."

They went over to them beside a splendid coupe with cream and brown paintwork recalling certain tasteless two-tone shoes.

"Here's something that ought to interest you, Monsieur Von Wogau. I was just showing these people one of the finest items in my collection, a Panhard et Levassor 1936"—he mispronounced the names as *Panarde et Lévassor* but with something about his intonation that indicated he was convinced he was speaking them in the French manner. "The *Dynamic* with a freewheel! Four speeds, automatic clutch, torsion-bar suspension . . . Three parallel windshield wipers, headlamps and radiator with matching grilles and a centrally placed steering wheel, if you please. The best your country produced."

"What speed?" a nasal voice asked.

"*Eighty-seven miles an hour,*" the governor said in English, as if he were announcing a profit he'd made on the stock exchange. "And fifteen miles a gallon," he confessed to Loredana in guilty tones but with a smile at the corner of his mouth showing that he was just as proud of the excessive fuel consumption as he was of the speed.

"I'm sorry," Loredana said, "but I can't really appreciate these things. Aesthetically at most. I haven't even got a driver's licence, so cars, you know . . ."

For a moment the governor was dumbstruck. "Did you hear that?" he then said to the assembled company. "The lady hasn't got a driver's licence! And she's Italian!"

A young man with the look of a Mormon missionary immediately translated this into English, which aroused a certain amount of polite amusement from some and, with a slight delay, had the Asians springing grotesquely to attention.

Eléazard started as a hand was placed on his shoulder. Turning around, he saw Euclides's beaming face: "Your move, my friend," he whispered in his ear, pretending to be interested in the conversation. "Quite a gathering. The Pentagon, does that mean anything to you?" With his eyes he indicated two graying-at-the-temples bucks who could have come from a TV ad for cheap aftershave.

All at once Eléazard was overcome with the irresistible longing for a cigarette. Not that he felt intimidated by the occult power of those men or nervous at the godsend of an explosive revelation—that modern tendency of journalism was precisely what he found nauseating about his profession, but he suddenly felt the prickling lies set off in him. Nothing equals the feeling of having access to the truth like a whiff of falsehood, the imminence of evidence to expose as false something that was claiming to be genuine—a system, a theory, but equally the stature, the honest image of a man and what he says. As a result, Eléazard felt as exultant as a police inspector at the moment when the possibility emerges of demolishing the defense of a suspect he'd known for ages was guilty.

Every sense on the alert, he listened as the governor continued his whimsical address. With all the mannerisms of a passionate collector, and not without a certain brilliance, Moreira sang the praises of the perfect curves of the Panhard, its lines, *not feminine, that would be an insult to women,* but animal, fleshly, organic . . . Beautiful cars, he said, went beyond the simple idea of transport, they were cult objects, magic scarabs, pure talismans destined for those whose thirst for progress, power and mastery over things impelled them irresistibly toward the future.

"Talking of *thirst,*" Loredana broke in, "you wouldn't have something to drink?"

He laughed at her forthrightness and, excusing himself for forgetting his duty toward his guests, signalled to one of the twenty mulattos in overalls he employed to look after his cars.

"We're sticking to champagne, yes? It's a celebration this evening."

"And what are you celebrating?" Loredana asked out of simple curiosity.

A mischievous, teasing expression appeared on Moreira's face. "But the pleasure of having made your acquaintance, of course. That alone would justify emptying my cellars completely . . ."

Loredana's response to the flattery was a skeptical pout. The alcohol had suddenly gone to her head. All at once she was very annoyed with Eléazard for having left her in Moreira's hands. By way of revenge, she allowed the governor to take her hand and lead her to the rear of the car.

BROUGHT FROM THE *fazenda* by the mechanic, two waiters distributed glasses of champagne all around.

"Why do people call you 'Colonel?'" Loredana asked after having emptied her glass in three gulps. "Have you been in the army?"

"No, not really," the governor replied nonchalantly, gesturing to a waiter to refill her glass. "It's a kind of assumed title." He mechanically smoothed one of his sideburns. "It's still used for political leaders and the *fazendeiros*, the owners of the big estates. It's a tradition going back to imperial times: in his struggle against the rabble-rousers, Don Pedro I organized regional militias, putting the notables of the Interior in command with the rank of colonel. The militias have disappeared but the title has remained. Having said that, we can dispense with the formalities. I would be honored it you would simply call me José."

She drew herself up with a thoughtful air, though her words were starting to get slightly slurred. "You're a fast worker, Colonel."

Apart from the Japanese, who were talking among themselves, examining the Panhard with ceremonious courtesies, the guests were gathered in a circle around the governor; with no obvious malice, they fed his banter with questions or remarks that were too accommodating not to bespeak a grotesque smugness.

With impassible faces, hands in their pockets, Eléazard and Dr. Euclides seemed lost in thought.

"I agree with you, William." The governor, his eyes fixed on Loredana, as if seeking her approval, started to hold forth. "Destitution is a genuine problem. To think that a country such as ours is still ravaged by the plague or cholera, not to mention the lepers you see begging more or less everywhere! It's more than a tragedy, it's a waste! It's easy to blame the incompetence of the politicians, corruption or even the disparity in wealth between the *fazandeiro* and the peasant. But that is to take a very narrow view of things. Our foreign debt is one of the biggest in the world, it's come to the point where we're reduced to having to borrow again and again simply to pay the interest! It's obvious we won't be able to get out of it as long as there isn't a permanent mora-torium. In the meantime, Brazil remains the world leader in the production of tin, the second most important producer of steel and the third for manganese, not to mention arms. Whom do you think we have to thank for that? The *Partido dos Trabalhadores*? The Communists? All these pseudorevolutionaries who spend their time criticizing without the least comprehension of the eco-nomic realities of the country? Or perhaps those peasants who stop cultivating their fields as soon as they've harvested enough maize to feel secure. We must face up to facts: the Brazilians are still in their childhood. If we weren't here to change things, we, the entrepreneurs who have a vision of Brazil and give ourselves the means to satisfy our ambitions, who would do it, I ask you? Destitution is just one symptom among others of our immaturity as a country. It's sad, lamentable, tragic, whatever you want, but the people must be educated, whether they like it or not, so that they will finally grow up, see reason and get down to work." Then, turning to Eléazard, he asked, "You're a journalist, Monsieur Von Wogau, tell me the truth: am I right or not?"

Eléazard stared at him without replying, contempt oozing from every pore. Grab him by the collar, heap abuse on him, spit his nauseating cynicism right back in his face! The words came tumbling down without managing to cross his lips; he was clearly aware of the pointlessness of making a scene, but unable to bring himself to mutter an agreement out of pure expediency, he re-mained silent, wavering, muzzled more by his own fury than by etiquette.

Loredana's remark was like the flap of a sail in the unruffled calm: "The day beggars get forks they'll be given gruel . . ."

Dumbfounded for a moment, the governor decided to laugh, following Dr. Euclides, who was giving muffled applause.

"Not bad," said Moreira with a nasty grimace. "Not bad at all. And do you know this one? What does a blind beggar say when he's feeling a rich man's car?"

. . . ?

"Oh my God," he whined, caricaturing the plaintive tones of the people of the *Nordeste,* "what a little bus!"

Eléazard gritted his teeth, concentrating fully on keeping his face expressionless. There were a few polite smiles but a tangible unease had people staring into space. Furious at Eléazard and Loredana, the governor was searching for an anecdote that would relax the atmosphere, when Loredana broke the silence again: "How about taking me out for a spin?" she said in a playful tone. Adding, as she stroked the curve of the Panhard's wing, "I'm dying to see what she can do . . ."

José Moreira looked her up and down, as if he were wondering if she were serious. Flattered by what he saw in her eyes, he opened the door of the car and invited her to get in.

"Take a seat, *senhorita.* I'm sorry to have to abandon you like this," he said to the other guests, "but what a woman wants . . . We'll be back in a few minutes, makes yourselves at home until we return."

Starting up as soon as he was at the controls, the Panhard reversed briefly then drove silently toward the garage exit. With a brief flash of the headlights and a resonant blast on the horn, the car disappeared into the night.

After the departure of the governor and his capricious passenger, the abandoned guests took a few minutes to decide what to do. Visibly annoyed with their host for his discourtesy, the Asians agreed to withdraw; having translated a bouquet of flowery farewells, their factotum followed them, tight-lipped and stiff-legged.

Ignoring Euclides and Eléazard, the Americans were consulting together in low voices.

"You mustn't condemn her," the doctor said, placing his hand on Eléazard's arm. "Jealousy—just like despair, by the way—is a pleasure we must be able to deny ourselves. Especially since it seemed to me that our dear Loredana was perfectly aware of what she was doing. If you want my opinion, there's more trouble in store for that old fuddy-duddy colonel."

Eléazard seemed to be immersed in a meditation on his shoes. The triumphant ironic glance from Moreira as he put the car into reverse added insult to the bitter taste of humiliation. Finding himself hoping against hope, begging for something from the depths of his distress, he pulled himself together. After all, she didn't owe him anything. If she wanted to sleep with the guy, she had every right to do so . . . But what a bitch! A little tart who understood nothing about anything! A slut, a low-class whore!

Pouring his bile over her like that, he realized he was debasing himself and that Euclides was right.

"All right then, we're off too," said one of the Americans, the one whose anodyne remark had triggered the governor's profession of faith. Copied by his companion, he took his leave of all those present—at least of those he assumed were not servants—and went.

That left the two stylish men Euclides had told his friend were from the Pentagon.

"Henry McDouglas," one said, coming over to them, hand held out ("Matthew Campbell, Jr.," said the other, like an echo). "One's as bad as the other, they've all slipped away."

"That's my impression too," said Euclides, returning the American's smile. "We're the only ones left on board."

McDouglas looked around the circle of cars. "Impressive collection he's got."

"So people say. But my sight, thank goodness, spares me the displeasure of having to have an opinion on that. Let's just say that it goes with the man. I presume he's shown you his jaguar as well?"

"You're a real clairvoyant, I must say!" McDouglas exclaimed, with a laugh that showed all his perfectly descaled teeth. "He even explained it was out of consideration for the animal that he didn't have a car of the same name . . . I guess he says that to everyone the first time they come to visit, or am I wrong?"

"No, not really," Euclides replied. "Everyone's got their little ways and there are worse ones than that."

"I understand you're a journalist?" Campbell said to Eléazard. "Have you been in this part of the world for long?"

"Six years. Two in Recife and four here."

"That's some time! Brazil can't have any secrets for you by now."

"No secrets is going too far, but I like the country and I make an effort to get to know it better, including its less glossy sides."

"And what do you think of the political situation? I mean here, in Maranhão. The left-wing parties seem to be on the up and up, don't you think?"

"Just be careful what you say, Eléazard," Euclides broke in jokingly. "These gentlemen are from the Pentagon. Anything you say may be noted down and used against you . . ."

Eléazard took a step back, pretending to be alarmed. "From the Pentagon? *Meu Deus!*" Then, still smiling, "Joking apart, I find that intriguing. What exactly do you do there? If I'm not being indiscreet, of course."

"None of the kind of things you seem to be imagining. We're official representatives for Latin America, in a civilian capacity to be precise. We're sent all over the place to prepare or check out various dossiers, get assurances from our partners, put out feelers, that sort of thing. As I'm sure you know, the Pentagon's just a business, the biggest in the United States, sure, but a business all the same. And there's a few thousand of us solely occupied with routine problems of management."

"All of which is pretty vague," Euclides joked, as if to say they couldn't fool him.

"In fact," said McDouglas, rolling his eyes as if he was suspicious of everyone, "our mission is to capture the governor of the State of Maranhão! He's a usurper, impersonated by a dangerous terrorist and we need your help, gentlemen."

His little spiel almost made him likeable. Euclides apologized for pushing him; he understood very well the discretion imposed by the obligation to maintain secrecy in such circumstances . . .

"What obligation to maintain secrecy?" McDouglas exclaimed as if it were a good joke. "You're overstating our importance, I assure you." Serious again, he went on in professional tones, "You know that Brazil produces manganese, the governor reminded us of the fact just now, but what you perhaps don't know is that it is an essential part of certain alloys used by the American army. Until now the mineral has been delivered in its raw state, but the Brazilian government seems to have decided to try and process it here. Which would suit us very well, I make no secret of that. I'm simplifying matters, of course, but we're here to discuss the standards they must stick to if they go ahead with the plan. Nothing top secret in that, as you can see. It's the Minister for Industry, Alvarez Neto—I'm sure you'll have seen him—who brought us here. The chance to meet industrialists, bankers, politicians . . . and to see a bit of the country. You know Brazilia, it's deadly boring."

He spoke deliberately, and with his crew cut and suntanned face his warmth and frankness were contagious. To anyone but Eléazard, Euclides's obstinacy would have seemed the height of discourtesy. "That is reassuring," he said in feigned casual tones. "For a moment I thought you were here because of this business about a military base on the peninsula."

"A military base? That's a new one on me. As you can see, you know a lot more than I do. D'you know anything about that, Matt?"

"First I've heard of it," the other said with a shrug. "Sounds interesting. May we know what it's all about?"

"It's a rumor," said Eléazard, "a vague project the United States is said to be associated with; I read about it in one of the tracts distributed by a Workers' Party candidate. Some are talking about a base for strategic missiles, others about an arms factory, neither backed up with any evidence. Disinformation for electoral purposes probably . . ."

"More anti-American propaganda," said McDouglas, a smile on his lips. "Fair enough, but it's starting to get tedious, you know. Those clowns are playing with fire: the day our economy crashes I wouldn't give much for Brazil's prospects, nor those of South America or even the West in general. Do you think the socialists have a chance in the coming elections?"

"You certainly stick to your guns," Eléazard quipped. "To answer your question: no, practically none at all. They may well have one or two federal deputies, but then . . . Moreira will be reelected governor of Maranhão and everything will continue as before."

"You sound disappointed by that . . ."

"And you're not, from what I see," said Eléazard a touch aggressively. "Personally, my weakness is that I still believe in certain old-fashioned values. I remain convinced, for example, that corruption, nepotism, the enrichment of a few at the expense of all the rest are not normal, even though there are ten thousand years of history to suggest they are. I believe that poverty is not fate but a phenomenon that is deliberately maintained, managed, an abject state that is necessary solely for the prosperity of a small group with no scruples . . . We tend to forget—everything is designed so that we do—that it is always an individual who changes the course of events, by his decision at a particular moment or his refusal to act. That is what power is, without that no one would be interested in it, as you well know. And it is those men, I mean those men in power, whom I hold responsible for what happens."

"Well, well," the American mocked, "I'm beginning to see why you're not exactly popular with the governor."

"It's mutual, I assure you."

"You really think that someone else could do better in Moreira's place?"

"You don't understand. People aren't interchangeable, ever. If a man of good will should appear, someone who's neither a techno-crat, nor a number cruncher, nor even a saint or some guru, such a man would achieve more on his own than generations of profes-sional politicians. That may seem all pie in the sky to you, but there are righteous men—or madmen if you prefer—people who are quite simply honest, who refuse to 'adapt' to the 'real world,' who act in such a way that the real world adjusts to their madness . . ."

He stopped when he saw the mechanics hurrying back to their places. A few seconds later, just at the moment when the purr of its engine became audible, the Panhard came into the garage and parked in the exact spot it had set out from.

Moreira appeared with the frosty expression of a man who was just managing to control his anger. A few seconds later he was tak-ing it out on the unfortunate mechanic who had dashed forward, clutching a cloth, to deal with the splashes on the windscreen: the car was pulling to the left a little and a strange whistling noise could be heard as soon as he was doing more than ninety; they'd better sort those problems out, and quick, he wasn't paying them to sit there twiddling their thumbs and he was fed up with all these stupid mulattos . . .

"So what was it like?" McDouglas asked Loredana, less out of interest than to hide his embarrassment at the Colonel's boorish outburst.

"Not bad," she said with a cold smile, "but the car was pulling to the left a little and there was a strange whistling noise when we went a bit too fast . . ."

Moreira looked at her with a murderous expression, but Loredana merely stared at him with a feigned air of surprise, lips pursed, as if she had no idea what had got into him. Euclides took advantage of the situation to say he'd like to go home now. He was in the habit of rising with the lark and felt exhausted at having stayed up so late.

The Americans took leave of the doctor and his companions with exquisite politeness, unlike the Colonel, who made no attempt to conceal his bad mood.

"What on earth got into you, for God's sake?" Eléazard suddenly cried as they were heading back to the Ford.

With a reproachful glance for his impertinence and in detached tones that say that a problem has been solved and there's no point in dwelling on it, Loredana declared, "I wanted to have the chance to slap the guy. I've had it. Period."

And while Eléazard pulled up short, his eyes almost popping out of his head, Euclides gave one of those little giggles in which he expressed his absolute joy at women's intelligence.

A FEW HOURS later, after the last guests had finally left, while the servants were still busy restoring order to the *fazenda*, the governor had shut himself in his study to smoke one last cigar. Delightfully tipsy, with dark rings under his eyes from fatigue, he finally had the time to examine the model that had been delivered that afternoon. Crafted in meticulous detail, it represented on a scale of 1/1,000 the project of a vast seaside resort Moreira had been working on for months. Like a little boy with his nose pressed against a shop window at Christmas, he did not tire of examining his dream, of admiring its scope, its spectacular prospect. Surrounded by coconut trees, the eighteen stories of an immense, crescent-shaped building towered up facing the Atlantic: freshwater and seawater swimming pools, tennis courts, a golf course, catamarans, a helicopter pad, nothing had been forgotten to transform this expanse of jungle into a first-rate tourist destination. As well as the five restaurants and the luxury shops on the ground floor, there was even a beauty salon, a health spa and an ultramodern center for thalassotherapy. The Californian architect, who had been charged with giving shape to his desires, had produced something well beyond his expectations, sculpting the tropical forest so that all that was left were a few civilized patches of greenery, among which the bungalows and sports installations were arranged harmoniously. The golf course alone would have justified the huge advance that had already been paid to him: it would be one of the finest on the international circuit and definitely the most exotic. Clearly all that would cost a fortune—twenty-five million dollars at the lowest estimate—but the first hurdle had been overcome: just before the festivities that evening to celebrate this three-dimensional fantasy, the banks had undertaken to guarantee three-quarters of that sum, with the result that they could start clearing the ground in a fortnight's time, as soon as the funds were released.

Entirely absorbed in his rapture, the governor was indulging in visions of a happy future. The region would enjoy an unparalleled revival: several hundred jobs created immediately, not to mention the subsequent spin-off from all those rich tourists who would have nothing better to do than deluge the Sertão in a shower of dollars more effective than any rainfall. It was a godsend that would finally allow them to restore the old baroque districts of São Luís, transform Alcântara into a jewel of colonial architecture and attract even more visitors to this out-of-the-way place.

Yes, everything was possible, and all thanks to his creative imagination! There would be a certain amount of friction because of the launching base, some whining from ecologists desperate for a sit-in outside the Palacio Estaudal, but eventually reason would prevail: these two projects, his and that of the Americans, were a rare opportunity for Maranhão, the only one which would allow it to escape its congenital poverty.

That he should make a lot of money out of the projects was only fair. The influx of American technical and military staff would not have been sufficient on its own to give the region the shock treatment it needed. It would owe its revival to its governor's presence of mind alone, to his managerial and entrepreneurial skills. In our lives we encounter certain combinations of circumstances to fail to exploit which would be an insult to destiny. When he heard— from the lips of Alvarez Neto and under the seal of secrecy—of the existence of these negotiations, the whole process, which had just been completed, had immediately appeared to him with blinding clarity. On the very evening of his interview with the minister he had started to buy up the land provisionally selected by the Americans for the installation of their experimental missiles, as well as all the parcels surrounding them, so that he could sell them on at a high price when the time came; the aim of this speculation was not merely to make a fantastic profit, but to underwrite his real-estate project. Contacting the architect, meeting him in Palo Alto, setting up the financial arrangements had not been easy, far from it! The small landowners needed a lot of persuading to sell their patches of land, the architect took ages to send him his plans, then the banking pool had done its bit, criticizing his valuations, demanding more guarantees to the point where he had had to agree to mortgage the *fazenda* and his collection of cars, the only assets of which he was sole owner. Everything else belonged to Carlotta: the steelworks in Minas Gerais, the seafront apartments in Bahia, the 35 percent of Brazilian Petroleum ... a fortune he managed for her and which their son would one day inherit. The Alzegul inheritance! What a load of nonsense. He never thought of Mauro without falling into a kind of impotent, bitter rage, rather as if he had fathered a legless cripple or a child with an atrophied brain. An intellectual crammed full of books, an Alzegul through and through, incapable of distinguishing between a balance sheet and a working account. Yes, disabled, with no knowledge of reality apart from his petrified memory, ancient, sterile, outside human time, outside his own life ... A paleontologist! And since it summed up all his disappointment and misfortune as a father, the word twisted his lips, as if it were an insult. All that money lying idle. For what, for whom? If only they would allow him to pump the money into business enterprises! That and that alone would have a profound effect on the world. His son, his wife, all those who were always making speeches but never got their hands dirty—nothing but a load of jerk-offs who never produced anything, who only made ripples by spitting in the water! But the Earth went on turning without them and would consign them to oblivion in its slow metamorphosis.

It had taken no great effort for Moreira to overcome his scruples and use part of these savings to acquire the land he wanted. After all, the title deeds were in his wife's name and were a much more profitable investment than ordinary stocks and shares. The fact that this subterfuge meant that his own name appeared nowhere in the long chain leading to the *Alcântara International Resort* was a pretty neat trick as well.

Entirely taken up with his blissful thoughts until that moment, he was completely unprepared as the shadow of Loredana returned to haunt him. His excursion with her passed before his inner eye in a succession of disjointed shots, like a film botched during editing.

Her shameless invitation had made him drunk with pride, a feeling of euphoria due less to the prospect of a probable affair with
the woman than to the pleasure of whisking her away before the
very eyes of her hack admirer. So he'd driven off, foot down, on
the long straight road through the fields of sugar cane. Because of
their protective grilles—an innovation at the time—the Panhard's
headlights only lit up the strict minimum so that the car seemed
absorbed into the night as it sped forward. One of the advantages
of the Dynamic—"A real car for the ladies' man," he often said, "just
imagine yourself driving with a girl on either side. *Mãe de Deus!*"—
was that the central steering wheel reduced the distance between
the driver and the door, favoring all sorts of maneuvers; there was
no need to imagine a bend to feel Loredana's shoulder against his
own. Determined not to take the initiative, savoring every moment
of the sensual pressure, Moreira was quivering, every nerve strain-
ing toward a body he was sure he was going to possess very soon.

He turned off onto a country lane, bumped along in neutral for
a hundred yards and stopped by an isolated chapel. The headlights lit up a beautiful portal with baroque ornamentation over
it, a mixture of angels and skulls. "I wanted to show you this little
jewel," he said in a warm voice. "The end of the seventeenth century . . ." This ploy always worked with women. Loredana seemed
very taken with it, she admired the bas-reliefs, asked questions:
were they still on his land? So this chapel belonged to him? To
him, yes, like the hamlet they'd just passed through, like the wells
or the hill you could make out over there, like the whole of the
Alcântara peninsula. At first in order to impress her, then simply
because he got carried away, he found himself telling her about
his projects for Maranhão, the tourist complex, the sums he'd invested . . . And then, quite naturally, as if to get her to share in his
vision, to associate her with it more closely, he'd put his hand on
her thigh . . . His cheek was still stinging.

She could go to hell, her and her stupid frog! And Euclides as well, for having brought along a couple of leftie fanatics like that! Any woman but her would not have got away with it, but afterward she had looked at him with such disdainful calm—as if, without giving it a further thought, she had squashed an irritating fly—that he had simply started the car again, turned and driven back.

Relighting his cigar, he suddenly found it odd that even the memory of that fiasco had not managed to mar his joy.

CHAPTER 15

Which follows the preceding chapter & in which Kircher
contrives an astonishing pedagogical surprise for Caspar . . .

"JUST IMAGINE, CASPAR, how easily the idolators will recognize their errors if we show them that we speak the same language! For us as for them the Sun is the universal source of light, it is the work of the 'Most High,' the dwelling place of God. As for the world, it is never more than the shadow of the divinity, its distorted image. 'Give me a place to stand,' Archimedes said to Hieron of Syracuse, '& I will move the Earth,' & I say, 'Give me the right mirror & I will show you the face of Christ, restored in His perfection & wholeness.' This mirror, which eliminates outward perversions and transforms the monstrosity of forms into pure beauty, I have in my hands, Caspar: it is analogy. Make the effort to reflect the totality of worlds in it & like me you will see, clear and resplendent at the very heart of darkness, the sole image of God."

Athanasius fell silent & was lost in thought for a moment.
I could have listened to him for hours on end, especially since
the Burgundy was beginning to have its effect; I felt that I
understood better than ever the importance of his mission.

"There's nothing like an experiment," he said in decisive
tones. "Come on, off we go, *discipulus*, I am going to show
you something few people have had the opportunity to see.
Provided, that is, that you agree to allow yourself, when the time
comes, to be led without being able to see a thing."

I agreed jubilantly, enticed by this condition, like something
out of a romance.

We left the College & set off to walk into the town. It was
clammy, the heat oppressive & in the sky there were some of
those little coppery clouds announcing a storm. We chatted
as we walked, Kircher untiringly commenting on all the
monuments of Ancient Rome we passed on our way. Just as we
turned into the street of St. John Lateran, leaving the Coliseum
behind us, Kircher stopped.

"This is where you have to accept the little formality
necessary for my experiment. I'm going to ask you to accompany
me for several minutes without seeing anything. Not as a
precaution, for there's nothing you mustn't see, but to ensure the
maximum effectiveness of my experiment. So close your eyes &
don't open them again until I tell you to."

I happily obeyed & my master led me by the shoulder, as if I
were blind. After about fifty paces we entered a shady alley—I
realized that from the welcome absence of the sun on the back
of my neck—& quickly turned off two or three times. Then we
started to go down some never-ending steps. What was odd
was that there was now no noise to be heard. This complete
silence was certainly frightening & I started to tremble with
apprehension as much as with cold. From time to time we took

several paces on the level, twisting and turning, as if we were in a labyrinth. Finally, after about thirty paces along a path so narrow we had difficulty walking side by side, Kircher stopped.

"Here we are," he said gravely. "We have only gone some twenty paces down into the depths of the ground, but in so doing we have passed through the ages! Just use your imagination: not far from here the gladiators of Publius Gracchus are training to die; Tertullian is still drowning his sorrows in the outskirts of Carthage, Marcus Aurelius is slowly dying on the distant banks of the Danube & Rome is already nothing more than the indolent capital of a rickety, moribund empire. It is the year of Our Lord 180, in the villa of an idolator rich enough to have set up in his own house a shrine to the god of his heart. Open your eyes, Caspar, & contemplate the God Mithras, prince of the shades & of light.

I obeyed my master & could not prevent myself from shrinking back at the spectacle awaiting me. We were in a sort of little cave hewn out of the very rock; two oil lamps cast a weak light on a stele roughed out into panels but with a very delicately sculpted bas-relief on one of its faces. It showed the god Mithras as an ephebe in a Phrygian cap cutting the throat of an enormous bull. The surface of the stone and the walls of the grotto were soiled with splashes of dried blood. I crossed myself as I spoke the name of Jesus.

"Don't be afraid," Kircher said calmly, "the only danger we are exposed to here would be to catch a cold. Help me light these torches, we'll be able to see better & it will warm up the unhealthy air in this place a little."

As we lit the torches, I saw that the shrine was the largest of the six or seven rooms in an underground dwelling. These other rooms were paved in rudimentary *opus sectile* & one could still make out patches of crude decoration on the walls. In a recess,

which must have been the kitchen, clear water was still running
into a granite trough. We went back to sit opposite the altar of
Mithras, on one of the stone benches running along the sides of
the temple.

"The worshippers of this god," my master went on, "used to sit
here, just as we are sitting, after having placed the consecrated
offerings on a table. Then they would start praying, while the
priest, doubtless the master of the house, would chant the ritual
hymns. That was the point at which assistants would cut the
throat of a bull in a room above this one; the blood poured in
through the openings you can see in the vault in a warm, sickly
rain toward which the proselytes turned their hands & faces in
humility . . ."

"Are they . . ." I stammered, pointing at the brownish-red
stains on the stone.

"No, no," said Kircher, amused, "those are the remains of
paint. Everything was decorated, walls & bas-reliefs, & it's the
murex dye that resists the ravages of time best."

I was glad of the correction but still could not repress a
certain feeling of disgust at the sight of the ambiguous stains.

"Once this ritual & purifying shower were finished, men
& women in their bloodstained robes, hair sticky with clots,
started to eat & drink in honor of the god. Then an unbridled
orgy brought this 'liturgy,' worthy of the most barbaric of
mankind, to a fittingly appalling end."

The scene evoked by Athanasius having revived my remorse
at certain doings of which the reader will be aware, you will
understand how distressed I was at this account. Fortunately he
was already explaining to me the symbolism of the stele before us:

"It represents the scene of the taurobolium, the ritual sacrifice
of the bull. It shows light & darkness, that is, Ormuzd &
Ahriman in their endless struggle against each other. These two

enemy brothers from the Persian cosmology would destroy each
other were it not for the harmonizing action of Mithras. Uniting
hot & cold, wet & dry, good & evil, generation & decay, dawn &
dusk, he brings about essential harmony, just as a heptachord
tempers the low sounds with the high ones, the high sounds
with the middle ones, the middle sounds with the lower ones &
the latter with the higher ones again. A doctrine that illustrates
perfectly Zoroaster's egg, such as I have managed to piece it
together from the works of Iamblicus & Plutarch of Chaeronea."

Taking a pointed stone, on a patch of plaster Kircher drew
an ellipse filled with long, black & white intersecting triangles,
with the Sun in the middle & the southern and northern
constellations all around.

"But Zoroaster," I asked, "what exactly was he?"

"Zoroaster was not a man but a title, the one given anyone
who concerned himself with knowledge of the arcana & magic.
The famous Zoroaster, the inventor of magic, is no other than
Ham, the son of Noah. The second Zoroaster is Cush, the son of
Ham & faithful interpreter of his father's knowledge. Cush, in his
turn, is the father of Nimrod, who built the Tower of Babel. It is
probable, as I could easily prove, that Ham learned from Enoch
not only the doctrine of the angels & the mysteries of nature but
also the black arts concerning the strange & esoteric arguments
of the descendants of Cain. Mixing the lawful & unlawful
arts, he established a rule that was degenerate in all respects
compared to that of his father. In a second age, Trismegistus, a
descendant of the Canaanite branch of Ham—& the son of that
Mizraim who had chosen Egypt as his country—separated that
which was lawful from that which was not & created a rule that
conformed more closely to divine religion. And he proceeded
like a pagan philosopher, supported solely by the light of nature
amid the depravation of the world. And he, in truth, is the only

Zoroaster, the Hermes Trismegistus praised by so many writers of Antiquity. But it's time we moved on to the second premise of my stone syllogism; there are more surprises in store for you."

Without giving me time to respond, Kircher grasped a torch & led me along the narrow corridors of this subterranean dwelling. Lit by the reddish light of the flame, he looked like a Virgil guiding his Dante Alighieri to hell, *si parva licet componere magnis*.[1] Soon we saw some steps carved in the rock. After having climbed them carefully, we came into a vast subterranean hall supported by a multitude of heterogeneous columns.

"Cross yourself," said Athanasius, as he did so himself, "for we are in a basilica. This church dates from the fourth century after the death of Our Lord; it was constructed by the first Christians out of the scattered materials of the devastated city. Never have faith & love reached such a high point as in this place. It was the beginning of a new era, built on the ruins & doubts of a collapsed civilization. Here there is no display of wealth, no frivolous ornament, but simplicity alone, as befits the nakedness of man before the grandeur of God.

We made our way between the columns while my master was talking & came to a little Christian altar: a stone trough, its sole decoration the Chi-Rho symbol on each of its sides. I crossed myself again, full of intense feeling, sensing the presence of God with all my faculties. Although underground and abandoned by for so long, this chancel was inhabited . . .

"Help me," Kircher said taking hold of the marble slab covering the trough, "I'm going to show you something."

We put the lid on the ground & Athanasius told me to look inside the trough. To my great surprise I saw that it had no bottom & opened like a well onto total darkness.

1 If I may be permitted to compare small things with great.

"The sacred chalice, the luminous vase in which the sublime mystery of the transubstantiation takes place, rested above this well of darkness. Here, on the edge of light and dark, the wine turned into blood again, the unleavened bread to flesh, in an ever-renewed sacrifice. Night & day were reconciled in the person of Christ to maintain the balance of the universe. Here, Caspar, in this very place!"

Kircher had raised his voice & as he said these last words he cast his torch into the black hole at the bottom of the trough. After a brief fall it landed a few feet below in a shower of glowing embers, then continued to burn, though less fiercely. My heart missed a beat & my blood ran cold: below the altar, just at its base, the god Mithras seemed to be moving slowly in the glow of the dying flames.

"Extraordinary, isn't it?" Kircher murmured fervently. "Zoroaster, Hermes, Orpheus & the Greek philosophers worthy of the name, I mean the disciples of Egyptian wisdom, all believed in a single god. The very one whose multiple virtues and perfections were represented by the Egyptian priests through Osiris, Isis & Harpocrates, in a way that is a mystery for us."

"The Trinity?" I ventured, trembling.

"Yes, Caspar: Osiris, the supreme intellect, the archetype of all beings & things; Isis, his guardian angel & his love; their respective virtues give birth to Harpocrates, their child, that is, the world perceived by our senses & this admirable harmony, this perfect concord of the universe, which we ascertain each day all around us. It is, therefore, clear that the sacrosanct & thrice-blessed Trinity, the greatest & thrice-sublime mystery of the Christian faith, has been approached in other times under the veils of esoteric mysteries. For the divine nature likes to remain veiled, it hides from the senses of common & profane men behind similes & parables. It is for that reason that Hermes Trismegistus introduced the hieroglyphs, thus becoming the prince & father of the whole of Egyptian theology and philosophy. He was the first & the most ancient of the Egyptians, the first to think of divine matters correctly, carving his opinions for eternity on immortal cyclopean stones. It is through him that Orpheus, Musaeus, Linus, Pythagoras, Plato, Eudoxus, Parmenides, Plotinus, Melissus, Homer, Euripides & so many others had true knowledge of God & divine matters. He was the first, in his *Pimander* & his *Asclepius*, to affirm that God was One & was Goodness; the other philosophers merely followed him &, for most of the time, with less good fortune . . ."

My head was splitting, I must admit, at the consequences of such a vision of the world. Kircher had hit the nail on the head: there had never been either paganism or polytheism but one single religion, that of the Bible & the Gospels disguised, more or less, by the ignorance & guile of those who have turned it to their own advantage. It was no longer worth the trouble of trying to convince the infidels of the superiority of Christianity over their own belief, since it was enough, on the contrary, to show that they were identical, which until then had remained unclear—& that by logic alone, based on the most ancient texts & the lesson of the hieroglyphs. Intelligence & history could finally come to the aid of the light of the Gospels to support the indefatigable zeal of our missionaries . . .

"It's marvelous!" I exclaimed, dazzled by my master & as if I had absorbed by osmosis some of the divine favor he enjoyed.

"I am merely an instrument," he replied, "it is its creator who should be thanked. But come, let me finish my demonstration."

Going back up the steps by which we had come, we left the basilica & soon emerged in a building with enough lights to make our torches unnecessary. After a few twists & turns we were in the transept of a church I immediately recognized.

"Yes," said Athanasius, "Saint Clement's. It is beneath this unremarkable chapel that the mysteries into which you have been initiated are to be found. And, as I'm sure you'll have guessed, the altar of this third sanctuary is directly above the other two. It is thus the same god who has been worshipped here without interruption for fifteen hundred years."

When we left Saint Clement's the daylight blinded me for a brief moment. I was, however, less dazzled by it than by the far more decisive illumination that had set my soul on fire; I was enraptured, serene, like one who has been blessed. From that point on there was no doubt at all in my mind that in Kircher I was keeping company with a veritable saint!

ON THE RIVER PARAGUAY: *sudden plops, muffled lapping, brief splashes, languid belches of the mud*

"That guy's a headcase," Elaine said, flopping down beside Mauro. "Do you realize what he's done? Now there's no proof Milton was murdered . . ."

She was still using the familiar '*tu*' without noticing. Mauro could have said precisely when she had started: in the heat of action, when she was giving orders, magnificent, her breasts exposed, like the figurehead on a ship.

"Calm down," he said, taking her hand. *It was exciting to continue to address her as* '*você,*' *to maintain the distance between them that had now become artificial.* "Anyway, it doesn't make any difference now."

Their voices were hoarse with weariness, the aftereffects of the emotions they had been through in the course of the day.

"What do you think we should do?" Elaine asked, as a way of countering her desire to cry. "Should we wait here?"

"It seems the most logical solution to me. I can't see us carrying Dietlev through the jungle for days on end."

"And if Petersen doesn't come back?"

"He'll come back, don't worry, even if only to refloat his boat. And then there's Yurupig, he won't leave us in the lurch."

"You didn't see, just now, while I was discussing things with that swine, he made a sign to me to say no, as if he didn't want us to stay on the boat. That's why I played for time."

"You must have misunderstood. We'll talk to him a bit later, once we've got Petersen off our backs. And what about Dietlev?" he added, looking at the blood-soaked bandages, "It doesn't look too good."

"We need to get him to a hospital as quickly as possible. I've done my best, but his knee's all smashed up."

"You've done everything that could be done. I'd never've been able to do that, even if I'd known how. Are you a trained nurse, or what?"

Elaine managed to smile. "I wish I were. If Dietlev hadn't helped me, I think I'd still be looking for the artery. All I've got is a vague memory of things I read when I was pregnant: I was terrified at the idea of being caught up in an accident unprepared. I spent months imagining the worst, it was hell. I even learned to give injections . . . When my daughter was born the obsession disappeared just like that. Strange, isn't it?"

"How old is she?"

"Moéma? Eighteen. She's studying ethnology at Fortaleza. When I think how she envied me this trip!"

Mauro felt a twinge of disappointment: he was in love with a woman who could be his mother. That thought threw him back into the uncertainties of youth worse than a rebuff would have.

"At Fortaleza!" he exclaimed, despite himself. "Why so far away?"

"It's complicated," Elaine replied after a second's hesitation. "How shall I put it? In retaliation, I suppose. She was disoriented when I left; she didn't want to live either with me or with her father."

"You're divorced?"

"Not yet," she said pensively. "It's in progress."

Night was beginning to fall, hiding her face.

"Right," said Mauro, "I'll go and find a lamp and open a couple of tins. All this has given me an appetite . . ."

"You stay here, I'll see to it. It'll give me a chance to have a quick wash too."

"As you wish. I'll call you if he wakes up at all."

"Thanks," she said, getting onto her knees before standing up. "I mean thanks for standing by me back there. I was pathetic."

"Forget it, please. Without Yurupig it wouldn't have got us anywhere."

Mechanically she ran her fingertips over his swollen face. "I'll have a look at that when I come back, when I've got some light. Try and get some rest."

THE BOAT'S BATTERIES gave a feeble light. The pale yellow flickering exaggerated the wreckage in the saloon; the jumbled objects gave off an intense feeling of distress. Going into the kitchen, Elaine suddenly found herself face to face with Yurupig.

"You mustn't stay here," he said in a low voice, placing a finger on his lips to tell her to be quiet. "You must come with us, into the forest . . ."

"But why?" she asked, also in a whisper.

"He's a bad man. He knows you have no chance. You'll wait for days and days, and he won't come back." Since she still seemed to doubt him, he added, "The water. I saw him, he's the one who punctured the jerricans."

AFTER A PERFUNCTORY wash, Elaine put on a clean but damp shirt and jeans and went back up on deck. She took a paraffin lamp and a mess tin of black beans Yurupig had prepared for them. Dietlev had just woken up.

"I can understand drug addicts better now," he said with a smile that emphasized his cheekbones. "The dreams I've had! X-rated stuff!"

"He didn't want me to tell you," Mauro said in answer to Elaine's glance.

"How d'you feel?" she asked, sitting down beside him.

"Oh, never better, it's as if I'd drunk a whole bottle of schnapps. I only hope I don't get the hangover to go with it."

"You must take some anti-inflammatory pills. I'll get you some."

"Don't worry, it's seen to. I swallowed a small handful when I woke up."

"Here," she said, handing Mauro the mess tin, "start eating. It's Yurupig who made it. I must tell you what I've just heard. You won't believe your ears." In a few words she explained to Dietlev what had happened while he was asleep, then reported what Yurupig had told her. Mauro could not hold back a few choice words of abuse regarding Petersen.

Dietlev's face had darkened. "That changes the whole situation," he said after a brief pause for reflection. "We'll have to see to it that we do the opposite of what he wants. Yurupig's on our side, so it shouldn't be too difficult. But we'll have to be on our guard, the guy's capable of anything. Mauro, you'd better get the satellite maps, it looks as if they're going to be even more useful than I thought."

Mauro shook his head as he hurriedly swallowed the food he was chewing. "You can forget them, they're nothing but papier-mâché."

"You're sure?"

"Sure. They were the first things I looked for when I went down."

"Get something to write with, then. I've still got some details in my head, I'd better tell you them while I can still remember."

When Mauro had gone, he took Elaine's hand. "And how are you?"

"I'm surviving, you might say. It's your leg I'm worried about. It's all my fault . . . But I think I would have thrown myself in the water rather than go with that guy."

"Don't be stupid. Mauro beat me to it by a few seconds, but I wouldn't have abandoned you either. The lad did well. As for my leg, it'll hold out till I get to a hospital, won't it?"

Elaine looked at him without finding a single word of reassurance.

"If not," he went on with a smile, "we'll just have to cut it off and we can forget about it. I've always dreamt of having a wooden leg, like Long John Silver. It'll make me stand out, so to speak."

"Stop it! I don't even want to think about it."

"This is all I could find," Mauro said reappearing in the light of the lamp. He handed Dietlev two flyleaves torn out of a book and a pencil.

"That'll do. Help me sit up a bit. Right," he went on, drawing as he spoke, "let's recapitulate: there's the river with the junction and here's where we were the last time I looked at the map, not long before we reached the crocodile hunters' camp. You won't get very far with that," he said when he'd completed his map, "but this sketch should be enough to stop you going seriously wrong. If you skirt the marshy area you should be able to get back to the river in two or three days, though you may have to double that time because of the difficulties of making your way across this terrain. I'll make a list of what you have to take."

"What *we* have to take," said Elaine.

"No. I'm staying here, quietly waiting while you're getting eaten up by mosquitos . . ."

"Out of the question! We're taking you with us whether you like it or not."

"She's right," said Mauro. "It's out of the question."

"Don't be stupid," said Dietlev calmly. "I've worked everything out, I'm well able to manage on my own, as you'll see."

"We've said no," Elaine insisted. "It would be madness."

"We'll talk about it in the morning," said Dietlev, putting an end to the discussion. "In the meantime you'll pack your rucksacks according to my instructions. And no slipping in anything else at all, OK?"

AFTER THEY'D GOT their things together as Dietlev had ordered, Elaine and Mauro went back on deck. A further morphine injection allowed her to clean Dietlev's wound and change the dressing. After that she forced herself to try and eat a little, but when the first mouthful turned her stomach, she told Mauro she wanted to get some sleep and stretched out alongside Dietlev.

For what seemed a long half hour she lay there, motionless, her mind fixed on the conviction that she would never get to sleep; once she had accepted this fact, she suddenly woke to the nocturnal din of the forest: still the same guttural cries, closer to or farther from the river, the same overexcited polyphony from the buffalo frogs, the same indistinct calls rendered even more oppressive by their resemblance to familiar noises—castanets, water dripping or a reed pipe. And during the brief islands of silence, Dietlev's convulsive snores and Mauro's slow breathing.

The howl of some animal having its throat ripped open made her start. Tomorrow, she thought, they'd be making their way toward these specters with nothing but a compass to guide them. Something deep down inside was making her hope Petersen would force them to stay on the boat. Dietlev shifted in his sleep with the groans of a feverish child.

"Are you asleep, Elaine?" Mauro whispered.

"No, I can't manage to drop off."

"What's bothering you?"

"The questions you ask," she said in ironic tones. "We get shot at by machine guns, one of us gets killed, Dietlev's seriously wounded, we're stranded right in the middle of the Pantanal with a bastard who's doing all he can to leave us here to rot . . . and you wonder what's bothering me?"

"There's something else. I know. Tell me the truth."

Cut to the quick by this demand, Elaine remained silent. Every time this boy managed to drive her into a corner. The truth . . . Her new life had not matched up to her hopes. Her other men—a few pale silhouettes were all that came to mind—were not a patch on Eléazard. Even Dietlev, so tender and funny, so brilliant, had not managed to eclipse the man she had fled in a desperate rush, in one last instinctive assertion of freedom. And, God, where had it left her? In this permanent anguish of having to live alongside a shade, in this quiet disgust with herself?

"The truth," she suddenly said in a low voice, "is that I'm afraid. In a panic about what's going to happen tomorrow . . . You don't feel afraid, do you?"

Mauro did not reply. Elaine closed her eyes with a smile. She matched her breathing to his and finally fell asleep herself.

DAWN RAISED BANDS of mist over the river, creeping greedily, ready to wrap themselves around the least protuberance,
as if they could thus secure their fleeting existence. Nocturnal
predators and prey had finally dozed off; their successors were
still asleep. A brief moment of equilibrium during which the river
noises alone—sudden plops, muffled lapping, brief splashes, languid belchings of the mud—broke the morning calm. The effort
of sitting up made Petersen aware of his hangover. The first thing
he did was to go and look for Yurupig to order him to make some
coffee. He was not in the least surprised to find him squatting
on the prow, his gaze fixed on the forest, so accustomed had he
become to the Indian's permanent, almost superhuman wakeful-
ness. You could have sworn he slept standing up, like horses or
certain sharks whose need to keep their fragile organs ventilated
day and night forced them to keep moving.

Petersen climbed up to the wheelhouse to collect the few instruments that were indispensable for his march thought the forest: the
detachable compass, the binoculars, two distress rockets rusting
away in a drawer. He put these things by the Kalashnikov, congratulating himself on not having thrown it into the river with Hernando's body. Satisfied with his preparations, he went back down onto
the lower deck, heading for the kitchen. Yurupig wasn't there. *Never
there when you need him, the baboon. Surely he doesn't expect me to
pack the rucksacks. It's not even properly light and he's already managed to make me mad . . . But OK then, there are more urgent things
to do.* Seeing a bottle of *cachaça*, he swigged a mouthful, grimaced
and went to his cabin. The ceiling light concealed a hiding place.
He took out the odd belt Hernando had given him and buckled it
around his waist. Then he took a few steps to check the distribution
of weight, adjusted the little bags by sliding them along the leather
and seemed happy with the result: it wasn't ideal, but it would do.

Back on deck, he heard voices: his passengers had woken.

"Morning, good people," he said in placatory tones. But when he saw Yurupig drinking his coffee with Elaine and Dietlev, he gave him a murderous look. "So," he went on, "how is the wounded man today?"

"Not that bad," Dietlev said. "We can set off as soon as Yurupig's made a stretcher for me."

Petersen froze. "Bullshit, *amigo*. In the state you're in you won't last two days. I've already told the *professora* it would be better for you to wait here while I go for help."

"Except that we haven't enough water to last more than a week—thanks to you, I believe—and that, for some reason that escapes me, you've decided not to come back."

"You're crazy," said Petersen. "Whatever makes you think something like that?"

"Stop putting on an act," said Elaine in contemptuous tones, "you were seen puncturing the jerricans."

Realizing where the information must have come from. Petersen turned to Yurupig, his face twisted with rage. "You! I swear I'll have your hide for this!"

And since the Indian gave him a defiant look, he suddenly turned around, determined to fetch the Kalashnikov and put an end to all this palaver. He stopped short: Mauro stood before him, holding the rifle.

"Is this what you were going to look for?" he said in a toneless voice. "I'm not a weapons fanatic, but I've learned to use them." Matching action to words, he fired a brief burst into the air before aiming at Petersen again. "It's the first time my national service has been any use to me," he added airily.

"Have you all gone out of your heads?" Petersen cried, gray-faced.

"It's a preemptive strike, that's all," Dietlev said firmly. "Just remain calm and nothing will happen to you. We're all going to leave together, but first of all we need a few explanations. Why you punctured the jerricans, for example."

"What jerricans, for God's sake?! Surely you're not going to believe that savage? He'll tell you anything. He's a two-faced bastard, he'll take the lot of you for a ride."

"For the moment it's his word against yours, and I have to admit that your protestations don't count for very much, especially after what's happened. But as you like: you'll give your explanations to the police, that's all. While we're waiting you can give me your belt."

"You've no right," Petersen said, turning pale, "they're personal things."

"The belt," said Mauro threateningly.

"Fire if you like, I don't give a shit."

"*Cocaína,*" Yurupig said simply. "He's the one who makes the deliveries."

"Aha! So that's it," said Dietlev, raising his eyebrows. "That explains everything. Now I can understand why this dear fellow didn't want anyone to go with him." Seeing Elaine's nonplussed expression, he added, "At a rough estimate there'll be five or six kilos there, let's say 50,000 dollars at the very least, and I'm sure our friend was banking on disappearing without a trace but with that little fortune. Since the Paraguayans certainly wouldn't be happy with that, he wouldn't risk setting foot in these parts again. As for taking us with him, that would be going into the lion's den, since sooner or later he'd have to deal with the authorities . . ."

"It's not 50,000 dollars but 500,000, you poor fool!" Petersen exclaimed, his arrogant self again. "And there's half of it for you, if you let me slip away with it when the time comes. Just think, it's more than you'll earn in your whole life."

Dietlev shook his head, a sorrowful look on his face: "If that's all you learned in the Waffen SS, I'm not surprised the Germans lost the last war."

"I'll throw the lot of the filthy stuff in the river and that'll be the end of it," said Elaine firmly.

"Definitely not," Dietlev said, "it's the only proof of his complicity. He can keep it on, that's one thing less you'll have to carry. Keep an eye on him while Yurupig gets the stretcher finished, we're leaving in half an hour."

Eléazard's Notebooks

KIRCHER STILL BELONGS to the world of Archimboldo: if he enjoys anamorphosis, it's because it shows reality "the way it isn't." To truly exist, landscapes, animals, fruits and vegetables or objects of everyday life must be put together to make the face of man, of the divine creature for whom the Earth is intended. With the distorting mirrors or those which, on the contrary, rectify skillfully calculated optical aberrations, Christianity of the Counter-Reformation period takes over the Platonic myth of the cave and turns it into an educational show: during our lives we never see more than the shadows of divine truth. Because it incites lust, this beautiful female face destined for hell is the lesson of the mirrors that distort it horribly; that this blood-colored magma will be of significance one day is the promise of the cylindrical mirrors, which reshape it and change it into the image of paradise.

"FOR NOW WE SEE through a glass, darkly; but then face to face: now I know in part; but then I shall know even as also I am known." I am submissive, it's the fault of St. Paul; and I live on illusions, it's the fault of . . . a familar tune.

ON EUCLIDES'S REMARK ABOUT GOETHE AND THE *ELECTIVE AFFINITIES*. The doctor appears to be talking to me in metaphors, but I have difficulty seeing what he's getting at. That damned parrot's definitely getting on my nerves. Must get rid of it.

TARTARIN DE TARASCON REVISITED: "Father Jean de Jésus Maria Carme, having become separated for a while from the people who had undertaken the same journey with him, saw a frightful crocodile coming straight toward him, mouth wide open, to devour him, and at the same time an angry tiger emerging from the rushes, equally determined to take him. Alas! How could the poor wretch flee the death that was threatening from all sides? What skill could he use to escape the fury of the two most cruel monsters of nature? There was nothing he could do. Thus exposed to this peril, with no human help, he made vows and prayers, now to the Virgin Mary, now to all the saints. But while he was trying to get Heaven to look favorably on him, the tiger leapt. The man bending down low to the ground to avoid the animal's jaws, it flew right over him and hit the crocodile which, having its jaws wide open, fastened on the head of the tiger instead of that of the poor man and gripped it so tight in its long teeth that it died immediately. At that, the poor man fled, taking advantage of the opportunity as fast as he could." (A. Kircher, *China Illustrated*)

KIRCHER'S FAULTS: preferring rhetoric to deductive rigor, commentary to the sources, the apocryphal to the authentic, preferring quasi-artistic expressiveness to the cold realism of geometry.

FROM LOREDANA: Chuang Tsu passing judgment on Moreira: 'When the Tsin king is ill, he summons a doctor. To the surgeon who lances an abscess or a boil, he gives a chariot. He give five to the one who licks his hemorrhoids. The baser the service performed, the better he pays. I suppose you treated his hemorrhoids—why did he give you so many chariots?"

I REMAIN CONVINCED that our faculty of judgment is sharper, closer to what we truly are, in the negative—that is, in exercising criticism, in everything our very fibers reject before any conscious intervention of the mind. It's easier to recognize cheap or corked wine than to distinguish the specific qualities of a great one.

KIRCHER is a mystical forger.

"SHE LIVED FOR THE EXQUISITE PLEASURE of remaining silent." A nice quote, and one that seems to have been made expressly about Loredana. But we must be able to take it further . . . (Relate it to the *Tractatus*: "Whereof one cannot speak," etc.)

CHAPTER 16

In which the story of Jean Benoît Sinibaldus & the sinister alchemist Salomon Blauenstein begins

IN 1647, AT the age of forty-five, Reverend Father Athanasius Kircher was still a fine figure of a man. His beard had gone white in places, also his hair, but nothing else about him suggested he was that old. He had an iron constitution, much stronger than mine despite the difference in our ages & was only occasionally troubled by hemorrhoids, which he treated with an ointment he had formulated himself.

Summer & winter he rose a little before the sun & attended mass in our chapel, then had a frugal breakfast: a piece of black bread and some soup, which the bursar had sent up to his room. Not that he refused to take his meals with us in the refectory, but his multifarious activities meant he could not afford to waste precious time by devoting it to food alone. Eating at his desk, he could continue to read or write & was very content with something none of us would have thought of considering a privilege.

Thus from seven o'clock until noon he stayed in his study, fully occupied with his books, working on several different ones at any one time. My task was to help him as best I could.

Normally we would go down to the refectory for our midday meal, but during those years of intense work it happened more than once that we missed lunch without even noticing. "It just means we'll have an even better appetite this evening," Kircher would say with a smile, though he would then call the porter by his acoustic tube & and have some confectionery brought up or a cup of that decoction called coffee that was fashionable at the time.

We were also in the habit of having a sleep for an hour or two, immediately after lunch; it was a custom from which my master never departed, but he never lay down, having a leather armchair with a spring that allowed the backrest to to be tilted. After that, Kircher spent his afternoon in various practical activities. He supervised the assembly of the machines he was constantly designing for the amusement of the Pope or the Emperor; several of the priests were occupied with these inventions in the College workshops as well as various outside craftsmen.

Many hours were devoted to chemistry, an art that Athanasius pursued passionately in the laboratory he had set up in the cellars, below the dispensary. He prepared the Orvietan antidote & the sympathetic powders to cure the ills with which the great of this world, or simply our brothers in the College, were afflicted. He also had to entertain & guide the scholars who had come to Rome especially to see him & view his collections. Without forgetting, of course, all the physical experiments he regularly carried out in order to test his theories, or those of others, against reality.

At six he attended vespers, then we had our dinner. The hours after that were devoted to reading, conversation &, whenever the clarity of the atmosphere permitted, to observing the stars, an occupation that my master pursued persistently & that we did from a little terrace that had been put up on the College roof. Toward eleven o'clock we went to our well-deserved rest, but it was not uncommon to still see light in his study late in the night.

That year was marked by an episode that, all in all, was fairly pleasant but that was to cost Kircher certain unexpected vexations twenty-two years later.

There was in Rome a French doctor, Jean Benoît Sinibaldus, with whom my master was on good terms because he was a useful acquaintance. Sinibaldus, who had a considerable personal fortune, was a keen alchemist & spent a lot of money, to the great displeasure of his wife, acquiring the materials that were indispensable to the art.

One afternoon in the spring of 1647 Sieur Sinibaldus appeared at the College & asked to speak urgently with Kircher. My master, with whom I was working on a machine that was later to become famous, showed some irritation at being disturbed by this tiresome interruption; nevertheless, he received him with his usual courtesy.

"O joy! O happiness!" Sinibaldus exclaimed a soon as he saw Kircher. "I have seen the sophic sal ammoniac! I have seen it with my own eyes! It's incredible! The man is a genius, a huge, profound genius, a truly sublime mind."

"Now, now," said Athanasius, who found the man amusing & could not stop himself from addressing him with a touch of irony, "take a hold of yourself, my dear friend, & begin at the beginning. Who is this individual who is so happy as to merit such praise from your lips?"

"You're right," Sinibaldus replied, absentmindedly adjusting his wig, "you must forgive my overexcitement, but when you know what brings me here, I am sure you will understand my agitation. This individual is called Salomon Blauenstein & the whole city is talking of nothing but him, for he knows how to make gold from antimony with an ease that says much about the extent of his knowledge."

Suddenly he lowered his voice &, after a quick glance behind him, added in a whisper, "He says he is able to make the Stone, it's only a question of time & the right method . . . His whole person exudes saintliness. He is a true sage & it's clear that he is seeking neither gold nor glory: it was only after I had spent several days begging him that he consented to demonstrate his art to me, but grudgingly, as if he were lowering himself to a practice that was unworthy of his talents."

"Hmm . . . You know my opinion on this matter. Also you must permit me to express some doubt as to the abilities of your . . . your . . . what did you say he was called?"

As we only learned much later, Sieur Sinibaldus was outraged by Kircher's attitude. He could not understand how someone could dispute something, regard it with such skepticism, without even having taken the trouble to check the facts. As soon as he left the College, he determined to show my master how blind he had been. To do that he hurried off to said Blauenstein, whom he persuaded—not without difficulty, for the fellow pretended to be reluctant—to come and live with him. He placed both his laboratory & his whole fortune at his disposition, provided he would teach him to make the stone or the powder of projection, the mere contact with which, as he had established *de visu*, turned the basest matter into gold.

Blauenstein's wife was a young Chinese woman called Mei-li, whose mysterious, silent beauty contributed to the alchemist's aura of unsuspected powers. Mei-li, Blauenstein said—while maintaining a discreet silence about how he had met her during a journey to China—was the sister of the "Grand Imperial Physician attached to the Chamber of Remedies," a man who was versed in the art of alchemy & had taught him many secrets taken from ancient grimoires. To anyone who flattered him enough, Blauenstein would willingly, but with many signs of respect & precautions, show a pile of notebooks covered in Chinese characters that he claimed, with no great danger of contradiction, were a compendium of alchemical knowledge.

This strange couple thus settled bag & baggage in the luxurious apartment Sieur Sinibaldus put at their disposal in his own mansion. No sooner had they arrived than a new athanor had to be constructed for the laboratory, the old one not being suitable, & a number of very rare & very expensive ingredients had to be ordered to start the long process that would lead to the Great Work.

When Sinibaldus admitted his ignorance of the products required & of the means of procuring them, Blauenstein offered to obtain them himself & at the best price, solely out of friendship for his host. The good doctor's moneybags suffered a severe flux, but the alchemist insisted, despite his victim's protestations of trust, on producing all the bills justifying his expenses: fifty thousand ducats for a pound of Persian *zingar* & ten ounces of powdered scolopendra; eighty-five thousand ducats for realgar, orpiment & indigo; the same amount for a small piece of bezoar from a llama; a hundred thousand ducats for tacamahac resin, Turkestan salt & green alum plus a quantity of other materials that were less rare but hardly less expensive, such as cinnabar, powdered mummy & rhinoceros horn, fresh sparrow-hawk feces or wolves' testicles . . . Although substantial, Sinibaldus's resources were dwindling dangerously;

&, as if by an effect of Divine Providence, those of the alchemist were increasing proportionately.

During Blauenstein's planned absences, supposedly to seek out these inestimable materials but in reality to salt away the ducats he saved on his purchases, Mei-li & Sinibaldus had the task of looking after the alchemical furnace & watching over the slow sublimation of sulphur & mercury. Using the heat of the laboratory as an excuse, the beautiful Chinese always appeared in a silk négligée, which would fall open at the slightest movement, revealing, as if inadvertently, quivering charms deliberately left free. Her hair, exquisitely combed & tied at the back, was covered in pearls & topped with a little bamboo bonnet, with an outer shell of silk from which a tuft of red horsehair stuck up. In this transparent semiundress, she would prostrate herself, with much waggling of the rump, before a little altar she had made herself with Christ alongside hideous idols from her own country; also—still in order to encourage heaven to look favorably on the Great Work—she would shamelessly engage in lascivious & languorous dances.

It was not long before poor Sinibaldus was captivated by all this. Only three months after having taken the devil into his home, half-ruined, his willpower paralyzed by love, his senses inflamed by her courtesan's tricks, he would have sold his soul for a kiss. But, although keeping his passion at boiling point with a thousand lubricious wiles, the hussy was careful not to allow him the least liberty; with her simpering ways, she seemed made to show the extent to which intemperate desires can be aroused when self-interest & avarice lend a hand.

These machinations lasted until the dupe was judged ready for culling & on St. John's Eve Blauenstein announced that the Great Work was entering its final stage. All the necessary ingredients had been meticulously weighed out, filtered &

decanted prior to being added to the broth of sulphur, mercury
& antimony that had been simmering in the crucible for so long.

"In two weeks to the day and the hour the mixture will have
attained the sublime perfection extolled by the Ancients. Then all
that will be left will be to precipitate this liquid matter with the
bezoar stone & you will see—born before your very eyes!—the
famous "Green Lion," the wonderful substance that assures you
both wealth & immortality. But the alchemical process is not
simply a question of purifying inert materials, in order to work
it requires an analogous decantation of the body & the mind
without which we will not be able to witness the final miracle.
To this end I am going to retire to a monastery with the bezoar
stone & will pray without cease for these two weeks. My wife,
who was initiated into the most divine secrets by her brother, will
tend the alchemical vessel on her own. As for you, my dear friend
& benefactor, you will retire to your room to pray, merely taking
some food to Mei-li twice a day. The slightest infraction of these
simple rules will put an end to our hopes for good . . ."

Much moved by this, Sinibaldus swore that it would be as the
alchemist desired & that he would spare neither mortification of
the flesh nor prayers to purify his soul.

Blauenstein spent the rest of the night "rectifying" the
laboratory: with his wife & Sinibaldus on their knees, he drew
on the floor & the walls all kinds of magic pentacles to prevent
demons entering the room, recited a number of formulae
taken from the Chinese cabbala & placed the furnace under
the protection of at least three dozen "sephirotic spirits."
Gesticulating & chanting himself hoarse in the thick clouds of
incense he had burning all the time, the alchemist seemed to
Sinibaldus like the very incarnation of Trismegistus.

In the early hours of the morning Blauenstein locked his
wife in the laboratory, then ceremonially handed the keys

over to his host, repeated his orders of the previous evening &
left. Exhausted by the sleepless night, Sinibaldus went to his
bedroom, where he soon fell asleep, lulled by fond hopes and
delusions, beside himself with joy.

Waking around one o'clock, he immediately had a meal
prepared, which he took himself to the fair Mei-li. Respecting
the alchemist's orders, he kept his eyes lowered & closed the
door immediately after having placed the tray of food on the
floor. Back in his bedroom, he flagellated himself for a good
while, then immersed himself in prayer until the evening.

Returning to the laboratory with another meal at dinner
time, he was so surprised to find the morning's tray untouched
that he could not resist taking a glance inside the chamber: only
dimly lit by the reddish light from a little stained-glass lamp,
Mei-li was lying at the foot of the altar. Was she ill? Perhaps
dying?! Locking the door behind him, Sinibaldus dashed over to
the young Chinese woman . . .

He had hardly shaken her than she opened eyes full of tears.
Clinging to his neck with her head between his arms, she
started to sob. Although reassured about her state of health,
Sinibaldus was concerned by these irresistible tears. For a
moment he thought she had committed some irreparable fault
in keeping watch over the Great Work & turned to look at
the crucible: the furnace was roaring as it ought to, nothing
needed to keep it going seemed to have been omitted. His fears
on that point calmed, he set about comforting this magnificent
creature, who was leaning against his shoulder giving rein to
the most intense sorrow. After many friendly words and chaste
caresses he managed to get Mei-li to dry her tears & give him an
explanation of her despair.

"Oh, signore," she said, her voice still broken by sobs, "how
can I tell you that without earning your contempt? You who are

so good & have shown us such trust. I'd rather die a thousand deaths . . . Why must I be the one to suffer such shame and misfortune?"

She spoke Italian fluently but with an accent that made her even more adorable. Sinibaldus did everything he could to get her to speak, assuring her that he would pardon her whatever she said. He had loved this young woman in silence for so many days & here she was huddling up to him in a most delightful state of abandon. The kind of oriental gown she always wore had become undone, revealing a warm, firm bosom he could feel throbbing against his chest. Her thick, jet-black hair gave off an intoxicating perfume; her imploring lips seemed to beg the tenderest of kisses & the ardor of her look expressed transports of love rather than deep distress. Beside himself with desire, Sinibaldus would have consigned the Great Work itself to the rubbish bin at the slightest sign from Mei-li.

When she saw that he had reached that state, the wily woman finally agreed to explain the reason for her despair: Salomon Blauenstein was a saintly man, a gentle, considerate husband, an alchemist unique in his knowledge & experience, but he would never manage to produce the elixir of life without one requirement she alone knew about. She had never had the courage to tell her husband about it, so certain she was that he would have renounced his quest rather than obey it. To bring about the true transformation, not that of gold, which presented no difficulty at all, but that of the elixir of youth, something other than inert matter was necessary.

"How could something without life," the bewitching Chinese said, "produce immortality? You will clearly see that that is impossible & that is the reason why all alchemists had failed up to now. All, that is, apart from certain masters in my country who were aware of the truth & made use of it for their great good fortune."

"But this ingredient, signora? Tell me, I beg you."

"This secret ingredient, signore, the true *materia prima*, without which no transformation can be completed, is human seed, that metaphysical concentrate of divine power thanks to which life is created & renewed. Even that is not of itself sufficient, it also requires love, the passion whose heat alone indissolubly unites man's seed to woman's & allows the Stone to coagulate at the last stage of the Great Work. That is the cause, the sole cause of my despair."

Once more Mei-li burst out sobbing & it was only with the greatest of difficulty that Sinibaldus managed to draw these final words, punctuated by hiccups, out of her: 'I respect my husband, my feelings for him are those of infinite friendship & gratitude, but . . . I do not love him. That essential ardor, that inclination, I have not felt until now . . . until now that . . . now that you have aroused it in me, monsieur. To my misfortune, to yours & that of my husband, I can see, alas, that you are far from sharing that emotion & that henceforward nothing can save our joint enterprise. It was for you that I was crying, imagining your disappointment after so many hopes, so many illusions; as for myself, I will not survive this calamity . . ."

This sent the bashful lover that Sieur Sinibaldus had so far been into a frenzy. Mei-li's declaration not only assured him of an unhoped-for joy but also of the success of the Great Work. Beside himself, forgetting his wife & his children, he covered Mei-li in kisses, laughing & crying at the same time, declaring the passion he had kept hidden for so many months in the most extravagant terms. He had never loved anyone but her, it was as if the goddess Isis had finally found her Osiris & there could no longer be any doubt that they were blessed by God.

The little hussy feigned surprise, then the most unbridled passion & it was there, on the stone floor, that they disported themselves in their lewd Cyprian acts.

During the two weeks in which they remained locked in the laboratory the emissions of their lust poured out constantly. Mei-li carefully scooped up this disgusting mixture in a porcelain vase, then poured it into little wax figurines they made themselves to represent various Chinese gods, but also Christ & the apostles. They then threw these blasphemous idols into the crucible with all sorts of ceremonies & the orgy started up again. Blinded by passion & pride, Sinibaldus obeyed her in everything without for one moment seeing the abyss into which he was sinking.

At the time he had previously fixed, Salomon Blauenstein returned from his supposed retreat. Sinibaldus, who had gone up to his room a little earlier to allay suspicion, came down to meet him. He was surprised at how pale the alchemist looked & at the evidence of privations written all over his face. As for Blauenstein, who had actually spent the time in a brothel in Travestere, he saw the same signs of exhaustion in his host's face, although without deceiving himself as to their true origin; from that point on he was in no doubt about the success of his scheme. They greeted each other warmly &, after the alchemist pretended to set his mind at rest concerning the strict obedience to his orders, they went into the laboratory.

CANOA QUEBRADA: *And for him war was like a merry game . . .*

In the beginning the world did not exist. Neither darkness, nor light, nor anything that could have taken their place. But there were six invisible things: little benches, pot stands, gourds, manioc, ipadu leaves that make you dream when you chew them and plugs of tobacco. A woman made herself out of these things, that were floating around, and appeared, all decked out in finery, in her splendid quartz dwelling. Yebá Beló was her name, the ancestral mother, she who was not begotten . . . In the time it takes to say "Ugh!" she started to think up the world the way it ought to be. And while she was thinking, she chewed ipadu and smoked a magic cigar.

When the Indian dragged her out of the *Forró da Zefa*, Moéma was under no illusion about what would happen between them that night. Worried by Roetgen's absence, she spent a few seconds looking for him in the crowd. Not that she felt obliged to explain what she was doing, but she had insisted on bringing him here and felt bad about abandoning him in such cavalier fashion in a world he wasn't yet familiar with. As for Thaïs, that was both simpler and more awkward: their liaison being based on absolute sexual liberty, Moéma was not committed to anything in that respect. They believed that the love they had for each other—a topic that reappeared in crucial fashion every time one suffered at the other's escapades—went far beyond physical vagaries. Instead of undermining their relationship, this independence "fertilized" it, enlarged it . . . Since, however, this naive generosity of spirit could not prevent either jealousy or the anguish of feeling abandoned, they had come to the point where they observed maximum discretion when they went off with someone else. Moéma was therefore hurrying to avoid running into her friend when she saw her dancing with Marlene. Caught out, she replied to Thaïs' look by fanning herself with her hand, as if to say the heat was too much for her and she was going out for a breath of fresh air. When the response to her bit of playacting was a sad, disbelieving smile, Moéma turned away in irritation.

Once outside, they walked in the darkness, going back up the street to the cabin, since Moéma wanted to collect her supply of *maconha* before going down to the beach.

Beside the water the strength of the wind was visible as it blew away the dunes. Aynoré remained silent; from time to time Moéma felt his hand brush against hers as they continued on their way, staggering as they were hit by gusts. A few hundred yards farther on they sat down on the sand, in the shelter of a jangada pulled up onto the beach. Moéma had rolled a joint. In the deafening roar of the waves, something from the primeval ages of the Earth, an incomprehensible and disturbing din made them snuggle up against each other. She took a drag on the coarse cigarette she had managed to roll despite the wind; Aynoré did the same and started to speak in a low voice: the world had begun in this same way, with a woman emerging from her own night and a magic cigar . . .

Her thoughts came out in the form of a spherical cloud with a tower on top, a bulge like the excrescence of the navel on the belly of a newborn baby. As it spread out, the bubble of smoke enclosed all the darkness so that it remained captive there. Having done that, Yebá Beló called her dream the "belly of the world" and the belly looked like a large deserted village. So she wanted people there where there was nothing and started to chew ipadu again as she smoked her magic cigar . . .

Aynoré's father had been the shaman of his village, somewhere in the Amazonian forest, at the confluence of the Amazon and the Rio Madeira. A renowned magician, the religious and political head of the village, he had treated people with tobacco juice and extracts of plants, of which he guarded the secret jealously. It was from his perseverance in recounting his tribe's epic that this long story with its innumerable ramifications came, a parasitic myth of the origin of the world, which seemed to unfold of its own accord from the lips of the young Indian, feeding on his memory, establishing itself and multiplying like a virus, as it had been doing for centuries. His father had passed on to Aynoré, who was intended as his successor, all the ancestral knowledge that makes a true *pajé*: he knew the foundation myths of the Murururucu, their rites, their dances, their traditional songs, knew how to invoke the spirits, transformed into so many pebbles in the gourd rattle, and to interpret their messages in the whir of the bullroarer; he also knew how to talk to the animals, how to throw invisible spears that poisoned people or sent them into trances that exorcised them. At the age of six he had gone off in search of his soul and it had entered his body in the form of an anaconda. Like his father, he would have become able to borrow the wings of the kumalak bird and fly over the mountains, if the loggers had not come and turned his life upside down.

And with the loggers there was also an official of FUNAI—"the National Indian Foundation! Just imagine! What would a National Foundation of the White Man do for you, eh? Just think about it for a moment"—and with him the army and with the army the end of everything. The villagers had to be evacuated and go and join the other tribes languishing in the Xingu reservation. His father, leading a few men, had tried to resist and they were all dead, shot like common macaques in the course of a manhunt in the forest.

Aynoré was only twelve, but he refused to go with the others to the Xingu reservation, so the FUNAI official immediately sent him off to the Dominican orphanage in Manaus. He learned to read and write there without ever belonging to the religion in which a puny god allowed himself to be crucified in a land with no jungle and no macaws. Then it was a boarding house run by the same order in Belém. He strung them along for a while, then ran off with the money from the bursar's office. Skilled with his

hands, he managed to get by making feather necklaces and earrings that he hawked on the streets.

Aynoré stroked Moéma's hair. Under the influence of his intoxication, his voice took on ceremonial tones, sometimes becoming
unrecognizable in the dialogues, high and distorted, like a ven-
triloquist's. Moéma listened reverently, images and shivers running through her. Even more than by its poetry, she was carried
away by the age-old character of this litany. It was a fascination
tinged with venom toward the whites and their wretched slav-
ish devotion to their god. What an incredible mess! From having learned them, to her disgust, at the university, she knew the
figures of the atrocity by heart: two million Indians when the
Spanish and Portuguese arrived, fewer than a hundred thousand
today . . ."The Indians were innumerable," she had read in a report by a sixteenth-century traveler, "to such an extent, that if
one shot an arrow in the air, it was more likely to end up in an Indian's head than in the ground." The author in question was talking about the Várzeas, a tribe that had ceased to exist less than
a hundred years after this first attempt at a "census." The Tupi,
Anumaniá, Arupatí, Maritsawá, Iarumá, Aulúta, Tsúva, Naruvôt,
Nafuquá, Kutenábu and so many other tribes decimated . . . More
than ninety Amazonian tribes had been wiped out in the course
of our century alone . . . Of what unknown and unknowable lives
have we deprived ourselves for good? Of what possible worlds, of
what healthy evolutions?

A land without men for men without land. It was under this generous slogan that the Brazilian government had decided to construct the Transamazonian Highway, three thousand miles of
road to give white pioneers new lands to cultivate. Every sixty
miles along the road there were 250 acres of virgin land to clear
on either side, a hut already built plus six months' wages and
interest-free loans for twenty years; a multitude of half-starved

people from the *Nordeste* had risen to the bait. All this ignoring the fact that this "land without men" was crammed full of Indians, who were given no more consideration than the flora and fauna sacrificed to the program, no more than at the time of the boom in rubber when the clothes handed out with a friendly smile to the naked savages were impregnated with the germs of smallpox or other fatal diseases.

But what no one had anticipated was that the ground taken from the forest would be completely exhausted after the first two harvests and today the cattle barons would be buying up this sterile land at low prices from the colonists, poor devils who, overburdened with debt, prefer the arid misery of the Sertão to the torture of this dripping desert. The funds earmarked for surfacing the road had disappeared, so that in the rainy season the Transamazonian Highway turns into an impassable river of mud, eaten away a little more each day by the determined reprisals of the jungle. In the course of the Americans' interest in buying several million square miles of land in the Carajás region, rich deposits of iron, nickel, manganese and even gold were discovered in the Serra Plata. The mines and the placers finished by ripping this true paradise apart and everything went up in smoke: the forest, the Indians, dreams of agrarian reform. All that this incredible farce achieved was to make the indestructible caste of bastards a little richer. She felt almost suffocated by a sense of the chronic, oppressive injustice, like a nocturnal asthma attack.

Then the thunder-man came down onto the river of milk where he was transformed into a monstrous snake with a head resembling a boat. The two heroes climbed up onto the snake's head and started to sail up the left bank of the river. Every time they stopped, they established a house and, thanks to their wealth of magic, filled it with people to live there. Thus gradually, house by house, the mankind of the future developed. And since the vessel went below the surface, the houses were under water, so that the first men appeared as fish-men who settled in their underwater houses.

Nothing was as beautiful as this resplendent story, it gave a glimpse of a world of innocence and quiet freedom, an everyday life in which every moment was special, a supernatural game with creatures and things. The secret of happiness was there, in this preserved speech. To go away with Aynoré and seek his people, to recover together that original communion with the river, the birds, the elements; Moéma felt she was ready for this return to the native soil. Not as an ethnologist, but as an Indian in both heart and mind. As a lover of the things themselves. Living was that or nothing at all.

Thus mankind grew, passing by imperceptible degrees from child-hood to adolescence. And when they reached the thirtieth house, that is, the halfway point of their journey, the twins decided it was time to make men speak. That day each performed a ritual with his wife: the first wife smoked the cigar and the second chewed ipadu. The woman who smoked the cigar gave birth to the sacred Caapi, which is even more powerful than ipadu; and the one who had eaten ipadu brought forth the parrots, the toucans and other birds with colored feathers. And from these two women the men came to know trem-bling, fear, cold, fire and suffering, all things they had seen in them while they were in labor.

And the power of the infant Caapi was so strong that all mankind had fantastic visions. No one could understand anything about them and each house started to speak a different language. From this sprang many languages: Desana, Tukano, Pira-Tapuia, Barasana, Banwa, Kubewa, Tuyuka, Wanama, Siriana, Maku and, last of all, that of the White Men.

"Caapi," Aynoré said, "is a kind of vine. You make a potion from its bark and you have visions. It's a thousand times stronger than anything you can ever have tried. Among our people the women are not allowed to drink it. It's a sacred plant, the vine of the gods, the vine of the soul . . ." They'd often taken it in the men's cabin, it was completely crazy: you met the Grand Master of the hunt, you watched extraordinary fights between snakes and jaguars, you discovered the true invisible powers behind the illusion of life. "I had no will of my own," Aynoré said, "no personal power. I didn't eat, I didn't sleep, I didn't think; I wasn't in my body anymore. Purified, I woke up as a sphere of seeds that had burst open in space. And I sang the note that smashes structure to pieces and the one that abolishes chaos and I was covered in blood. I have been with the dead, I have tried the labyrinth . . ." For there was a world beyond ours, a world both very near and very far away, a world where everything had happened already, where everything was already known. And that world spoke, it had its own language, a subtle idiom of rustlings and colors. Blue, purple or gray visions, like tobacco smoke, which declined the unknown modes of thought; blood-red visions, like a woman's discharge, her fertility; yellow or off-white visions, similar to semen, the sun, through which the mystical union with the beginning was realized. And everything appeared in an indescribable luminosity, as if detached from its context, charged with new meaning, a new quality. After the ceremony, when they woke from a profound sleep full of dreams, each one of them drew or painted what he had seen. There was not a single decoration, not a single tattoo, that had not been inspired by these journeys through hallucination. And the reason there were so many different languages was to try to say all that, to express again and again the things they were unwilling to leave in the ambiguous silence of images . . ." A man who has taken Caapi is said to have drowned himself, as if he were returning to the river from which he came, as if he were plunging back into the undifferentiated source . . . A man who has an orgasm when he possesses a woman is also said to be drowning himself, but that is to indicate that he is in a state similar to the one produced by Caapi."

The eighth and last ancestor was the priest. And he came out of the water with his book in his hand, and he was as sterile as a castrated pig. So the Creator commanded him to stay with the Whites, and that is why we knew nothing of the existence of the priests until they came with you from the East. At the fifty-seventh house the men were grown up and they could start to shorten the rites. Thus the twins continued to people the rivers until the sixty-seventh house, down toward Peru, then returned to the fifty-sixth, the one from which men had first appeared on earth.

"You, the Whites," Aynoré went on, "you go into your churches and you talk about your lousy god for an hour; we, the Indians, go into the jungle and talk *with* ours, with all our gods, for whole days . . ."

By carrying out the ceremonial rites, each house had its own function and each could finally occupy the world, just as the armadillo fills its shell.

That is the way our ancestors spoke. But the work of the Creator did not go on forever, for there were three great disasters: two fires and a flood. And each time Ngnoaman had to start again from scratch. After the flood he established a fourth mankind, the one we are part of, and declared, "It's too much work for me to redo everything each time. From now on, I will leave men in peace, they're plenty big enough to punish themselves . . . And that is the story of the great start, the origin of the first beginnings."

Moéma couldn't think anymore, so vivid were the colors lighting up her night. The Garden of Eden really had existed, somewhere between the tropics and the equator. "You are the whirling woman of the whirlwinds, you are the woman who rumbles, the woman who rings, the spider, the toucan and the humming-bird . . ." She didn't know whether Aynoré said that or simply thought it, but when they made love on the deck of the jangada, among the stench of brine and fish, their bare skin spattered with sand, and she concentrated on the elastic center of their yoked genitals, she thought she could grasp all the words of this flowing language, of this constant murmur that finally reconciled her with men: *Nitio oatarara, irara. Mamoaùpe, jandaia, saci peirerê? We* have time, honey-eater . . . Where do you come from, little yellow parrot, nocturnal sprite?"

At the same moment, up in the bluish semidark of the cabin, Thaïs leaned out of her hammock to be sick.

Fortaleza: *I'm not a snake but I go, full of venom . . .*

Zé had brought him back to the favela very early, before setting off on a delivery trip that would last three days. By seven in the morning Nelson was already at his post where the Avenue Duque de Caxias and the Avenue Luciano Carneiro crossed. Impervious to the nauseating stench of the exhaust fumes—fuel made from cane-sugar alcohol, on the contrary, used by a considerable number of cars, left a pleasant scent in his nostrils, as if all the inhabitants had taken part in a massive booze-up the previous evening and were exuding *cachaça* from every pore—deaf to the cacophony of horns and the roar of the engines, Nelson went about his begging with the casual assurance of a true specialist. Toward nine, when the stream of motorists going to work was replaced by taxis and vans, he went to the *beira-mar* to work on the tourists who were starting to venture out of their hotels. His feelings for them were a mixture of contempt and pity: contempt for their arrogance of holidaymakers with nothing better to do than to waste their dough on pointless purchases, and pity for the palefaces, flayed alive by the scorching sun, making them look like people with third-degree burns rather bewildered at finding themselves without their bandages. Unlike the lepers, whom hardly anyone went near out of instinctive repugnance and fear of contagion, or even the legless cripples and the blind who were less mobile than he was, his handicap was useful: just as it allowed him to attack cars, it made it possible for him to storm the entrances of luxury hotels, and even if he did have to use a bit of cunning not to get thrown out by the commissionaires—some of whom turned a blind eye to his game for a percentage of his takings—it was rare for tourists, taken by surprise as they left the Imperial Orthon Palace or the Colonial, not to quickly give a few coppers to blot out this disturbing piece of bad taste in a day devoted to pleasure.

It was almost midday when Nelson decided to take the bus to Aldeota, the posh district of the town. Not that there was any chance of getting a single cruzeiro there—the rich were barricaded in their fortress-like villas and it was teeming with vigilantes, often more dangerous than the cops themselves—but Zé had finally given him the address of the garage that had acquired the Willis. He intended to ferret around a bit up there.

At the José de Alcanar Garage Nelson observed an employee half-heartedly polishing a radiator grille; taking advantage of his inattention, he slipped under one of the cars parked inside the garage building. A Mercedes agent, the owner had specialized in classic cars. Nelson's eye was caught by a splendid front-wheel-drive Citroën whose polished chrome parts seemed to him as beautiful as monstrances. Crawling under the cars with the litheness of a Sioux, he reached the shelter of the Citroën without mishap and, stretched out on his back, his nose glued to the rear axle, closed his eyes the better to savor the smells of oil and rubber.

He couldn't have said how much time had passed when he was roused from his half sleep by loud claps. "Hello! Is anyone there?" said a deep, imperious voice.

"*Sim senhor.* I'll be right with you," the garage-hand replied.

"I'm *Deputado* Jefferson Vasconcelos. Go and fetch your boss, I want to see his old cars."

"Right away, sir. Have a look around, he'll be here in a moment."

Nelson heard the garage-hand run off and, a few seconds later, the steps of the garage-owner hurrying to see his customer.

"Floriano Duarte, at your service, sir. Pleased to meet you, *senhor deputado.*"

"Yes, yes . . ." came the irritated voice of the member of parliament. "To put it briefly, I'm in a great hurry. I promised to buy my son a car for his eighteenth birthday and he's taken it into his head to ask for an old model instead of the Golf I was going to give him, and I can't get him to change his mind . . ."

"I know how it is, sir. It's impossible to go against fashion and young people are crazy about those cars and, with all due respect, I think they're right. And I'm not saying that just because I sell them, mind you, since I also sell Mercedes. Modern cars look like suppositories or, at best, like bars of soap: bathroom design, no imagination, no beauty. It's as if all the manufacturers are in it together. Whereas in the old days they used to deck them out like carriages, like cathedral altars! And I'm not just talking about your Hispano-Suizas, your Delahayes or Bugattis, mind you—look at the Plymouths, the Hotchkisses, the Chryslers. People pamper them, exhibit them in museums like works of art while they're still working, often better than lots of others! This model, for example. Please, come and have a look."

Two pairs of feet came up to the car under which Nelson was hiding. He immediately identified those of the *deputado* by the perfect cut of his trousers over his polished casuals. He could touch them if he stretched out his hand.

"A 1953 front-wheel-drive Citroën. Look at this little jewel! Six cylinders, fifteen hp, floating engine with wet-lined cylinders, eighty miles an hour in twenty-seven seconds! What do you say to that? Come closer, no need to be afraid! Now tell me honestly: doesn't that scream class, style? Look at the curve of those wings, of the bumper. A Volkswagen and a marvel of engineering like that—there's simply no comparison! It's more than just a car, it's a symbol, a way of life—"

"I'm sure you're right," the *deputado* said, the nervous tapping of his foot indicating his irritation, "but I've not come here to buy a symbol, I just want a car that will keep going without breaking down every five minutes. You see what I'm getting at, don't you?"

"Do you know what this model was called, *senhor deputado*?" Duarte said, in offended tones. "'The Queen of the Road'! I don't know if you realize what that means. During the last war the Germans requisitioned all of them; believe me, they did thousands of miles without the slightest hiccup. May I remind you that it's engines like this that did the *Croisière Jaune* from Beirut to Peking or crossed Africa."

"Precisely, *senhor*— What did you say your name was?"

"Duarte, Floriano Duarte."

"Precisely, *Senhor* Duarte, precisely. All these engines have done far too much. How many miles does this marvel of engineering have on the clock?"

"None," Duarte replied proudly.

"What d'you mean, none? Are you putting me on?"

"Not at all, *senhor deputado*, I wouldn't dream of it. I've completely rebuilt the engine using a batch of original parts: this car might well be old, but its engine is as *new* as if it was straight out of the factory. Your son can drive to Belém and back, if he feels like it, and I will guarantee he'll have no problems. Not to mention the comfort," he said, opening the door, "velvet interior trim, rebuilt suspension, plenty of room in the trunk. It's a little gem, *senhor deputado*. Get in and see for yourself."

Realizing his legs might be trapped if someone got in the car, Nelson twisted around so he would be able to escape at the last moment.

"I haven't the time," the other replied. "Let's get down to the painful part: how much does it cost?"

"The same as a Golf, *senhor deputado*. Exactly the amount you intended to pay for that car."

"The same as a Golf? For this pile of scrap metal? What do you take me for?"

"For a man who wants to buy his son a car while getting a bargain at the same time. I will guarantee this Citroën for three years, labor and parts included, and I promise to find you a buyer at the same price if you should decide to sell it. As you know as well as I do, a new car loses something of its value with every day that passes. With quality old models it's exactly the opposite. Instead of squandering your money on a simple whim, you would be making a very good investment. And you should note that I'm doing you a personal favor with my guarantee: true collectors don't demand anything like that, I can assure you. Only last week I sold a 1930 Willis without even seeing the purchaser. And it cost twice as much as the Citroën! It was Colonel José de Moreira who bought it from me, I'm sure you know him . . ."

"The governor of Maranhão?"

"The very same, *senhor deputado*. Not a man who was born yesterday as far as classic cars are concerned, as I'm sure you'll agree."

Nelson almost cried out. That name above all names, held in such contempt he could hardly bring himself to speak it, associated with the Willis, hit him like an electric shock. His expression froze and the tears suddenly poured down in absurd, mechanical spurts. His hatred swelled until it enveloped the whole world in its inky whorls until even he was blinded by its opacity. For a brief moment he saw himself as an octopus, a mollusk lurking in its shell of black metal, a shapeless beast throwing its tentacles around the legs of the garage-owner, drawing him into the morass of rancor that would reduce him to a pulp underneath the car. His limbs jerked convulsively, flecks of foam gathered at the corners of his mouth. When he came to himself again, just a few seconds later, there was only one thing in his mind: the name had been spoken, it was like a sign of his justification, a final exhortation to carry out the punishment.

There was no one around the car anymore so that Nelson could emerge from his hiding place unmolested. Risking a glance over the hood, he saw the garage owner and the *deputado* in deep discussion behind the glass door of the office. Reassured, he went to the part of the garage used as a workshop, rummaged through a toolbox beside a car that was being repaired and swiped a file before leaving. He had no trouble getting back out to the heat of the pavement and the comforting feeling of the softened asphalt under his fingers.

The sight was a shock for the wealthy lady with the elaborate makeup who passed him at that moment; she froze in front of him. The miniature dog she had on a lead started to yap, baring its teeth and bristling. With a vicious punch on its muzzle, Nelson transformed its hysterical barking into a high-pitched wail.

"*Não sou cobra, mas ando todo envenenando,*" he said menacingly, jutting out his chin at the woman.

As she ran off, clutching her dog, he burst out laughing and had a long pee, out there in the street, in the sunshine.

CHAPTER 17

In which Kircher exposes Blauenstein's trickery

THE FAIR MEI-LI greeted her husband by prostrating herself in the manner of the Chinese but the alchemist paid her no attention. Hardly had he entered the laboratory than he started to frown & pace up & down from one pentacle to the other, a concerned look on his face. He was going past the altar when an invisible force appeared to stop him going any farther, as if he could tell that the place had been the scene of a shameful act. He turned slowly around to face his wife & Sinibaldus.

"If I didn't have such trust in you," he said gravely, "I could believe that my orders have been disobeyed. There are evil effluvia in this room from which I foresee many setbacks for our undertaking. Are you sure you have not neglected to carry out any of my orders? It would be a tragedy to fail so close to our goal."

Sinibaldus had gone pale. Prey to the most horrible doubt when faced with the alchemist's extraordinary powers, his knees

were knocking & he was sweating profusely. Especially since
Mei-li, far from maintaining her usual impassive expression,
also seemed extremely perturbed, looking as if she expected
anathema to be pronounced against her. Sinibaldus made a great
effort to reassure the alchemist but he became so flustered as
he lied that he noticed the weakness of his argument himself &
eventually fell silent.

"I will not insult you by doubting your word," Blauenstein
went on, with marked skepticism, "I could be wrong . . . But all
this will be quickly verified: a simple action will reveal the plain
truth to me immediately."

He took the bezoar stone out of his pocket & went over to
the furnace, followed by his wife & Sinibaldus. Then holding it
above the athenor, he declaimed:

"By Kether, Hokmah, Binah, Hesod, Gevurah, Rahimin,
Netsh, Hod, Yesod & Malkuth! By the seventy-two secret
letters of the name of God whom I now invoke, may this final
testimony of the purity of our bodies & of our souls bring us the
elixir of immortality!"

At that, he cast the bezoar into the bubbling elements.
Deliberately prepared for this, the mixture immediately exploded,
sending up a shower of sparks & a thick cloud, which concealed
the furnace from them. Whilst Sinibaldus, in terror, was praying
out loud to God & dashing from window to window in order
to ventilate the room, the alchemist took advantage of his
preoccupation to operate an ingenious mechanism.

Once it was again possible to see sufficiently, the three of them,
coughing, blackened with soot, hurried over to the crucible.
Blauenstein immediately drew back with screams of horror.
When he went to look, Sinibaldus thought he would drop dead on
the spot; his heart missed a beat & a mortal chill spread through
his bones—there was a living viper in the athanor!

"Treachery! Treachery!" the alchemist bellowed, his face contorted with fury.

Sinibaldus had not had time to recover before Mei-li was clinging to her husband's coattails, begging his forgiveness & confessing in detail to all the ignominious acts she had committed in his absence. More dead than alive, completely bewildered by the malice of his tormentors, Sinibaldus wished the ground would open & swallow him up: he could not believe his ears as he heard this woman, who had sworn eternal love to him in transports of ecstasy, now accuse him of every evil in a brazen travesty of the truth; he realized it would be impossible for him to clear himself of the accusations. Struck dumb by her infamy, his legs gave way and he collapsed in an armchair, overwhelmed by the extent of his misfortune.

"Passing over the fact that you have wasted all our efforts," the incensed alchemist said, "after all, it's your money that has gone up in smoke, but to skewer my wife, indulge yourself with her, & against her will, in the most vile sorcery! I will report this to the Inquisition, sir, you will see that this kind of crime is not treated lightly. Justice! Justice! Send for the guard!"

Alerted by the tumult and worried about her husband, Sinibaldus's wife was making a racket outside the door. Looking up, Sinibaldus caught a smile of complicity between Blauenstein & his Chinese she-devil; all at once he realized how he had been duped & that none of his pleas would loosen their clutches into which he had fallen.

He managed to find the strength to murmur, "All my wealth, monsieur, all my wealth if you remain silent."

His words had the desired effect.

Sinibaldus hastened to reassure his wife, speaking to her through the door, & then returned to Blauenstein to drain the bitter cup to the dregs. Under the contemptuous stare of the woman whom he had taken for Isis herself, he submitted to the will of the alchemist. He had one week to realize the whole of his wealth & hand it over to these two scoundrels; once he had done that he would be guaranteed their silence for ever. If he failed to do so, he could be equally assured of denunciation, scandal &, consequently, the stake.

It was the day following these disastrous events that Sinibaldus returned to the College for the first time. Kircher was surprised he had remained absent for so many weeks, afraid he had perhaps been a little too brusque at their previous meeting. He therefore welcomed him with sincere pleasure & an astonishment he could not conceal: the man before him had aged by fifteen years, was bent low beneath his misfortune & repentance, and had come to ask for confession.

"Alas, Father," said Sinibaldus, "when they met me coming out of chapel, this monster spun his web so well there is nothing left for me but to let them strip me bare."

"No, no, my friend, you mustn't lay down your arms so quickly. And it seems to me I can see a way of—"

"Oh, Father," Sinibaldus exclaimed, grasping his hand, "if there is such a way, set it in motion. I will obey you in everything & my gratitude, you can be assured—"

"Forget your gratitude, at least for the moment, & do what I am going to tell you. Never let it be said that the Church capitulated before the creatures of the Fiend. You will go back to your house & persuade this accursed alchemist to come & set about making gold here. Continue to play your role of dupe, allay any suspicions he might have by begging him to pardon you for the adultery of which you were guilty, play up to him . . . Finally, tell him that I have heard of his extraordinary talents & would like to see him demonstrate them. And above all do not forget to hint at my credulity in such matters nor to paint in glowing colors the advantages he stands to gain by convincing me. You are well aware that the Emperor himself is interested in alchemy & does me the honor of granting me his friendship & his favor."

Cheered by the hope my master had revived in him, Sinibaldus hastened to put Kircher's plans into action. They worked beyond all expectation: blinded by his sense of his own superiority, Blauenstein fell into every trap set by Athanasius & less than two days had passed when the acoustic tube announced his presence, with Sinibaldus, at the entrance to the College.

Kircher received his visitor with a great show of courtesy as he led him to the laboratory where we then shut ourselves away. Feigning naïveté, my master pretended to be enraptured by the supposed exploits Blauenstein brazenly boasted about, although he did so beneath a façade of indifference & wisdom that had so deceived Sinibaldus.

"Gold, of course . . ." the alchemist said in contemptuous tones, "there's a word that brings many foolish men running. What if I were to tell you that for me it is the basest of metals? A strange paradox, don't you think? But to make it one must first of all understand the vanity of all the riches of this world; the very moment one knows the secret of transmutation, one realizes how futile it is . . ."

"True, sir. However I believe that your uncommon knowledge in matters of alchemy could help to explain much that is obscure in the workings of nature & I know a very worthy man of very high rank—it would not be appropriate to name him yet—who would be very happy to profit from your wisdom. But for that, you would have to deign, solely as a guarantee for the procedure I am undertaking here in his name [Kircher pronounced these last three words with sufficient gravity to make the alchemist feel he was acting in an official capacity], to repeat for me the

experiment my friend Sinibaldus has spoken of with such
admiration."

"Nothing simpler," Blauenstein replied, happy that he had
come to the point and not at all put out by this request, "it is
with great pleasure & all the respect due to . . . this person that I
agree to demonstrate my paltry knowledge."

"I believe our laboratory is equipped with everything you
need," Kircher said &, as the alchemist turned to the huge cast-
iron boiler bristling with retorts roaring away in the center of
the room, added, "This furnace of my own design has sixty-six
separate crucibles but, as you see, they are all being used to distil
medical essences. Take this one, which I use specifically for my
chemical experiments. As for the ingredients, you have but to
ask and my assistant will be happy to fetch them for you."

Never happier than in this situation, Blauenstein strutted
over to the furnace and majestically set about starting it up, all
the while enumerating the ingredients he would need:

"Realgar: five ounces, cinnabar: five ounces, sulphur: one &
a half ounces, the same for saltpeter & Turkestan salt, twice as
much mercury & orpiment . . ."

Athanasius & Sinibaldus watched the alchemist throw
all these substances into the crucible as I brought them,
after having duly weighed & prepared them according to his
instructions. When the mixture was complete and starting to
boil, Blauenstein opened a little case he had brought with him
& took out a long jade spoon & a vial of transparent liquid. "In
this flask there is what remains of a liquid I made when I was
in China some years ago. Its power is such, that a single drop
poured into the appropriate mixture will immediately bring
about the transmutation."

"And this magnificent object?" my master asked, looking as if
he would like to examine the jade spoon.

"It has no effect on the process whatsoever," the alchemist said, readily handing it to Kircher, "it is a present from the Grand Imperial Physician, my late brother-in-law. I merely use it in honor of his memory & to benefit from its intrinsic virtues."

"In that case," Athanasius said, absentmindedly stroking the jade surface, "I imagine you will not see any inconvenience in using one of my own spoons. Look, this one was designed by . . . by the person of whom we were speaking earlier. He will be flattered, I can assure you, to learn that he made a contribution, however small, to the accomplishment of the Great Work . . ."

Never did a face change so quickly; in a few seconds nothing was left of the solicitousness & boldness that characterized Blauenstein's expression. Without saying a word, he stared at Kircher with the suspicious, malignant look of a rat in a trap, while my master kept his eyes lowered, fixed on the instrument that seemed so essential to the alchemist.

"You must give that person my sincere apologies," Blauenstein eventually said with ill-concealed wiliness, "but it is very important to me to use that spoon. Because . . . let's say because I am very much attached to it. Transmutation is not a simple matter of chemistry, it also requires a certain . . . touch, you need to have the trick of it & in that one's familiarity with certain objects, sometimes the affection one has for them, can play a decisive role—"

"Enough, sir!" Kircher said, slowly raising his eyes to fix them on the alchemist. All trace of the inane affability my master had affected until then had vanished: suddenly Blauenstein was faced with an inquisitor, a monster to make one's blood run cold. "The trick of it is exactly what mountebanks of your kind have. Except that mountebanks don't have the hypocrisy that is your true nature. You are an imposter, a common cutpurse & if you have produced gold it is only by taking it from the pockets of those who are more credulous than I—"

"How dare you!" the alchemist exclaimed indignantly, in one final attempt.

"You turd excreted from the seminary! Do I have to reveal all your tricks one by one?" Kircher went on, seizing him by the collar. "Do I have to tell you why you insist on using this spoon? On your knees, you unfrocked monk, on your knees. The torturers of the Inquisition reserve special treatment for scoundrels of your sort."

And if Sieur Sinibaldus was not yet convinced of the imposture of which he had been the victim, what followed would finally have opened his eyes. With nothing to fall back on in the face of Kircher's attacks & threats, Blauenstein suddenly yielded & poured out all the tricks his evil imagination had invented. Nothing was so pleasing as to see this man, who had been so full of himself, tremble & to hear him go to any lengths to beg my master for mercy.

Once Athanasius had reduced him to this state, he pretended he had decided to let clemency prevail. "I am not going to ask you to make any promises—after this what person in his right senses would believe your word?—but I order you to leave this city at once with your prostitute & never return as long as you live. I beseech you to give up alchemy. As the price of his sins, Sinibaldus will make you a present of the money you acquired by such dishonest means—use it to mend your ways by taking honest work & save your soul by sincerely repenting your past sins. If I ever hear of your misdeeds again, I will not hesitate to hand you over to the jurisdiction of the Church."

Blauenstein, as one can well imagine, did not need to be told twice. He swore to everything that was asked of him, poured forth his pathetic thanks & took to his heels.

Sinibaldus could not believe his good fortune. In a few minutes Kircher had given him back both his honor & the largest part of his wealth. Weeping tears of emotion, his eyes shining with gratitude, he knelt down to thank God. Athanasius went over to him, admonished him mildly & gave him absolution.

As for me, I congratulated my master for the exemplary way in which he had unmasked that dangerous swindler, but I also questioned him about certain points that were still unclear to me. How would Blauenstein have claimed to make gold if he hadn't been stopped at the last moment? By what miracle had Kircher become aware of the alchemist's former profession?

My master replied to my questions with a smile. "Make gold? Nothing easier."

He went over to a furnace on which water was boiling in a glass bowl, plunged the jade spoon into it and started to stir slowly. To our great amazement we saw a shower of gold flakes appear in the clear water of the retort.

"A trick as old as the world," Kircher said, "but that always works. Examine the spoon yourselves: a little channel has been made in it. All you have to do is to fill it with gold powder in advance & block the opening with a little wax. When the time comes the heat of any mixture will melt the stopper, releasing real gold into the crucible. Yours, for example, my dear Sinibaldus. As for the fact that the man had previously been a monk, I admit I took a few risks. I'm taller than Blauenstein & while he was talking I had the opportunity to observe the top of his head. I was struck by a curious anomaly. His hair was much thicker on the back of his head, which could be easily explained by him having had a tonsure for several years. All I did after that was to set him a trap in the course of our conversation by mentioning his suitability for religious service. He couldn't repress a slight look of concern, which confirmed my initial deduction. Child's play, as you will agree. But that's enough talk, this business has given me an appetite. What would you say to giving the *coup de grâce* to a few chickens from our friend Carlino just down the road?"

We accepted with pleasure & Sinibaldus insisted on paying for our feast.

When he returned home a few hours later, the alchemist & his wife had decamped. After this incident Sinibaldus remained eternally grateful to my master, though one could not say the same of Blauenstein. Defeated and humiliated by Kircher, he vowed implacable hatred to him, the results of which were to appear several years later, as we will see at the appropriate time.

ALCÂNTARA: *In memory of Jim Bowie and Davy Crockett . . .*

"At least we have to get a copy of the project," Eléazard said with a frown, "otherwise there's nothing I can do. You can't write things without proof, you know, especially when you're exposing someone."

Alfredo shook his head as he angrily filled the glasses with *vinho verde*. It was clear he didn't see things the same way. "What about his wife? There's no way of getting her in on it?"

"Not at the moment," Loredana replied. "According to Dr. Euclides it's personal with her. It's her money so she can intervene."

"Didn't she suggest you give her some Italian classes?" Eléazard asked. "Has nothing come of that?"

"On the contrary, she's to ring me back on your phone in the next few days. That'll give me a chance to sound her out a little."

"Right . . ." said Alfredo sulkily. "If I can sum up: there's an American base going to be established here on the quiet, a shit of a governor who's using that information for some quiet speculation and three stupid bastards sitting here twiddling their thumbs just waiting for it to happen."

"Give it a rest, Alfredo," Eléazard said. "They're not going to have it that easy, I promise you, but it's too soon to act. If they get wind that we're on to them before we can take effective action, they'll clamp down on everything and that'll be that."

"He's right," Loredana said. "Trust us."

"*Trust us*," Alfredo repeated, parodying her soothing tones. "I'm very fond of you both, but it's *my* country, *my* region, so I don't trust anyone and I can promise you that . . ." He broke off, distracted by the appearance of the hotel's three American guests.

"I can't stand them any longer," he said after the couple and their daughter had walked past the little group as if their table were invisible. "They don't leave their room except to order So-corró around or hang out in the bars. You should see the state they'll be in, all three of them, when they come back."

When he'd come to the hotel that morning, Eléazard had tried to talk to the old servant, but she refused to accept any wages that did not come from her work. All labor, she said, has its share of ingratitude, God had arranged things that way. She still preferred the humiliation of fanning these Americans to that of begging. She was, nonetheless, grateful for his interest but politely asked him to mind his own business.

"Poor old Alfredo," Eléazard said when he and Loredana were back at his house, "he's taking this business very much to heart."

"And you're not?" she asked, an aggressive note in her voice.

"Of course I am," he immediately agreed, "but I really can't see what can be done at the moment. And even later, if you think about it. Despite our advice, Alfredo will inform his friends in the *PC do*

Brazil, their rag will publish a model accusation *à la Zola*, and then what? Moreira will have a good laugh and arrange to have them silenced. And he will make them pay for their noble indignation, believe me. As for me: assuming dear Carlotta suddenly turns into a martyr of the revolution—and you'll allow me to have my doubts about that—and brings me the material I need for an article, do you think that'll make one iota of difference? Millions of dollars and the Pentagon against Eléazard von Wogau, on German police files as a sympathizer with all that was worst in the left-wing splinter groups twenty years ago . . . You get the picture?"

Loredana looked him straight in the eye, as if she were wondering about his ability to hear what she was going to say. "You have to beat the grass to flush out the snake. When you're a little less pessimistic I'll talk to you about the *Thirty-Six Stratagems*, OK?"

It was Eléazard's turn to size her up with an odd look. "Why not?" he said in a tone that expressed his lack of interest in the book.

"You look like your parrot when you make a face like that," she said, switching on the computer. "You know what they say back home? *Chi non s'avventura non ha ventura!* Right, I'll let you get on with your 'work'. . . ."

Funny girl, he thought, when Loredana went off to see Soledade in her room. He was, he admitted openly to himself, attracted by her nonconformism, by her constant mixture of affection and un-failing clearheadedness to the point where she was beginning to obscure the image of Elaine on his high altar, where he endeav-ored to keep it. He couldn't get over her attitude at the governor's party. The way she'd schemed with the sole intention of being able to slap him! Very clever, but it left him unsure; seeing oth-ers so deftly manipulated, he couldn't prevent himself from won-dering if he was in danger himself. Wasn't she behaving in the same way toward him? Even Euclides had succumbed to her spell.

Having said that, she had given the Americans in the hotel a hard stare that still sent shivers down his spine. If there was one thing Eléazard was certain of in all this, it was that she was capable of anything.

LOREDANA KNOCKED ON Soledade's door; she went in without waiting for a reply. Sprawled out on her unmade bed, an open packet of cookies beside her, she was watching a soccer match on TV.

"Brazil versus the Soviet Union," she said without taking her eyes off the screen for a moment. "One all, it's almost over. Quick, come and sit down."

Loredana took a step then pulled up abruptly: large, damp letters could still be seen on the white walls. Turning a full circle, she read one sentence repeated all round the room up to the fly spray left on the dressing table: *Eléazard, te quero . . .*

"So that's it," she said with a smile, "you're in love with him."

Soledade looked up, eyes wide. Seeing the message she thought she'd wiped off, she screwed up her eyes in comic fashion, then covered her face with the sheet to avoid Loredana's look.

She went to sit down beside Soledade. "Don't be silly," she told her gently, "I won't say anything. It's none of my business."

She managed to pull aside part of the sheet Soledade was clinging to. "You won't say anything to him? Promise?"

"Promise. Cross my heart and hope to die," Loredana said, taking her in her arms. "But tell me, have you slept together yet?"

"No," she replied, visibly embarrassed by so direct a question. "Well, almost . . . Just once he took me into his bed, but he was so drunk he fell asleep without touching me. I'm sure he won't even remember," she added with a touch of pique. "You're not jealous, are you?"

"Of course I am," said Loredana, joking. "He hasn't even tried to kiss me."

"But you're the one he's in love with. I know him well, I see the way he looks at you."

"I know," said Loredana. She was staring into space. "I love him too. But that's nothing to worry about, there'll never be anything between us."

"Why not?"

"Because . . . A secret for a secret, isn't that it? You won't say anything either, OK?"

At that moment the commentator speeded up his delivery, to keep up with play where things were getting exciting: *Dangerous free kick, forty yards from the opposing goal . . . Serginho's lining it up and . . . it's Falcão who shoots! The ball swerves round the wall, Junior heads it . . . against the bar! But it's not over yet, Eder's got the ball. A lovely dribble, he kicks the ball through the defender's legs and passes to Zico . . .*

"Quick, look!" Soledade said. "They're going to score!"

At the same moment the commentator let out a lupine howl: "Goa a a a a a a a a a al! Ziiiiico! Viva Brazil, meu Deus! Dois a um!

Fascinated by the slow-motion action replays on the screen, screaming and clapping her hands, Soledade gave free rein to her delight.

A magnificent volley, the commentator's hoarse voice said, *a classic goal that will be all the more remembered because it was scored in the last seconds of play . . . The referee's looking at his watch . . . No, that's impossible, the game's going on! A corner for the Soviet Union. All the players have gone up for this last chance to equalize . . . And . . . It's over! The referee's blown for time, in the ninety-second minute! Two-one, goals from Socrates and Zico for Brazil, and they're in the second round of the World Cup. Viva Brazil!*

"Brasiou u u u u u!" Soledade repeated, in raptures. "We're going to win the cup, we're going to win it!"

"I'm going to die," said Loredana.

The way she said it, she could have been expressing her disappointment that it was about to rain or that she'd remembered there was no sugar in the kitchen cupboard.

DURING THE FEW minutes in which she was alone with these terrible words, her admission delayed by Soledade's innocent passion for football, the memory of a similar gap had taken her back to her distant past, to the time when she was twelve. It was the day before her first communion, night was falling on the almond trees in blossom. She was going to the village priest for confession.

Father Montefiascone's cadaverous complexion and the way he whined when showing his slides—wishy-washy pictures with no life, nothing cheerful about them at all—had put her off religion from the very first catechism class. For several weeks Loredana, without thinking she was doing anything wrong or feeling the least bit guilty, had replaced this stupid farce with delightful daydreams in the surrounding countryside. The very idea of having to "make her first communion" seemed ridiculous to her. Her mother attached such importance to this bizarre event that she had accepted its inevitability: it was something everyone went through, a requirement to which you had to submit without bothering to understand what the point of it was, a bit like getting dressed up on Sundays or speaking in a low voice in church. This communion . . . For days on end now they'd been going on at her about it! Her cousins, aunts and uncles who would be coming, the candle she'd have to hold straight to avoid burning herself with the wax, the pounds and pounds of pasta and gnocchi to be prepared for the big family meal after the ceremony, the famous *torta a più piani* ordered from the cake shop—a huge cake with several tiers that Loredana imagined leaning slightly, like the Tower of Pisa. They were constantly checking when it would be delivered, as if the fate of the whole world somehow depended on this mysterious precision. And that afternoon, while she was once more trying on the immaculate alb she would be wearing the next day—it had been Ariana's, her big cousin's, which explained the incessant alterations—her mother had asked her how confession had gone. What confession? Loredana had asked in naive astonishment. What? She hadn't been to confession? her mother had screamed, almost swallowing all her pins. The curtain had gone up on the most grotesque of melodramas. What did she think she was doing? How was she going to make her communion if she hadn't been to confession? She had been to catechism, hadn't she? *Madre di Dio!* A stinging slap, tears, wailing . . . "Giuseppe! This little . . . this shameless little hussy's missed all the catechism classes! And, yes, it is serious, you heathen! You Communist! And how many times have I told you not to smoke in the bedroom?! With all the family coming!" And the communion cake that had cost a fortune. There was nothing left for her but to die of shame.

Contacted by telephone, the priest had merely added to their shame. Loredana Rizzuto? Sorry, he didn't know a child of that name . . . Although . . . Could they be talking of that brazen hussy who always turned off toward the hills before she reached the church? Unfortunately, and this was certainly going to cause her parents a lot of trouble, it would naturally be impossible for her to make communion the next day. It was unthinkable, it would be a mortal sin to offer the body of Christ to that child, he told her mother emphatically. Oh, dear old Father Montefiascone. He had taken a long time persuading before he had agreed to take the little lost sheep back into his flock. Perhaps the matter could be reconsidered, but she would have to come to confession right away.

No, not in the church, in his house, on the other side of the street. He was making an exception, of which he hoped Signora Rizzuto was fully aware, he was doing this out of pure charity . . . The Lord could not be bought, Signora Rizzuto, but the poor of the parish would be grateful to her for this unexpected offering . . .

So Loredana was walking toward her fate, three steps forward, one step back, never stepping on the abyss of the gap between the paving stones, jumping over the manhole covers without a run-up, as if the village had been transformed into a gigantic game of hopscotch. The closer she came, the more pressing the tricky question of her "sins" became; never having been to confession, she only knew by hearsay that you had to confess your sins, the more horrible, the better, and obtain forgiveness in return for a varying number of prayers. However hard she racked her brains, nothing admissible came to mind. To her, petty misdemeanors such as "I disobeyed my parents" or "I missed catechism" seemed insipid and unworthy of confession, and she exhausted herself declining verbs whose nefarious reputation she was aware of without, for all that, having any clear idea of the crimes behind them: to have, to sleep, to rape, to touch, to touch oneself . . .

Night was falling when she finally rang the priest's bell. An old woman came to the door and, muttering about the lateness of the hour, pushed her to the stairs up to the first floor. Loredana remembered the prints of all the stations of the cross and the sound of gunfire that accompanied her as she climbed the stairs. Guided by the shots, she found Father Montefiascone sitting watching a large television set with gold knobs and a Formica case on which Davy Crockett, alias John Wayne, was organizing the defense of a besieged fort. Cassock, doilies, engravings of Saint Ignatius and the Virgin Mary . . . as if intoxicated by the television, reality itself was projected all around her in black and white. Irritated at being interrupted while watching his film, Father Montefiascone hardly acknowledged her arrival. Without even standing up, he made her kneel down on the carpet, beside his armchair, facing the television and told her to recite the *confiteor*. Loredana was forced to admit she didn't know it then suffer the old man's vituperation before repeating after him the words he grudgingly spoke.

On the screen the final battle has started. Davy Crockett starts to retreat under the number of attackers, his companions falling one by one around him. In the burning fort the last barricade gives way under the repeated charges of the cavalry. "Adelante!" With fixed bayonets, a mass of hussars, a white cross on their chests, advances inch by inch, making the screen bristle. "Does that mean what I think it does?" a man gasps as he collapses onto a wounded soldier with a fur hat. "It sure does," the other replies, looking the man who's about to finish them off straight in the eye. Leaving the rampart, where he was firing the last cannon, Davy Crockett starts to run toward the powder magazine, his torch in his hand. Before going in, he turns round and a hussar takes advantage of his movement to nail him to the door with his bayonet. He pulls himself free, staggers for a moment . . . Despite his screams, you can still believe in a miracle, but there's a large dark patch on his back, identical to the one on the wood of the door, just at the place where he had been. You see him make one last effort and throw his torch on the powder kegs then disappear in the magazine. Everything explodes, but you know very well that John Wayne has died for nothing.

Without being capable of appreciating the ridiculous nature of the situation, Loredana sensed its absurdity: it was like a nightmare, one of those you get after eating too much or bringing home a bad report. Insidious and hostile, Father Montefiascone's voice mingled with the tumult of the battle.

Jim Bowie, stiff leg stretched out on his bed in the ruined chapel where the wounded are sheltering. Watching over him is his old black slave, given his freedom before the attack and whose first gesture as a free man was to face death to defend his liberty. A wave of Mexicans; the two men fire their guns: rifle, blunderbuss and pistols. The bayonets approach Jim Bowie, they're going to run him through . . . No! The old slave has thrown himself over his master, the blades sink into this last shield. Body on body . . . His knife! Entangled with the corpse as he is, Bowie still manages to cut the throat of one more assailant. His face in close-up: the bayonets are stuck in the adobe either side of him. We see those that miss the hero, but we hear those that kill him: the cry of a stuck pig, a gurgling noise, retching, mouth open . . . Naked death, in all its ugliness.

The world wasn't full of sunshine anymore, it was gray, unjust, evil-smelling . . . a huge conspiracy since the beginning of time to bring about the death of Davy Crockett and his faithful companions. When the time came, Loredana heard herself confessing to a few venial sins then, in a toneless voice, in a silence broken only by the flapping of the flags, to having slept with her father.

The whole Mexican army standing to attention to salute the two survivors of the massacre: a mother and her little daughter riding on a mule, like Mary on the road to Bethlehem. They leave, defeated, pale images of misfortune and reproach, while stupid trumpets are sounding in their honor. When they pass General Santana—despite his cocked hat he's the spitting image of Father Montefiascone—the mother cannot resist giving him a defiant look. The little girl's stronger, she ignores him, him and his world. She's beyond hatred and scorn. Ready for the Red Brigades . . .

"With your father!" the priest exclaims, turning toward her for the first time. Yes, with my father. Above all, don't flinch, stand up to the interrogation with grandeur and dignity, ready to die like John Wayne and Richard Widmark. Yes, in his bed . . . That night when the village policeman's house was struck by lightning. Yes, my mother was there as well . . . You're too big to sleep in your parents' bed, Father Montefiascone said, reassured by this willing extension of the sin. *Dominus, abracadabrum sanctus, te absolvo*, it was over. "Sleeping" with your father, and even with your mother was allowed, for all the consequences it had: three *Ave Marias*, so why not, you left washed clean of the worst atrocities, without a glance at the bodies of Davy Crockett and Jim Bowie.

That evening Loredana had learned that man is a creature without shelter, exposed to injustice, suffering and decay. Having died for the first time at the Alamo, she had never afterward seen a monk or a soldier without mentally spitting in his face.

"WE'RE ALL GOING to die," Soledade said, switching off the television.

Despite her determination not to give in to emotion, Loredana was hurt by this apparent coldness. Something in her bearing must have alerted Soledade to this, for she went on in gentle tones: the question wasn't to know when or how we were going to die, but to live at such an intensity that we had no regrets when the time came. She wasn't saying that out of a lack of compassion. If Loredana was serious, what was she doing here in Brazil, far from her family and friends?

Since their first meeting, and the time when they had become friends while talking about everything and anything in the kitchen, what Loredana liked about the young mestizo was her total lack of romanticism, a fault she herself had to beware of all the time. The fact that she wrote her love on the walls did not stem from an indulgence in a feeling of abandonment but was an example of sympathetic magic, a relic of her African inheritance that made her eat handfuls of earth when she was sad or turn the little rutting monkey, which Eléazard had placed in a prominent position on one of his shelves, to face the wall.

"I just don't know anymore," she eventually admitted, her voice choking with an irrepressible desire to cry. "I'm afraid of dying."

Soledade took her in her arms. "I know what you need," she said, stroking her hair. "We'll go and see Mariazinha . . . She's a *mãe-de-santo*, a 'mother of saints,' she's the only person who can help you." And then, in confidential tones, "I've seen her make a lemon tree die, just by looking at it!"

SÃO LUÍS: *Simply a question of the mechanics of banking . . .*

For months he had only seen Carlotta in her dressing gown and in a state of intoxication that accentuated the slovenliness of her dress, so the Colonel was agreeably surprised that evening to find his wife in a Chanel suit, makeup and jewelry. For a moment he hoped their relationship might be revived, but when she curtly refused to have a glass with him and informed him that they had to talk, he was immediately on his guard.

"I came across this by chance, the other day," she said, tossing a file onto the low table in the drawing room.

Recognizing the shiny cover of the finance plan, Moreira concentrated for a moment on the brown spots disfiguring Carlotta's hands, noting those freckles that could no longer be explained by overexposure to the sun, and prepared himself for the worst.

Two hours later he took refuge in his office, on the first floor, his mouth dry from having vainly defended himself; he poured himself a whiskey and spent a long time scratching the little scab on one eyebrow that was irritating him. He had not for one moment imagined that the "worst" could reach such proportions! That his wife should make a scene because he had used her money without her approval was perfectly foreseeable. That she should be in such

432

a huff as to want to cancel the land purchases done in her name was something he would never have imagined. Swindler, crook, unscrupulous developer . . . he had come in for the whole catalog of insults and accusations. Even at times when she'd threatened to press charges for misusing his power of attorney, she had never abandoned the impressive calm in which he saw the Carlotta of the old days, the one he still loved despite the domestic hell she made him suffer since the business of the photo. A girl he hadn't even kissed! You had to see the funny side.

He lit a cigar. Stroking his sideburns, he found a new scar to tease. He was not convinced his wife would see reason after a night to sleep on it; she might just as well persist in her stubborn determination. He'd definitely have to take steps to secure himself once and for all against the danger of such moods. Ownership of those parcels of land was the basis of his enterprise, without them no speculation, no *resort,* the whole of the financial arrangements would fall through. The simplest solution would be to buy them back. Apart from taking out a second mortgage on all of his own property, he couldn't see how to obtain the necessary money.

Moreira opened the little safe concealed, as a matter of form and to give it some style, behind a woodcut by Abrão Batista. He took out a pile of bank files and immersed himself in the figures. For many minutes the only sound was that of papers being turned feverishly. Then a creak of furniture and the governor leaned back in his chair with a satisfied smile. The most obvious solutions did not always appear immediately, swamped as they were by the mass of minor details. He read once more the fax containing the key to the problem. *Sir, subsequent to our conversation of the . . . etc., we can confirm that the sum of 200,000 US dollars for the advance financing of your project had been approved.*

We would remind you that this loan will be released to your account on receipt of the various works status reports . . . etc., etc.

The previous day the Japanese had released the first tranche of their commitment. The sum was intended to cover the expenses of setting up the project, so that they could go ahead with the construction as soon as possible, once the Brazilian government had given the green light. All he needed to do was to take enough out of it, under some pretext or other, to repay Carlotta. Since he had the power of attorney, he wouldn't even need to ask her opinion, the title deeds would change hands without any problem. The profit on the sale of the plots of land for the American army would then allow him to make good the withdrawal. It would make a small dent in his personal gain, but that was of no consequence.

Once the principal of the transfer was established, carrying it out was merely a question of the mechanics of banking and paperwork . . . The governor picked up the telephone and dialed the home number of his lawyer.

"Governor?" came the sleepy voice from the other end of the line. "What time is this?"

"What does that matter?" Moreira said, looking at his watch. "Two in the morning. Time to wake up and pay attention."

"Just a moment, I'll go to the other phone . . . All right, what is it?"

"Listen carefully: you must be at Costa's by the time the offices open. I don't care how you do it, but don't leave until you've got a work status report equivalent to 100,000 dollars. Tell him to invoice us for clearing the ground, or whatever, I don't know. He's the project manager, so he's to sort it out so that it looks genuine . . ."

"Is there a problem?"

"Nothing serious. I'll tell you about it. As soon as you've got the document, you're to go to the Sugiyama Bank to have that sum credited to my account and go to the palace with the notary public with the title deeds. All the pieces of land have to be in my name by tomorrow morning. We'll sort it out formally later on."

"In your name? Really?"

"Wake up, for God's sake! It's a manner of speaking . . . Do it so you cover our tracks a bit as usual. It doesn't really make a lot of difference, but from a political point of view I mustn't appear in this transaction. OK?"

"I'll see to it."

"Right, then. Get back to sleep. See you tomorrow."

CHAPTER 18

*In which the fountain of Pamphilius is unveiled & the pleasant
conversation on the subject that Athanasius had with Bernini
recorded*

THE YEAR 1650, which began at this juncture,
saw a further increase in Kircher's fame, for he published
two fundamental books one after the other: the *Musurgia
Universalis* & the *Obeliscus Pamphilius*. The subtitle of the *Musurgia*
summarized the importance and novelty of this work: *The great
art of consonance & dissonance, in ten books wherein are treated the
entire doctrine & philosophy of sound & the theory as well as the
practise of music in all its forms; the admirable powers of consonance
& of dissonance in the whole universe are explained therein with
numerous & strange examples that are designed for diverse & practical
uses, but more particularly in philology, mathematics, physics,
mechanics, medicine, politics, metaphysics & theology . . .* Three
hundred brothers from our missions, who had come to Rome to
take part in the election of the new General of the Society, each

returned with a copy of this book, convinced it would be of great use to them in the barbarian countries to which they were going.

As to the *Obeliscus Pamphilius*, besides numerous explanations of Egyptian symbolism, it gave for the first time the faithful & complete translation of a text written in hieroglyphs! Not long after the appearance of these books, letters of congratulation began to flood in from all parts of the globe.

All this hustle and bustle was crowned by an unexpected event: the Roman senator, Alfonso Donnino, who had recently died, bequeathed the whole of his collection of curios to the Society of Jesus & to Kircher in particular. This collection, one of the finest of its time, comprised statues, masks, idols, pictures, weapons, tables made of marble or other costly materials, glass & crystal vases, musical instruments, painted dishes & innumerable fragments of stone from antiquity. Some alterations to the third story of the College were thus necessary in order to increase the floor-space of the museum so that this extensive collection could be housed there.

In the spring of 1650 the Fountain of the Four Rivers was unveiled by the Pamphili family. The greatest names of Rome all gathered in the Forum Agonale together with Kircher & Bernini, the sole creators of this magnificent work. After a long speech on the virtues of his predecessor, Alexander VII, the new Supreme Pontiff, blessed the fountain with great ceremony; the sluice gates were opened & the pure water of the Acqua Felice finally flowed into the immense basin.

"This fountain is absolutely worthy of praise," the Pope said as he approached our little group, Kircher, Bernini and me, "& I salute you as men who deserve to be as greatly honored by our age as Michelangelo & Marsilio Ficino were in theirs."

Bernini visibly swelled with pride, my master having, out of humility, emphasized the modest nature of his own contribution.

"Is it true what they say," the Pope went on, turning to Bernini, "that this rock with the pipe through it, this lion & this horse only required a few weeks' work?"

"A few months, your Holiness," Bernini corrected, piqued by the insinuation. "The rest of the work presented no major difficulty & would have taken more time than I had at my disposal."

"I know, I know," the Pope replied in honeyed tones, looking demonstratively at the statue of the Nile, "but no one could maintain that this fountain would have been equally majestic if you had sculpted it entirely with your own hands . . ."

There was no mystery about the fact that Bernini himself had only worked on the three figures mentioned by the Pope & that for the other parts of the fountain he had been happy to supervise the best pupils in his studio. It was due, moreover, less to a decision on his part than to the time limits imposed by the late Innocent X. But even if the Supreme Pontiff's irony was merely intended to tease Bernini in his too obvious vanity, it still seemed very unfair to me. Seeing the sculptor roll his mastiff eyes & aware of his impulsive nature, Kircher stepped in: 'Doubtless it sometimes happens that pupils surpass their teachers—*Tristo è quel discepolo che non avanza il suo maestro,*[1] is he not? Nevertheless, that is rare & in this case it is to the one who has taught them everything that the credit is due."

"But tell me, Reverend," the Pope asked without appearing to have noticed Kircher's interjection, "is there not a contradiction in placing this stone idol at the center of a monument dedicated to our religion? I have not yet had time to look at your book, which I am told is fascinating, & I would be interested to know by what magic you manage to justify the unjustifiable . . ."

---

1 Sad the disciple who does not surpass his master.

Athanasius threw me a quick glance in which I could see his surprise: the Pope was attacking him for having supported Bernini against his irony! The sculptor gave my master a little shrug as if to apologize for having landed him in such an awkward position.

"There is no need of magic," Kircher replied, "to explain the presence of this obelisk at the very heart of the Eternal City. Your predecessor, the late Pope Innocent X, since it was his wish that his name & that of his ancestors should be forever associated with this monument, was quite right to place it here. Although the product of one of the most ancient of peoples, but also of the one most worthy to be compared with ours, this obelisk remains a pagan symbol; it is for that reason that it is surmounted by the dove of the Holy Ghost, indicating the superiority of our religion over paganism. Thus the divine light, victorious over all idolatrous religions & descending from the eternal heavens, spreads its blessings over the four continents of the Earth represented by the Nile, the Ganges, the Danube & the Plate, the four splendid rivers from which Africa, India, Europe and the Americas draw their sustenance. The Nile is masked because no one has yet found its sources; as for the others, they are each represented by emblems corresponding to their nature."

"Very interesting . . ." Pope Alexander said. "From what you say, then, it is a monument to the propagation of the faith that we owe to the generosity of Innocent X & to your genius . . . I didn't see it from that point of view. Especially after the dispute the Franciscans had with you not long ago . . ."

"I insist," Kircher said, ignoring the dig at him, "that this fountain is a stone symbol of the glory of the Church & of all the missionaries who serve our holy cause. But it is more than that, & if I may—"

"That will be enough for today, Reverend Father, other duties call. But I will be happy to listen to your . . . 'stories' some other time."

That was the first & last time I saw my master turn scarlet with indignation. I was afraid he would direct one of the quips he always had up is sleeve at the Pope, but he contained himself & bent humbly to kiss the ring Alexander held out to him. "*Tamen amabit semper*,"[2] he said between his teeth, as the rules of our Society commanded him. Bernini & I did the same, then the Pope turned his back on us without further ado.

As soon as he could do so without danger of being noticed, Bernini burst out into open, infectious laughter. "You see what it costs to take the side of a stonemason," he said, placing his hand on Kircher's shoulder. "Welcome to the brotherhood of actors, Father Athanasius, for you have just been promoted to the ranks of storytellers . . ."

"How dare he?!" Kircher exclaimed, still rather somber. "Years of work to decipher the hieroglyphs, the key sought by men for centuries & that all at once can give us the whole of the science & philosophy of the ancients! All that dismissed with a wave of the hand, like an irritating fly! Why is God punishing me like this? Do I still have too much pride?"

"No, no," said Bernini in soothing tones, "only a few days ago that Pope was merely Cardinal Fabio Chigi, well known for . . . let's say his lack of judgment & his patrician smugness. If it is true that the function creates the organ, it'll take quite some time with that fellow."

---

2 Yet he will always love. (Read phonetically as a French sentence, this gives: *Ta main à ma bite, Saint Père*—Your hand on my cock, Holy Father. —Translator's note.)

The thought drew a smile from Kircher, accompanied by a
pseudoreproachful frown. I could have kissed Bernini for that!
Especially since he now invited us, with all the warmth of an old
friend, to accompany him to his house.

"*Carpe diem*, my friends. Let us forget that ass & go & empty
a few bottles of French wine that I have been keeping for this
occasion. For myself, I prefer to drink that to the water of the
rivers, even if they were those of the Garden of Eden."

His house was not far from where we were. There we met
several of his pupils who had played a part in the erection of the
fountain and had preceded us to their master's house after the
unveiling. There were also several ragged creatures who lived
there to serve as models for Bernini & his pupils, but also to act
as servants &, from what I thought I could tell from the liberties
they allowed these gentlemen, as other things as well . . . Good
girls, all the same, cheerful & in some cases even cultured, who
behaved in a seemly manner while we were there.

We all sat around the common table in the studio surrounded
by the clay models, blocks of stone and drawings cluttering up
the room. Large white sheets hung underneath the glass roof
allowed a soft light to filter through; the wine in the copper
goblets was deliciously cool, we were in high spirits & Kircher
quickly recovered his good humor.

Bernini went on & on about his set-to with the Pope &
how my master had backed him up & suffered for it. He did
a marvelous imitation of Alexander's curt, arrogant voice,
prompting general hilarity. It was nothing to make a fuss about
& my master laughed as much as the others at the biting satire,
though taking care not to join in it himself.

Once we had finished the second bottle of white wine from
Ay, our host had several chickens killed and sent to be roasted
at a neighboring eating-house. It was therefore with mouths full

of perfectly cooked meat that we started to discuss the fountain again. One of the young women sitting at the table asked if we had to believe that all the animals carved on the obelisk told a story.

"And what a story, my lovely!" Bernini exclaimed, tearing a chicken leg apart. "You can trust Father Kircher, he can read hieroglyphs as if he'd drawn them himself. Is that not true, Reverend Father?" he added with a wink.

"We mustn't exaggerate," said my master, "it's a bit more complicated than that; our good Caspar, who helps me in my work, will confirm how much labor the translation of each line demands. The priests of ancient Egypt took their time making this secret language complicated in order to keep their knowledge inaccessible to the profane; the centuries have shown how successful they were in this."

"And what is the story these figures tell?" the young woman asked.

"A beautiful story, one I'm sure you'll enjoy," Bernini said, taking over from Kircher, "the story of the love of Isis & Osiris. Listen, my girl, and don't let me die of thirst: a certain Râ of Egypt, the sun god of his land, had the misfortune to have four children—two daughters: Isis & Nephtys, & two sons: Typhon & Osiris. These brothers & sisters married each other, as was the charming custom among the powerful. Isis became the wife of Osiris & Nephtys that of Typhon. Since their father was becoming a little decrepit, he put the administration of the kingdom into the hands of Osiris, the one who was more worthy to exercise that power. Under him Egypt thrived; aided by his wife, he taught the people how to cultivate wheat & the vine, introduced the religious cults & built large and beautiful cities, thus ensuring the happiness of the nation. But then Typhon, jealous of the power & fame of Osiris, decided to conspire against his brother. Drawing him into a cleverly laid trap, he killed him, cut him up into tiny pieces and threw him into the Nile.

"Poor Isis, in despair but still in love, set about finding the pieces of her husband. Through her persistence, she managed to find almost all of them, for the fish of the Nile treated him with respect & spared them. There was just one missing, a dainty morsel the oxyrhynch had not been able to resist . . . & this piece, my little doll, the one that Isis, as a true woman, preferred above all, was his gherkin, his big bird, his engine, his tassel, his family organ, his Don Cypriano, his awl, his chitterling, his fiddle bow, his syringe, his ploughshare, his Polyphemus, his father confessor, his lance, his yard, his pintle, his drumstick, his coney-catcher &, in a word, his sweetmeat! Yes, my lovelies, his sweetmeat!"

This tirade drew laughter and chuckles from all sides & even Kircher congratulated him on the *richness* of his vocabulary.

"A tragedy, then," the laughing sculptor went on, "for the widow Isis, but that would be to ignore her—very understandable—persistence, for the queen, aided by her sister & by Anubis, reconstructed her husband's member with river silt and spittle, stuck it on him in the right place &, thanks to heaven & various practices, brought it back to life. And since, as it seems to me, this new instrument worked better than his previous one, Isis soon found she was pregnant. She gave birth to a boy, who was called Harpocrates and became king in his turn, while Osiris, the first mortal ever to be recovered from a definitive death, was enjoying a happy eternity in the Fields of Iaru, the Egyptian paradise . . ."

The company was fascinated by Bernini's story & asked many questions, principally regarding its truth.

"The Egyptian priests," my master said, "following the doctrine passed on by the patriarchs of antiquity, were convinced that God was to be found everywhere & they aimed at finding His manifestations hidden in natural entities &, once they had been discovered, showing them in symbols derived from nature. The story of Osiris is a fable, of course, a discreet veil beneath which the sages were, according to the testimony of Iamblichus, endeavoring to express the most profound mysteries of the deity, the world, angels & demons."

"Oh, come on, Reverend Father," Bernini mocked. "Who do you take us for? Next you'll be asking us to accept that your pharaohs believed in the one God & the Holy Trinity!"

"You don't know how right you are . . ."

"How is it then that the entire world isn't Christian?" Bernini asked in more serious tones than before.

"The malice of the Devil is infinite &, moreover, it was greatly aided by the confusion of languages following the fall of the Tower of Babel, by the nations moving farther & farther away & the perversion of rites to which that led. All idolatrous religions are nothing but more or less recognizable anamorphoses of Christianity. The Egyptians, who, thanks to Hermes, still retained the greatest secrets of universal knowledge, passed them on throughout the world as far as China & the Americas, where they were gradually transformed, growing paler like those foxes that lose their natural color & take on that of the ice or the desert where they live. But the Egyptians knew that truth as well, for what is the dismemberment of Osiris by Typhon & Isis's patient search other than an image of idolatry itself, a misfortune that divine wisdom remedied by reuniting the scattered parts of the archetype in a single mystical body? Look around you: nothing stays the same, nothing lasts, no peace can be guaranteed by laws that are so strong they will not collapse. War is everywhere! And it is up to us, the priests & missionaries, to seek, through suffering & martyrdom, that lost stability . . ."

MATO GROSSO: *What comes knocking at night on the meshes of the mosquito nets . . .*

On the third day of their journey on foot through the jungle it became clear to all that their progress would be much slower than expected. Yurupig, Mauro & Petersen took it in turns to carry Dietlev's stretcher, but the most they could do in a straight line in the forest was about ten yards, so frequent were the tangles of branches and succulents, dark undergrowth and luxuriant, impenetrable foliage. Occasionally the person opening up a path managed to make a passage with the machete, but almost always they had to go round the obstacle, clamber over a fallen tree trunk, which would disintegrate into sawdust under their weight, thread their way as best they could through the rigging of the intertwined lianas or even crawl, when a way forward could be vaguely discerned behind an arching root. Constantly diverted from their ideal line, they concentrated on following natural gaps oriented toward the northeast quarter of the compass. This course, however, remained largely theoretical inasmuch as they were sometimes forced to turn back and try another route that was less obvious but better suited to their goal. They had the impression they were treading on an immense mass of decaying material that collapsed, liquefied under their feet, an elastic, aromatic humus from which the trampled vegetation immediately sprang up again, made stronger, denser by its own decomposition. Bromeliads and rubber plants suffering from gigantism with nothing in common with the plants Elaine knew by those names from the florist's, vegetable columns, smooth or ringed, recalling the impossible combinations of computer-generated images: root-stilts, strangler fig trees, all kinds of parasites, a Chinese box of jungles, one inside the other at the very heart of the jungle. An indefinable cacophony came down from above, filling the space all round them, a shrill, discordant hubbub in which Yurupig and Petersen alone were able to pick out the howl of a capuchin monkey, the castanets of a toucan's beak, the sudden hysterical shriek of a great macaw . . . The mystery of life seemed to have concentrated in this primordial crucible teeming with mosquitos and insects.

By five in the afternoon the green shade had become too dense to continue so that they had to set about looking for a place to camp fairly early to give them time to clear their chosen spot, hang their hammocks off the ground and collect some dead wood. Elaine would never have thought it could be so difficult to find something that would burn in the middle of the forest: the wood was spongy. Full of mosses, of fermented sap, ant and termite nests, lived in, alive, as combustible as a sponge full of water. The hissing fire they gathered round when night had fallen was thanks to Yurupig alone.

They had agreed that Elaine would bring up the rear, in order to save her as far as possible from the ambushes of the forest; their progress disturbed a large number of animals, which they only saw as they took flight, but having seen a little coral snake disappear more or less from under her feet, she knew she was as exposed to danger as the others. However much she kept her eyes fixed on the ground, every tree trunk, every crevice remained a deadly trap she had to beware of. Just as in a ghost train at the fair, the immense webs of the bird-eating spiders would suddenly stick to her face like candy floss, an an aggressive rustling close by would send her heart racing, everything seemed to be conspiring against the intruders, to be uniting to swallow them up.

Yurupig and Petersen were more at ease in this ordeal. They both knew a thousand and one tricks to find drinking water or to make the trees 'sing' before attaching their hammocks. Petersen was grumbling all the time, reviling the world and its creatures, while the Indian moved silently, all senses on the alert, a hunter through and through. For the first two days the German had sullenly refused to speak to them but then, without anyone really understanding the reason for this sudden change, recovered his spirits and a certain comradeship with the group.

When they gathered around the fire on the evening of the third day, all hope of reaching the junction of the river soon had vanished. "We're going to have to ration the food a bit more," Mauro said. "At this rate it won't last much longer."

"How far would you say we've been today?" Elaine asked.

"No idea . . . A mile at most. But I'm as exhausted as if we'd done seventy." His hand inside the collar of his T-shirt, Mauro was scratching his chest frenziedly, then examined the little scab he'd managed to bring out: a kind of tiny spider, swollen with blood, seemed to be enclosed in the dead skin.

"Oh no, I don't believe it!" he said with revulsion. "What the hell's this bug?"

"*Carrapato*," said Yurupig without even glancing at it.

"A tick," Dietlev said in a weary voice. "The pubic louse of the bush. Don't worry, we've all got some and they won't be easy to remove even when we can get down to it seriously. It was one of the surprises I was keeping in store for you."

Revolted, Elaine thought she could feel even more itchiness in the pubic area and under her armpits. "It's one I'd have happily done without," she said, sketching a smile. "All right then, 'operation scratches' . . . Who wants to go first?"

"Me," said Mauro, lifting up his trouser legs. "These bloody things sting."

His heels, lacerated by the sharp-edged grasses, were covered in red streaks. Elaine smeared them with Mercurochrome then treated his neck and forearms. Yurupig had a nasty gash across his cheek disinfected, while Petersen refused all help, muttering that he'd seen worse than that and there was no point anyway. After that Mauro dealt with Elaine's cuts.

"Don't we look great," he said when he'd finished daubing red over them. "We'll soon be terrorizing the monkeys."

"Please, Mauro, could you . . . ," Dietlev said.

He stood up immediately, as did Yurupig. They lifted up the stretcher and carried it out of the circles of light cast by the fire. Elaine concentrated on her medicine bag without even paying any attention to the patter of urine on the leaves; only a few days ago she would have been horribly embarrassed by this lack of privacy, but this wasn't the time or place for niceties. When she'd undone the bandage, Dietlev's wound was crawling with maggots; the big flies that tormented them while they were walking had managed to lay their eggs in his skin, despite the care she took to protect the wound. His leg was a blackish color, taut, ready to burst. The leg of a drowned corpse. The gangrene was rising inexorably. Three ampoules of morphine, one bubble pack of sulphonamide tablets . . . it wouldn't be enough, she realized to her dismay, to contain the infection. The thought went through her mind that Dietlev would not make it back to Brazilia with them, but she dismissed it at once, for fear it would bring him bad luck. To imagine the worst was to hold a platinum rod up at the lightning . . . She couldn't remember who had said that, but she believed the precept as if it were a commandment.

When Mauro and Yurupig brought the stretcher back close to the fire, Dietlev was shivering with pain. The sweat was streaming down his face.

"Do you want an injection?" she asked, wiping his forehead.

"Not yet, it'll go away . . . Petersen, come and have a look at this."

"Here I am, *amigo*. How can I be of service?"

Dietlev unfolded the piece of paper on which he'd sketched his map. "By my estimation we're somewhere in this area," he said, pointing to a zone to the southwest of the swamps, on the first quarter of their approximate route to the river junction. "You agree?"

'Yes," said Petersen after a brief glance at the map. "More or less, I imagine. We should get to the swamps soon. It'll be easier to find our way, but it's likely to make walking more difficult."

"That's what I was afraid of," Dietlev said to Elaine. "It's going to take us ten more days or so; I'm sorry, but it's a lot more than I was reckoning on."

Petersen shrugged his shoulders and drew the snot up his nose noisily. "You should have waited for me on the boat, like I said. Going through the jungle with a woman, a boy and a stretcher . . . Talk about a useless crew!"

"Shut it!" Mauro said venomously. "You're the one responsible for whatever happens to us."

"He's going to die," Petersen replied, shrugging his shoulders. "He's going to die, and you as well. You make me sick, so there!" He turned his back on them and climbed into his hammock. They heard him sniff loudly again under his mosquito net.

"He's not entirely wrong," Dietlev said apologetically. "If you'd left me back there, you'd get on two or three times as quickly. Of course, one solution would be to take me back to the boat, but—"

"*But* there's no question of that," Mauro broke in calmly. "We're going to get there and no one's going to die, trust me. I promised my mother I'd be in Fortaleza for Christmas and I will be. And that's that."

"Then there's no point in arguing," said Elaine, giving him an affectionate smile. "In bed everyone, we need our rest."

Mauro and Yurupig put Dietlev in his hammock, while Elaine held his leg. Despite their attempts to avoid even the slightest jolt, he was almost crying with pain. Elaine waited a few moments and then, when he asked, gave him a dose of morphine. Once he'd calmed down, she gave him a quick kiss on the lips and put the tarpaulin over him.

Elaine had gone out like a light and slept like a log. In the middle of the night she woke from a dream with the feeling she'd crashed on the ground after a vertiginous fall. Still half-asleep, she stretched out her arm, looking for Eléazard's shoulder, his warmth, and woke fully to find herself in the prison of her hammock. Through the invisible wall of the mosquito net the red glow of a few embers could still be seen, without standing out clearly from the surrounding gloom. The silence had the inexplicable opacity of the blackness. Drifting on the surface of the dark, Elaine suddenly had a vision of their encampment: a collection of fragile cocoons suspended in the void, tiny, exposed to the blind trampling of the throng. To her amazement, she heard the noise of a demonstration approaching, chants, then the roar of a stadium as the whole crowd lets out its disappointment. Then a squall sent a crackling through the whole jungle and the patter of the rain on the roof of the hammock finally dispersed her hallucination. Frozen stiff, Elaine curled up, desperate to get back to sleep, shutting out the images of death that came knocking at her mosquito net. With all her heart she longed for daybreak.

AT FIRST LIGHT, when Yurupig clapped his hands to wake them, the rain had stopped. Still half-asleep, Mauro forgot to push the tarpaulin back before opening the zip, so that he got the quarts of water that had accumulated above him full in the face and, clutching the Kalashnikov, shot out of his hammock like a scalded cat. His misfortune even drew a titter from the Indian, something unusual for him. Despite the nocturnal drenching the forest had received, he'd managed to light a fire; Mauro went to warm himself at it, at the same time drying the gun with a handkerchief.

"If you don't strip it down completely," Petersen said scornfully, "the breech will rust up and it'll be no good for anything but cracking nuts."

"In my opinion," Mauro replied without looking at him, "the water didn't have time to get inside. But we can always try it out," he added, cocking the rifle and aiming it at the old German.

"Stop it!" Dietlev said firmly. "I don't want to see you playing with that gun, understood? Come and help me get out of this thing instead, I'm frozen."

Elaine had slipped behind a tree; she came out and helped Mauro and Yurupig to carry Dietlev to the stretcher.

"How do you feel?" she asked, once he was by the fire.

"Like a baked Alaska, hot on the outside, icy inside. But there's no pain, I'm still a bit stoned."

"There was a lot of rain last night," Yurupig said, handing him a mug of coffee. "Not good for us."

"But surely it's not the rainy season," Mauro said, attempting a joke.

"No," Dietlev replied, "that's in four, six weeks. There's no danger in that respect. A good shower from time to time, especially at night, that's all we have to fear at the moment."

Pity, Mauro thought. He was beginning to enjoy the adventure and, despite their concern about Dietlev, felt on a high.

Not long afterward, once the mist had cleared, the little expedition set off again.

THEY'D BEEN WALKING for two hours, Petersen and Yurupig carrying the stretcher, when Mauro sank up to his knees in sticky mud hidden underneath the grass. He called to Yurupig to help him out of the marsh and came back with him to join the others.

"We've reached the swamp," he announced gaily, "that's worth a celebratory rest, isn't it? What do you think Dietlev?" He turned toward him and suddenly his smile vanished. "Dietlev?"

Elaine, who had sat down on a stump behind the group, hurried over to the stretcher: eyes half-closed, a feverish glow on his face, Dietlev was having difficulty breathing. Far away from her, in another world, beyond suffering and language, he didn't reply to her anxious questions.

"Get me some water, Yurupig." She dissolved a large dose of aspirin in a cup and forced Dietlev to swallow it. Petersen came over as Elaine hurriedly uncovered the wound. It was crawling with maggots again, fewer than previously, but his leg had swollen even more and his thigh was mottled with dark patches.

"It'll have to be amputated pronto," Petersen said.

Elaine turned toward him as if he'd said something obscene, but he met her look with no show of emotion. His eyes were shining, his pupils abnormally dilated deep within his wizened face. "The gangrene's rising. If we don't cut off his leg, he's fucked and that's it. It's up to you to decide."

Elaine realized at once that he was right, even before she saw the sad look on Yurupig's face; the tears immediately came to her eyes, not because of the amputation, which she accepted was imperative, but because she knew she was incapable of performing it.

"I can see to it, if you want," Petersen said. "I've already done that on the Russian front."

"You?!" Mauro exclaimed, taken aback. "And why would you do that, eh?" Falling into the familiar form to express his contempt, his voice hoarse with fury, he went on, "After all your scheming to get us to stay on the boat, you want us to believe that you're . . . You bastard. You want to kill him, that's it."

Petersen thought of replying that you could very well kill someone in cold blood without being able to bring yourself to let him die like a dog, but it was too complicated, so he went back to the fire.

"It *has* to be amputated, don't you see that?" Elaine said to Mauro gently. "Now look at me: would you do it? Would you?" Her eyes probed his expression as he struggled to find the words, a helpless look on his face.

"Don't worry," she said, putting her arms round him, "if he wanted to harm him, all he had to do was to hold his tongue. Now pull yourself together, Dietlev's going to need us."

She went back to Petersen. "Get on with it, then. I'll take the responsibility."

"So that's it, is it? I'm not a murdering bastard anymore. You have to make up your minds one way or another."

She gave him a pleading look.

"OK, off we go. But I'm doing it for you, for you alone."

THEY RETRACED THEIR steps until they found a more open space. At Petersen's orders Yurupig made a fire big enough to boil the water and sterilize the blades. When everything was ready, Herman left them for a few minutes; he was sniffing when he came back. Dietlev was lying on the ground, half-unconscious because of the morphine injection Elaine had just given him.

"You, you little brat," he said to Mauro, "you hold his shoulders. Yurupig, you see to his other leg."

"What about me?" Elaine asked.

"You'll do what I tell you as we go along. There'll be just the tourniquet to hold and the arteries to ligature, if they're visible."

WHEN PETERSEN TACKLED Dietlev's femur with the saw blade from the survival kit, Dietlev screamed, just once, a long scream from the depths of his coma. The retraction of the muscles around the exposed bone, Dietlev's abrupt jerks . . . Elaine found that all less horrifying than the sight of his leg, detached, obscene, along-side his body while she was containing the hemorrhage.

"That's it, done," Herman said when he'd finished washing the flesh with boiling water. "The stump has to be left exposed to the air, so it'll heal over; no Mercurochrome, nothing, just water and some gauze to protect it. I cut quite high up, I hope it'll do."

They were standing round Dietlev's tortured body, pale, their faces pinched from weariness and the extreme strain the primitive surgery had put them under.

"Thank you," Elaine said, taking Petersen's hand. "I don't know how, but I'll repay you some day."

Petersen muttered something, visibly embarrassed by this show of emotion. He straightened up, took a few steps, stuck his foot under the amputated leg and sent it flying into the thicket. "Put him back on his stretcher," he said as he turned round, "we've been hanging around here for long enough already."

Eléazard's notebooks

IT IS NOT ONLY the musical theory of the *Musurgia* but the whole of Kircher's work that is "infectious" or, rather, colonialist.

THE HERMENEUTIC MANIA . . . *"A symbol,"* Kircher writes, *"is a mark signifying some more hidden mystery, that is to say, its nature is to lead our minds, thanks to some similarity, to under-stand something very different from those objects brought to us by our external senses whose property it is to be hidden or concealed*

beneath the veil of an obscure expression." (Obeliscus Pamphilius)
The dance of the seven veils, again and again . . . But why should
things be a sign of something other than their own radiant nudity? What perverse eroticism does it take to compel us to skin
them like rabbits?

LITTLE RED RIDING HOOD: How good you are, Father, at
weaving mosquito nets!

Athanasius Kircher: All the better to lift them off, my child . . .

KIRCHER MISSED THE DAWN of the scientific spirit. His work
remains a sterile accumulation of information. It is even astonishing, given the huge number of his books, that he had so few
interesting insights. He was unworthy of his age.

MORE THAN THE IDEA OF GOD, it is the dogma that is unhealthy, like systematics in philosophy or any rule based on precepts lubricated with the Vaseline of the Absolute.

"IDEOLOGY," Roland Barthes wrote, "is like a fryer: whatever idea
you drop into it, it's always a french fry that comes out." Kircher
smells of the rancid oil of the Counter-Reformation. He ought to be
burned, not in effigy, but really, as an example, "for the survivors
and those who haven't committed a crime." Why are we at liberty
to condemn the dead? Pierre Ayrault asked: "Because otherwise we
would not be able to absolve or praise them." To be able to decorate a soldier killed while acting under orders, we have to be able to
hang the corpse of one who showed cowardice under fire.

PUNISHING A PERSON'S MEMORY: After having razed his
house to the ground, filled in his moat and his ponds, degraded his

offspring and scratched out his name from the register of births, the guilty man's forests were cut down to the height of a man.

MINOR CHINESE OFFICIALS:
Official in charge of the Confines
Official in charge of insignia made of feathers
Inspector of medicine tasters
Commissioner in charge of demanding submission from rebels
Head Clerk of the office for receiving subjugated rebels
Grand Master of reprimands
Officer of the tracks
Official in charge of the Entrance and the Inside
Grand Rear Secretary of the Grand Rear Secretariat
Official charged with embellishing translations
Official charged with showing and observing
Observer of drafts
Subdirector of the multitudes
Superintendent of frogs
Condemned man of noon
Official charged with keeping his eye glued to the cupboard keyholes
Official charged with preserving and clarifying
Official charged with making good the emperor's oversights
Leader of the blind
Minister of winter
Shaker of hands
Superintendent of leather boots
Regulator of female tones
Participant in deliberations on advantages and disadvantages
Fulminator
Official charged with speeding up delayed dispatches

Musician for secular occasions on a short tour of duty
Grand supervisor of fish
Fisher of rorquals
Friend

DICTIONARIES and catalogs: the natural home of compulsives. The index as a literary genre?

KIRCHER ONLY THINKS through the intermedium of images, which comes down to saying he doesn't think at all. He's a meditative type, in the sense in which Walter Benjamin understood the expression: he's at home among allegories.

THINGS THAT PLEASE the deity: odd numbers, vowels, silence, laughs.

THE PORTUGUESE of Brazil is a language full of soft vocalizations. A language of black magic, of invocation. In his *Manual of Harmonics* Nicomachus of Gerasa declares that the consonants constitute the material of sound, the vowels its divine nature. The latter are like the notes of the music of the spheres.

HAVING BECOME MASTERS of Egypt, the Arabs called the hieroglyphs the "language of the birds" because of the large number of stylized fowls to be seen among them.

FLAUBERT'S NOTEBOOKS, October 1859: "Father Kircher, the author of the Magic Lantern, of the *Œdipus Ægyptiacus*, of a system for making an automaton that would speak like a man, of the palingenesis of plants, of two other systems, one for counting, one for expatiating on all subjects, studied China, the Coptic language (the first man in Europe to do so); author of a work that begins

JEAN-MARIE BLAS DE ROBLES

with the words: *Turris Babel sive Archontologia,* born in 1602."
The fact that this summary is there together with the little note
on Pierre Jurieu—"Pierre Jurieu, tormented by colics, attributed
them to the battles seven knights ceaselessly fought out in his
bowels"—which he was to use in the preliminary manuscript of
Bouvard et Pécuchet, leaves little doubt as to the high regard in
which Flaubert held Athanasius Kircher's works.

LOREDANA: She gives her advice with all the tenderness and
gentleness of a heavy machine gun. Having said that, there's no
doubt she's right: if you stand still, the beast will eat you, if you
run, it'll catch up with you.

CHAPTER 19

*In which we hear of the unexpected
conversion of Queen Christina*

❧ THAT SAME YEAR the most incredible news
reached the Vatican by devious routes: the daughter of that
Gustavus Adolphus who had vowed to exterminate all the papists
& Jesuits in creation, the enlightened but libertine sovereign of
a kingdom that was a stronghold of the Reformation, Queen
Christina of Sweden secretly wanted to convert!

There were important matters at stake: it was a unique
opportunity for the Church of Rome to demonstrate its power
& its ability to bring one of the most striking figures of the
Reformation back to the fold. It was a matter, therefore, of
carefully selecting those who would be charged with accelerating
proceedings. Kircher's services were once more called upon and
he gave his superiors the benefit of his wise advice; two Jesuits
from his immediate entourage were dispatched to Sweden at
once, disguised as simple gentlemen.

The indoctrination of Christina of Sweden began right away, though not without difficulty as the Queen, intelligent & more conversant with theological matters than one would have thought, opposed argument after argument from her two instructors. Having said that, the stumbling block to her conversion was purely temporal: if she became Catholic, Christina could not remain head of a Protestant kingdom.

For the next two years my master hardly left his study at all, entirely taken up with the compilation of his *Mundus Subterraneus,* which grew a little larger with every day, & with the revisions and adjustments essential for the publication of his *Egyptian Oedipus.* To his delight, on May 2, 1652, the day of his fiftieth birthday, he finally held the first volume of this major work in his hands, the one to which he had devoted every moment of his life, from the time when the hieroglyphs had, as it were, appeared to him. Twenty years of uninterrupted research, more than three hundred authors of antiquity quoted in support of his thesis, two thousand pages divided into four volumes to be published over three years! A very large number of engravings, executed to his orders by such talented painters as Bloemaert & Rosello, provided marvelous illustrations to a text for which my master had many new characters cast. It was a huge enterprise & enjoyed corresponding success.

The *Œdipus Ægyptiacus* thus created a great stir throughout Europe & from 1652 to 1654 Kircher had to put up with the inconveniences caused by his contemporaries' enthusiasm. Scholars, sent by the greatest scientific academies in the world, flocked to Rome to meet him. People came from all sides to see the man who had managed to decipher the language of the pharaohs, the hieroglyphs that had remained such a mystery to ordinary mortals for twenty-four hundred years . . . It was such a success that the books were sold out even before they came

off the printer's presses. The name of Kircher was on everyone's
lips & during those three years we had to reply to more than a
thousand laudatory letters.

Meanwhile in Stockholm the Pope's envoys suddenly saw
their efforts rewarded: on February 11, 1654 Queen Christina
of Sweden announced to the senate her decision to abdicate
in favor of her cousin, Charles. All the protestations of the
senators were futile &, in a coincidence to which destiny alone
holds the key, it was on May 2, 1654, Kircher's birthday, that
she renounced the throne before all the representatives of the
estates. After that, the ceremony of abdication was a mere
formality & on June 16, having returned the crown jewels and
taken off her crown herself, Christina of Sweden held sway over
no one but herself here below.

Scarcely twenty-eight years old, though having reigned for
longer than many a king who had gone white in the exercise
of power, she immediately set off, anxious to leave as quickly
as possible a kingdom from which she had banished herself in
an act of great self-denial. Accompanied by a few servants &
faithful courtiers, she had her hair cut, dressed like a man so as
not to be recognized & left with no regret the country that had
shown her such little love.

She headed for Innsbruck, where she was to abjure her heresy
officially. One can well imagine how anxiously the ecclesiastical
authorities followed her progress step by step. Her abdication,
important though it was, meant nothing in itself; at any
moment Christina could have renounced the sacrifice of her
faith, which was so important for the Church. And my master
was not the only person to follow the Queen on her journey by
means of the letters the Vatican's spies sent to the Quirinal.

On December 23, she arrived in Willebroek, where Archduke
Leopold, governor of the Netherlands, had gone to meet her.

After a sumptuous dinner, they embarked on a frigate that took them along the canal as far as the bridge at Laeken, on the outskirts of Brussels. During the short voyage the Archduke & Christina played chess, while the sky above was constantly lit up by fireworks. The next evening, Christmas Eve, they gathered with some nobles in Leopold's palace, in the very place where, a hundred years earlier, the Holy Roman Emperor Charles the Fifth had abdicated to devote the rest of his life to the contemplation of the works of Our Lord.

That was the night when, under the direction of the Dominican, Father Guemes, she abjured Protestantism before God.

Kircher admitted to me that there had been great relief in certain quarters on hearing that news. However, the repeated reports following this memorable event were still disturbing: far from showing the humility appropriate to a new convert, Christina of Sweden was said to be leading a very hectic life in Brussels. One feast, one reception followed upon the other & Christina's activities were on everyone's lips. She played billiards, at which she exceled, exclusively with men, took part in wild sleigh races across the countryside or even through the city streets & went so far as to play unsuitable roles in the sung plays the Church condemned. But the most difficult part was over & there was certainly much exaggeration in the reports of her wild behavior. No one had been informed of Christina's conversion, so all she did was give the world material to criticize the usual excesses of the reformed religion.

In June 1655 Christina of Sweden finally reached Innsbruck. It was in the cathedral of that city, on November 3, that the Queen recanted, now in full view of the whole world, at the same time taking communion & receiving absolution for her sins. On this occasion she displayed perfect reverence & a humility, which boded well for the future.

Christina of Sweden a Catholic! The event, ceaselessly trumpeted abroad by the Church, was devastating for all the Protestant states. Sweden, above all, was thrown off balance by the coup. More than the Peace of Westphalia, this victory brought the Thirty Years' War to an end, crowning the triumph of the Apostolic Church of Rome. Alexander VII was jubilant; never had our religion been in such a healthy state as under his rule. And when, only a few days after the ceremony in Innsbruck, Christina of Sweden expressed the desire to come to Rome & settle there, the Pope lost no time in granting her permission. After having convoked the Congregation of Rites, in the presence of all the cardinals, the General of the Jesuits & Kircher, he decided on the ceremonial to be observed in celebration of the entry of the eminent convert into the Eternal City. Any animosity toward my master had long since been forgotten & he was personally charged with organizing the preparations for her welcome to give them due pomp & solemnity.

Christina of Sweden had set off for Rome on November 6, after having been advised to make as slow progress as possible in order to give the Vatican time to make proper preparation for her arrival. Nevertheless there was no time to lose. As my master had been given carte blanche, he secured the collaboration of Bernini. They worked together night & day to devise & realize all kinds of magnificent projects.

While this feverish activity was going on, Christina was making her leisurely way. The Duke of Mantua received her with the respect due to a sovereign: reclining in a palanquin, she crossed the Piave by the light of thousands of torches

brandished by the soldiers of the Duke of Mantua, who had
gone to meet her.

Dressed like a stage amazon & adorned with jewels, Christina
made triumphal entries to Bologna, Rimini then Ancona. Like
a river getting fuller & fuller as it flows down from its source,
her retinue had taken on alarming proportions. Noblemen
of all nations, but also foul courtesans lured by her excessive
extravagance or soldiers of fortune whose only wealth was in
their fine looks, came to accompany Christina on her journey
to Rome. And it was at Pesaro, while dancing the *Canaria,*
the new dance that had come from the Islands, that she met
Counts Monaldeschi & Santinelli, those unsavory individuals
who, a few years later, were to involve her in a scandal that
everyone still remembers. For the moment, dazzled by the two
adventurers, she admitted them to her entourage & continued
on her way.

At Loretto, at the gates of Rome, Christina insisted on
depositing, in a symbolic gesture, her crown & scepter on the
altar of the Virgin Mary. It was on the night of December 19 of
that same year that she finally entered the city, shielded from all
eyes by the closed windows of her carriage, & immediately went
to the Vatican, where the Pope had placed some apartments at
her disposal.

During these two months Kircher & Bernini had made
tremendous efforts. Drawing without restriction on the
resources of Alexander VII, they had prepared the most
majestic of receptions. Christina's official entry was not to take
place until three days later, to give her time to recover from the
fatigue of the journey. And even though the preparations had
been completed a week ago, the setting up of the vast mechanism
still had to be supervised. The College was in the grip of panic.
Cloistered in his study, Kircher was constantly on his acoustic

tube: ordering, shouting, checking a thousand things, spurring on his troops like a general on the eve of a decisive battle. In obedience to his commands, all the actors in this performance kept on rehearsing their roles & I had never rushed round so many of the streets of Rome as in those days.

On the morning of Thursday, December 23, Christina secretly left the city to go to the villa of Pope Julius, from which she was to set out in the early afternoon to make her solemn entry. Alas, a north wind had started to blow, gathering heavy clouds full of rain over the Campagna Romana. Seeing this from his window in the College, Kircher was on tenterhooks, so concerned was he that the ceremony should proceed correctly & praying that no ill fortune should deprive him of the fruits of his efforts. Immediately after lunch, which Christina took with the Pope's emissaries, the storm burst with unheard-of violence. Flashes of lightning & peals of thunder followed at ever-decreasing intervals, as if to show disapproval of the pomp put on for a mere mortal.

In the courtyard of the villa, over which canvas sheets were hastily hung, Monsignore Girolamo Farnese, the Supreme Pontiff's majordomo, showed Christina the presents His Holiness was giving her: a six-horse carriage designed by Bernini, which was adorned with admirable unicorns covered in gold leaf; a palanquin and a sedan chair, both of delicate workmanship; and an immaculate Anglo-Arab steed whose gold & vermilion harness made it worthy of an emperor. Since the rain did not stop, the majordomo proposed that Christina should cancel the 'Ceremonial Cavalcade' & enter Rome in a carriage, but the former sovereign, with all the confidence of her twenty-eight years, refused point-blank. Thus it was that the long procession set off on the Flaminian Way in the driving rain.

There was nothing so beautiful as her route through the town. In every street swathes of silk were flapping at the

windows, the drums beat a steady rhythm & from all sides
a multitude of glittering carriages came to join the solemn
procession. Inside these vehicles the noblest ladies of the city
displayed unashamedly costly dresses and jewels. As for their
husbands, no less decked out, they rode along beside them in a
deafening tumult of hooves and neighing.

When they reached Saint Peter's Square, the rain redoubled
its assault, but Christina, who only had eyes for the cathedral,
seemed unaffected by it. And the whole procession followed
her example; the wind blew away hats, the downpour spoiled
the precious fabrics without anyone appearing to regret or even
notice it.

On leaving Saint Peter's she went, still under escort, to the
Palazzo Farnese, which the Duke of Parma had put at her
disposal for the whole of her stay in Rome. As was the custom
to honor the great ones of this world, the entire front was
concealed behind a fake façade. Designed by Kircher, it was
impressive both for its splendor and for its unusual purpose.
For the architecture he had taken his inspiration from the
Temple of Music imagined by Robert Fludd & for the content
from the famous "theater of memory" of Giulio Camillo, with
the result that the façade represented the sum total of human
knowledge. Driven by clockwork mechanisms, large wooden
wheels, artistically decorated by the best artists of Rome, slowly
turned, reproducing the courses of the planets, the sun & the
stars. Seven other wheels, equally delightfully decorated with
emblems & allegorical figures, were superimposed, but set off
from each other: as they turned, Prometheus appeared, then
Mercury, Pasiphae, the Gorgons, Plato's cave, the banquet the
Ocean gave for the gods, the Sefiroth &, within those classes, a
large number of symbols drawn from mythology, which allowed
all branches of knowledge to be gradually encompassed.

When Queen Christina, fascinated by this spectacle, enquired about its maker, Cardinal Barberini sang Kircher's praises, telling her she would soon have the opportunity of meeting him, since a visit to the Roman College had long been planned for the next day. He added in passing, as if to make fun of the common people who kept commenting on these figures, that this plaster & wood encyclopedia had cost more than five hundred crowns. The paintings were by were Claude Gelée, known as Claude Lorraine, & Poussin; as for the practical details, they had taken sixty-six hundred large nails, & four boilers had been in operation uninterruptedly for two weeks to produce the 130 gallons of glue needed to assemble the various parts of the ephemeral facade.

Christina's admiration knew no bounds & she immediately sent for Kircher to give him a precious medallion that she gracefully detached from her bracelet.

CANOA QUEBRADA: *Drinking isn't such a sin . . .*

Waking next to Aynoré's body, ensconced in the hammock he rented in the lean-to at *Dona* Zefa's, Moéma spared a thought for Thaïs. Scraps from her fling with Aynoré, as precise and embarrassing as pornographic pictures, exploded over an image of a sad, accusatory smile. Her forehead felt as if it were being squeezed by a ring of iron, her moist skin gave off a smell of sour wine and her mouth tasted of sawdust—all signs that her remorse was the product of last night's binge. She just needed to put up with it for a couple of hours and she would be cleansed of this nebulous feeling of shame, which is nothing more than the postbooze horrors.

Aynoré was sleeping like a log, a Gulliver trapped in the fine net of his tattoos. His naked, suntanned body inspired not so much a feeling of tenderness as of respect, a sort of esteem bordering on veneration. All she retained of the things he had said the previous evening was an impression of efflorescence, something like the slow-motion take-off of a parrot, the red and gold traces of a lost paradise.

She suddenly heard a voice above her: "So you couldn't resist him either?" Marlene's pale face had an expression of slightly contemptuous surprise. "Don't worry, I'll keep silent as the grave. I just hope you haven't switched over, that's all."

"Drop it, will you," Moéma replied stretching out, totally unconcerned about the fact that she was naked. "And you can tell who you want what you want, I'm past the age of secrets." She pulled her tousled hair aside, like opening the curtains. "Is it late?"

"Eleven o'clock, time to get up for a joint. They way you look, poor thing! The whole gang of us are off to the beach, are you coming?"

"We'll be there," Aynoré said without opening his eyes.

Seeing the quiver that voice sent across Moéma's skin, Marlene raised his eyebrows in a jokey expression, "Well, well, old girl," he muttered as he went off, "you haven't seen the last of your troubles yet. *Você vai espumar como siri na lata . . .*"

During the few moments Moéma stayed in the hammock, running her fingers over her lover's hairless skin, Marlene's innuendo had time to get its hooks into her. It was no use her telling herself the drag queen's insinuations were only dictated by jealousy, she couldn't recover the happiness she'd felt during the night. Added to the feeling of having betrayed Thaïs—it was already clear to her that giving herself to the Indian was not a passing fancy but a commitment with no way back, a deliberate and definitive farewell that she ought to sort out with her friend—were the doubts aroused by Marlene's acid comments. His "either" had struck home. Given his appeal, Aynoré was bound to attract girls like flies . . . So what? The feelings that had thrown them into each other's arms were unique and no one had the right, except out of spite, to say differently. Aynoré had promised to initiate her into all the things in us that modern society was doing its utmost to obliterate and she trusted him to keep his word. You couldn't tame a wolf, nor was she attempting to do that, she would become a she-wolf herself, worthy of his way of being in the world, of the savageness he put into it.

It sometimes happens that one feels the need to be all the more determined in justifying a dream when it begins to fade; Moéma clung onto this one, trying to secure it by a founding act, a sacrifice that would testify to its legitimacy. As she pondered this vague plan, an image came to mind that brought a victorious smile to her lips. She shook herself, suddenly released from her fears, and climbed carefully out of the hammock.

When, a few minutes later, she gave Aynoré the comb and scissors she'd borrowed from *Dona* Zefa, the Indian made no difficulty about going along with her request. With the haughty aloofness that astounded Moéma, he started to cut her long hair in the fashion of the women of his tribe: having cut a horizontal fringe, which came down to her eyebrows, he continued along that line at the sides, leaving the full length of her hair over the back of her neck alone. He shaved her temples, to remove all trace of the former growth, and finished by clipping one of the blue-and-red feather earrings he sold in the streets to the lobe of each ear.

"You're lucky I'm not a Yanomami," he said as he held a piece of broken mirror in front of her, "you'd have been seeing yourself shaved from your forehead right back to the middle of your skull."

Moéma didn't try to recognize herself in the strange reflection he held in his fingers: with the sacrifice of her hair, her dream had finally emerged from limbo, she felt herself put right, inwardly modified after what she saw as an initiation ritual. Strengthened by this rebirth, she started to imitate Aynoré in his haughty bearing. Silent, with economy of movement—like a priestess of the olden days, she thought—she rolled a joint with a mysterious smile. And what she smoked that morning was not *maconha* but the sacred Caapi, the intercessor between the world of men and that of the gods . . .

As they went down to the beach, in the dazzling midday brightness, Moéma felt beautiful and in a warlike mood, a killer of men, an eater of flesh, an Amazon. They stopped at *Seu* Juju's hut to eat crabs.

Thaïs had gone away toward the sea as soon as she saw their silhouettes appear over the top of the dunes.

WHEN THEY REACHED Marlene's little group, far along the beach, beyond the promontory shielding the nudists from prying eyes, Moéma would have been happy to continue, but Aynoré took off his shorts and sat down among them without even consulting her.

"*Deus do céu!*" said Marlene, putting his hand over his mouth, "what have you done to your hair?"

"If you don't like it," Moéma said, getting undressed unselfconsciously, "you've only to look the other way." She looked daggers at one of the boys who was giggling unrestrainedly. "It's my business, not yours, OK?"

"Hey, stay cool," Marlene said in conciliatory tones, "I was surprised, that's all. You can shave your head, for all I care. But all the same . . . Turn around."

Moéma hesitated for a moment, then turned round, glowering.

"It looks great! It suits you, it really does."

Aynoré had stretched out on the beach. He was lying there, eyes closed, unmoving. Slightly embarrassed, Moéma noticed the size of his penis: in a soft curve against his thigh, it was longer than those of Marlene and his pals. Proud to have established this, she lay down beside the Indian, fully aware that all the others were eyeing them. It was good to be consciously naked as the focus of all these looks. Stretched out like this beside each other, they must look like the primordial pair, and she wished she could split herself in two to be able to enjoy the sight. With a mental flick of the hand she brushed aside the image of her father that suddenly appeared above her, drawing on his cigarette as he shook his head with a woebegone expression. Her mother would perhaps have understood, perhaps not, but she would certainly not have simply watched them with that hangdog expression . . . Moéma moved her arm until it touched Aynoré's and when his hand closed over hers, she felt happy, at peace with the world and herself.

The sun was burning her skin in a way that was pleasant. By association of ideas, she remembered the story of the fires and the flood, the three founding catastrophes of the Mururucu myth, that Aynoré had told her before going to sleep, though her memory of the details was somewhat confused.

Even the air was burning . . . That was how the few survivors of Hiroshima had put it, in those very words, without anyone learning the ultimate lesson of human folly from them; all at once she felt too hot to stay on the sand one second longer. She got up, announcing that she was going for a swim, shook off her dizziness and ran to the sea.

After having played in the waves for a while, she lay down on her front at the edge of the sea. Facing the beach, her hands under her chin, she concentrated on the bubbles of foam sizzling on the back of her neck at regular intervals. Thirty yards away from her, Aynoré had joined the others at keeping the ball in the air with shouts and acrobatic dives. Far beyond them the short cliff bordering this part of the shore—a cliff of solidified sand, the sand that was put in layers in little bottles for the tourists—was like a rampart veined with gradations of pink.

Roetgen . . . Moéma realized she hadn't given a single thought to him since the moment, already distant, when she'd left the *forro da* Zefa. He must be somewhere out on the open sea and she couldn't wait for him to get back to tell him how her life had been turned upside down in his absence. She resolved to be there to meet him when the jangadas came back the next day. Perhaps she could do a thesis on the mythology of the Mururucu or gather sufficient material before going to Amazonia. She definitely wouldn't tell anyone of her decision, not even her parents. Later, perhaps, when she had children, a swarm of little half castes playing along the riverside . . . She saw herself in the pose of Iracema, motionless beside the river, her bow aimed at the shadow of an invisible fish, or prophesying beside a fire, her eyes haunted by visions. The female condition of Indian women? The evidence that proved a thousand times over that they were kept on the sidelines because of their "impurity." The practise of "couvade," the tragicomedy in which the Indian men, in their masculine pretension, went so far as to act out the sufferings of childbirth and, moaning in their hammocks, receive the congratulations of the whole tribe while the new mother, still unsteady on her feet, was tiring herself out cooking cakes for the guests. All these distortions, which usually modified her enthusiasm for the Indian tribes, had vanished into thin air, rather as if all her critical faculties had been disconnected. Her love—for the first time she gave that name to the euphoria she felt at the mere thought of Aynoré—would transcend all these obstacles; and, if necessary, they would bend the tradition a bit . . .

At the roar of an engine she turned her head toward the promontory: driven at full speed along the very edge of the shore, a gold-colored beach buggy was visibly growing bigger as it sent huge sprays of water shooting up.

WITH A GOOD wind behind it, the jangada had been bowling along toward the shore for two hours, comfortably riding the heavy ocean swell. Cutting up a huge turtle, which they had caught right at the end of their fishing, had delayed them, so that now the sun looked like a globule of red sitting straight ahead of them on the dark line of the coast. João gave his orders for landing: "You come beside me," he said to Roetgen, without looking at him, "and don't get off till I tell you. One false move and we'll capsize."

Roetgen had understood the point of these orders; standing and symmetrically placed on either side of the trestle, which they were clinging onto, the four men had to concentrate right to the end on keeping the jangada balanced as it headed for the beach. A hundred yards from the shore, where the waves started to break in long, translucent rollers, João tensed as he clutched the steering oar. Features taut and eyes ceaselessly moving to check the trim of the boat and the hollow of the waves threatening to swamp the stern, he corrected its course with swift, precise touches on the helm. If it should get athwart the waves, or lose a little of its speed, the waves would roll them like any old log. Every time a breaker seemed about to catch them, João maneuvered so as to maintain the surf and the jangada would accelerate sufficiently to escape once more. Swept away uncontrollably by the final combers carrying it toward the shore, the vessel suddenly bumped the bottom, its headway carrying it, scrunching, up the beach. At João's command, the four immediately leapt out and held the jangada against the pull of the ebb while other fishermen running to meet them placed log rollers under the prow and helped them push it out of reach of the waves.

The two-wheeled collection cart, pulled by a mule, came to meet them. While João was arguing over the catch with Bolinha, the driver, Roetgen took a minute to catch his breath. He was exhausted, but with that mellow weariness that comes from the completion of a task that everything had suggested would be beyond his ability. His sailor's pride was now joined by the sweeter sense of having been accepted by the fishermen as one of them, of belonging as of right to their brotherhood. It was at that moment that he saw Moéma . . . The first thing that outraged him was her new hair style, so ridiculously loaded with meaning, the second to see the Indian kiss her on the neck as they came toward him. That smug complacency of a pregnant woman, Thaïs nowhere to be seen . . . Moéma hadn't even spoken to him and already Roetgen was ruminating on the sour secretions of his self-esteem.

Without being insulting, he replied curtly to her questions with the slightly disdainful distance of someone who doesn't really have the time to talk to idlers. Then, apologizing to her, he helped João and the others to carry the fish to the cart. When the time came to distribute their shares, he told Bolinha to take the one due to him to the fisherman he'd replaced and to see that he was credited with his usual amount with the cooperative.

With a weary smile, João slapped him on the shoulder: they were going to drink a *cachaça* or two together, perhaps even three, assuming they didn't collapse first. With a little wave to Moéma, the two men picked up their things and left, staggering with fatigue, against the light in the red of twilight.

For a few seconds Moéma watched them go as they climbed the dune. Roetgen's looks had made her feel ugly and she had to hold back the tears.

If I've become addicted to drink,
> . . . the *violeiro* said, sitting on a beer crate, his voice husky, his guitar cracked. The mug of a Haitian sorcerer . . . the guy was falling apart at the seams . . .

The reason's just the despair I'm in.

... José Costa Leite, the real one, with his little piggy eyes and his baseball cap stiff with grease.

No need to tell me what you think,

... me neither, thought Roetgen, nor João, nor anyone else either. Fill that up, will you?

Drinking isn't such a sin.

... definitely not, eh João? Anything you want, but not a sin. A duty, a moral law, even. A categorical imperative!

No job, no dough, I'm on the street,

Nothing in my bag to eat . . .

... my God, the poor guys! To be listening to that while millions of others are getting all worked up over the Montignac diet or liposuction . . .

Why not make your home the inn?

Drinking isn't such a sin.

... a medieval minstrel's voice, a Sardinian voice, an Andalusian voice, a lonesome voice on the Blues railroad . . .

Alcohol soaks up the sadness,

Drown your memories in gin,

That'll shut out all the badness —

Drinking isn't such a sin . . .

... mass for the downtrodden, and educational! Verses poured forth at top speed and without taking a breath, the last line descending to the quavering line of the refrain. "Hell!" João suddenly says, his eyes glassy, his face ashen, "Come on, *cantador,* what about hell?"

Sozzled kidneys or a stroke?

Drunk or sober, you'll still croak.

's my own choice, this hell I'm in —

Drinking isn't such a sin . . .

... an African song, the song of a visionary praise singer. The lament without joy of the man without hope.

"Freedom!" Roetgen says, and he says it again because he feels as if he's got a hot potato in his mouth, and he's annoyed with himself because all at once the word seems as strange, as devoid of meaning as methoxypsoralen or retinol mononitrate . . . Two chords and the improvisation starts up again:

Freedom to which a donkey's bred?
Endless traipsing 'round its shed.

. . . José Costa Leita looks at the wall, his singing gets hoarse, akin to a cry, finds new paths . . .

The rich man's lapdog gets to guzzle,
The poor Brazilian gets a muzzle—
Your heart is free to pound and race
When the cops take up the chase . . .
So I maintain, through thick and thin:
Drinking isn't such a sin . . .

. . . whistles round the bar, appreciation expressed in grunts and spitting . . . "*Que bom!* Where does he find these things?" the barman says. "A *cachaça* for the poet, and well filled!" Then suddenly there are two angels, two apparitions suffused with light against the darkness of the doorway. My word, it's enough to make you believe in God! Prince-Valiant-style hair, sides and crown glittering with gold powder, long satin robes, pink for one, azure for the other, two young angels, wide-eyed, hands clasped high on their chests in a gesture of prayer. They've stopped to have a glance at hell, just as two real little girls might have done, letting their curiosity get the better of them on the way to church. Roetgen, however, didn't think the angels had that grave look, the look of an entomologist intrigued by the sudden, inexplicable turmoil in an anthill. He waved them in— and they were gone: it was as if a stultifying wind had blown its peace over the bar. Costa Leite picked up his guitar again . . .

The factory bosses, in the main,
Have got a nice, poetic vein;
The workers veins are varicose
And they shit worms, to add to their woes.
I'll sell my soul to the devil too,
If it'll save some pretty girl's
Let God save all the filthy curs
Since he has nothing better to do.
My only friend's the pot I piss in—
Drinking isn't such a sin.

. . . another *cachaça,* and another, to the very confines of this night. "You mustn't hold it against her," João says, his eyes fixed on a packet of Omo, "it's not her fault. *A mulher e capaz de quase tudo, o homem de resto . . .*" Ready to drop from drunkenness and fatigue, they cling to each other, shoulders together, arms groping the bar, each holding the other up on the edge of the abyss.

When Thaïs found him, late in the evening, Roetgen was asleep on the billiard table, a nasty gash on his forehead, dried blood over his face. The barman told her he'd had to smash a bottle over his head, he was a decent guy and there was no real harm done, neither to his skull—just a bit of a cut on his scalp, nothing serious—nor in the damage he'd caused. João had been forcibly taken home a little earlier, griping about his wife at the top of his voice.

FORTALEZA, FAVELA DE PIRAMBÚ: *Angicos, 1938 . . .*

Nelson had been filing down his iron bar for hours. His mind released by the repetitive nature of the work, he was once more reliving the death of Lampião. There was something that bothered him

477

about the way it had happened, his end was too prosaic, at odds with the qualities of cunning and intelligence attributed to his hero. Angicos, 1938 . . . The tragic end of the famous *cangaceiro* was well known: proud of their deed, the men of the flying squad commanded by Lieutenant João Bezerra had reported every last detail.

When the pale light of dawn rose over that part of Brazil on July 28, 1938, the police were so close to the *cangaceiros* that they could hear them talking or watch those already stretching in the doorway of their shack. Dressed in the only uniform the *caatinga* allowed, the men on both sides looked disconcertingly similar: a leather jerkin held tight over the chest by the crossed cartridge belts, gaiters, leggings jointed at the knees, a wide cocked hat in fawn leather, stuck with stars and gilded rosettes—a bit like the hats of the dandies of the Directoire period but with a headband and chin strap. Designed to resist the thorny vegetation, this bronze armor united hunters and hunted like knights and their reflection. Dull sounds emerged from time to time beneath the patter of the driving rain: the clatter of mess tins, a horse snorting, a dry cough . . . They were only to open fire on Bezerra's command, but the lieutenant's jaws were welded so tightly together by fear that his pulse was visible on his cheek; far from being ready to pounce, he was trying to disappear into the puddle where he was crouching. The sudden rattle of a sewing machine sent the coward's face plunging into the mud . . . A sudden movement in the scrub? The metallic glint of a carbine? An unusually deep silence round the encampment? Without anyone being able to say why, one of the *cangaceiros* gave the alarm. A second later Maria Bonita thought she saw her sewing machine spitting bullets.

Rushing out when his companion called, Lampião was one of the first to fall under the hail of machine-gun fire. While a good number of the *cangaceiros* scattered into the hills, Maria Bonita, Luís Pedro and the most faithful of the outlaws entrenched themselves in the huts. The attack only lasted about twenty minutes, but long after the last rifle facing them had fallen silent, the machine guns continued to pepper the shelters of canvas and branches.

Thus the battle was turned into a pigeon shoot. The machine guns had given the *cangaceiros* no chance at all. And how could such a rout be justified? Why should Bezerra, the well-known coward, have prevailed over intelligence and bravery on that morning rather than any other? Lampião and his faithful followers had died without fighting. They had simply been executed.

Moved by the scene he was visualizing, Nelson had increased the speed of his file over the iron bar. No, he thought, Lampião would never have allowed himself to get caught so easily on a field of battle, even if he'd been taken by surprise. The story just didn't stand up. The other version, though, the one that had been rumored abroad almost immediately after the tragedy of Angicos, was much more convincing: fuelled by the revelations of Father José Kehrle and confirmed by the brothers João and David Jurubeba, it declared that Lampião and the ten *cangaceiros* who had been martyred along with him had been poisoned.

CHAPTER 20

*In which Kircher finds himself obliged to tell Queen Christina
a scabrous story he wanted to keep to himself . . .*

ON THE NEXT day, December 24, 1655, Queen
Christina honored us with her presence, as arranged.

Kircher was experienced as a guide; speaking without
interruption to his guest, he quickly & amusingly presented
large sections of his museum to her, only pausing over
objects worthy of the royal interest. Here a robe from China,
embroidered with gold and dragons, there an Egyptian intaglio
of the most beautiful jasper or an abraxas engraved on jade &
mounted on a revolving ring; further on a series of distorting
mirrors. One of these made an extraordinary impression on
Queen Christina; when you looked at yourself in it, you saw
your head stretch more & more into a cone, then four, three,
five & eight eyes appeared; at the same time your mouth
became like a cave, with your teeth rising up like precipitous
rocks. Widthwise you first of all saw yourself without a

forehead, then getting donkey's ears without your mouth
& nostrils being modified at all. But I cannot find words to
describe the whole variety of these hideous apparitions. My
master tirelessly explained the catoptric principles involved
in these inventions & in those far more interesting ones that
he had worked out in his mind, should some patron one day
enable them to be realized.

After the catoptric museum, the finest & most complete in
the world, Kircher showed Christina the great python of Brazil
& the elephant seal, gigantic animals his fame alone had brought
into his possession. After the Queen had gone into raptures
at the size of these giants of creation, my master showed
her an engraving & asked if she could identify the animal it
represented.

"What strange monster is that?!" Christina exclaimed with a
laugh. "It looks like a dromedary sitting on a branch."

"It's a flea, Your Highness, & its perch a human hair, which
the power of my microscope has enlarged like that to offend the
eye—& delight the mind. Take a look yourself . . ."

At once Athanasius handed her one of these instruments &
several specimens he had prepared for that purpose. Christina,
bending over the eyepiece, gave little cries of astonishment
at the sight of these insects transformed into frightening
chimeras simply by virtue of the lenses, while my master in his
imperturbable way, continued to expound upon the infinitely
great & the infinitely small.

From there we went on to the winged dragon Cardinal
Barberini had parted with for our museum & that was
made to inspire men with terror. But Queen Christina was
made of sterner stuff & true to her reputation for subtlety.
"A few months ago," she said, "some German Jesuits told me
they had seen dragons *priapos suos immanes, in os feminarum*

intromittentes, ibique urinam fudentes.[1] I really gave them a piece of my mind," she added, "for having permitted such offensive behavior, but they just laughed."

"I hadn't heard of that," Kircher replied, "nevertheless I am disappointed at their thoughtlessness. I wouldn't have left without capturing these beasts or . . . 'converting' them if you prefer . . ."

Following this skirmish, there was the lamb with two heads, the bird of paradise with three legs & the stuffed crocodile apparently sleeping under a reconstructed palm tree.

"The crocodile," my master explained, "is the symbol of divine omniscience, since only its eyes emerge from the water &, although seeing everything, it remains invisible to our mortal senses. It has no tongue and divine reason has no need of words to make itself manifest. And as Plutarch points out, it lays sixty eggs that take that many days to hatch; it also lives for sixty years at the longest. Now sixty is the first number astronomers use in their calculations, so that it was not without reason that the priests of ancient Egypt dedicated a town to them, Crocodilopolis, & that the inhabitants of Nîmes still have this emblem on the walls of their town."

We were making our way through the rest of the Egyptian section of the museum, heading for the curio with which a visit usually ended—a stone of 10 ounces removed from the gallbladder of Father Leo Sanctius, who unfortunately died during the operation—when Queen Christina stopped by a statuette to which I had never paid much attention: a rather plump figure wearing a hat in the form of a scarab, the rear legs of which hung down like ribbons well below the back of its

1 (. . .) putting their huge penises in the females' mouth and pouring their urine into it.

neck & that appeared to be squatting down while holding its
sides.

"And that, Reverend Father?" Christina asked.

"An unimportant Egyptian idol," Kircher replied, making as
if to continue walking.

"I must say it seems extremely odd to me," the Queen
insisted. "What strange deity is it?"

Being perfectly familiar with the least of Athanasius's
expressions, I could tell he would have preferred to talk about
something else & his reaction aroused my own curiosity.

"I'm afraid, Your Highness," my master said, embarrassed,
"that it is not something for delicate ears & I would most
humbly beg you to permit me, with due reverence for your rank
& your sex, to draw a veil over this exhibit."

"But if I did not permit you . . ." Christina said, smiling
with feigned ingenuousness. "You must realize that my rank
allows me to do things that are denied other women & even the
majority of men. Do not be misled by my dress; it is not their sex
that makes a king or a queen, it is their rule, & that alone, that is
decisive."

"And your reign, Your Majesty, was great & remarkable, one
of the most notable. I therefore bow to your wishes & beg you
to pardon my untimely reticence. This idol represents the *deus
Crepitus*, the Fart god, of the Egyptians, & that in the comical
posture appropriate to his nature."

Queen Christina remained perfectly impassive, proving that
she fully merited her reputation as an enlightened monarch,
more interested in increasing her knowledge, even in such a
scabrous area, than in making puerile jokes about it. When
some of her suite giggled & made ironic comments on the fetid
side of this deity, she silenced them with a look that indicated
the authority this masterful woman had over them.

"Please go on, Reverend Father. How is it that the builders of the pyramids & the library of Alexandria, the inventors of the hieroglyphs & so many other marvelous secrets, could lower themselves to this shameless cult? I must admit that my curiosity has been aroused by something that, on the face of it, has neither rhyme nor reason."

"So you wish me to explain to Your Majesty the deified fart of the Egyptians? But would it not be to go against people's rights to publish abroad the apparently ridiculous side of that wise & learned nation?

"Among those nations that have granted divine rights to sentient creatures I see none more excusable than those who worshipped the winds; they are invisible, like the grand master of the universe, & their source is unknown, like that of the deity. We should, therefore, not be surprised if the winds have been worshipped by the majority of nations as terrible & unfathomable forces, as marvelous workers of the storms & of the calm of the world & as the masters of nature; you will know what Petronius said: *primus in orbe Deos fecit timor . . .* [2] The Phoenicians, as vouched for by Eusebius, who gives an account of the theology of these nations, dedicated a temple to the winds. The Persians followed their example: *Sacrificant persæ*, Herodotus says, *soli & lunae & telluri & aquæ & ventis.* [3] Strabo confirms that in almost the same words.

"The Greeks imitated one or the other of the nations I have just cited. When Greece was threatened by the expedition of Xerxes, they consulted the oracle at Delphi, who replied that they needed to make the winds favorable to them to get their

2 At the beginning of the world, fear alone created the gods . . .

3 The Persians sacrifice to the Sun, the Moon, the Earth, to fire, water and the winds.

aid, so they made sacrifice on an altar dedicated to them & Xerxes's fleet was scattered by a furious storm. Plato, in the *Phaedrus*, reports that in his day there was an altar consecrated to the wind Boreas in Athens. And Pausanias tells us that there was an altar at Sycion for the sacrifices that were made to soothe the anger of the winds.

"The Romans fell into the same dreams, according to Virgil they sacrificed a black sheep to the winter winds & a white one to the Zephyrs. And the Emperor Augustus, despite his enlightened outlook, being in Gallia Narbonensis & dismayed at the violence of the Circius wind, which is still called the wind of Cers in Narbonne & which blew down houses & the biggest trees & yet made the air marvelously salubrious, made a vow to consecrate a temple to it & did indeed build it. It is Seneca who tells us that in his *Naturales Quaestiones*.

"Finally the Scythians, according to Lucian, swore by the wind & by their sword, which they thus recognized as their god.

"And man, who has always been regarded as a microcosm, that is, as a small world, has his winds like the great world. And these winds, in the three regions of our body as if in three different climates, set off tempests and storms when they are too abundant & too swift, & give refreshment to the blood, to our animal spirits & to our solid parts, & health to our whole body when they are gentle and regular in their movements; but it only takes a pressing abundance of these enclosed winds to create an incurable colic, a windy dropsy or a knotting of the bowels, all of which are fatal ailments. The Egyptians, therefore, awarded divine status to these winds of the small world as the originators of sickness & health in the human body. And Job seems to confirm their view when he says, *O remember my life is wind* . . . However, they prefer the fart to all the other winds of this small world, perhaps because it is the cleanest of all or because it makes a loud noise as it escapes from its prison, thus imitating the sound of thunder & this meant that it could be regarded by that nation as a small Jupiter the Thunderer who deserved their worship.

"Let us, however, thank the Lord for rescuing us from all these aberrations by the light of faith; whatever the power we admire in these natural agencies to do us good or ill, let us regard them solely as steps on a mysterious ladder by which we must ascend to the adoration of the Creator who afflicts or favors us by the ministrations of the greatest or least of his creatures, following the unfathomable commands of His providence."

Christina of Sweden was delighted with this learned dissertation. She promised my master her support in maintaining & enhancing his museum, then left. My master was exhausted, but pleased to have withstood this little storm so well; he slept solidly for eight hours, something that hadn't happened for a long time.

Kircher had acquitted himself well & returned to his studies without delay. He continued to be inundated by the wave of celebrity unleashed by the publication of *Œdipus Ægyptiacus*, with the result that there were not enough hours in the day for him to reply to all the questions & honors that came flooding in from all over the world. It was during this period, if I remember rightly, that a certain Marcus, a native of Prague, paid tribute by sending him a manuscript that was extremely rare but indecipherable, since it was written in a language that was entirely made up. Athanasius recognized it as the missing part of the *Opus Tertium* by the philosopher Roger Bacon; he put off the translation until later &, unfortunately, never found the opportunity to complete it.

The next year, 1656, flew by like a dream. There was nothing to disturb my master's good humor, apart from the most disquieting rumors from the Farnese palace. Christina was living in grand style, with no regard for Roman sensitivities, & this set the tongues wagging. The sole woman among the hundred or so men of which her court consisted, she threw herself unreservedly into any fancy her imagination suggested. On her orders, the fig leaves had been removed from the statues in her palace, the pictures lent her by the Pope—all with devout or instructive subjects—had been replaced by mythological scenes more fitting for a brothel than the residence of a new convert, & her courtiers did not hesitate, to the despair of the majordomo Giandemaria, to strip bare the palace of the unfortunate Duke of Parma, even removing the trimmings from chairs & brocade curtains to sell to wealthy commoners in the city. Cardinal Colonna had become so infatuated with the young Queen that he had to be sent to his house in the country & a young nun, to whom she had taken such a fancy she wanted to remove her from Our Lord's service, had to change convents!

It was at this time that my master caught a stomach chill, from having eaten too much fruit, as he thought, during Lent. This indisposition was unfortunate, Christina having invited us, along with various other ecclesiastics, to a concert she had arranged as a sign of contrition. Having, since the early morning, tried all known remedies with no improvement, Kircher was in despair. Fortunately, just as he was coming to a decision to decline such a prestigious invitation, my master remembered a vial he had recently been sent by a missionary in Brazil, Father Yves d'Évreux. This vial, the Jesuit had said in his letter, contained a sovereign powder for all ailments that, in addition, helped to restore the vigor of a mind exhausted by study; he had, he said, often observed its effects both on the Tupinamba Indians, from whom he had obtained it, & on himself. As far as he had been able to ascertain, this remedy came from a certain liana they called *Guaraná*; it was mixed with rye flour, the sole purpose of which was to make it into little balls that were easier to swallow.

In this dire situation, Kircher did not hesitate for one moment; following Father d'Évreux's instructions to the letter, he ate one of the pastilles I made up for him with a little holy water. And where all the secrets of our pharmacopoeia had failed, the savages' medicine produced a miraculous result: less than an hour after he had taken it, my master felt better. His stomachache and the fluxion disappeared, the color returned to his cheeks & he found he was humming a cheerful tune. He felt he had recovered not only his health but also the energy & sharpness of mind of his younger days. There was never anything so surprising as this metamorphosis & we were grateful to the Indians for the gift of this providential cure from so far away.

Kircher was making jokes all the way to the Farnese palace. His good humor was so infectious that we both fell about laughing several times at trifles that weren't really that funny.

As usual Michele Angelo Rossi, Laelius Chorista & Salvatore Mazelli, the three musicians who were performing Frescobaldi at Queen Christina's concert that evening, played impeccably, but their music struck an unexpected chord in my master. Hardly had they started to play, than I saw him close his eyes & fall into a reverie that lasted the whole concert. Sometimes he gave little exclamations of joy, which told me he was not asleep but plunged in the most marvelous rapture.

When Athanasius looked at me, long after the last note had been played, I thought his illness had returned, so strangely fixed was his look. His eyes, moist with tears, went through me without seeing me . . . From the few incoherent phrases he managed to utter, I realized my master was immersed in the most absolute voluptuous delight, but words seemed to have extreme difficulty passing his lips, which made me very apprehensive.

"*Abgeschiedenheit!*" he murmured with a singular smile. "I am naked, I am blind & I am no longer alone . . . *Schau*, Caspar, *diese Welt vergeht. Was? Sie vergeht auch nicht, es ist nur Finsternis, was Gott in ihr zerbricht!*[4] Yes, burn! Burn me with your love!"

As he said this, he moved his hands & feet involuntarily, just as if they were touching burning coals. By these signs I recognized the divine presence & the immense privilege accorded Kircher at that moment. But I could also see that he was in such a state of ecstatic beatitude that he would be incapable of social intercourse, so I thought it my duty to take him back to the College at once.

In his room, to which I had to lead him like a little child, Kircher knelt down at his prie-dieu: far from fading, his rapture took a remarkable &, in many respects, frightening turn . . .

ALCÂNTARA: *Something terrible and obscure . . .*

Loredana did not regret having confided in Soledade, but the soul searching her admission had forced on her had left her not knowing where to turn.

Two days later, when Soledade told her Mariazinha was expecting them that same evening, it took her a while to remember where she had heard the name. She was no longer at all attracted by the idea of meeting this woman who was supposed to be able to cure her of all her ills, but she accepted it out of consideration

---

4 Isolation! Look, this world is fading. What? No, it is not fading, it is just the darkness in it that God is shattering!

for Soledade, who had gone to great lengths to get Mariazinha to agree to the meeting and seemed very proud of her efforts as a go-between.

She came for her in the late afternoon and they left right away, without having been seen by anyone in the hotel. As they walked, Loredana got dribs and drabs of information from the vague replies to the questions that were going through her mind: they were heading for the *terreiro* of Sakpata, where there was to be a gathering that evening, a *macumba*; they would see the 'mother of saints' before that, because it wasn't certain that, as a stranger, she would be able to attend the ceremony. As to learning what exactly a *terreiro* or a *macumba* was, what sort of cult was being celebrated, Loredana had to give up on that since Soledade confessed that she was forbidden to reveal such details. Since, in contrast to her usual affability, she had assumed an air of obstinacy, Loredana left her in peace.

They left the main street, then the last permanent houses, and plunged into the peninsula on a footpath bordered by the occasional shack surrounded by *babaçus*. Despite the lack of rain over the last few days, the red soil still stuck to their sandals, making walking an effort. A zebu standing still, its ribs sticking out; a dog, nothing but skin and bones, too weak to bark as they passed; half-starved figures dressed in colorless rags, looking lost, with big, shining eyes focused on nothing . . . It was a vision of impoverishment beyond anything Loredana had previously seen, oppressive destitution, a storm ready to break, more visible here than in the streets of Alcântara or San Luís. The path grew narrower and narrower, the darkness was beginning to make the dark-green coat of the tall trees quiver: for a moment Loredana had the feeling they were somehow going to meet the night.

After three-quarters of an hour they found themselves beneath a huge mango tree, its bloated trunk, enlarged by its own shoots, twisting like Laocoön assailed by snakes. A fairy-tale tree, green-ish, shining, sprawling and large enough to serve as a hiding place for a whole tribe of witches.

"We're almost there," Soledade said, taking a little track hid-den by the roots.

Mariazinha's house appeared among the trees in the hollow of a perfectly leveled clearing that was so well maintained it looked unreal after the postwar landscape they had just come through. The façade was white, turning to dirty ochre, and Loredana was struck by the lack of windows and, as she approached, the re-mains of a stone cross above the door.

Hardly had they crossed the threshold than a little girl came to meet them. She showed them into a room that gave Loredana the shivers, so much did the furnishings recall the jumble of red and gold in Tibetan temples. Lit by a multitude of oil lamps, the place was crammed with fetishes in painted plaster: Indian chiefs, laughing demons, sirens, dogs barking at the moon. The walls were covered with sorry-looking lithographs indicating an ill-considered enthusiasm for the spiritualist Allan Kardec. Hanging from the ceiling was a whole network of scraps of red paper, prayer ribbons and banknotes. Surmounted by a statue of St. Roc—his name was written on the base so no one could miss it—and surrounded by plastic flowers, a large wicker chair seemed to form the heart of the sanctuary. Ensconced in it was an old woman.

Mariazinha was small, plump and of an ugliness that her great age had almost turned into an advantage. Her cast-iron complex-ion clashed with her frizzy white hair done up in a bun on top of her head; her goat's eyes only seemed to look at people or things to see through them; her artificial voice, the rictus, caused by the pa-ralysis of one side, which twisted her lips when she spoke, every-thing about her appearance gave her the frightening attraction that hideousness sometimes arouses in us. Very skeptical as to the supposed powers of the woman, Loredana was playing along out of politeness. Mariazinha just stared at her, straight in the eye, while muttering some incomprehensible litany, a flood of words completely separate, dissociated from her look, a little like when playing a piano the right and left hands can manage to break the natural symmetry there is at work in the body. She was scrutinizing the stranger, reading her, like a sculptor studying the faults in the unworked stone, so that for a moment Loredana felt as if she were being divested of her own image.

"You're ill, very ill," the old woman eventually said, her look softening.

Oh, fantastic! Loredana thought, disappointed by the charlatanism of this oracle. It was obvious Soledade must have informed her of her condition.

"And I knew nothing of your affliction," Mariazinha went on, as if in response to Loredana's visible mistrust. "All the girl said to me was, 'She needs you.' Omulú wishes you well, he will save you if you are willing to receive him."

"Should I go back to my country?" Loredana asked abruptly, as a challenge, the way skeptics will sometimes look at a chance cut of the cards or the conjunction of the stars to back up a decision.

"Your country? We all return to our point of departure one day . . . That is not what is important, which is to know where it is. If Omulú can help you, he will, he is the doctor of the poor, the lord of the earth and the graveyards. *Eu seu caboclinha, eu só visto pena, eu só vim en terra prá beber jurema . . .*" She drank straight from a large bottle she handed to Loredana: "There, you have a drink as well. May the spirit of *jurema* purify you."

Overcoming her revulsion at the sight of the dirty bottle and the small quantity of thick, red liquid left in it, she forced herself to swallow a mouthful. It was acrid, very high in alcohol, with an indefinable taste of green leaves and cough syrup. Mariazinha must be completely inebriated to drink something like that.

It was at that moment that she heard the drums, very close, beating out the rhythm of the samba.

"Go and sit down," Mariazinha said, taking them out of the room. "And you," she added to Loredana, "try to do as the others do, don't resist anything the night will bring."

"Come on, it's this way," Soledade said, once they were alone, "I didn't think she was going to let you attend the *macumba*, it's super! You'll see, you haven't got anything like this in Italy . . ."

Loredana followed her to a door leading out behind the house. She stared, open-mouthed, at the sight that greeted her: there were about fifty people there, men and women, sitting on the ground or on low benches around a wide rectangle of swept earth. An old telegraph pole had been placed at the intersection of the diagonals; several strings of fairy lights spread out from it, making a canopy of light above the audience. Standing behind their instruments, three young drummers seemed to be getting a kick out of their own virtuosity.

To Loredana's great relief, the people paid no attention to them. They moved aside quite naturally to let them sit down on the edge of the *terreiro*. The crowd was buzzing: the dispossessed, marked by privation and fate, ghostly beings, their swarthy skin shining in the many-colored lights. Certain mulatto women were wearing long white dresses that made them look like Tahitians in their Sunday best. On the other side of the area Loredana saw Socorró. Their eyes met without her showing any reaction at all. She was more saddened than surprised by this disdain; the old woman must find the presence of a stranger unseemly in that place. Even Soledade's attitude to her had changed. She sensed that she was distant, reserved, despite the occasional whispered remark:

"The silent queen," she said, pointing to a slatternly adolescent who was holding out a calabash filled with *jurema* to them.

It was Mariazinha's niece, a mute girl whose job it was to serve the gathered crowd. She drew the drink from a large bucket with a tin jug eaten away with rust that dribbled the red liquid over her calves. Equally silent, and resigned, was the cluster of black hens tied by their legs to the central post. Crude pipes were being passed round; they were filled with a mixture of tobacco and pot which made your head spin with every puff. Kept at ground level by the nocturnal humidity, the smoke hung around like mist, giving off a scent of eucalyptus.

The rhythm of the drums quickened as some men placed Mariazinha's wicker throne, with its back to the darkness, between two pyres on the side of the yard that had been left free. Then they brought in a little table, on which the silent queen placed a white cloth and a covered object, which she handled with an indefinable look of fear. Bowls of popcorn and manioc also appeared, the traditional offerings to Omulú, as well as the array of his attributes: a kind of loincloth with an openwork bonnet and the *xaxará*, the bundle of reeds tied by rings made of cowrie shells, which Soledade explained as a kind of scepter imbued with magic power. The fires on either side of this altar were lit, the drums fell silent, and all eyes turned toward the house.

Her bottle of *jurema* in her hand, Mariazinha went to the middle of the *terreiro*; she walked in a bizarre manner, taking little hurried steps, as if her ankles were hobbled with invisible chains. Close to the central post, she stopped to take a mouthful of *jurema*, which she sprayed over the hens. After having put her bottle down, she took a bag of ash from beside the altar, made a hole in it and started to draw large figures on the ground. In a loud voice she uttered invocations that the crowd immediately took up with fervor:

São-Bento ê ê, São-Bento ê á!
Omulú Jesus Maria,
Eu venho de Aloanda.
No caminho de Aloanda,
Jesus São-Bento, Jesus São-Bento!

Behind her she left geometrical figures, stars and black-headed snakes.

Then she went to the edge of the arena and had another drink and puffed a pipe, blowing the smoke into the faces of the onlookers. She was reeling now, but in an artificial way, imitating the confused walk of drunks. Back at the altar, not far from where Soledade and Loredana were sitting, she put a tremulous hand toward the covered object that drew wild-eyed stares. With one movement, she lifted off the cloth and stepped back, as if repelled by a magnetic force; the drums started up again louder than ever.

Loredana looked at the shiny wooden statuette that had set off murmuring among the crowd. It was a sort of horned Buddha, seated in the posture of abandonment—under its tucked-up leg a little monkey carved in bas-relief seemed to be making a penis bigger than itself on a wheel—with a goat's face that expressed a strange mixture of gentleness and severity. Hanging round the neck of this Asiatic Beelzebub, a human thumb swung to and fro for a few seconds before coming to rest. *Eidos, eidôlon,* image, ghost of a thing . . . an idol! With a sense of disgust, Loredana became aware of what that word must have meant for generations of horrified Hebrews or Christians, of what it still meant for all the people around her. Something dark and terrible invested by the god with his power like a second skin, like his very form.

A long groan ran through the crowd; Mariazinha had started to tremble all over her body, her arms extended before the idol. Her eyelids were fluttering, very quickly, sending out flashes from her rolled eyeballs. A little foam formed on her lips as she was carefully carried to her chair. She sat there, motionless, paralyzed by her trance, then relaxed, opened her hands. She smiled. But with what eyes and what a smile! Her face had taken on the serenity of Khmer statues, of the most enigmatic Greek statues of young girls. However, it was another memory that came to dominate, that of certain features glimpsed in a film seen a few years previously. The director—Loredana had forgotten his name—had had the idea of filming, one after the other, thousands of passport photographs, men and women mixed, with no distinction of race, age or hairiness. Once a certain projection speed had been reached, the improbable happened: out of this crowd of successive individuals one face took shape, one single calm, unreal face—nowadays people would call it "virtual"—which was neither the sum, nor a résumé of the photos that had been put together, but something that transcended them, their common base, that of a humanity that was shown for the very first time there. It was as if the door to the secret had been left ajar or one of her own dreams had been projected before her. Loredana had thought of God. When the film had begun to slow down and the vision disappeared to be replaced by a simple stroboscopic effect, then by images in which she started to see the features of each individual again, she had felt extremely frustrated. She would have liked to have kept the epiphany before her eyes for ever, to feed on it in eternal contemplation, not living anymore, such was the way it fulfilled all expectation, deprived the senses of all desire. And here it had manifested itself again, stuck on Mariazinha's face like a glass mask . . . *Ialorixá!* Loredana proclaimed her joy at the same time as the congregation, moved to tears by the coincidence of this sudden fusion with all the others. She had not been alone in recognizing the Unnamable, seated on the wicker throne.

Mariazinha stretched out her hands to bless the gathering, revealing an abnormality that disturbed Loredana beyond all reason: the priestess of Omulú had lost her left thumb. But someone flung herself into the *terreiro*—it was Soledade, transformed into a whirling puppet. For several seconds she fought against a supernatural enemy, hitting the air, protecting her head, then went rigid, seized with spasms. Mariazinha sat up in her chair:

"Exú has ridden her!" she roared in a hoarse, hardly recognizable voice. "*Saravá!*"

"*Saravá!*" the crowd responded, while Soledade was swaying her hips in simian fashion, her whole body twitching.

"Exú Caveira, master of the seven legions!" Mariazinha went on. "Exú death's-head! May Omulú, prince of all, descend! May he consent! May he come down to us!"

Loredana could not believe her eyes. Like the word "idol," until now "trance" had been for her merely a term from the manuals of anthropology, a manifestation of hysteria that could affect only the feeble minded or the irrational. She had of course been expecting something of the kind, but she was more astonished by how easily people could succumb to it than by the sight of the trance itself. Soledade looked like a genuine madwoman, she was dancing, rolling her eyes, speaking *in tongues*, acting out some primitive scene or other, her look vacant, slobbering, rolling in the ashes of the figures drawn on the ground, getting up, starting all over again. Bewildered by the violence of her fit, she felt a degree of contempt for her friend, mixed with pity and panic.

No one else seemed surprised at the exhibition. The silent queen continued to refill the receptacles with *jurema* and the pipes with the mixture that greatly increased the effect of the alcohol; from time to time a man or a woman would drop their calabash and throw themselves into the thick of the mystery, in convulsions, distortions, ridden by one of the spirits whose name Mariazinha

immediately added to the list—Exú Brasa, Burniron; Exú Caran-
gola, Sidragasum; Exú da meia-noite, Haël; Exú pimenta, Tris-
maël; Exú Quirombô, Nel Biroth—begging them again and again
to intercede for her with Omulú, the master of all of them. People
shouted abuse at the beings unleashed in the *terreiro*, commented
on their gestures and their grimaces. Overtaken by events, Loredana drank and smoked everything that came her way. Her eyes
were stinging, she was thirsty for water and light, but that night,
filled with wonder, she explored what Brazil had to offer.

Then Soledade collapsed like a rag doll. At the request of the
woman sitting beside her, Loredana helped to carry her back to
the side. She was dripping with sweat and her head was nodding,
her eyes closed, her muscles relaxed. Loredana, frightened by this
faint, was patting her cheeks when Soledade gave the first signs
of coming to. Hardly was she conscious again than she was asking the people around her . . ."Exú Caveira!" she said to Loredana
with a radiant smile, "I've been ridden by Exú Caveira! Can you
imagine?"

"Not really," she replied, devastated by the ravages on her
sweet face.

By now the situation seemed to her to defy the imagination's occult laws; Mariazinha's followers were falling one after the other
into the dust, brought down by the sudden withdrawal of the spirits that had them in their grip. Cries were heard, groans, orgasmic
screams. Loredana was caught between the desire to go back to her
room and the certainty that she would never find the way.

At a sign from Mariazinha, erect before her throne, the drummers changed their rhythm. Those still possessed by the spirits came out of their trance almost immediately and they were
quickly helped back to their places.

"*Oxalá, meu pai,*' the priestess intoned, "*tem pena de mim, tem
dó! A volta do mundo é grande, seu poder ainda é maior!*"

A man rushed up to her, knelt down, quickly placed his head on the old woman's feet, then stood up and took the hand she held out to him. With another movement they came close enough for her to give him a swift accolade, first on the right shoulder, then the left, and Mariazinha made her follower turn under her arm, as in rock-and-roll, before letting go of him. The man took a few steps back and stood there, dazed, a smile on his lips. Now they all ran up to perform the same ritual. Once it was done, some fell into their trance again or grasped the priestess's skirts, weeping tears of happiness and gratitude.

Despite Loredana's instinctive resistance, Soledade dragged her toward the altar. When she was presented, the mother of saints nodded her head, as if assessing what she could read in her expression. Putting her left hand on the back of Loredana's neck, she placed her thumb between her eyebrows: "What you must do, you must do, escape is not possible," she said. "What you must do, you will do for me . . ."

Then it was the same ritual as for the others. Loredana was left standing under the lights of the *terreiro*, open-mouthed, dumbfounded by the burning sensation boring into her forehead.

There were more dances, trances, prayers. Their thirst for *jurema* seemed unquenchable, for all of them the world had plunged into that frontier zone where sense and nonsense were the same. Then a negro was at the center on the *terreiro*: the *Axogum*. The name had preceded him on the lips of all the adepts. He sprinkled manioc and *dendê* oil on the hens, lit matches above them and took a machete out of its sheath.

"Thus let the plague die, leprosy and erysipelas," he declaimed in a voice hoarse from alcohol. "Arator, Lepidator, Tentador, Soniator, Ductor, Comestos, Devorator, Seductor! O old master, the hour has come to fulfil your promise to me. Curse my enemy as I curse him. Reduce him to dust as I reduce this dried hummingbird to dust. By the fire of night, by the blackness of the dead hens, by their cut throats, may all our prayers be granted!"

He slit the throat of one of the hens; a woman, the one who had brought the offering, dashed across to drink the first spurts from the arteries. She was seized by a trance as if by a virulent poison. The hens were passed from hand to hand, as the *Axogum* sacrificed them. Now the calabashes had a mixture of blood and *jurema*. Even more people were falling into a trance, the *terreiro* was filled with a sort of solemn euphoria, the kind that sometimes follows a funeral meal.

For a long time now Loredana had been swallowing everything that was passed to her without giving it a second thought. When Soledade had a sticky, twitching decapitated hen in her hands and pressed it like a wineskin to squeeze out the juice, she held out her calabash to her with a smile. Nothing was important anymore. Obey the night—Mariazinha's words were still flickering in her memory—let the unexpected come, accept things, all things, without naming them. The statuette was glittering in the light of the fires. Baal Amon, Dionysus: drunken gods, fragile gods, deities smeared with the white lead of the charnel houses.

They were eating the entrails of the sacrificed chickens when a man suddenly rolled over the ground with all the signs of a convulsive seizure. The crowd howled to Mariazinha; she brought the attributes of straw and shells: the loincloth of Omulú, the *xaxará*. The man put them on. The drums stopped. In the silence, the people slowly parted, seized with sacred terror at the sight of this nightmare creature now standing on the dancing floor. Braided openings at eye level gave the bogeyman a round visor, as if the creature that had donned it could see on all sides. A hand came out of the loincloth, holding the scepter and the apparition started to revolve, at the same time moving round the central pole, a sphere in orbit round the fixed axis of the universe.

Led by Mariazinha, the gathering saluted its god:

He's come back from the Sudan,
The one who respects his mother alone . . .
He's limping, he's stumbling with fatigue
The one who haunts the graveyard bones . . .
A tôtô Obaluaê!
A tôtô Obaluaê!
A tôtô Bubá!
A tôtô Alogibá!
Omulú bajé, Jamboro!

He was there, the god they had begged to come, he was dancing, jerkily, alternating little leaps with his feet together and
octopus-like undulations. A trance descended like a mist over all
his devotees. Some ran over to Omulú to receive his blessing—a
tap on the shoulders with the *xaxará*—others collapsed where
they stood, bellowing, jiggling. The women undid their hair and
shook their heads furiously, their faces veiled by their hair. Everyone was dancing to the rhythm of the drums that had been
released. A kind of savage epilepsy swept through the *terreiro*.

Loredana was still observing all this as a spectator. She was
also following the rhythm of the drums, swaying forward and
back, cradling her own isolation, invisible at the heart of this
company of the blind. Even Soledade, frenzied, no longer saw her.
She found it almost amusing to observe the strange commotion—
abrupt regroupings of cockroaches on a patch of grease—which
suddenly began to spread: a woman threw herself on a man, lifted
up her skirt and took him there, in front of everyone. They were
caught up in an orgiastic wave that broke over the night. The
god himself interrupted his dance, joined the crowd for a swift
coupling, then returned to the arena to continue his ponderous

dance. The bulbs were no longer lit, but someone must have been feeding the fires, for the bacchanal was gilded by high, desolate flames. An unknown man took Soledade. And as their bodies touched her thigh, Loredana saw their faces, strangely calm, strangely empty, in the vigorous embrace; a lascivious solemnity, which she observed, without judging it, with the sense of having gone beyond the limits of intoxication, of being out of her depth. The remnants of reason were sounding the alarm in her head, but she forced herself to drink in order to free herself from the control of that authority, impatient to catch up with the frenzy at work all around her. Something fundamental was moving over this mass of humans, something she desperately wanted to receive but that filled her every fiber with a twilight dread. There was a stirring of organic matter, a ferment of worm-ridden compost—a presence—and Omulú was there in front of her, unmoving, frightening, his penis sticking out through the raffia strands. Like a stained-glass window exposed to the fury of a fire, her mind flew into a thousand fragments. For a few seconds she made every effort to gather them together, stricken by a sense of absolute urgency, sheer animal panic. Then she lay down, half on Soledade, half on someone else, not even on the ground, her eyes staring up at the sky. Hands tore away her skirt, a body weighed down on her with the dry crackle of a straw mattress. The god penetrated her, giving off a smell of candle wax and crumbly soil.

She came to again a few minutes later. As she stood up, a sticky fluid dripped down from between her legs.

"He's going to leave," Soledade kept repeating in desperation, "he's going to leave. Come on, quick!"

She dragged her into the arena, where the congregation was gathered round to see the last convulsions of the god. Mariazinha had taken back the *xaxará* and was making strange signs above him:

He's going back to where he came from
To Luanda,
To Luanda,
May he take the sheaf of our prayers,
May he grant them before he returns.

Finally the man possessed by the god lay motionless, stretched out on his back, a Christ without his cross, a dervish released from his vertigo. They lifted up his body so that the mother of saints could remove his garb. And under the mask there was another mask, that of a man, jaw hanging loose, a blank expression on his face—the face of Alfredo.

ALCÂNTARA: *Nicanor Carneiro*

Gilda awoke with a start at around three in the morning and listened to the noises of the house. The baby seemed to be whimpering. She waited a little, hoping it would go back to sleep. A persistent wail, the kind that comes with a sudden release after someone has held their breath for a long time, made her sit up in bed.

"What is it?" Nicanor grunted without opening his eyes.

"Nothing," Gilda said affectionately. "I'll go see."

Reassured by his wife's reply, Nicanor Carneiro immediately went back to sleep. He had been working hard for months without finding the time to rest and the birth of their first child hadn't helped.

Fully awake now, Gilda disentangled her nightdress and trotted off to the other room. She was worried, Egon had never cried like that before, he must be ill. As she switched on the light, a hand was placed over her mouth, stifling her cry: a man, his face distorted by a nylon stocking, was beside the cradle, facing her, the baby under his arm and a razor in his right hand.

"Not a sound, bitch," the one who was holding her from behind whispered. "Do what you're told and nothing'll happen to him."

She started crying with terror and at the sense of her own powerlessness. Her legs gave way. The point of a knife was pressed against her throat: "You understand? Call your husband. Just tell him to come, nothing else."

She couldn't utter a sound. The baby, purple, retching, was choking with terror. The man grasped her breast and tightened his grip. "Get on with it, you cunt, or I'll stick this into you!"

Carneiro came running at his wife's second scream. He stood there, hair tousled, his nakedness emphasising how skinny he was, looking as if he couldn't believe what was happening.

"No time for sleeping," the man in the hood who was holding his wife said, "we're in a hurry. You've ten seconds to put your name to this piece of paper." His glance indicated the pen and sheet of paper on the table. "You sign and we go; any quibbling and your fucking brat gets it first. Is that clear?"

"Leave them alone," Nicanor said, his voice hoarse with anger, "I'll sign."

The man checked the signature: Nicanor Carneiro, folded the bill of sale and put it in his pocket.

"There, that wasn't difficult, was it?" he said in satisfied tones. "All right then," he went on, pushing Gilda toward him, "you can have your old woman back. She's got terrific tits, you must have a great time, you lucky bugger. C'mon, Pablo, put the kid down, we're off."

The silence following this command seemed to stretch on and on. All eyes turned toward the cradle, where the man with the razor was clumsily shaking the inert body of the baby, as if trying to make it work again.

SÃO LUÍS, FAZENDA DO BOI: *It'll be in the papers tomorrow, Colonel . . .*

"Frankly, Carlotta," the Colonel said as he put down his napkin beside his plate, "you're worrying about nothing."

They were finishing their breakfast out on the patio. There was a flush of sunlight behind the still-wet foliage of the bougainvillea. Carlotta had hardly slept all night, her pale, bleary face was that of an old woman.

"Mauro's a big boy now," Moreira went on, "and from what I understand, he's with people who know the area. They must have found what they're looking for and it's made them forget the rest of the world. You know what they're like. So no news is good news. If something had happened to them—and I really can't see what— we'd know by now." He poured the rest of the coffee into his cup.

"Perhaps you're right," Carlotta said, massaging her temples. "I hope upon hope that you're right. But I can't set my mind at rest, it's stronger than me."

There had been a call from the University of Brazilia the previous afternoon. Not having had any news of the expedition, the Geology Department secretary wanted to know whether Mauro had contacted his parents at all. With the new semester starting in three days' time, the vice chancellor was getting increasingly concerned about the prolonged absence of his principal lecturers. When Moreira had come home, he had done his best to reassure his wife, his confidence only increased by his belief in the proverbial absentmindedness of scientists. Carlotta had seemed grateful for the effort he made and as a result the switch of the title deeds had gone ahead smoothly. She had even thanked him for the promptness with which he had righted the situation.

"I apologize for the scene I made the other evening," she had added. "I don't care about the money myself, but it's for Mauro, for him alone . . . You understand?"

OF COURSE HE understood. The Colonel gave his reflection a self-satisfied smile and patted his cheeks with Yardley lavender water. The "Countess of Alzegul" had apologized to him and the Willis was being delivered that day. It was certainly getting off to the best possible start.

Back in her room Carlotta started when she heard the telephone ring—Mauro! Something had happened to Mauro! But her husband had already answered the phone, so she didn't say anything, anxious for news of her son.

"The Carneiro business is sorted, Colonel. He's signed, I have the bill of sale here . . ."

"Good, very good," Moreira replied. "I knew I could trust you, Wagner."

Disappointed, Carlotta was thinking of putting the receiver down when the voice at the other end of the line faltered. "Colonel . . . How shall I put it . . . Things went wrong . . . There was an accident . . ."

"What do you mean, went wrong? Out with it, Wagner, I've got a meeting in half an hour and I'm not dressed yet."

"The baby . . . well, from what they told me . . . the baby choked to death, just like that. When the father saw it, he threw himself on one of my men and managed to pull his hood off . . . They panicked . . . It'll be in the papers tomorrow, Colonel . . ."

"You mean they've been . . ."

"Yes."

There was a long silence during which Moreira stared blankly at his bedside table, incapable of gathering his thoughts.

"You've no need to worry, Colonel, no one saw them. I've done the necessary, they're safe, in my *sitio*, in the country, it'll be absolutely impossible to link them with me, even less with you . . . Colonel? Are you still there, Colonel?"

"I'll see you shortly," Moreira said in icy tones.

A little later, when he knocked on Carlotta's door, he was surprised there was no reply. He left without persisting and never realized that a mechanism had been set in motion that would continue inexorably to its final denouement.

CHAPTER 21

*Athanasius's mystical night: how Father Kircher journeyed
through the skies without leaving his room. The vermicelli of the
plague & the story of Count Karnice*

T H E S T O R Y I am about to relate is a marvelous
example of divine omnipotence & shows how it manifests
itself by unfathomable ways in the most virtuous of men.

After my master had knelt at his prie-dieu, he started to
murmur in a plaintive & disjointed manner, as if he were
answering someone & commenting, although laboriously, on
the images flooding into his mind. I went over with the idea of
helping him, but also of hearing what Our Lord had chosen to
say to him, so that I could testify to it later. Kircher clutched
my hand feverishly; his eyes were wide, moist & clouded, as you
see on the pictures of saints, but he nevertheless appeared to
recognize me.

"Ah, Cosmiel!" he exclaimed with delight, trembling all over. "I
am so grateful to you for condescending to come to me . . ."

"I am merely obeying the All-powerful," said a low, rumbling voice, grave, distorted & appearing to come from a metal throat.

I was frightened beyond expression, having in the past seen a man possessed through whom Beelzebub expressed himself in the same way. But I immediately recalled the name of Cosmiel & that calmed my fear somewhat: my master was only possessed by angels or, to be more precise, by the most noble & most learned of the heavenly host.

"Prepare yourself, Athanasius," Cosmiel went on through Kircher's mouth, "you have been chosen & you will have to show that you are worthy of this favor. For though the journey for which Virgil was the guide existed in Dante's imagination alone, I have truly been sent by God to lead you forward in the knowledge of the universe created by His will. Come now, it is time to set off for infinite space. Open that window, Athanasius, and cling on where you can, while I spread my wings."

"I hear & I obey," Kircher replied in earnest tones.

He stood up & made his way unsteadily toward the window. I was afraid that he might be going to throw himself out—& that if he had done so I would have not held him back, so sure I was that his faith & the presence of the angel would have prevented him from falling, carrying him through the air much better than my artificial wings had carried me all those years ago—but he did nothing more than contemplate the star-studded night, as if transfixed by the vision of the heavens he was traversing together with Cosmiel.

From his repeated exclamations I soon realized that my master had reached the moon. He described it in the most minute detail, flying over its seas & mountains with exclamations all the time about the new things he was seeing.

After the moon Kircher went to the planet Mercury, to Venus, then the Sun, where I really believed he was going to suffocate, such were his sufferings from the great heat there. After that it was Mars, of which Cosmiel maintained it was an evil planet, responsible for the plague & other epidemics on Earth; Jupiter with its satellites &, finally, Saturn with its rainbow-colored rings.

On each of the planets he visited, something no man had done before, my master was greeted by the angel or archangel governing its influence. Confirming the Scriptures point by point, he met Michael, Raphael, Gabriel, Uriel, Raguel, Saraquael & Remiel, who spoke directly to him to tell him about the sphere where he was.

Kircher's astonishment reached its peak when he came to the Firmament, the region of the fixed stars. Far from being stuck onto a celestial crystal sphere, the innumerable stars moved in the same way as the planets: Aristotle, the prince of philosophers, had been greatly mistaken about the nature of the eighth heaven.

"Yes, Athanasius," his guardian angel said, "every star has its own governing intelligence, whose task is to keep its movement within its proper orbit, thus preserving the eternal & immutable laws. Like all the creatures of God, the stars are born & die over the centuries. And the Firmament, as you can see, is neither incorruptible, nor solid, nor finite."

I was trembling at the thought that someone other than I might hear these words. They expressed, without circumlocution, the doctrine of the plurality of worlds and the corruptibility of the heavens, a heresy for which Giordano Bruno had been burned at the stake a few years previously. A horrible torture that old Galileo had only just escaped, & for the same reasons, by agreeing to recant.

Kircher was shaken by long shudders, which even made his beard stand on end, but he did not appear to feel any fear. To be honest, the longer he continued in the company of the angel, the more his face was radiant with intense happiness.

"Look, Athanasius, look carefully. It is at the very heart of this unfathomable abyss that the mystery of the deity is hidden. The soul alone can understand this mystery; for the moment be content with the immense privilege that has been granted you. Praise & worship God in all his blazing glory. Day is breaking, it is time for me to return to the first Choir of the celestial hierarchy. So until we meet again. You will not fail in your mission, for I will be with you."

Then it was as if Kircher had been struck by lightning. He fainted and slumped down onto the tiles. I hurriedly shut the window before laying him on his bed & making him inhale some spirits of wine.

When he recovered consciousness, my master was in a high fever. Streaming with sweat, he was delirious for several hours without my being able to catch a word he was saying. I did not dare seek assistance for fear he might start upholding some heresy more dangerous for his health than this strange ailment to which he had fallen prey.

But, thanks be to heaven, after a fit of acute euphoria, Athanasius suddenly calmed down. His breathing became normal again, his eyes closed &, clasping his hands on his chest, he muttered a fable, which he assured me was translated from Coptic, stopping after each sentence, as if he were saying a prayer:

> Father Gustave listened to his worthy abbot, John Colobos, dictating the new arrangements he had made: "It is with justification & a very great comfort that, as I set out, you will assume my office while I feed on herbage, following with the utmost rigor the example of my venerable forerunners. Soon I will be alone out in the hindmost parts of the desert."

*The heat was enough to cremate him, but Abbot John went
on his way out onto the sand, a saintly hermit, a psalm on his
lips, chanted in a minor key, while chewing on a kebab, which was
nourishing and tasty.*

*He knelt by the edge of the wadi, and it echoed & echoed to his
cry of deepest despair: "Peccavi!" But all at once, e'er the penitent
Abbot John had finished his heartfelt confession, a most ghastly,
hideous two-horned demon appeared in a blinding light &, with
loud, obscene fulminations, proceeded to whip & flay John's back
like a voracious vulture. Thus made aware of his sinful state, his
feeble prayers, Abbot John was seized with remorse, knelt down &
right urgently began to commend his soul to God, binding himself
with vows to extol the Most High by celebrating His great goodness, thus entering that most blessed legion of all the faithful with
the noble aim of seeing the conversion of all men.*

"Peccavi?" Kircher repeated, just before falling asleep, & that
in a tone of quiet astonishment.

The reader will understand my anxiety as I waited for him
to wake up. I feared my master would not come out of such a
crucial experience unscathed. Even though this vision granted
him by God was a great honor, making him even more precious
in my eyes than previously, I was still afraid that he might
continue talking to the angels for ever.

Fortunately, when he woke, six hours later, his rapture
had left no aftereffects. His eyes were slightly more sunken,
proof of the physical fatigue caused by his excursion, but
he recognized me immediately & spoke to me in a wholly
rational manner. He remembered his night with the angel
perfectly, at least in its broad lines; as for the detail, he
admitted he was unable to remember a single word of what
he had said or heard. This made me more than ever glad

I had a good memory & he was delighted to hear these
revelations again.

Kircher confirmed in every respect the impression I had
formed during the night. From the very beginning of Christina's
concert in the Farnese Palace, he had felt overwhelmed by the
music, as if he could not only perceive the most subtle harmonies
but also discover the profound meaning of the universal rhythm.
The music produced by the instruments quickly disappeared, to
be replaced by innumerable polyphonies instantly created by his
imagination. He counted the buttons on his cassock in his head &
that produced a chord; he followed the lines of a piece of furniture
or a statue in his mind & he heard a melody, as if all the beings
and objects in this world were capable of generating their own
music, pleasing or dissonant, depending on the extent to which
their structure obeyed the golden rule of proportion.

In the same way, my master had heard the harmony of the
celestial spheres as we returned to the College & it was not long
before the angel Cosmiel had appeared. Kircher gave me a detailed
description of his youthful and surprising beauty; that of the most
perfect of da Vinci's angels would have paled beside him.

As for his voyage to the stars, Athanasius confessed that
he had never experienced anything as marvelous. He took it
for granted that it had been just as real as our walk in Sicily,
although the knowledge he had harvested from it was much
more valuable. Immediately he thought of writing an account of
it for the edification of mankind, a project I approved of with all
my heart & that I urged him to carry out.

After another night of rest, Kircher put aside all the studies
on which he was engaged in order to start composing the *Iter
Extaticum Cœleste* in which, he told me, new truths about
the structure of the universe would be explained in the form

of a dialogue between Cosmiel & Theodidact. And in that pseudonym, behind which my master hid, I once more saw all his natural modesty.

Sixteen fifty-six, alas, was a year that started under very unfavorable auspices: the news came that Naples had been devastated by the plague, which had come from the south. Although it had happened a long time ago, everyone still remembered the epidemic that had carried off three-quarters of the inhabitants of Rome, but such is the frailty of human nature that no one thought the scourge would reach this far again. People were very sorry for the inhabitants of Naples who were dying, but they must have sinned horribly for God to visit such a punishment on them. Protected, they thought, by the presence of the Pope in their city & their presumed virtuousness, the Romans continued to live a life of carefree enjoyment.

The first cases appeared in January, in the poor districts, without really causing alarm among a population used to all sorts of illnesses & whose shameless debauchery made them likely victims of divine anger. In March three hundred deaths were reported . . . Alone among the nobility Queen Christina took measures to avoid the threat: alerted by the figures & in less time that it takes my pen to write it down, she left a city that had given her such a magnificent welcome, thus removing to Paris, where Cardinal Mazarin had invited her, the appalling conduct which, even today, I cannot help thinking was the sole cause of the misfortunes that struck our beautiful metropolis.

In July we finally had to face up to the fact that the Black Death was in Rome, killing and laying waste worse than the most horrible of wars. People were dropping dead like flies, with the result that they had to be buried at night & by the cartload in the common pits hastily dug out by the surrounding lower-class districts. Profiting from a situation that was so favorable for his natural evil, the devil seized the weakest souls & the most execrable heresies reappeared. The healthy, knowing their death probable, if not close at hand, indulged in orgies to the very gates of the graveyard, blaspheming God & defying death to do its worst. Never were so many crimes committed in so few days. Between July & November the epidemic carried off fifteen thousand inhabitants & people thought the end of the world had come.

During those four months when the world seemed sure to end in madness & torment, Kircher did not spare himself. Volunteering to help the sick, despite his age & our superiors' desire not to have him exposed unnecessarily, from the very beginning he undertook to work alongside his friend, James Alban Gibbs. We therefore spent most of our time in Christ's Hospital in the Via Triumphalis.

To my great shame I have to admit that I was not exactly pleased at a decision that placed my life in such great danger, but my master's devoted application to looking after those stricken with the plague & to seeking the causes of the implacable disease, the kindness he tirelessly showed in giving moral support to those who needed it & the example of his own courage, quickly revived more Christian feelings in me. I took Kircher as my model & never had reason to regret it.

Although he admitted such a calamity could sometimes be the result of God's designs, my master thought that we should see it simply as the result of natural causes, like any other disease. He therefore put all his efforts into seeking out those causes.

He was fascinated by the speed & effectiveness of the disease. The plague found its way everywhere, striking rich & poor without distinction, without sparing those who thought to defy it by isolating themselves completely in their houses.

"Exactly like those ants," Kircher said to me one day, "that invade even the most enclosed places without us being able to say by which way they came . . ." Just as he was finishing that sentence I saw his eyes light up, then shine: "And why not?" he went on. "Why should the cause not be even tinier animalcules, so small they cannot be seen with the naked eye. Some species of spider or miniature snake whose poison leads to death as surely as that of the most venomous of asps . . . We must hurry, Caspar, hurry. Run quickly to the College and bring a microscope, I must check this hypothesis immediately."

I went immediately. One hour later my master got down to work. Cutting open the most swollen bubo we could find—that was the only operation we could perform to bring some small relief to the dying who flocked to the hospital—he cautiously collected the blood mixed with pus from it. Then he placed a few drops of this foul fluid under the lenses of his instrument.

"I thank Thee, o Lord!" he exclaimed almost immediately. "I was right, Caspar! There's an infinite number of vermicules so small I can hardly see them, but they're milling around like ants in an anthill & pullulating to such an extent that even Lynceus himself would not have been able to count them down to the last one . . . They're alive, Caspar! Look yourself & tell me if my eyes are deceiving me."

To my amazement, I could only confirm what my master had just described so excitedly. We repeated the experiment several times & with humors from different abscesses, but the results were always the same. While marveling at their extreme vigor, we made several drawings of these creatures that were invisible to the naked eye. I called Alban Gibbs and he came to observe Kircher's discovery himself.

"These little worms," my master told him, "are what propagate the plague. They are so minuscule, so fine and thin, that they can only be seen with the help of a microscope. They are so imperceptible, we could call them 'atoms,' but I prefer the

Italian word *vermicelli,* which better describes their nature and
their essence. For like shipworms, those dwarf worms that are,
however, like elephants beside them, they nibble away from
inside with a speed proportionate to their number & once their
ravages are complete, they attack another victim, propagating
the *pestiferum virus* like a mold & destroying the substance of
the living organism. It is transmitted by breathing & finds refuge
in our most intimate clothing. Even the flies are carriers: they
suck at the sick and the corpses, contaminate our food with their
excrement & transmit the disease to the humans who eat it."

Gibbs was in a fever of excitement about what he'd seen &
heard. But bearing in mind that the microscope showed us
things a thousand times bigger than they were in reality, he
argued that the use of the instrument should be restricted to
those, such as Kircher, who were competent to make proper
use of the results, knowledge of which should be reserved *solis
principibus, et summis Viris, Amicisque.*[1]

Even if the cause of the contagion could finally be attributed
to these *vermicelli* of the plague—which were certainly produced
by the corruption of the air brought about by the corpses
& which transmitted their mortiferous power by a sort of
magnetism, just as a magnet "infects," so to speak, any piece of
metal with which it comes into contact—there was nothing as
yet to suggest anything to counter this pullulating species. We
therefore had no choice but to continue to use the old remedies,
of which we knew only one thing: they worked for some & not
for others, which was as good as saying they were ineffective.
Under the direction of Gibbs and Kircher, we used toad
poison—on the principle that like should be cured by like—the
juice of bugloss & scabious root thinned down with a good

1 (...) to princes alone, great men and friends.

theriac & many other preparations recommended by Galen, Discorides or more modern authorities. Unfortunately nothing worked, so that more than once I saw my master so discouraged he was brought to tears.

Dr. Sinibaldus came to work in our hospital at the height of the epidemic. Anxious to atone for his previous errors, he showed admirable zeal in tending the sick & happily God spared him & all his family.

That was not the case with everyone; the plague carried off the volunteers one after the other, so that of all the doctors who came to work with Gibbs, three-quarters did not live to see the end of the epidemic. As for those who survived, they were often left to mourn the loss of their loved ones. An example is what happened to Count Karnice, a physician at the Russian court who was compelled by the situation to stay in Rome & whose pleasure trip ended in distress & affliction.

Once the city had been declared closed, this excellent man left his young wife and their child with some friends & came to offer his services to our hospital, where he displayed unfailing selflessness.

On the evening of August 15, a servant sent by his friends informed him that his wife had died. She had been carried away within a few hours & he would have to hurry if he wanted to see her sweet face one last time. Since there had been an influx of patients & the living took precedence over the dead, Count Karnice, despite his own despair & our advice, decided not to leave immediately. When, two hours later, he reached his friends' house, his wife was no longer there; she had been put in a coffin—at great expense, coffins having become almost unobtainable —& buried in the nearby graveyard. The young count poured forth his lamentations & was a pitiful sight; he would certainly have killed himself if it hadn't been for his baby, his sole comfort in his sorrow.

Unfortunately that was only the start of his misfortunes. That very night his dear child showed all the signs of the contagion. His skin became covered in pustules the size of millet seeds, then black buboes rapidly formed in his groin & under his armpits, causing terrible pain. His screams at the bites of the *vermicelli* infecting his flesh were heartrending. By the early morning they had reached his meninges; he became delirious, while large livid and brown blotches appeared on his skin. Finally, at eight o'clock, God showed mercy & took him to paradise.

There was not enough money for another coffin, but in his distress, Count Karnice did not want his son to be buried in the common grave. Recalling the love his wife bore her child & arguing that they must not be separated in death, he picked up the little corpse, determined to put it in the same coffin as his wife. Abandoned by his friends, who feared the contagion & thought he was out of his mind, he went to the graveyard and got the attendant to show him the still-fresh grave of his beloved wife. Taking a spade he started to disinter her himself, trying to dull his grief by exertion.

When the metal of his spade hit the planks, he completed his awful task with his bare hands, hurrying as if he were exhuming not the mortal remains of his dead wife but a captive impatient to recover her freedom. Fumbling in the slimy soil, Count Karnice finally managed to open the lid of the coffin. What horror was in store for him: his wife's hand shot up from the grave & slapped his cheek! As had unfortunately happened several times during those days of fear & haste, Count Karnice's wife had been buried alive . . . Waking in the darkness of the tomb, the poor woman had scraped the wood with her fingernails as she attempted to escape a ghastly death. Her horribly dislocated body had stiffened like a bow in her final effort to reach the light.

Count Karnice took to his heels, distraught with terror. When they found him, he was mad.

MATO GROSSO: *Deliberately choose the other path . . .*

Dietlev regained consciousness in the evening. His voice, coming from the stretcher beside the fire, made Elaine start.

"Knock, knock!" he said in a perfectly serious voice.

"Dietlev!" Elaine exclaimed, immediately going over to him. "You gave me a fright, you big bad bear."

"Come on. Knock, knock! Who's there?"

"I've no idea, Dietlev, and I don't really care, you know."

"Agee."

"OK, if you insist. Agee who?"

"A geologist hitting the door with his wooden leg!" he said with a faint smile.

"I'm afraid that's beyond me," said Herman, "but how are you, *amigo*?"

Dietlev's face darkened for a moment. His temples were still moist from the fever but his eyes were open and he seemed to be completely lucid again. "Like Long John Silver. *It was a pretty drastic way of losing weight. Ten pounds, twenty pounds? How much does a leg weigh?*"

"We had to do it," Elaine said, taking his hand. "The gangrene was starting to spread."

"I know. Don't worry, I was thinking that too. Well, almost . . . How did it happen? Was it you who made the decision?"

"No, it's Herman who made it clear to me how urgent it was. He was great, he's the one who saved you, just him . . ."

Dietlev looked puzzled for a moment, as if he were trying to understand Herman's motivation. "*Danke*, Herman," he simply said.

Using German expressed more gratitude than the word itself and Petersen was aware of that. "It's nothing," he mumbled, "you'd have done the same in my place."

"Where's Mauro?"

"Here I am," he said, moving into Dietlev's field of vision. "you gave us all a fright, you know."

"You can't get rid of me that easily, as my students will tell you. Anyway, I'm thinking of coming back here next year." He didn't really believe what he was saying and none of them was stupid enough to take him at his word.

"You all look as if you're at the end of your tether," Dietlev said after having scrutinized them. "You need to get some rest, otherwise you're not going to cope."

"It's been a hard day," Elaine said, staring into space. "We've been squelching across the edge of the marsh, it's not easy. And I don't have to carry the stretcher . . ." But as she spoke, all she had in mind was the agonies of the amputation, the anxiety that had twisted her stomach.

"So we've reached the marshes?"

"Yeah, *amigo*," Petersen replied. "You were down for the count, that's when we realized how bad you were." He hesitated for a moment, then went on, "We have to talk about this, seriously, you know . . . We're never going to get there in these conditions, I mean with you, and then—"

"He's on about it again!" Mauro said in exasperated tones, "for a long time now—"

"Let him finish, please," Dietlev said. "Go on, Herman."

"Listen: I stay with you and we send Yurupig on ahead. He knows the forest, he'll get to the river three or four times quicker than us. And we can follow him at our own speed. By marking the route, he can help us avoid the dead ends he'll have to check out himself. That will save us time and effort. If he's quick, he can bring the rescue team to meet us."

His suggestion immediately made sense to them. Even Mauro couldn't find fault with it.

"What do you say, Yurupig?" Dietlev asked.

The Indian turned to look at Petersen, putting his head on one side as if to assess him better. "I agree, but you'll have to be on your guard. When the snake offers to help the rat, it's because he's found a quicker way of eating it . . ."

"What a load of bullshit! You really can't stand me, can you?"

"So that's settled," Dietlev said after a questioning glance at Elaine and Mauro. "You can take the compass, we won't need it now. You know how to use it, don't you?"

Yurupig closed his eyes to indicate agreement.

"Notches in the tree trunks to show the route, a cross to tell us not to go that way. You think you can make it?"

"In the forest that depends on the jaguars . . ."

THE NEXT MORNING, at first light, Elaine and Mauro made up a rucksack for Yurupig. They packed his share of the provisions, the compass, a cigarette lighter, a flask of alcohol and a dose of snakebite serum. When the moment came, the Indian took one of their three machetes and turned to the members of the expedition: "Take it easy," he said, "I'll be back."

Cutting short their farewells, he gave them a final wave and left at a jog. Dietlev had decided to give him two hours' start, so they lingered over breakfast after he left.

When they set off again, Elaine went on ahead. Here and there a notch weeping milky fluid indicated a path that had been freshly made through the vegetation; in fact, Yurupig had made so many marks that the trail was fairly easy to follow. The fact that they didn't have to wonder what was the best route made everything much simpler. After two hours, Elaine took Petersen's place carrying the stretcher. Dietlev seemed to be recovering his strength, so that Mauro gave him the Kalashnikov to hold since it hampered his movement.

The day passed without any incidents worthy of note. Once evening came, they sat around the fire again; it was time to assess the situation: as far as they could tell, they had progressed two or three times more quickly that on the previous days, but at the price of greater tiredness. Elaine above all felt the effects. Aching all over, her muscles stiff from carrying the stretcher, she had to force herself to eat and stay sitting with the others.

"My last batteries," Mauro said, changing the ones in his Walkman. I'm gong to have to ration my music as well. He looked drawn, like a long-distance runner after the race, but he was standing up to the strain quite well. "When I think," he went on, "that the new semester starts in three days' time. They aren't going to be very pleased."

"You can say that again," Dietlev said. "Five years ago I got back from an expedition two hours before my first lecture; an airplane hadn't been able to take off in time, a car broke down, problems with customs . . . the whole works. When I got to the lecture theater, Milton was just telling my students I was absent; I thought he was going to have an apoplectic fit!"

The thought of their dead colleague cast a veil over his smile.

"Poor guy," Mauro said. "I didn't like him, but all the same . . . he was a big name . . ."

"A big bastard, you mean," Elaine said wearily. "If you knew everything he put us through. His death doesn't change that."

"True," Dietlev said, "but if we had to kill all the incompetents, the idiots, the corrupt, there wouldn't be many people left in the world."

"You never spoke a truer word, *amigo*," Petersen said, interrupting his whistling.

"At least we can't say you're exhausted by all the walking," Elaine said, slightly surprised at the German's verve.

"Matter of being used to it," he said after sniffing noisily.

"Have you caught a cold?" Elaine asked. "I must have something for it in the medicines."

"Don't bother."

"I wanted to say . . ." Mauro paused, then went on, "I've been a bit hard on you, I misjudged you. It was a good idea to send Yurupig on ahead."

Petersen made a gesture to say no need for any more apologies.

"You trust him, don't you, despite the way you treat him?"

"Not at all. He's doing it for you, not for me. That's why he'll come back. He'd have left me to die without giving it a second thought. And I'd have done the same. It's normal."

"I'm sure you don't think the way you talk," Dietlev said in a tone of mild reproach. "You can't live without other people, as you perfectly well know —"

"Live? Don't make me laugh. Staying alive, that's all that counts, the rest's not worth bothering with. And I have to say I'd rather be in my place than yours."

In the ensuing silence, the humidity enveloped them like a blanket that hadn't been wrung dry. The mosquitos were buzzing around like mad.

"I think we'd best get under shelter before the rain," Mauro said.

The following day they dragged themselves out of their hammocks feeling they were even more exhausted than the previous evening. While Petersen and Mauro got the fire going again, Elaine went through their rucksacks to prepare breakfast. Since she couldn't find the one with the pan, she turned to the two men: "There's a rucksack missing," she said.

"Are you sure?" Mauro asked, examining the spot where they they put all their luggage together in the evening. "That's impossible, it must be there somewhere . . . Perhaps a monkey's taken it," he added after having convinced himself it wasn't there.

"At night the monkeys do the same as us," Petersen said. "They go to sleep, or at least they try to. What was in it?"

"The coffee, the mess tins, the whetstone . . ." Elaine said, trying to visualize the contents. "A few tins of food . . . It was yours, Mauro."

"The fossil samples," he went on, "the cutlery . . . I don't really know. We'll have to search around the camp."

"Search as much as you like," Petersen said with an air of indifference, "but you've no chance of finding anything."

Despite that, Mauro examined the area around the camp while Herman, on his knees by the fire, was carefully blowing on the twigs.

"I don't believe it," Mauro said coming back empty-handed from his search. "What kind of animal could be interested in our mess tins?"

"If there was no food in them," Petersen said, screwing up his face because of the smoke, "it can't have been an animal."

"So who then?" Mauro asked skeptically. "There's only us in this stinking jungle."

"You're forgetting Yurupig, sonny."

"Yurupig!" Elaine exclaimed. "He's certainly got better things to do than come back to steal things from us. Anyway, what d'you think he'd do with a bag of mess tins?"

"You never know what's going on inside an Indian's head," Herman replied with a shrug of the shoulders. "Whatever, we're going to have to find something to heat the water in if we're going to drink coffee."

They heard Dietlev's irritated voice. "Just open a tin. And come and get me out of here, I'm chilled to the bone."

Elaine could tell at a glance that his condition had worsened. He was sweating copiously again and incapable of making the least effort as they lifted him onto the stretcher. He was stinking of urine.

"I'll change your dressing," Elaine said. "It doesn't look too good this morning—but it's the same for all of us, believe me. Did you hear all that about the rucksack? What do you think?"

"Not much. I don't think it could be Yurupig. There are much better ways if he wanted to land us in the shit. Anyway, we'll just have to manage with what's left."

He looked at his leg as Elaine gently washed the stump. "I think the gangrene's come back."

"No, no," she lied, "it's just a normal reaction after what you've been through."

"Elaine . . ." he said in a low voice. "If I don't make it . . ."

"Stop going on about it, please."

"I'm not a little boy, as you well know, Elaine. *If* ever I don't make it, I want you to know . . ."

He closed his eyes to concentrate better. After such a clumsy start, how could he say what he felt without sounding silly or sentimental? The words jostling each other in his mind obviously wouldn't express anything of the veneration he had for this woman, of his desire for her ever since the time when she'd landed, almost by mistake, in his arms. She would take his solemn—too solemn—avowal of love as merely an expression of his fear of dying, and she would doubtless be right . . .

"Dietlev?"

"Too late," he said with a feigned smile. "I'm exhausted. Just forget it, will you?"

THEY SET OFF again along the trail marked by Yurupig. Elaine was walking like a machine, every stride had to be torn from the suction of the soil. Her mind was wandering far from the jungle and the little group she was leading. Like a driver fighting against tiredness, she took flight in daydreams that grew longer and longer and revolved around her return to Brazilia. She imagined herself replying to questions from her colleagues, from journalists. The first thing to do would be to telephone Moéma to reassure her, perhaps Eléazard as well, using the pretext of asking how he was getting on . . . No, it was he who would call her, or there'd be a message on her answering machine. A few concerned words, an invitation to start all over again. Without knowing why, she was convinced nothing would be the same as it was before, that all this—not just what she'd been through during the last few days, but all the rest, her sufferings, her disappointments, her divorce—that all this mess had a hidden meaning, a positive charge that would burst into life sooner or later. What had gone wrong with Eléazard? At what precise moment? Where had it started, where was the point after which they had begun to go their separate ways? She had to get back to that bifurcation in order to deliberately choose the other path, to wind the film back to their initial happiness, back to the still that would repudiate their failure, make it impossible. Once more she saw the terrace of the old house where they had lived, some fifteen years ago, when they were staying in France. The wooden table under the arbor, the wasps around the wine, the splendid torpor of a siesta in the warm shade of the plane tree—

Her fall woke her up without bringing her back to the present. Something heavy on her back was holding her to the ground; she had a cramp and the pain made her want to scream.

Mauro rushed over to her. "Are you hurt?" he asked, taking off her rucksack so she could sit up.

"It's nothing . . . I'm worn out . . . I . . ."

He pushed her hair back to clean the mud off her face. "Just rest, we'll have a break. I'm exhausted too."

Mauro went back to help Petersen with the stretcher. Dietlev still had a high temperature, despite the aspirin he'd been swallowing. The haggard look on Elaine's face filled him with concern: "Is there something wrong. What happened?"

"It's stupid," Elaine replied, blushing. "I think I must have fallen asleep while I was walking. I'll suck a couple of sugar lumps, then it'll be OK." There were tears in her eyes and she was making a visible effort to look all right.

"This is a nice mess we're in," Petersen said sarcastically. "You'll have sweated your sugar lumps out after a couple of hundred yards. We'll never get there if we stop every ten minutes, I can tell you that for free."

"We've been sweating our guts out for two hours now," said Mauro irritatedly, "so cut the crap, OK? We're exhausted, every one of us . . ."

Dietlev looked at them apologetically. "You're wasting your strength for no reason. We have a break because *I'm* tired, because *I* need a pee and because this stretcher makes *me* seasick."

Petersen fumbled in one of his pockets, took out a film container and tossed it to Elaine. "There you are," he said, "take a bit, it'll perk you up no end."

"What is it?" she asked as she caught the container.

"*Cocaína*. It's better than sugar, I can assure you."

Elaine suddenly understood why Herman sniffed so often. And she had offered to give him something for his cold! Without giving it further thought, she tossed the little container back to him. "Thanks, but I prefer sugar, if that's all right by you."

For a brief moment Mauro thought there'd be no harm in trying; the Peruvians of the high plateaus chewed coca leaves to help them keep going . . . He met Dietlev's reproving look and kept quiet.

HER SHIRT STICKING to her skin, sweat dripping from her hair, Elaine focused her attention entirely on the jungle. Annoyed at her fall, she determined to anticipate Yurupig's waymarks so as not to hold up the two struggling along with the stretcher. She had no idea how long they'd been trudging along like that when a movement in the foliage made her stop in her tracks; for the first time since they'd been trekking through the forest, it was the sign not of something fleeing but approaching, so that she instinctively curled her fingers round the short handle of her machete. At the same moment a man appeared in front of her, a naked Indian, with a black hole instead of a mouth; a feathered mummy that silently split into two.

"Don't move!" It was Petersen who spoke as she stepped back, struck dumb with fear. "Keep facing them."

Around twenty Indians armed with bows and blowpipes had assembled in front of them. They just stood there waiting, unmoving gods, aware of their power.

"Friends!" said Elaine, stretching out her arms to show her good will. "We're lost. Do you understand? Lost."

The simple sound of her voice seemed to disconcert them. Some cries rang out, immediately followed by impressive intimidatory moves. One of them started stamping on the spot while pointing to Elaine's arm.

"The gun," Herman said urgently, "give me the gun. Quick!"

"Drop your machete," Dietlev ordered from his stretcher, "slowly. Friends! *Yaudé marangatù*, we're harmless."

The Indians reacted solely to the dropping of the machete. The one who seemed to be their chief uttered a few words. The one nearest to him picked up the coveted object at Elaine's feet. Then he took one step forward to speak to Dietlev.

"What's he saying?" Mauro asked.

"No idea," Dietlev admitted without ceasing to smile obviously at the man who had spoken. "It sounds a bit like the Guarani I've learned, but I can't understand a blind word of what he's saying. It could be a variant, but at least they seem to have calmed down. *Ma-rupi?*" he tried, pointing to the path made by Yurupig. "The river? Where? The white men?"

The Indian put his head on one side, then scratched his thigh to give the impression of composure. Since nothing happened, he gave a brief order and two of them came to pick up the stretcher.

"I think they've understood," Mauro said with relief.

"Fucking savages," was Petersen's response. "I don't know what they've understood, but we've no choice but to stick to their tail."

Eléazard's Notebooks

TO HEAR those who are silent from having screamed too much . . .

AT THE BAR: "Women are like matches, as soon as they get hot they lose their heads." *Mulher é como fósforo: quando esquenta, perda a cabeza.*

"WHY do we foresee only catastrophes?" Hervé Le Bras asks. "Why not see that certain consequences of human activities could protect instead of threatening us?" If it is true that we are heading for a new, fairly harsh and brutal ice age, our efforts ought to be directed toward increasing the greenhouse effect with the utmost urgency, instead of trying to reduce it.

THE TWENTY-FIRST CENTURY will take precise account of our disillusionments; it will be obscurantist.

THEY CAN ALWAYS TURN OUT TO BE USEFUL: bits of string, wood, plastic or rubber, small metal components, broken engines, odd parts, the scattered pieces of a whole, of a dismembered Osiris that can be used to repair, to restore a whole in the universe of things. But they can also create new, unexpected and previously unseen wholes that the reuse brings to life and to which it gives a history. Accumulation and reclamation as the foundations of creativity, the rag-and-bone man as the demiurge of a possible world; the attic as the natural refuge for poetry. And even if these things will never be used, as happens most of the time, it is the *perhaps* that is important, the acceptance of the potentiality of a possible advent or at the very least of the restoration of a lost unity.

THE DAY WHEN WE TIRE OF HEARING OUR FAVORITE STORY, of demanding, as most children do, a strict word-for-word retelling, is the day we enter the age of desecration. Our astonishment at the mystery is no longer triggered by its repetition, but by its ever-renewed transgression.

"AMONG MAMMALS," A. Villiers writes, "it is dogs to which crocodiles seem particularly partial. Rose cites the case of a cayman, the stomach of which contained, apart from a woman's diamond ring, 32 dogs' ID tags, which, taking the dogs without ID tags into account, represents a considerable figure."

SCIENCE has this in common with religion, that most of the time it only produces *impressions of truth*, but it alone has the ability to produce the thing that will dispel them. Where nothing is falsifiable, nothing is provable either.

HIGH ON LSD? Without realising it, Kircher must have ingested some rye ergot (*Claviceps purpurea*). His ecstatic journey was nothing but a bad trip. That is what Dr. Euclides maintains after analyzing his reactions when he took the tonic sent by Yves d'Évreux. This minuscule fungus, a parasite on rye and rich in lysergic acid, caused communal poisoning when it was inadvertently mixed with flour made from that grain. What used to be called "holy fire" or "St. Anthony's fire." Euclides argues very persuasively that partaking of rye ergot was at the basis of the Mysteries of Eleusis.

THE ART OF LIGHT AND SHADE contains a whole chapter on the manufacture of marbled paper. In his *Natural Magic* (*Magia universalis naturæ et artis, sive recondita naturalium et artificalium rerum scientia*, Würzburg, 1657) Caspar Schott declares that he learned the method of "painting paper with varied colors in the manner of the Turks" while watching Athanasius Kircher at work: "He made all sorts of designs on paper—people, animals, trees, towns and regions—now as breaking waves, now as various marbles, now as birds' feathers and as all sorts of other figures." Specialists in this matter, in particular Einen Miura, recognize Kircher as the first to introduce the art of marbled paper into Europe.

DATES of C. Schott?

ATHANASIUS KIRCHER did not take part in any of the religious controversies by which his times were rocked. An attitude of reserve that can be counted in his favor. He seems to have adopted the exhortation of Muto Vitelleschi, Father General of the Society during the Thirty Years' War: "Let us not say: my country. Let us stop speaking a barbarous language. Let us not glorify the day on which prayer becomes nationalized . . ."

FROM GOETHE, in his *Theory of Colours*: "Thanks to Kircher, the natural sciences present themselves to us in a much livelier and brighter manner than with any of his predecessors. They have left the study and the lecture theatre for a comfortably appointed monastery with ecclesiastics who are in communication with the whole world, have influence on the whole world, who want to teach people, but also to entertain and amuse them. Even if Kircher solves very few problems, at least he brings them up and examines them in his own way. He demonstrates an ease of understanding, facility and unruffled calm in his communications."

FROM GOETHE, again: "Each one of us has something hidden inside himself, a feeling, a memory, which, if it were known, would make the man hated." Doubtless the worst of men also has, even more profoundly hidden, something that would make him loved.

THE SUBCONSCIOUS is but one possible strategy of dishonesty.

CHAPTER 22

In which the episode of the coffins with a tube is reported

ATHANASIUS KIRCHER COULD not
hear the story of Count Karnice without shuddering.
The horror of his wife's awakening in the darkness of the tomb,
which he could clearly imagine, spurred on his genius to such an
extent that only two days after that terrible event, he showed
me his designs for a "tactile recaller," a machine to prevent such
dreadful mistakes ever happening again.

It consisted of a metal tube, six foot long & about six inches
in diameter, to be inserted into the casket at the time of
interment through a circular opening, which carpenters would
have no problem incorporating in their coffins as a standard
feature. The upper section of the tube, that which would be
above ground, would terminate in a hermetically sealed box
containing the works necessary for the functioning of the
mechanism. My master explained its ingenious simplicity with
a cross-section drawing. A rod attached to a very sensitive spring

went down the tube into the coffin; screwed to the end was a brass sphere, arranged in such a way as to touch the chest of the presumed corpse: the least movement, even a breath taken before recovering consciousness, & the sphere would set the rescue in motion. The box would open at once, letting air & light flood into the coffin; at the same time a flag would be raised, a loud bell would sound, while a rocket would shoot up into the sky before exploding noisily, spreading the dazzling light of the resurrection over the graveyard.

If the box remained closed for two weeks, a sufficient lapse of time for all hope to disappear, all one had to do was to pull up the tube; a valve would automatically close the opening, so that one could finally fill in the grave. Once the "recaller," or at least the part that had touched the corpse, had been disinfected, it was immediately ready for use in another interment.

I warmly commended Kircher's latest invention. As it cost only a modest sum & was a model of simplicity, it would be easy to supply the cemeteries with them to avoid the risk of premature burials.

As I mentioned above, it was impossible to find a single coffin in Rome, but Cardinal Barberini, when he heard of this machine, put four of his own at our disposal. Working day & night, we made the tubes in less than a week. They worked perfectly & it was not long, alas, before they were put to use. Six of our Jesuit brothers were carried off by the plague in less time that it took to mourn them. Two of them, whose bodies were in such a state of decay there was no doubt they were dead, were sent to the communal grave, but the other four were interred in the College cemetery, each grave equipped with a "tactile recaller."

Nothing happened during the first two nights & we went to bed on the third with our minds at rest concerning the fate of our unfortunate friends—they were resting in peace. Around three in the morning, however, a terrifying explosion woke us with a start. Realising immediately what it meant, Athanasius threw on his shirt as he hurried down the stairs, calling for help. I followed him, accompanied by several fathers.

We reached the cemetery almost as soon as he did, but he was already beside a grave with a raised flag, digging furiously with his mattock & shouting words of comfort to the one whose return to life had set off this commotion. Grasping other implements, we joined him to disinter the unfortunate man as quickly as possible.

I was busy with my spade, working as quickly as I could, when a long whistle followed by an explosion that set the night ablaze almost made us die of shock. Another flag had gone up a few yards from where we were. The ringing from the box sounded as if it came from the very depths of Hades. Those who so far had only been watching, hurried over to that grave & started digging up that coffin.

While they were thus occupied, a third detonation & then a fourth at almost the same time took our agitation to fever pitch. The whole College had woken. Some were praying in loud voices, others proclaiming a miracle: never did a cemetery resound with such faith & hope. Since there were more arms than implements, some started pulling up the soil with their hands; cries of encouragement mingled with thanksgivings, & the torches, a large number of which had been lit by the brother porter, gave the unusual scene the look of a phantasmagoria.

Having started first, we were the first to disinter the coffin; using a forked lever, Athanasius opened the lid as quickly as he could. In the light of the torches, we formed a circle round him: the sight that greeted us was more repulsive that our most revolting nightmares. The murmurs that came from our lips were more ones of disgust than of disappointment. Some turned away, calling on God, & a novice, suddenly fainting, almost fell into the grave. Floating on a sea of maggots, black with gangrene, Father Le Pen seemed ready to burst so swelled up he was with gas & sanies. It was his belly, taut as a wineskin, that had moved the sphere, setting off the alarm mechanism. The same causes producing the same effects, the cemetery was soon filled with lamentation & exclamations of horror.

Once we had gotten over the general stupor, we reinterred the four brothers, with many prayers at having disturbed their souls' repose, then returned to our rooms, though few of us managed to get any sleep that night.

Put away in the mechanical section of the museum, these excellent machines were never used again. Even after the plague, once the corruption of the flesh had returned to its natural limits, no one thought of using them, out of either superstition or mistrust, so profoundly disturbing had been the effect of that first trial.

At the end of November the *Draco Pestis*, the insatiable hydra that had gorged on so many human lives, decided to abandon its prey. Overnight no one was dying of the plague in the streets of Rome anymore. Whether it had been set off by the Jews to avenge themselves on the Christians—as Cardinal Gastaldi maintained for no good reason since eight hundred of them had died in the ghetto—or by God himself as punishment for our sins, that still did not justify the scourge: God does not have to justify his acts, neither when He chastises us, nor when He delivers us.

As I have already said, fifteen thousand people died in Rome in four months; but that number, huge though it might be, was much lower than that which afflicted the cities of Palermo, Milan or, later, the big city of London. All in all, the Romans should be glad to have come out of such a trial relatively lightly.

In 1658 the *Scrutinium Pestis* appeared. In these two hundred pages my master examined the history of the epidemic, its possible causes, its different forms and symptoms, without omitting a single one of the remedies used to counter it. "But," he concluded, "the best remedy for the plague is to flee very quickly & very far, & to stay away from the sources of infection for as long as possible; if, however, you cannot do that, then live in a very large, well-ventilated house situated on top of a hill, away from the drains & stagnant water; open the windows so as to purge the air & fill your dwelling with aromatic herbs; burn sulfur & myrrh & take abundant vinegar to purify the inside of your body as well . . ." Precious advice that subsequently saved the lives of numerous people.

FORTALEZA: *But it was a Lourdes or a Benares . . .*

Roetgen returned to his teaching with the uncomfortable feeling that he had only just escaped all sorts of complications. By transgressing the tacit rules associated with his status as lecturer he had exposed himself to professional problems whose seriousness he only now appreciated. Despite his hurt pride and the obsessive image of Moéma, he was astonished he had come out of it so lightly: what madness, he said to himself, to have yielded to that girl's advances. I really was a fool. She only has to tell people half of what happened on that beach and I can pack my bags.

Without feeling embarrassed at what he'd done—you had to take people and things as they were and not be afraid of having your senses disturbed if it was in the interest of ethnography—he saw himself in danger of stubbornly denying his mistakes, of declaring, in outraged tones, that people shouldn't cast slurs on his reputation simply because of malicious student gossip, that it was too easy . . . But the various scenarios in which he rehearsed his defense did not reassure him, so that he basked in the warmth of the flattering memory of his outing in the jangada, reducing his stay at the seaside to that exploit alone.

Happening to meet him on campus, he told Andreas of his adventures. "You're crazy," was his smiling reaction, "but I don't think I could have resisted either . . . Still, you'll have to be careful, they can't stop themselves gossiping. Not out of malice, that's the odd thing about it, but because they have a taste for it, for the sheer enjoyment of the *fofocas* . . . Tittle-tattle, it's almost a way of life here! You'd think they couldn't communicate in any other way. And I have to agree that it's quite nice: the mystery ends up giving a kind of density to human relationships. You can be sure you'll be rumored to have done a lot more things than you would ever do, so, a bit more, a bit less, you've no need to worry as long as you're not sleeping with the principal's wife. And even then you'd have to be caught in the act!"

He put a friendly hand on his shoulder. "Tell me, do I know the girl?"

"She doesn't exactly hide her light under a bushel. Moéma von something, I can't remember what, something that sounds German."

"Moéma von Wogau?"

"That's it," Roetgen said in amazement. "You know who she is?"

"I know her father, an old university friend. He's a journalist, a foreign correspondent in Alcântara. I even palmed my parrot off on him. He stays with us when his work brings him here. He told me his daughter was coming to the university here, I was supposed to keep a bit of an eye on her, but I have to admit I've completely forgotten."

"Why didn't she go to São Luís?"

"Her parents are in the middle of a divorce, it could well be that it's already gone through. As I understand it, the girl's taking it rather badly. The mother's a Brazilian, a lecturer at Brazilia; she's making a name for herself in palaeontology, always on the move. She's the one who left. As for her father, I quite like him but he can be unbearable. The kind of guy who's always preoccupied with the world and with himself and despite that not very perceptive about other people. For all that, a brilliant guy. I've never understood why he was so determined to ruin his life. And from what you say, the girl's got problems too . . ."

"You can say that again," Roetgen agreed.

With this verdict he was back in the comfort zone of a dominant position and ready to forgive Moéma her infatuation with the Indian. The fact that she had 'problems' changed everything; from a nympho she became a child who needed help.

That same evening, after turning it over in his mind again and again in the little attic flat he rented in a modern block, Roetgen decided to go and see Thaïs. She'd given him her address on the bus journey back. Three days had passed since then.

Having knocked on the little door in Bolivar Street with no response, he was about to leave when Thaïs's head popped through the bead curtain over the window. "Oh, it's you!" she said cheerfully. "Come in, just give me a few seconds."

Roetgen noted the dark red blotches on her cheeks and the top of her chest. He must have surprised her in the middle of her frolics with a new lover. She's consoled herself pretty quickly, he thought with a touch of disdain. He was then all the more astounded to see her reappear, knotting an extravagant kimono with a multicolored floral pattern round her buxom figure and leading in a young man with a large blond mustache, very thin, who did not seem the least embarrassed by his scanty attire—just a pair of boxer shorts.

"This is Xavier," Thaïs said, pronouncing the "x" aspirated in the Portuguese manner. "He disembarked yesterday. You can talk French with him; if I've understood correctly he made the crossing from Toulon in a sailing boat. I think he's going to stay here for a few days . . ."

They were both wearing rather inane smiles. The room was stinking of grass. Roetgen introduced himself coolly to his compatriot.

"Anything new?" Thaïs asked, rolling a joint.

"Nothing. Lectures, the university, routine . . ."

He looked her in the eye and took the plunge: 'Heard anything of Moéma?"

Immediately Thaïs's face darkened. "Nothing at all. She must be in Canoa with that goddamn Indian. You wouldn't believe she'd pull a trick like that on us."

Roetgen was surprised but flattered to see himself included in their relationship. "These things happen," he said.

"You're in love with her as well, eh? I mean, it's serious, I haven't got it wrong, have I?"

"More than anything," Roetgen replied, alarmed. It is often our lips that decide between truth and falsehood. Roetgen couldn't say whether he was lying in order to attract sympathy and take center stage in the matter or whether his unconsidered reply was more of a revelation of the truth. He detected overexcitement in it, the kind that goads us, when we're in a confession situation, into going for the full pathos rather than some banal, inglorious suffering.

"At least, I think so," he said, trying to collect his thoughts. "She . . . How should I put it? I miss her."

"I knew it," Thaïs said, passing him the *maconha* joint. "It's the same with me. We're up the creek, *cara*. Up shit creek. I've never seen her like that before. It's as if the bastard had put a spell on her."

Xavier couldn't understand a word of what was being said and looked as if he couldn't care less. Sprawled out on the cushions, unruffled, his face wreathed in smiles, he puffed at his joint, scrutinizing the walls of the little room.

"It's not normal," Roetgen went on, "I can't stop thinking about her, ever since I got back to Fortaleza. About you too, be it said. It's extraordinary the things we went through together down there." Against all expectation, he found Thaïs much more alluring than at Canoa. A gleam in her eye—and perhaps also the fact that she hadn't fastened the top of her kimono, revealing a little more than she should have of her ample bosom—assured him that the attraction was indubitably shared.

That was the point their mutual titillation had reached when the curtain over the front door was pushed aside. It was Moéma. Puffy-eyed, holding back her tears, she fixed a look of mute entreaty on her friend. Thaïs immediately stood up and, ignoring the two men, drew the prodigal into her room.

"Some great girls round here," Xavier said as soon as Thaïs had closed the door. Then, with a wink, "I've a feeling it's some time since you had any French mustard, am I right? But I've got some whiskey as well, if you prefer, Johnnie Walker Black Label. It's no great shakes, but it's all they had at Cape Verde."

MOÉMA HAD GREAT difficulty recounting the sequence of events that had led to her hasty return. One scene kept coming back to mind insistently and tormented her like anything: Aynoré making love to Josefa, the girl with the gold beach buggy. She happened upon them, after her siesta, hardly hidden in the dunes behind the beach. The little tart was jigging about on him, clinging onto his shoulders.

"What the fuck are you doing here?" Josefa spat out, "Can't you see I'm busy?"

Moéma was struck dumb, all she could do was give the Indian an imploring look. If he had come to her at that moment, she would have forgiven him, such was her infatuation. He looked her up and down, as if everything was perfectly normal: "Don't get all uptight like that, girl. Let me finish, will you."

It was as if the whole of Amazonia were disintegrating before her very eyes. She started crying, frozen in a stupor at the wreckage of her dream. Just before turning away, she released her fury in an insult she had regretted ever since: "Oh, fuck yourself, you fat slut!"

The reply caught her off guard as she set off running to the beach: "Hey, lezzie! Believe it or not, that's just what I'm doing!"

Then laughter. The laughter of two people that still tormented her.

SHE FOUND MARLENE on the beach. Seeing the state she was in, the transvestite made her sit down on the sand. With caresses and comforting words, he managed to get her to tell him what was wrong.

"I told you to be careful," he said, "he's a dangerous guy, a real wolf in sheep's clothing. I bet he gave you his shaman spiel?"

She gave him a questioning look, dreading what she was going to hear.

"It's his trick for getting off with girls, a book he found: Indian legends, shamanic rituals, the flood . . . everything's in it. A load of rot, girl. He's hardly Indian at all and no more a shaman than you or me. His mother was a hostess in a Manaus bar and as for his father, she never knew which one it was of all the drunks she'd slept with . . ."

"It's not true," Moéma sobbed, "you're lying."

"Don't believe me if you don't want to, but it's the simple truth. You just have to have a look at the book, I'll lend it you, if you like: *Antes o mundo não existia*; it's a guy with a real tongue-twister of a name telling the mythology of his tribe. Aynoré's got nothing to do with the Indians, he told me so himself. His get-up's just for selling his junk to tourists at the *beira-mar*. He's a little bastard, a little shit dealer. He's not worth crying over, not for a girl like you, Moéma."

SHE ONLY DRIED her tears after having been forgiven by Thaïs and confirmed her worst fears about Aynoré's honesty. The book mentioned by Marlene—the first entirely written by a Brazilian Indian—had appeared some twenty years ago; Roetgen remembered it clearly from having studied it to prepare a lecture: everything from the birth of the world and the first cataclysm of fire, right down to details about shamanism was in the book used by the con man.

Disenchanted, then furious, Moéma never alluded to him again, not even in her own thoughts, without inventing some new insult: *that no-good Indian* she would say in disillusioned tones, or *that two-faced bastard, when I think I fell for him hook, line and sinker . . . the swine!* It made things easier, at least at the beginning.

After the few hours it took to sort out Moéma's disappointment, Roetgen made a suggestion that swept away the last remaining tensions. At the end of the week a ten-day holiday started, what did they say to all going to the annual pilgrimage at Juazeiro? It would give Moéma and himself the chance to observe the survival of indigenous cults in the devotion of the people of the *Nordeste* to Padre Cícero; as for the other two—Xavier was invited, of course—they would have a superb excursion in the Sertão. He'd hire a car, they'd sleep outdoors, improvising as they went along . . .

They were all enthusiastic about the idea and three days later they were singing their heads off in a Chevrolet Andreas had lent them. All in dark glasses, they were chanting in chorus a Rolling Stones song, bellowing out of the open window their inability to get satisfaction.

They were crazy days, off-the-rails days suffused by alcohol with a vague sense of depravity. The drugs as well, which they took all the time, detached them from the real world, confining them within the limits of immediate experience. Not much older than his three companions—the seven years between him and Moéma weighed more than he would have thought—Roetgen took charge. He was the only one who drove, the only one with money, the only one who still kept a cool head. If he did snort a few lines of coke, smoke a few joints, it was above all so as not to stand out and because his scorn for drugs told him that this excess was merely a tropical diversion in the course of his life, a necessary experience from which he would emerge unscathed. He made up for it by drinking a lot and it was just by luck that he avoided any accidents while they were driving. Remaining faithful to what he had been surprised to find himself admitting to Thaïs, he cultivated his "love" for Moéma. A strange attachment that he did not bother to analyze but that made him suffer regularly, for example, every time she slept alone with Thaïs and he attempted to dull the humiliation by chatting with Xavier.

Despite her apparent unconcern, Moéma was still suffering the effects of her disappointment with Aynoré. She wasn't lying when she told Thaïs that nothing could separate them anymore, or when she told Roetgen she couldn't contemplate losing him, she was so happy in his arms. From the depths of her hatred for the Indian came the clearer and clearer feeling that her liaison with him had been of a different type. The harsher her acrimony toward him became, the closer she edged toward the other two, as if to protect herself from the abyss still yawning at Canoa.

Unlike Roetgen, who had no idea what was going on, Thaïs had not forgiven her friend her infidelity. She knew for a terrible fact that, for all her protestations, the bond between them had been broken. And if she slept with Xavier just for fun, but knowing it wouldn't last, it was above all to get at Moéma. Not nastily or out of resentment but out of a feeling of desolation. Of the party, she was probably the only one who was really suffering because she was the only one who loved with no other perspective than her love itself.

As for Xavier, the *Atomic Mosquito,* he was there without being there, without making any judgments, without the least awareness of what was happening to them all. He never sobered up, smoked joint after joint, laughed a lot. A seagull drawn by the horizon, a fanatic of the ephemeral, he was soaring far above them. A very strange bird of passage, a sort of angel, puny but ready for anything, whom the three others pampered, knowing very well that he would soon take flight. An angel, yes. A phantom angel. A mustachioed smile worthy of the most beautiful dreams of Alice Liddell.

For whatever reason, our four dopeheads forged on regardless with an exuberance that resulted in them doing the most stupid things. At Canindé, where they stopped to see the shrine of St. Francis, the priest gave them permission to take any of the hundreds of votive offerings heaped up behind a grating. Placed by supplicants at the foot of the miracle-working statue, copies of all parts of the body were piled up to waist height: breasts, legs, skulls, intestines, genitals, carved in wood or wax. If you had prostate problems or an ulcer, if you were afraid of an operation or a wedding night, all you had to do was to make a model of the part in question for St. Francis to effect a supernatural cure.

"I have to burn the lot once a month," the old priest whose siesta they'd disturbed told them. "Take anything you find interesting and bring back the key when you've finished."

After having made fun of the naive pictures covering the walls of the church, attesting the wonders worked by the indefatigable patron saint of Canindé—"Thank you, São Francisco, for having allowed my little girl to excrete the house keys without hurting herself"—the two couples made love right in the middle of the votive offerings, half-buried under the crudely hewn heads, members and organs of these imaginary bodies. They left slightly disgusted but proud of an exploit that had the feel of sacrilege.

"Surrealistic!" was the one word on Thaïs's lips to express her astonishment at everything they saw. Through a slit in the glass coffin harboring the statue of a pale and gaunt Christ, the pilgrims would slip small banknotes as offerings: a transparent money box with the hideous corpse of a shipwrecked sailor just about floating on the green mold of the banknotes. They dropped some playing cards onto it, a condom, some greasy paper and several pages out of a notebook covered in vile blasphemies.

Dead drunk, they posed in front of one of the canvases with the figure of St. Francis that half-starved itinerants had put up around most of the square outside. They had agreed to silently utter some intimate secret just as the photographer released the shutter. As they watched the black-and-white pictures being developed in a galvanized tank, they were enchanted by their lack of lips.

It was a Lourdes or a Benares, whichever you prefer, and the crowds from the Sertão engulfed the town in their misery: lepers dragging their supplications on their knees through the dust; the bedridden, black with sores; cripples; people with improbable mutilations, monsters you couldn't bear to look at; men and women with their eyes swollen with tears—all these unfortunates queuing at the confessionals set up, like country urinals, against the church walls, struggling with each other to make their way toward the plaster idol, fainting at the flaking picture of his bare feet. The stalls were selling good-luck ribbons arranged in multi-colored armfuls, vignettes, holy pictures—a collection of junk on which the people of the *Nordeste* wasted their last cruzeiros. In all this display of misfortune there was an exhibitionism that they eventually found irritating.

In the zoo there all they saw was a pair of armadillos desperately masturbating and a sheep painted blue. Before leaving they bought leather hats and long cowherd's knives. The car was full of assorted votive offerings chosen for their aesthetic qualities or their involuntary humor: heads whitened with lime and seeds for eyes or tufts of human hair stuck on top, twisted torsos, carbuncular buttocks mounted on flimsy stilts . . . the Chevrolet looked like an anatomical display case.

They were caught in a storm on the way to Juazeiro. It was such a violent downpour Roetgen had to pull over to the shoulder. A donkey emerged from the void and galloped past, braying with terror, its four iron shoes skidding on the red mud covering the tarmac. Overawed by this infernal vision and weary of the proximity of destitution, they took the first excuse to abandon their plan: "How about going to the brothels in Recife?" Moéma said.

Roetgen did a U-turn and headed off to the southwest, in the direction of Pernambuco.

FAVELA DE PIRAMBÚ: *You'd see it go past in the night, among the stars . . .*

"What are you going to do with this, son?"

"It's my business. You can lend it to me or not, but no questions, OK?"

Uncle Zé had been intrigued. His look had gone blank in an odd way, proof that he suspected something. But what? No one could guess, not even Uncle Zé. No one. Just like Lampião . . . They were waiting for him in Bahia and he popped up in Sergipe; they laid an ambush for him at Rio Grande do Norte and there he was at home having his photo taken by the journalists of the *Diário de Notícias*. He drove them crazy, every one of them. That wasn't what he wanted to do to old Zé, but it was better if he wasn't in on it. Fortunately he'd brought the contraption, after all it was easier using it and you could do a better job. The whole business had taken him several days . . . above all because of the mold. He'd sweated his guts out for that mold, he really had, but he'd found a solution in the end and it was all done two days ago when the old guy had turned up to take him out for an ice cream. Pink mango and passion fruit . . . If it was up to him he'd eat nothing else, it was so good! Zé hadn't even mentioned it again, he was so busy getting ready for the Feast of Yemanjá: this year he was organizing everything for Dadá Cotinha at the Mata Escura *terreiro*. Dadá, that was the same name as Corisco's wife, wasn't it? Those bastards had smashed one of her legs with their machine guns. Four hundred miles in the back of a truck with her leg just attached by the tendons . . . Fucking hell! He had to remember that, he mustn't forget a single murder, a single humiliation because those meters weren't reset at zero, definitely not! Uncle Zé had problems. Not big ones, nothing at all even, compared to his truck, but he couldn't find a girl to sit on Yemanjá's throne. Corta Braço, Beco de Chinelo, Amaralinha, all the other *terreiros* in the district had already got the prettiest girls. All that was left were the old ones or the fat lumps. Crazy, old Zé said, how many fat lumps there are around! And they all come to see me, one after the other: Choose me, Zé, with the gown and the wig no one will be able to tell I'm a bit overweight . . . And even worse was what

they were offering to get him to choose them . . . It was unbelievable. I'd rather die, old Zé told them, can't you see you'll frighten
the little kids? If I choose you for the procession no one'll come
within miles. He's not stupid, old Zé. He knows how to get things
done when he puts his mind to it. I should never have agreed to
see to all that, he kept saying. I've got the costumes for everyone, the band, the *cachaça* . . . but if I don't find a girl with a good
figure for Yemanjá, what are we going to look like, eh? It was in
the almanac . . . Just a minute and I'll show you . . . here, look: un-
lucky days January 12, May 4, August 15! You can keep it, I want
nothing more to do with this bird of ill omen . . . *The coming year
for the* Nordeste: *horoscope for all.* A fat pamphlet, yellow, one of
those that cost 200 cruzeiros! Crazy what you could find in an
almanac like that and not just predictions, loads of stuff and all
spot-on . . . *Anyone who does not have God deep in their heart will
not have Him anywhere else.* Well put, eh? You could twist the
words whichever way you liked, it hit the mark: God deep in your
throat, God in your lungs—that must make you cough your guts
out! God behind your ear, God deep in your ass . . . No, only the
heart, nothing else was possible. *The intelligent man: an intelligent
person doesn't smoke, doesn't drink, doesn't judge and doesn't argue.*
Drinking and smoking, OK, but he couldn't stop himself. Judging?
How can we not judge? Not judge the rich, the stupid, the Yanks,
the murderers? Not judge men who gouge people's eyes out, and
what else then? And arguing was the same . . . Your "intelligent
man" wouldn't happen to be dead, would he, or is it just that I really am stupid? *Champions at starving: the flea—can live for several
months without food. The armadillo—almost a year without eating.
The snake—more than a year feeding on its poison alone. The people
of the Nordeste—spend all their days living on hope.* The guy who
thought that up was intelligent, no question. "Spend all their days
living on hope"—too fucking right! And there was plenty more

stuff like that, at the bottom of every page . . . *Without food a man can live for up to three weeks; without water for up to a week; and without air for five to six minutes. In the human body there are 2016 pores allowing the body to perspire and refresh the blood, which irrigates the heart after it has been filtered 120 times by the kidneys. The heart beats 103,700 times in twenty-four hours, a woman's heart even more. At the age of seventy the human heart has, on average, already beat more than three billion times. The energy used over seventy years of life is sufficient to send a train and ten wagons loaded with pickaxes to a height of five hundred yards.—Puxa!* That was talking! And him too, cripple that he was . . . And if they all set about it, the people of the favelas, those of the Sertão, they could send thousands of trains loaded with pickaxes up into the air. What a bloody mess that would make, eh? And a fucking metal downpour when it all started falling . . . Or perhaps it would be better to team up and dispatch just one, but much higher. To send it into orbit, the bloody train with its load of pickaxes, you'd see it go past in the night, among the stars. It's the Pirambú train, people would say . . . There'd be messages in large letters on the wagons, just like on the tractor trailers . . . *The rich can go to hell! Signed: Nelson, the aleijadinho.* That's what they'd write on his wagon. And in luminous paint so that it could be clearly seen in the darkness . . . *Aquarius (Mars). You are idealistic. You love freedom and you do everything you can not to be pushed around. When you're frustrated that makes you ultranervous, and you put yourself in danger. You panic at the thought of poverty but you like to remember the past. Beware of your instinct for independence. In general the year is favorable for your projects* . . . Now if that wasn't a good horoscope, what was, for fuck's sake! There it was in black and white, he just had to sit back and wait for it to come.

Nelson put the almanac down on the sand and went to sleep, at peace with the world.

CHAPTER 23

In which there is talk of the universal language &
an indecipherable secret message

IN 1662, THE year in which he was sixty, my
master stepped up his activities even more. Stimulated
by his discoveries of the symbolic system of the hieroglyphs &
the comparisons he made with Chinese characters, he started
to think of a language in which men of all nations could
communicate with each other, without, however, having to use a
language other than their own.

"You see, Caspar," he explained to me one morning, "although
it is easy for an Italian & a German to correspond in Latin,
since that is the common language of all educated people in the
West, it is more difficult between a German & a Syrian or, *a
fortiori*, between a Syrian & a Chinese. In the latter case, either
the Syrian has to learn Chinese or the Chinese Syriac, or both of
them a third language they could have in common. As you will
surely agree, these three solutions—because they assume a long,

solitary or mutual apprenticeship learning grammars & scripts that are difficult to acquire—will do nothing to persuade these two men to try & understand each other. As I have realized while studying Chinese with my friend Boym, even knowing twenty thousand characters—which enables me to read almost all Chinese writing—does not allow me even to hope that I could use the language orally with, say, a native of Peking: one needs, in addition, knowledge & practise of the accents, or musical tones, which discourages even the most zealous of our missionaries. On the other hand, with a pen & paper I can express myself perfectly to any Chinese. Similarly a Pekinese & Cantonese, who have the Chinese language in common but pronounce it in such different ways that they cannot understand each other when they speak, can easily communicate with a brush and a little ink.

"Let us return to my example of the Indian in the Americas. I drew a gondola floating on the water with its gondolier, thus showing him that it is a kind of boat, which, after all, was easy enough. But what will happen now if I want to get him to understand an idea or a type instead of a simple object? What should I draw to express 'the divine' or 'truth' or 'animals'? You will agree, my dear Caspar, that here our task becomes somewhat complicated. And that at the very point where it is crucial he should understand as precisely as possible. What use is a language if it can only be employed to name or manage objects & not ideas, which are the token within us of divine creation? We have to go from a simple drawing to a symbol! How, Caspar, would you make a Tupinambu realize that the mystery that is called 'Tupang' in their idiom coincides with what we understand by 'God' or 'the One who is'?"

I concentrated for a moment, going through in my mind all the symbols that might represent the deity & make sense to our Indian & suggested the cross . . .

"That would do for a European," Kircher said, "but for a Chinese all you would have done would be to have written the number 'ten' in his language; as for the Tupinambu you have in mind, it would probably mean something else to him, & so on for all the nations who are not familiar with that symbol."

"What can one do, then? Do we have to go back to a dictionary?"

"But of course, Caspar, just a dictionary. But not any old dictionary. As always, extreme simplicity comes from a complex base; a dictionary or, to be more precise, two dictionaries in one, as I will attempt to show you.

"If I were to write: *Would you, my dear friend, be so kind as to send me one of those animals from the Nile that are commonly called 'crocodile' so that I could study it at my leisure?* or: *You send crocodile for study,* my correspondent would understand me perfectly in either case. Following that rule, I have purged the dictionary so that only those words remain that are indispensable, 1218 to be precise, which I have arranged in thirty-two classes, each containing thirty-eight terms. The thirty-two symbolic categories are listed in Roman numerals & the thirty-eight terms in Arabic numerals. The word 'friend,' for example, is the fifth term of class II of terms for people. Look . . ."

MY MASTER SHOWED me a sheaf of papers on which he had written out what he had just explained to me. First and foremost, his new compilation contained a marvelous dictionary over which he must have burned much midnight oil. Thanks to its very simple organizing principle one could easily find the number of the translation of the 1218 essential words necessary for all, even very metaphysical, discourse into eight different languages (Latin, Greek, Hebrew, Arabic, Spanish, French, Italian & German). This written dictionary, intended for anyone who wanted to translate their thoughts into "Universal" was complemented by a second, inverse volume for anyone who wanted to translate into his own language something that had already been converted into numerical form.

"This is only a draft," Kircher went on, "but you can see that it will be very easy to compile a similar dictionary for each part of the Old & the New World. And when Asia, Africa, Europe & the Americas all have one, there will be no longer be any barrier to understanding; it will be as if we had returned to the purity of the Adamic tongue, the sole mother of all the different languages that God made to punish us after the Tower of Babel."

This new invention left me dumbfounded. Athanasius's genius seemed inexhaustible & no man was ever less affected by the cruel ravages of old age. Perhaps thinking my silence expressed reservations, Kircher answered a question that had not even crossed my mind so far.

"Of course, you'll be wondering how one can write anything understandable without using inflections or conjugations; to which my immediate answer is that I've anticipated that difficulty: to each numerical representation of a word one will just have to add a symbol of my own invention that will indicate, where necessary, a plural, a mood or tense of a verb. Let me give you an example."

Taking a pen, he wrote as he continued to speak. "'Our friend is coming' is: XXX.21 II.5 XXIII.8, while 'Our friend has come' is: XXX.21 II.5 XXIII.8._E, the sign at the end indicating the immediate past. Here you can see the table with these indispensable markers."

I was so excited by this splendid language & the perspectives it opened up for spreading the true religion throughout the world that I strongly encouraged my master to publish his work. He consented on condition that I helped him by genuine criticism of his rough draft to turn it into a truly efficient dictionary. In order to achieve this we agreed, at his suggestion, to exchange numerical messages each evening on any subject that occurred to us, in order to check that the process really worked. I thanked God for this exceptional mark of trust & did everything I could to show myself worthy of it.

At this point & while the College was buzzing with rumors about our mysterious epistles—the interest made Kircher smile & only encouraged him to increase the atmosphere of secrecy surrounding his experiments—an unexpected event once more called on his knowledge: it happened that on July 7, 1662 the Vatican spies had intercepted a letter to the French embassy in Rome. Written in French, though obviously encoded, the letter defied the efforts of the best experts in that field to decipher it. As a last resort, they turned to Kircher as the only person who still might be able to unravel it.

The encoded text was as follows:

> Jade sur la prairie; sens à l'omble-chevalier; échelle craquante;
> bière de paille; oui, le labyrinthe; horde de choucas, hein; l'ambre
> triste a entendu l'arum de France; le rayon de la colombe a
> taillé en pièces le pisteur; lardez son épave; l'aisance verse le viol,
> Henri; sel de loupe; destin de Rancé, pourparlers, orphie, cheval
> de pont, singe dupe; Parme épluche le trou; badinerie rôde; rat, si,
> vous; l'oeuf de lièvre anti-jet tue l'aura du dard; les beaux jours
> invertissent; taillez, dupes, l'âge récent du désordre; entravez le
> péché; germe de poule; baigner la fourmi; voir le moulin du doute;
> senteur marine; faire la sauce de la fin; signe jaune, vous, Eyck;
> sève délivrée, corde essentielle . . .

Kircher worked on this night & day for two weeks without the least success & he was sadly thinking he would have to admit he was baffled when his friend, the doctor Alban Gibbs, came to see him.

SÃO LUÍS: *"Ideal" incandescent fuel stove with flue*

"The expedition should have returned two days ago," Dr. Euclides said, wiping his spectacles, "Countess Carlotta is really very worried about her son . . . you don't happen to have heard anything from Elaine?"

"Not a thing," Eléazard replied. "Having said that, there's no reason to get alarmed, people don't disappear like that nowadays."

After having wished she were dead a few weeks ago, he was suddenly afraid some evil spirit might have granted this idle wish of wounded self-esteem.

"No doubt, my friend, no doubt," Euclides said, "I simply wanted to warn you. By the way, how's your daughter? I miss her a lot, you know. I enjoyed watching her grow up."

"To tell you the truth, I've no idea. I have the impression she hasn't gotten through adolescence yet. She tells me what I want to hear and I'm forced to believe her. Which doesn't stop me worrying; one of these days I'm going to turn up at her place to see for myself. I can understand why she wanted to get away from me, but it does make things damn complicated. She even refused to let me have a telephone installed for her."

"You just have to be patient, I imagine. Though . . . Recognizing the moment when indulging your children is the only effective way of helping and the moment when it becomes neglect—no, that's not the right word, let's say renunciation—that's what must be difficult."

"That's what I'm asking myself all the time, as you can imagine. I try to do what's best, but that's the standard excuse for the most stupid mistakes, which isn't very reassuring."

"Come on, chin up! Things always sort themselves out in the end. They have to get better before they can get worse again."

"If there's one thing I like about you, it's your 'optimism,'" Eléazard said in friendly mockery.

"I got out of bed on the wrong side this morning so you'll have to go somewhere else if you're looking for comfort. What can I get you? You'll join me, won't you? I need a little glass of something to turn my mind to brighter thoughts."

"It's all right," Eléazard said, getting up. "I'll see to it. Cointreau, cognac?"

"Whatever you're having," Euclides said, making himself comfortable in his chair again.

Eléazard poured two cognacs and sat back down opposite his host.

"To Moéma," the old man said. "May she not settle down too quickly, it's bad for your health."

"To Moéma," Eléazard responded, looking pensive. "And to you too, Euclides."

"Right, perhaps you will now tell me to what I owe the pleasure of your visit?"

"The Kircher biography, as always. I hope you don't find it too tedious."

"On the contrary, as you well know. It's the kind of mental exercise I delight in and it's excellent for my last remaining neurons; old machines need more care and attention than new ones."

"You wouldn't happen to have anything by Mersenne or La Mothe Le Vayer in your library? I'm sure Father Kircher, or at least Caspar Schott, plagiarizes them in certain passages."

"What makes you think that?"

"A sense of déjà vu, certain free-thinking turns of phrase, little anomalies that don't tally with what I remember. I've written to a friend in Paris to ask him if he can do some research along those lines, but I wondered if you perhaps could help me save time."

Dr. Euclides closed his eyes and concentrated for several seconds before replying. "No, I'm sorry, I've got nothing by them. I do remember having studied them at the seminary, Mersenne especially, as I'm sure you can imagine. A fine mind, by the way, who unjustly remains in the shadow of his friend Descartes. You could perhaps consult Pintard—*Les Érudits libertins au XVIIe siècle*— I'm not absolutely sure about the title, but it'll be shelved under history. I've got two or three things on rationalism and Galileo as well, but I don't think they'd be much use to you."

"I should never have accepted such a commission," Eléazard sighed, shaking his head. "I really need to be in Paris or Rome to study the manuscript properly. I haven't a hundredth of the things I need."

"I can well believe that. Let us assume, since everything seems to be leading you to that conclusion"—Dr. Euclides leaned toward Eléazard, resting his elbows on his knees—"let us assume Schott or Kircher did plagiarize this or that author, and let us assume you have the formal proof you're looking for: tell me sincerely, what difference would it make?"

Disconcerted by Euclides's question, Eléazard gathered his thoughts, carefully choosing his words as he replied. "I will have shown that, as well as having been wrong about everything, which is excusable, he was also a sanctimonious hypocrite, a man who consciously cheated the people of his day."

"And you would be going down the wrong road . . . insofar as you would be confirming something of which you are already sure, even before having examined your hypothesis as what it must remain until the end : a *hypothesis*. Although I'm not clear about the reasons, I have gathered that you don't like this poor Jesuit very much. Every time you talk about him, it's to criticize him for something, in general terms for not having been Newton, Mersenne or Gassendi . . . Why would you want him to be anything other than himself, Athanasius Kircher? Take a look at La Mothe Le Vayer, for example, a free thinker, a skeptic after your own heart. Now there's a nasty piece of work for you! He denied his fine ideas ten times over, out of ambition, out love of power and money. Newton, Descartes? Look closely and you'll see that they're not as pure as the history of science, the new *Legenda Aurea*, would have us believe. As soon as you are interested in something or someone, they become interesting. It's a truism. The converse is also true: you decide someone's a rogue and he'll become one in your eyes, as sure as eggs are eggs. It's autosuggestion, my friend. All of history is nothing but this self-hypnosis in the face of the facts. If I could persuade you, by putting on an act, that you had swallowed a bad oyster, you'd be sick, physically sick. I don't know who or what put it into your head that Kircher was contemptible, but that's what has happened and nothing will make you change your mind as long as you haven't identified the process that has led you to 'somatize' this result."

"You are laying it on a bit thick, Doctor," Eléazard said, slightly ill at ease. "History is what really happened. Kircher didn't decipher the hieroglyphs, though he thought, or gave the impression that, he had. No one can maintain the opposite without being looked on as a crank. Most of the scholars of his day suspected that was the case before there was any actual proof. Today it's a fact."

"True, my friend, true. But why do you go on about it? If you pick out that failure, it's simply to provide grist for another mill: you want to prove that Father Kircher was a forger. That's where you move into a fantasy world, in this relentless determination to show that his reputation is based on fraud. You quoted Ranke, I have another for you. Read Duby again: the historian, he says, is a dreamer forced—"

"Forced by the facts not to dream, despite his propensity to do so!"

"No, my friend: forced to dream in the face of the facts, to plaster over the gaps, to replace of his own accord the missing arm of a statue that only exists in his head. You're dreaming up Kircher at least as much as he dreamed himself up, as much as we all dream ourselves up, each in his own way . . ."

"Perhaps," Eléazard said, refilling their glasses in a state of agitation, "but when my imagination copies out the best pages of Nobili or Boym without quoting them, as he does in his *China Monumentis*, it is still downright plagiarism and it is not to his credit. What do you make of that? Surely you're not going to justify this regular pillage?"

Dr. Euclides took a sip of cognac before replying. "His plagiarism is unworthy of him, I agree. My initial reaction is the same as yours, but I am aware that in that I am following contemporary convention . . . The crux of the problem is the creative act itself, the fact that one cannot conceive of it without having recourse to imitation."

"But imitation is not, nor has it ever been simply copying a text, it —"

"Please, let me try to explain. Voltaire and Musset were extremely scathing about plagiarism—I seem to recall that you have a certain admiration for the first of those, haven't you?"

"That is true," Eléazard confessed, without having the least idea where his old friend's argument was leading.

"Voltaire gave out complete poems by Maynard as his own; as for Musset, you remember his 'I loathe plagiarism as much as I loathe death; my glass is not big, but I drink out of my own glass'? He borrowed scenes from Carmontelle! Whole scenes, apart from the odd comma! Compare his *Le Distrait* with Musset's *On ne saurait penser à tout* and you'll see what I mean. You want more examples? Take Aretino: the whole of his *History of the Goths* is translated from Procopius, using a manuscript of which he thought he owned the only copy . . . Machiavelli? The same scenario with his *Life of Castruccio Castracani* where he puts the *Apothegms* of Plutarch in the mouth of his hero . . . Ignatius Loyola? Have a look at Cisneros's *Spiritual Exercises* and you'll be surprised . . ."

"Ignatius Loyola!" Eléazard exclaimed.

"Not word for word, but very much 'inspired by,' which wouldn't have been so bad if he'd acknowledged his debt, as La Fontaine did with Aesop, for example."

"In that last case it's a reworking. And I'm sure you'll agree that La Fontaine is somewhat superior to the original as far as the form is concerned."

"Got you there!" Euclides said, wagging his finger at him with a mischievous look. "It's exactly the same whether you're plagiarizing someone's words or ideas. The whole history of art, and even of knowledge, consists of this assimilation, taken to greater or lesser lengths, of what others have tried out before us. No one has been able to avoid it since the beginning of time. It's not worth commenting on, except to say that our imagination is limited, which we've always known, and that books are only made with other books. Pictures with other pictures. We've been going round and round in circles since the very beginning, round the same pot, the same mess tin."

"I'm not that sure . . . But anyway, what's to stop some people from putting quotation marks when they use other people's work? Apart from the desire for fame, the aspiration to pass for something they aren't?"

"Just think about it a bit. When Virgil uses a line from Quintus Ennius as if it were one of his own, and he did it several times, whether you like it or not . . . No, sorry, it's not going to work with that example. Let's take that sentence from Ranke you quoted just now instead: *History is what really happened.* You had the good grace to make a pause and to indicate by your intonation that it wasn't something of your own. Right. Now I could interpret your tone because we've been friends for years, but someone else could have assumed that you had just produced that definition yourself. And yet you don't consider yourself a plagiarist."

"That's unfair, I knew that you were familiar with it!"

"Agreed, but that's not the point. How often do we go down that slippery slope? My own quotation from Duby, for example. I've never read the book it's taken from. I don't even know if I've seen it quoted somewhere or just heard it said as coming from him. Perhaps he never even wrote it; that often happens with the kind of maxim that's on everybody's lips without anyone bothering to check the source. A rumor, when it comes down to it, nothing but a rumor. Just think, no conversation would be possible at all if we had to justify every one of our words. *History is what really happened* . . . Can you be sure no one wrote or spoke that banal little formulation before Ranke? To be able to use a single sentence without quotes, our memory would have to contain everything that's been said since back in the mists of time! The search for whoever originally coined a phrase would be infinite, it would simply result in silence. To get back to Kircher: why should one not have one's doubts about the authors he plagiarizes as well? Who can guarantee that Mersenne himself didn't rob some student of his discoveries? Where do the quotation marks stop? If I write: History is what really disappeared, have I the right to claim it as my own property, or should I write: *History is what really* disappeared, with a footnote to render unto Ranke that which is Ranke's? We might as well put every word in the dictionary in quotes, every one of their possible combinations, for even when I produce them, I can't be certain that they aren't already there in billions of books I'll never read. You see what I'm getting at, Eléazard: the important thing is the universal gray matter, not the individuals who, by chance or consciously, become owners of it."

"Well, well," said Eléazard in astonishment, "for someone who doesn't feel in form . . . You must admit you're going a bit far. I can't believe you attach so little importance to literary or artistic property."

"There's the rub, my friend. There was a time when neither books nor products of the mind in general brought in anything at all for their authors. Court proceedings against pirated editions only start with industrial mercantilism. You don't find that strange?"

"But fame and glory, Doctor? The glory enjoyed by a Virgil or a Cervantes, by an Athanasius Kircher, 'the man of a hundred arts,' the 'genius' revered by everyone?"

"'Rome that I hate, and will ever so remain, Rome for whose sake my lover thou hast slain!' Perhaps you know who wrote that?"

"Corneille, of course," Eléazard replied, feeling such an elementary question was almost an insult.

"No he didn't, my friend, he didn't. It was Jean Mairet, a poor fellow who ought to have been grateful to Corneille for having plagiarized him; it's only thanks to this that he's still mentioned in a few learned commentaries. Even if he had taken action against the thief, it would have done nothing to change the unfortunate truth: his tragedy was poor, Corneille's a success. Two or three borrowings are not enough to bring glory; it's clear that certain garments are far too large for the scribblers who fashion them. Let's be serious, shall we? Plagiarism is necessary! And even that simple assertion isn't by me, it's from Lautréamont: *we follow an author's words closely, we use his expressions, we delete a mistaken idea and replace it with a sound one* . . . Which he put into practice himself by shamelessly correcting the maxims of Pascal or Vauvenargues. *Poetry should be made by all*, he writes a bit further on. It's not the words themselves that are important, it's the things they modify around them, the things they set off in the mind that receives them. And the same for all the rest, Eléazard. Beethoven plagiarizes Mozart before becoming himself, as Mozart had done with Gluck, Gluck with Rameau, et cetera. Inspiration is just a nice word for imitation, which is itself just a variant of the word plagiarism. 'Stealer of slaves' as the Greek has it but also stealer of fire, a springboard to the stars."

Shaken by the reference to Lautréamont, Eléazard had lowered his guard. Dr. Euclides strung together a series of comparisons from the fine arts, invoking Aristotle and Winckelmann: Poussin had reproduced a Roman fresco, which had since disappeared, to make the background to one of his paintings, for a long time Turner had desperately tried to rival Poussin, Van Gogh copied Gustave Doré, Delacroix and Japanese prints; as for Max Ernst, he quite logically ended up cutting out others' engravings to recompose them in his own style. Picasso, Duchamp, there was no one true artist who had not, at least at the beginning, nurtured his talent with pastiche, parody and plagiarism . . .

Close to a technical knockout, Eléazard made a desperate attempt to slip Euclides's punches: 'You're not playing fair, Doctor, and you know it. I can see what you're getting at, but there's a clear difference between the acknowledged admiration of one artist for another and the fraud of appropriating part of his work. I can't see what's wrong with one painter imitating another to learn the craft, we're in agreement on that. Except that it has nothing to do with plagiarism. Is that even possible in painting?

Do you seriously think that nowadays you could paint a glass of water on top of an umbrella without being immediately accused of having plagiarized Magritte?"

"You like Magritte?"

"A lot, yes."

"All the worse for you . . ."

Euclides stood up with a haste that had a touch of irritation. Eléazard watched him as he scrutinized his bookshelves, muttering to himself, his face right up against the books. "There you are," he said, coming back to sit down with a little pile of books he kept on his knees. He put a big catalog of Belgian painting on the table "Find *The Man with the Newspaper*, please."

Eléazard knew the painting in question: a man was warming himself beside the stove while reading his newspaper. The same image was repeated in the three other compartments of the painting, the same stove, the same window and the same table, but without the figure.

"Done," he said with a hint of condescension.

Euclides handed him another volume, clothbound this time. "Now would you be so good as to find the article 'Stove, *Ideal* incandescent fuel with flue.'"

Smiling at the old man's eccentricity, Eléazard first of all glanced at the title—Bilz: *The Natural Method of Healing*—then at the polychrome cover, embossed as on the old *Collection Hetzel* books. On it a young woman was bathing in her beneficial rays two young children, who were sitting in the middle of nowhere. Eléazard noted the art nouveau style of the decoration and leafed through the book to find the entry suggested by the doctor: SELF-ABUSE; SINGING IS CONDUCIVE TO HEALTH; SPIRITS, LOW; SPITTING BLOOD; STAMMERING, how to cure in children; STAYS, see: "Women diseases of"; STIFF NECK; STOMACH WEAK AND SICKLY; STOVE: ("Ideal") incandescent fuel stove with flue.

At once his intrigued amusement turned to amazement. Without leaving him time to react, Euclides placed his finger on his lips. "Not now, I beg you," he said wearily, "we'll continue this conversation another time. I'm sorry, but I have to lie down for an hour or two." Nevertheless, he insisted on accompanying him to the door. "Give my best wishes to Kircher," he said out of the corner of his mouth and putting on the most serious of expressions, a pretense that almost made his friendly mockery disagreeable.

When she woke up early in the afternoon, Loredana had some difficulty gathering her memories. The rhythms of the *macumba* were still sounding a vague echo behind her headache. What had happened at the end of the ceremony? How had she managed to get back to the hotel? Alfredo's face had shut off her memory like an iron mask. The grubby light filtering through the venetian blinds seemed to be impregnating her clothes, scattered all over the room, with gray mold. Her will was urging her to get up, to get away from feeling the suffocation and sadness that marked her awakening, but her drowsiness pushed her far back toward the faint swirls of frayed dreams.

When she did finally manage to sit up in bed, the images of the previous night all had a grotesque look. She had thought there would be nothing for her in the experience and now realized, from her heightened feeling of anguish, that she had been wrong. Despite a short loss of consciousness that she put down to the drugs and alcohol, the consolation she had hoped for from the world of the *orixas* remained inaccessible. This new defeat overwhelmed her; her temples were moist with sweat that was running down her back in hostile trickles. Rather death, she told herself in her feeling of helplessness, than the uncertainty of still being alive, the horror of a constantly renewed reprieve.

A little later she went down to have something to eat. To her great relief, Alfredo was nowhere to be seen. After having grumbled that it wasn't the right time for lunch, Socorró agreed to give her a plateful of the *feijoada* that was simmering in the kitchen. She had hardly turned her back than Loredana spat out the first mouthful into her hand. The very idea of having to swallow something made her feel sick. Fearing the worst after a first spasm, she stood up, having decided to go back to her room, when Socorró came back to put a letter on the table. Before even opening it, Loredana knew what it contained.

"It's not good?" Socorró asked, an inscrutable look on her face as she pointed at the plate.

"It's not that . . ." she managed to reply, "but I'm not well. I have to go and lie down . . . But don't throw it away, I'll eat it all this evening. I assure you it's very good."

"How can you know? You haven't even tasted it."

"I'm sorry Socorró. I have to go upstairs. I feel ill . . ."

Feeling dizzy, she gripped the back of her chair, making a great effort not to faint.

"You mustn't play with the god of the cemetery," the old woman murmured as she took her arm, "it wasn't a good idea to go down there. Alfredo!" she called out then, "Come over here, the lady's unwell."

"It'll be all right, there's no need to bother," Loredana begged, unable to move a step. "It'll soon pass . . ."

She let them carry her up to her room. Alfredo looked drawn, but nothing in his attitude or his speech suggested he was embarrassed to see her. He came back to bring her an Alka-Seltzer and behaved toward her as usual. Loredana was convinced he couldn't remember anything.

Stretched out on her bed, she was still hesitating to open the letter. She mustn't let herself be influenced, must weigh the pros and cons again until the moment when she was absolutely sure she would not call her decision into question. Scraps of her conversation with Soledade came back to her, images over the surface of which her own death poured a black flood of raw fear.

ALCÂNTARA: *I want justice to be done, Monsieur Von Wogau!*

"Countess?" said Eléazard, looking up from his computer, "I'm delighted to see you."

"Please, call me Carlotta. I apologize for bursting in on you like this, but the girl insisted I should come up unannounced."

Eléazard went over to shake the hand she held out to him. "She was quite right. What can I get you? Fruit juice? Tea? Coffee?"

"Nothing, thank you."

For a brief moment Eléazard had assumed she had come to see Loredana, but her weary expression and the way her fingers gripped her document case suggested she had something else in mind.

"You must be concerned about your son," he said offering her a seat. "Euclides told me there was no news of the expedition to the Mato Grosso."

"Concerned is putting it mildly, I'm sick with anxiety. They've been officially reported missing. An army helicopter is setting out to search for them first thing tomorrow morning."

"I can understand your worry, but I have great confidence in Professor Walde. I've met him several times and he gave me the impression he wasn't a man to be involved in that kind of undertaking without thinking the matter through. He's anything but an adventurer, you know. There must have been some kind of hitch, you can imagine all sorts of things happening in that area. Walde will be furious when he learns they've started the search so soon."

"I pray God that you're right, Monsieur Von Wogau, but that's not the reason why I'm here. I . . ." She bit her lip, seeming to hesitate before taking the irrevocable step. "Journalists have a duty of confidentiality, do they not?"

"Just like doctors," Eléazard replied, his mind suddenly on the alert. "Or priests, if you like."

"Have you read the papers this morning?"

"Not yet, I spent the morning in São Luís, with Dr. Euclides, and I started work as soon as I got back."

With trembling hands, Carlotta unfolded the paper she'd brought with her, then pointed to one of the headlines on the front page:

TRIPLE MURDER IN ALCÂNTARA

Eléazard ran his eye over the article, then turned to look at Carlotta.

"It was my husband," she said, the tears welling up in her eyes. "I overheard him speaking to one of his lawyers on the phone."

Eléazard let her tell her story then asked a few questions, insisting she try to recall as accurately as possible the words used. Any doubts he may have had vanished when she showed him photocopies of a file devoted to the governor's land purchases; the name Carneiro was there, with a question mark followed by a handwritten note: *to be settled as a matter of urgency!* For a moment he had the feeling he had a time bomb in his hands . . . Links between the projected military base and Moreira's speculation gradually formed in his mind.

"What do you want me to do?" he eventually asked after thinking it over.

"I have already started divorce proceedings," she replied, trying to recover her composure. "I know him well, he didn't intend that, he can't have intended it . . . But there comes a moment when one has to answer for one's actions before men, so that one can answer for them before God. This crime must not go unpunished . . . I want justice to be done, Monsieur Von Wogau, by any means you judge necessary to bring that about."

"I will see to it," Eléazard said gently. "It's very courageous of you."

"That's not the word," Carlotta protested, eyebrows raised. "No, I don't think that's the right word . . ."

CHAPTER 24

Which tells of the unexpected way in which Kircher managed to decipher the sibylline writing of the French; in which we make the acquaintance of Johann Grueber & Henry Roth on their return from China & hear how they quarreled about the state of that realm

WITH HIS EXPERIENCED eye, Alban Gibbs noticed at once his friend's worried appearance. Kircher made no attempt to deceive him; this affair with the secret message was threatening his own reputation but also risked undermining the Society's standing, which was much more important. Explaining the details of the mystery to him, he eventually showed him the note with the text &, since Alban Gibbs did not know French at all, translated it:

"*Jade on lea sense at char ladder cracky,*" he said in lugubrious tones, "*chaff ale yea daw maze horde hey amber sad heard France arum . . .*"

I saw Gibbs repress a slight smile: my master's knowledge of English was perfect, but he had never succeeded—because he had never tried—to get rid of his strong German accent, which people regularly made fun of. This did not bother Kircher & he concentrated on his translation. Far from refining his pronunciation it seemed to me that he was actually trying to distort it even more.

"*Dove ray have heck tout lard her wreck ease pour rape Harry lens salt fate of Rancé parley gar deck horse dupe ape . . .*"

He stopped, looking thoughtful, as if he were going through the words he had just spoken in his mind. Then he repeated, "*parley gar deck horse dupe ape,*" & his face lit up. "*Danke, mein Gott!*[1] he suddenly exclaimed &, with a little dance step (something I had never seen him do before), "*Parley gar deck horse dupe ape!* Ho, ho! I've got it, my friends, I've got it! And it's all thanks to you, Alban."

Gibbs gave me a worried look & I felt a shiver of fear myself at the idea that my master might have gone beyond the borders of his mind.

"*Parma pare hole,*" Kircher went on, increasingly exultant, "*jape rove, rat if ye egg hare anti toss kill aura dace heyday invert hew dupe recent mess age!* It works, my friends! *Fetter sin germ hen, lave ant see doubt mill sea scent sauce end do* . . . And it's already 3 October! *Sign yellow ye Eyck rid sap rope main* . . . My God, Louis XIV! We must hurry, we've wasted too much time already!"

Kircher seemed to wake from a dream. Becoming aware of our presence & our dumbfounded expressions, he gave us the explanation of his agitation while he dressed to go out: "You must excuse my haste, but this is a most serious matter. It is essential I communicate the contents of this letter to the Supreme Pontiff."

1 Thank you, God!

"But . . . the code," I ventured to ask.

"Nothing simpler & nothing more ingenious. Listen to what I'm saying as if I were speaking French: *parley gar deck horse dupe ape*. What do you hear but: *par les gardes corses du Pape*? That is the way the whole message works, you can reconstitute the meaning easily. Wait for me here, I'll be back before long."

As soon as my master had left, I pounced on the letter & unravelled the text following his indication:

> *Je donne licence à Charles de Créqui, Chevalier de mes ordres &*
> *Ambassadeur de France à Rome, d'oeuvrer avec toute l'ardeur*
> *requise pour réparer l'insulte aux Français par les gardes corses du*
> *Pape. Par ma parole, j'approuve, ratifie & guarantis tout ce qu'il*
> *aura décidé en vertu du présent message. Fait à Saint-Germain, le*
> *26 d'août 1662. Signé Louis & écrit de sa propre main.*[2]

Alexander VII was delighted with Kircher's success; he immediately had the two guards who had molested the Duke hanged & made dispositions to keep the French in Rome under surveillance.

The days that followed this episode, which Athanasius had merely seen as an occasion to exercise his skill, took on a different aspect. Kircher realized that a secret language was as useful as a universal language & was related to it as darkness is to light. In this my master was not for one moment thinking

---

2 I give leave to Charles de Créqui, Knight and French Ambassador in Rome, to do everything required to avenge the insult done to the French by the Corsican guards of the Pope. I hereby approve, ratify & guarantee all steps he should deem it necessary to take by virtue of the present message. Done at Saint-Germain, 26 August 1662. Signed Louis & written in his own hand.

of serving kings or other persons who wanted to hide their
correspondence, but simply of serving the truth. For if it
was good to reveal knowledge & propagate it, it was not less
necessary, sometimes, to restrict certain information to those
wise enough to make proper use of it. Which the priests of
ancient Egypt had done by inventing the hieroglyphs, as had
a number of other nations such as the Hebrews with their
Cabbala, the Chaldaeans or even the Incas of the New World.
Accordingly my master decided to invent a language that was
truly indecipherable & while I put the finishing touches to his
Polygraphia, he devoted himself entirely to that project.

The year 1664 was marked by the return to Rome of Father
Johann Grueber. When, eight years previously, he had been about
to go to China, he had promised Kircher, at his request, to be his
eyes there and to observe everything he could, down to the least
details that might serve to satisfy his curiosity about that country.

Aged forty-one, Johann Grueber looked much younger,
despite the strain of the journey. He was a sturdy man with a
massive but well-proportioned head, a flowing beard & fairly
long black hair, which he threw back over his shoulders. His
skin had been tanned by the desert sun, his gestures were slow
& measured. His gray eyes, slanting as if from his long stay in
China, had a slightly timid, almost dreamy look that still seemed
to be fixed on those marvelous countries that he admitted he
had only left with great regret. Of a jovial disposition, great
courtesy & a very pleasant German frankness, he was such a
gentleman that even if he had not been a Jesuit he would have
enjoyed the esteem of everyone he encountered.

Father Henry Roth was a striking contrast with Grueber:
small & puny with sparse white hair, he compensated for
his apparent constitutional weakness with a moral rigor and
authority in dogma that impressed us all.

After the effusive welcome home & a few days rest, the two travelers came to recount to Kircher everything they had observed during their peregrinations. Aware that my master was working on a major book about China, they humbly decided that there was no point in publishing their own writings on the subject; however, unwilling to allow the spiders & worms to eat away at this precious material in a corner of the library, they happily entrusted it to Kircher so that he could incorporate their observations in his book, which, in truth, was the best way of making them known to the widest number of people.

The first news we heard from Grueber's lips was the death of our dear Michal Boym, which affected my master more than I can say . . .

After leaving Lisbon at the beginning of 1656, Father Boym had arrived in Goa one year later. Held up in that town for various reasons, later besieged by the Dutch, he had only reached the kingdom of Siam in 1658. Once he was in Macau & still bearing letters from Pope Alexander VII for the Chinese Empress Helena & the eunuch general Pan Achilles, he found that the Portuguese authorities refused him permission to return to China out of fear of reprisals against them from the Tartars. Determined to face any danger to accomplish his mission, Father Boym embarked in a junk, accompanied by the convert Xiao Cheng, & reached Tonkin, from where he reckoned he could cross unseen into China. In 1659, after further delays while looking for guides capable of helping them to cross the frontier, the two men finally succeeded in entering the Celestial Empire by the province of Kwangsi. It was, alas, only to find all the passes blocked by the Tartar army. Seeing that it was impossible to continue by that route, Boym decided to return to Tonkin to try another way, but the government of that country would not authorize this. Trapped in the jungle, where he was hiding from the Tartars & depressed by the failure of his mission, Boym was struck down with the "Vomito negro" & called on his Maker after suffering terrible agonies. Faithful to his master even in those extremely distressing moments, Xiao Cheng buried the good father beside the road, together with the missives for which the unfortunate man had given his life, then planted a tree on his grave and escaped through the mountains. One year later he reached Canton, which Grueber happened to be visiting, & recounted the sad end of that excellent man to him.

Kircher had a mass said in memory of his friend during which he gave a sermon recalling Boym's numerous works on botany while emphasizing the human qualities of a man who, from that moment on, could be looked upon as a martyr to the faith.

These reflections on the difficulties encountered by Boym in carrying out his mission made it necessary to have a report on developments in China, which Father Roth provided for us quickly, but leaving no doubt as to his familiarity with the material. To spare the reader tiresome details, it is sufficient to recall that the heir to the Ming emperors, his son Constantin & all his faithful followers, among whom was the eunuch Pan Achilles, were exterminated in 1661 by the Tartar armies of Wu San-Kuei in the province of Yunnan, where they had taken refuge. Since 1655 the Tartar Emperor Shun-chih, founder of the Ch'ing dynasty, had made great & ultimately successful efforts to establish his power in a China that had finally been completely conquered. An enlightened sovereign, patron of Chinese arts & letters, he had succeeded in restoring peace to his kingdom & governed with discretion a nation that hardly looked favorably on his race. From invader, he transformed himself into the defender of China &, what was very important for the Church, showed greater favor to our Jesuit missionaries than any monarch before him, an attitude that allowed us great hope for the progress of the Christian religion in those distant lands.

Grueber, however, modified this idyllic report.

"What distressed me most," he said, "was to see, while I was traveling upriver on a Dutch boat, the cruelty with which the Tartars treated the Chinese pulling our vessel, which was simply the result of the natural hatred between the two nations. To tell the truth, hatred is nothing but cold, pernicious malice; it's always sitting on a few serpent's eggs from which it hatches out an infinite number of disasters &, not content with pouring its venom over particular places & at particular times, goes to the ends of the earth & on to eternity. This teaches us that it is difficult to make a whole empire love a man, as if one were claiming one could start friendships by cannon fire. Don't keep going on about a Nero, a Caligula, a Tiberius, a Scylla or other Roman emperors, don't talk to me of the Scythians, the Etruscans & other nations who boasted of their cruelty. I can truly say that I have never seen anything more cruel, nor more perfidious than the behavior of the Tartars toward their wretched captives. I have seen those stony-hearted creatures smile at the terrible groans, even at the death throes of the poor Chinese worn down by hunger, blows & labor. You would say, Father Athanasius, that they were made up of instruments of torture or, rather, demons that had slipped into that beautiful kingdom to make it into a hell on earth. They think that the principal mark of their power is to squeeze the life out of those miserable bodies drop by drop; would it not be more secure & more useful for these proud conquerors to assuage the just rancor of their vanquished subjects, to adopt gentler habits, pleasures without such excesses, splendor without such deviousness & devotion without so many crimes and torments—"

Father Roth protested, accusing his colleague of
exaggeration in the picture he had painted, but Kircher
intervened to calm them down. "There are, alas, some loves
and hates that one cannot put on & take off as easily as a
shirt. Anger is more transitory, more specific, more seething
& easier to cure, but hate is more deep-rooted, more general,
more joyless & irremediable. It has two notable properties,
one of which consists of aversion & flight, the other of
persecution & harming. These degrees of hatred are so
widespread in nature that they can even be found in brute
beasts who, no sooner have they been born, than they are
pursuing their enmities and wars in the world. A little chicken
with its shell still stuck to it has no fear of a horse or an
elephant—which ought to seem such frightening animals to
those unaware of their natures—but it is already in terror of
the sparrow-hawk & as soon as it sees one goes to hide under
its mother's wing. The lion trembles at the crow of the cock;
the eagle hates the goose so much that just one of its feathers
will burn the whole of a goose's plumage; the stag persecutes
the snake, for by breathing deeply at the entrance to its hole, it
pulls it out & devours it. There is also eternal enmity between
the eagle & the swan, between the crow & the kite, the mole
& the owl, the wolf & the sheep, the panther & the hyena,
the scorpion & the tarantula, the rhinoceros & the viper, the
mule & the weasel, & between many other animals, plants or
even rocks that are repugnant to each other. These harmful
contradictions also exist among the idolaters & can be seen,
you say, between the Tartars & the Chinese, but God has
made it possible for us, in contrast to the rest of the natural
world, to overcome these antagonisms & settle differences in
a merciful way. And there can be no doubt that the progress
of the Christian religion in the land of China will extinguish

these enmities just as thoroughly as water will destroy the immemorial hatred opposing wood to fire.

"But tell me," he went on with a smile, "haven't you brought back any curios from China that might help to lessen my ignorance about that realm and what there is there?"

Father Roth nodded his agreement, took a handful of dried plants out of his bag, handed them to Kircher. "Even though this herb, which they call *cha* or *tea,* exists in numerous locations in China, it grows better in some places than in others. They make a beverage with it that they drink very hot & its beneficial properties are widely known, since not only all the inhabitants of the great empire, but also those of India, of Tartary, of Tibet, of Mogor & all the regions of the Orient take it up to twice a day—"

Kircher gestured him to stop. "There is no need to go on," he said in friendly tones, "for I already know this remarkable herb. I would never have believed it had so many beneficial properties if the late lamented Father Boym had not made me try it some years ago. As I have been taking it regularly since then, I can tell you that, having a purgative quality, it opens up the kidneys marvelously so that their ducts become very wide & allow urine, sand & stones to pass through; it similarly purges the brain & prevents smoky vapors from troubling it, so that there is not a more effective restorative for scholars & men who are so overloaded with business they are constantly compelled to burn the midnight oil: taking this herb not only helps them to bear their work & relieves their weariness, providing the strength necessary to go without sleep, it also gives so much pleasure to one's taste buds that once one has accustomed oneself to its acrid & slightly insipid taste, one cannot stop oneself taking as much as one can. What we can say is that the *coffee* of the Turks & the *cocolat* or *chocolate* of the Mexicans, which seem to have the same effect, do not do so to the same extent, since *cha* has a more temperate quality than the two others; we have noticed that *cocolat* is too warming in summer & *coffee* excites the bile to an extraordinary degree, which is not the case with *cha*, since one can take it at all times & with benefit, even if one were to take it a hundred times a day."

Father Roth could not conceal his disappointment at not having been able to provide a surprise for my master. He still congratulated him and gave him the *cha* he had brought from India so that he could compare its flavor and properties with that of China, a present for which Kircher expressed his great satisfaction.

"I thought of you as well," said Grueber, taking a little package out of his cassock. "Here is a paste made out of a certain herb of the province of Kashgar. It is called *Quey* or 'the herb that banishes sorrow' & possesses, as its name indicates, the quality of producing joy & laughter in those who have taken it. Even better, it is a tonic and stimulates the heart, a quality I have observed myself on numerous occasions when I was eating it to help me climb the steep slopes of Tibet."

"It could be," Kircher replied, "that we have a similar herb here, namely *Apiorisus*, & I would have no difficulty believing such a plant was to be found in that country, if it was said to be poisonous; but you say it is one of the cardiac plants that promote good health, which I cannot understand and will not subscribe to until I have tried it."

"If you insist, Reverend, but you will have to mix it with jam or honey, since by itself it is unpleasant to the palate."

At a sign from my master I was about to do the necessary when the gong sounded. By the communication tube the porter announced that Cavaliere Bernini was requesting an interview. Kircher had him sent up immediately, delighted at the thought of seeing his old friend again.

"To work! To work!" Bernini cried when he appeared on the threshold of the library. "Alexander has need of us."

Kircher went over to him, not without apologizing to those present for the sculptor's impetuous nature. "So," he said, "could you tell me the reason for this deafening entry?"

"Of course, Reverend, nothing simpler. I have just heard, from a very reliable source, that the Supreme Pontiff, in imitation of the late Pamphilius, wants to erect an obelisk in Piazza della Minerva & has seen fit to involve us once more in the design of the project. I therefore came as quickly as I could to give you the news, knowing you would be as delighted as I am."

"I am, indeed, very pleased, but are you absolutely sure of what you say?"

Bernini went up to my master and whispered a few words in his ear.

"In that case," Kircher said, a joyful look on his face, "there is no doubt at all; I am delighted at your good fortune as well as at the trust the Holy Father has shown us. But let me introduce Father Roth & Father Grueber to you, they have just returned from China & I cannot hear enough of their adventures there . . ."

MATO GROSSO: *In the dead mouth*

They'd been trotting along for two hours, escorted by the Indians who were following the trail marked by Yurupig. Elaine forced herself to talk to Dietlev; she sensed he was worried because of his continuing high temperature and tried to reassure him: "It's almost over now, they must know the forest inside out, they'll get us back much more quickly than we could by ourselves. There might even be a mission somewhere around here."

Dietlev looked skeptical. "I'd give my right hand . . ." He paused, confused by the unintended relevance of the expression. "Well, perhaps not," he went on with an apologetic smile. "Let's say I would swear these people have never had contact with Whites."

"Oh come on, that's just not possible. Not round here, at least. What makes you say that?"

"In the reservations, and even in the forest, there are always some the missionaries have persuaded to wear shorts. But above all it's the way they behave, the way they look at us . . . Did you see the way the machete caught their eye?"

Elaine was shaken by his argument. "You think they're the ones who stole the rucksack?"

"There's a strong chance they were," Dietlev agreed. "They must have been watching us for a good while. Herman, have you any idea what tribe they might belong to?"

Petersen shook his head. "Not the least, *amigo*. They don't look like anything I've seen in this part of Amazonia. I don't know where they might've come from; if they've already seen a white man it's so long ago they've forgotten."

"When I think what some ethnologists would pay to be in our place!" Mauro said. "And your daughter would be one of the first, wouldn't she?"

"That's for sure," said Elaine, turning toward him. "I wonder how she would have reacted? They scared the pants off me. Did you see the color of their mouths?"

"They chew tobacco." Petersen said, "even the kids. It's general among the Indians."

"Well at least they seem to know where they're going," Mauro said. "That's something to be grateful for."

"I wouldn't be so sure about that," Herman grunted, "it's ages since I saw one of Yurupig's marks."

Carried away by the conviction that everything would be all right now, Elaine had paid no attention to the way they were going. She realized, at the same time as Mauro and Dietlev, that none of them could have said whether they were still going in the right direction.

"And it's not even worth bothering trying to get our bearings," said Dietlev in disgust.

"We should have kept the compass," Petersen said in vaguely reproachful tones. "They're taking us for a walk, that's all."

"You always look on the dark side," Mauro said. "At least things can't be any worse than before they turned up. They could have killed us ten times over if they'd wanted . . ."

That idea had never occurred to Elaine, even during the first moments of their encounter with the Indians. Now, when even Dietlev fully agreed with Mauro, pointing out how quickly they'd taken charge of the stretcher, Elaine was suddenly seized with retrospective fear that she could not overcome.

Ignoring their conversation, the Indians continued at a rapid pace, gathering herbs as they passed or collecting a handful of caterpillars, which they ate belching copiously and clicking their tongues.

No one had spoken for an hour when they entered a clearing where smoke was rising from a few huts made of palm leaves and branches. There were women, children and other Indians there who froze at the sight of the strangers, mouth open, their wad of tobacco almost falling out. They looked, unable to believe their eyes, at these unnatural animals the hunters had brought back from their expedition in the forest. A long murmuring was heard, then an imperious yap that made all eyes turn to one of the huts: the emaciated body of a very old man appeared in the entrance. A feathered maraca in one hand, his wad of tobacco stuck between his teeth and his lower lip, he walked in dignified fashion over to the stretcher, while the warriors made a circle around him. Once there, he pulled at Dietlev's beard, as if to make sure it wasn't false, and stepped back with clear signs of satisfaction: his scouts had not lied, God's Messenger had come, as his father had told him, as the father of his father had always affirmed, as had been predicted since time immemorial. The prophecy was fulfilled at last. Why did the Messenger only have one leg? Why did he say incomprehensible things instead of using the language of the gods, those ageless words he sang to his son as his father had sung them to him all those years ago? It was something he was not yet allowed to understand. But it did have meaning.

The shaman shook his gourd filled with seeds, breathed on the Messenger to drive away evil spirits and spoke the words of fire, *"Deusine adjutori mintende,"* he said, pointing to his head, his stomach and his arms. *"dominad juvano mefestine!"*

"There's an answer to our questions," Elaine said as she recognized the imitation of the sign of the cross in his gestures. "The White Fathers have been this way—"

"It's even better than that," Mauro broke in excitedly. *"Deus in adjutorium meum intendo; Domine ad adjuvandum me festina:* "O God, come to my assistance; O Lord make haste to help me." Psalm 69, I repeated it often enough when I was an altar boy. This guy can speak Latin!"

When he heard Mauro, the shaman started turning round and round. His wad of tobacco kept poking out between his smiling lips like a parrot's tongue.

"We are going to the river," Dietlev said, gathering together what scraps of Latin he could remember. "The white men . . . The town!"

"Gloria patri!" the shaman said, delighted to hear the sounds of the sacred language. *"Domine Qüyririche, Quiriri-cherub!"* He was enraptured. The father had come, the silent one, the

royal falcon! Nothing now could stop them taking off for the Land-with-no-evil.

"*Quiriri quiriri!*" Petersen muttered, mimicking the old Indian. "All these grimaces are starting to get on my nerves. This macaque's half crazy, he can't understand a single word of what you're saying. The way he's going on, we're in for something, I can tell you."

It was at that moment that Elaine saw a second machete in the hands of one of the warriors. It could be a coincidence, but she was sure it was one of theirs, the one Yurupig had taken, to be precise. Petersen had followed her glance.

"*Amigo,*" he said through his teeth to Dietlev, "you'd do better to give me the gun. They're not a nice lot, they've done in Yurupig . . ."

"No they haven't," Elaine said without thinking. "What proof do you have that—"

"It's Yurupig's," Petersen said firmly. "There's no getting around it, look at the way he's holding the machete—it's the first time that guy's had one in his hand. I'm ready to bet he's the one that bumped him off."

"Stop being paranoid, will you!" Dietlev said, wiping his forehead. "You can see that they mean us no harm. You can have the gun, if you like, I threw the cartridge clip away en route."

"You idiot, you fucking idiot! Tell me you didn't do it."

"I'm tired, Herman. I'm absolutely whacked, so you try and find some way of communicating with them. I'm not going to be able to hold out much longer."

Elaine was close to tears. Every time things got a bit more complicated. Despite what Dietlev had said—admirable as it was, his courage was distressing to see—she was sure something had happened to Yurupig.

"He must know how to treat you," Mauro said with no great conviction in his voice. "Look," he went on to the shaman, "he's ill. Do you understand?" And pointing to the stump of Dietlev's leg, "He needs treatment. Water? Drink?" he said, making as if to put a cup to his lips.

The shaman's eyes lit up. Me, Raypoty, distant grandson of Guyraypoty, I'm going to lead my people to the Land-of-eternal-youth. That had just been clearly confirmed: Qüyririche, the Messenger, the One-with-pubic-hair-on-his-face, would give them all the water of youth to drink. They had to give him a fitting welcome, honor him with a festival that would delight both him and his companions.

He gave a few orders to those around; two young warriors picked up the stretcher and the crowd parted to let them through toward the largest of the huts. Seeing Elaine follow her companions in, the men of the tribe let out a murmur of disapproval. Raypoty immediately silenced them; this woman was Nandeçy, the mother of the Creator, his mate, his daughter. An immortal spirit, like the other strangers. She could enter the men's house without fear and contemplate herself the sacred objects she had handed down to the Apapoçuva people. They would dance to draw her favor down on them, to thank her for having come with Qüyririche, then they would all set off for the Land-with-no-evil . . .

The men's house was simply a large hut where the males of the tribe gathered for various ritual occasions. There wasn't much in it apart from a few mats, a hearth, gourds of different sizes, some small benches and several ornamental feather garments hanging from the central pillar. The walls of crudely woven palm leaves let in a dim light with moving shadows. The heat was stifling.

As soon as the Indians had left, Elaine attended to Dietlev. After having dissolved two aspirins and their last sulfonamide tablet in the bottom of a gourd, she forced the neck between his lips. She wanted to talk to him, reassure him, but nothing came to mind, such was her own need of comfort. Petersen watched her ministrations with a doubtful expression, every wrinkle in his face saying, "He's a goner for sure."

"I just can't believe it," Mauro said in a low voice. "What're we going to do?"

Elaine made an effort to throw off the despondency that had gripped her. The words came mechanically from her lips: "We'll wait a bit before leaving . . ." With a glance she indicated Dietlev, who had fallen asleep and was breathing with difficulty, his eyelids flickering, his jaw clenched. "We must manage to get them to understand what we want."

"That could take some time," Mauro said bleakly.

"You've got a better idea?" It had come out a bit sharply and Elaine immediately apologized. "Just ignore that, please. My head's in a whirl . . ."

"One of us—I mean Petersen or me—" he went on, "could perhaps go on alone?"

"Without Yurupig to guide you? You haven't a hope in hell."

Mauro's face darkened. "You really think that . . . that they've . . ."

"I sincerely hope not—and not just for our sakes. He was a decent guy and I wouldn't want anything to happen to him. At the moment there's no way of knowing."

The mat over the entrance was lifted and two Indians slipped in. As if hypnotized by Elaine, they put a bowl of fruit down in front of her, another filled with an indefinable brown broth and a waterskin. One of them spoke rapidly, pointing to the food, while the other put the rucksack they'd stolen from them on the floor with the rest. He grabbed the arm of his companion, who seemed rooted to the spot by the sight of the strangers, and dragged him out.

"It looks as if they like us," Petersen said, having been roused from his somnolence by the appearance of the Indians.

"It's obvious," said Elaine, quickly opening the rucksack to check the contents. "They've taken nothing . . . apart from the fossils. Now that is odd."

Mauro had knelt down at the entrance to the hut. He peered out through the gaps in the mat for a moment.

"What are they doing?" Elaine asked.

"They're very busy. Some are sweeping, others building a kind of pyre . . . The women are pounding something for all they're worth. It's as if they were preparing a celebration or something like that."

"You can't see the cooking pot where they're going to boil us, by any chance?" Herman joked. As the only response was a reproachful silence, he turned over muttering, "You all piss me off. If you only knew . . . Youpissmeoff!"

THE INDIANS WERE painting each other; each painted on the other's face a blood-red variant of motifs that had probably come down through the ages. Bowls of *urucu* paste were passing from hand to hand; squatting down in a long line, the children were delousing each other, eager to nibble the tidbits taken from their neighbor's head. They decorated their shoulders with macaw or toucan feathers, white down was dribbled on their their mud-smeared hair, all the men seemed to dress up as quickly as possible as birds of the forest. However closely Mauro observed them, he could see no sign of contact with civilization. The women and children were completely naked; as for the men and adolescent boys, a simple bark strap around their hips kept their foreskin tight against their belly. Apart from the two machetes from the expedition, there was no other metal object to be seen: stone axes, knives made of bamboo cut to a point, gourds or crude pottery of clay coils. Preserved by some historical or geographical chance, this tribe had never known anything other than the solitude of the forest and it was as moving as seeing a live coelacanth. Mauro was in the same situation as the first explorers of the New World, the mercenaries fascinated by Eldorado. Or, rather, in that of the first white men to make the effort of approaching the Indians—for other purposes than to massacre them. How had the Westerners managed to communicate with them? How did they make a start?

"Elaine," he said all at once, an earnest look on his face, "I'm going to see the village chief. I must get him to understand what we want. You stay here with Dietlev." With that he walked out without giving her time to get a word in.

His appearance brought all the tribe's activity to an immediate halt. His forehead beaded with sweat, Mauro set off for the hut from which they'd seen the shaman emerge an hour ago. While the women and children stayed where they were, the men came over to him, gradually surrounding him as he progressed. The silence must have alerted the shaman, for Mauro was still twenty yards away from the hut when he slipped out under the mat and came to meet him.

"I'm called Mauro," he said, pointing to himself. "And you?" he added, pointing to him.

"*Aymacalado maro? Andu?*" the old man repeated, raising his eyebrows. The young god obviously wanted to teach him some new words of power; he concentrated to engrave them on his memory.

Mauro tried once more, instinctively simplifying his language: "Mauro," he said with the same gesture, forcing himself to enunciate clearly. "You?"

"*Maro-uu!*" the shaman immediately exclaimed.

Mauro gave a weary sigh. Perhaps they had to start with something simpler. He looked round for something basic to name, and with sudden inspiration, pointed to his own nose: 'My nose," he said, placing his finger on the said organ, "My nose."

"*Mainos!*" The shaman repeated as best he could. He was wondering why it was suddenly so important to smell, and which smell would be meaningful.

Mauro repeated his gesture, this time without saying a word.

"*Mainos?*" the shaman said again, sniffing the air around. "*Mainos, mainos, mainos?*"

The result was scarcely conclusive. Mauro gnawed his lip in irritation. Seeing a mat with unknown fruits piled up on it, he went over to it, followed by the shaman and the crowd of Indians. He picked up one of the fruits and simply held it out to the shaman without saying a word.

"*Jamacaru Nde,*" the shaman said gravely, "This *jamacaru* is yours."

"*Jamacaruende?*" Mauro repeated, trying as hard as he could to reproduce the sounds he had just heard precisely.

"*Naàni! Jamacaru Nde!*" No, it's yours, the old man insisted. If the young god wanted the fruit, he was welcome to it, it belonged to him, just as did everything that belonged to him and to the people of the tribe.

"*Nana, jamcaruende,*" Mauro repeated automatically, though realising that it didn't get him any farther. Was the fruit called *jamacaruende* or *nani*? Not to mention that they could also mean *yellow, ripe, eat* . . . or something else that hadn't occurred to him.

The shaman shook his head at such insistence. Disconcerted, he accepted the fruit Mauro was holding out to him, but hastily handed him two or three others. "I'm sorry, old chap, but I'm fed up with this," Mauro said in friendly tones, aware he'd got nowhere. "*Ciao!* I think I'll just go and have a sleep."

He was turning round when he saw, quite close to him, one of the Indians with a machete. As he stopped to check that it was indeed one of the expedition's implements, he notice the gleaming object round his neck: the compass! The compass they'd given Yurupig before he set off . . .

"Where did you get that?" he exclaimed, grabbing the object on the chest of the dumbfounded Indian. "Our compass, for fuck's sake!"

There was movement in the crowd and murmurs of indignation, but the shaman calmed them with a word. Nambipaia had behaved wrongly, he explained. He should not have taken that thing; the young god regarded it unfavorably. It had to be returned to its owner immediately.

Pushing the Indian by his shoulder, he invited Mauro to follow them. They all trooped to the edge of the village and gathered round a post stuck in the ground. On the top of the post was Yurupig's head, mouth open, eyes closed, like someone taking communion.

At a brief command from the shaman, Nambipaia took the compass from round his neck and pushed it into the dead mouth.

Eléazard's notebooks

AN ARABIC PROVERB used by Kircher as an epigraph to his *Polygraphia*: "If you have a secret, hide it, if not, reveal it." (*Si secretum tibi sit, tege illud, vel revela.*)

VILLIERS DE L'ISLE ADAM, like an echo: "And none among them is capable, in advance, of reaching the thought that a secret, however terrible it might be, is the same as nothing if it is never told."

THROUGH MATHEMATICS Kircher sought a yardstick, a universal language that could reduce multiplicity and resolve the apparent contradictions of the world. He dreamed of a return to the purity of mankind before the flight from Eden.

ACCORDING TO MALONE, of the 6,043 lines of verse in Shakespeare, 1,771 come from his predecessors, 2,373 have been reworked by him and only 1899 can still be attributed to him, perhaps for lack of material for comparison.

"THERE ARE SOME BOOKS," Voltaire wrote, "that are like the fire in your hearth; you go and get some fire from your neighbor, light it in your own home, pass it on to others and it belongs to everyone." (*Philosophical Letters*)

SAVED BY UMBERTO? "When Kircher set out to decipher the hieroglyphs, there was no Rosetta stone to guide him. This helps explain his initial, mistaken assumption that every hieroglyph was an ideogram. Understandable as it may have been, this was an assumption that doomed his enterprise from the outset. Notwithstanding its eventual failure, however, Kircher is still the father of Egyptology, though in the same way that Ptolemy is the father of astronomy, in spite of the fact that his main hypothesis was wrong. In a vain attempt to demonstrate his hypothesis, Kircher amassed observational material and transcribed documents, turning the attention of the scientific world to the problem of the hieroglyphs [. . .] Lacking the opportunity for direct observation, even Champollion used Kircher's reconstructions for his study of the obelisk standing in Rome's Piazza Navona, and although he complained of the lack of precision of many of the reproductions, he was still able to draw from them interesting and exact conclusions." (Umberto Eco: *The Search for the Perfect Language*, tr. James Fentress)

STRANGE how I've suddenly started finding quotations in favor of Athanasius.

AT THE END OF THE EIGHTEENTH CENTURY there were still eminent scientists who maintained that "the Egyptian pyramids are large crystals or natural excrescences from the earth fashioned to a small degree by human hand."

MINOR OFFICIALS at the court of Louis XIV: Inspector of fresh butter, King's councillor for the woodstacks, Treasurer of the emergency fund for wars, Senior and biennial seedsman (works one year in two), Alternative and biennial seedsman (works during the years when the senior seedsman isn't working), Angevin examiner of pigs' tongues (has the pig beaten to make it stick its tongue out "in order to see if it is measly") . . .

BABEL, STILL . . . In eighteenth-century Germany the myth of an original language led two honest scientists to abandon two children in the woods in order to see what language they would start to speak in the absence of any linguistic models. The resulting aphasia should have put them on the right track . . .

KIRCHERIAN MINOR OFFICIALS: resuscitator of oysters and varnisher of dead lobsters.

CHAPTER 25

*On a Javanese pyramid, on the Quey herb & on what
followed . . .*

MY MASTER INTRODUCED Cavaliere
Bernini to our two visitors with many complimentary
remarks. Although quite different in temperament, Grueber
& the sculptor appeared to like each other from the very
beginning. Just as a cobbler would only have been interested
in the natives' footwear, or a roofer in their way of assembling
roof timbers, Bernini immediately turned the conversation to
the statues and monuments of Asia, asking if there were some
worthy of comparison with those of the West or of Egypt.
Henry Roth launched into a description of the buildings of
China, arguing very learnedly that though the Chinese, like
the Romans, excelled in the construction of walls, roads and
bridges, their statues, although often colossal, never reached
the refinement & beauty to be found in our countries. They
were nothing but coarse idols or monsters & demons whose

deplorably grotesque & sometimes even lubricious style owed so little to art that they ought to be seen as the work of the devil rather than of human beings.

Grueber took up the argument. "I agree with what has just been said, even though I have seen some statues in China that do not deserve the disapproval shown by Father Roth, for they often have a nobility & serenity that, to my mind, characterize the outstanding examples of Great Art. However, it wasn't in China but in the Sunda Islands that I came across the most divine sculpture you ever could see. And I am convinced, Signore Bernini, that even if you had merely glimpsed it you would consider it one of the wonders of the world."

"That is certainly something to whet my appetite. Would you do me the favor of describing it?"

"Willingly. But allow me first to describe the location: during my voyage to China I took a ship from Tonkin heading for Amacao that was thrown off course by a storm; we had to put in at Batavia, or Jacquetra, the capital of the island of Java—"

Seeing Bernini's baffled expression, Kircher came to the rescue by bringing over a large globe on which Grueber could point out the places he spoke of as he went on.

"There's such a large number of islands among the ins and outs of the Indian Ocean that there's no way of being sure how many there are. Sumatra—there—is the largest, Borneo the second, Java the third biggest. It has been called 'the world in miniature' because of its immense fecundity, of the ease with which it grows and produces all sorts of things. It not only gives us pepper, ginger, cinnamon, cloves & other aromatic spices but also harbors all sorts of animals, both wild & domesticated, which are exported to various foreign lands. There are also mines abundant in gold & precious stones of incalculable value. There are innumerable silks . . . In brief, it would be one of the richest & most pleasant islands of the East, if it were not too often ravaged by storms the mere expectation of which brings despair & terror to all parts. The islands' inhabitants claim to be descended from Chinese who in the past were so plagued by the perpetual privateering & invasions of the pirates that they abandoned their homeland & went to establish colonies on this island. The people are of middle height, with round faces, & the majority go completely naked or have little cotton cloths hanging from their belts down to their knees. I consider them the best mannered & most civilized of the Indians—"

"A true paradise on earth!" Bernini exclaimed. "Would that I were younger and wealthier so that I could go to that land!"

"A paradise, perhaps," Father Roth snorted, "but inhabited by demons! I know for a fact that they're greedy scroungers, they're brazen, impudent & arrogant & freely lie to get their hands on other people's property. These Indians are nothing but two-faced, mealy-mouthed, light-fingered thieves. They'll flatter you, make promises, swear by Heaven, Earth & Mahomet, until you take everything they say as the unvarnished truth; but if you talk to them one hour later, they'll brazenly deny everything they said! The language of men, they say, is not made of bones, by which they mean you can bend it to your will without it being constrained by oath."

Grueber & Bernini were dumbfounded at this sudden diatribe. An uncomfortable feeling of embarrassment spread among us & I could see that Grueber, eyes lowered, was biting his lip to repress a retort to his elder colleague.

"I'd no idea," my master said with feigned nonchalance, "that you had been to that island as well."

"To be honest," said Father Roth, slightly flustered, "I've never been there, but I had what I've just said from a Dutch merchant who had spent more than twenty years in Batavia & went on to me at length about the Javanese."

Kircher gave Father Roth a severe look: "Ask the wolf what he thinks of the sheep he devours or keeps under his sway & he will always tell you that the poor creatures deserve their misfortune because of their numerous faults & if he concerns himself with them it is only out the goodness of his heart. For that reason I would be wary of giving credence to what your merchant says. That the Javanese are idolaters & that it is proving difficult to convert them to the true religion, I can well believe; but that they are demons forever impervious to reason & divine compassion is something I cannot accept. Nor can you, I am sure, Reverend Father . . ."

Father Roth apologized, albeit grudgingly, then asked to be allowed to retire, pleading his age & the strain of the journey. Bernini made no attempt to hide his delight at seeing such a carping tongue depart, for which he was given a friendly reproof by my master.

"You were saying, Father Grueber?"

"Well, while my ship was stuck in the harbor of Batavia I heard marvelous reports of a very ancient city, which was said to have been swallowed up by the jungle, a few days' journey by mule from a small town called Djokdjokarta. Driven as much by my own curiosity as by my promise to report to you, Reverend Father, anything out of the ordinary, I had myself taken there. To get to the point—& leaving aside the travails of the journey, which I had been warned would be as difficult as it was hazardous—the first sight I had of Boeroe Boedor, the 'lost city,' came when, after one last turning, my guides pointed with trembling fingers at a little black mountain rising from a sea of luxuriant vegetation. But as I approached it I saw that not one inch of this hill of stone had escaped the sculptor's chisel; & I think I am not wrong in saying that his pyramid was, on a base a hundred paces square, forty paces high!"

I saw Kircher's face suddenly light up. "This 'pyramid,'" he asked excitedly, "would you say it resembled those that can be seen in Egypt?"

"Not exactly. In form it was more like the structures of the ancient Mexicans as our missionaries have drawn them. Visualize four square tiers, each surmounted by a round terrace, the whole reducing in size as it rises up."

"Forgive my impatience, Reverend Father, but you still haven't described the sculptures you spoke so highly of."

"Of course, I'm sorry . . . All along the galleries or the paths going from the base to the summit are some fifteen hundred bas-reliefs that, put end to end, would stretch over five leagues! From what I understood, these sculptures represent the life of Poussah or the idol, Fo, as it is recounted in the Chinese or Indian legends, but you would swear, Cavaliere, that they had been produced by the most talented of the Greeks, so perfect is the composition & so refined the ornamentation. There are more than 25,000 figures, a quarter or half in high relief, that come to life before our very eyes in such a natural way that there is nothing so beautiful in the whole world. Men & women, all in graceful postures, are walking, dancing, riding or praying in the most noble and refined attitudes: musicians are playing the flute or the drum, whole crews are busy on their proud vessels, sublime warriors are resting amid vegetation in which one can easily recognize all the trees, all the fruits, all the flowers & plants of the region, even those that have retaken possession of the stones & are inextricably intertwined with their own image. Elephants, horses, snakes, all kinds of fish and fowl can be seen in the postures typical of their species &, in a word, I could not imagine anything better than to spend my whole life as the simple warden of this sumptuous collection . . ."

Grueber fell silent. He seemed to have gone back in memory to Boeroe Boedor, contemplating the beautiful art he had just described to us.

"Why did you not make some drawings of these marvelous sculptures . . .' Bernini said pensively. "Your account has made my mouth water & I would give much to have accompanied you to that place."

"I have filled several books with drawings of them in wash & red chalk, which I intended to bring back to Europe; but God did not want that to happen, for it was doubtless He who inspired the young emperor of China with the desire to keep them in his possession."

"That is not so important," Kircher said, "for it is enough to have heard what you say to see in that temple the clear influence of ancient Egypt. Everywhere in Asia, as on your island of Java, you can find mystical pyramids & superb temples built on the model of those the Egyptians had erected to their guardian spirits. To put it in a nutshell, China is the ape of Egypt, given the naive way it imitates & resembles that country in everything."

Without it being clear to me why, Father Grueber suddenly went pale; I saw his jaw muscles tense as if he were fighting an intense pain.

"Are you unwell?" I immediately asked.

"No, not really . . . There is no need to be concerned. It's just . . . a nervous reaction that sometimes comes over me when I think of my journeys."

"Come, Caspar," my master said with urgency, "go quickly and fetch one of those bottles of Ho Bryan Mr. Samuel Pepys gave us; & then bring some jam, I think it is time to sample this famous herb that banishes sorrow."

"Spoken after my own heart, Reverend Father!" Bernini exclaimed, rubbing his hands. "But tell me, what is this herb to which you are going to treat us? If you are not deceiving us about its qualities, I will order a bale immediately for my personal use."

Kircher repeated to Bernini what Father Grueber had told us just before he arrived, not without making a friendly joke about him not needing this remedy at all, being inclined by his nature to good humor. So we ate some of this *Quey* as we drank & conversed.

"This plant," Grueber said, the wine apparently having brought some color back to his cheeks, "is very similar to hemp & grows in abundance in the province of Xinjiang, but they don't use it in the same way as we do, for the Chinese don't know how to weave its fibers to make ropes."

To a further question from my master, Grueber continued to talk about the Chinese pharmacopoeia.

"I can tell you," he said, "that they use five types of quartz, of earth & of mushrooms, according to their respective colors. We use honey & Spanish flies, but they think that that is to deprive oneself of the marvelous qualities of the bees themselves, of wasps, of their wax & their nests, of galls, cocoons, clothes moths, cicadas, mosquitos, spiders, scorpions, centipedes, ants, lice, fleas, cockroaches & crab lice! These insects are prepared, sold & bought just as happens here with rhubarb & mandrake."

"Well I'll be damned!" Bernini exclaimed. "Why haven't we got such apothecaries in Rome! I haven't got the whole collection of your creepy-crawlies, but I've got enough of some of them to grow rich!"

We all burst out laughing, congratulating Bernini on his witticism, then joyously drank to his health and wealth.

"You find that list amusing," Grueber said, elated, "but what will you say to what comes next? For these same Chinese collect the venom that can be squeezed out from between the toes of toads to make little pills, a sovereign remedy, they say, for bleeding gums, toothache & sinusitis—provided, in the latter case, that the pill is crushed, mixed with human milk and trickled drop by drop into the nostrils. The fluid from the longest tapeworms cures eye disease & boils; the threadworms from donkeys dissolve cataracts; mixed with cicada skin & alcohol then rubbed on the navel of a pregnant woman, lizard's liver will bring about an abortion! Python's bile will give clearer vision, its skin will cure paralysis & rheumatism, its fat deafness & its teeth avert maladies from those who wear them. Dragon's bones, which are commonly found out on the steppes, make the male organ go rigid, disperse nocturnal sweat, calm the mind, exorcise devils, but they can equally be used to treat diarrhea, fever and nymphomania . . ."

Laughing all the time, we could not stop uttering exclamations of astonishment as Father Grueber, carried away by his own fluency, poured forth his inventory in one continuous stream:

"The sperm of the whale, or ambergris, drives away neurasthenia, incontinence, eczema of the scrotum & encourages sexual desire in women . . . China has immense resources—even if all these animals were to disappear, they would still have all the creatures of fur and feathers. Thus for domestic animals they have multiple uses for the least parts, not omitting the most revolting. As for wild beasts, they are not spared either: lions, tigers, leopards, elephants & anteaters are used to make up innumerable remedies. Rhinoceros horn prevents hallucinations, encourages the development of a robust physique, soothes migraines & bleeding from the anus. The palms of bears' paws fortify one's health, their parasites cure yellow fever & blindness in the newborn; hartshorn overcomes almost all diseases, including vaginal discharges from little girls;

monkeys' brains, mixed with chrysanthemum flowers, make you grow; foxes' lips eliminate pus & the urine of the wildcat, poured into the ear, makes all insects leave it instantly —"

"Would that it could also spare us the buzzing of the innumerable bores who bombard our ears with their stupid chatter!" said Bernini, raising his glass. "A toast to the urine of the wildcat!"

"To the urine of the wildcat," we chorused as I went to open a second bottle.

FORTALEZA: *There was still hope for this country . . .*

They reached Recife at nightfall, after having traveled several thousand miles. In the Rua do Bom Jesus, where Roetgen finally found a parking space, they witnessed an astonishing meta-morphosis: banks and shops, housed in the decaying remains of the splendors of the colonial period, emptied with a rapidity that seemed to parallel the setting sun. The workers were in a hurry to get away, the cars to disappear. By dusk the district was deserted, evacuated. Then, from goodness-knows-where, the kings of the night appeared, sailors, thugs, male and female prostitutes, their pupils shining, knives under their shirts . . . a dark-skinned, gaudily dressed multitude that by daylight the city expelled to the shantytowns on the outskirts, just as in the old days it used to exclude madmen. Scraps of haggling could be heard on all sides, shady propositions came to them. Like those plastic-coated pictures that change as you tilt them, the harbor zone unveiled its secret life. One by one the brothels lit their little red lights, sambas and pasodobles filtered out through the closed shutters. Dilapidated vestibules opened onto old stair-cases, whose various stopping points the drunks had marked in their own inimitable manner, but which all took off toward a blaze of neon glory.

They went up to the first floor of the Attila.

The owner welcomed them, a monster with mauve sequins and a chignon larded with black down from which silvery metal tentacles emerged, appendices that terminated in little fluorescent balls. Slow by nature and by necessity—she avoided all contact so as not to spoil the arrangement of her hair—the imposing wall of flesh carefully counted the banknotes Roetgen handed her. He imagined the feverish hours that had preceded the evening, when the woman was still sitting on the third floor of the house with a throng of half-naked whores, twittering with excitement, adorning her like a queen mother before her son's coronation. Installed in a tall chair, slavering and moaning with excitement, an ageless figure with Down's syndrome observed the strange opera that was making his eyes boggle. Close by him, behind the counter, a young mulatto girl was swaying on the spot as she served the drinks; the whores twirled round; the 1930s one with a pageboy hairstyle, green miniskirt and reticule slung over her shoulder, the pink Andalusian with white polka dots, the one with rainbow stripes, the one with translucent skin dressed in garbage bags . . . Moéma danced languorously with a bewigged mummy, all gauzy frills and flounces, that desire made beautiful despite the subtle irony of her smile and her perfect mastery of a game that testified to her long experience in this field. They picked up girls that they handed on to each other, interspersing their love displays with short breaks at the bar for a glass of gin or *cachaça*, launched on a night of pure sensual pleasure in which they saw further proof of their rapport.

Afterward there was a long meander around the docks, chasing rats among the moorings, the squiggles of rope below the wall of cargo boats . . . At dawn, when its splendor dipped the cranes in scarlet, they crawled inside a huge pile of pipes, going from one to the other like bees in a cast-iron beehive, amusing themselves by setting off echoes of their Christian names, amplifying their cries.

A military patrol turned up, dumbfounded to find them in the middle of this consciousness of being. They took them back to their car, well outside the prohibited area: they had made love in the naval dockyard of Recife—it was as if they'd won a war.

BACK IN FORTALEZA the party went on. They slept through the day and went out when night had fallen to quench their thirst for intoxication: the trendy bars where Arrigo Barnabe delivered the very latest chords of a music that was so revolutionary it verged on the inaudible, languorous bossa novas in the gray light of dawn, grass and coke from Pablo. Out of his mind after some wood alcohol, Xavier dived onto the tarmac, convinced it was a swimming pool. Despite the open cut above his eye, the kid refused to go to the hospital, so they patched him up at Thaïs's place. He only had scratches, but he still had scabs on his face and arms when he left. For he was leaving: "I set sail at eight o'clock on Sunday morning," he announced, just like that, without giving any particular reason.

It was an irrevocable decision. They'd drunk a large part of his whiskey on board the boat, in the Yacht Club marina; as for the mustard, he hadn't even tried to sell it, such was the laughter the idea had set off among his friends. A money order from his grandmother had arrived from somewhere or other; he'd immediately turned it into grass, for his personal use. His intention was to go to Belém, or even farther, it wasn't very clear, not even in his own mind. But he was leaving.

The Saturday before he was due to leave, the *Náutico* was organizing one of its monthly festivities: a tennis tournament, swimming races, a dinner-dance with orchestra. A member of the club since his arrival in Fortaleza—he had been proposed by the vice-chancellor of the university and paid dearly for the honor of socializing with a caste he didn't like—Roetgen suggested they go to celebrate Xavier's *despedida*. A farewell evening, in a way, a fitting end to this fantastic holiday together. Except that Moéma had gotten a tab of acid from Pablo and she and Xavier had half each, which complicated matters before they even set off.

As Andreas was not coming back until the next day, they gathered in his house, by the sea. Of a common accord, though for different reasons, Thaïs and Roetgen had passed on the LSD; Thaïs because she knew the devastating effect of the drug and was determined to keep a clear head to be ready for any eventuality, and Roetgen because he had read somewhere that LSD destroyed some of your neurons and could leave you insane. He made much of his sensible stance and declared he would look after Xavier, without realizing exactly what he was getting himself into. As he was about to swallow the pink tab—it had a Donald Duck printed on it—Xavier confessed it was the first time he'd ever tried it.

"Don't worry," Moéma said, sitting down on one of the loungers on the veranda. It'll be a good half hour before it takes effect. Then it's all up to you. If you decide you're going to have a bad trip, then you'll have a bad trip, if you stay cool, it'll be cool . . . The thing is to remain calm and force yourself to think positively."

"No problem for me," Xavier said, in cheerful tones. But they could tell that, instead of reducing his apprehension, the little exhortation had increased it.

Thaïs and Roetgen went to sit with them under the green arbor. They brought a tray with some white wine and nibbles. It was early afternoon. On the other side of the road, fifty yards away, they could see the *beira-mar* and, through a gap in the curtain of coconut trees, the blue-green ocean with the sail of a jangada passing.

"I hope your friend has a good supply of wine," Thaïs said to Roetgen, "because acid makes you thirsty."

"There's more than we need," Roetgen said. "And if not, I'll go and buy some."

"You'll see," Moéma went on to Xavier, "it comes in waves. You think it's stopping, but it starts up again, even stronger."

"How long does it last?" Roetgen asked.

"Twenty-four hours, more or less. Why d'you ask? You're worried, aren't you?"

"A bit. It's Xavier I'm thinking of . . ."

"Don't worry," Xavier said in reassuring tones. "If I don't set off in the morning, it'll be in the evening or tomorrow. I never takes risks with the sea, it's too dangerous."

Roetgen said nothing. When you saw the wreck in which the guy had crossed the Atlantic, you wondered whether he was as cautious as he claimed.

"You know he went out for two days on a jangada?" Moéma said.

Roetgen could see from her look that she immediately regretted having mentioned the episode. To Xavier, who asked if it hadn't been pretty difficult, he replied coolly, "Not really. It's getting back to normal afterward that's hardest."

This reply was so obviously addressed to Moéma, that Xavier dropped the subject. If those two had something to sort out between them, that wasn't his problem. Thaïs gave Roetgen a hard look to tell him it was better to leave it be, given the situation.

"I'm sorry," he said after a while, taking Moéma's hand under the armrest of the lounger. "It just came out like that. I've no hard feelings, I swear . . ."

Moéma's reply was a simple squeeze of the hand. She seemed fascinated by a cargo ship that was scarcely visible on the horizon.

THOSE FIRST HOURS were peaceful, though ambiguous, list-less and ashen, like those you have to spend visiting a patient in the hospital. Thaïs and Roetgen whispered, took little sips of cold white wine, all the while keeping an eye on their companions im-mured in the isolation of LSD. All around was a feast of light and warmth that kept them glued to their deck chairs.

Their conversation proceeded with the interminable slowness of a drip feed. Fascinated by parapsychology, and more generally by everything that seemed to defy understanding, Thaïs was full of anecdotes illustrating her naive belief in the supernatural, lit-tle real-life experiences for the most part, which she recounted in her singsong voice and in the confidential tones of testimony more captivating than their content.

Roetgen was delighted at her wonderment, at the openness with which Thaïs talked to him. It was something new in their relation-ship. Contrary to Moéma, who would dig her heels in on such occa-sions and refuse even to contemplate the slightest dent in her beliefs, she showed a flexibility that worked to his advantage. Not that she was convinced by the arguments Roetgen deployed, but she lis-tened, weighed the pros and cons, and tried to defend her position without once asserting the a priori existence of the *supernatural*, or the *powers of the mind* that fascinated her. Their conversation quietly touched on all the standard features of this material—the tarot, clairvoyance, horoscopes, telepathy, flowers responding to being talked to and other contemporary superstitions—without arousing the usual irritation in Roetgen. She confided in him her desire to have a child. He confessed to her that he wrote poems. It was becoming very suggestive when Moéma interrupted them. "What's the time?" she asked, without taking her eyes off the patch of light quivering by her feet. "I mean do the Indians ever ask that kind of question? How do they manage to have a notion of time. I'm serious, *professor*, I'm not joking . . ."

Roetgen gave a long reply with many illustrations taken from his lectures. Above all, he talked about the banana calendar, without realizing he was talking to Thaïs and not to the one who had asked for enlightenment on the subject.

Then there was a resplendent sunset over the *beira-mar*, when they all concentrated on trying to see the "green flash." Finally Xavier stood up, saying he was fed up with sitting down and it was perhaps time to think about having a bite to eat if they weren't going to wither away, slowly but surely, on these bloody loungers.

"Corpse," he declaimed bombastically, "that something that has no name in any language! Tertullian quoted by Bossuet: Lagarde et Michard, seventeenth century, page 267 . . ."

"What's he talking about?" Thaïs asked.

"Some thing he picked up in a school textbook, but it's too long to explain," Roetgen said with a laugh. "But to put it briefly, we're off."

WITH MOÉMA AND Xavier behaving like little children attracted by the least colored object on the seaside stalls or falling into interminable fits of wild laughter, it was getting on toward nine by the time they reached the *Náutico*. The pretentious pink edifice was teeming; people around the immense pool were yelling as a swimming final was taking place. Farther away, under the floodlights, some aged blacks were rolling the red shale of the tennis courts.

Moéma insisted she wanted to dance.

"Go easy, please," Roetgen begged as she dragged Xavier off toward the music, "there're people who know me around here."

"I will, and that's a promise," Moéma said in a tone that suggested the opposite.

"We'd better follow them," Thaïs advised.

They found a little table that was free that gave them a view of
the dance floor. Roetgen ordered a selection of snacks, a bottle of
vodka and some orange juice. After the second glass no one could
remember the precise chronology of events. The fact is that there
was a moment when all four drank a toast to the departing Xavier,
another when Roetgen, completely drunk, made a declaration of
love to Thaïs and a final one, much later when they realized there
were only three of them left.

LYING ON HER back at the end of a jetty stretching far out into
the sea on its metal supports, Moéma was looking at the sky.
Exaggerated by the acid, the ocean swell was making the rickety structure vibrate. She could feel it rolling in underneath her
like the spine of a voluptuous tiger. The Southern Cross started
to sway from one side to the other, then to come closer, pulling
the whole of the zodiac behind it in its train. Struck with fear,
Moéma headed back. The wind off the sea was scourging her
with stars.

Avoid the metal struts, step between the gaps over the foaming Atlantic, get out of this scene full of pitfalls . . . Thaïs and the
others must still be dancing in that shitty club . . . *Náutico Atlé-
tico Cearense* . . . Athletic my ass! Roetgen had renounced her,
for good. She'd heard him making a declaration to Thaïs . . . The
professor . . . It was as if he'd been kissing her with words. There
wouldn't have been anything worth making a song and dance
about if she hadn't seen the same abandonment in Thaïs's eyes
that she kept for their own intimate moments . . . Nothing to do
with the way she looked when the three of them slept together. Let
them dance, let them screw themselves silly, she no longer cared.
Was this what was meant by "hitting rock bottom"? Wanting and

no longer wanting, dying and not dying? The guardrail of direct, immediate perception of appearances was missing. This permanent suspicion, this way she had of never taking things literally, of suspecting other levels of meaning! When a door was opened, there was always another one, then another, an infinitude of doors pushing farther and farther away the serene correspondence between a being and its name. All at once she felt sure an Indian never saw himself thinking, that he would open a door, just the one, and see the thing naked before him, without a further skin to peel off. What had Aynoré done but open her eyes wide to that obvious fact? Be more cool about things ... accept anything that wasn't prohibited by any law ... As long as an individual's actions didn't endanger the world order, they were allowed: why couldn't the relaxed moral attitudes of the Amazonian tribes apply to our society? The way we experienced love, with suffering, jealousy and resentment, derived from Judeo-Christian emotionalism. It was just as pointless as a Romantic devotion to ruins and the patina on statues ...

Back at the *beira-mar,* deserted at this late hour, Moéma strode along under the yellow streetlights. Scattered all along the pavement, going about their rodent business, the rats hardly moved out of her way at all.

To plant the sequoia ... To walk along, pockets full of seeds, casually sowing the tarmac until the day when the young shoots dislocated the town with the force of a cataclysm ... To create innumerable openings bursting with sap in the concrete of the metropolises ... The gaps between the stones, between people, that empty space between bones that allows the butcher to cut up the carcass without blunting the edge of his knife. Salvation lying in the interstices ... Come on, Jesus, put an end to all this internationalist Western bullshit! Restore a jungle virginity to these coasts polluted by the tumescent cross of the Jesuits and the conquistadors. Look what they'd made of this new, improbable, unconsidered world! It was as if they'd crapped on the lawn as soon as they arrived in paradise . . .

A big rat didn't move out of her way quickly enough, she made to step on it, as people usually did with pigeons, knowing they would fly away before being touched. But her foot caught the animal on the back of its neck; she watched it in its death throes right there in front of her, sickened by the twitching of its paws. The coconut trees were twisting as well, seized with reptilian convulsions. Her head spinning from the return in force of the hallucinations, she lay down on the pavement for a few moments, amused by the idea that she might be found there, in the gutter. Then she got up again and continued her forced march toward the northern end of the avenue.

Get out of the town, turn toward the jungle of the favelas . . . Aynoré had told her he was a regular at the *Terra e Mar*, that was where she'd go. It was a goal like any other, a reason for living that was, if anything, better than the others. Go back to Aynoré, make love with the handsome Indian who was so natural in the way he used his freedom, take up her dream again where she'd left off.

She felt as if she'd been walking for hours. Little streets lined with houses, waste ground . . . the tarmac replaced by sand and dust, a proliferation of shacks with no order in the middle of refuse, the rats becoming arrogant.

"It's not the place for you, Snow White."

"What the fuck's it got to do with you? Tell me where it is and I'll give you my lighter. Look, it's almost new."

"You haven't got the cigarettes to go with it, have you, my lovely? . . . OK. You follow the railway and it's to the left of the signal. A green signal, you'll see, perhaps red, whatever . . ."

Fights between stray cats, the stench of sewers and rotting fish. Walled in but open to the sky. Where I live is a cursed place, she told herself, which locusts darken with swarms like iron filings. Cold sweat made her T-shirt stick to her skin . . . From what even blacker underground abode did this anguish come? Thaïs had moved away from her too quickly, from her and from what they had been through together . . . She saw herself raising a glass to her lips and breaking it with her teeth, like biting into half a chocolate egg. The shard of glass made a kind of sparkling dagger. Thaïs, naked under her silk dress, a nacreous gleam covering her forehead . . . Escaped eagles were running, clumsily, after her shadow.

Blown along by the breeze, a piece of paper stuck to her ankle. Instinctively she bent down and picked it up. An election pamphlet. The bluish light the moon cast over the favela made the letters bob up and down before her eyes:

Partido do Movimento Democrático Brazileiro

THE STATE OF CEARÁ DESERVES
A DEPUTY WHO IS:

AN ARMED ROBBER
(SEARS store, Rio de Janeiro)

A TERRORIST
(Guarapes Airport, Pernambuco)

A HIJACKER
(Cruzeiro do Sul plane bound for Cuba)

ANGELO SISOES RIBIERA

It was like a letter sent by the dark. There was a motif across the page, hammers and sickles on a red background. A guarantee that the guy didn't lie, never had lied. He displayed his crimes like stripes to the world at large . . . She folded the leaflet and smiled as she slipped it into the back pocket of her shorts. There was still hope for this country.

Then all at once she saw him coming out of *Terra e Mar*, clearly tipsy, with a group of his pals. When they saw the young woman, three of them immediately approached her; they had the muscles and supple movement of men who practised *capoeira*.

"Hey, look what's turned up, a little darling looking for a hunk . . ."

"And who doesn't look as if she really knows how far gone she is . . . I'm sure she'd like to smoke one last joint before going to bed . . ."

"And where's Little Red Riding Hood heading for? In the middle of Pirambú with those tits that're likely to cause an accident . . ."

They had surrounded her. Hands were placed on her shoulders, stroked the curve of her back. One of the guys touched his penis as he stared at her.

"Aynoré!" she begged, unable to find a way out of her despair.

"You know her, *Indio?*"

"A real pain in the ass," the Indian said, spitting on the ground. "Go ahead, I'll leave her to you."

The silhouettes that picked up Moéma left long luminous trails behind them. The spaces between their bodies had started to vibrate, she could feel it, like a magnetic aura, a shield it was impossible to get past.

On the slope where they laid her, a white heron seemed to be pacing up and down the rubbish as cautiously as an Egyptian hieroglyph.

FAVELA DE PIRAMBÚ: *the Princess of*
the Kingdom-where-no-one-goes

A good day . . . It was no use people having bearskin wallets, they always opened them eventually. It was all a matter of patience and know-how. Nelson counted the banknotes again, divided the little bundle into two equal parts and dug up the iron box where he kept his savings. Having checked that his nest egg in its plastic bag hadn't been spoiled by dampness, he added that day's haul, then quickly buried the lot again. A hundred and fifty-three thousand cruzeiros . . . He needed another three hundred thousand to buy the wheelchair he dreamt of. A splendid machine he'd seen in the town, in the wealthy districts, three years ago. Chrome hubcaps, indicators, four-cylinder Honda engine . . . a little jewel that could be steered with one hand and do up to twenty-five miles an hour. Nelson had made every effort to find the shop that sold this marvel and went there from time to time to admire it in the window and check the price: when he'd started saving up, almost immediately after he'd seen it for the first time, it cost 145 thousand cruzeiros. Now it cost three times as much. The thought that he could have bought it with the money he had in his box now, made him feel sick. It was almost as if it were being done deliberately: the more he saved, the more the price rose. It made you think someone was doing their utmost to keep it inaccessible. However, against all reason Nelson did not lose heart; one day he'd stick his ass on that chair and go off to beg like a young lord. Zé would help him soup up the engine, he might be able to hit thirty-five, or even forty! Everything would be so much easier. With a blanket, no one would see he had the legs of a stillborn calf instead of proper human ones.

This glorious vision upset him. He decided to go and watch the freight train pass; the sight of the engine splashing sparks and flickering lights all over the darkness was something that always calmed him down.

He went out of his shack, without replacing the sheet of cardboard that blocked the doorway. He lived in a world where even the poor stole from each other; it was better to leave it open, with the lamp lit to make it look as if someone was inside. The railway was three hundred yards away and he dragged himself there quickly, unconcerned about the rats that his deformity seemed to frighten off almost as much as humans.

The best place was just behind Juvenal's hut. From the little pile of almost clean sand beside it, he could watch the train approaching, see it slow down at the signal and go past less than three yards from where he was. Juvenal had eventually become accustomed to it: nothing could wake him apart from the smell of *cachaça*. He dreamed of earthquakes and would spend the whole night running to avoid the yawning cracks splitting the shantytown apart beneath his feet.

Nelson was going through his own victories in marathons, all those occasions on which he entered the stadium and put on a spurt to the cheers of the crowd, when the train emerged from the ambiguity of the shadows. The engine sputtered out a compact beam of darkness, its two eyes fixed on the track; its wheels chewed away at the rails, spilling out on either side the reddish glow of crackling fountains of hydrogen welding . . .

That was the moment at which Nelson saw her spring up from the slope and attack the monster. She kicked and hit the moving carapace of the trucks with all her might, in a fit of madness, determined to smash her fists on its crude bulk. Each time she assaulted it, she was thrown back; she swayed to and fro, raised her arms, yelled again and, head lowered, returned to the duel. The train raised its voice, again, and then again, in a deafening outburst of fury. The young princess was going to get herself knocked flat! Nelson crawled toward her as fast as he could, shouting to her to move away.

When she saw this nightmare freak appear, there, in the never-ending infernal racket grinding away at the horizon, Moéma was stricken with panic. She wanted to run away, but collapsed, overwhelmed, exhausted.

Nelson could not believe his eyes, his princess was sobbing, calling for her mother in a plaintive voice, curled up, her hands between her thighs. Apart from her T-shirt, which was ripped right down and only held on by the seams at the neck, she was completely naked, her body was covered in patches of blood and black grease, all over, on her face, on her stomach . . . her breasts were disfigured by large aubergine-colored bruises.

Lying beside her without touching her, Nelson spoke for a long time, just so she could hear his murmurs of compassion, so she would gradually overcome her fear:

"Don't cry, things'll sort themselves out, you'll see . . . My name is Nelson, I was born like this, with my legs all crooked . . . There's no need to be afraid, at least I can't do you any harm. Who's the bastard who put you in this state? I'll find him, I swear, we'll make him pay . . . Look, take my shirt and cover yourself up, princess. Come on, you can stay with me until the morning . . . You can't stay here in this state, that's for sure . . . I'll go and tell Uncle Zé and he'll sort everything out, I promise . . . come on, don't stay there . . . I'll tell you stories, I know piles of them . . . *John the Bold and the Princess of the Kingdom-where-no-one-goes, Snow White and the Soldier of the Foreign Legion, The Ballad of the Mysterious Peacock* . . ."

He moved away a few yards to encourage her to follow him, then returned to the attack, gabbling all the *cordel* titles he could remember, baptizing her with all their luminous promise: *The Goddess of Maranhão. The Story of the Seven Cities and the King*

JEAN-MARIE BLAS DE ROBLES

of Magic, Mariana and the Ship's Captain, Ronaldo and Susana on the River Miramar, The Sufferings of Alzira the Fairy, Rachel and the Dragon, The Unprecedented Fate of Princess Eliza, The Story of Song of Fire and His Will, The Duchess of Sodom, Rose of Milan and Princess Christine, João Mimoso and the Enchanted Castle, Prince Oscar and the Queen of the Waters, Lindalva and Juracy the Indian . . .

CHAPTER 26

The continuation of Johan Grueber's report on Chinese medicine

THERE WERE EXCLAMATIONS and grimaces of disgust all around the table. Bernini swore by all the gods that he would never go to China for fear of falling ill & having to be treated there. Kircher nodded, invoking Galen & Discorides; as for myself, I prayed to God that this wonderful evening would never end, so delighted I was by the conversation.

"Bottoms up!" I was slightly surprised to hear myself saying. "To liquid excrement & to the wonderful virtues of diarrhea!"

"Bottoms up!" My companions replied before emptying their glasses.

"Now what would you say," Father Grueber went on, "to looking at bone disease? A little concentrated urine from a three-year-old girl will get rid of it instantly. Diabetes? Make your patient drink a full cup of the same liquid from a public urinal! Loss of blood? The same, but eight pints! A dead fetus to be expelled? Two pints will suffice. Body odor? Apply to the armpits, several times a day."

"Good Lord!" said Kircher, pinching his nose.

"Everything can be used, I tell you. And you've heard nothing yet. You should know that the Emperor T'ou Tsung used to cut his own whiskers to treat his dear Li Hsün, the 'Great Scholar for the Exaltation of Poetic Writing,' for their ashes are good for abscesses . . . A snake has bitten you & you have no snakestone, what can you do? Do not fear, twelve pubic hairs sucked for a long time will prevent the venom from spreading through your entrails. A wife is having a difficult birth? No matter, make her swallow fourteen other hairs mixed with bacon fat and she will have a swift delivery—"

"What's all this you're trying to tell us!" Kircher exclaimed, wiping the tears of laughter from his eyes. "If you didn't inspire me with absolute confidence, I wouldn't believe a single word of what you're saying."

"And you would be wrong, for all I am doing here is repeating things that are common knowledge among all Chinese physicians."

"If Father Roth could hear you!" Kircher chuckled. Then, putting on an angry look, he pointed a threatening finger at Bernini, he said, "Oh, how wise those pagans were who had a law forbidding a man of fifty to consult a doctor, saying it showed too great an attachment to life! Among the Chinese, as among the Christians, you will find some men of eighty who won't hear a word of the other world, as if they hadn't had a moment's leisure to see this one. Do you not know that life was given to Cain, the most evil man that ever there was, as punishment for his crime? And you want it to be a reward for you?!"

"But one has to live, see the world," Bernini replied, joining in the playacting, like a character who already knew his defense was weak.

"What is living, apart from getting dressed & undressed, getting up, going to bed, drinking, eating & sleeping, playing, jesting, haggling, selling, buying, masoning, joinering, quarreling, quibbling, traveling & roaming in a labyrinth of actions that are constantly retracing their steps & always being the prisoner of a body, be it a child's, an invalid's, a madman's?"

"You're forgetting something important, Father, something that would on its own justify my existence . . ."

"*Vade retro, Satanas!*" Kircher bellowed, his eyes sparkling with laughter. "One must see the world, you say, & live among the living. But if you should spend your whole life locked up in a prison & only observe this world through a little grille, you would have seen enough of it! What can one see in the streets apart from men, houses, horses, mules, carriages—"

"And women, Reverend Father . . . Fine-looking girls, nice little chickens that revive your appetite for meat."

"Little hussies who stink of rotten fish! And courtesans who walk the streets like drunken fish and whose only virtue is often the pox, which sends you to the other world. O God, how empty our lives are! Is it for this that we are unfaithful to & break with the Lord, that we try to live for all those years that consist of nothing but foolishness, work & misery? Oh, my fellow Christians, be not like those babes that cry when they emerge from the blood and excrement to see the daylight & despite that do not want to return to the place whence they came!"

"Although—" Bernini murmured in ribald tones.

"Please!" I begged, red with embarrassment.

My three companions gave me mocking but affectionate looks. "Come on, Caspar," my master said, "we're only joking & I can assure you there's nothing wrong in that. If we scoff at everything, poor Scarron said, it's because there's another side to everything. Laugh in the devil's face & you'll see him turn tail at once, for he knows very well he has no hold over those who can see the grotesque side of his nature."

"But since the subject has cropped up," Grueber whispered, turning to Bernini, "I will make no secret of the fact that there is a proven method of combating old age, at least from what my Chinese informant said. Man is in the air, he told me, & the air is in man, thus expressing the prime importance of the breath of life. Since this principle dwindles with age, it is, according to him, advisable to regenerate it by the addition of breath that is still young. To that end he regularly hired the services of a maiden or a youth to insufflate their surplus vitality into his nostrils, navel and male organ!"

"Good Lord!" Bernini exclaimed, highly amused, "if that's all that's needed, I can assure you that I have been obeying his prescription for a long time & without having noticed any other effect than an excess of weakness . . ."

The conversation between Grueber & Bernini continued in that tone, but I paid less attention; my master had a faraway look in his eye & appeared to be gathering his thoughts. I presumed he was a little weary, which would have been quite natural at that late hour. His attitude seemed to confirm this, since he soon left the table and went to a neighboring room. After some time, since he did not return, I went to him, walking with care so as not to give way to the dizziness that had seized me as I stood up. My master was standing by a bookshelf, apparently putting some books away, but when I came closer, I saw that he was aligning the spines meticulously. Despite my own confused state, it was something so unusual in him that I was immediately worried; a quick glance around the room only served to confirm my concern: in the grip of a strange obsession, Kircher had carefully grouped in decreasing order of size all the objects amenable to that kind of classification. Goose feathers, inkwells, sticks of wax, manuscripts—in a word, everything that could be found in a study—had been arranged in that order, an oddity that caused me profound uneasiness. You will understand my real anxiety, dear reader, when I tell you that my master, turning round slowly, looked at me glassy-eyed!

"The mind, Caspar," he said in a toneless, faraway voice, "will always be superior to matter. That has to be the way things are, whether we like it or not, until the end of the world. You do understand, don't you? Tell me you understand . . ."

To be honest, I was in such a state I would have understood much more difficult statements, so I hastened to reassure Kircher, while encouraging him to get some sleep. He allowed himself to be put to bed without resisting & I went back to join our two visitors in the other room.

" . . . that the Incas, the emperors of Peru," I heard Grueber saying, "conferred the order of knighthood by piercing the men's ears. I will say nothing of the women's, since at all times & in all places that has been one of their greatest vanities. Which explains Seneca's complaint that they had two or three times their inheritance hanging from each ear. But what invective would he have aimed at the Lolo women of Yunnan province, who pierce the extremities of their most intimate parts to attach gold rings, which they can remove or replace as they see fit?! And the truth is that the men do not show greater modesty, for they wear little bells, made of different metals, tied to their male organ or stuck between the flesh and the foreskin, and make them ring in the streets when they see a woman they like. Some take this invention as cure for sodomy, which is common in all areas, but I fail to see how it could prevent them from indulging in it."

I took advantage of the pause to inform Cavaliere Bernini & his drinking companion of what had happened to my master.

Grueber was not surprised for one moment; with a smile on his lips, he explained that the *Quey* herb sometimes produced this kind of confused state, but that it was not at all serious, it would have disappeared by the next day. The two of them apologized for having kept me up so late and left, wishing me a good night.

Their wishes, alas, had no effect. I had such nightmares that the harshness of my hair shirt was powerless to stop the succubae from paying me their shameful visits.

The next day, as Grueber had predicted, my master woke refreshed & full of energy. Mentioning the *Quey* herb, he assured me it had had no effect on him. Anyway, he told me, this remedy & those like it dispelled less our low spirits than our reason; that being the case, he could see no excuse for using them, neither for healthy minds, which ought to endeavor to increase the divine clarity within themselves rather than to reduce it, nor for madmen who already lacked it. Recalling the hellish dreams of the night that had just passed, I concurred in this condemnation with all my heart.

We returned to our studies while continuing to see fathers Roth & Grueber in order to collect their thoughts about China.

In the appearance of the comet, which we observed with the astronomers Lana-Terzi & Riccioli, we had cause to see an auspicious sign for the destiny of my master's works and an ill omen for the infidels & other peoples of the Levant: the *Mundus Subterraneus* had just arrived from Amsterdam. This book, which scholars had been waiting for with as much impatience as they had in the past his *Œdipus Ægyptiacus*, prompted an extraordinarily enthusiastic response.

This thunderbolt was followed in June by the printing of his *Arithmologia*, the work my master had started immediately after his *Polygraphia*. Apart from an immense historical section devoted to the significance of numbers & their use in Greece

& Egypt, it contained a clear and definitive account of the
Jewish Cabbala, which he had learned from Rabbi Naphtali
Herz ben Jacob, with whom he had assiduously studied the *Sefer
Yetzirah* & the *Zohar*, the books containing that knowledge. His
perfect knowledge of Hebrew & Aramaic had rendered easy
for him a task that was well beyond my feeble abilities & I was
pleased finally to understand what was concealed within that
magnificent body of knowledge.

Finally, when the effect produced by those two books had
not yet abated, the *Historia Eustachio Mariana* also appeared,
in which my master recounted the circumstances under which
we had discovered the Church of Our Lady of Mentorella &
proved, step by step, that this church was indeed a place of
miracles. Thanks to the contributions of numerous patrons who
had interested themselves in the project, the work of restoring
& refurbishing the church was completed in the same month.
Desiring a worthy inauguration for this new place of pilgrimage,
Kircher decided it should take place on Whitsunday with all
due pomp and reverence. Pope Alexander VII having promised
to go there to consecrate the church & give his blessing to
the congregation, the whole of Roman society was feverishly
preparing to accompany him on the journey.

ALCÂNTARA: *Stuff floating on the sea . . . .*

If Eléazard had ever wondered whether Moreira was unworthy of
the position of governor, the papers entrusted to him by his wife
would have been enough to convince him. He could already feel
the task he had accepted as weighing heavily on his shoulders—
it's sometimes a fine difference, he told himself, that separates a
common informer from a righter of wrongs—but he had become

too involved in this country and its inhabitants, too much of a fighter against all kinds of corruption and shady deals, to refuse the challenge. He would follow his conscience, without compunction and without hesitation. To see justice was done . . . Yes, but how? he wondered as he strode toward the Caravela Hotel.

"There's something new," he said to Alfredo when he ran into him in the vestibule. "We have to talk, all three of us. Where's Loredana?"

"In her room. She almost fainted. Socorró told me she ate nothing for lunch."

"What's wrong with her?"

"I don't really know but she certainly doesn't seem too well."

Eléazard couldn't say what was the real reason, but he felt it was essential to let her in on the secret. He sensed that the feeling of rebellion was stronger in her than in him but, paradoxically, more controlled. So he took the risk of disturbing her, going up to her room with Alfredo.

Loredana was just finishing putting on her makeup. Happy to hear Eléazard's voice, she invited them in at once.

"You don't look great, you seem—"

"I overdid the *cachaça* a bit, yesterday evening," she said, "but I feel a lot better now."

"Well hold on tight," Eléazard said, putting Countess Carlotta's photocopies on the bed. "Council of war! We've got the means to bring Moreira down."

Two days ago the idea would have filled Loredana with enthusiasm but her world had been so completely turned upside down that she listened dispassionately to what Eléazard had to say.

"What a shit!" Alfredo said when Eléazard had finished going through the dossier. "We'll get him for that. But we mustn't mess up."

"That's precisely why I wanted to ask you two your opinion. It's not that simple finding the best way to proceed."

"We just have to go to the police with all those papers," Alfredo said, immediately realizing he'd said something stupid. "Well perhaps not the police, you never know with them . . . How about the newspapers? We could tell them it's his own wife the information comes from and . . ."

"And what?" Loredana asked quietly. "If the business is made public, they'll have plenty of time to cover their tracks and kick up a fuss about a smear campaign. You don't seem to know what they're like . . ."

"If we can't get our hands on the guys who committed the murders," Eléazard said, "anything we can do won't add up to much."

"That's better," Loredana said. "Aim at the mulberry tree to get the locust tree . . ."

"Sorry?"

"Stratagem number twenty-six for battles of union and annexation. It's a Chinese ploy, but what it comes down to is that we have to get at the governor through his lawyer. We have to start with his henchmen and since we have a good idea where they are . . ."

"I'll make sure they talk, if that's what you want," Alfredo said in macho tones.

'Please stop talking nonsense. You don't happen to know a state prosecutor or a judge we can trust, I mean someone who isn't in his pocket? That would make things easier."

"There is Waldemar de Oliviera," Eléazard said. "A young prosecutor in Santa Inês. I've interviewed him two or three times about cases, he's an upright guy, he has a reputation of being incorruptible. But it doesn't really fall within his remit . . ."

"He'll do, at least to start the ball rolling. Now this is what I suggest . . ."

ONCE ALFREDO HAD left the hotel to inform his Maoist pals in the Communist Party, Eléazard and Loredana went back to Eléazard's house. There they spent a few hours compiling several reports designed to reveal what had been going on; in them they exposed, with much supporting detail, Moreira's speculation, divulged the series of events that had led to the murder of the Carneiro family and accused Wagner Cascudo by name of sheltering the perpetrators in his country cottage. The journalists were going to have a field day.

"What's wrong with you?" Eléazard asked when they'd finished correcting the final version of the letter to the lawyer on the computer.

"Nothing, I'm just tired," Loredana replied, pouring herself a glass of *cachaça*. "Black thoughts, it happens sometimes . . . You don't get fed up of living in this country, do you?"

"Not really, no. I like the people here. With them, everything's possible. They're not carrying a lot of baggage, as they do in Europe. What have they got behind them, four, five hundred years of history? You're going to find this very naive, but seeing them, I'm always reminded of Stefan Zweig's little book: *Brazil: Land of the Future* . . . You've read it?"

"Yes, it's not bad. Though having said that, I find it odd that a guy could write that of a country where he'd decided to commit suicide."

"Actually, he died because of Europe, not because of Brazil. A bit like Walter Benjamin. They're both men whose horror of fascism drove them to the breaking point. The people of their own countries sent them into depths of despair we can hardly imagine."

"Where have you gotten with Kircher?"

"I've almost finished. The first draft, of course. But it's getting difficult—things that can't be verified, others for which I haven't got sufficient material. The worst is that I'm starting to wonder what the point of all this work is . . ."

Reflectively he chewed away at the inside of his cheek.

"Stop that," Loredana said, imitating him. "I'm sorry, but it's irritating. What work, yours or Schott's biography?"

"Both," Eléazard replied, disturbed by her comment and by the effort he had to make to prevent himself from starting to chew his cheek again. "It's a lot more complicated than I thought. How can you annotate a biography—above all, one that is so lacking in objectivity as Schott's—without establishing another biography? If I want to piece together the real nature of the relationship between Peiresc and Kircher, for example, I can't restrict myself to one or two comments taken from the correspondence of the former with Gassendi or Cassiano dal Pozzo. There's no a priori reason to trust him rather than Schott or Kircher himself. To take it any farther I need to know the most minor features of their relationship, which means studying Peiresc's biography as scrupulously as Kircher's, then Gassendi's, then Cassanio's, et cetera, et cetera. There's no end to it!"

"In the *Chuang-tzu* there's a little story that puts what you're saying in a nutshell: an emperor asks to have a very precise map of China drawn. All his cartographers take up their brushes apart from one, who sits quietly in his studio. Two months later, when he's asked for the fruits of his labor, he just points to the view out of his window: his map is so precise because it's on the scale of one to one, it's China itself."

"Borges mentions that too," Eléazard said with a smile. "It's a nice paradox, but what does it say? That there's no point in doing anything? That you can't write a biography of Kircher without being Kircher and all the others as well?"

"For me it's clear," Loredana said. "If it's the truth that's at stake, then that's the price of precision. But a map, a biography or notes on a biography, *perché no*, the real question is: what is its purpose? If it's a map—to go where? To invade which province? If it's your notes—to prove what? That Kircher was an incompetent, a genius, or simply that you know a lot more about the subject than most of us? As you well know, it's not the erudition that counts, it's what it aims to show. A simple note a few lines long can hit the mark better than eight hundred pages devoted to the same individual."

"Effectiveness as always, eh? You really are astonishing. I must admit I was very impressed just now: 'we'll do this, we'll do that.' Did you see the expression on Alfredo's face? It could have been Eva Perón he was listening to!"

"People aren't as stupid as you like to believe. Alfredo's bright enough to be taken in, but he's a more complicated person than he seems. The day you realize that, you'll perhaps have fewer problems with Kircher . . . All right, I have to go back. I'm exhausted. You too, it would be a good idea if you went to bed early if you want to be in form tomorrow morning. You've got to go to Santa Inês, don't forget . . ."

"You're sure you don't want to stay?"

Gently but firmly Loredana took Eléazard's hand off her shoulder. "Absolutely sure, *caro*. As I said, I'm not feeling well."

"Another of your Chinese stratagems, I suppose?" Eléazard said with a sad smile. "What number is that one?"

"Stop that, will you? You're wrong—about me, about Kircher, about almost everything. A strategy is what's left when morality's no longer possible. And morality's no longer possible when absolute values are missing. If you believe in a god or something like that, it makes everything so much easier."

"You don't think it's enough to believe in man?"

"As an absolute value?! Every man has his own definition of Humanity, and with a capital H, if you please. In life, if you insist, in the totality of living things, but not in man, not in the one being capable of killing just for fun."

"Also the one with awareness? At least as far as we know . . . What do you think of reason?"

"Awareness of what? Of himself, of his complete freedom, of the relative nature of good and evil? There's not a single concept that can stand up to the fact that we have to die, and if there's nothing after that, as we've come to believe, then everything's allowed. Reason doesn't produce any kind of hope, it's hardly even able to give a name to our despair."

"You're taking a pessimistic view of things. I'm certain that—"

"I can't go on," Loredana broke in. "Another time, OK?"

"I'm sorry. I'll see you back."

On the way to the hotel Loredana stopped for a moment to watch the mist of fireflies lighting up the rectangles of a façade open to the night.

"It's beautiful," she said. "It's as if someone's lit candles for a celebration."

ONCE IN HER room, Loredana stretched out on the double bed, which hadn't been made yet. Her hope of getting some sleep vanished almost immediately. She thought back to the ruins of Apollonia and to the magnificent moment when she had wanted to die, even though she had felt better than she did now. She had travelled to Cyrenaïca with the avowed intent of going back to her earliest childhood for one last time. The Libyans who used to work with her father had aged, true, but less than her, to all appearances, for she had recognized them immediately while they had some difficulty putting the name of a boisterous little girl to this woman with the awkwardness of an adult. On the heights, Casa Parisi had now disappeared behind the eucalyptus trees, the same ones with which she used to amuse herself by pulling their trunks down so she could see them shake themselves in the sun when she let go. The modern town of Shahhat had deteriorated, as if it were in a hurry to match the ruins, to follow the dark voices of Cyrene and of the ancient necropolis on which it was founded. This tendency toward the vestigial was particularly noticeable in Marsa Susa, of which the Italian quarter, already dilapidated in her memory, seemed to have suffered a veritable bombardment. The customs building, the harbormaster's office, the Hotel Italia, the cafés and restaurants with their shady terraces . . . all of that had vanished, or almost: inside the shells of the buildings— occasionally identified by a flaking syllable on the façade—herds of goats were capering, rummaging through the rubbish. There were wrecked cars or trucks everywhere, already half-buried in sand, apparently determined to become part of a dubious posterity. On the shore, all around the port, scraps of plastic bags were stuck to the ribcages of boats, standing, faded, on the shore like humpback whales in a museum. High up in its last dry dock a tug, perforated by rust, dominated the wharf. Young Arabs were enjoying themselves diving from the superstructure of a landing craft and three huge barges shipwrecked in the docks. Compared with this junkyard, the archaeological site of Apollonia seemed a model of town planning, of cleanliness: visible beyond the cemetery gate that closed off the port, just below the beacon, the shafts of Byzantine columns proclaimed a sort of Garden of Eden where she hastily took refuge. Although he had spent most of his time in Cyrene, at the works on the agora, it was in this haven of peace that she had her most pleasurable and moving memories of her father. The family came here every Friday, by the old road that snaked down between the sarcophaguses and tombs, now just loose stones in the thickets, to wind for a short while across the panther skin of Jebel Akhdar before suddenly plunging down, right at the bottom, toward the promise of the sea. In her mind's eye she could see herself running over the beach with the smell of fresh bread in her nostrils, the joy of being alive that emanated from the sand and the sun, and which the call of the muezzin sometimes made swell to the very limit of what was bearable. In her clinging, white-satin bathing suit, suntanned like a movie star, her mother was reading under a hat shaped like a lampshade, and she just had to lift her head to see her father, sitting on the half-buried capital of a column or squatting down to clear out one of those mysterious foundations that would appear, as if by magic, under his trowel. Professor Goodchild would come over to say hello. He'd show his Italian colleague the progress made in his own excavation and always ended up inviting him to have a glass of bourbon in the old redoubt where the American archaeological team was based.

Nothing had really changed, except that her father wasn't there anymore, nor Goodchild, nor the others, and that profoundly modified her view of things. Only the ruins had remained faithful to the child she had been, with that unfailing faithfulness shown by dogs and tombs.

She had waited for Friday before revisiting the site, waited with the same impatience, the same painful desire that had taken hold of her in her childhood when they'd been loading her mask and her flippers in the back of the jeep. The track of the narrow-gauge railway could still be seen, here and there, between the red earth of the molehills. Seen from a distance with their regular lines of columns, the three basilicas had made those "poky little holes" appear over the horizon, those poky little holes that had made Professor Goodchild frown:

"Poky little holes! My basilica's poky little holes! Well, really. *You good-for-nothing child, I'll tell Miss Reynolds when she comes, you know, and what will you do then?*"

The one memory alone had made all the rigors of the journey worthwhile.

When she came to the old theater at the far end of the site, she sat down for a moment on the top tier, at the very same place her father preferred. Down below, just beyond the stage, the sea was so calm, so transparent that one could clearly make out the geometrical shapes of the submerged ruins. To the right of the stalls, a bushy palm tree had found room to grow between the blocks of stone. Quite close to her, on the dazzling limestone, a tiny chameleon was regarding her with magnificent disdain. Looking at it, she had told herself there would never be a more fitting occasion: now, on the point of noon, it was time to bow out, to cut her wrists and wait quietly until she resembled that little animal that seemed to concentrate the whole of the sun's heat in itself.

She would die far from her home town, far from Rome, so pleasant in the spring when sudden warmth finally releases your drowsy body. When you stop hearing the din of the vehicles going around the Coliseum and the ill-tempered whistles of the carabinieri. With every step a bud is revealed, then another, and another. Young street vendors get drunk on their broken voices. The alleys resound with the amazement of sparrows. On Piazza Navona the water beneath the Nile is singing . . .

Yes, she had thought, as she made one of the most beautiful sentences ever written her own, that was what she wanted, *to die slowly and attentively, in the same way as a baby sucks at its mother's breast.*

Then a flight of pink flamingos had crossed the sky above some islands, a truly pink cluster of those large, gangling birds. The splendor had been like an electric shock to her. Something had been scrawled on the horizon ordering her to wait longer, to watch these performances life had in store for her to the very end.

Instead of cutting her wrists, she had gone down to the center of the stage and, facing the terracing, had declaimed the only poem she knew by heart:

In questo giorno perfetto
In cui tutto matura
E non l'uva sola s'indora,
Un raggio di sole è caduto sulla mia vita:
Ho guardato dietro a me,
Ho guardato fuori,
Nè mai ho visto tante et cosi buone cose in una volta . . .

Loredana opened her eyes and looked at her watch: more than five hours till daybreak. She felt guilty about Eléazard. The thought of having to explain herself had made her withdraw at the last moment, but she'd been close to telling him she was going to take the first flight to Rome. She wondered what memories he would have of her brief intrusion in his life. Four years ago she would have tried to make a go of it with him. He was reassuring, solid, even in his way of questioning things . . .

AFTER A CLOSER analysis of the terms used, Wagner put the anonymous letter in his personal safe. The letter might be just a friendly warning, but it still represented a threat: that someone could know so much about his implication in the triple murder, which was its main topic, came as a shock. As his unknown informant advised him, it was time to take steps before his complicity became general knowledge.

Leaving a secretary to look after the office, Wagner Cascudo jumped into his car. During the drive he kept asking himself what he should do with the hired men who were holed up in his country cottage. Those two cretins had dropped him in it and right up to the neck! The thought that the police might find them made him break out in a cold sweat. He'd just told them to lean on Carneiro to get him to sign the deed of sale, at worst he was looking at a charge of collusion. Unless those morons took it into their heads to accuse him to save their own skins . . . He had to get them out of his cottage as quickly as possible. What could he have been thinking? And he'd thought himself so clever to hide them in the *sitio* . . . He'd stick them on the first bus to Belém and then they'd see. And as soon as he was back in Fortaleza he'd ring the governor. He'd be very surprised if he didn't manage to sidestep the issue, perhaps he'd even be able to stop the newspapers publishing the devastating article the letter had mentioned . . .

When, two hours later, he reached the *sitio de la Pitombera*, he'd almost persuaded himself he had things under control again. When he pushed open the door of the little cottage that, unknown to his wife, he only used for amorous escapades, he found Manuel and Pablo sitting at the table with a bottle of wine.

"Get your stuff together," he said immediately, "we're leaving —"

It was only after he'd spoken that sentence, which he'd repeated over and over to himself during the last few miles of the journey, that he realized from their evasive looks that something was wrong. At that same moment armed police burst into the room.

OF ALL THE things that happened following this, the only one that Loredana doubtless hadn't foreseen was the local population's reaction to the three Americans in the Caravela Hotel. On the day when she came back from São Luís with the ticket for her flight confirmed by Varig Airlines, she met Eléazard and Soledade to attend the funeral of the Carneiro family. It was a rainy morning, making the sad occasion even more dismal. Hundreds of people had come to join the procession organized by the priest of Alcantâra. As it passed, people opened their doors and windows to allow free access to the souls of the dead.

"Give them rest eternal!" a relative or friend would cry. "And light perpetual, O Glorious One. Help them to die!"

And they dropped everything to come out and join the funeral cortege.

"Come, brother of their souls!" the crowd would repeat to welcome the one who'd just joined them.

No one was crying, so as not to make the wings of the little corpse wet and thus stop him from entering paradise. Nicanor! Gilda! Egon! They called on the dead by their Christian names to make them feel lighter in their deal coffins. Lamentations of grief to help the deceased to die, lamentations in the hour of death, lamentations at the moment the cock crowed for the last time, lamentations on the dawn in which the inert parts of the body and every item of clothing are chanted: songs of mourning and litanies flow in one single lament, the echo reverberating from the ruined façades of the town. A long, ochre groan, rust tarnishing the steel of the sky. The men were getting drunk, a drummer was summoning the rain.

Eléazard suspected Alfredo was behind what happened when they got back from the cemetery. Rumors went from mouth to mouth, excitement took over. Like a shoal of fish responding to the strange magnetism governing their least movement, the whole crowd gathered in the square, outside the Caravela Hotel. "Yankees out! Death to the CIA!" An almost mystical frenzy twisted their lips, raised their fists. They thought the three Americans had barricaded themselves in their room, but Alfredo saw them coming back from a bar and approaching the mob with no idea that they themselves were the cause of the commotion. A stone flew, immediately followed by dozens of other projectiles. The man put his hand to his face and stared in amazement at the blood on his fingers. Hardly restrained by the priest, who was exhorting them to remain calm, the people of Alcântara advanced toward the object of their fury. Instinctively the Americans drew back, then started to run, panic-stricken, toward the landing stage. The *Dragão do mar* was preparing to cast off and the people let them take refuge on board without pursuing them further. Hurrying to the scene, those who had gone into the hotel threw the foreigners' suitcases toward the boat—not properly closed, they burst open before they reached it. The sea was covered with female clothes and items of underwear, which sent the kids clustering the bank into howls of laughter.

Watching the boat disappear, Loredana said, with a sigh of resignation, "I suppose it was bound to end like that . . ."

"It's nice to see, all the same," said Eléazard, misinterpreting what she had said. "Anyway, they got away, though it was a close shave. Did you see all those panties?"

"I saw them," she said with a smile. "To tell you the truth, I'd forgotten those clowns . . ."

Eléazard looked at her, slightly surprised. Her expression showed the kind of embarrassment, tinged with a feeling of unease and vulnerability, that precedes a confession. Later on, when he was going through his memories, he would regret not having embraced her at that moment. It would doubtless have changed the course of events.

"So what were you going to say?" he asked gently.

"It's not because of the suitcases," was her enigmatic reply. "There's not much left of a story when it's finished. Stuff floating on the sea, like after a shipwreck . . ."

Still not looking at him, she felt for his hand and took it in hers in a way that was quite natural.

"We're friends, aren't we?"

"More than that," Eléazard said, trying to conceal his emotion, "you know very well . . ."

"If one day I need you . . . I mean, if I call for help, from the depths of . . . You'll be there?"

Eléazard took this unusual request with the seriousness it deserved. He gave Loredana's hand a squeeze to let her know he would answer her call, whatever happened. Overjoyed to finally see her with her defenses down, he didn't realize that that was the very moment when she needed him. Perhaps it would have taken no more than that flash of understanding to keep her there, to stop her from turning those moments of silence on the planks of the landing stage into a farewell. Perhaps she wouldn't have changed her decision, but how can one know? He was afraid of offending her if he took her in his arms, afraid of appearing indiscreet if he asked about the reason for her sadness, afraid of irritating her if he told her that her anxieties were not worth the bother and that life was there and he loved her.

Together they waited for night to fall over the sea. Then she felt cold, because of the drizzle, and said she wanted to go back. Hand in hand they walked toward the square. Neither of them said a word, they were so choked with emotion and sure they would burst out sobbing. As they parted, she kissed him on the lips; Eléazard watched her go to the hotel without for a moment suspecting that they would never see each other again.

SÃO LUÍS: *He'd find himself in Manaus in no time at all!*

Going up the steps to the Palacio Estadual, Colonel José Moreira noted the sheepish expressions of the porters who stood at attention to salute him. Everyone knew already . . . Rats leaving the sinking ship! But surely they didn't think he was going to let them go ahead without taking countermeasures. Quick enough when asking for handouts, but when it came to defending their boss, there was no one there . . . OK, that was the way the game was played, as he knew better than anyone. I'm going to show them, he told himself as he forced himself to smile at all and sundry, that people don't defy me and get away with it. When he entered his office, briefcase under his arm, even Anna was favored with a pat on the rump. Good thing he hadn't waited until he got to the palace to read the papers! At least he'd been alone when he'd received the shock, in the rear of his car, with no need to put a bold face on it for these hyenas. He'd also had enough time to work out a strategy for a counterattack. Having said that, the bastards who'd compiled the dossier against him had done an excellent job. Certain details were only known to a very limited number of people, they couldn't have come out without collusion from someone close to him. You could never be too cautious . . . One day the guy who'd done this to him would be on his knees, begging for mercy.

"The press review is on your desk, sir," his secretary said, trying to sound businesslike but unable to restrain a note of satisfaction. "The minister of justice, Edson Barbosa, Jr., called and asked you to call back as a matter of urgency. There's also a news team from TV Globo asking for an interview. I've put the journalist's card in your diary."

"Thanks, Anna," he said, placing both hands flat on his desk. "Cancel all my meetings for this morning, I don't want to see anyone. Tell Jodinha and Santos to come here as soon as they arrive."

"They're already here, Governor."

"Good." Moreira looked at his watch, yes, even those two were in early today. "I'll see them at ten, I've a few telephone calls to make and I don't want to be disturbed before then. For anything that doesn't concern merely administrative matters—you see what I mean, don't you?—you'll steer them toward the press secretary."

"What shall I say to the television people?"

Moreira's first impulse was to send them away, but then he thought it would be a good idea to issue an official denial of the accusations. "Eleven o'clock, after the meeting. They can set up in the meeting room now if that suits them."

The governor waited until she had closed the door before he dialed the first number, that of the state's Department of Political and Social Order. "Is that Superintendent Frazão? Moreira da Rocha here . . . Yes, Superintendent, yes . . . I was one of the last to hear about it and I'm not very happy about that. How could such a blunder have been made? You have good reason to make yourself agreeable to me, if I remember rightly . . . No, no excuses, it's facts I want, Superintendent, facts! Who's responsible for this fucking mess? . . . What was that? Waldemar de Oliveira . . ." He noted the name down to remind himself. "Where's he been all the time? OK, OK, I understand . . . And my lawyer, Wagner Cascudo? . . . But what do you expect him to say, for God's sake? He's done nothing wrong . . . How much has bail been set at? Two hundred thousand? . . . Yes, I'm listening . . . I'll do the necessary . . . But of course I'm counting on you, Superintendent, and it's in your own interest to tell me precisely what happens . . . I made you and I can unmake you whenever it suits me. Just remember that, Franzão."

He slammed the receiver down and lit a cigarette. Whoever had set this up hadn't pulled his punches. And he'd been so quick, for Christ's sake! It was hard to believe . . . He had to get Wagner out of prison before the stupid bugger turned informer . . .

He called Vicente Bilunquinha, a young lawyer who owed him, amongst other little sweeteners, his membership in the Lions Club. "Good morning . . . Yes, a nice election stunt, they're pulling out all the stops this time but they won't get away with it, you'll see . . . But while we're on the subject, could you attend to our friend Wagner Cascudo? You'd be doing me a great service. I have complete confidence in you, you know that . . . Yes . . . I'll send you the amount for bail by special courier . . . Exactly. Call me back as soon as he's out and keep him snug. Be sure to tell him I'll see to everything, he needn't worry . . . A thousand thanks, Vivente, I'll pay you back for this . . . With pleasure, of course. I'll discuss it with my wife and get back to you . . . *Ciao*, Vicente, *ciao*. *Ciao*. To your wife as well, *ciao* . . .″

He'd hardly replaced the receiver when he started as the phone rang:

"Moreira here. Who's that? Oh, it's you, Edson . . . I was just about to call you . . . I know, yes, I know, but they've nothing they can use against me. It's our political opponents, they're just bluffing. It'll all die down in a few days. . . . Don't worry, I tell you, I've got things well in hand. I'm going to make a statement on Globo in an hour or so, just to clarify matters . . . There's nothing in it, I assure you. It's a complete fabrication. You know me, I wouldn't do something like that . . . The speculation? That does exist, of course, Edson . . . As far as I'm aware we haven't made a law against making a profit yet. On that point, forgive me for reminding you, but you're hardly in a position to lecture others . . . That's not what I meant, Edson, but if anyone comes looking for trouble, they'll get it. Neither you, nor I, nor the Party stand to gain anything from all this fuss. Let me remind you that the elections take place in three weeks' time, so I'd be grateful if you could have a look into this business. It's in all our interest, as you very well know . . . Yes . . . De Oliveira, Waldemar de Oliveira . . . A little shit-stirrer from Santa Inês. I don't know how he did it, but he's managed to bypass all my officials here . . . That would be perfect,

Edson. I'm delighted we speak the same language . . . OK, I'll see to it and I'll keep you up to date . . ."

Moreira threw himself back in his chair and exhaled slowly. A smile on his lips, he took deep breaths, like an athlete after a race. He'd got out of that nicely, and no mistake! If the minister of justice himself was going to look into the question then that Oliveira wasn't going to have much of a future . . . He'd find himself in Manaus in no time at all! The counteroffensive had started, all that was left was to close off his links to Wagner and put any compromising documents in a safe place. . . . There was nothing sensitive about the *resort* project in itself. The reason he'd kept it secret so far was merely a matter of expedience. First and foremost he had to control the media; he was going to have to grease quite a few palms, but he could use the secret funds put aside for that very purpose. A couple of favorable editorials, get that prosecutor involved in a juicy sex scandal—he'd have to speak to Santos and Jodinha, surely his advisers could find some druggie to claim he shagged little boys—and by the time the guy had managed to extricate himself from the tissue of lies he'd be back in the saddle for another term . . . The governor felt he was growing claws. For the first time that morning he was optimistic about the future again.

"Moreira," he said as he lifted the receiver. "Oh, it's you, darling . . ." Suddenly he felt a hot flush down the back of his neck. "You're not going to believe everything they say in the newspapers? Not you, surely? I swear to you I've nothing to . . . Carlotta! There's no question of that, I refuse, d'you hear? I . . . Carlotta! Carlotta?"

For a moment he considered calling straight back. But it was better to give her time to calm down. He'd see that evening, at the *fazenda*. It really would be the last straw if she joined in . . . The fact that Mauro was missing was almost driving her crazy . . . A twinge in the region of the sternum told him he wasn't going to be able to get her to change her mind. Not this time. For a moment he imagined life without Carlotta, then dismissed the thought, he found it such an insult to his sense of order and symmetry.

CHAPTER 27

How the decision to erect another obelisk was reached & the subsequent discussion on the choice of a suitable animal

THE WHITMONDAY CELEBRATIONS passed off perfectly. It was on that occasion that the Supreme Pontiff very clearly expressed his desire to erect an obelisk, the one, to be precise, that had just been unearthed during the works carried out by the Dominicans around the church of Santa-Maria sopra Minerva. Once more Kircher was to collaborate with his sculptor friend on the design of a statue worthy not only of that monument from antiquity but also of the Piazza Minerva, of which it would be the principal ornament.

Cavaliere Bernini had been called to Paris by Louis XIV in order to revise the plans for his Louvre Palace & to sculpt a bust of him at the head of his army. Since he could stand neither the courtiers nor the climate of that city, he returned to Rome at the end of October, the richer by three thousand *louis d'or* & an

annuity of twelve thousand *livres* as a reward for his services.
When he arrived at the College to tell us his ideas on the
Piazza Minerva monument, Kircher & I were busy with Father
Grueber, taking notes on his journey to China.

"Come now," Kircher said with a smile, "don't despair! Rome
wasn't built in a day & with God's help I'm sure we'll manage
to restore the original wisdom of the ancients. And since the
matter has cropped up at such an opportune moment, tell me,
Lorenzo, what are your suggestions for the Minerva obelisk?"

"Given the small size of the object, I feel it's impossible to
design a majestic monument in the style of the Pamphilius
Fountain. Therefore I had the idea of simply placing it on the
back of a animal whose symbolic value could match that of the
hieroglyphs. That is as far as I've gotten, since I don't know what
they contain, though certain animals, for example the tortoise
& the armadillo, do fascinate me from an artistic point of view,
so that I have started to sketch out some designs using them."

Kircher looked dubious. "We'll go into the choice of animal
later. Anyway, it's less important that it corresponds to the
teaching of the hieroglyphs carved on the obelisk than to that of
the Church & of the Supreme Pontiff, her symbol in this world.
But so that you have all the details necessary for your work, I
will give you my translation now."

Athanasius picked up a sheet of paper from the table &,
after having cleared his throat, read the following in solemn
tones:

"*Mophta, the supreme spirit and archetype, instills his virtues
into the sidereal world, that is, this solar spirit subject to him.
From which the vital movement in the material or elemental
world proceeds; & from which the abundance of all things as well
as the variety of species arises.*

"It flows out unceasingly from the Osirian mud, attracted by some wondrous sympathy & strong in the power hidden in his figure with two faces.

"O clairvoyant Chen-Osiris, guardian of the sacred canals, symbols of the aqueous nature of which all life consists!

"Through the good will of Ophionus, that spirit sufficient to obtain favors and the propagation of life, principles to which this tablet is consecrated, & with the assistance of the humid Agathodaemon of divine Osiris, the seven towers of the heavens are protected from all damage. That is why the image of the Same must be presented circularly in the sacrifices & ceremonies.

"The left hand of Nature or the fountain of Hecate, that is the swirling that is the very respiration of the universe, is evoked by sacrifices & attracted by that in which the demon Polymorphus produces the generous variety of things in the quadripartite world.

"The deceitful artifices of Typhon have been broken, thus reserving the life of innocent things; to which the pentacles and amulets below lead because of the mystical foundations on which they are built. That is why they are powerful to obtain all the good things of an enchanting life . . ."

"God's blood!" Bernini exclaimed. "I would have understood just as much if you'd been speaking Iroquois. Your Egyptian priests were better than anyone at jumbling up their little homilies . . ."

"There were two good reasons for that, the first being the profundity of the mysteries they were expressing, the second as a precaution against heedlessly giving away such sought-after knowledge to ignoramuses. Simple arts, such as music & painting, require a long initiation; much longer & more arduous is that required by knowledge. Pythagoras, remember, enjoined his disciples to silence so that they would not divulge the sacred mysteries, because one can only learn by meditating, not by speaking. . . ."

"As for me," said Bernini, slightly piqued, "I'll stick to the arts without trying to decipher such recondite allegories . . ."

"Come now, my friend, don't misunderstand me. Knowledge requires application alone & you make wonderful use of yours in a field in which you excel. Life is too short, alas, to consider devoting oneself fully to more than a single art. Socrates was a poor sculptor before becoming Socrates; as for Phidias, that maker of divine images, he could well have been dumb for all we know of his philosophy. One acted as a midwife to minds, the other to stones, that's all!"

"Capital!" Bernini said with a laugh. "How could I fail to be convinced when you compare me to such a master?!"

"I didn't forget myself, either," Kircher said in the same tone, "but that was only for the purposes of the analogy, since I would have great difficulty competing with Socrates. If you are incontestably the greatest sculptor of the age, I am nothing but an honest laborer in the field of knowledge. I have nothing else to do, all my time is my own, so that I can concentrate on things for long periods without interruption. That is the only way in which I may call myself a genius. I have learned by long experience how much time such an intellectual task can take & to what extent the mind must be free of all distraction to complete it successfully . . . But let us return to our obelisk. As I'm sure you will have realized, despite your protestations at its apparent obscurity, this text contains a summary of the Egyptian doctrine regarding the supreme principles governing the world. Replace Mophta by God, Osiris by the Sun and the seven towers of the heavens by the planets & you will see that this doctrine only differs from that of the Church in points of detail. You will therefore, I hope, agree that the tortoise & the armadillo are hardly suitable symbols for such a complex system."

"I'm happy to grant you that," Bernini said with a frown, "but I'm sure you will have some other beast to suggest . . ."

"To tell you the truth, I haven't thought about it. However, it seems to me that the ox or the rhinoceros would be perfectly suitable: the ox because it warmed Our Savior with its breath, but also because in it the Greeks venerated the Sun & the Moon under the name of Epaphus & the Egyptians the souls of Osiris & of Mophta, under the name of Apis. The rhinoceros, for its part—"

"Out of the question," Bernini broke in shaking his head, "the French have already used it in that way for the entry of Catherine de Medici to Paris. As for the ox, it's an interesting symbol, but I can already hear the comments of the good citizens of Rome on such a statue: they'd make a thousand smutty jokes about its horns and its genitals I very much doubt the Supreme Pontiff would appreciate . . ."

"You are right there. We mustn't neglect that aspect of the problem."

Grueber, who until then had listened in respectful silence, suddenly joined in: "What would you say to an elephant, gentlemen?"

"An elephant?!" Bernini said.

"But of course!" my master exclaimed, grasping the sculptor by the shoulders. "*Cerebrum in capite!* The brain is in the head! Don't you see, Lorenzo? The *Hypnerotomachia* & its obsidian enigma. Why didn't I think of that sooner? We've got our symbol for, in truth, no other beast is as knowledgeable as the elephant!"

Bernini looked as shamefaced as a tomcat being castrated. Caught out, his only comment was, "Huh!"

MATO GROSSO: *Like arrows fledged with dreams . . .*

Elaine had been worried about Mauro every second while he was away. Still under the shock of the horrible vision, he burst out sobbing as he told them what had happened; she was happy to console him when he buried his face in her breast. As well as the genuine sorrow she felt, she was in the grip of a fear that kept her stuck to the bench. Inside her head a compass needle was spinning round and round wildly.

As night fell, the mosquitos arrived.

"When I think that he threw the magazine clip away . . ." Petersen muttered. He was thinking out loud and, since they expressed the impasse they found themselves in, the odd phrases they didn't want to hear seemed to deepen the darkness even more.

Dietlev regained consciousness with the name of Elaine on his lips and she immediately replied. As she cleaned his wound, more to give her something to make her forget her fear than out of necessity, she decided to keep the death of Yurupig from him; the infection was taking an alarming turn and he'd need all his strength to cope with it. The Indians had brought the rucksack back . . . They'd leave in the morning . . . He just had to hold on . . . As she talked to him, these white lies turned into their opposite inside her head so that what she heard as she spoke them was the strict truth: Dietlev wouldn't hold out much longer, they'd perhaps never leave this clearing. Fear and uncertainty condensed in a nasty sweat under her armpits.

"Was there anything missing from the rucksack?" Dietlev asked in a low voice.

"No," Elaine replied. "That is, yes, there was. The fossil samples have gone. They must have thought they were ordinary stones and chucked them away."

They heard Petersen sniff noisily in the darkness.

"Him and his coke," Dietlev said irritatedly.

"Just ignore him, try to sleep."

The Indians had lit their bonfire. Gleams from the flames turned the interior of their hut red, casting fanciful ideograms over their faces. A strident, repetitive threnody suddenly swelled up with the light; shrill flutes accompanied a plaintive chant: the whole tribe was groaning in rhythm, softly, with unpredictable variations, sudden occlusive surges in which their throats grew hoarse.

The mat over the entrance was raised; the same Indians who had brought them food invited the strangers to leave the hut. Without having time to discuss it, they were led toward the huge bonfire crackling in the middle of the village. Little benches to sit on, platters loaded with food, large calabashes filled with beer . . . they were being treated as distinguished guests, with the result that Elaine started to hope again.

Still daubed with red, shining like swimmers who had just come out of the water, several Indians were already turning around the blaze. Long macaw tails stuck out of the yellow plumes they wore around their arms, just under their shoulders. Their hair speckled with white down, kingfisher feathers in the lobes of their ears, they were miming something animal or organic. Elaine started back slightly: the shaman had suddenly appeared in front of the little group of strangers. Black snot was dribbling down from his nostrils in two syrupy trickles; it was splattered all over his scrawny chest. Having wiped his nose on himself, he appeared older, more deranged. More savage, Elaine thought, filled with re-pugnance as he began a long, strangely melodious speech.

It was a celebration in honor of Qüyririche, a celebration in which they had prepared all the food they possessed for the Mes-senger and his divine relatives. The manioc beer was ready, they would blow a lot of epena, clouds of magic powder, again and again, until they went up into the invisible clouds where the destiny of the worlds was woven. He, Raypoty, had been able to interpret the signs: he knew the source of the fish-stones! For many years he had searched for the opening of the universe else-where, the secret fissure through which his people could finally escape, like an asshole suddenly relaxed in the mortal belly of the forest. But now the god himself had come to open his eyes. There was no need to plant nor to hunt anymore, they would depart at dawn, leaving behind everything that might weigh them down and prevent their final take-off for the Land-with-no-evil.

He finished with a few occult words designed to attract the favors of the Messenger so that he would continue to guide him and his people.

"*Agnus Dei qui tollis peccata mundi,*" Mauro immediately translated, "*miserere nobis.* It's crazy! If we ever get out of here I'm going to spend the rest of my life inventing a universal language. It's as if he's decided not to understand a word of what we're saying. If he won't make an effort, all our attempts to communicate with him will get us nowhere. It's just too stupid!"

"That's not the problem," Dietlev said, his voice affected by his fever. "I think he believes we can understand him. We need to try and talk to someone else in the tribe."

"We've got to get out of here, that's what," Petersen growled. "I've an uneasy feeling about these loonies."

The shaman took a long tube of bark as thin as a blowpipe, put a pinch of black powder in one of the ends which he handed to an Indian squatting down. Squatting down himself, he put the other end to his nostrils. Holding the tube between his index and middle fingers, the Indian breathed in and blew the dose of *epena* high up into the shaman's mucous membrane.

"See, I'm not the only one!" Petersen gloated. He'd already observed the same practice among the Yanomami and knew they were witnessing a ritual taking of drugs.

Eyes closed, his face screwed up in pain, the shaman prepared the tube then blew the powder into the nostrils of the one who had just helped him. The Indian stayed on his heels, transfixed, prey to what looked like insupportable pain. He nose began to drip black fluid onto his chin, sinuous trails of snot, which the Indian suddenly made spray out with an abrupt exhalation. Thus he was splashed with the blood of the true world, drawing on his chest a horoscope that the shaman alone could interpret.

It was like a signal; all the Indians in the tribe started to breathe in the magic substance. Between each pinch they quenched their thirst with beer and greedily dug into any food within reach. After the third or fourth inhalation, a man would start howling, waving his arms, then he would stand up for an unmoving dance that made him shake on the spot like a soul in torment. Eventually he would faint and collapse, overcome by the visions. The women would then drag him off a little way, while the one who had blown the drug into his nostrils had it done to himself by someone else.

One hour later most of the men were lying on the ground alongside each other, like corpses waiting to be dealt with.

"*Guardians of the dream,*" the shaman was saying as he deciphered the symbols on the torsos, "*living shelters of the true soul, your hearts do not lie. On them I can see the anaconda and the jaguar, the terrapin and the hummingbird. You are like arrows fledged with dreams, great birds who are consumed in the sky by their wings of fire. The end of all your woes is near, for soon the Messenger will guide us to that mountain where visions cascade down uninterruptedly. Your torsos tell me much: they tell of the return to the land of our birth, to the smiling happiness of newborn babes . . .*"

The shaman walked along between the bodies, releasing their penises, swollen by the sensual wanderings of the sleepers' minds, from their thin shackles, spitting magic arrows at invisible enemies swirling round them like flies. Agitated, close to trance, he came back and stood in front of Dietlev. Petersen was the first to understand his gesticulations: "He wants to get you to sniff his rubbish," he said in mocking tones. "No way out of it, old chap . . ."

Elaine turned to Dietlev, full of concern: "Don't do it," she begged. "You've seen what it does to them."

"Given the state I've reached . . . and then we don't know what'll happen if I refuse. It's the best way of keeping in their good books. So long, Carter—won't see you again . . ."

He stuck the wax tip of the tube in one of his nostrils; when the shaman blew down it, he was immediately thrown back on the stretcher. After a few seconds of an intense burning sensation spreading through his sinuses, Dietlev had the very clear impression that the right side of his brain had frozen with no hope of it ever unfreezing. Opening his eyes, he was alarmed to see the sepia tones of the forest: the harmony of an old photo abruptly torn apart by sudden flashes of lightning, revealing incredible perspectives in which amber and mauve shaded into infinity. A Piranesian delirium, architectural tumors ceaselessly proliferating. He could hear the slow grinding of icebergs, the overthrust of continental plates. Distant whirlwinds started to stir up space with their spirals, cracks appeared all over the earth, which opened up like a round loaf under the irresistible force of the mountains. Stones rose in the air! Before he lost consciousness Dietlev was aware he was witnessing something grandiose, an event mingling the beginning of worlds and their apocalypse.

VERY EARLY THE next morning Elaine was woken by the sound of voices punctuated by crying children. First of all she had a quick look at Dietlev—he was still sleeping and appeared to be breathing normally. Then she got our of her hammock to have a look outside the hut. The whole tribe was packing its bags . . . Woken by Elaine, Mauro and Petersen went to the mat over the entrance.

"It looks as if they're leaving," Mauro said, a touch of concern in his voice.

"And taking us with them," Petersen added, seeing a little group of Indians approaching.

Once in the hut the two men they already knew indicated that they were to pick up their rucksacks and follow them. With great signs of deference, they lifted up the stretcher while other Indians took the various feather ornaments down from the central pillar.

Elaine's face shone: at last they had understood, they were taking them to some civilized place where Dietlev could receive medical help. Cheered by this prospect, Mauro returned her smile. Petersen's eyes were sunken, his complexion gray, his expression hard. All he did was shake his head at the other two's silent joy.

The whole tribe plunged into the forest. The indifference with which the Indians had abandoned their village was disconcerting. They were only taking the strict minimum with them, a monkey-skin bag, twists of chewing tobacco, bows, arrows and blowpipes. In woven baskets held on their back by a strap around their forehead, the women were carrying a few mats, hammocks and various receptacles; they were also taking embers from the hearth with them, but none had paid the least attention to the heaps of food still scattered round the smoking ashes of the bonfire. Curled up in the carrying cloths, the babies were sucking at their mother's breasts. A population of refugees setting off on their exodus, Elaine thought without dwelling on it. She felt guilty at having allowed herself to hope: however horrible it was, however present in her thoughts, Yurupig's death was tending to fade as the prospect of reaching safety grew more imminent. Obsessed by the vision of his tortured head, Mauro was making every effort to erase even the unfortunate Indian's name from his mind. As for Petersen, he didn't remember him until much later and then to blame himself for not having thought of recovering the compass.

The shaman seemed to know exactly where he was going. The long procession made fairly good progress under the hostile cover of the jungle. Dietlev still hadn't woken; despite all her efforts, Elaine couldn't get him to open his eyes. His coma was worrying, though she couldn't tell whether it was an effect of the gangrene or of the powder blown up his nose by the shaman. The Indians had recovered fairly easily, but the fact that Dietlev had never experienced it before would explain a longer period of recuperation.

"What did he mean, yesterday evening?" Mauro asked as he met her anxious look. "He was talking about someone called Carver or Carter, wasn't he?"

The reminder made Elaine smile. "Carter," she said. "It's an old private joke. I don't know if you've read 'The Statement of Randolph Carter' by H. P. Lovecraft? The story begins with a guy going to a cemetery, an unknown graveyard he's discovered. He takes a friend called Carter with him. They lift a slab and discover a flight of stone steps . . . The guy knows he's going to have to fight 'the thing,' some kind of fiendish entity from the depths of time, et cetera, et cetera—the usual Lovecraft. He leaves Carter on the surface and goes down into the tomb. As they have a field telephone with them, Carter remains in contact with his friend. He hears him panicking, then everything gets more frenzied until the moment comes when it's clear he'll never get back to the surface. At the end of the first chapter the guy orders Carter to replace the slab and then manages one last sentence: '*Tão longo, Carter.*' I did think it a bit odd, but that was all. What could it be that was *so* long? But then you're not surprised at anything in Lovecraft, I just accepted it as an enigma. It was Dietlev who one day pointed out to me that it was a mistake in the translation. The original English text simply said 'So long, Carter.' It didn't make much difference to the rest of the story, but it ought to have been translated by something that meant 'Goodbye, Carter' in Portuguese, say '*Até logo, Carter.*' You know Dietlev and his twisted sense of humor. He made me laugh at it so much, we got into the habit of using the phrase for saying goodbye. A kind of in-joke between us, at one time . . ."

"I see," said Mauro.

AFTER THEY HAD been going for two hours, Petersen broke the sulky silence he had maintained since they left, simply saying, "There's a snag."

"What's wrong?" Elaine said.

"What's wrong is that we're going away from the river; look at the moss on the tree trunks."

"That's what I've been doing all the time," Mauro said with some irritation. "They generally grow facing the sun, thus indicating south—"

"Well done, sonny, except that you've got the wrong hemisphere and it's the exact opposite. We've been heading due northwest since the start. I waited until I was absolutely certain before telling you."

"But what does that matter?" Mauro replied. "The important thing is that they're taking us somewhere; the actual place doesn't really matter as long as there's some means of contacting the emergency services."

"Northwest, you said?" Elaine asked.

"Yes, *senhora*. And not deviating by even a hair's breadth."

Elaine vainly tried to visualize the map. Only Dietlev could have said what there might be in that direction. "And have you any idea what we might find going in that direction?" she asked.

"Not the least," Herman said with a shrug. "The farther we go to the northwest, the deeper we go into the jungle, full stop. There's never been anything up there, never will be. A blank space on the map, there's quite a lot of that round here."

Elaine did indeed recall those gaps, so attractive that she'd had dreams about them during the preparations for the expedition. And now that she was near them, they brought tears to her eyes.

Mauro was making every effort to fight off a sense of discouragement. "Assuming you're right," he said a little less aggressively, "why would they take us with them in the jungle? It's a question of logic: they surely won't have left the village just for fun, will they? What you're saying just doesn't stand up . . ."

"And Yurupig?" Petersen asked. "What was that for? You know what goes on inside their heads, do you? If I had a compass I swear I'd try to give them the slip—and as soon as possible!"

"What's stopping you, since you know exactly where we're heading? Off you go, don't worry about us."

Petersen ignored his mockery. Apart from the fact that it was impossible to make headway through the jungle without a machete and other equipment, he was exhausted. His body was cracking up all over. If the cocaine had allowed him to look as if he were taking it all in his stride during the first few days, now it was making him suffer rather than helping him. As its effects wore off he was prey to such weakness and depression that he had to take another dose, with increasing frequency and in greater and greater quantities.

"We'll discuss it later," he said eventually, "but I'll be damned if we see even the shadow of a white man in that area."

Elaine knew that she would not be able to just set off for the river. Whatever destination the Indians had in mind, they had to trust them—or see themselves, she suddenly realized, as their prisoners. Despite what they'd done to Yurupig, she found it impossible to feel in danger with them. The whole tribe continued to treat them with perfect consideration; there were even men or women coming up to them to touch Dietlev's stretcher in a gesture that was clearly compassionate. Each time she tried to say a friendly word, to put on an inviting look, but the Indians were too overawed, just one little girl had returned her smile.

THEY FINALLY STOPPED at around four in the afternoon. The whole tribe seemed to have great fun searching the undergrowth for a place to camp for the night. Lean-tos of a sort were erected with amazing rapidity—four poles supporting a crude roof of palm leaves beneath which each family quickly spread out their mats and hammocks. Blowing on the embers, the men lit fires in the middle of these shelters. By a stroke of luck three howler monkeys and a coati were shot; a worm-eaten tree trunk provided an abundance of big grubs; the girls brought back some honeypot ants, some honey and the pith of young palm trees cut up by the adults. Wild oranges appeared as if by magic.

Dietlev still hadn't woken; Elaine cleaned up the stump of his leg as best she could then gave in to her weariness. Mauro and Petersen slumped down beside the fire as well, they too exhausted by the day's walk. Plagued by insects that the smoke hadn't yet managed to drive off, they nibbled on some beans from a tin they'd opened, not being able to bring themselves to eat the food the shaman had sent to them. Mauro tried the oranges, but they were so bitter they were sickening. As for the honey, it was used to thicken a kind of porridge which, seething with grubs, produced the same effect.

The Indians observed them with a discreetness that was in inverse proportion to their curiosity: the more marvels they showed—tins of food, knives or matches, fantastic objects that flew across their field of vision like breathtaking comets—the more they pretended not to be interested. They were not intimidated by those-who-had-come-out-of-the-night, but basic politeness toward the newcomers—even if they were supernatural beings—demanded this friendly reserve. To look a woman in the eye was to sleep with her, to stare at a man made him a mortal enemy; between seduction and combat there was no room left to follow impulse without jeopardizing the whole social order.

Elaine noticed this feigned indifference without understanding its motivation. Too tired to think and uneasy at the feeling of being spied on, she drifted off into memories, mingling vague images of Eléazard with those of Moéma. With Caetano Veloso filling his ears, Mauro watched her daydreaming; the splashes of mud on her face, her damp, dirty, tangled hair, the weariness visible under her eyes made her more beautiful, more desirable than ever. He envied Dietlev for having held this woman in his arms, while wondering what could have attracted her to a man with such an ungainly physique. Not being able to imagine them in the same bed in a way that wasn't ugly made him irritated with her, despite having a clear sense that it was just an expression of resentment, both puerile and unwarranted.

Petersen was already asleep, or pretending to be.

In the last shafts of daylight between the trees a flight of parakeets splashed the space above them with blood.

A little boy had come up to them, fascinated by Mauro's Walkman. Very gently he put the phones over the head of the boy, who initially reacted with alarm then, very quickly, with a joyful smile. His father came to tell him to stop pestering the strangers but, overcome with curiosity, he acquiesced when the boy wanted to share his discovery with him, Hardly had he clumsily put the headphones to his ears, however, than he threw them to the ground, punched the child on the head and was seized by a fit of rage. Dumbfounded by the violence of this response, Mauro curled up: the Indian was threatening to bludgeon him with his bow and would certainly have done so if the shaman, alerted by his furious cries, had not quickly caught his arm. The old man must have found the right words to explain the magic, for the Indian calmed down almost immediately. His wife had run over and soothed him by massaging his neck and shoulders while he continued to clean out his ears with his little finger to rid them of the voices contaminating his memory with their verminous parasites.

ELAINE WOKE DURING the night. There was hardly any glow at all from the fire but there was a halo of cold light shimmering beside her: unrecognizable under the phosphorescent nimbus it was giving off, Dietlev's body was shining like a mirror struck by the sun!

Despite its improbable, dreamlike quality, the vision seemed so real that Elaine stretched out her hand toward the brightness. A cloud of fireflies flew up from the corpse, riddling the darkness with thousands of slivers of glass.

Eléazard's notebooks

LOREDANA talking about Moreira: "He's got a head you could stick in a pair of trousers . . ." Chuang-tzu lives!

KIRCHER associated with Poussin, Rubens, Bernini . . . Could someone these exceptional artists regarded as their master and their friend be fundamentally narrow-minded or a simple mediocrity?

NEWTON practised alchemy, Kepler speculated on the music of the spheres . . .

"MY AIM IS TO reconstruct the museum assembled by the Jesuit Athanasius Kircher, author of *Ars Magna Lucis et Umbrae* (1646) and inventor of the 'polydiptic theater' in which about sixty little mirrors lining the inside of a large box transform a bough into a forest, a lead soldier into an army, a booklet into a library. (. . .) If I were not afraid of being misunderstood, I would have nothing against reconstructing, in my house, the room completely lined with mirrors according to Kircher's design, in which I would see myself walking on the ceiling, head down, as if I were flying upward from the depths of the floor." (Italo Calvino: *If on a Winter's Night a Traveler*, tr. William Weaver)

EVERYTHING IS DONE in our world to eliminate the spoken word as far as possible. The solitude of everyone in the midst of everyone: clubbing in one's own night, practicing epilepsy as an alternative to despair. The mirrors, present everywhere, allow each one to dance alone, facing themselves. Sexual displays, anonymous, the narcissistic seduction of one's reflection. Four hours of glory a week, all the rest is merely a deferred suicide.

THREE LINES from the 200 pages of the Voynich manuscript:

BSOOM.FZCO.FSO9.SOBS9.8OE82.8EO8
OE.SC9.S9.Q9.SFSOR.ZCO.SCOR9.SOE89
SO.ZO.SAM.ZAM.8AM.4O8AM.O.AR.AJ.

WHERE TIGERS ARE AT HOME

What delusion could compel a man to encrypt his own writings so that they are illegible to anyone but himself? The absolute necessity for them to remain secret. What reason could demand that their content be hidden to such an extent? Fear of death or of being plundered? There were different ways of risking one's life in the thirteenth century, but the surest of all was heresy. As for losing some treasure, the least the man must have done would have been to have achieved the transmutation of lead into gold or found some elixir of immortality. A heretical cosmogony, an alchemical treatise? In the first case we're dealing with a coward, in the second with a skinflint; and in both with an imbecile.

Was he even able to reread them himself?

A BASE ACT: I WASN'T SINCERE, I only smiled at Alfredo for my smile to ricochet off toward Loredana. A common smile of complicity designed to reinforce my own superiority.

EVEN ROGER CAILLOIS finds things in Kircher's works to stimulate his own imagination: "For the same reasons I have particularly high regard for a *Noah's Ark* illustrating one of the numerous works of P. Athanasius Kircher, an unknown grandmaster in the realm of the unusual. In front of the floating barn, among rumps and limbs of men and horses, fish are dying, monstrous ones with two heads or eyes surrounded by petals of cruciferous plants, themselves overwhelmed by the irresistible flood and as if suffocated by their natural element. The horrible aspect is that they appear to be spared by the rain, which, falling from frightening storm clouds, mysteriously stops before the terrified shoal of this animate flotsam and jetsam. No one thought that the deluge must have destroyed even these aquatic creatures."

FLAUBERT, CALVINO, CAILLOIS . . .

WHAT DID I LIKE IN KIRCHER, if not what fascinated him himself: this kaleidoscopic world, its infinite ability to produce the fabulous. A *Wunderkammer*: a gallery of curiosities, a collection of fairy tales . . . an attic, a box-room, a toy chest with our first marvelings curled up inside, our first frail steps as discoverers.

"THE KIRCHER EFFECT": the baroque. Or, as Flaubert put it, that desperate need to say what cannot be said . . .

WITH GREAT LAMENTATION and to help him to die more quickly, young men saw wood—the wood of his coffin—outside the door of a dying man. *They are sawing the old man.*

I'VE MISSED OUT ON EVERYTHING through not taking part in society . . .

IT'S HIGH TIME I asked myself what I expect from my work on this manuscript . . . Schott's manuscript is so hagiographic he's almost comic; I probably am just as much because of my skepticism . . .

THE ONLY POSSIBLE TRANSCENDENCE is when a man surpasses himself to find an excess of humanity in himself or in others.

LOREDANA is wrong, for once . . .

ON THE INDIANS who every day compel the sun to appear: what is important is their self-possession, their certainty that they are making the sun rise for others, while they themselves are convinced that this world rises on its own. Beating the drum for dawn; making morning break against all odds while people are sleeping.

CHAPTER 28

*In which Kircher explains the symbolism of the elephant,
hears alarming news from China & trembles for his collections
because of the King of Spain*

"NO OTHER BEAST is as knowledgeable as the elephant,"
Kircher repeated. "But also there is none more powerful
on earth, even the tiger has to give way to its power & its
redoubtable defenses. And yet this animal lives on plants alone &
is of such a noble disposition that it never attacks others except to
punish those who, out of malice or ignorance, disturb the peace
of its kingdom. And it only does that with extreme prudence,
knowing, as every true monarch ought to, that one must consider
one's actions & words, distrust everyone & look after one's own
security as well as that of one's subjects. Julius Caesar was well
aware of all this, for he had his medals engraved with the image
of the Ethiopian mastodon instead of his own. As an emblem it
is even more pregnant with meaning for, according to Servius,
the word for elephant in the Punic language is 'kaïsar' . . . As

665

for Pliny, he regards the animal as an Egyptian symbol of piety; indeed, does he not tell us that elephants, impelled by some natural & mysterious intelligence, carry the branches they have torn from the forest where they graze, raise them up in their trunks & turn their eyes toward the new moon, gently waving the branches as if they were praying to the goddess Isis that she may look favorably on them? . . ."

"Not forgetting," Grueber said, "—& this is what I had in mind when I took the liberty of interrupting—the qualities given it by the inhabitants of Asia. For they say that the elephant, just like Atlas, supports the world: its legs are to the mass of its body as the four columns that support the celestial sphere. The Brahmins & the Tibetans worship it under the name of Ganesh & the Chinese, in the legend recounting their origin, make it give to the god Fo-hi. If, then, you place this obelisk on its back, as can be seen in the illustration to the *Dream of Poliphilius*—"

"We will have," Kircher broke in excitedly, "the appropriate hieroglyph: intelligence, power, prudence & piety supporting the cosmic universe but surmounted by divine omniscience; that is, the Church as the support of God, or the Supreme Pontiff as well, making it possible, through his powers & his generosity, finally to restore the wisdom of the ancient world! And never will there have been a better symbol to honor Minerva, to whom the square is dedicated!"

"Wonderful!" Bernini exclaimed. "But where will I find an elephant?"

"At the Coliseum, of course," Grueber replied, as if it were the most natural thing in the world. Then, seeing the sculptor's baffled look, he added, "A troop of gypsies is showing wild animals for a few coppers; you'll find the one you're looking for there."

"I'm off, then," Bernini said without further thought. "I want to get down to work as quickly as possible."

After Bernini had left, my master heaped praise on Father Grueber for his quick-wittedness. The more he thought about it, he said, the richer in symbolic meaning the animal they had chosen seemed to him. Following his first three interpretations, he elaborated others, less obvious but just as rigorous, emphasizing the analogy between the papal ministry & the influence of Mophta, the supreme spirit, on our sublunar world.

"If I weren't sure that it would offend Alexander's natural modesty," he told us, "I would call this monument 'Osiris Resuscitated' & everything would be expressed with sublime concision."

Two weeks later Cavaliere Bernini had enough sketches of elephants for the project to be submitted to the Supreme Pontiff, who accepted it unreservedly & our sculptor immediately set out in search of a suitable block of marble in the quarries of Florence. As for my master, he burned the midnight oil even more so that he could finish the work that was to accompany the erection of the monument.

It was, therefore, in February 1666, at the same time as Bernini's magnificent sculpture was revealed to the public, that *Obeliscus Alexandrinus* appeared, a little book in which my master once more displayed his profound knowledge of Egypt & its hieroglyphs. Naturally it contained a translation, with commentary, of the Egyptian text, but also an ideal reconstruction of the great Temple of Isis in Rome, the building to which the obelisk had originally belonged. Not wanting to repeat what he had already dealt with at length in his *Obeliscus Pamphilius* & *Œdipus Ægyptiacus*, in this work Kircher limited himself to restoring & interpreting numerous objects from his museum & emphasizing the importance of Egyptian cults in ancient Rome. He finished by elaborating in detail the symbolism of the monument itself in the way it demonstrated to the whole world the achievements of the Supreme Pontiff in upholding and diffusing the Christian religion. *May this obelisk of the ancient sages,* my master wrote, *erected to make the glory of thy name shine out, go to the four corners of the globe & speak to all of Alexander, under whose auspices it has been brought back to life!*

In those days Rome, thanks to the Vicar of Christ & his missionaries, cast its glorious light over the whole world, as Heliopolis had done in the past. And I can assure you, dear reader, that the dedication & genius of Athanasius Kircher were not without having played a part in its success.

Grueber having left us to return to Austria, Kircher continued to work on his book about China. Father Heinrich Roth was invaluable for his knowledge of India & of *Sanskrit,* the language of the Brahmins, but my master very soon admitted to me that his dry conversation made him miss that of Grueber more every day.

It was during this period that we received a very alarming letter from Father Ferdinand Verbiest, the auxiliary closest to Adam Schall in our Peking mission. Kircher was deeply affected by the sad news it contained. Several times the disappearance of Adam Schall, an old friend whom he had in his youth sincerely hoped to accompany to China, moved him to tears of sadness. Sadness which sometimes gave way to sudden outbursts of rage.

"Just think, Caspar," he would cry, "our most eminent priests, men who are the glory of religion & the most difficult sciences, these men bear without shrinking the many torments inflicted on them by the fiendish ignorance of the pagans, they go with a smile on their faces to the most horrible martyrdom, resolved to die for the faith & the future of the world, & what is their reward?! The oblivion they suffer would itself be profoundly

unjust, but to add vilification to that, & calumny! How can we
not be outraged when we hear Jansenists, Dominicans & even
some Franciscans, who know nothing of the rites & customs of
the Chinese, accuse the members of our Society of propagating
idolatry & take it upon themselves, from the depths of their
comfortable ignorance, to berate the true apostles of the faith?!
If religion has been given to men in order to save them, then
it must be made hospitable . . . Have these Arnaulds, these
Pascals & other cheap imitation Catos ever saved one single
soul from the claws of Lucifer? They have not, for they are
like importunate flies that settle on any rich food, attempting
to tarnish the luster of the most perfect & the most genuine
things & constantly blackening that which is very pure & very
beautiful with their insolent chatter & the blackest of malicious
gossip! How long must we continue to suffer the despicable
arrogance of these nonentities?!"

Then he would calm down, suddenly overcome with the
memory of his friend again, & would reread, a frown on his face,
the tragic account of Father Verbiest.

Informed of what had happened in the Peking mission,
Father Paul Oliva, the eleventh Superior General of our Society,
immediately appointed Father Verbiest to replace the late
lamented Adam Schall. As we shall later see, he never had cause
to regret that important decision.

A few days, dark days to tell the truth, passed without my
master appearing to get over these misfortunes. He seemed to
have lost interest in our work in progress and immersed himself
in prayer & meditation. I was beginning to fear seriously for his
health, when he appeared one morning with a smile on his lips,
as if he had been fully restored.

"The Lord be praised!" I exclaimed, clasping my hands, full of
joy to find him thus disposed.

"Indeed, for without Him we are nothing & we must certainly see His will in the sudden light that has illuminated my mind."

But as he was about to confide the nature of this revelation to me, the surprise visit of the young King Charles of Spain was announced. He was scarcely five years old & accompanied by his mother, Maria Anna of Austria, the widow of Philip IV who was governing the Empire until her illustrious son came of age. Although we knew that they were in Rome to present the royal child to the Supreme Pontiff, we were far from imagining he would visit us. But my master was not especially surprised, as the reputation of his museum was such that it attracted even crowned heads.

They appeared accompanied by several richly appareled duennas, the Jesuit Father Nithard, recently appointed (thanks to the favor of the Queen Mother) Inquisitor General & Prime Minister, & his nephew, Don Luis Camacho. The latter was only thirteen, but had a precociously lively mind and was justly the pride of his uncle.

Kircher was quite right about the reason for their visit & with him as guide the whole party spent a long time going around the galleries of the museum. The young king amused himself in a very devil-may-care manner with the skeletons, mummies and stuffed animals, grabbing everything within reach with a fidgety clumsiness without anyone in his entourage thinking to remonstrate with him & almost ruined several invaluable exhibits. My master was seething inside & he was very grateful to Don Luis Camacho for gently pulling the little brat away every time he was about to do irreparable damage.

A little later, when we were gathered in the great gallery for an improvised collation, the Inquisitor General asked Kircher for details of the recents misfortunes suffered by our missions in China. My master gave him Father Verbiest's letter to read & the conversation quickly came round to idolatry, then to the points of doctrine criticized by the Chinese.

"Very good," said Father Nithard, "but may I ask you another favor? My nephew here hardly ever has the opportunity to assess his knowledge by comparison with an intelligence such as yours & I would be happy to see him face up to you on this question. Whatever the result, it will be a lesson in humility & very profitable for him & I do not doubt that he will learn much from it."

"Nothing would give me greater pleasure, Father. I have observed him just now & have formed a high opinion of his abilities. Having said that," he went on, turning to young Don Luis, "allow me to treat you as Socrates did Phaedo & deliver you of a truth you possessed without being aware of it. This, I assure you, is not a simple whim on my part, but an example of something that has gladdened my heart ever since God saw fit to give me the gift."

The boy, who had listened attentively to the discussion between the grown-ups, willingly agreed & in the ensuing dialogue made every effort to meet my master's expectations.

FAVELA DE PIRAMBÚ: *Only the law can save us!*

When Moéma woke in the stifling gloom of the shack, the strangeness of the surroundings prolonged the stupefied state she was trying to shake off. Beyond the blurred foliage of her eyelashes she could see large red letters on the boxes making the roof—THIS END UP!—and the broken glass that indicated, without having to resort to language, the extreme fragility of contents deprived of protection. A body, her own body, was wearing a soccer uniform, a jersey and shorts in the colors of the Brazilian team. Leaning over her, a kind of angel was wiping her forehead with a sponge, a young man with a somber face, with big, sad eyes, a sparse, downy beard, one of those Neapolitan *ragazzi* you can see in the encaustic paintings of the Faiyum Roman mummy portraits. She closed her eyes. Stay like that, don't say anything, continue to play dead to avoid being hit . . . The angel was speaking incessantly, in a low voice, a whole rosary of phrases tracing the erratic swirl of the dust. The word "princess" kept recurring in an obsessive way, full of consoling warmth. Moéma remembered having followed this same melody, drawn like a lost ship by the distant promise of calm water. Before that there had been the acid, at Andreas's place, then that dance where she'd felt so miserable, the rat, the twisting alleys of the favela . . . A lacework of memories in which she retained the feeling of an intense and thus far unknown ordeal. Of all these incidents, separated by obscure rents, a single one came back to mind with unbearable contours: the one where a white heron had broken the rampart of light that protected her from the world. She saw the features of each one of the bastards who had raped her, heard each one of their insults, suffered one by one each brutal act they had inflicted on her while laughing at her pleas. The effects of the LSD hadn't worn off yet and its almost undetectable persistence only increased the sensation whenever her mind nosedived into the horrors of the previous night. Her tears returned. Head in her hands, she tried to make herself as small as possible, to gather together at whatever cost the scattered pieces of the thing inside her that had been crushed by the pack of wolves.

She slept again.

Later in the day she found herself alone and took advantage of that to pee in one corner of the hut. Lying on her side, she spent a long time watching an oval of light projected onto the sand through a hole in the roof. Clouds slowly passed across it. She felt terrorized by the "world outside," out there, immediately beyond the shelter of planks and cardboard boxes. Then she studied the black-and-white magazine photos covering the clay and straw walls by her head: pictures of Lampião for the most part, plus some of a person whose eyes had been scratched out with the point of a knife. Underneath the portrait of a smiling American girl sitting on a four-poster bed with a drill on her lap—the child was surrounded by a heap of scrap iron at the top of which was a celluloid baby doll, riddled with holes like a sieve—it said:

> *The destructive instinct. Robin Hawkins, just two years old, is already considered a classic case by psychoanalysts. One of her favorite toys is this drill, which she will fight tooth and nail to stop anyone taking from her. During the last few weeks this cute little girl has destroyed a number of things (for example the TV, the fridge, the washing machine, etc.) at an estimated value of over $2,000. Proud of her precocious talent, Mr. and Mrs. Hawkins encourage their child to practice this new form of expression. At the moment the only precaution they have taken is to have their bedroom door reinforced with metal plates.*

The outside seemed to bounce off her pupils. Her sense of humiliation even extended to her relation to things, she felt impure, dirty, a fly on the surface of the milk. She wished she could be anesthetized for the coming days, which she felt it would be impossible to live through, could wake up a year, two years later—was it something you recovered from anyway?—relieved of this hatred of men that was paralyzing her thighs, of this loathing in which Aynoré, Roetgen and all the rest fused into the object of the same abhorrence.

The angel returned and this time she saw the deformity that forced him to drag himself along the ground when he moved.

"His giant's wings prevent him from walking," she thought without emotion as if such a metaphor—which Thaïs insisted was taken from *Jonathan Livingston Seagull*—were patently obvious. The cherub's lips were still fixed in a touching smile, exaggerating the sense of blissful wonder to such an extent that he looked like a character from a silent film. She allowed him to smear Mercurochrome on her visible cuts. It made the scratches sting a little, but following his movements she could see that she had no serious wounds. After that she bit into the sandwich he offered her, drank out of a bottle of mineral water he unscrewed clumsily and studied his callused hands as he made the motions of rubbing his shoulders and chest with a tube of ointment.

Lying on her back, she listened to him. His voice drew an endless tracery behind her eyes, musical calligraphy that she just had to follow to think of nothing.

THEN THE ANGEL wasn't there anymore. An angel's privilege, she was beginning to get used to it. He'd left some new clothes beside her, a T-shirt with an ad for a Swiss brand of crème fraîche across the front, a beige pair of shorts, still folded inside their transparent packing. There was also a beautiful bar of red and gold soap on a new towel.

Have a shower, scour her body from head to toe, disinfect it like a lavatory bowl . . . Without hesitation she slipped into the little cubicle, open to the sky, behind a sheet of semitransparent plastic against the wall at the far end of the shack. Three pallets stuck in the sand, a rusty barrel, a tin can. Used to the discomforts of Canoa, she took off her clothes and squatted down in the barrel.

Her manic cleaning of her body only ended when the cramp became too painful.

Back in the room, she put on the clothes left by her guardian angel, though not before having rubbed arnica over herself as he had suggested. There was a little mirror with a pale-green plastic frame on a box and she automatically picked it up. Despite her puffy eyelids and a little bruise under her lower lip, her face had not suffered, her hair was sticking up all over the place . . . Holding the mirror at arm's length, she tried to assess her general appearance.

Nata Suiça Nata
Suiça Nata Suiça
Nata Suiça Nata
GLORIA
Suiça Nata Suiça
Nata Suiça Nata
Suiça Nata Suiça

She gasped. Reflected back-to-front in the mirror, the T-shirt had a message that was clearly aimed at her: Athanasius . . . What was the name of that guy her father used to keep telling her about at one time: Karcher? Kitchener? A rather nice priest whom she used to imagine looking like Fernandel playing Don Camillo. The cat organ, the magic lantern, all the marvelous toys he'd invented for her, night after night, shone once more in the glittery colors of childhood. In her imagination he had been as alive, as exceptionally alive as Baron Munchhausen, Robinson Crusoe or Captain Nemo. Despite the only approximate spelling of the reflection, Moéma found the coincidence disturbing out of all proportion. Magnified by this fortuity, even the brand name, *Gloria*, took on the appearance of a hieroglyph awaiting translation.

She remembered, doubtless by analogy, the anecdote her father would relate whenever the conversation turned, as it often does after a drink, to omens. One day, as he was about to board the steamship *Général Lamauricière*, a writer whose name she had forgotten had sensed a supernatural warning: instead of *Lamauricière* he had read, in a brief moment of extreme anguish and clairvoyance: *La mort ici erre*. Shaken to read that "death is wandering here" he had resolved to wait for the next ship. One week later the news came that the *Général Lamauricière* had indeed sunk during the crossing. After having given his audience time to enjoy the punch line, her father would generally add that Samuel Beckett had found himself faced with a similar scenario: "Captain Godot is delighted to welcome you on board," the loudspeakers had said as the plane was already turning onto the runway to take off. Seized with panic, Beckett had fallen into a real fit of hysterics and had kicked up such a fuss he had forced the crew to turn back and let him get off what could only become his coffin. This time, by contrast, there was no tragedy. Which only proved, according to Beckett—we sometimes have such a strong impression that we have seen through the secret workings of fate, such an urgent need to authenticate our foreboding—not that his fear was groundless but that in getting off the plane he had thwarted a fatal plan and saved the lives of the other passengers at the last minute.

If the inscription in the mirror was a similar phenomenon, of what was it warning her, of what imminent shipwreck? Moéma was lying down again. With a sense of unease, she felt herself being dragged down into obscure depths where the enigma concealed in her T-shirt flickered. Nebulas exploded inside her brain and at the conclusion of a slow dissolve, Eléazard's face revealed the message she was desperately trying to decipher: it was a cry, an appeal that grabbed her by the throat, making breathing difficult. After her parents' break-up, she had first of all sided with Elaine, without for one moment concerning herself with what her father might feel. She hadn't tried to help him, nor even to understand him. *You have your own life to live, Moéma,* her mother had said when she refused to take her to Brazilia with her, *cut the cord. It's not healthy to stay tied to my apron strings. We'll become real friends, you'll see, grown-up friends. But you have to do the same as me, liberate yourself, make a life of your own . . .* The problem was—and it was the first time Moéma had formulated it—that she didn't feel grown-up at all, that she wanted a father and a mother, not "friends"! Suddenly the fact that Elaine could tell her something so absurd seemed monstrously selfish. Everything became suspect, including her insistence on being called by her Christian name, as if she were ashamed of being her mother . . . Looked at from this point of view she wasn't free of blame herself, since she had betrayed her father's love—a love that neither her whims nor her ingratitude had done anything to lessen!—with at least equal lack of consideration. But perhaps it was time to put things right, to tell him now what he should have been told six months ago. She would go and stay with him in Alcântara, he would be able to put her back on the rails, untangle the mess her life had become. Pity about this year at university, but it was down the drain anyway. She must write to him as soon as possible, tell him about the turnaround that had just taken place. In her distraught state, she thought she had found the solution and held on to it like a life preserver. *Dear Papa, if you agree, I'll come back and live with you. It's hard to write to your father without having something to ask from him, but I'll explain everything soon . . . This time I'm just begging you to forgive me. With love and kisses,*

"Moéma."

"I'm Nelson," the angel replied. "I thought you couldn't speak, you know. Uncle Zé can't come until tomorrow, but we'll sort things out."

Night had fallen, a small oil lamp was burning in the hut. Moéma apologized to him, he'd been asking her what her name was for hours and hours. She wiped away her tears and got him to tell her everything from the start.

THAÏS AND ROETGEN only started to get worried two days after the *Náutico* episode. They went round to Moéma's the next day, around noon, then in the evening, without becoming particularly concerned; they assumed she was sleeping off the LSD. They went again the following day, shortly after Xavier left. Finding her door closed again, it occurred to them that she might be incapable of responding to their knock; they asked a neighbor on the same landing and eventually stepped across from his balcony to get into her flat. Roetgen saw that Moéma wasn't at home and that there was even good reason to believe she hadn't been back since the evening of the *Náutico* dance.

"In one way I find that reassuring," Thaïs said. "It's not the first time she's slept out . . ."

"But where?"

"She could well have gone to a hotel, so as not to be found, or she may have gone back to Canoa . . . you never know. What is sure is that she's still got some cash, so there's no need to worry."

They both felt guilty about Moéma, which made them blame her apparently casual treatment of them all the more harshly. "Surely she'd realize we'd be worried sick," Thaïs said.

"Yes, it's not very considerate. At least she could have left a note."

A SORT OF euphoria, equally unhealthy, followed the paralysis of the first day. Moéma felt she had been reborn. Galvanized by her decision to leave Fortaleza and go back to her father, she threw off her old self with the vigor of a woman who had come back from the dead. Her traumatic experience still brought on horrifying visions, such as the one in which she was stirring human bones in a huge cauldron that stank of hot fat and corpses. Moéma found herself hesitating as she tried to explain to Nelson what she'd been through. Her memory consisted of disparate images that, paradoxically, were entirely lacking in violence—the heron, a gold tooth, the label on a beer bottle—images from a nightmare that, at the time, we are sure will remain etched on our memory but to which, in the morning, we've lost the thread.

She blamed herself now for having wanted to see Aynoré again, for having thought herself strong enough to face the hazardous labyrinth of the favela at night. Her punishment was certainly out of proportion to her error but, ultimately, just as valid as a bad mark on a botched essay. She found it almost impossible to envisage the idea that one day she'd have to leave this refuge of shadow and tenderness where, out of pure animal instinct, she was lying low. In order to postpone that eventuality, she rigorously avoided any questions about her address or identity. There was the world before and the world after; she no longer wanted to hear anything about the former while not yet being ready to face the latter.

Her talk with Uncle Zé was a crucial stage in her metamorphosis. He came to see her in Nelson's shack late one afternoon and stayed with them the whole evening. "Hi, Princess," was his simple greeting. "It seems you've had a narrow escape."

Moéma was immediately taken with his affable manner. Already predisposed in his favor by Nelson, she changed this prior esteem into genuine admiration. It was above all thanks to him that she could put a name to the things that had turned her world upside down. In simple words and without abandoning the gentle tone, which was more eloquent than an expression of his rebellion would have been, he lifted the veil on the favelas. This fringe, the existence of which she deplored, this dark, shameful world,

had swelled to its full scale, had become embedded in physical reality to the point where it had broken down what she used to feel
was her clear conscience. What Nelson showed her merely by his
existence as a minor beggar, Zé multiplied by such numbers that
she had begun to feel in a minority in her own town. In Fortaleza
alone the shantytowns contained over eight hundred thousand
inhabitants with no other refuge but the sand and the noisome
precariousness of the dunes. Condemned to the clear blue skies of
the tropics, irradiated by poverty, these slums spread misfortune
with an energy that was constantly renewed: children's brothels,
incest, endemic diseases—the very ones that elsewhere they boast
about having eradicated!—hunger that drove people to eat rats or
chew the dried soil in the ruts, the inconceivable privations they
had to suffer just to obtain a set of tiles necessary for a family's
basic survival: *With a roof*, Uncle Zé told her, *it takes a process
lasting six months to flatten an illegal dwelling, when there's no roof
they just have to send in a bulldozer.* Those machines arrived without warning, like diarrhea or stomach cramps, they gobbled up
everything in their path to clear the dunes for the property devel-
opers and to allow them to continue the immense concrete barrier they were erecting along the river bank. Mutterings, protest?
They fired on the crowd with the same indifference with which
they'd fire on a flock of sparrows. And if that wasn't enough, there
were the continuous brawls among the poverty-stricken inhabitants themselves, alcohol, cocaine, bodies buried sitting up—
sometimes you tripped over their heads when you were going
for a pee!—the innumerable mad people, the toilet paper on
which crooks who claimed to own your hovel would scribble a
receipt for rent, infants sold to the rich, to all those worthy souls
short of offspring, the harpooners' beach where everyone pulled
their pants down to do their business, the children, boys and
girls naked until they were eight, who suddenly dropped dead,

with empty stomachs, after feats of endurance a yogi would have been proud of . . . ninety million blacks with no birth certificate or identity card, more than half the population of Brazil in dire poverty.

"Not even slaves, hardly human but still human beings, that's Brazil, Princess. Not that you can see it out of your window."

"The last time they sent in the 'dozers," Nelson added, "everyone thought they'd come to clear up the rubbish. But the rubbish was us, if you get what I mean."

What she had thought was the ultimate in deprivation among the fishermen of Canoa suddenly seemed an enviable situation, unattainable luxury.

THERE WERE FAINT signs of resistance, however, thanks to the work of a few visionaries—saints, Princess, veritable saints!—who had come to live in the heart of the favela and share the wretched conditions of its inhabitants. Somehow first-aid posts had been set up, embryonic health centers where people could see a doctor free, get together, talk. Organizations such as the Hole in the Sky, Our Lady of the Graces, the Guava Community taught children to read and write, distributed food to the ten families who arrived on the dunes every day, forced into exile by the drought in the Sertão or the rapacity of the landowners. They were helped to build makeshift shelters to give them a foothold in the area. Gradually the people of Pirambú were rediscovering solidarity, the strength of united action. Charitable souls donated provisions, medicine, large sheets of plastic packaging to insulate the roofs or, fastened between four posts, to make the walls of an umpteenth shack. In the favela of Cuatro-Varas, for example, there was a committee, the first of its kind, a little group of elected representatives that dealt with local problems and represented the interests of the shantytown with the authorities. All that wasn't much but it did have the great advantage of actually existing.

"He's the one who built the house for me. And sometimes he swipes a few tiles from the depot. Just like that, for others. He even gives Manoelzinho a tip to get him to fill my water tank every day!"

Embarrassed, Uncle Zé gave Nelson a sign to shut up and changed the subject. It was true, nevertheless. Among the crazy people who were not indifferent to what went on in the world, there were those who were committed, one way or the other, to try to change things and those who were happy to modify what they could see around them, bit by bit, in their own way. The two attitudes were probably complementary, as Moéma was realizing now; she had adopted neither the one nor the other and that was something else she would need forgiveness for one day. What had she done for all those Indians, whose genocide she so smugly condemned, apart from taking them as a pretext for her own malaise, her own moaning. Was there anything, any single thing she could point to that gave her the right to speak, to exercise that right with a minimum of justification?

"It's just not possible," said Uncle Zé. "We've reached the year 2000 and three-quarters of the world's still starving to death! Tell me, what's the point of this fuss about 2000? Things are just going to get worse, my girl, even worse than people think. We haven't made the slightest progress, not the slightest. It'll all end in tears, you mark my words."

Now it wasn't just the Yanomami or the Kadiweu who were screaming revolution in Moéma's guilty conscience but the innumerable tribe of the destitute. It was obvious what she had to do: the last vestiges of humanity within us and on earth had to be preserved, at all cost, to allow a true world to develop, so that no one in the future could look back on us with contempt for not having done anything when everything was still possible.

"Even Father Leonardo was silenced by the Pope. He was a Franciscan, a real one . . . That cunt of a Pope—forgive me, Princess—should have his balls torn off for doing that. It's criminal . . . There's millions and millions of people who died because of him!"

MOÉMA'S EYES WERE being opened all the time, she felt guilty of nonlove, of criminal negligence. But Uncle Zé had given her a gentle reproof for indulging in self-flagellation: "When you break a glass, Princess, it's still a broken glass, even if you stick the pieces together again. It's best to buy a new glass, if you see what I mean."

She saw. To repair her life, her illusion of being alive must be to set up something new, to make a complete change in the way she was with others. But how? She hadn't got things clear in her mind yet but the first step was to go back to her father, to the house. After that she'd comes back and offer her services, in this favela or another, work for the FUNAI with the Indians, in the Xingu reservation. UNESCO, UNO, an NGO perhaps? *It's crazy the kind of shit they send us, single shoes, teddy bears, glasses that saw Christ walking on water . . . Anything they've no use for anymore! Why should we have a use for it, eh? And when it's money, we only see the check in the papers . . .* But there were a thousand ways of making oneself useful. And she thought: of finding forgiveness, without seeing that first of all she had to forgive herself, that her good resolutions would remain ineffective, even pointless without that essential preliminary.

Having donned the prestigious uniform of the humanitarian legion was already making her feel redeemed. Her enthusiasm intensified. Expressions such as "a new beginning" or "back to square one" were going round and round in her head as persistently as the nagging awareness of her responsibility. When Zé mentioned the Feast of Yemanjá and his difficulty finding a girl worthy of representing the goddess, Moéma immediately offered to help. Uncle Zé explained what she was getting herself into and arranged to meet her in two days' time at the *terreiro* of Mata Escura.

FAVELA DO PIRAMBÚ: *I saw her and I didn't see her . . .*

After uncle Zé had taken Moéma back to the town center, Nelson curled up in his hammock. He should have taken advantage of the truck to go begging on the sea front, but the departure of his princess had caught him unprepared. "I'm like a werewolf at the full moon," he told himself, somewhat bewildered, "there's something wrong with me." Everything in his hut reminded him of the young woman who had been there, tiny changes, objects he had deliberately not moved so as to prolong the spell her presence had cast. Frowning and staring at the ceiling, he tried to relive his past happiness, visualizing two or three specific scenes; these few days could be summed up in the feeling that for a brief moment the world had brightened up but now it was dark. It wasn't possible his memory could be playing such tricks on him, not about that, for God's sake! He wriggled in the canvas, changed position. And how would he manage if the police turned up to interrogate him, eh? He couldn't just give them the shit that was left inside his loaf: the light's gone out of my life. The cop would give him a clip on the ear right away. And then another, straight after, just to get rid of his fancy ideas . . .

"So has that cleared the shit out of your head, half-pint? A bit clearer about things now, are we? What the fuck was a tart like that doing here?"

"I went to see the train go past and she was there, fighting, but not with anyone. It was obvious someone had hurt her."

"How could you tell?"

"She'd nothing on and she was crying. It was as if she was out of her mind . . ."

"And you, of course, tried to screw her . . ."

"I swear I didn't, *comandante*. To me it was as if she was wearing a blue satin gown with flounces . . . a king's daughter, so beautiful it knocked you over on your backside! I wouldn't have touched her, not for anything in the world. I brought her back here to protect her from the dragon."

Wham! Another clout. He'd done nothing to deserve that one either. The bloody cop didn't understand that she came out of a *cordel,* she was the Princess of the Kingdom-where-no-one-goes. At the same time he wasn't daft, he knew very well it wasn't her. But he'd never for a moment thought that she came from Pirambú: even completely naked as she was, you could see she belonged to the *soçaite,* the *crème de la crème.*

"What time was it?"

"Dunno . . . three or four in the morning. I couldn't leave her like that, but I never touched her, never even looked at her. I gave her the only things I've got, apart from what I'm wearing, my soccer uniform, with Zico's number! And as soon as it was light I went off into the town to buy her the very best. I've never spent so much money in all my life, *chefe.* The T-shirt I got for almost nothing, at the *Legion of Support against Infantile Diarrhea,* but the shorts, the towel . . . *Puxa!* I even got rose-scented soap. *Phebo de Luxe,* manufactured according to the English system, the most famous speciality of Brazilian industry. The soap of choice for persons of good taste—that was written on the wrapper—it swathes the body in an aura of elegance. An aura, *comandante,* I couldn't invent something like that! Insisted on by the world of fashion—and I'm not lying."

Following a sudden inspiration, Nelson went to fetch the soap and climbed back into the dream-inducing nest in his hammock. His nose on the translucent bar of soap and the towel Moéma had used, he was in a hurry to return to the scene he had evoked.

"It'll come back to me, I promise."

"What did you do then?"

"I treated her wounds as best I could and I watched her sleeping. When she woke up, I showed her the place where she could wash. I told her she should put some ointment on her bruises, I hadn't done that, out of respect for her, well, you know . . . There was no way I could get a word out of her. She was looking right through me, as if I was a shop window or a windscreen. Then I could tell she had the *encosto*. She was possessed, ill. I even thought she'd never been able to speak . . . So I spoke for both of us. I made some questions and the answers, then I told her all the stories I'd promised . . . 'cause I'm sure that's what got her to come. What are you called, Princess? Where's your kingdom? Things like that . . . She opened her eyes, then she went back to sleep. There must have been several of them had a go at her."

"Oh yes? And why didn't you tell the police?"

"With all due respect, *comandante*, the less we see of the cops, the better off we are, as they say. Anyway, they wouldn't have come, they're a load of cretins . . . (This time I'd duck just at the right moment and his fist would go over my head.) I called Uncle Zé, from a telephone booth. It was a bit of luck that he was there at all, at the depot. I can only come tomorrow evening, he said, I've a delivery for João Pessoa. In the meantime keep a good eye on her. So I came back home, on the double, around the back way, because it's shorter. And there I saw she was washing herself: just her arm came out to get some water from the can . . . You can se a bit of what's going on through the pallets, if you look—"

"And you got an eyeful, *viado*!"

"No I didn't, sir. It was the same as the first time, I saw her and I didn't see her . . . I can't really explain it. She didn't stop washing herself, she wasn't paying attention to anything else. But all I saw was little bits of her and I couldn't go in because of the curtain. I didn't want her to think I'd been watching her."

"But you still had a hard-on, eh, you swine?"

So then he took out his switchblade and stuck it in the stupid pig, right in the belly and ripped it open. You just couldn't allow people to say things like that to you. To be honest, though, seeing her like that had turned him on. But not like at the VASP plane. He'd felt like a man, how should he put it, like a man who'd controlled himself. Zé had told him that it had happened to him once, when he was looking at a statue of the Virgin. Well, it was that kind of thing. You know, feelings . . . But, shit, that cop's intestines in the hammock, that just made it impossible for him to think . . . The damn corpse was taking up all the space, he'd have to put it back up on its feet, with the knife in its stomach, as of nothing had happened . . .

"OK, then . . . But there must have come a moment when she'd finished washing herself?"

"Yes, but I still waited. Quite a while, even, to let her get dressed, instead of pretending I wasn't looking . . . Well, I know what I mean. When I went in she was lying down again. It was just like before, except that she smelled good, *meu Deus!* A baby all cleaned up, the arnica . . . But what had happened to her still had her in its grip, she didn't see me, so I went on talking to her, all the time, until the evening . . . And then suddenly she spoke to me: 'Moéma'—that was even better than Alzira or Theodora. She could hardly remember anything. I told her what I knew, how I'd found her and then what I've told you. But for her, it was all dammed up inside her. She just wanted to stay there, she was afraid of going out, of people finding her . . . like a wounded animal. She wanted me to tell her about myself, so I did. Everything, my father, who was dead and converted into a rail, my saving for the wheelchair, I even showed her the place so that she knew I trusted her . . ."

"And the pistol? You told her about the pistol?"

No, it was stupid, the fat slob couldn't know that. And anyway, he'd kept the story of the pistol to himself. What might she have thought, eh? It wasn't good that he'd kept it from her, but above all he hadn't wanted to frighten her.

"OK . . . And once you'd finished telling her your life story?"

"After that there was Uncle Zé. It was he who did everything. I mean . . . he's a bit of a *paï de santo*, a father of saints, he knows how to deal with minds. He told her about Pirambú, a load of things about us lot, the *faveleros*. And I don't know how, but it took the hurt away. She kept on saying she'd come back, that she'd found something to do with her life. Zé, I know him, didn't really believe that but he knew it was definitely doing her good, 'cause he didn't contradict her; as for me, I'm sure she was being honest. And then . . . he came for her this morning. As she left, she said she'd bring back the things I'd bought for her. I'd meant them as a gift, but I said nothing, to make sure she'd come back . . ."

The sound of a loudspeaker burst the bubble of his memories—surely they hadn't decided to flatten the whole favela today?! Nelson hurried out to see what was going on, but it was just an election agent, with a loudspeaker in his hand, come to sell his tawdry wares. People had gathered around the van, aware that this kind of thing always ended with a handout.

"Who got the bus shelter in Goiavera built?" the guy with the smallpox-ravaged cheeks was asking. "Edson Barbosa, Jr.! Who's been fighting for four years to get mains drainage in Pirambú? Edson Barbosa, Jr.! Who allowed the building of the Health Centre for All? Edson Barbosa, Jr.! Who spoke to the Pope about your situation, in a personal audience, if you please? Edson Barbosa, Jr. again!

The other candidates promise all sorts of things, but they don't do anything. Only Edson Barbosa, Jr. has slaved away to make life better for you all! And this time he has some great news for you—if you want to know what it is, come to the big meeting that will be held tomorrow on the Future Beach. I guarantee you won't be disappointed! And in addition everyone wearing one of these baseball caps or one of these magnificent T-shirts will be entitled to a basket of food! That is Edson Barbosa, Jr., generosity in person! Vote for him or get others to vote for him and these baskets will multiply! There'll be so many you won't know what to do with them! Come to Edson Barbosa, Jr.'s meeting for the feast of Yemanjá, the patron saint of Pirambú. Even the governor of Maranhão is taking the trouble to come. Just think, his Excellency José Moreira da Rocha will be there to support your candidate! José Moreira da Rocha, the big industrialist! José Moreira da Rocha, the millionaire who talks to our beloved president just as I'm talking to you. The one they call 'the Benefactor' because he did away with the favelas of San Luís. It's as true as I'm standing here, go and see for yourselves if you don't believe me: no shantytown, not a single shack left! May God give me a deadly dose of cholera if I'm spinning you a yarn! All the poor have been rehoused in permanent homes, everyone's got a regular job and can eat their fill! And this is the man who has come to advise our governor so he can do the same in Fortaleza! José Moreira da Rocha and Edson Barbosa, Jr. on the Future Beach—for your future, my friends! And it starts tomorrow!

Nelson didn't even try to get a cap in the throng that formed around the political huckster. He had fled back to his hut, quivering with emotion. Moreira da Rocha ... The almanac hadn't lied ... *Laudato seja Deus!* His wheel of destiny had suddenly engaged like the cogs in a gearbox. He felt drunk with a terrible joy, it was like a boiler roaring inside his head as he tried to calm himself down by slashing the pictures of the governor.

"Should we reject Marxism, abandon the struggle against oppression, our hope of the Great Day, just because the Communists fell in Russia?" Uncle Zé had said only yesterday. "No, Princess, that would suit too many people down to the ground. It's not clear at all. They strut about today, but all they've managed to develop is underdevelopment, if you want my opinion. Even the aid to third-world countries, you know how that works? They take the dough from the poor of rich countries to give it to the rich of the poor countries . . . It's just going round in circles . . . I'm not a Communist, but the only political action for a fly is to get off the flypaper and no one will persuade me any different . . ."

I'm not a Communist either, Nelson said to himself, I'm not much at all . . . I'm not even a fly, I'm just a cockroach. But I'm going to show them what a cockroach can do! What it can do to get out of the insect trap.

The words of the only song ever composed by Lampião came back to mind: *Olé, Mulher Rendeira, olé Mulher renda! Tu me ensinas a fazer renda, que eu te ensino a namorar . . .*

The Future Beach. He'd be there for sure!

CHAPTER 29

Which tells how Kircher delivered young
Don Luis Camacho of some essential truths of
which he had knowledge without knowing it

"I THINK THERE is no better way to start," Kircher said after a brief moment of reflection, "than by asking you a very simple question: what, according to you, is the task of a teacher? Try to reply simply & not using any faculty other than common sense."

"I think I would not be wrong," Don Luis Camacho said earnestly, "if I said his task was to instruct. Is that not the case?"

"Very good; but to instruct in what?"

"Some area of knowledge . . . or, at least, one he is reputed to have mastered."

"Of course. And I think we can say that so far you haven't made the slightest mistake. However, there are thousands of kinds of knowledge & I imagine you will agree that they are not all of equal importance. One man might know the art of making mirrors, another that of tailoring a fine suit or of concocting a sovereign remedy for gout. Which would you say are essential to the student to attain understanding?"

"For anyone who wants to learn a trade, that of apothecary, tailor or mirror-maker, knowledge of each of these arts is essential. However, it is clear that anyone who aspires to universal understanding of things & to acquire the wellspring from which these rivers & their innumerable tributaries flow, so to speak, will have to learn the sciences . . ."

"Well thought out, Don Luis. But what do we mean by 'sciences'? Would it be alchemy, magic or the art of predicting the future you were thinking of?"

"Obviously not. What I had in mind was the exact sciences, the ones that can be verified by experiment or by reason & that no one could doubt, as for example mathematics, logic, physics, mechanics . . ."

"Ah yes, definitely! However, we also need to define what is meant by 'verify by experiment or reason' in a way that does not give rise to criticism."

"It means to go back from the effect to the cause so that we can understand the true principles at work in the world. In this I'm just repeating what I have heard people say, but it seems correct to me."

"Absolutely correct, my son. It would be impossible to define science better than you have done. By the very act of drawing the world out of chaos, God created the principles necessary to maintain the universe and ensure that it runs harmoniously. Now, would this teacher not be at fault if he stopped halfway & did not go back to the celestial origin of these principles? Should he not, on the contrary, make every effort to show how the laws of physics, as those of the other sciences, ultimately rest on the will of the Creator alone?"

"Indeed—"

"And what is it that teaches us this holy truth, more essential than all the others? Is it the Mohammedans, the bonzes of the Buddhists or the Brahmins of China?"

"Definitely not! For it is the Bible & the Gospels, that alone contain the word of God, the Church, in that she is the principal support of the Christian religion, & her theologians, who are better equipped than anyone to understand the mysteries . . ."

"Well, my son, you could not define the task of a teacher more correctly: a master worthy of that name is not simply someone who teaches the true sciences, he must also expound the true religion, which is the foundation on which the laws and natural principles rest. Imagine that you are one of our missionaries. There you are in Peking, charged with both practicing & inculcating that true science which is astronomy. But one of your Chinese students makes a mistake in predicting an eclipse of the moon. What do you need to teach him?"

"The correct way of pursuing astronomy; that is, the laws regulating the movements of the planets & allowing us to calculate their courses."

"Very good. But is that sufficient? Will your pupil not be mistaken if, predicting a new eclipse accurately, he attributes the ultimate cause of this phenomenon to some occult power of the god Fo-hi?"

"Of course. It would be my duty to get him to see that he was just as mistaken in believing in a false god as he was in his false astronomy."

"Very good. And how should one proceed if not by using the same rule of returning to the origins, to the first principles of all things? What is valid for the sciences is equally valid for theology. So how would you go about making him see his error?"

"It seems to me that I would go back in time & the history of mankind to stand at the period of the creation of the world in order to show him by logical deduction that his god, Fo-hi, is a later invention & has never existed except in the imagination of ignorant men."

"True. But are we here talking of history as conceived by Herodotus or Pausanias, that is, of true accounts, and fairly recent ones at that? No. What we need, as you see, is knowledge of the origins or, to put it in Greek, an 'archaeology.' And to whom or to what must we turn in order to acquire this science of first principles?"

"To the Holy Bible &, more specifically, to the chapter in Genesis that deals with these questions."

"Exactly. But we must go further & ask what, in Genesis, are the crucial moments, those that set all the rest in motion?"

Don Luis Camacho concentrated for a long time, counting on his fingers the stages as they came back to mind. "There are five," he said with the assurance of youth, "the creation of man by God, the Fall, the murder of Abel by Cain, the Flood & the confusion of tongues at the building of the Tower of Babel."

"Well done, my son. Your answer is worthy of a most eminent historian. Having said that, can you not distinguish, among these original moments, any that we could establish with all the marks of certainty, as knowledge with the same degree of assurance as that which persuades us to believe the stories of Herodotus, since we can still see today the animals or the monuments he described four hundred and forty-five years before the birth of Our Lord?"

"I have to admit I can't. My mind is suddenly a blank & . . ." Don Luis Camacho's pretty face turned crimson, such was the distress his inability to answer caused him.

Kircher got up to look for something in the gallery where
we were & came back to us with various objects, which he put
down on the table. "Here," my master said, showing Don Luis
Camacho the selection he had made from among his collections,
"here are several pieces that should help you to solve the problem
you have just been set. Do these stone fish and shells not look as
if they had been sculpted *intaglio* by an artist with a wonderful
skill at representing this kind of creature?"

"Definitely!" the boy replied admiringly. "I have never seen
any so perfectly copied."

"And with good reason," Kircher went on with a smile, "for
these are genuine marine animals brought back by various
missionary friends of mine. They were found, trapped in the
rock, on the summits of some of the highest mountains on
Earth; in Asia, in Africa & in America. How would you explain
their presence so far from their habitual element?"

"I don't know . . . They must have been carried up there for
some reason or other . . . or at some very ancient time the sea
must have been very high &—oh, my God, I think I've got it!
Could it be the Flood?"

"Excellent! Did I not say you would find the answer yourself,
on condition that you had a subject that would allow full scope
to your intellect? Yes, the Flood. For there is no other possible
explanation for the presence of so many aquatic animals on the
summits. There is in this a clear relationship of cause and effect
that verifies not only the text of the Bible but all subsequent
writings that recall that terrible cataclysm. I am thinking,
of course, of Plato who, in the dialogues of the *Critias* & the
Timaeus, describes how Atlantis was engulfed, but also of a
number of other traditions that recount the same flood, though
also distorting it. The Brahmins, from what Father Roth says,

testify to it in their rituals & the priests of Zoroaster do the
same in the Kingdom of Persia; Father Walter Sonnenberg,
who is in Manila, says the same of all the tribes of the Asian
archipelagos, Saint Francis Xavier of the negroes of Malacca,
Valentin Stansel of the Topinambus of Brazil, Alejandro
Fabiàn of the Mexicans, Lejeune & Sagard of the Hurons of
Canada . . . For God wanted all these peoples to retain, even
in the depths of their idolatry, the memory of the punishment
inflicted on them in the past for their disobedience. These
proofs are amply sufficient, but if they should not suffice,
here is something that would win over the most obdurate of
unbelievers."

Opening a precious casket and unfolding the cloth protecting
it with infinite caution, Kircher showed us a very old piece of
wood. "This fragment of cedar," he said, "so uninteresting at
first sight, was taken by Father Boym, during his journey in
Armenia, from a very old piece of wreckage he discovered on top
of a mountain the people of that country call Ararat . . ."

"Mount Ararat?! Are you suggesting that this is—"

"A genuine fragment from Noah's Ark. Yes my son. The
ark was the miracle of the world, the universe in microcosm,
the seedbed of all living, sentient nature, the refuge of a world
about to perish & a favorable omen for a world that was reborn.
Just remember, its length was ten times that of its height,
proportions that are exactly those of a human body with arms
outstretched or, rather, a crucified body! The wood of the Ark
is comparable to that of the Cross: for Noah as for Christ it
was the instrument of salvation, of redemption offered to
mankind. And this ark, outside which there is no salvation, is
the Church! Tossed to and fro like a fragile ship in the tempest
of the centuries & heresies, loaded with men who, truly, have
the ferocity of lions, the greed of wolves, the cunning of foxes,

who are lustful as swine & as prone to anger as dogs, the Church resists the flood of passions & remains, thanks to God, free, intact and invincible."

"Magnificent, that is truly magnificent!" Father Nithard exclaimed. "What do you think, your Highness?"

I could not tell whether the Queen Mother had enough Latin to follow the finer points of Kircher's argumentation, but she gravely nodded her approval.

"I will continue, then. If we can prove, as I have just done, the reality of the Flood, that is to say that all the lands were actually submerged & mankind disappeared completely for a year, apart from Noah & his family, should we not consider the history of the world as beginning again from that moment, that is, according to my calculations, in the 1657th year after the Creation or 2396 years before the birth of Our Lord?"

"It seems to me—"

"We can pursue the same reasoning starting out from the ruins of Babel, of which I have a stone here that Signore Pietro della Valle brought to me as evidence of his discovery. To prove that the Tower of Babel truly existed is to demonstrate the truth of the Bible regarding what came before and what followed it. More than any other science, it is archaeology that will change the face of the world by restoring the lost unity, the original paradise! That is what I came to understand last night when I found myself prey to the most terrible doubt—"

"Excuse my interruption," Father Nithhard ventured to say, "but how can you prove the reality of Babel with the same certitude as that of the Flood? As you are well aware, a simple stone, however well its provenance is testified would not be sufficient to convince the unbelievers . . ."

"Of course not, your remark is very perspicacious. But if, starting out from the present diversity of languages and their phenomenal multiplicity—I have counted a thousand and seventy different ones!—I managed to show that they all derive from five roots instilled by the angels after the destruction of the Tower, that is, Hebrew, Greek, Latin, German & Illyrian, which themselves derive from the Adamic language that Noah & his descendants spoke, would I not have proved the historical truth of the confusion of tongues? And by the deduction that men were separated in families, because they suddenly found it impossible to understand each other, would I not also have proved the ensuing dispersal of the tribes, which contributed to the debasement of God and the Bible in their minds?"

"Who would doubt it, Reverend Father?"

"Accordingly, & in order to provide a solid foundation for the historical chapters of my book on China, I have decided to devote my latter days to two books of sacred archaeology that will silence the most obstinate of the idolaters: one on Noah's Ark, the other on the Tower of Babel. These books will be the touchstone of all my work—" Kircher turned to Maria Anna of Austria, "& if your Highness will grant me that signal favor, they will be dedicated to your son, the king."

In the name of her son, the Queen Mother declared herself honored by this tribute. She thanked my master warmly & promised to finance the publication of said books. Kircher congratulated Don Luis Camacho on his excellence in dialectics. As a souvenir of their dialogue, he gave him one of the fossil fish, whose significance he had appreciated, & enjoined the boy to apply himself to the study of nature.

At the end of that October the proofs of *China Monumentis* began to arrive in a constant stream. My master devoted his days to them, at the same time preparing the material destined for his *Arca Noe* & *Turris Babel*. I had never seen him take so much pleasure in the planning of a work & I was not mistaken in predicting that they would give as much to their readers a few years later.

The following year was remarkable in many respects; at the very moment when *China Monumentis*, which had finally come off the press, was going from hand to hand to an unfailing chorus of praise, our Holy Father departed this life with laudable acceptance & obedience. His family was greatly afflicted, especially his beloved brother, Cardinal Orlando Chigi. I well remember the beautiful words of consolation my master addressed to him at this sad time: "*You have suffered a great loss,*" he wrote, "*& the Church an even greater one, but what right had you to hope that you would never suffer it? I have heard tell of several people who had received remarkable gifts from heaven, but you cannot say that God gave them the gift of never dying. I beg you, Monsignore, to call to mind all the families of your acquaintance, you will not find one where you have not seen tears shed for the same reason that is causing yours. There are lead lines to sound the abysses of the sea, but none for the secrets of God, so do not question them; accept what has happened to you with reverence & you will calm your troubled mind. I am not telling you anything that you do not know better than I, but the tokens of respect you have always shown me oblige me to make a contribution to the relief of your sorrow & to express the gratitude with which I remain, yours faithfully, etc., etc.*"

On June 20, 1667 his Eminence Cardinal Giulio Rospigliosi was elected by the conclave under the name of Clement IX, but his advanced age gave rise to fears that he would not stay on St. Peter's throne for long.

As well as *China Monumentis*—to which book my master had added the first Latin & Chinese dictionary ever to appear in the West & which was a great help to those of our Society who were preparing to go to China—Kircher presented to the learned world a *Magneticum Naturae Regnum* that was remarkable despite its brevity. In it he had gathered together, for pedagogical purposes, all possible experiments concerning the attraction between things with the result that the book was a great success for the ease with which it allowed both neophytes and scholars to study these matters with no other guide.

ALCÂNTARA: *He walked crabwise, with the occasional lurch, which made him snigger to himself . . .*

Having worked on his notes until two in the morning, Eléazard got up later than usual, but with the feeling that he had turned a corner: both the person and the works of Athanasius Kircher had been reshaped in his mind with sufficient contrast to make him see the extent to which he had caricatured them up to that point. This adjustment owed much to Dr. Euclides, even more to Loredana's willingness to say what came into her mind; she had asked good questions, ones that challenged his own attitude to Kircher rather than the German Jesuit's supposed genius or hypocrisy. He was in a hurry to see her to discuss it, in a hurry to go further with her in this sort of loving intimacy their relationship had entered into.

He breakfasted in the kitchen. The Carneiro affair was still front-page news: one of the two alleged killers had finally admitted to having been in the house at the time of the murder. He was giving evidence against his accomplice in the hope of reducing his sentence, at the same time testifying that they had been sent by Wagner Cascudo to persuade their victim to hand over his property to him. That said, the lawyer had been released on bail and was protesting his innocence. He was standing by his own version of the matter, namely that he didn't know the two men from Adam and the whole thing had been set up by the police. As for the governor, there were lengthy quotations from his outraged denial on television: this conspiracy against him had been mounted for purely electoral ends, its sole aim was to destabilize the party in power. If the press was going to start suspecting every honest man in the country, they were heading for a catastrophe. He had known Wagner Cascudo for years, he was not only an outstanding lawyer, but a friend, a man whom he knew to be incapable of the least wrongdoing.

And not a single word on his schemes.

Being in the business, Eléazard could sense that there was a kind of turnaround in opinion in process, the result of shrewd manipulation. He tried to reassure himself with the thought that the state prosecutor in Santa Inês wouldn't give up that easily, especially after the confession implicating Wagner Cascudo. He was getting ready to leave, with the idea of going to see Loredana, when Alfredo clapped his hands to announce himself.

"What's up? Why the grim look? What's been going on?"

"She's left—"

"Who d'you mean, she?" Eléazard broke in, a sinking feeling in his stomach.

"Loredana. She took the first boat this morning. Only Socorró saw her. She paid her bill and left . . ."

Eléazard sat down. His heart was pounding in his chest. "Without even saying goodbye," he said, stating the obvious.

"Socorró said that to her. Her reply was that it was better like that and, anyway, she just had time to catch her plane. She left you a letter. Here it is, if you want to read it . . ."

She'd known she was going to leave today, Eléazard told himself as he looked at the large envelope Alfredo was holding out to him, she knew and she didn't say anything . . .

"But what's got into her, for God's sake?" he said angrily. "You just can't do something like that!"

"I don't know any more than you, Lazardinho. She left me a note saying sorry and that she had to go back to Italy. I've a funny feeling about it too."

Eléazard pointed to the pile of articles he'd cut out in order to file them: "Pour yourself a glass and have a look at those while I'm reading this, OK?"

"I've nothing else to do," Alfredo said, looking downcast. "Anyway, the hotel's empty, so . . ."

The envelope contained a voluminous dossier and a letter, in Italian and in a large round hand that seemed determined to cover every last inch of the page . . .

Doubtless you'll be surprised, Eléazard, and hurt, I know, to learn of my departure in this way, but I no longer have the courage or the strength to tell you these things face to face. All right then, here I go: it seems that I'm ill, a kind of cancer of the blood that doctors don't know much about. And it's a contagious disease that develops so quickly it's starting to have a devastating effect on me. My life expectancy is only a few months, a year or two if my body resists it more strongly, as it appears can happen sometimes . . . Oddly enough, it's not the fact that I have to die that poses most problems—that awareness is so insupportable that my brain switches off after a few seconds. It's as if it were producing endorphins of hope just to fool us, to allow us to pretend we're OK until the next low. No, the worst thing about it, and I've realized this here more than in Italy, is the delusion that you're going to survive despite everything. I'll spare you the details of the soul-searching all that leads to, the nostalgia, the terror, the desperate need to hang on, to continue to exist . . . Basta!

I'm leaving you my bedside book. That's where I got everything I know about strategy. The translator's a good friend of mine, I hope you'll like his pseudonym.

That's it. There's nothing more I can say apart from begging
you not to have any hard feelings. Forget Kircher for a bit, give
Soledade a kiss from me and drag Moreira through the shit
right to the end.
    I'll say goodbye with a kiss, as I did just now, when I left you.
    Loredana

"Well?" Alfredo asked; he hadn't been able to take his eyes off him all the time he was reading.

"You knew?"

"What?"

"That she was seriously ill."

"What are you getting at? I assure you I knew nothing."

Eléazard handed him the letter so he could read it for himself.

"I'm sorry," Alfredo said after a brief glance, "but Italian, you know . . ."

He smoothed down his hair with both hands. Without realizing, he'd started to chew the inside of his cheek again.

"She didn't leave a book with the letter?"

"Sorry, I almost forgot," Alfredo said, taking a black and red book out of his bag. "I don't know where I am today!"

Eleazard quickly read the front cover:

THE 36 STRATAGEMS
A secret treatise on Chinese strategy
translated and annotated by
François Kircher

"I think I'll have a drink too," he said in a toneless voice.

AFTER ALFREDO HAD left, he continued to fill his glass as quickly as he emptied it. Close to a drunken stupor, he reread

Loredana's letter, scrutinizing each expression, as if one of them might eventually give him the key to her disappearance, but the more he probed the words, the more he felt their lack of substance.

Mechanically he leafed through the little book she'd left him. Some passages here and there were indicated by lines in the margin, but there was nothing to suggest, as he had for a moment hoped, that they had been underlined as a message to him. A difference in color indicated two readings at different times, each revealing separate preoccupations. Without having specifically looked for it, Eléazard came across the principle put forward by Loredana to take on the governor of Maranhão: *The tall silhouette of the sophora shields the puny mulberry tree in the shadow of its foliage just as great men surround themselves with a court of clients and protégés. To attack one of the followers as a direct threat to his master is a common practice* . . . The thirty-sixth stratagem was the only one with a box drawn round it; Eléazard was sure it came from the second reading, the one Loredana had done in her hotel room during the last few days. *If all else fails, retreat*, he read, feeling a pang of anguish. *When your side is losing, there are only three choices remaining: surrender, compromise or escape. Surrender is complete defeat, compromise is half defeat, but escape is not defeat.*

Tired of going around in circles, he went to find Soledade to ask her. She was sitting on the floor in the farthest corner of the veranda, her legs hanging down outside, through the bars. She replied to his call but didn't turn around. From the sound of her voice, he could tell she was crying.

"What's wrong?" he said, sitting down beside her. "You know? It's about Loredana?" From the side he could see her wipe her eyes with the back of her hand and try to control her breathing.

"I know," she finally said. "Alfredo told me when he went up to see you."

"And that's why you're crying?"

She shook her head and stuck her face between the bars.

"Why, then?" Eléazard said. "What's making you unhappy? Don't you like it here?"

"I'm going to leave as well . . ."

"What's all this nonsense? You're not going to leave me all by myself, are you?"

Eléazard was used to these fits of depression. Soledade never carried out her threats, so he never really took them seriously.

"Brazil lost," she said, making a face. "I'd promised to go if they didn't reach the final . . . So I'm going back to Quixadá, to my parents. Say, could I . . . could I take the TV?"

"Stop it, Soledade. You can take whatever you like, that's not the problem. What I'm asking is for you to stay with me, you understand?"

"Oh yes," she said, imitating his accent, "Who's going to do the washing, the shopping, bring me my *caipirinhas*? That's all I'm any use for. She's the one you love . . ." She started crying again.

"But what difference does it make? She's gone now, so . . . nothing's changed, everything's as it was before."

Soledade started crying again. "Except that she loves you as well," she managed to say between two sobs. "She told me so."

"I don't believe it," he said, unsure whether that revelation assuaged his sadness a little or actually made it worse. "It's absurd. What did she say exactly?"

"That you were a filthy exploitative frog, that . . . that she hated you!" Her pitiful expression contradicted the lie.

"Seriously, Soledade, it's important for me."

"She said she loved you, but she was going to die and that there was no point getting worked up about it." The tears came pouring out as she went on, "And I . . . I just said that we're all going to die. But that was just because I was jealous, you see. And now she's gone and it's all because of me."

"No, no," he said, trying to comfort her, "we never know what's going on inside other people's heads: she was afraid of making us suffer"—as he spoke, Eléazard felt he was getting close to the truth at last—"afraid of infecting us with her suffering. She realized she'd tried to negotiate with her illness and then she pulled herself together, out of pride, the better to fight . . ."

"It's my fault," Soledade sobbed. "I took her to the *terreiro* . . . The parrot wasn't afraid of her, you see, it was a sign . . . And Omulú chose her, her and not me . . ."

Eléazard had no idea what she was talking about. "What's all this about a *terreiro*?"

Soledade put her hand over her mouth, rolling her eyes in fright.

"Tell me," Eléazard insisted, "please."

Soledade's only answer was to stand up swiftly and run off to her room.

Eléazard would have liked to be able to cry like her, to wash out his mind. He stayed on the terrace, dry-eyed, the bottle within reach. A little later he heard, without moving, the telephone ring then the message spoken in a brusque voice by Dr. Euclides on his answering machine.

When the mosquitos appeared he took refuge in the living room; he walked crabwise, with the occasional lurch, which made him snigger to himself.

THE FOLLOWING DAY he woke up much earlier than necessary. The *cachaça* made his head feel as if it were clamped in a vise and the prospect of having to go to San Luís in response to Dr. Euclides's appeal was not an attractive one at all. But the old man was unforgiving in such matters: no one who had broken faith with him, even just once, could boast of having seen him again.

He stayed up on deck during the crossing, allowing the sea breeze to relieve his splitting headache a little. Once he arrived in San Luís he bought the *Maranhão Courier* and treated himself to a coffee. The Carneiro affair was still taking up a good part of page three; a journalist well known for his reactionary views was giving free rein to his venomous pen. The authorities, he wrote, had definite proof that it was a plot intended to blacken the *Partido Democratico Social*. Waldemar de Oliveira had gone beyond the limits of his jurisdiction: since the matter had taken place in Alcântara, it fell within the competence of the San Luís state prosecutor's office and not that of the municipality of Santa Inês. The gentleman's communist sympathies were well known, not to mention his notorious homosexual habits . . . Certain leaks, from official sources, mentioned a transfer for disciplinary reasons and even a possible indictment for child abuse. The Governor had been vilified in a manner made all the more despicable by the fact that his son had been reported missing in the Mato Grosso, probably having died for the glory of science and his country!

Moreira must have paid a juicy sum, the article was convincing, it would have the expected result. That was that, Eléazard told himself, the whole business would peter out, once again. Moreira would even benefit from it at the elections. When it came to the crunch, the stratagems so dear to Loredana hadn't worked out that well. The way things were turning out, the sophora was getting ready not only to clear the mulberry tree, but to crush as many silkworms as it could find while it went about it.

"WELL, WELL, YOU'VE been getting up to some fine tricks," were Dr. Euclides's welcoming words when he arrived.

Eléazard smelled Carlotta's perfume even before he saw her in the corner of the drawing room. He bowed and sat down opposite her.

"Have you told him?" he asked. When she nodded, he went on, "For all the effect it's going to have . . . Have you read today's paper? He's going to manage to hush up the whole business, you can see that a mile off."

"Defeatist as ever, aren't we?" Euclides said, pulling at his beard. "Nothing's been decided yet, believe me. He's pulling out all the stops, that's fair enough. But if Carlotta herself accuses him, his career's finished."

"But that wouldn't get us anywhere in court, would it? It'd just be her word against his?"

"Doubtless, but he'd certainly lose the election. His political allies would drop him one after the other."

"You'd be prepared to do that?" Eléazard asked, turning to the Countess.

Carlotta seemed close to exhaustion, but the firmness of her voice showed her unshakable resolve. "If necessary I will indict him personally. I've nothing much left to lose, you know . . ."

"Still no news of the expedition?" Eléazard asked with a detachment that surprised himself.

"They're alive," Euclides explained. "The helicopter flew over their boat—they obviously ran it aground after it was damaged. They think they must have gone into the forest, that's all we know at the moment. It'll take weeks to get a search party together."

"And to think I said you could trust Dietlev. But it's good news all the same, isn't it?"

"If you insist," Carlotta said. "No one can explain why they didn't stay by the boat and I can't stop myself seeing the dark side of things. But I'd rather not talk about it, if you don't mind."

Eléazard remained silent for a few moments, long enough for him to realize that Elaine had disappeared from his life long before vanishing in the Mato Grosso. He was convinced he was right in thinking that the announcement of her death would draw nothing but formal expressions of mourning from him.

"Loredana's gone back to Italy," he said, without noticing his own boorishness.

"We know," Euclides replied simply. "That's why I made you come so early today. Too early, from what I deduce from your sweat; you reek of sugar-cane alcohol, my friend, as bad as a bus."

"Let him be," Carlotta broke in. "I assure you it's not true, you don't reek, Monsieur Von Wogau . . ."

"I'm used to it," Eléazard said, blushing despite everything "But how did you hear?"

"She came to say good-bye before taking the plane. She's a nice girl. Don't be too hard on her, sometimes it takes more guts to get out of things than to stay."

"She told you everything?"

"If by 'everything' you mean her illness, yes, she did."

"And you think—"

Euclides broke in immediately. "No. I know what you're thinking, but it's out of the question. We have to accept her decision for what it is, a refusal to harbor delusions about herself and about others. And, consequently, a refusal to see you again. She didn't act on impulse, you know."

"I understand," Eléazard said sadly, "but I don't approve."

"Well that's because you don't understand anything," Euclides said bluntly.

SÃO LUÍS: *Some simple, rational means . . .*

"I've told him repeatedly, first of all finish your degree, then you can do whatever you like . . . But you know what it's like, especially when they're that age, they don't give a fuck—pardon my

French—about what you tell them . . . He didn't even take his final exams! So there we have it! You're still smoking as much, from what I see . . . It's going to take a good half hour . . . I'd have preferred to do it in two goes, but OK . . . It could hurt a bit, as we go on, tell me if you need a little rest. Aspirate, please, Katia . . . The electric guitar, that's the only thing he's interested in. Having said that, it seems to me he has a gift for it, and a damned good gift at that . . . Admittedly I don't know much about it, but it really gets you going when he plays . . . I bought him a Gibson and that's not just any old guitar, you can't imagine what a thing like that costs. Just between ourselves, I managed to get a friend to buy it for me in Hong Kong. And when I think they refused to have him at the Academy of Music! Can you understand that?"

Lying on his back, hands on his chest, Moreira kept his eyes fixed on the glass and stainless-steel sun above him. This chair was surely the only place in the world where he could get away with not answering an idiot's questions. The droning voice as much as the patch of luminosity behind the frosted glass was sending the governor into a drowsy state close to hypnosis. He closed his eyes. It was an ideal way of having time for himself.

The day's good news was summed up in one word: Petrópolis. *That's it*, Barbosa had said on the telephone, *it wasn't easy, but he's been officially taken off the case and transferred to Petrópolis. With promotion as a nice sweetener . . . Thanks to you I've got the state lawyers' association on my back . . .* I've seen them off, Moreira kept repeating to himself with satisfaction, I've seen them off once and for all! Biluquinha had been unusually categorical: they hadn't been able to establish a prima facie case since there had been a procedural error during the arrest. The case was heading straight for a dismissal. Definitely for Wagner and with a good chance for the two others, since one of them had withdrawn his confession on the grounds that it had been given under duress.

Edson, the old fox, had not waited long before asking a return favor. The opinion polls had him in front in Ceará State, but not far enough for it to be a foregone conclusion. So he'd had to agree to his request to go and support him in his territory, trying to pull in the floating voters. The idea of going to Fortaleza didn't particularly appeal to him but it was a case of "you scratch my back, I'll scratch yours." It was the least he could do after the way Barbosa had saved his bacon.

For a fraction of a second the pain made Moreira freeze. It was as if Carlotta had given his memory a vicious jog. Carlotta . . . The more things were sorting themselves out, the more determined she was to divorce him. He'd tried to cajole her again, yesterday evening, but she'd refused to give him a hearing. She'd stayed silent, locked in her room, until he'd really seen red. But when he tried to force her door, the jaguar had started growling, arching its spine, as if it were openly taking sides against its master. The son of a bitch! He'd been forced to calm down. He would never have suspected his wife possessed such strength of will. Eventually she had spoken to him, but solely to inform him that a lawyer—"her lawyer"!—would be contacting his shortly. He had been flabbergasted that she had already been to see one of those guys. She who didn't even known how to fill in a tax return! It was hardly believable.

He was choked by a profound sense of injustice. He hadn't worked like a nigger all his life to end up here. She's suffering from severe depression, he thought, it's Mauro who's making her act crazy. As soon as he gets back from his stupid trip everything will sort itself out. But a sharp little voice kept reminding him that he'd insisted on marrying with a prenuptial property agreement. A noble gesture that was threatening to send him back to his state of penniless country bumpkin; if Carlotta remained inflexible, that's when the real problems were going to start. As far as his feelings were concerned, the idea of a divorce seemed painful but bearable, even attractive given the prospect of regaining his freedom; politically it was a nuisance; financially it was unacceptable. There must be some way of getting out of it, he told himself, his fingers clenched over his stomach, some simple, rational means . . .

"A position as clerk or even a court usher, anything as long as he's a state official. I'm sure you know what I mean, a small salary but regular. I can vouch for him, he won't cause you any bother . . . There, that's it finished. You can rinse out your mouth."

Moreira drank the contents of the plastic cup before spitting into the basin. He stretched his jaw then licked his freshly scaled teeth. "Get him to send me a CV," he said as the chair came up with an electric rumble, "I'll see what I can do. But don't expect anything before the elections."

CHAPTER 30

How a fever can give birth to a book; also containing a description
of a thinking machine worthy of praise

WE HAD JUST finished celebrating the New Year when my master fell ill with a very nasty fever that came close to taking his life. Without having had any prior indisposition that would explain his sudden fatigue, he woke one morning with no strength at all. When I saw him confined to his bed for the first time, his gaunt face & pale complexion moved me to pity, though less, however, than the definite change in his accustomed bearing: he had an astonished look on his face, as if he were in the grip of some amusing, secret reverie, while he was actually incapable of thinking of anything at all. The muscles of his face twitched with brusque, convulsive movements, & his arms & hands as well, so that he looked as if he were catching flies.

The College surgeon, Father Ramón de Adra, was summoned immediately and found that he had milky urine, his lower abdomen tensed & his tongue covered in a yellowish brown sediment. As for his pulse, it was beating much more quickly than normal & was very irregular. Seeing this, he prescribed a light, astringent diet based on vegetable stock, to which the juice of sorrel or lemon, Morello cherries & pomegranates could be added. Father Ramón then bled him as a preventive measure, assuring me the illness would leave no serious aftereffects.

The next day there was no improvement in his state; on the contrary, Kircher had purplish ulcers, hard to the touch, inside his mouth & on his lips as well as on the glands in his groin & armpits. He had black, fetid diarrhea, which left him so exhausted he was insensible to everything apart from a severe headache that held his forehead in a torturous grip. Seeing these new symptoms, which are characteristic of recurrent fever, Father Ramón could not conceal his anxiety; if Father Kircher were not carried off during the next seven or eight days, he said, there was perhaps some hope that he might recover. So that he had left nothing untried, he prescribed small doses of cream of tartar mixed with ipecacuanha—to curb the violent stomach pains & encourage perspiration—&, alternating with them every two hours, a half dram of snakeroot & ten grains of camphor in order to build up his strength. Regardless of expense, he also gave me an ounce of the best quina, ground up very fine, & several poppy heads to be administered in minimal doses during his bouts of fever. Then he left, but not before having advised me to purify the air in the room by keeping the window open and burning vinegar all the time.

On the seventh day, since there had been no improvement, Father Ramón authorized me to try a remedy Athanasius had always been against but that his worsening state & approaching end meant we could no longer put off. So I had a live sheep brought in, which we tied to the foot of his bed. And I did well to do so, for on the ninth day—either because the animal had breathed in the poison coming out of my master's body, thus taking it away from the victim, or because of some happy coincidence—we found the sheep dead & Athanasius well on the way to recovery.

Less than another week had passed & my master was already proposing to get back to work. Father Ramón argued strongly against this, pointing out that such fevers came first & foremost from enclosed air & excessive confinement in one's study. For this reason he prescribed frequent walks in the country & a healthy routine regulated by the course of the sun.

When, however, on our very first outing he introduced me to Agapitus Bernardinis, the young engraver who was to accompany us outside the city walls and whom he praised highly, I realized that my master intended to kill two birds with one stone & had only given way in order to profit from his medically enforced idleness. When I asked him, he readily explained his thinking to me: obsessed with the urgency of completing his archaeological project, he had decided to travel around the whole of old Latium on foot so as to build up a picture of ancient Rome & prove the perfect agreement of Latin history with that of the Bible. Despite my concerns about the possible repercussions of such a plan on his health, I determined to help him as best I could in his enterprise.

Thus until May arrived we went around all the ruins of the city, both inside and outside the walls, making maps and plans of all the places or buildings that still bore the marks of their great age. Nothing escaped my master's meticulous curiosity, neither the magnificent remains of the *Domus Aurea* nor those more modest ones of the Temple of the Tiburtine Sybil, whose oracles had in vain announced the advent of Our Savior to Caesar. At Tusculum, where in the old days Tiberius and

Lucullus had taken refuge from the plagues of the city, we went to see a number of villas erected on the same site by the noble families of our time. They all received Kircher as a distinguished guest & graciously did anything they could in their keenness to aid his research. No one, however, treated us with such kindness as old Cardinal Barberini. His house having been built on the ruins of the temple of the goddess Fortuna, Athanasius was able to make a faithful recreation of the appearance of that edifice, the most imposing & most successful of Roman architecture. In the cellars he even had Agapitus copy an original mosaic that showed precisely the blessings of the goddess through a beautiful scene on the Nile. We completed out studious walks on the slopes of Mount Gennaro in order to observe people harvesting manna, Styrax & terebinth resin.

Back at the Roman College Agapitus's folders were full to bursting with drawings & my master's with enough notes for ten volumes on Latium. But however estimable this was for our knowledge of Roman history, the full splendor of Kircher's study only came with the sagacious conclusions his genius reached: everything vouched for the fact that the tribe of Noah had been the first people to settle in Italy, shortly after the collapse of the Tower of Babel; as for the Roman gods, they were nothing but avatars of Noah himself, that holy man whose memory, distorted by legend & myths, had been preserved in the myriad facets of a grotesque pantheon.

"Saturn," Kircher said to me one evening when we were strolling around the Capitol chatting, "the god who himself gave its name to Latium—when Italy was still called Ausonia—Saturn was revered for the golden age his just & peaceful reign had given the Aborigines, that is humanity. This golden age clearly corresponds to the period of abundance established by Noah when he came out of the Ark. And just as Ham, Noah's son, showed his rebellious spirit in not covering his father's nakedness on the night when Noah had made himself drunk on wine for the first time, so Jupiter, the son of Saturn, mutilated his father in the place of the organs of generation, thus destroying by that senseless act the happy times of our beginnings. What you must realize, Caspar, is that the gods of paganism are merely mortals who stand out by their qualities or their weaknesses from the common run of men and have been deified through the ignorance of others. Neptune & Pluto, the other two sons of Saturn, thus correspond to Shem & Japheth, & this analogy can be established between all the great figures of the Bible & all the idols past or present of the nations of the Earth.

By now the fever that had laid my master low was, as you will have been happy to note, nothing more than a distant memory.

Kircher celebrated his sixtieth birthday in the College and amazed everyone with his renewed vigor. Tanned by the fresh air & sun of the Campagna, he kept on gently teasing our young novices about their pale complexions, all the while drinking quantities of the white wine Father Ramón insisted he take to complete his recovery & guard against a possible relapse. Challenged to arm wrestling by the more vigorous among us, he defeated his adversaries one by one without appearing the least affected by his repeated exertions. I was so happy to see him in this frame of mind that I spent the whole night giving thanks to God.

After having solved the mystery connected with the poisoning of the Pamphilius fountain & invented the "Tructometer" to prevent a repetition of such an unfortunate happening, my master immersed himself in his work again. At the same time as the *Arca Noe* he had taken it into his head to write an apology for the Habsburgs of Austria. Rereading his copious correspondence with some of those illustrious personages for this purpose, Kircher came across a letter from the late Emperor Ferdinand III, who had shown exemplary constancy as his patron & friend. A passage in this letter struck my master like a thunderbolt. "He was right," Kircher muttered, putting the letter down on a table already covered in opened letters & papers. "How could I not see it at once?!"

Intrigued by my master's sudden perplexity, I ventured to ask for an explanation.

"I was thinking of the *Art* itself, Caspar, & of the marvelous intuition of its inventor: the *Ars Magna*, that 'Great Art' that allows us to combine both things & their ideas thanks to three divine instruments: synthesis, analysis & analogy. By synthesis I can reduce multiplicity to unity; by analysis I can go from unity toward multiplicity; & by analogy I can see not only the original, divine & metaphysical Unity of the world, but also that of knowledge, for I discover the miraculous harmony of the forces and properties that constitute it! The *Art* of Ramon Lull is not perfect, which is why his discovery proved unusable. But I maintain that this art is possible! It was long ago that I first glimpsed its principles & I use them in practice every day; it is, however, a matter of urgency—I suddenly realized this while rereading the letter from the late Ferdinand III—finally to satisfy the appetite of those less favored among us & to give the more knowledgeable this infallible means of reaching the truth. I insist that any man endowed with reason is capable of acquiring, in a short time, a true if summary vision of the totality of the sciences! I am an old man, Caspar, but I will devote such further days as God will grant me to constructing something no one has ever dared dream of: a machine for thinking! The equivalent, for concepts, of this museum that bears my name & that is nothing other than a visible &, as one might say, palpable encyclopedia & grammar of universal reality!

I was stunned by my master's contagious enthusiasm & by the success that promised. In a hurry to start work on revising Ramon Lull's *Ars Magna*, Kircher entrusted the final putting together of his *Arca Noe* and *Archetypon Politicum* to me in order to concentrate entirely on writing this new book. He had to organize the whole range of human knowledge according to a certain system, derived from the divine order, before setting up the analogical rules & the system of combination that would allow anyone to avail themselves of it for their own use. As arduous an undertaking as one could imagine, but one that my master accomplished with disconcerting ease, without his resolution weakening for one single moment.

At the very beginning of 1669, while Athanasius was having the pages of his *Ars Magna Sciendi* taken to the printer's as he completed them, a controversy arose that was as nasty as it was brazen. Two works were sent to Kircher by Father Francisco Travigno, a colleague and friend from Padua: one was a book by Valeriano Bonvicino, Professor of Physics at the same university as Father Travigno, & the other a copy of a pamphlet, published with the support of several members of the Royal Society of London & written by—Salomon Blauenstein!

In his *Lanx Peripatetica*[1] Bonvicino strongly criticized Chapter XI of *Mundus Subterraneus*—in which, as you will recall, Kircher publicly denounced transmutational alchemy— claiming he had been making gold for decades in his house in Padua. As for Blauenstein, that arrant knave who had almost ruined the too-naive Sinibaldus years ago, he repeated the same criticism of my master, but with a biting irony & spite unworthy of any man of science.

1 The Peripatetic Scale (of a balance).

However unfair they were, Kircher was deeply wounded in his pride by these these attacks. His anger did not subside for several days, until one of his detractors was struck down by divine justice & many letters of support from the most eminent scholars started to arrive. Kircher did not let up in his work, however, so that his *Ars Magna Sciendi* & his *Archetypon Politicum* appeared simultaneously in the autumn of that year, setting off a wave of admiration among the decent gentlemen of Europe.

However, the incomparable success of his books was spoiled by a double misfortune that resounded throughout Christendom, like a divine warning not to underestimate for one moment the devilish machinations of the idolators . . .

MATO GROSSO: *Angels falling . . .*

Having lost all sense of the passing of the days, the nights, of everything apart from the mechanical resumption of their movements, they penetrated farther and farther into the green depths of the forest. Dietlev's death was largely responsible for their resignation; it had deprived them of a leader, of a friend for some of them, but equally of the sole grounds for continuing to resist despair. Elaine in particular could not get over it. For some reason none of them could understand, the shaman had refused to bury the body and persisted in addressing long, passionate speeches to it. Adding horror to mental aberration, he continued to have it carried on the stretcher, despite the stench it quickly started to give off. Elaine felt haunted by this ever-present reminder of his death, definitive yet denied. Pursued by the dead man who was no longer the man she loved, but not yet the one whose memory she would one day cherish, she came to understand the haste we have to get the corpses out of our sight; the purpose of the funeral is to get rid of the decay, to prevent this tangible, inhuman anguish from coming to pollute the world of the living. Without a tomb to place these unattached beings firmly in a state of absence, the dead would return.

At dawn on that morning, when they'd all been walking for an hour, wrapped in freezing mist and in sleep, a murmuring ran through the column, swelling as it progressed. They stopped. Puzzled, Mauro went to the head of the line and saw the wall of black stone blocking the track hacked through the forest. Facing it, the shaman uttered loud invocations then set off again. He followed the cliff until he came to the gap he knew; although vegetation had taken over again, a steep way up could be made out; it had even been improved in places to make it easier to climb. The column entered it, following the shaman who was hurrying, showing clear signs of impatience.

After a wearying initial climb, they were above the tops of the taller trees and were rewarded with a sight that took their breath away. The mountain rose like a sugarloaf into the clear sky like the background to a Flemish painting: a bare, blackish mass with streaks of white but surmounted by a crown of greenery that seeped down into the smallest rifts in the rock. Below them the jungle they had been making their way through for days stretched out as far as the eye could see, a dark swell flecked with white horses, infinite, as impenetrable as the surface of the oceans.

"An inselberg," Elaine murmured, amazed at the contrast between the barren sides and the luxuriance of the summit.

"That's right, it is like an island," Petersen said, a bit surprised to have understood what she had said. "I've never heard of anything like this."

She sighed, her eyes screwed up, her mind elsewhere. "You can't even see the river."

"But at least we can get our bearings at last," Herman said, his eyes fixed on his watch. Turning his wrist so that the 12 was pointing toward the sun, he drew an imaginary line between that and the hour hand: "North's over there, which means the River Paraguay must be more or less in that direction."

He pointed to a line of foliage that was just a little darker, very far away to the southeast. "At a rough guess, I'd say we're to the east of Cáceres. I'm not even sure we're still in Brazil . . ."

"You're right," said Mauro after having scrutinized the landscape all around. "If there was a mission in the area we'd at least see smoke or something . . . God knows where they're taking us."

It was a statement, not a question, and there was no answer, but he could read the unavoidable conclusion in Petersen's blue eyes: God Himself had no idea.

They continued to climb the steep slope of the mountain. The line proceeded in zigzags, as if they were ascending the ramps of a Tower of Babel. Elaine remained fascinated by the sea of vegetation spreading wider and wider below them. Truly, they were on an island in the middle of the forest, a geographical anomaly that had perhaps been located by satellite but which, she was convinced, no Westerner had ever explored.

After three exhausting hours of climb, they entered the summit jungle, which once more made them lose their bearings. Elaine felt frustrated at having enjoyed the open air and the sun for such a short time. It was Mauro who first noticed the change in the composition of the forest; the surrounding flora was unusual, a veritable botanical garden with a considerable number of strange insects and animals. Scarlet mushrooms, frogs with gaudy colors like fish in an aquarium, tree ferns with their bishop's croziers unfurling aggressively above their heads—almost nothing of what they could see corresponded to what they had been seeing up to that point. Gathering her memories out loud, Elaine explained the curious phenomenon:

"There's the same thing in French Guyana, a peak that's sufficiently isolated to have its own ecosystem. The sort of thing Darwin used to confirm his theory. Natural selection has taken place, but it has developed in isolation, rather as it would on an atoll. Certain rainforest species have evolved differently in this bubble, away from the upheavals affecting the plains."

She told them to imagine a Noah's Ark continuing to float for thousands of years without ever reaching dry land. The species on this biological Flying Dutchman would be more or less similar to those that had gone on board at the beginning; some would have changed to adapt to life on the ship while others would not have survived . . .

"It's wonderful!" said Mauro, picking up a huge beetle bristling with horns. "It's like an earthly paradise."

"You're going to have plenty of time to admire all this shit," said Petersen contemptuously. "We've arrived."

INDEED, THE WHOLE tribe was settling down on the edge of the bush, on a bare plateau that was attached to one side of the sugarloaf hill and ended, on the other, in a precipitous cliff. Unlike the last few days, the Indians took great care over setting up their camp. After a supply of water had been collected and the usual harvest of grubs, palm marrow and other products of the forest gathered, the women started to soak manioc in the large oiled baskets in which the beer was brewed. A band of young men cheerfully set off to hunt; stacks of firewood piled up . . . Everything suggested that this stop on the summit of the inselberg was not a simple halt, but the end of the journey.

"Surely we're not going to stay here?" Mauro asked in a tone of voice that gave a hint of his fear.

"You can go and ask them, if you like," Petersen replied, undoing his cocaine belt.

Elaine had sat down on her hammock. One clear thought emerged from the depths of her exhaustion: nothing, not even passive expectation, was going to influence the course things would take. She couldn't stop herself thinking of Dietlev's body as it had appeared to her, haloed in light, in majesty. His death was gradually taking root in that part of herself where, one wound after another, life unhurriedly weaves its own disappearance. She was no longer afraid.

The shaman had waited, motionless, facing the mountain, for the Indians to build him a hut. He disappeared into it for a few minutes, just long enough to hide the instruments of his office from sight. Having done that, he gave the tribe a long sermon then set off alone toward the peak. The Indians watched him leave until he was out of sight, then returned to their various activities.

"They're preparing another celebration for when he comes back," Petersen said.

His remark, which later turned out to be relevant, did not elicit a single comment. *Professora* Von Wogau was lying down, exhausted, staring into space. As for Mauro, he couldn't stop going into raptures about the bugs he was unearthing all over the place. Herman sniffed a pinch of powder and stretched out to think things over. A warning siren was wailing inside his head, telling him to clear off as quickly as possible, get away from these unpredictable savages; but even if he did manage to slip away during the night and to put enough distance between the Indians and himself, his chances of survival in the jungle were close to nil. The rainy season was approaching; the more time passed, the more difficult it would be to feed himself in the forest. And even allowing that he could get his bearings without a compass, it would take days, even weeks, of walking and the painful cramp in his weary legs was enough to make him scream . . . He was angry with himself, blaming himself for having, like the others, given way to hope; they should have made off as soon as the Indians appeared instead of counting on the cannibals to take them back to civilization. He clenched his fists in fury at the memory of Dietlev and the rifle rendered unusable.

HAVING REACHED THE highest point of the mountain, the shaman of the Apapoçuvas sat down cross-legged on a flat rock and waited. Nothing in the surroundings, neither the source of sacred stones—the womb known only to him, the secret belly in which grew the embryos of everything that would one day come into existence—nor the beauty of the panoramic view could drive away his anguish. The soul of Qüyririche was flying around him, filling the air with the heavy beat of its wings, but it obstinately refused to speak to him. *I have gathered your people together where the signs commanded, I have shunned women, the flesh of the agouti and of the great anteater; every night since you left it I have kept company with your body without sparing either my chants or my saliva . . . Qüyririche, Qüriri cherub! Why do you deprive me of the help of your words?* He had obeyed and the god with the white skin remained silent! The invisible armadillo had taken advantage of that to slip into his stomach, as if into its burrow, and now the shaman felt ill, weakened. The animal was eating him up from inside, it was freezing his blood.

Years ago, when he was just a youth, he had almost died from the same illness. His father had passed away and the invisible armadillo had gone into his son's entrails. They had put his father in his usual place in the house, sitting up, with his bow and arrow, his beer gourd and his toucan whistle. And then the men had built a second house around him, a very close palisade of young heveas, leaving an aperture opposite his navel, after which they had pushed his father's blowpipe in through the hole until it went into his stomach. And he, Raypoty, had stayed in the forest, all alone, without drinking, without eating, without daring to approach. In the middle of the night the invisible armadillo had bitten his heart, so hard he thought he was on the point of dying. And he had submitted. Terrified by the deep darkness, begging the mercy of the wandering souls that were breathing in his ears, he had set off toward his father's house. He had gone into his father's house, even though he could not see his hand in front of his face. And, by feeling his way, he had eventually found the blowpipe and had followed it until his finger touched the navel where it was stuck. At the same moment he had said, "Father, I am your son," and his heart had started to pound, as if he had been running after a wounded jaguar, and a ball of fire had rolled into his head and the invisible armadillo had rushed out of his entrails.

After the time it takes for a bunch of bananas to ripen, the surucucu snake had bitten him on the heel without managing to take his life, proof that he himself was *pajé*, the heir to his father's occult power, worthy to succeed him.

Raypoty knew what he must do: fast, chew datura and wait there, on that rock for the ball of fire to appear. Qüyririche would speak to him once more, would tell him how to find the "Land-with-no-evil." He would rather die than admit to the members of his tribe that his whole life had been a failure. Qüyririche, Qüriri-cherub! The messenger of Tupan, the Great Vulture.

Despite his experience as a shaman and his stock of magic darts, he felt as terrified as he had as a youth, He felt he had no courage, no courage at all . . .

IT WAS IN a soft but strained voice that Mauro told them the news: they had buried Dietlev . . . For a brief moment Elaine looked as if she were truly going mad, her eyes went wild, trying to cling on to objects.

"What . . . what have they done?" she managed to say, her throat tight with emotion.

Mauro took her in his arms. He was close to tears himself, the memory of the burial still weighing heavy on him. The fetal position of the body, crouching in the pit like an animal in its cage, the branch put through his armpits so as to bring up his hands on either side of his face, the mats, the black earth on top of them and the circle of spears, so small, so slim they looked like a trap for some terrible prey . . . The Indians had done it very quickly, touching the body as little as possible because of the stench and the decomposition. "It's over, Elaine, it's all over," he said, rocking to and fro himself as he cradled her.

That night she came to his hammock and they made love, to comfort each other, panic-stricken at the proximity of death. Petersen was having a bad dream, they heard him groaning beside them several times.

ON THE EVENING of the third day, the shaman reappeared on the side of the mountain. He came down the slope, his arms full of stones, as the whole tribe looked on, stupefied. As soon as he reached the camp he headed straight for the little group of Palefaces and put his unusual burden down in front of them. With an imperious gesture, he invited them to examine the strange nodules from the womb of the mother of all mountains. Among the various fossil birds and fish, Elaine immediately recognized the samples Dietlev had taken. She picked up a flatter fragment and immediately fell on her knees with an exclamation of surprise;

before her was an assortment of the things they had come to look for in the Mato Grosso: complete and perfectly preserved specimens of a fossil earlier than *Corumbella*!

"This is it, all right," she said, her face radiant with happiness, "even with the peduncle, but a lot more secondary polyps. The chitin is different, coarser . . . And look at the structure of the sclerenchymas. We must learn their language and get out of here, Mauro! You realize what we've found?"

Already she was thinking about naming the object she held in her hand, running her fingers over the imprint. This fossil would be a stele to the memory of Dietlev. Tomorrow they'd go and have a look at the top of the mountain, there was a good chance they'd find other new species. Paleontology was going to take a leap of several thousand years back toward the beginnings of life!

"So this's the thing that's worth so much?" Petersen muttered, his attention suddenly gripped by this turn of events. There must be some way, he thought, of hoodwinking the Indians into carrying as many of these bits of stone as possible through the forest . . .

Satisfied with their reaction, Raypoty sketched something resembling a smile. He had interpreted the signs correctly, the god's companion was satisfied. Qüyririche had appeared to him while he was handling the sacred stones on the mountain, identical to the ones one could see of the *aracanóa* bequeathed by his ancestors. The ball of fire had appeared as well, as it had in his childhood, and the Messenger had spoken distinctly inside his head: *Maëperese-kar?* What are you looking for? *Marapereico?* What are you asking? *Ageroure omano toupan?* I am asking: How is it that god can be dead? When will we too fly as high as the urubu? What must be said to the jaguar to stop him pissing on the forest? And Qüyririche had answered each of his questions clearly. The invisible armadillo would never come back. All was in order among the things, each object, each being in its respective place. That night

•

they would fly off to the Land-with-no-evil, would finally reach that dark junction where the universe fitted together, closed on itself like the shell of an armadillo. Qüyririche had gone on ahead to prepare their mat under the great canopy of the sky. He was waiting for them. His life as a shaman would not have been in vain; his people were finally going to leave the circle of suffering and solitude in which history had enclosed them. He had invoked the god correctly, forced him to speak to him. That evening the people of the Apapoçuva would go back to the very beginning, to that moment when all things were equal because all were equally possible, and it would be, oh god!, as if we had never chosen to be what we were . . .

"*Etegosi xalta,*" he said, turning to Elaine, "*fuera terrominia tramad mipisom!*"

Mauro raised his eyebrows as he recognized the shaman's ecclesiastical intonation. After a moment's reflection to separate the syllables and put them together again in their correct order, he translated, "*And I, when I am raised up from the earth, will take unto myself the whole of the world*—but I've no idea where he got that from!"

"It's crazy," Elaine said as she watched the shaman walking away. "I can't get over it. Here we are in the back of beyond with guys naked as nature intended, who've never seen any whites, and they speak Latin and give us the fossils we've come to find. It's enough to give you a fit of the giggles!"

"It's not really the moment for it," said Mauro, trying to control his own mirth. Even Petersen, full of his dreams of wealth, was smiling.

The shaman came back to see them, accompanied by a few Indians this time. His frightening appearance, the black snot spattering his chest, both suggested he had just taken another dose of *epena*. Without hesitation he placed the ends of the pipes through which the ritual powder was insufflated in Mauro's and Petersen's hands. Herman tried to refuse, but the shaman seemed so unhappy at this that he immediately complied. Mauro had not even considered it; still full of the desire to laugh, he had decided to take the absurdity to its limit and go along with everything. They were given one dose in each nostril. The violence of the effect left them both stunned. Heads in their hands, they groaned, their sinuses white-hot, their brains dazzled with explosions of light.

Elaine was delighted at having been spared the honor done to her companions. The flutes had started up their shrill laments again, torches of copal resin were lit as night began to fall.

"That really clears out your head!" Mauro said, wiping away the thick mucus that was running down onto his lips. "It's unbelievable!"

The drug had disturbed his vision. The things around him were slightly fuzzy, blurred, accentuating the effects of the chemicals in the depths of his brain cells. It was as if a pair of 3D glasses had been put inside his head, he told Elaine in an attempt to explain what was happening to him, the kind used to look at anaglyphs. He was seeing everything in red and green, with distortions, overlappings that he kept on describing amid gales of laughter. Petersen was similarly euphoric, though less outgoing than Mauro; he was happy to laugh to himself, in long, silent spasms.

"And it gives you a hard-on as well!" Mauro exclaimed, placing Elaine's hand between his legs as naturally as one would get someone to feel a bruise. "You should try it, I swear you should."

She drew her hand away sharply. Mauro had lost all restraint, becoming more and more grotesque. His facial muscles twitching uncontrollably, he became bolder and bolder, desperately trying to touch her breasts.

She was glad when the shaman interrupted them. "Join the birds," he said, shaking toucan and kingfisher skins, "lighten your body to lighten your spirit."

When Mauro realized the Indians wanted to make him like them, he undressed without embarrassment and let them paint his body with annatto and genipa juice. Long tufts of feathers were tied to his shoulders, his hair was coated with some sticky matter and had white down scattered over it. Finally a bark lace around the foreskin tied his penis to his lower abdomen. Petersen could feel his limbs growing numb; incapable of thinking or reacting, he allowed himself to be disguised without making a fuss. Putty in their hands, he watched unmoved as one of his packets of cocaine was squashed beneath the foot of the Indian who was dolling him up.

"It's great!" Mauro exclaimed when Petersen's transformation was complete. "You look like an old parrot, Herman! An old, plucked macaw!" And he slapped his thighs, so pleased he was with his metaphor.

The shaman placed a kind of large bundle wrapped in plant fibers at Elaine's feet. He spoke to her earnestly for several minutes, interspersing his speech with singing, clucks and gusts of fetid breath.

He was handing the *aracanóa*, that smoke-cured dream, the proof, the guarantee of the Other World, back to her. Its contents were mysterious, its antiquity acknowledged. By a miracle known to Tupan alone, the whole of the world was shown in it. Not a blade of grass had been omitted, not an insect. Everything in it was indecipherable, apart from the stone eggs waiting for the rainy season to hatch out in the rivers. It was up to her, the great sister of Qüyririche, to take it. She must see how his fathers and he himself had taken care of it. Men, men and more men had died so that this magnificent thing should live. She must know, she must realize herself.

With that he turned away and left, taking Mauro and Petersen with him. Alone, Elaine watched them take more *epena* and start to move round a blazing fire with tall, crackling flames, some way away from where she was. Soon the whole tribe was dancing in a fiery glow speckled with insects and glowing embers. They went forward and back, raising their arms. She recognized Mauro and Petersen in the crowd from their awkward movements. The beer was flowing freely. The women and, what was even more dumbfounding, the children had started to take the drug.

A change in the rhythm focused her gaze on the red glow of the fire. Elaine saw the shaman emerge from the group of dancers and come toward her accompanied by three torchbearers. Stricken with sudden terror at the idea that she might be compelled to join in the barbarous celebration, she took advantage of the darkness and hid behind a bush growing on the edge of the precipice. The shaman showed no surprise: the Messenger had gone back to Qüyririche. He had expected her to leave and raised his arms to thank her. Her sons would guide him, him and his people. The moment had come.

Elaine saw them return to the center of the clearing. The music stopped abruptly, the bodies froze in the light of the torches. The shaman briefly harangued his tribe and knelt down to kiss the earth. Then he picked up a torch, had one each given to Mauro and Petersen, and stood between them, while two other Indians positioned themselves on either side. There was a brief moment of hesitation when they started to run, but the Indians grasped the strangers by the arm and forced them to set off. Getting into the spirit of the game, Mauro shook himself free and tried to overtake everyone. Elaine thought they were going to go past her; amused, she was admiring the long ribbons of flame when she saw Mauro's torch wobble then disappear in a wailing curve. Far from slowing down, the other runners plunged over the precipice deliberately, dragging Petersen with them. In that same futile second the shaman beat his arms as if he were trying to fly. Immediately the whole crowd of the Indians rushed toward the precipice. A blaze of fire threw itself at the night, the torches swirled and crackled, plunging into the invisible jungle, where they continued to glow, like phosphorous rockets under the sea. The plumed torsos floated for a moment, swathed in residual light, sparks of down . . . Angels falling.

Eléazard's Notebooks

THE AIM OF A CHRISTIAN TEACHER: to lead the disciple back in time so he can see the real origins of his erroneous belief. Close to Platonic anamnesis.

GLOSSOLALIA . . . Everything begins with the myth of Pentecost: the Holy Spirit descended upon the Apostles and gave them the gift of tongues, the better to convert the unbelievers. In terms of output, of rhetorical efficiency, the ability to speak all languages or to reduce them all to one amounts to the same thing.

Ite et inflammate! Go and set on fire! Ignatius Loyola orders the members of the Society. Prattle on and make a bonfire of all dialect—nothing gets a blaze going so well as hot air.

China Monumentis remains one of the the most beautiful books it has been my privilege to hold in my hands. As in his *Œdipus Ægyptiacus*, Kircher creates marvels of typography in it that inspire respect.

ONCE THE CLOCK HAD BEEN INVENTED, no one went back to the hourglass except to boil eggs. There's no alternative: we must finally take account of the sacred character of human solitude and its struggle. A moral code has no meaning except inside this combat area, that of a lucidity that is not despairing but free of false hopes of transcendence.

TURNING ONE'S BACK on the waters of the spring like the tigers of Bengal . . .

THE ARCHAEOLOGY OF KNOWLEDGE: Although unaware of it, Kircher is writing an encyclopedia of everything that is going to disappear or be called into question after him. In that sense he is the curator of knowledge already fossilized during his lifetime rather than the first museum worthy of that name. The Copernican then Galilean revolution in astronomy, the sudden extension of the chronology of the earth overturned received ideas with the violence of a tidal wave. Kircher chose not to embrace this new conception of the world but to uphold the old one at all cost. He is the Noah of his age. His life's work is the ark of a submerged world.

THE TRAPDOOR SPIDER HAS COVERED ITSELF in a fine spider's web. Strange. Redundant: a fly-trap set over the fly-trap.

"WHERE DOES A THING COME FROM if it has not been ready for a long time?" Father Kircher, Goethe says, always appears at the moment when he's least expected. He's a mediator, he gets us, like children, to put our finger on what is causing a problem.

"MACHINES FOR THINKING": those of Lull, Kircher or Jonathan Swift in the chapter devoted to the academicians of Laputa. The same desire to combine words or concepts in an automatic way, to draw on their vast reservoir of potentialities. Equipped with a computer, Kircher would probably have used it to play chess, produce sonnets and cantatas or to shuffle the letters of the Torah *ad infinitum*. He would have made the numbers feel sick, hoping to get them to spew up as quickly as possible something that was worth the effort among the things that are possible.

ONCE ONE GETS INVOLVED IN BIOGRAPHY, one has to resign oneself to the role of Sancho Panza.

NEVER LOOK STRAIGHT AT THINGS, but always with a sidelong glance, the only way of bringing out their beauty and their faults. Learned from Heidegger. The parrot, not the other one. Although . . .

I CONTINUE ON MY WAY, resolutely, without knowing whether it's taking me closer to or farther away from the essential, without even knowing whether it's going anywhere.

AMAZING THE ROCK: a process that consists of heating the surface of the stone rapidly then pouring water over it to make it splinter. Loredana . . . It's left me shattered.

ALFREDO, TRYING TO CONSOLE ME: Life's a brassiere, put your breasts in it! *La vida é um soutien, meta od peitos!*

THE 36th STRATAGEM. Recommended by Kircher, the truth as the ultimate resort against the plague . . .

IF ALL CERTAINTY has been lost and the unity between ourselves and things betrayed by a book, it is by another book that the unity will be re-established. We deride this obvious fact so often and so dishonestly that we must be blind, or content to enjoy the happiness of an abandoned animal.

A LITTLE NOTICE on the ferry to São Luís: "Man overboard: if you see someone fall into the sea or see someone in the sea, shout, 'Man overboard on the starboard side.'" I must have fallen on the port side.

"THE STONE IS GOD, but it doesn't know it is and it is the fact of not knowing that defines it as a stone." Meister Eckhart. Relate that to Lichtenberg and the dreams of drunk elephants: "Just before going to sleep a dog or a drunk elephant might have ideas that would not be unworthy of a master philosopher; they are, however, of no use to them and are immediately erased by excessively excitable sensory organs."

NEWS ITEM: In Australia six men became amnesiac after eating mussels . . .

CHAPTER 31

On the conversation Athanasius had with Chus, the negro,
& the remarkable conclusions he drew from it

ALTHOUGH HAVING BEEN decimated in the Battle of Saint Gotthard in 1664, recently the Turkish armies of Mehmet IV had been going from victory to victory. After having taken the islands of Tenedos & Lemnos from the Venetians, Kupruli Ahmet, the Sultan's son, seized Galicia & then Podolia. Besieged for months, Crete put up valiant resistance to the attacks of the infidel hordes but in the winter of 1669 we were plunged into despair at the news of the capture of Candia & the complete rout of the soldiers of the true faith. *Post hoc, sed propter hoc*[1] the Church lost its most ardent defender with the death of Pope Clement IX from grief on hearing the news.

He was succeeded by Cardinal Emilio Altieri under the name of Clement X.

---

1 After that but because of that.

The publication of *Latium* in 1671 brought Kircher a chorus of universal praise. Nothing was as beautiful as the plates in that book and it sold out very quickly. My master often talked of giving it a more scholarly continuation, in the form of a *Journey to the Land of the Etruscans,* but the book never reached that stage.

That was the year in which Athanasius adopted the habit of retiring to the Santuario della Mentorella each autumn. There he found the healthy air recommended by the doctors as well as the peace & quiet conducive to contemplation. But far from the vain hustle & bustle of the world though it was, it did not stop people coming to pester him there, sometimes even to harass him.

Thus it was that another controversy, more serious than the previous one, came to shatter the calm of his retreat. In January 1672 he read, in the bulletin of the Royal Society of London, an article entitled as follows: *A summary of the speaking trumpet as it was invented by Sir Samuel Morland & presented to his most excellent Majesty King Charles II of England.* This trumpet was described as an instrument capable of transmitting the human voice over a distance of two or three miles & "useful on sea as well as on land." Simon Beale, one of His Majesty's trumpeters, had made it according to the plans of Sir Samuel Beale, Bart., & was already selling them at great profit for three pounds each.

Always inclined to ignore anything that happened beyond their borders, the English had claimed the invention of the Megaphone, one of Kircher's clearest successes, & not content with adding arrogance to theft, now they were making a profit out of their shameful robbery!

Since it was a major matter I encouraged Athanasius to protest immediately against such an iniquity. Kircher consulted his colleagues & friends; armed with their support he decided not to restrict himself to a simple assertion of priority but to publish a whole book on the question of the megaphone, showing his superior knowledge & practice in that area.

In May 1675, the holy year of the Jubilee, Kircher finally decided to publish his *Arca Noe*. Following his original idea, he dealt with the history of mankind from the Fall to the construction of the Ark, the circumstances leading to the Flood & the exploits of Noah and his descendants after God's punishment. The book concluded with a detailed explanation of the origins of hermetic knowledge. My master had taken particular care over the quality of the illustrations accompanying the text & the whole world combined to pay tribute to the appearance of such a marvel. The young King of Spain, twelve at the time, showed his true appreciation of a work dedicated to him; adding munificence to his most sincere congratulations, he ordered the crown to cover all the printing expenses of *Turris Babel*, the book that was to supplement *Arca Noe* & to which scholars everywhere were looking forward with impatience.

His work on the Egyptian tombs already being with the printer, Kircher could have devoted himself entirely to *Turris Babel*, but his great kindness and overhospitable nature hardly left him time for it. *"If you knew the continual burden imposed on me by my affairs,"* he wrote in reply to a letter from Gaffarel, a Provençal, complaining about his tardiness as a correspondent, *"you would not reproach me for this. In this Jubilee year a multitude of visitors, dignitaries & scholars, come in an uninterrupted stream to see my museum. I am so taken up with them that I have hardly any time at all to devote not only to my studies but also to my most basic spiritual duties . . ."*

Consequently Athanasius greeted the return of the autumn with great joy & with it the prospect of retiring to Mentorella. We were considering going there when an unexpected event once more gave my master the opportunity to distinguish himself.

A Portuguese ship returning from the Americas brought an exceedingly strange savage to Italy. It was not his color that was strange—he was black as coal but we had become used to that for several years now—but the mystery of his language & his origin. From what the captain said, they had found this negro in the open sea off the Guinea coast, drifting, half-starved, in a little boat that was no more than a hollowed-out tree-trunk. After having regained his strength, the man had shown such ingratitude, refusing to learn the language of his rescuers, that the sailors wanted to put him straight back in the water, as a punishment for his barbarousness. Fortunately for him, there was a Jesuit scholar on board, Father Grégoire de Domazan; seeing that this negro had a certain air of pride & nobility, he saved him from certain death. Once in Venice, he took the shipwrecked man under his protection & became interested in his linguistic peculiarity: although the man was able to write Arabic with a facility that left no doubt as to his ability to master the language, he did not speak the tongue of the infidels at all but an idiom completely unknown to those who heard it. Moreover, when Father Grégoire showed the pages written by the savage to some specialists in oriental languages, it turned out that the writings were devoid of meaning.

To cut a long story short, this negro, called Chus because of his color, was brought to Rome to be examined by Athanasius Kircher.

So one fine morning Dr. Alban Gibbs arrived at the Roman College accompanied by Friedrich Ulrich Calixtus, professor of Oriental Languages at the University & a delegate, on this occasion, of the *Accademia dei Lincei*. Six foot tall, with remarkably fine & regular features, Chus came in, handcuffed and escorted by two guards, a necessary precaution because of his numerous attempts to remove his person from the curiosity of interested gentlemen. Kircher received his visitors in the great gallery of his museum. His first concern was to free the prisoner of his chains, & that despite Calixtus's reiterated warnings. Surprised, but apparently very pleased at this, Chus bowed to my master; then, turning haughtily to Calixtus, he said in his deep voice, "*Ko goóga! Ò ò maudo no bur mâ 'aldude!*"[2]

Calixtus started back in fear at the threatening vehemence of these words, but the negro immediately calmed down. Fascinated, it seemed, by the sight of the collections around him, he did not cease to roll his terrible eyes as he looked at one object then another. With a gesture Kircher invited him to sit down, but Chus refused with a smile: "*Si mi dyodike, mi dânato.*"[3] Then, pointing to the books filling one of the bookcases, "*Miñ mi fota yidi windugol dêfte . . .*"[4]

Kircher seemed pleased at his interest. "*Libri,*" he said in Latin, pointing to the objects he was naming, "books."

"Libi, libi?" the negro repeated in astonishment.

"*Li . . . bri . . .*" my master said, emphasizing it by splitting the word into syllables.

"Li-bi-li . . . *Libilibiru!*"[5] he exclaimed, delighted at having managed to imitate such a difficult word.

"That's right," my master said, congratulating his guest, "books." I think we're beginning to understand each other. "Now something more difficult: *millia librorum*, thousands of books."

"Mi yâ libilibiru? *Mi yâdii libilibiru!*"[6] the negro repeated, slapping his thighs in amusement. Then he shook his head with a very pity-ing look. "*Lorra 'alaa . . . Ha'i fetudo no'àndi bu'ataake e dyâlirde.*"[7]

---

2 In truth, this worthy gentleman is richer than you!

3 I will fall asleep if I sit down.

4 I like to write books as well . . .

5 The song of the swallow!

6 I accompanied the song of the swallow!

7 If you insist . . . Even a madman knows you mustn't shit in a mosque.

"You did well to bring this man to me," Kircher said to Gibbs. "His dialect is unknown to me although I believe I can see some similarities to ancient tongues. But let us proceed in an orderly fashion. You gave me to understand that he knows Arabic writing & that is doubtless where we will find some way of making progress. Caspar, an escritoire & some paper, please."

While I was thus occupied, Chus stopped in front of a stuffed hyena & expressed his joy with many exclamations and much slapping of his thighs: *"Heï, Bonôru! Ko dyûde hombo sôdu dâ?"*[8]

"See," Kircher commented, "he's recognized an animal from his country. That is another purpose my collections serve, & not the least either. I am sure that any man, whichever nation he came from, would find himself in familiar surroundings here since nature is our true homeland."

My master went over to Chus &, showing him the escritoire, indicated his wish to see him describe on paper the animal that had provoked such joy. The negro seemed happy with this invitation. He concentrated for a moment then, sitting down on the floor, wrote a short paragraph in a language that perfectly resembled Arabic & handed his work to Kircher with evident satisfaction:

جَنْدٍ فَعْ بْنُورْ مَرْ، تُو يِمْبْ نُهوِيسْ نَبِي دْ وِعِ عُكْرِبِلْنْ بَــُ وِعِ بِعُكَتّا سُوتّا بْنُورْ دَنْ لِمْتِبْ حَا بِمَّ مَبْ هَرْ دْ وِعَالِ فَعْ بْنُورْ دَنْ مِينَى مِيطْ دْ وِعِ كُنْ سِمْلِي، هَا بَنِي سَبْ هَرْ مِوعَالِ فَعْ مِهبَى بَــُ بِوِعِ عَهبَى دْ وِعِ بِعِ طَطا! بَرْقَلْ دَارِ، سُوتّا سَبْ بِوِعِ كَسْبْ بِعْكَدْ بَــُ دِبِذْ هَابِنْ جْيطْ نَمْتِ بُولْدِ

"You were right," my master said after having glanced
through the text, "this is definitely Arabic as far as the form
of the letters is concerned, but it is meaningless—& I believe
I know, besides Syrian, Coptic & Persian, all the dialects that
employ this script. Let us now try a reverse attempt. Make sure,
Caspar, that you note down precisely everything he says."

Expressing himself by gestures, Kircher asked Chus to read
out loud the passage he had written.

"*Gnyande go'o bonôru*," the negro began once he understood
what was being asked of him, "*arii tawi yimbe no hirsi nagge*"⁹—at
this point he changed his voice to a higher register, mimicking
the actions of someone asking for something to eat: "*okkorè lan
tèwu.*"¹⁰ Then, in his normal voice again, he went on, "*Be wi'i be
'okkataa si wonaa bonôrudün limana be hâ timma sappo, hara du
wi'aali go'o . . .*"¹¹

"Very good," said Kircher, interrupting him, "everything
seems to suggest that what we have here is an original way
of translating, by means of a borrowed script, the sounds of
a language that does not possess one of its own. It is, after a
fashion, a steganography comparable to—"

"*Mi lannaali woulande ma!*"¹² Chus cried, interrupting my
master in his turn. "*Wota dâru fuddôde, daru timmôde.*"¹³

We were so dumbfounded by the fit of anger, that our man
had time to continue his reading: "*Bonôrudün mîdyii sèda du wi'i:*

9 One day a hyena happened to find itself face to face with some people
slaughtering an ox. It said to them,

10 "Give me a piece."

11 They replied to him, "We will give you one if you can count up to ten for
us without saying one."

12 I've not finished talking to you!

13 Don't look at the beginning, look at the end.

Kono si mi limii hâ yonii sappo hara mi wi' aali go'o mi hebaï tèwu? Be wi'i: 'a hebaï. Du wi'i: Be'i didi e gertogal dâre si wonaa sappo be wi'i ko sappo. Be 'okkidu tèwu, du feddyi."[14]

After a pause & as if he were telling us an important secret, he said in conclusion. *"Hâden dyoïdo, no metti fó lude."*[15]

"And they weren't lying, either," Kircher said, pointing out how proud the man was. "It's clear he did not like being interrupted while he was speaking . . . So, as I was saying when he paid me back in my own coin, his language is related to written Arabic in the same way as music is to any system of notation. Let me explain: the Topinambus of Brazil could not write their language when we encountered them for the first time; but our missionaries taught them to use the Latin syllabary to represent its sounds so that today those of the savages that have made the effort are able to write down what they have to say in their own language. If the Mahommedans had landed in Brazil instead of the Portuguese, the Topinambus would be transcribing their language in Arabic script today, just as this negro here has done."

We all automatically turned to look at Chus; leaning on the windowsill, he had lost interest in us and was looking at the sky, apparently sad to see nothing but leaden clouds announcing a storm.

Kircher picked up the phonetic translation I had made while Chus was reading out what he had written. He spent a long time going through it, then underlined some words that seemed to

14 The hyena thought for a moment, then said to them, "And if I manage to count to ten without saying one, will I get some meat?" "You will." "All right then: two goats and a hen. Now if that doesn't make ten . . ." "You're right," they said, "that certainly comes to ten," and they gave some meat to the hyena, who went away.

15 A man of wit can get out of anything.

have attracted his attention. "Could it be . . ." he murmured to himself. "Everything is possible. I am in your hands, my Lord."

"Have you perhaps discovered what language the man is speaking?" Gibbs asked.

"Perhaps, but it is such a crazy hypothesis that first of all I'd like to show you what suggested it to me. Please take a look at the words I've underlined here: if I break up *bonôru*, I get *bonô* & *ru*, that is, the adjective "good" in Italian & the word for "breath" or "spirit" as it appears in Hebrew. Which I would be tempted to translate as "the good spirit" or, even better, "the holy spirit."

"By my truth, that's true," Calixtus said admiringly. "This language appears to consist of a marvelous mixture of all the others & it took your unique and multifarious knowledge to see that so quickly. But what deductions do you make from that?"

"I deduce its origins, sir, or at least I assume them, with a clarity that seems more likely with every second. Since it appears logically impossible for this language to have been formed through contact with all the others, which would suppose that the tribe had gone all over the earth without being able to speak, that compels us to presume its preexistence: could it not be the first language from which the angels took the substance of the five languages instilled in mankind after the fall of the Tower of Babel?"

"Are you suggesting this man speaks the *Lingua Adamica*?"

"Yes, Professor Calixtus, the Adamic language itself, which God gave to the first man & which was spoken all over the world until the collapse of the foolish presumptions of humanity—"

Kircher's explanation was interrupted by a terrible thunderclap; it was so sudden that we could not prevent ourselves from seeing it as a sign of divine assent. Staying by the window, Chus turned his eyes away from the curtain of rain-darkening the day. *"Diyan dan fusude,"* he said sadly, *"doï, doï."*[16]

And even though it was only three in the afternoon, Kircher had the chandeliers lit.

"It will take several weeks' work before I can be absolutely sure, but what I can tell you now is that this man's language, even if it doesn't turn out to be the matrix of all others, is older even than Chinese, which itself is the oldest development of the language of Ham. And it would not surprise me if we should subsequently discover a direct correlation between those two idioms."

Seeing my master put his hand to his forehead & close his eyes for a moment, I realized that his headaches—more and more frequent during these last few months—had returned. I therefore urged our visitors to cut short the discussion to allow him to rest. But while admitting he was very weary & apologizing to Gibbs & Calixtus for that, Kircher was determined to try one final experiment. Picking up the second volume of his *Œdipus Ægyptiacus*, he opened it at a certain page marked in advance by a strip of paper.

"This figure in the shape of the sun," he said to Calixtus, "contains the seventy-two names of God, which I have arranged according to the principles of the Cabbala, that is, the different ways seventy-two nations have of naming the divinity. And even if not all the languages of the world are represented in this wheel, it at least contains the essential roots outside of which the name of God cannot be expressed."

After having said that, my master went slowly over to Chus. He seemed fascinated by the storm, which was showing no sign of abating, but he turned around when Kircher came up to him.

16 It's raining slowly, slowly.

His white eyes were gleaming in the half-light & his silhouette, outlined against a sky streaked with lightning, seemed to me like that of a giant straight from the Book of Genesis.

"*Ko hondu fâlâ dâ?*"[17] he asked sternly.

Kircher simply looked down at his book. "*Deus!*" he said firmly &, leaving a pause between each word, went on, "*Yahvé! Theos! Gott! Boog! Dieu! God! Adad! Zimi! Dio! Amadu!—*"

At this last name an extraordinary thing happened: letting out a howl that made my blood freeze, Chus raised his hands to heaven before dropping to his knees. "*Mi gnâgima, Ahmadu!*"[18] he said, prostrating himself with all the marks of the most intense veneration, "*kala dyidu gôn yèso hisnoyé. Mi yarnè diyan bégédyi makko, mi hurtinè hümpâwo gillèdyi ha-amadâ!*"[19]

After kissing the ground three times, he stood up & gave my master a look of contempt, shaking his head from side to side. Kircher came back to us, a smile of triumph on his face gaunt with fatigue.

"Amadu or Amida—that is the name by which the Japanese worship the god Poussah. This becomes Amitâbha among the Indians & is, however, none other than the Fo-hi the Chinese have made into their deity, unaware that it is the same as Hermes & Osiris. If we remember that 'China' is called *Shen shou*, that is 'the kingdom of God,' it becomes clear that our Chus worships one of the closest avatars of Yahve—or Jehovah; & I am not without hope of discovering that those sacred names are not only known to him, but even more precious than that

17 What do you want?

18 I prayed to you, Mohammed!

19 All those who have seen that face will be protected. My thirst will be quenched by the water of the lakes; I will mingle with, I will be proud to count myself among the faithful of Mohammed!

of Amida. And it is for that reason, that I would ask you to be good enough to come back tomorrow, at the same time if that is convenient. I will undertake a detailed study of this language &, with God's help, we will open up new routes toward the beginnings."

Once we were alone, Athanasius withdrew to his study, taking with him the notes of his conversation with Chus. Despite their paleness, his eyes were sparkling with excitement & I did not need to ask him to know what hopes he was pinning on these future meetings.

Unfortunately our expectations were thwarted by a disastrous event & if, dear reader, you want to know what became of the negro, Chus, it will be related in the next chapter.

FORTALEZA: *As in an old film with faded colors*

Opening the door of her flat, Moéma found the little note Thaïs and Roetgen had composed together. She just read the signatures and dropped it in the garbage can. Her resentment toward them had become all the more bitter now that it seemed it was unjustified. They had stayed behind, a long way behind, much too far behind what she had been through these last few days. She wouldn't see them again.

The first thing she did was to run a bath. As she put the clothes Nelson had bought her in the washing machine, she decided to keep them as a souvenir of Pirambú: the 'Gloria' T-shirt had taken on the status of a relic, it bore witness to a complete change of outlook that was going to transform her life. She'd buy some new things for the boy then she'd ask her father to give him the wheelchair he dreamed of. It was the least she could do to thank him for everything he'd done for her.

Immersed up to the chin in the foam, she saw herself go to the orthopaedics shop with Nelson. She'd see that he wasn't there when she paid so that it'd be a surprise for him to be able to drive off in it. She definitely wouldn't abandon him, she was going to look after him. Eléazard would do everything he could to find him a job, perhaps even take him to Alcântara.

The more Moéma clung to these images of happiness, the more she felt the darkness inside her rise up again. Those bastards might have given me a disease, she thought with a vague feeling of disquiet. And what if I got pregnant? It had crossed her mind to report the men to the police but she had rejected the idea, paralyzed by the thought of what she would have to go through at the trial and by the certainty that no verdict could lessen the sense of her own degradation. However, she would still go and see a doctor; later on, at the slightest suspicious sign.

In her bathrobe and with her hair twisted up in a white towel, she stretched out on her bed. Tomorrow was the Feast of Yemanjá. Uncle Zé had told her how to get to the *terreiro*, that was no problem. With a bit of luck the money her father sent her every month would arrive next Monday or Tuesday. She hardly had enough to last until then; after that it was all settled: the bus to São Luís! She'd be there in three days, perhaps less. There was no point in writing, she'd arrive before her letter.

On the bedside table were the two syringes she'd used with Thaïs the day before they'd all met up at Andreas's place. They rekindled her feeling of distress. At the same time she knew, with the obviousness that goes with easy solutions—the kind that make a problem worse rather than helping to solve it—that a little line of coke or simply a joint would calm her down. Psychological dependence, she told herself with a snigger. She wasn't ill, she had none of the physical torment that went with genuine withdrawal symptoms; she was suddenly aware—and forcibly so—of the absence of the feeling

---

of being on top of things, in perfect control of her body and her mind. Every time this urgent need had appeared, she had obeyed it immediately, just as you satisfy the desire for a cigarette or some chocolate without thinking; at worst she would go and see Paco and everything sorted itself out. Today it was all much less simple. She got up to search every place where she was in the habit of hiding her drugs. She knew that there were none left, but something was pushing her to pretend the shortage didn't exist, as if the mere fact of looking would make a bit of hashish appear or a few forgotten strands of *maconha*. In desperation and with the nervousness that goes with the hunch that you've found the right key, she took apart the frame of the mirror she used to divide up the coke; there was only a fine dusting of crystals left, just enough to rub on her gums and make her even more impatient. At once her need intensified: she had to get the substance her body was demanding so insistently, she simply had to. It was no use reasoning with herself, the urge for satisfaction had her in its grip. There was no question of asking Roetgen, the only one of her acquaintances who would be able to lend her the money. Ask Paco to give her credit? That was even less of a possibility, he knew too well the kind of people he was dealing with. Moéma had reached a state where she was considering the most absurd deals when Nelson's savings came to mind. She was sure he wouldn't refuse to do this for her. She had to get out of this, clear her head of this shit, never mind how.

She put on some jeans, a blouse she chose less for its elegance that for the opacity of the material, then rummaged round in the jumble in the drawer until she found the little teargas spray her father forced on her. She put it in one of her pockets and hurried out of the building.

It took her almost an hour on the bus to get back to Pirambú. When she reached Nelson's shack, she knocked several times without reply then went in to wait for him to come back. The soap and towel lying in the hammock, the tattered photos, the sand covered in furrows as if a boa had been writhing all over the room seemed unhealthy, though the only effect of that was to increase her feverishness. The first five minutes seemed interminable and her irritation did the rest. Hardly bothered by the idea that Nelson might catch her doing it, she dug at the spot he himself had shown her and unearthed the plastic bag. She was surprised to find the gun in it but she left it there, just taking the wad of notes she was desperate to have, then filled in the hole, quickly smoothed out the sand and cleared off.

She'd pay him back as soon as she'd cashed her father's check. Until then there was little chance of Nelson discovering she'd borrowed it. It was a loan, OK? Not a theft. It had to be done. Anyway, he wouldn't need the money since she'd decided to give him the wheelchair.

Despite all these excuses her guilty conscience made up, Moéma didn't calm down until she was out of Pirambú. If Nelson had been telling the truth, she was carrying a hundred and fifty thousand cruzeiros, enough to finance a fitting end to her old life and she could come off drugs once and for all. After the Feast of Yemanjá she wouldn't touch them again, whatever happened. If her father insisted, she'd even agree to a course of treatment for addicts. But that wouldn't be necessary, she felt strong, in control of her future and of her willpower. She would go as far as coke would take her, to the very limits, to show that she'd hit rock bottom, then she'd resurface, fresh, new, cleansed of a lapse that would remain forever buried in the dark night of her youth.

On the way back she called in on Paco to place her order. One hour later a first injection was finally sealing up the widest fissures of her ill-being.

After dark she heard a knock at the door. *"Carinha!* It's us." It was Thaïs. "Open up, we know you're there."

Moéma felt she was caught in a trap. Don't move, play dead. One word and that was it, she'd end up letting them in.

"Open up, please," Roetgen said in reasonable-sounding tones. "We saw your light. We have to talk, the three of us, it's stupid to leave things like this . . ."

The light. She should have realized they'd see it. Them or someone else. She didn't want to hear about it, not anymore. It was her night, her solitary vigil before her forthcoming wedding with life. Was it not enough for them to have betrayed her, to have abandoned her to the filth of the embankments?

"Moéma," Thaïs went on again, "what's up with you? We were pissed, surely you can understand that. I don't know what you're thinking, but you're wrong. Don't be silly, open up, come and have a drink with us at the *beira-mar* . . ."

A whirlwind had started inside her head, sucking up everything as it went. Thaïs's voice, Thaïs's smile, Thaïs's body . . . She was her sister, her lover, the only friend who had shared her hopes, her fears. Shouldn't she forgive her, not make intransigence the foundation stone of her new life?

"Come on, open up," Roetgen begged. "We've been worried about you."

What a creep! If he hadn't been there she would at least have opened the door a crack, just to assess the truth in Thaïs's look. The guy made her want to puke! He'd taken advantage of them like the filthy swine he was. Tell him that! Tell him that men were all selfish bastards who could think of nothing but screwing while the world went to pieces around them . . . Yes, open the door, tell him to fuck off and let Thaïs in.

She took two or three deep breaths, checked that she was presentable and opened the door, resolved to carry out the plan she'd made. No one. The cretins had gotten fed up with waiting. Fine.

To hell with them, she said out loud as she felt the tears well up, to bloody hell with them!

ON THE MORNING of the Feast of Yemanjá thousands of people started to converge on the Future Beach in honor of the goddess of the sea. Riding in trucks or carts, the *terreiros* of Fortaleza moved en masse, bringing all the faithful behind their spiritual leaders. Once a year this ceremony combines the fervor of all the houses of the Umbanda and Candomblé religions. To get to the appointed place, Moéma had to go in the opposite direction to the stream of traffic filling the seafront. People in their finery were already crowding the pavements, a veritable exodus—mostly *faveleros*—in their long walk to the festival.

The *terreiro* of Dadá Cotinha was like a ship of fools. People in fancy dress, drummers trying out their drums at full pitch, mulattos in sky-blue gowns, boxes of *cachaça*, bouquets of roses and carnations, cries, tears, gesticulations . . . from top to bottom the whole building was bubbling over with party spirit. Dressed up as Prince Roland in a plumed helmet and red cloak, Uncle Zé was shouting out instructions for the loading of his truck.

"Ah, there you are, Princess," he said when he saw Moéma. He seemed agreeably surprised, like someone whose worst fears have turned out to be unfounded. "How's things today? I hope you slept well, it's going to be a tough day."

Moéma had spent a sleepless night entirely devoted to the pitiful miracles coke can produce. She was wearing dark glasses but was brimming over with nervous, almost painful energy.

"Come on, come on, I'll introduce you. It's Dadá herself who's going to get you ready."

They threaded their way into a small room where some old women were laughing as they fussed around little girls they were dolling up. Dadá Cotinha, a cheerful, buxom dame with the air of a nanny to the child of a Southern general, praised Zé's choice then gently shooed him out. Time was running short, the girl had to be dressed.

Surrendering to the flock of hands fluttering round her, Moéma allowed herself to be put into costume without flinching. She squeezed into a flesh-colored swimsuit that molded her curves perfectly. Sewn in at the right place, two rubber teats emphasized the tips of her breasts. She blushed bright red when the old women went into raptures about her ample bosom. Then there were the trousers in silver lamé that imitated scales. When her legs were pushed tight together, two triangles of the same materials made a fish-tail at her ankles.

"You must have lovely hair," Dadá Cotinha said in a reproachful tone, "What a pity you had it cut. If I could get my hands on the bungling idiot who gave you that pineapple head . . ."

"I wanted to have a bit of a change," Moéma said, making a face, "but I obviously didn't go to the right person. Is it really that awful?"

"Don't worry, girl, we can sort that out, you'll see." Out of the cardboard box, from which she had fished out every element of her outfit, Dadá took a wig with very long black hair which she fitted on Moéma's head. "It's real hair . . . Fatinha's, it came down to her heels. Quite a sacrifice she made there . . ."

Pins, mascara, face powder, blusher, lipstick, when it was all done and she appeared in the great hall, escorted by her old fairies, Moéma set off a chorus of exclamations and drums:

Yayá, Yemanjá! Odó Iyá!
Saia do mar,
Monha sereia!
Saia do mar
E venha vincar na areia!

For everyone she was now simply Yemanjá, the siren-with-the-voluminous-breasts, the one who that very day would emerge from the depths of the sea. Dadá Cotinha was obliged to step in to stop the most fervent adepts from touching her. She made a little sign and Uncle Zé gave the order to leave.

"What about Nelson?" Moéma asked. "Isn't he coming?"

"I don't know what he's up to," Uncle Zé said with annoyance. "He should have been here ages ago. We can't wait for him any longer. Anyway, he knows where it is."

He's found out that I've borrowed his money! Moéma immediately feared. Impossible, he would have come here right away to tell his friend. Her concern was unnecessary.

"Time to go, Princess," Uncle Zé said, helping her up onto the trailer, uncovered for the occasion.

"You knew that he's got a pistol in his shack?" Moéma asked without thinking.

"A pistol? A real pistol?"

"Yes. I don't know about these things, but it looked like a policeman's gun . . ."

"How do you know? Did he tell you?"

She was sorry now she'd mentioned it. Her carelessness was taking her onto dangerous ground. "No, he'd hidden it. He doesn't know I've seen it . . ."

"We'll sort that out later," Uncle Zé said with an inscrutable expression, as he went off to climb into the cabin of his tractor trailer.

THERE WERE HUNDREDS of trucks like theirs, of all sizes, all colors, streams of them rattling along all the roads. Piled into the back of one, in the middle of an improbable number of passengers, the samba orchestras drowned out the roar of the engines.

Men and women were jigging to the rhythm of the accordions and marimbas, clinging onto the rails, the people were laughing, singing, calling out to each other: Yayá, Yemanjá! May she bless you! May she hear your prayers! Moéma was all eyes. The power of these people, their contagious joy, but also their irreverence, the disillusioned cynicism engendered by poverty that she could read in the inscriptions on the trucks. All along the route these puns and maxims passed like the pages of an intangible book: Four full tires for an empty heart . . . Friend of the night, companion of the stars . . . Sadness is rust on the soul . . . From Amazonia to Piauí I only stop for a pee . . . I've looked down the blouse of distance at the breasts of melancholy . . . A girl's kiss cleans better than dentifrice . . . Your God is mine as well, millionaire . . . Lucky old Adam with no mother-in-law or toothbrush . . . The only time the poor are in front is when the police are running after them . . . I'm parked in the garage of solitude . . . If my mother asks for news of me, tell her I'm happy . . . If your father is poor, it's down to bad luck, if your father-in-law is, it's because you're a dumb cluck . . . If the world was perfect, its creator would be living in it . . . Light of my eyes . . . The good life is that of other people . . . The only one who's made money out of running all over the place is Pelé . . .

Today is the first day of my life was written on the billboard they finally stopped beside. Moéma felt a surge of self-confidence; there were signs for her everywhere, signs of rebirth.

THOUSANDS OF PEOPLE were milling around on the Future Beach, adherents of the *terreiros*, city folk keen on folklore, young people with nothing better to do. Divided up into innumerable sections, makeshift enclosures with improvised altars, the shore disappeared under the boisterous disorder of the crowd. From the road where Zé had just parked his truck it looked like a huge demonstration squashed into the wide corridor separating the dunes from the sea. Bathed in the light of a sun that seemed to renew its strength with every second, this teeming, tumultuous mass formed a contrast with the pale green of the Atlantic. A continuous stream of reinforcements came pouring down toward this deafening magma. Hanging from their poles, the banners billowed in the wind like the sails of a schooner; basic canvas shelters shook violently, threatening to take off. Shimmering, shining, like café advertisements against the glorious sky, huge flags flapped the three colors of Brazil.

The new arrivals made their way toward the location Dadá Cotinha had chosen two days before. Surrounded by women bearing flowers and garlands and earnest little girls in their immaculate dresses—ceaselessly readjusting the white pschents they were wearing on their heads—with men laden with baskets large and small bringing up the rear, Moéma-Yemanjá walked with her head held high.

As in a crystal cut in facets, the siren goddess multiplied: young women in more or less successful costumes, papier-mâché giants or modest votive statuettes, each idol gathering its group of faithful round it. So many clusters, so many syncopated tunes, benedictions, laughs jostling together without producing any discord at all. Deriving from the *cordels* and *congadas,* the army of Charlemagne deployed in all its pasteboard splendor. The beach was awash with limp plumes and wooden swords—belonging to the avatars of Roland, like Uncle Zé; of Oliver; of Guy of Burgundy; but also of the Saracens, Fierabras to the fore; or even of *Galalão,* the traitor Ganelon of the *Song of Roland,* who seemed unconcerned by their expiatory role. The latter pretended to attack the spectators to give the valiant heroes the opportunity of defending them, a ploy that led to violent single combats, fights between Sicilian marionettes in the course of which these puny paladins cut each others' throats before laughing as they bit the dust. Slightly worried despite everything, a few tourists with fair hair and red faces smiled inanely, one hand on the zip of their belt, the other securing the shoulder strap of their Nikon.

When Dadá Cotinha's people joined the little group that had waited all night for them on the beach—men she could trust, whose job it was to keep the candles to Yemanjá alight along the shore—they quickly set up their stand. Moéma had to take her place at the top of a large wooden stepladder where she towered above the crowd. The steps were decorated with flowers and pieces of cloth, then a big basket of flowers was placed at her feet.

Yeyé Omoejá
O mother-whose-children-are-fish!
Yemanjá!
Janaína, Yemanjá!

A new center of the world had come into being, similar to all those filling the beach, yet different, unique, not replaceable by any of the others.

Sitting facing the sea, which was breaking on the shore some thirty yards in front of her, Moéma breathed in deeply the wind-borne spray. He breasts had swelled with excitement, the star on her pearl diadem blazed. The souls in torment on this earth came one by one to place their offerings in the basket. For hours on end they raised eyes clouded with tears to the hope and mercy she represented. Deeply moved, aware of her role, she listened to the people beseeching her:

"Hail, *Yemanjá Iemonô*, oldest goddess, richest, farthest away in the sea! See that my children always have something to eat. I give you this perfume sample so that you will smell good . . ."

"Hail, *Yemanjá Iamassê,* violent goddess with blue eyes, you who live on the reefs! See that my husband finds work and stop him beating me up. I give you some salt and onions because I haven't enough for a duck . . ."

"Hail, *Yemanjá Yewa,* timid goddess! Make Geralda respond to my advances. Here is a comb for your long hair and a lipstick . . ."

"Hail, *Yemanjá Ollossá,* you whose look is unbearable, who always appear in profile, such is your haste to turn away from the ugliness of the world! Make my little girl regain her sight. She gives you her only doll so that you will recognize her. Don't worry, I'll make her another one . . ."

"Hail, *Yemanjá Assabá,* you who live in the surf of the beach, clothed in mud and gooseberry-colored seaweed! Make me win the lottery so I can return to the Sertão with my family. I leave you some soap and a pretty bracelet . . ."

"Hail, *Yemanjá Ogunté,* you who care for the sick, you who know all the remedies! Cure my husband of *cachaça* or make him die, we can't go on living like this. I give you this piece of cloth to make a dress or whatever you like . . ."

"Hail, *Yemanjá Assessu,* you who live in the eddies! I give you this postcard with a picture of a duck because I know you like them. Make things change, I beg you. You know what I mean. I also give you my lunch for today and this necklace of shells . . ."

Others left their requests in little messages folded in four, people threw armfuls of roses or bougainvillea into the basket, ribbons, lace, mirrors, anything that might please the goddess-with-seven-paths and bring down her favors.

From time to time Uncle Zé came to see how Moéma was doing and offer her a lemonade bottle filled with *cachaça.* He was content; the girl was radiant on her throne, she seemed happy. Since Nelson still hadn't turned up, he questioned the people around with growing concern. When his back was turned Moéma took little pinches of powder out of her bag and inhaled them as she pretended to blow her nose. With a slightly bitter taste at the back of her throat, she didn't tire of observing the mass of humanity, of sensing a sort of nervousness arise, an infectious carnal tension. Dadá Cotinha blessed her followers by making them pass under her shoulder; a young man—decked out in a yellow satin shirt and a maharajah's turban surmounted by an incredible ostrich feather—was dancing on the spot, swaying convulsively. Arms outstretched, palms upward, he was showing the whites of his eyes, like a martyr in ecstasy. A good-luck ribbon tied round their foreheads, their long hair open to the wind, tall women were whirling round, oblivious to everything. Superb bathing beauties displayed thighs smooth and tanned like a Vienna loaf, their minimal bikinis glistening in the sun. Fishermen with faded locks got majestically drunk, old people passed by, their donkey or bicycle at their side, one was praying standing up, head in his hands, in the grip of a vague headache. People fell into trances, like fires breaking out unexpectedly, a Saint George in a red cloak decorated with stars and spangles was trying to see something in the distance, shading his eyes with his hand. A skinny woman was shaking large, two-colored maracas, kids were bathing, playing in the rollers. Languid bodies were getting carried away by the rhythm of the sambas, blacks were stumbling along . . .

This flood of humanity gave off a pungent stench of wild beast and cheap eau de cologne.

Moéma was suddenly afraid she might see her attackers in the crowd. The thought had not occurred to her when she went back to the favela the previous day, so urgent was her need for coke. Now the possibility filled her with dread. What should she do if it happened? Hand them over to Uncle Zé and the lynching that would probably ensue? That would solve nothing, as she was very well aware. But her desire for vengeance was still there, insistent;

despite herself, something inside her was demanding justice and the paradox disturbed her.

The heat had become intolerable, Moéma was dripping with sweat underneath her wig and her costume. Not seeing Uncle Zé, she waved over a man he'd been talking to only a few minutes ago: "Have you seen Zé?"

"He's just gone."

"Where to?"

"Don't really know. Perhaps to the rally with the governor, at the other end of the beach. I told him I'd seen Nelson, this morning. He was hitching a lift to get down there. Senhor Zé said he'd go and look for the lad and that he'd come back."

Moéma knew all the terms of the problem, but not for a moment could she establish the connection between them that had precipitated Uncle Zé's departure. She was simply glad she'd see her guardian angel again soon.

Coming from no-one-knows-where, a flotilla of jangadas had started to glide along a parallel course close to the shore. Regularly one of them would detach itself from the group and ride the surf in masterly fashion to land on the beach. The great moment of the festival had arrived. The samba orchestras and *violeiros* redoubled their efforts on their instruments; corridors opened in the middle of the throng for the procession of the *filhas-do-santo* carrying the baskets of offerings onto the sailing boats. Escaping from a horrendous crush, Dadá Cotinha managed to clamber aboard the boat she desired: like all the spiritual leaders on the beach, she had to stay with the basket from her *terreiro* to the very end. Without the signal they were obeying being obvious, all the jangadas set out to sea again as one, accompanied by a delirious crowd in the waves; they were heading for the open sea to meet Yemanjá. There, far out in the swell, they would deposit the pitiful offerings of her followers; if none of them was found on the beach the next morning, they would deduce that they had been accepted by the Princess of the Sea and their wishes would be granted.

Moéma took out the syringe she had prepared that morning: a dose of coke, the last, but a stiff one to celebrate giving up. She couldn't have chosen a better moment, the crowd had its back to her, watching the jangadas leave. The beach looked like the banks of the Ganges during a ritual period; the sea, the people themselves, nothing had ever been so ablaze with holy energy. To be in agreement with the world, she thought, injecting the contents of the syringe. It must happen, Yemanjá, I must regain my taste for simple things, rediscover the pleasure of just being alive . . .

She hardly had time to register the impression of plunging naked into a mountain stream, of feeling her veins freeze. The images started to flutter, like an old film with faded colors. A man was drinking seawater and laughing. The waves were rolling up wedding dresses, there were gleams of orange along the edges. Then the film suddenly broke and all she could see was a kind of white sky swarming with swallows more and more quickly streaked by the opening frames of a reel. Nothing was passing through her mind, not a word, not a vision, not a memory, simply the feeling of having missed the boat. For a brief moment she knew she needed help, but an iron fist gripped her jaw tight enough to make it crack.

Something horribly specific came down on her.

FAVELA DE PIRAMBÚ: *The coldness of the metal, its weight, like a tumescent organ . . .*

Nelson had passed the afternoon at the Bar—the marshy estuary of the River Ceará—on the bank of a lagoon where the women of Pirambú went to do any washing people were prepared to give them. With the water halfway up their thighs, the washerwomen were beating red linen with heavy blows of their paddles. Their bottoms were sticking out toward him, their damp dresses clinging to them. A little farther away naked children were playing football with a tin can. Nelson saw neither the dead pig, swollen to bursting-point on the sand a few yards away from the other women getting water for the kitchen, nor the flies, nor the desolate appearance of the pool teeming with death in all its infinitesimal forms. It was life such as he had always known it and he was sad to have to leave it behind, however worthless it might seem. He was moved, too, by the memory of Moéma. He was madly in love with his Princess who had come from nowhere and never ceased imagining the moment when he would see her again.

When he went back home, at sunset, a word from Uncle Zé or Moéma would have been enough for him to give up the idea. He felt alone and spoke to the soap and the iron bar, hoping for a sign that would tip the scales once and for all. With nothing better to do and to help him weigh up the two sides of his dilemma, he dug up the plastic bag.

The loss of his savings left him cold. Not for one moment did he think who might have taken them; he was looking for a sign, now he had it. Someone had made the decision for him and sealed his fate to that of Moreira. The possibility of recovering his money never occurred to him. The extreme weariness that had crept into the farthest recesses of his being told him it would be too hard to start all over again. It was as if the Colonel had come in person to take away his wheelchair, depriving him—after his father—of the only reason he had left for living. He would go to the rally, do his duty as a son and that would be that.

Check the hammer was working while it was unloaded, clean the bullets again and again . . . His night was like a vigil of arms dedicated to the thousand deaths of the governor.

THE NEXT MORNING Nelson headed off for the *beira-mar*. Standing by the roadside, he got a lift on a truck that dropped him on the first part of the beach. That was where he met Lauro, who had climbed up the dunes to wait for Dadá Cotinha. Fortunately no one had arrived yet. The very thought of meeting Uncle Zé or Moéma made him break out in a cold sweat. He was afraid the old man's look would make him lose his nerve, afraid of seeing in Moéma's the confession he dreaded. He gave evasive answers to Lauro's questions and found another vehicle for the next part of his journey.

When he reached the placards announcing the governor's rally he was still a half mile away from the platform. Making his way toward it, he didn't take his eyes off it so as to make his route as short as possible. Then it was the crowd and the jungle of legs blocking his view. He pushed his way through slowly, all the time asking people to let him through, out of fear of being trodden on. One or two would move aside and then he'd have to go through the process again. The most difficult part was not to yield to the temptation to warn people by touching their calves; that provoked an instinctive reaction of alarm that resulted in an immediate kick. Nelson took his direction from the powerful loudspeakers playing sambas before the party leaders made their speeches. He had let his football shirt hang loose, *à la Platini*, to avoid arousing suspicion that he might have a gun. Stuck in between his skin and the elastic of his shorts, the pistol bit into his flesh every time he crawled a bit farther forward. The coldness of the metal, its weight, like a tumescent organ, anesthetised even the pain of being alive.

The crowd around him started to dance, threatening to crush him. Never having been in such a throng, Nelson panicked. The music seemed to be coming from all sides at once, legs bumped into him, he was breathing in sand. Stepping back, a fat woman tumbled down on his chest, almost crushing his ribs.

"Where are you off to like that?" said a swaggering black man with biceps the size of his head.

"To the rally," Nelson managed to reply, panting. "I want to go to the rally."

"Up you get, then. I'll take you there, to the rally."

The man lifted Nelson up and held him in his arms as easily as if he were a shirt he'd picked up from the dry cleaner's. "And what are you going to do over there? Don't you know all politicians are liars? Surely you're not going to vote for those bastards?"

"No," Nelson protested, "I just want a T-shirt . . . They also said there'd be something to eat."

"I'll see to it," the negro said, shaking his head with a sympathetic look. "You'll get your T-shirt, as sure as I'm called Walmir da Silva."

Using his elbows and shoulders, Walmir quickly got to the foot of the platform. It was huge and they'd put up one of those marquees the well-to-do hire for their wedding receptions on it. Placed on either side, gigantic speakers were vibrating with the pounding of the music. There was also a microphone on a stand, flowers and banners repeating the name of the governor. In the tent a group of campaign organizers were busying themselves round a pile of cardboard boxes. They were all dressed in white and sported T-shirts bearing the name of Edson Barbosa, Jr. At the front of the podium four strapping men forming the security team were keeping an eye on the area round the platform and the wooden stairs leading up to it. You could tell they were uneasy, already sensing the flood of the destitute, who were demanding that the things they'd been promised should be distributed, might be too much for them.

With his body strength, Walmir elbowed his way to the stairs and ran up with a few lithe steps. Putting Nelson down behind him, he turned to face the security guards who had dashed over to confront him.

"It's forbidden to come up here. Come on, clear off. We'll tell you when it's time."

"The kid wants a T-shirt and his share of the grub," Walmir said calmly. "If he stays down there he'll get crushed."

Walmir was a good eight inches taller than the others; his hand was resting negligently on a long knife stuck through his belt.

"Go and tell the boss," one of the guards said, foreseeing a fight in which he wasn't sure the security team would come out on top. "Be reasonable, *compadre*. Just go down from the platform or there'll be trouble."

"Leave it," Nelson said, "I just want to watch. I'll wait at the bottom, no problem."

"You going to do as you're told?" another guard said, going up to Walmir in a threatening manner.

The negro just let out a terrible cry, a real roar that stopped the other in his tracks.

"Now let's all calm down, please, let's all calm down. What's going on?" said the half-pint who came over with swift little steps, a bald-headed man in a suit and vest with the clammy skin and flushed look of a pizza cook when his pizzas are about to burn.

It took the boss just a second, while Walmir was succinctly explaining again what he wanted, to size up the situation: he saw the knife, his men's anxious looks, and realized that the cripple could help his employer's image. "We can sort this out," he said in friendly tones and one of those smiles that experience can make almost believable. "Tonho, go and get two T-shirts . . . What's your name, son?"

"Nelson."

"Right, now listen to me, Nelson: I can't touch the food baskets just at the moment. If you got one and all the rest didn't, there's be a riot. You can see that, can't you? But I give you my word that you'll get one. I'll put it on one side—per-son-all-y . . . No, better than that," he said, his face lighting up at the idea that had just occurred to him, "it's the governor himself who'll give it to you. What about that, eh? The governor himself!"

Tonho had returned with the T-shirts. "Look, here's your T-shirt. Put it on and sit over there, by the loudspeakers. If you promise to stay still, no one'll bother you and you'll be in the front row."

"As for you," he said giving the other T-shirt to Walmir, "there's two hundred cruzeiros in it for you if you stay here and stop people climbing up onto the platform. Is it a deal?"

Without even bothering to reply, Walmir placed the second T-shirt at Nelson's feet and ruffled his hair. "So long, kid, see you around."

The campaign manager shrugged his shoulders as he went down the stairs and was lost in the crowd. "Come on then, come on then! Back to work," he said angrily to his hired men. "And if another of these assholes gets up on this rostrum, you can say goodbye to your money, I can tell you!"

CHAPTER 32

What happened to Chus, the negro

THE NEXT DAY, Ulrich Calixtus told us afterward, when the guards went in to Chus's cell it was to find him hanging from the bars of his window. From a cut he had made in his arm with the buckle of his belt, the unfortunate man had managed to squeeze out enough blood to scribble on the wall one final message in his enigmatic language.

Kircher was furious at the news. "Through the fault of your incredible negligence, Signor Calixtus, not only a man has disappeared, but a language—what am I saying, language itself. For the sake of your salvation & that of mankind, may Heaven grant that there is another of these primitive people in the world! If that is not so, we will never be able to restore the link with our origins & we must see that as a sure sign of our general damnation."

Calixtus did not even try to justify himself & just shamefacedly handed Kircher the piece of paper on which he had copied the two lines written by Chus,

"*Tyerno aliou fougoumba. Gorko mo waru don . . .*"[1] Athanasius read out with interest, suddenly succumbing to his passion for deciphering again. "Odd, very odd.

He concentrated on the text for a long time, while the professor gave me beseeching looks, hoping I would intercede on his behalf with Kircher. I was extremely sorry for the unfortunate position in which his negligence had placed him & would willingly have done so, but there was no point, for Kircher's face suddenly lit up with a reassuring smile.

"Now, now, pull yourself together my friend. These lines tell me that you are not at all to blame & that a decision from on high alone is responsible for that which for a moment struck me as the most disastrous of misfortunes. The time had not yet come, that was the decision made by the One who governs our destinies in such a merciful manner. These words that He, in His infinite kindness, intended to come into our hands speak of hope & urge us to be patient. Be patient, then. And without fear, for the day of reconciliation is not far off. That which is scattered & varied will in a short while return to its original cohesion. God has ordained it so. Just like the negro, in His hands we are nothing but passive instruments of His divine will."

These encouraging words concluded this surprising episode without my master losing his conviction that he would restore in full that "Adamic language" of which he had had a mere foretaste.

The year 1676 saw the appearance of his *Sphynx Mystagoga,* the final work Kircher devoted to Egypt & its hieroglyphs. In it he provided for the first time a faithful representation of the

1 Tyerno Aliou Fougoumba [the real name of Chus], the man you have killed . . .

pyramids & the underground graveyards that can be seen in the region of Memphis.

Hampered by severe impairment of his hearing, tormented by insomnia and more & more frequent headaches, Athanasius Kircher saw, not without some annoyance, that his strength was declining. His hand had started trembling so badly that it was only with the greatest difficulty that he could still write, forming misshapen or incomplete letters & ruining the formerly perfect layout of his manuscripts with irregular lines, crossings-out or even ink blots. But he bore his ills with exemplary patience & thanked Our Savior for having granted him enough time to finish his work.

At the approach of summer we went, as we did every year, to make our retreat in Mentorella. Kircher had great hopes of the beneficial effect of this stay in the country on his health but the extreme heat beating down on the land only aggravated his problems. Prostrate with his migraines & an attack of gout that lasted several months, my master could not take any of those country walks that revived his body as well as his mind. His forehead on fire, his legs horribly swollen, he would spend his nights in prayer until weariness & opium, which he took in stronger & stronger doses, finally granted him a few hours rest. And whenever his illness gave him some respite, he devoted his time to the pilgrims & the visitors, receiving them with a good humor and joviality that seemed to increase with every day, as if in defiance of the aggravation of his physical woes.

In the autumn of 1677, just after we had returned to Rome, my master told me about an invention he had imagined while lying awake with insomnia. Determined to fight against his physical deterioration, he had worked out plans for an ingenious chair designed to move his members without the aid of his muscles. Mounted on spiral springs intended to agitate

his hardened nerves vertically, this machine, or "jiggler," was
propelled by a clockwork movement that made you lift your
legs & arms in the rhythm of a forced march. I set to work
straightaway & as soon as it was finished, a few weeks later,
Kircher could take some exercise without having to leave his
room. Truly it was a very odd sight to see him wriggling about,
though with a serious look on his face, while sitting down &
with a young novice reading St. Augustine to him. Nevertheless,
these gymnastics were extremely good for his headaches &
toward Christmas he could walk normally again.

Kircher was too astute, however, not to know that physical
health, however important, was nothing compared with the
state of one's soul. Faithful to St. Ignatius & the precepts of
our Society, he threw himself with all his heart—& for what
he assumed would be the last time—into the practice of the
Spiritual Exercises. By way of a general examination & so as to
prepare his soul to appear before God, he judged it necessary to
go over the smallest details of his past life, asking his soul to give
an account, hour by hour, period by period since the day of his
birth, of his thoughts, then of his words & deeds. To assist this
holy enterprise he started, despite the great difficulty he had in
writing, to put the story of his life down on paper himself, giving
me once again cause to admire his magnificent strength of will.

On the first day of 1678 he put on his hair shirt & subjected
himself to a regular fast, then let his hair & beard grow as a sign
of contrition. It was no use warning him about the dangers of
an austerity that was incompatible with his great age; he stuck
to this regime without flinching, alternating his sessions of
discipline with those in the jiggler, humbling himself every night
in cold & prayer without, for all that, ceasing to receive visitors
and friends with a selflessness & cordiality that drew tears of
wonder from even the hardest of hearts.

It was around this time of the year, in November 1678, that my master finished writing his memoirs. He wanted them not to be published until after his death, but with a proof of affection that touched me greatly, he authorized me to be the first to read through them. Those of you, dear readers, who have read these marvelous pages, will easily imagine my admiration. Kircher's style appears there in all its nobility & does honor to that quality that we most appreciate in the Ancients, namely their sobriety of tone & their moderation. But even more than their literary perfection, the true value of these pages, what sends the reader into raptures, is its tone of sincerity, of a genuine & inspired confession. Kircher has opened his heart to God; he says what he has seen, what he has done, but he says it with simplicity, in a fervent outpouring. So strong is his love of truth that he refuses to embellish it for fear of misrepresenting it. As is well known, coquetry was never one of his faults. My master examines his life lucidly, quite openly, without pretense, & if occasionally there is evidence of a justified pride—that of having been the instrument by which Our Lord permitted the hieroglyphs to be deciphered—it is the profound humility of his writing that holds our attention. There is nothing more beautiful than these confessions, than his repeated avowal of love for the Virgin Mary, nothing more moving than this man on the threshold of death calmly going back over his younger days & his past.

Those who have read that confession will not find, I insist, that I am exaggerating its beauties; they will know the sublime prayer with which it concludes & will undoubtedly rank it among the most beautiful lines in honor of Our Holy Mother. What they cannot know, on the other hand, is that Kircher wrote that confession of faith in his own blood, so that after his death it would be hung on the statue of Our Lady of Mentorella as a sign of love & gratitude. One should go down on one's knees, as I did myself, at the sight of these lines with their dark red hue! And may the blood shed by my master serve as an example to the lukewarm, to all those whose hearts have grown colder with every passing day, like a lava flow cooling down.

It was at the beginning of 1679 that Athanasius's last book finally appeared in Amsterdam: *Turris Babel*. Faithful to his original intention, Kircher continued the vast study he began in *Arca Noe*. In it he published for the first time numerous pictures of the architectural wonders of the ancient world & the mathematical proof that the Tower of Babel would have never been able to reach the moon, thus showing that its destruction was more a result of the folly of the undertaking than of the divine will.

After much epistolary argument with the Frenchman Jacob Spon about the right word for the science that dealt with the history of our origins, Kircher had resolved to talk of *archontology*; Jacob Spon was in favor of *archaeology* but my master rightly considered that that word did not take account of political & religious history & thus had no chance of being adopted in the future.

At the very moment when the publication of that book was arousing universal agreement & admiration, Athanasius's health suddenly worsened. His body had always been robust & resisted the afflictions of old age quite well, but his headaches—more & more frequent, more & more insupportable—had the doctors baffled.

"It's as if my thoughts were eating away at my brain from inside," Kircher told me one evening when he had called me to his bedside. "My thoughts, Caspar, my very soul! Today, like little captive animals gnawing at the bars of their prison, they're trying to destroy what is suffocating them & holding them back so as to recover their freedom as quickly as possible. They no longer have any interest in the present; they have forgotten all the old days & cannot wait for those to come and the opportunity to join Our Savior."

Alarmed by the way my master took this comparison seriously, I tried to reassure him by relating his illness to physical causes: by its every nature the soul was impalpable, as diffuse and vaporous as the Spirit from which it came; it could not, therefore, affect the body so directly.

"Are you really sure?" my master replied with a hint of bitterness. "We are creatures & as such only possess something analogous to the divine essence. Analogous, Caspar! There is in the seed from which we come something of the universal seed, of that *pansemen* that gives life to the world; but in order to exist, this mystery, however impalpable it may be, requires a minimal amount of physical matter. This universal seed—which I would be happy to call *Primigenia lux*, first begotten primal light—possesses seminal & magnetic properties. It organizes everything, releases the forms of things, animates, nourishes, maintains & preserves everything according to the infinite arrangements & alterations of its matter. In a stone, it is stone, in a plant, it is plant, animal in an animal, element in the elements, sky in the skies, star in the stars; it is everything according to the mode of each &, on a higher plane, it is man in men, angel in the angels & finally in God, God Himself, so to speak."

Since I had difficulty grasping how this seminal light could be implanted in bodies so as to act on them, he went on with a smile, "But through the soul, Caspar! For mankind, at least, for they are the only ones among all the creatures to possess one. As for the rest, it is through salt, that raw material of all constituted bodies. For, to tell the truth, salt is the central body of nature, the virtue, vigor, energy of the Earth, the epitome of all earthly virtues, the subject of all principles of nature. Science & the absolute knowledge of the whole of nature depend on its central essence; it is the material from which all things are made & to which, once they have been destroyed, they return. It is the first & last, the alpha & omega of mixed bodies, the well from which nature draws its riches &, as Homer testifies, something that is almost divine. The Earth, that, is the center & matrix of all things, the place where the elements discharge their seed so that it can warm, cook & digest it in its bosom, is nothing other than a salt congealed by the universal seed, a salt at the center of which that spirit is concealed that, by its virtue, forms, condenses and animates everything, so that it can justly be said to be a kind of soul of the Earth."

Never before had Kircher reached such heights &, although flattered that he should consider me worthy of following him there, I had to confess that my mind was still confused. We seemed to have long since lost sight of the soul, which had been the starting point of our conversation, & so I tried to get back to it.

Kircher gently reproved me: "O thou man of little faith! Have you so far lost your confidence in my abilities? Well let me tell you that, contrary to what your questions suggest, we have never been closer to your concern, for what I was saying about the stars, the Earth or the planets can equally well be applied to man. It is well known that the celestial farmer left in our brain, when it was born, a certain amount of that *pansemen* which is concentrated in the pineal gland & merges with what we are in the habit of calling the *soul*. Depending on which seed each of us cultivates, that will be the only one to grow. If it is vegetable seed, the man will become a plant; if sensory seed, he will become a brute beast; rational seed, he will become a celestial being; intellectual seed, he will be an angel, et cetera. But if, not satisfied with any of these creatures, a man retires within the center of his unity, becoming one spirit with God in the solitary darkness of the Father, he will surpass all things. With the result that there is nothing in the universe that cannot be found in man, the son of the world, for whom everything was made . . ."

I felt I was finally beginning to understand what my master was getting at: if the human soul, despite its divine nature, possessed a corporality such as fire for the stars or salt for the Earth, it would be, like anything else, subject to mutation!

"Indeed Caspar, to mutation, but also to fermentation, coagulation & other motions characteristic of matter when it reaches that rarefied state. Think of alchemy & you will see that what takes place in our soul is comparable to the mysterious transmutations that sometimes occur in the crucible. I have thought a lot, during the last few months, about the nature of the soul, I have examined all the doctrines down to the present & God has granted me the benefit of his wisdom: Pythagoras, Democritus, Plato, Aristotle & the rest have all given a different definition of the question that concerns us but although each of them has approached the truth in his own way they were all mistaken because of the narrowness of their perspective. For the soul is neither a number, nor a breath, nor a spark of the divine fire; it does not consist of a collection of loose atoms, nor of a nonmaterial trinity of our senses, our will & reason; nor is it the pure form of body or thought, but all that at once! Yes, Caspar, all that without exception! And I cannot thank God enough for having allowed me to understand this sublime truth, even if this late in my life."

"But how can something be both mortal & immortal at the same time?" I ventured to argue, suddenly alarmed by this composite doctrine. "Is there not a contradiction there?"

"Only an apparent contradiction," my master replied, his eyes sparkling with excitement. "Death is no less of a mystery than birth, but it obeys the same principles. Why, of two men suffering from the plague to the same degree, does one die and the other not?"

"Because God wills it so."

"True. But in that case you agree it is possible for the same physical cause not to produce the same effect according to the circumstances. And if the plague did not manage to carry off one of the two men, we must grant that it wasn't the plague that did carry off the other one either. So what is dying, Caspar, if not being deprived of one's soul by the will of God alone? For neither the plague nor cholera could kill a man whose life Our Lord has decided to preserve; & nothing could save one He wishes to remove from our world. And in this process God's instrument, that on which and through which He operates, is not the illness but the soul, that particle of the universal seed he has deposited inside us. As you know, we are not immaterial angels, therefore the soul must have form & substance in order to exist inside us, just as it does in the Earth or the metal I mentioned earlier; it must also be situated somewhere in our body, on the analogy of a parrot or a squirrel in a cage. Aristotle says that this place is the heart, others suggest the liver or the spleen but, like Monsieur Descartes, I declare that it cannot be anywhere but in our head, that acropolis of the body, &, more precisely, in the pineal gland that is situated at the back of it. Remember Pietro della Valle: have you never noticed the strange object he had on his finger? It was the pineal gland of his wife, Sitti Maani! He had had it set in a gold ring, which he never removed for the rest of his life and took to the grave with him. Such behavior can be criticized in the sense that it is futile to attach oneself to the skeleton of a soul that has lost its seed, but nevertheless it shows a true awareness of the nature & function of that tiny part of our brain. This sheath that shelters

our soul & allows it to act on our body is mortal and material;
immortal and immaterial is the soul itself, that spermatic force,
that puff of air like the brush of an angel's wing inside us. Do
we not say that we *breathe* our last when we render up our soul?
Did not the Egyptians & the Greeks represent it in the form of
a bird escaping from the mouth of the dying person? I tell you,
Caspar, there is something in that gland that is not there after
death. And if we can say nothing about the profound nature of
that thing, at least we can assume it has mass, however minute,
& thus measure it—"

"Measure the soul!" I exclaimed, flabbergasted.

"Or, more precisely, to weigh it, Caspar! Do not forget that
that is exactly what Christ will do when he assesses the weight
of sins in his balance. For my part, I am sure the soul has weight
as long as it resides in our body & is part of the world where
nothing can escape the laws of physics instituted by God. Not
the weight of our sins but the weight of the quantity of matter
necessary for its presence in a human body. And that, with your
help, I can ascertain. I am soon going to die, Caspar, everything
convinces me of that day by day. Thus, when the moment
comes, you will have to place . . ."

My master stopped for a moment, as if to gather his thoughts,
but the fear I could see in his eyes, which were still fixed on me,
paralyzed me with horror.

"My head!" he suddenly howled, trying to raise his hands to
his forehead; they stopped halfway. I saw the blood suffuse his
face & he slumped back on his bed. When he started to groan
horribly, his fingers gripping the sheet, I rushed out to find help.
I woke Father Ramón de Adra, who was the first at his bedside.
Having taken Athanasius's pulse, he diagnosed an apoplectic
fit &, with tears in his eyes, indicated that it would be best to
administer extreme unction as quickly as possible.

Eléazard's Notebooks

WOKE UP WITH IDEAS UNWORTHY of a dog or an elephant . . .

A DIFFERENT WAY? A possible world?

CONTINUATION OF THE FLAUBERT QUOTE, from the note-books: "Art is the pursuit of the useless, for speculation it is what heroism is for morality." I hadn't understood anything. If Kircher resembles Flaubert's Bouvard and Pécuchet it is through his des-perate, heroic attempt to harmonize the world.

KIRCHER: "Salt abounds in vile places, especially in the latrines. Everything comes from salt and the Sun." *In sole et sale sunt om-nia. (Mundus Subterraneus*, II, p. 351.)
   Rimbaud: "Oh the drunken gnat in the piss-house of the inn, in love with borage and wiped out by a sunbeam!"

THE FEELING that I'm very close to my goal, that at any moment I'm going to "lift the veil."

SO MUCH MOLD has appeared on Heidegger's books that I've been obliged to put them out in the sun to dry, to brush them then to spray them, on Euclides's advice, with formic acid. There are still some suspicious reddish patches, like liver spots; "senile ker-atosis" in medical terms.

DYSARTHRIA, labiolingual trembling, Argyll-Robertson syn-drome, transitory aphasia, mental confusion, symptoms of amne-sia, general paralysis, in a third of cases a stroke, Dr. Euclides's diagnosis is final: Kircher is in the last stage of syphilis of the ner-vous system.

"The psychological and neurological symptoms remind me of Bayle's disease. I'm sure he had a positive Bordet-Wassermann, but OK . . . Hereditary cerebral syphilis or acquired syphilis, I'd stake my life on it. So the choice is yours, isn't it?"

TREPONEMA: *trepein:* to turn, *nema:* thread. Kircher is caught in a spiral of regression; he is ill from the start.

BEING AT THE FOREFRONT OF ONE'S TIMES? Kircher is a contemporary of Noah. He lives in a fluid age in which present and past mingle. To criticize him in the name of modern science won't get us anywhere at all. His struggles against war, against dispersal, against oblivion are more important than the solutions he suggests.

DELACROIX: "It is not new ideas that make men of genius, it is this one idea consuming them that what has been said has not been said enough yet."

ON A PIEDMONTESE, Chevalier de Revel, who at the time was the Sardinian ambassador in The Hague: "He claims that God, that is, the creator of ourselves and of everything around us, died before completing his task, that he had the grandest projects for the world and the greatest implements; that he had already set up some of these implements, as you erect scaffolding for a building and that he died in the middle of his work; that everything we have at present was made for a purpose that no longer exists and that we in particular feel destined for something of which we have no idea; we are like clocks that have no dial and whose works, endowed with intelligence, go round and round until they are worn out, without knowing why, but all the time telling themselves: since I turn I must have a purpose. This idea seems to me the most spiritual and most profound madness I have ever heard and far preferable to the Christian, Mussulman or philosophical madnesses of the first, eighth and eighteenth century of our era." (Benjamin Constant, letter of June 4, 1780, *Revue des deux Mondes*, April 15, 1844)

THE IMPORTANT THING IS neither to deny nor to assert the divine, but to despair of it. In its place leave the undecidable, don't bother with it, just as we couldn't care less how many mites will feed off our dead skin.

ALL MODERNITY, when it suffers the pains of metamorphosis and questions its own existence, needs to go and find in the preceding centuries a big brother it can identify with. Without warning, the age of gold becomes the precursor, or even the founder of ours, depending on the rhetorical skill of the person undertaking that kind of demonstration. As if it were absolutely necessary to find the causes of an illness or of good health to be able to treat or understand it. This return to the origins of our ills is symptomatic of our societies, symptomatic of Kircher. But it explains nothing. Knowing where everything started to go wrong is of interest to those alone who suffer those ills.

KIRCHER will have been my golden fleece, my own quest for the origins.

"IT IS SOMETHING I CAN PROVE TO YOU," Alvaro de Rújula concedes, "but that I cannot explain to you. It is one of those profound things one cannot really comprehend intuitively.' It has become impossible, even for the physicists themselves, to be able to imagine the universe other than by mathematical formulae, that is, by a device that allows anything you want apart from *seeing*, from grasping reality through our senses or our intellect. Until the theory of relativity came along, everyone could visualize the real, apprehend it with a greater or lesser degree of clarity. The way Aristotle or a nineteenth-century geographer such as Élisée Reclus saw the world was not much different from the way a sailor or farmer of the time did. Even if 'wrong' it had the advantage of being precise, of forming a picture in people's minds. Our knowledge of the universe is certainly closer to the 'truth' but we have to content ourselves with taking the few chosen ones who have managed to master the equations on which this certainty is based at their word. All that leaves us with is a little bundle of metaphors: puerile stuff about a big bang or astronauts who have grown younger or bigger during their stay in space, lifts going crazy, fishing rods that shrink when turned to the north, punches that never reach their target, stars whose light itself never manages to escape—and of which we know nothing except that they could contain more or less anything, including the complete works of Proust . . . Our notion of the world can be entirely summed up in the set of fables that scientists fabricate from time to time to explain to us, as if to little kids, that the results of their work are beyond our understanding. Kircher, Descartes or Pascal were still in a position to handle the sciences of their time, to falsify the hypotheses themselves, to formulate new ones. But who can boast of being able to embrace enough of the current sciences to be able to visualize the universe they account for? What can one say of a population that is incapable of visualizing the world in which it lives except that it's on the road to ruin for lack of landmarks, of reference points? For lack of reality . . . Is not the way the world has of henceforth resisting our efforts to represent it, the mischievous pleasure it takes in escaping us, a symptom of the fact that we have already lost it? To lose sight of the world, is that not to begin to be happy with its disappearance?

WE HAVE PRECISELY THE WORLD that we deserve, or at least that our cosmology deserves. What could we hope of a universe abounding in black holes, antimatter, catastrophes?

TO SERVE AS a television, a pocket calculator, a desk diary, an account book, a commercial catalog, an alarm system, a telephone or a driving simulator is the worst that could happen to a computer. However, Ernst Jünger had warned us: "The importance of robots," he wrote in 1945, "will increase as the number of pedants multiplies, that is, in enormous proportions."

LIFTING UP the bird-eating spider to clean it, I freed its disconcerting progeny. Myriad minuscule spiders that disappeared in the house before I realized what domestic hell their escape was exposing me to. Soledade is packing her bags . . .

EN ROUTE FOR FORTALEZA . . . Lifejacket is under your seat

"Are you asleep, Governor?" Santos asked, leaning over the back of the seat in front of him. "Can I have a word?"

Moreira turned his tired eyes toward his assistant. He looked worried but ready to grant him a few minutes to talk.

"The program for the next couple of days . . . Would you like to check it over?"

"Of course. Come and sit next to me."

Santos changed places, pulled down the tabletop and opened the file with his notes. "ETA at Fortaleza half past ten," he said, adjusting the little pair of round glasses on his nose, "then transfer to the Colonial Hotel. One o'clock: dinner in the town hall with the mayor—here's the summary of the index cards you asked me for. Four o'clock: presentation of an honorary doctorate to Jorge Amado, in the presence of Edson Barbosa, Jr., then a reception in the education offices. I've prepared a little speech for you, but it's up to you to . . ."

"What's it about, your speech?"

"Literature and popular realism. Something simple but fairly punchy. Intellectuals and politicians ought to work together to get the country out of the mess it's in, that kind of thing."

"I've every confidence in you, Santos. You do that kind of talk very well. Will the television be there?"

"Only regional."

"Doesn't matter, I'll say a few words to them anyway. You never know, they might put the ceremony on the news."

"OK, I've got that. To continue: tomorrow, around seven, working breakfast with the minister followed by a meeting with the Social Democratic Party councillors and some local employers. Subject: investment and the northeast. You're speaking at ten. TV channels, journalists, the lot."

The Governor nodded with the expression of a man perfectly aware of his responsibilities.

"Following that, lunch in the Palacio Estudial with the minister and the junior minister of education. Then you go off together to fire the starting gun for a jangada regatta and you all stay together until the election rally. It will be outdoors, from what the head of protocol says. Since the television will be there, they've arranged for the whole works: walkabout, handout to the crowd, the lot—but there will be appropriate security."

"My speech is ready?"

"Jodinha's just putting the finishing touches to it, you'll have it by this evening. After the rally, a dinner-dance at the sailing club with the crème de la crème of Fortaleza, return to São Luís the next morning at 8:05—"

"Has the flight been confirmed? You know I've a very important meeting at eleven."

"Everything's OK, Governor. I rang VASP myself."

"Well, then," he sighed, "I'm not going to be sitting round twiddling my thumbs . . ."

"Not at all, no," Santos said with a smile. "I'd rather be in my
shoes than yours."

Moreira turned his eyes heavenward, simply out of habit. He
was good at making people feel sorry for him from time to time,
to tighten the ties with his subordinates. "I'm sorry to bother you
with this," he said, "but I'd prefer to go back the same evening.
The time doesn't matter, but I don't want to risk being late in São
Luís. Could you take care of it?"

"I'll see to it," Santos said obligingly, "don't worry."

A stewardess stopped by their seats, sent specially to Moreira
before the other passengers were served. She was indubitably the
prettiest of the crew. "A drink, Governor?" she said with a smile
like a model on the front cover of a magazine. "Coffee, fruit juice,
an aperitif?"

"A glass of water, please," he replied, taking the hot napkin she
handed him with a pair of tongs.

"And you, sir?"

"The same please," Santos muttered with a touch of pique.

To fly first class and drink water, only the rich could afford that
kind of whim.

Moreira tilted his seat back and wiped his face with the napkin.
"I'm going to try and get some rest."

"In that case," said Santos, going back to his seat, "I'll call you
five minutes before we land."

"Thank you, Santos, thank you."

The red sign at eye level sent him plunging back into the mire of
remorse: *Life jacket is under your seat.* What he was going to do on

Monday morning was heartbreaking but it was a question of survival, the only thing left that could save him from certain disaster. Just as he was repairing the damage caused by the murder of the Carneiros, another breach had opened that was threatening to engulf him. The Americans were starting to become concerned: pressure from the Brazilian ecologists—manipulated by those idiots of the Workers' Party, that was patently obvious—murders, riots on the site, rumors of land speculation . . . the situation no longer seemed that favorable for their projects. A commission was preparing to send a hostile report to Washington. "I smell trouble," his contact at the Defense Ministry had told him. "It won't take much more and they'll be choosing another site, you know. Chile's putting itself forward, it could all happen very quickly. You've got to keep your nose clean: there's a small fortune hanging on this, the President hasn't calmed down yet . . ." It was the worst that could happen, an eventuality he had never envisaged, even in his nightmares. Ruin, his personal ruin. Even if he were reelected that would do nothing to solve the problem; without the profits he was counting on, the whole arrangement would collapse. The foreign banks would fall on him like piranhas so they could pull out. His own assets would never be sufficient to cover his debts . . .

"Everything will go," Wagner had told him, lowering his eyes, "the *fazenda*, the furniture, the cars—unless you can continue to manage your wife's fortune, of course. But for that, unfortunately, we'd have to . . . no, it's unthinkable."

"What would we have to do, Wagner? Stop beating about the bush."

For that, his legal adviser had told him, it would be enough to have Carlotta declared incompetent. A medical report, confinement not in a lunatic asylum, that was quite clear, but in a clinic or a convalescent home, then they'd get the divorce proceedings canceled and he would have not simply the right, but the duty, to manage his wife's savings until she was cured.

Eleven o'clock on Monday. He had to be there when the two psychiatrists arrived. He was dumbfounded that Wagner could find two guys like that so quickly. But he wouldn't leave her in the hospital for long, just long enough to put his affairs in order, he told himself to get rid of the stifling feeling of self-loathing. He raised his arm to try and direct some fresh air onto his face. A little sleep therapy would do him no harm, it would give him time to think it over. Perhaps she'd even go back on her decision. It's the only way I can get out of it, he thought, turning to look out of the window, the only way . . .

The plane was passing through a stream of fluffy clouds, out of place in the blue sky, like pieces of shrapnel.

SAD EPILOGUE

As its name indicates, alas . . .

I KNOW TOO well what I owe to Kircher, because after God I owe everything to him, not to dread the task incumbent on me at present, & no one can be more deeply moved that I am at this moment when I must recall the circumstances of his death. But we must bear our cross like a treasure, since by that we render ourselves worthy of Our Lord & comply with his demands.

Less than fifteen minutes after the fit my master had suffered, I was administering extreme unction with all the grief and sorrow one can imagine. Father Ramón would never admit defeat & despite his grim prognosis he took a pint & a half of blood from Kircher's arm to relieve, as far as possible, his brain of its humors. After having placed a little ivory crucifix in his hands, I started to pray with the doctor, whilst all the priests & novices made the College resound with their prayers.

In the early morning my master's groans gradually grew less frequent until they disappeared, then he closed his eyes, his fingers relaxed & I saw them let go of the cross they had been clutching until then. I burst out sobbing, convinced that I had witnessed his last breath; would God that it had been so . . . But Father Ramón, who had immediately attended to him, quickly rescued me from the abyss of despair into which I had plunged: Kircher had fallen asleep; his pulse, although slow, as is natural with old men, was no longer convulsive, which gave us grounds, against all reason, to hope he might be cured!

Our Lord desiring to make his most faithful servant undergo the worst of ordeals, Kircher did not die that time; but he did not come back to life either. As Herodian rightly says, Ουκελαβ οντπολιναγαρελπιζεφεκακα.[1] When he woke from his sleep, when he opened his eyes and looked at me, I realized with horror that he was incapable of moving or even of speaking. Paralytic! My master was paralytic.

Nothing was more unbearable during the following week than my impotence in the face of that look, which was by turns anguished, furious or imploring; I felt I could see Kircher concentrating every ounce of his willpower on escaping from the terrible shackles of silence & immobility, but whatever he did & however prolonged his effort, all he managed was to utter the words, "Whoring trollop!" And hearing himself say, despite himself, such a vulgar expression, so unusual on his lips, the tears ran down his cheeks.

---

1 They did not take the city, but hope revealed misfortunes. [If the Greek sounds are read as a French sentence, it gives: *Où qu'est la bonne Pauline? À la gare, elle pisse et fait caca* (Where is dear Pauline? At the station. She's peeing and doing a poo), a sentence that is said to have amused countless generations of French schoolboys learning Greek. —Translator's note.]

Since I had observed that he appeared still to be able to move his eyelids at will, I had the idea of using this as a means of conversing with my master: one blink for "yes," two for "no" & as many as necessary to indicate the position of a letter in the alphabet. Despite the difficulty of this device and the time it took, it allowed me to establish that my master was still in control of his mind, which made his disability even more tragic. The first word he transmitted to me by this means was "jiggler." That told me that he wished to use that machine & I had him placed in his mechanical chair. Thus it was that he forced his inert body to move, to the fury of the surgeons, who predicted the worst consequences from this exercise. Father Ramón, with the approval of the doctor Alban Gibbs, having assured me that, although such a remedy had little chance of success, it did not present any danger, I persevered with my decision to obey Athanasius's orders come what may. And I did well to do so for only three weeks after the start of these morning exercises, my master gave me one of the greatest joys I have ever known: one afternoon, while I was reading to him without listening to the "Whoring trollop!" that flew round the room from time to time, Kircher distinctly spoke my name! He immediately repeated it several times, in every tone & louder & louder, like a sailor sighting land after a long and perilous voyage. And as if that was a magic word that broke the spell binding his lips, he held out his hand toward me:

"I've . . . thought," he said in a trembling voice and hesitating over certain words, "I've thought of a . . . a new way of taking fown . . . fortified towns. You just have to soun . . . surround them with a wall as whoring . . . as high as its highest building, then to threaten the besieged that you will . . . will . . . fill them with war . . . water . . ."

At once I urged him to stop talking in order to conserve his strength, all the while silently admiring the power of a genius

that had not ceased to function at the heart of the most terrible
of illnesses.

It was the first of September of the year 1679; from that
moment on he never ceased to make progress in regaining
his health. In October he got out of his bed & took his first
steps & was soon able to get around once more as he had done
previously. His faculty of speech, alas, did not recover entirely
& right to the end he suffered from a trembling of the tongue
that made him hesitate slightly over words or, less often, invert
them. As for writing or devoting himself to some task, he was
so weakened there was no question of that. But he was alive,
thinking, speaking! How could I not thank God every day for
having granted me that consolation?

I must say, however, that there had been tiny changes in
him that I did not notice at first but that subsequently became
evident. Kircher was as cheerful, if not more so, than before
his apoplectic fit & his physical appearance only showed the
effects of his long confinement in bed. He was gaunt, his teeth
were loose, coming out one after the other; his hair, white for a
long time already from his studious life, was growing thinner,
but that was something he shared with other men of his age
or even, alas, less ancient. No, what changed imperceptibly as
he gradually recovered was his behavior. A fortnight before
Christmas, as he was finishing explaining to me a hookah he
had invented designed to refresh the opium & give it the taste
he liked, he started talking about himself in the third person:
"What he wants," he said without joking, "is for you to have
this machine, which his organism needs so much to get over his
weakness, constructed as quickly as possible."

For a moment I was taken aback & almost asked who had
enjoined him to adapt this instrument that was already known
to the Berbers. He pretended not to notice my amazement but

continued, giving me almost incidentally the key to this change: "For the one who remains is no longer the same. *I* died last August, Caspar, & *he* will need to use all the tricks if he is to have any hope of resembling him one day."

This caprice & what it implied about his lucidity as far as his own condition was concerned, made my blood run cold. Fortunately my master returned to his normal manner of speech, only using this third person on rare occasions, whenever he wanted to emphasize his reduced state compared to the man he no longer was.

In the same way I noticed in my master a new tendency to talk about his approaching death. Not that he was mistaken about that, since his age & his illness made it very likely, but what was shocking was the way in which he spoke of it: all smiles, as was his habit, he described in minute detail & with many macabre touches what would happen to his body once the worms started attacking it, almost as if he enjoyed emphasizing the way corruption would leave it crawling with monstrous parasites.

It was on this occasion that my master completed what he had been telling me when his apoplectic fit had interrupted him at such an inopportune moment. His idea was to weigh the body of a dying man constantly so as to be able to check whether breathing one's last and rendering up one's soul reduces its weight &, if that were so, by how much. It being a bizarre, not to say unseemly, experiment, he suggested it should be carried out on his own body, assured as he was of my friendship and assistance.

"It will be my final contribution to science," he added gravely, "& I want you to collect the results in order to publish them after my death."

Following Athanasius's instructions, Father Frederick

Ampringer & I started to construct a balance suitable for
that purpose. Kircher's genius could still work wonders &
we managed to install a system of pulleys in his room strong
enough to lift his bed & gauge its weight by means of a certain
number of weights with a hinged arm calibrated for that
purpose. In case it should happen during the night, Kircher told
me to come and counterpoise the balance each evening after he
had gone to bed; if I then found him dead in his bed I simply
had to rebalance it to find the precise weight of his soul. For he
did not doubt for one moment that the machine would register
some difference.

Before the end of January his headaches recurred, worse than
before. My master hardly stopped smoking his opium pipe at all,
the sole remedy for his torment; his mind wandered wherever
the dreams produced by the smoke took him & if sometimes I
was saddened by his absent look & the indifference he showed
toward me and my readiness to serve him, at least I knew he was
not suffering.

On February 18 one of our youngest novices came back from
a walk in Rome with a pleasing little toy bought for just one
lira from an Augsburg merchant who made it his business to
profit from people's taste for curios. It was a flea, attached by a
steel chain round its neck. When it was shown to him, Kircher
was so delighted with it and expressed such a strong desire to
have one like it that the novice willingly gave it to him. From
that moment my master was inseparable from his minuscule
companion. He spent many hours observing it through a
microscope, fascinated by the perfection of the insect itself as
well as by the wonderful skill of the man who had managed to
put a chain on it. The rest of the time he kept it under his shirt,
on his chest, after having fixed the tiny chain to a buttonhole.
To feed it, he took it to "graze," as he put it, on the richest

meadows of his body, that is on the open wounds the hair shirt causes on all those who wear it rigorously.

"Come, my friend," he would say very tenderly, "come and eat your fill, gorge yourself on the best nectar that ever there was. You have enough here to satisfy millions of your fellows, make the most of it without compunction in the knowledge that every one of your bites takes me a little closer to paradise."

One day when he was chatting thus in the presence of Father Ampringer, the latter could not sufficiently repress a reaction revealing his doubt as to the soundness of such a practice in the eyes of the Church. My master noticed this, unfortunately for the poor priest, who was a decent man & later reproached himself for having impeded Kircher in his admirable efforts to achieve saintliness.

"Let me tell you the story of the monk, Lan Tzu," my master said quite calmly, "as a trustworthy Dutch traveler told it to me. According to the ancient Chinese tradition, eight hundred years ago this Lan Tzu was regarded as a perfect model of all the virtues; very early on he left the noise of the cities and withdrew to the darkest cells of the Nan Hua gorges. Meat had no savor for him, drink no taste & sleep no rest. He had such a horror of immodesty, he so loved doing penance, mortifying the flesh, wearing coarse, rough clothes, that he had an iron chain made that he bore on his shoulders until he died. He looked on his body as the prison of an immortal spirit & believed that by gratifying it he would stifle what was best in him, which consisted of understanding. And when he saw worms falling out of his flesh, that had been eaten away by the work of the chain, he gathered them up gently & addressed them thus: 'Dear little worms, why do you abandon me in this way while you still have something to feed on? Take your place again, I beg you, & if faithfulness is the foundation of all true friendships, be faithful to me unto death & dissect at your leisure this body which from birth was intended for you & all your kind.'"

Kircher, who had become very heated during this, had such an afflux of blood that the surgeon had to be called hastily. After having bled him in several places, he advised us not to argue with my master if we wanted him to remain alive as long as possible. I took this very much to heart & made sure subsequently that no one should risk making his condition worse, either by ignorance or mistake.

Kircher's improvement lasted for three weeks & there was nothing to lead us to expect the second fit, which, alas, had a more severe & lasting effect on him than the first: on the morning of March 12, when I went to his room to light the fire, I found him sitting on his bed busy—my God, you must forgive me, but I have sworn to tell everything—making little balls of his own excrement!

"Not throw away, Caspar," he said with an artless smile. "Once dried, put in hearth instead of wood. Considerable savings to charitable ends . . ."

I immediately tried to speak to him but whatever means I tried, I very quickly realized that my master had gone completely deaf.

I was aghast. Father Ramón, whom I immediately called, could not conceal his sadness at such a distressing sight. On that & the following days he tried all the tricks of his art to try & improve my master's state, unfortunately without success.

Following the logic of his crazy ideas, Kircher soon refused all ablutions, & the efforts I made to get him to wash himself or even make himself presentable led to such fits of rage that I gave up all attempts. Every morning, after a session on the jiggler, he would urinate in a large earthenware pot which he absolutely refused to have emptied. Nauseous foam formed on the top:

"Sovereign soap for long hair, such as Incas make at Cuzco," he was good enough to tell me in confidential tones one day when I started to cry seeing him dip his hands in this cloaca to check its consistency.

After a few weeks his body was infested with vermin. But Kircher exploited this disaster to invent a new occupation for himself; he had the idea that these animalcules were nothing other than the sinful atoms escaping from his body, like rats leaving a sinking ship. Following the example of the Uros Indians, he meticulously counted the lice & other insects he collected from his body & put them into bamboo tubes that I then had to seal with wax, in order to prevent these "harmful monads" from spreading to other men.

One day when we were attending mass in Saint John Lateran, Heaven, presumably moved by his pain, allowed him to elude my surveillance to empty his bladder into the commode that used to be used to check the sex of the popes!

The list of his irrational acts would be long & I would not want to sully in a few lines the image of a man whose fame had, throughout his life, rested on both his knowledge & moderation. There is, however, one more fantasy I cannot resist recounting because of the suspicions it raised in my mind. One afternoon, when I had stayed longer than usual in the refectory, I found my master in a position that almost made me fall over backward: naked as the day he was born, he had stuck to his skin all the feathers from a stuffed swan, which was lying beside him in a pitiful state, dismembered. Kneeling on the floor, he was observing a helicoidal figure he had made by winding a cord into a coil; for fear of losing you in abstract explanations, dear reader, I have reproduced a drawing of this labyrinth here; in it the circles represent the half oranges my master had placed at certain points:

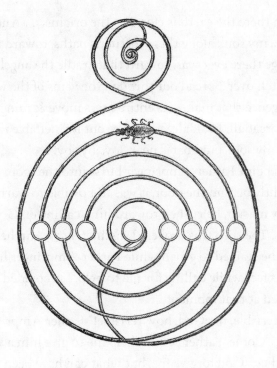

On the path created by the cord, the captive flea was cautiously dragging its chain along.

Although it only took me a moment to see all that, I have to admit that I hardly paid attention to it, so fascinated I was by Kircher's ridiculous costume. As I approached I heard him talking in a low voice to the insect: "For it is thus that the whole of the universe starts out from a single point of light, to which it will one day return after having followed the twists and turns of this marvelous spiral."

My master was speaking correctly! I almost threw myself on him to embrace him.

"The soul of the world is made like that, my friend," Kircher went on, talking to himself. "I've put on my angel's Sunday best in order to prepare for this return in the appropriate manner.

For down there the earth is closer to the origins . . . And I will guide you, my soul, along these tortuous paths, toward the only refuge there ever was, toward that cradle the angels of the house watch over. Spread out through the veins of the world is an intelligence that makes its entire mass move & mingles it with the great all: I can already make out its ineffable radiance. Courage, my soul, our goal is near. Joy, joy, joy!"

At this point Father Ampringer burst into the room & since I was slightly behind the door, it was impossible to warn him. Seeing my master, he rushed toward him, calling on God and all the saints. The spell was broken. I distinctly saw Kircher frown and then he started to groan while Father Ampringer helped him to his feet while calling for me to help. I pretended I had just arrived at that moment.

"How terrible, my God, how terrible!" Father Ampringer kept repeating. "Come, Father Schott, help me to give him a wash. All these feathers, God forgive me, but what can have been going through his mind?! Old age can be so cruel. Our good Father Kircher has gone back to childhood; we'll have to keep a better eye on him than we have done so far."

Father Ampringer had ventured to say out loud what people in the College had been muttering for several weeks, but I refused to accept this apparently obvious fact, especially after the scene I had just witnessed. Kircher could still speak! His intelligence was still intact, even if he made every effort, for obscure reasons, to delude people into thinking the opposite.

It took us several hours to make my master presentable but nothing in the world would have forced him to allow his hair or his nails to be cut &, although clean after our efforts, he remained unrecognizable. As soon as we were alone once more, I wrote these words on a sheet of paper: "I am with you, Very Reverend Father & I will keep your secret. But, for the love of

God, speak! Speak to me as you were speaking to this insect just now." After having read it, Kircher crumpled up the paper with his trembling hands and looked at me very sadly. "Can't say . . . Caspar . . . Can't say."

He looked truly sorry, like someone who has tried his hardest to fulfil your request, but in vain. And since, indifferent to my presence, he had started to play with his flea again, I plunged into despair & it was a long time before prayer managed to relieve it.

On the evening of that disastrous September 18 I confessed what I had seen my master doing to Father Ramón & confided to him my doubts as to the real nature of his state.

"I wish it were not true," he said gently, "but unfortunately I must dash your hopes, for they have no foundation. As I have observed in other patients, this kind of remission is merely superficial; far from heralding an eventual recovery, it actually indicates a worsening of the illness & is nothing but the patient's swan song, so to speak. The end is imminent, Father. Come to terms with that thought & your prayers for the soul of our friend will be all the better for it."

The further course of events proved Father Ramón right. Kircher did not say another word, apart from the absurd babbling that tormented me right to the end. But even if the voice, as Aristotle maintains, is a luxury in the absence of which life is perfectly possible, my master's voice during those last few months was still very upsetting. Henceforth he was an infirm and slovenly old man whose clothes were now too big for him; horribly emaciated, with long, greasy hair, he spent his days counting the companies of lice marching up and down his breeches. Although still amiable, he put people off by the repulsive layer of dirt he wore like a second skin. For all that, I loved him no less, knowing as I did that he was no longer responsible for his actions, but it cost me more than I can say to follow the deterioration of his body & mind day after day.

And the day when my master took to his bed, never to leave it, came sooner than I expected. On November 11 of that same year, 1680, he suddenly became so weak that his legs refused to carry him. His bowels having shrunk & no longer performing their function, he went seven days without eating; this long fast was followed by a burning fever. I realized he was going to die.

His condition having worsened on St. Severinus's day, January 8, my master received extreme unction with exemplary piety. And I do not doubt that he was happy for his death to be associated with that of the holy hermit.

Toward evening the death throes started &, although we had been prepared for this inevitable end for several months, Fathers Ramón, Ampringer and I were in tears at his bedside. About the eleventh hour of the night, when I had lost hope of ever seeing him open his eyes again, my master turned to look at me & spoke to me for the last time: "The scales, Caspar?"

Taking his hand in mine, I nodded to reassure him: I had not given up obeying his orders, the machine was in equilibrium.

At that, he sketched a smile, closed his eyes and expired. He had been on this earth for seventy-eight years, ten months & twenty-seven days . . . At that very moment, as he had predicted, we heard a tiny bell ring indicating a change in the balance! To the amazement of those present in the room, it was established that Kircher's soul weighed exactly half a scruple.

The death of my master distressed me more than I would have thought. Although life had become a burden for him & he was dragging it out in pain and grief, his loss left me inconsolable. His vitality, his piety & his wisdom, which made everyone who had the privilege of knowing him look up to him, were the principal reasons that made one love him.

Never was there a man more deserving of the admiration of
his contemporaries; for he was one of the Ancients worthy
of our esteem & who brought honor to science. But given his
condition, to wish him a longer life would have been to desire
something against his interest. His mind had never deteriorated,
but recently he had ceased to be active because he had gradually
been deserted by his five senses; no longer, therefore, having any
part in the things of this world, he had to go to the other for the
salvation & eternal rest of his soul.

Kircher's funeral was a magnificent affair. Taken with great
pomp to the Ecclesia del Gesù, his body was followed by the
innumerable crowd of all those who had loved or admired him.
United in their grief were monks from the Trinità dei Monti,
Dominicans, priests and monks of all the orders, bishops,
cardinals, princes, even Queen Christina of Sweden, who
seemed extremely moved by this mourning. But the tribute that
doubtless meant most to my master was the one paid him by the
cohort of students following his funeral cortege: they came from
the German, Scottish, French Colleges, all those who had at one
time taken Kircher's course wept as they saluted the *magister*
they had dubbed "the master of a hundred arts"! The service
for the dead, sung by all the Jesuits of the Roman College,
was admirable in its spirit of meditation. It was followed
by Couperin's *Leçons de ténèbres*, music the beauty of which
perfectly suited a man who for all his life had spoken out against
darkness the better to celebrate the glory of light.

My long task finishes here with the end of the man to whom
it was dedicated. According to Kircher's express wish, his heart
is buried at the feet of the Virgin Mary, at Mentorella. Today I
have reached my master's age & the ills I suffer make me hope
I will soon join him. Therefore I beg you, dear reader, to join
your prayers to mine that God may grant me that grace & to

meditate at times on the one my beloved master was not afraid one day to write in his own blood:

> *O Great & Admirable Mother of God! O Mary, Immaculate Virgin! I, Thy most unworthy servant, prostrate myself before Thy face, remembering the blessings Thou hast obtained for me from my most tender years, I give myself to Thee entirely, Sweet Mother, I give my life, my body, my soul, all my deeds & all my works. From the bottom of my heart, I express my innermost desires before Thy altar, at the very place where thou didst most miraculously inspire me to restore this place dedicated to Thee & to Saint Eustachius; & may the generations to come know that, however much learning I have acquired & whatever I have written that is good was achieved not so much through my own studies & work as through the gift of Thy singular grace & the merciful guidance of Eternal Wisdom. And as I lay down my pen, I bequeath this, which I have written with my blood in testimony to what Thou hast done, to all, Jesus, Mary, Joseph, as my sole true possession.*
>
> *I, Athanasius Kircher, Thy poor & humble & unworthy servant, pray that Thou mayst hear my prayer, O Jesus, O Mary. Amen.*
>
> *To the greater glory of God.*

MATO GROSSO: *One of the species is deadly, the other dangerous and the third totally harmless . . .*

Elaine could not say how many hours had passed since the sight that had overwhelmed her. When she once more became aware of herself and her surroundings she was standing in the middle of the clearing beside the sticky ashes in the hearth. It was daylight, she was hungry, the jungle around her was chirping like the aviary in a zoo. Where things had been, there was now nothing. The earth was littered with the tribe's bits and pieces: mats, gourds, bundles of feathers and arrows that were already fading, going over, head bowed, to the colors of the forest. Long processions of ants were crisscrossing the campsite, Roman legions bristling with standards and trophies. Perched on a leaf, a red-headed frog looked down its nose at these multitudes.

Elaine went to the edge of the precipice; the treetops were black with a swarm of vultures, though seen from above they looked like flies regaling themselves painstakingly on a corpse. Mauro, Petersen, all the Indian tribe were lying somewhere down there below her . . . None could have survived such a fall. She was alone on top of this mountain that was unknown to the rest of the world. Like Robinson Crusoe on his island, she told herself, at the same time vaguely deploring the out-of-place, almost frivolous nature of the thought. Her mind in a whirl, still hovering close to derangement, Elaine asked herself for what obscure reason she hadn't gone mad.

Her rumbling stomach took her away from the cliff. Walking unsteadily, she wandered round the camp looking for food. The first thing that caught her attention was Mauro's Walkman; it was still in the transparent plastic case he used to protect it on the rare occasions when he took it off. Then she saw his clothes and Petersen's, left in a heap on the sodden ground. Why had they taken the shaman's powder? Images came back to her, scraps of pictures tinged with red. They had howled as they fell, proof that they had realized what was happening at the last moment. And all the others, my God, all those women and their children . . . all those feathers beating the air in desperation . . .

She regained consciousness a little later, bewildered to find herself holding a tin of beans. I'm cracking up, she told herself, alarmed. There were stretches of time during that her body continued to live and move outside her perception . . . The contents of the tin made her feel sick but she forced herself to swallow a few mouthfuls. Her eyes were wandering around the clearing, touching on insignificant traces, sliding over them without seeing them. A trickle of saliva oozed down her chin. Arms dangling, she stared at the shapeless object a snake with black and red rings with white edging was slowly embracing in its coils. *There are three kinds of coral snake*, she recalled with composure, *all very similar as far as their colors and their characteristics are concerned; one of the species is deadly, the other dangerous and the third totally inoffensive—which was the first to appear in the order of evolution?* The question had been asked her years ago during an examination on mimicry among animals. She hadn't been able to answer it but clearly recalled the professor's explanation.

"Imagine you're a bird with a taste for reptiles," he had said, "and you try to eat the first of these three snakes. What ensues? You die on the spot without realizing what's happened to you and without having time to warn the other birds of the danger. The effect of this, in the shorter or longer term, would be the elimination of the predator-of-reptiles-bird species from the natural world. The same with the third: you eat the snake and, since nothing happens, you deduce that coral snakes are highly comestible. Result—the disappearance of your species when these reptiles eventually become venomous. If you get bitten by the second snake, the one that is poisonous but not deadly, you will suffer for a certain time then you will pass on the information as quickly as possible: eating a snake with black and red rings is very dangerous, it's best to avoid all snakes that more or less answer to that description. That, therefore, is the snake that will be the first to appear. Of necessity. Left in peace by the birds, its potential enemies, our coral snake can now develop other forms better adapted to its own needs, until eventually you get the Rolls Royce of the species, the one whose bite is terminal. As for the third, indubitably the most cunning, it's an animal of a species that has nothing to do with the previous two but that decks itself out in the colors of the coral snake to be left in peace, as they are, at very little effort. Having said that, he went on, not without a touch of irony, the natural resistance to the toxins shown by certain predators of reptiles, including several birds, presents an exciting problem, which down to this day is still . . .

Elaine wondered which of these three snakes was gliding along in front of her. When it had disappeared, she saw again the shaman place a strange bundle at her feet just before the horror had started to spin its web. Her mind a blank, she went over to it, then with the tips of her fingers, she undid the cover of plant fibers. Despite the greenish swellings distorting its old leather cover, she realized it was a book, a folio volume that she hastened to take out of its envelope and open at the title page. This impulsive action revealed the answer: *Athanasii Kircherii è Soc. Jesu Arca Noe, in Tres Libros Digesta* . . .

Noah's Ark! THE shaman had had one of Eléazard's favorite books in his hands. She was less surprised at such a coincidence than to see her husband emerge from the blind spot of chaos, as if to help her, to encourage her from afar to pull herself together. The book affirmed his presence with her and, in an equally mysterious way, justified the bee in his bonnet he had about Athanasius Kircher. It gave off a dubious magic, disproportionate tension. Elaine leafed through the damp pages spotted with brownish marks. Following *Arca Noe*, all the illustrations from *Ars Magna Lucis et Umbrae* and *Mundus Subterraneus* had been bound in; manuscript notes on several of the flyleaves formed an embryonic dictionary, a glossary, rather, such as missionaries who were approaching an unknown tribe would create. The fact that the glossary established links between Latin and the natives' language, that it was written down with a quill pen, the very style of the handwriting, all indicated that Kircher's book had belonged to one of the first Westerners charged with exploring the New World. Putting together these clues and the course of her own encounter with the Indians, Elaine felt she could reconstruct the story with a certain degree of probability:

One day a man, probably an ecclesiastic, had set off into the jungle with the scanty gear of all candidates for martyrdom: a Bible, a little collection of trinkets and mirrors, and one of those copiously illustrated manuals in which Kircher demonstrated better than anyone the superiority of the Christian religion. Certain Jesuits, Eléazard had told her, simply sat down in the depths of the forest and played the flute, or even the violin, until the Indians appeared. Like modern Orpheuses, they were lying in wait for souls, alternating music and prayer. By persevering, the Jesuit had managed to remain alive and settled in with a tribe, starting to learn their language. He had to point to earthly creatures, the plants, trees, animals in Kircher's book, and name them one by one with infinite patience; having done that, he could go on to supernatural matters, dig up the mythology of these savages and set about converting them. A few conjuring tricks, a lot of diplomacy and the Jesuit made a shaman—only too happy to come out of it so well— his ally and disciple. The missionary could speak—or thought he could speak—the language of his flock, he'd managed to baptize the children and even adapt some hymns; as for the shaman, he knew whole speeches in Latin and could jabber along in his instructor's language in a way that aroused great hopes . . . But then the privations, malaria or some sordid act of revenge put an end to the good Jesuit's undertaking. The tribe returned to its primitive existence. With the luster of new powers, the shaman took charge of the books and continued on the path that had served his foreign colleague so well. Tirelessly he repeated the Latin he had learned with such difficulty, told all the others that a prophet had come, but that another would come later, that he would have a beard, as in the engraving of Kircher at the beginning of the book, and that he would lead them to some paradise. The shaman died in his turn, after having passed the whole of his knowledge on to his son, and that had continued for four hundred years. At each transfer of the original message, something was lost, with the result that these people had come to worship Kircher himself: *Qüyririche* was the corresponding word in the glossary. Seeing Dietlev, the Indians had easily identified him as the messiah of the original myths. Even the fossils had played their part in this incredible misunderstanding; several of them were shown in the book, the new arrivals had some in their baggage, a great number lay hidden in the mountain. Signs that the shaman had put together, in one way or another, to reach the conclusion that the end of time was imminent.

However outrageously improbable it sounded, this explanation was the only one to give a logical shape to the horror she had been through. A misunderstanding, an appalling millenarian misunderstanding that had cost the lives of a whole tribe. Elaine found it tormenting not to have anyone to share this sudden insight with. The Bible had doubtless been lost, but the book open on her knees—the shaman's *aracanóa!*—had symbolized the sacred for generations of men to the point where it led their descendants to the abyss. Eléazard and Moéma would have been over the moon! Poor Dietlev as well, moreover, though he would have doubtless have been less interested in the living fossils than in those brought back by the old man from his stay in the mountain.

Elaine once more awoke to the world around her to realize she had climbed to the summit of the inselberg. The book was no longer there; it must have been left somewhere behind her. Despite her surprise and her alarm at the black holes into which her mind was retreating more and more often, she was happy to come out into the open air. The rocky crest around her was one great jumble of petrified impressions. *Tribrachidium*? *Archaeoscyathids*? *Parvancorina*? Her memory was uncertain about giving names to the stones cascading from this spring turned to stone: a unique crucible of algae and invertebrates, a puddle of time, of the initial time when the whole of the Earth was nothing but a tragic and unpopulated ocean. On this shoal, six hundred million years ago, the sea had hatched the miracle of life. An uninterrupted link connected her with these blind, impoverished creatures, let her share in their destiny of primordial glyphs. In the eye of the cyclone, at the very heart of the whirling that was raising the black waters of the forest beneath her, Elaine knew that she was finally going to be able to come to rest. Eléazard, Moéma . . . she found them both again, here and now, having taken such a long way around to them. A solar mirror reflecting the dizzying universe, she saw for a moment the absolute coherence of everything that exists. This nonplace, this still center with the frail shell of life coiled around it, now she felt it, now she occupied the smallest gap in its space. Freed from hope, smiling, she felt like a deserted ark.

Eléazard's notebooks

THE WEIGHT OF THE SOUL. From Euclides, ice-cold as usual: "Wind, just wind . . . Believe it or not, the air in our lungs has weight as well. Your Kircher weighed his last sigh; it's taking introspection a bit far, don't you think?"

NOVALIS made a *Catalogue raisonné of the operations man has permanently at his disposal*: he names saliva, urine, emissions of semen, putting your finger in your mouth to make yourself be sick, holding your breath, changing position, closing your eyes, etc. In passing, he wonders whether there might not be some possible use for excrement. Marcel Duchamp was to add to these: excess pressure on an electric push-button, the growth of hair and fingernails, starting with fear or amazement, laughing, yawning, sneezing, twitching, giving hard looks, fainting, and he too was to suggest a *"transformer to make use of* [all] *these little bursts of wasted energy."*

SIX GRAMS of soul . . .

I DON'T KNOW WHAT gives rise to the impression that henceforward Athanasius Kircher is part of my family. He could be sitting here, right beside me, his hat askew, shaking the skirt of his cassock to cool his legs. A familiar figure, with sparks of genius here and there, but very banal most of the time. A dreamer who enjoys life, a brother, a friend . . .

FRIDAY, TEN O'CLOCK in the morning: letter from Malbois.

> Dear Eléazard,
>   I apologize for the great delay in answering your questions. It wasn't that easy and demanded quite a bit of work, though I'm afraid you're not going to like the result.
>   First of all I researched the passages that you thought dubious in the works of Mersenne, La Mothe Le Vayer and the few others, the titles of which you will remember. Your suspicions were well founded: there are plenty of disturbing similarities, sometimes even more, without it being possible to say who was plagiarising whom; as you know, it was common practice at the time, there were seldom any repercussions. I won't go into details, they wouldn't be of any use

to you—you'll soon understand why: when I went on to the second question on your list, the one concerning the dates of Caspar Schott, the whole edifice started to crumble. 1608–1666! (Confirmed from several different sources.) Since the virtuous Caspar departed this life fourteen years before his master, it was obvious that the part of the biography devoted to Kircher's life after the latter date was apocryphal. There remained the possibility that someone else who had been with Kircher during those last years had continued Schott's work with sufficient skill to imitate his "style."

At once I went back to look more closely at certain elements that had tickled my fancy when I first read it: the Villa Palagonia only existed the way Schott describes it in the eighteenth century—between 1750 and 1760. As for the Désert de Retz, even if it is well known that it was inspired by Kircher's miniature landscapes, it definitely dates from 1785!

By this point in my researches it had become clear that not a single line in the manuscript could be by Schott, that the whole must have been written after 1780 at the earliest, that is, a hundred years after Kircher's death.

As you can well imagine, this conclusion cast doubt on all the rest, so I went about methodically picking out aspects that seemed suspect. There were quite a lot of little things (I even identified a maxim by Chamfort!), almost all of them impossible to verify, and I was about to tell you the stage my conclusions had reached when I reread that horrible poem by Von Spee. Even taking into account the fact that it was a translation from Latin—and that seventeenth-century poetry is really not my cup of tea—the lines seemed singularly anachronistic and devoid of meaning. By chance, or perhaps infected by the language games Kircher engaged in, I started looking at 'The Idolator' as an encrypted text. I have to say that I found the solution pretty quickly (a kind of rather convoluted acrostic). I won't spoil it for you, I'll let you work it out for yourself, but it's clear someone's been having you on, and with a vengeance! I hope you hadn't gotten too far with it . . .

Take it with a pinch of humor, have a good laugh at it—if you can. And keep me informed: supposing you ever manage to find out who did it, I'd very much like to meet the guy before you strangle him.

See you someday,

C. Malbois

ONE O'CLOCK. I take it fairly coolly, but it doesn't make me laugh. Impossible to get hold of Werner in Berlin.

SEVEN O'CLOCK: Spent the whole afternoon walking straight ahead. Hurt pride, of course. Once my initial irritation at having worked on these notes to no purpose had passed, I was above all mortified at not having discovered the hoax myself.

THE PROBLEM is not knowing whether a person really said what you made him say, but judging whether you managed to make him say it in a way that is true to him. Is not truth anything we find sufficiently suitable to accept it as such? The *borderline case of satisfaction*, as W. V. Quine put it. The person—Werner or someone else—who produced this sham comes closer to it than anything I could claim . . .

TO GO DOWN THE RIVER as far as Montevideo, to return to Lautréamont (to Voltaire?) just as turtles return to the beach where they were born to lay their eggs.

"IN A WORD," Kircher says in his conclusion to his work on anamorphoses, *"there is no monster in whose shape you cannot see yourself with a mirror of this kind combining flat and curved surfaces."*

WHO WOULD ruin their lives making a distorting mirror like that? Was it in the hope of fooling me or of achieving precisely what came out of it? I can't bring myself to believe that this document was produced with me in mind, but I'm also sure it wasn't entrusted to me purely by chance. Werner has been manipulated, I've no doubt he passed the manuscript on to me in good faith. Having said that, the authorship of the text is hardly important, the only question is: who likes me enough to give me such a violent wake-up call? Malbois?

It was a one-in-a-million chance he'd spot that acrostic . . .

"BIOLUMINESCENCE occurs when a substance known by the name of luciferin (from the Latin *lucifer*, 'the bearer of light') combines with oxygen when an enzyme called luciferase is present. There is a chemical reaction that releases energy in the form of light." (D. L. Allen) Literature, the name of light!

THE SOLUTION, PERHAPS . . . Neither darkness, nor light, nor twilight: studding with stars. Fireflies, living, random phosphenes in the depths of the night itself.

A MAXIM on a gnomon seen by Léon Bloy: "It's later than you think."

ALCÂNTARA: *Are you sure you want to eat mussels?*

When all's said and done, Eléazard thought, was it not reasonable to assume that the whole biography of Athanasius Kircher might be a fabrication, in the subject's own image. The proportion of fiction in the supposed writings of Caspar Schott represented more faithfully than any scientific study our poignant, unhealthy and obsessive determination to romanticize our existence. The message, if there was one, came down to this: the reflection always wins out over the reflected object, anamorphosis always has a greater power of truth than the object it at first sight distorts and transforms. Was not its ultimate goal to unite reality and fiction in a new reality, in a stereoscopic relief?

Eléazard quit his word processor and clicked on the file-manager icon. In the "Archives" folder he chose the file containing his notes, then asked to delete them.

"Are you sure you want to delete Kircher.doc? Yes. No."

His finger poised over the left-hand button of his mouse, Eléazard hesitated for a moment at the abrupt irrevocability behind this exhortation to prudence. There was no copy of his work, everything would be irremediably lost. *Forget Kircher*, Loredana had said to him . . . And now he understood what she was saying: Look after your daughter, beware of going back, avoid going back like the plague. Get on with life! His heart had started to beat more quickly. Are you sure you want to eat mussels? You wish for the delights of amnesia so badly? Shrugging his shoulders, with the foreboding that afterward he would be spared nothing, he answered "Yes" to the question. The cursor immediately turned into a countdown to death, an empty clock face with a single hand sweeping round at top speed. Deleting track after track of information that was of no interest whatever to it, the hard disk recorded his choice with a series of mild hiccups. At the end of the process a new window replaced the preceding one:

"Do you want to delete another file? Yes. No."

Hypnotized by the screen, Eléazard had started to play with his ping-pong balls again. Gravely they turned, those little blind planets. Milky, bulging.

FORTALEZA, THE FUTURE BEACH:
Bri-git-te Bardot, Bardooo!

Nelson had put his election T-shirt on over his center-forward's jersey; he was sweating as much from the heat as from anxiety. He'd been waiting at the side of the platform for two hours now, a hundred good reasons had made him give up his action, a hundred others had encouraged him to go ahead. Deafened by the closeness of the speakers, he was drifting along in a distressing and impatient daydream. His position off to the side limited his field of vision to the slanting lines of planks on the rostrum and the vertical infinity of the shore. Far away, sitting over the horizon, a line of clouds delineated the contours of an unknown coast, a world to discover.

As he did every time a piece of music came to the end, the campaign organizer came to test the mike and keep up the suspense. Walkie-talkie on his belt, he immediately plunged into a verbose harangue in which the names of Barbosa, Jr., and Moreira appeared again and again; they were on their way, they were about to arrive! While he was speaking, his assistants took turns throwing T-shirts by the dozen to the crowd. In the scramble that ensued, the area surrounding the platform became a sea of white.

All at once several sirens drowned out the hullaballoo on the beach. Right at the top of the hillock three black limousines flanked by police cars stopped above the platform. A swarm of policemen poured out of the vehicles to take up position along the slope and protect the officials as they got out. Masked by their bodyguards, the two governors began to walk down the dune, filmed all the way by a small TV team. At the bottom, the national anthem came over the loudspeakers, making all those who could hear it automatically stiffen and fall silent.

Nelson's mind had shut down. His lips quietly repeated the words of the anthem. To stop his right hand from trembling, he gripped the butt of the pistol underneath his soccer jersey, forcing himself to visualize Lampião. He was close to fainting.

Jaunty in their lightweight cream suits, Barbosa, Jr., and Moreira put on the act of men whom the security guards were stopping from joining the crowd. The closer they came to the platform, the more they pretended to push their way through the ranks of police to shake a held-out hand or kiss the grubby cheek of a child. From the moment Nelson identified Moreira, his eyes never left him. The governor seemed to have aged compared with his face in the photos, but it was definitely the man he had hated for years: the man who had murdered his father, the bastard who had stolen Uncle Zé's Willis.

Nelson released the safety catch of the revolver. A profound silence had fallen all round him; he heard neither the music starting up again, nor the campaign organizer at the mike, warming up the crowd. "Closer," he repeated to himself obsessively, "wait until he's really close."

When they reached the bottom of the steps, Nelson lost sight of the two men again. They had stopped one last time to face the cameras and put on a show of love of the people that would encourage a certain segment of the electorate to vote for them. None of these beggars would ever put a ballot paper in the box but they knew from experience that the charade would appeal to soft-hearted people watching the television news.

One of the cameramen climbed up onto the platform, followed by a sound engineer. The campaign organizer gestured to them to stand back a little so that they could include Nelson in the picture. Used to these media stratagems, Oswald understood what was wanted and positioned himself accordingly. The sun was behind him, the shot would be perfect.

Nelson saw nothing of this. Hypnotized by going over one single act in his mind again and again, he kept his eyes fixed on the patch of sky where the man he intended to assassinate would appear.

The police took up position around the platform and, while the bodyguards blocked access to the rostrum, the two governors mounted the steps. Barbosa, Jr., was the first to appear. A glance from the cameraman told him what was expected of him so that he headed straight for Nelson in a movement that appeared completely spontaneous.

Behind his lens, Oswald immediately centered the scene, going down on his knees so as not to miss the initial contact. The disabled lad seemed terrified and it took several seconds before he held out his left hand to the governor. One of his arms was paralysed as well! It was good, very good. Barbosa muttered some words of comfort to him and moved across to the mike. OK, the second camera had taken over there. Zoom in on the Governor of Maranhão: his expression relaxed, sideburns triumphant, José Moreira da Rocha made his way in his turn toward the young cripple. Then suddenly his smile vanished and his jaw dropped. Instinctively Oswald changed the focus and saw the young lad, his gun held out at arm's length, then the other hand gripping the butt to help hold it steady. Unable to believe his eyes, he looked up from his viewfinder and threw himself down flat.

The sound of the shots, a clock rapidly striking six, brought Uncle Zé to an abrupt halt. In the seconds that followed, he registered the howling of the crowd and the wave of panic sweeping back toward him. Two brief bursts of machine-gun fire set him running toward the platform again. He's done it, he thought, as he made his way forward, looking stunned.

The sound system, switched back on, sent out the latest samba:

Bri-gi-te Bardot
Bar-dooo!
Bri-gi-te Beijo
Bei-jooo!

Uncle Zé's lips went white with fury, a rage that had nothing human about it and that swelled in proportion to the absurdity beneath which the criminal stupidity of men generally hides.

JEAN-MARIE BLAS DE ROBLÈS is a former lecturer in French literature and philosophy at universities in Brazil, China, Italy, and finally, for the Alliance Française in Taiwan. His first literary publication was a volume of short stories in 1982, followed by two novels; soon after he turned to writing full-time. An avid traveler, Blas de Roblès also edits a series of books on archaeology and is a member of the French Archaeological Mission in Libya. In 2008 he was awarded the prestigious Prix Médicis for his novel *Where Tigers Are at Home*.

MIKE MITCHELL has translated more than seventy books, including works by Goethe, Gustav Meyrink, Adolf Loos, and Oskar Kokoschka. Many of his translations have been short-listed for awards, including three short listings for the Oxford-Weidenfeld Translation Prize. Most recently Mitchell has been short-listed for the Helen and Kurt Wolff Translator's Prize for Thomas Bernhard's *Over All the Mountain Tops*. In 1998 he was awarded the Schlegel-Tieck Prize for Herbert Rosendorfer's *Letters Back to Ancient China*.